catcHiNG
THe DriFT

catcHiNG THe DriFT

a.M.hartsocK

Bartleby Press
Washington • Baltimore

ISBN 978-0-910155-96-0
LCCN 2012941195

Published by:

Bartleby Press

8600 Foundry Street
Mill Box 2043
Savage, Maryland 20763
800-953-9929
www.BartlebythePublisher.com

Printed in the United States of America

For my sister, Missa

In gratitude for the artistry of
Heath Ledger, Nick Drake &
Kurt Cobain

CHAPTER ONE

Alex remembered nothing about the day he was rendered impotent or even the days or months before. He simply knew he was, and the realization settled on him like a heavy morning fog, clouding all details of the landscape, revealing only vague, gray shadows.

The impotence was not just sexual but extended to all aspects of his being, from his ability to exert any amount of energy into a single project to his capacity to feel deeply about any of the events of the past few months. He now sat in his parents' large green Bronco, speeding towards his new home in Kansas after spending the majority of his life in the mountains of Montana, and he felt . . . nothing. Not loss, not anxiety, not anger nor regret—nothing more than a dull ache in the pit of his stomach, an ache that began months ago when he lay recuperating in a hospital room from bullet wounds he did not remember receiving.

No one, not the few friends he had left nor his family, would discuss the incident, whatever it was, soon avoiding him altogether. Conversations would barely get past the weather and baseball scores before people would dart away nervously, like minnows startled by a plunking rock. As the weeks waned on, he let himself sink to the bottom of his murky existence, caught between a dark future and an even darker past. He believed in nothing he couldn't see or touch, and the summer sun wasn't enough to enlighten him.

Despite the car's air conditioning, he began to sweat as the sun's hot rays pierced the windows. The ache grew into a mild nausea, and he slouched in his seat, seeking a position comfortable enough to induce sleep. His father must have pulled over at some point, for the next thing he remembered was strolling through a field, following the path of a small stream in search of a bathroom.

The sky was still extraordinarily bright, the sun bathing everything in a blinding white glow. Up ahead was what appeared to be a small town, and he followed the stream as it widened into a canal that ran under the middle of a deserted intersection. The streets were lined with whitewashed adobe buildings. Each whitewashed adobe building was lined with deep green bushes, the small branches burdened with immense red, orange and magenta flowers. Wooden window boxes were full of the same lush flowers, dripping petals onto the deserted sidewalks.

Though the town appeared abandoned, he knew there were people nearby. He could sense them. And off in the horizon sat the beloved peaks of his home in Montana. So far off, that he wondered if they weren't really clouds - if he weren't really hallucinating.

Rounding the corner at the end of one of the streets, he stopped. Had he been there before, he asked himself. The landscape looked familiar. It was all beginning to look the same, street after street. Then he saw something up ahead, something colorful, flapping against the side of a building. Upon approaching the structure, he noticed a girl beating the dust out of a large red blanket. Tiny clouds of red dust settled over the flowers and walk below. He paused under her balcony.

She was a young girl with long dark hair and large brown eyes, who looked like someone he knew. She wore a soiled white blouse, and her expression was distant and gloomy. She pretended not to notice him and continued to beat her blanket furiously against the balcony.

"Hello," he thought he heard himself say.

"Why did you bring us here?"

"What do you mean? Do I know you?"

"We don't belong here. Wake up. Wake up before we both die."

"What do you mean? What do you mean wake up? Am I dreaming?" he asked. But she said nothing further. He then realized he was lost and began to panic. Spinning around, he grasped his head, not knowing which way to turn. His parents were waiting for him, but he could not remember where they parked, and now he could die, just as she said.

He walked quickly down the street, looking to the sky to determine the position of the sun. But he couldn't see the sun, only a bright light that enveloped the entire atmosphere. Shading his eyes, he strained to find the field through which he had walked earlier. If he could spot the field, he would surely find the road and the parked car. But the glare—

He heard footsteps. A person was walking close behind him, yet something told him not to turn around.

He felt the presence like one feels lightening before it strikes—a tingling sensation down the spine, the hairs of the neck and head standing on end. He walked faster, hearing the footsteps bearing down upon him. Just after the next street would be the car, or maybe the next. It had to be the next.

He saw something up ahead, something colorful, flapping against the side of a building. Upon approaching the building, he noticed a girl beating the dust out of a large red blanket—

He stopped, breathless.

He knew he shouldn't look, but he was tired and anxious.

He turned around.

For a split second, he saw black metal. And more horrifying, the face. The faceless face. The absence of face. And then there was an explosion, and he was bowled into the pavement by its force, his hands clutching his side in pain. His stomach felt wet. He knew it was blood, though when he looked at his hands, he saw none. But his stomach felt so wet.

The girl was directly above him, beating the blanket against the balcony. A rain of red dirt settled on and around him until a dirty veil covered his eyes. The world turned from red to black as his consciousness slipped away.

But I can't die . . . I can't die now. I'm not dead now. If I die now, I'll never wake up—

"ALEX—open the window! I feel sick—"

A hand shook his shoulder. He opened his eyes to dark green leather with two puffs of hair rising over the edge. The sun was blinding, and a musty odor permeated the car.

"Come on, Alex—it's hot in here. I'm going to die!" his sister exclaimed.

An intense pain shot through his body, concentrating in his loins. He instinctively put his hand to his stomach. It felt wet, his light blue cotton shirt soaked with sweat. He sat up, gasping for air and trying to get oriented. How long had he slept? Where were they? What state? What city? How much longer?

He ran his fingers through his shoulder-length, curly blond strands, peeling the hair away from his face. He then anxiously rolled down the window and leaned back in the green leather seat, still holding his stomach in pain.

"Thank you!" his sister sighed dramatically.

"Where are we?" His voice cracked, and he was barely able to speak, the pain heightening.

"On the eastern edge of Colorado," his dad answered. "We should hit Kansas in about ten minutes."

The pain sharpened to an unbearable degree. He looked out the window at the expanse of plains. Mile upon mile of field and dirt. Ahead, more field and dirt. Looking out the back window, he thought he saw an outline of the mountains. Maybe they were just clouds.

Catching his reflection in the rearview mirror, he saw a deathly complexion, the sharp hollows in his cheeks that usually gave him a healthy, rugged look now seemed only to define the bone beneath the skin. His brown eyes held a dull, blank stare like the pits of a skull. The pain shot through his stomach again followed by a wave of nausea.

He fell forward.

"Stop the car," he gasped. "I'm going to be sick—"

Outside, a hot, dry wind whipped dirt up into tiny clouds of stone and dust that stung his exposed skin and burned his eyes. He stood, hunched over a ditch, the parched grass scraping his shins, heaving air, water, bile and the sudden anguish he felt upon realizing he was leaving Montana, the first pronounced feeling that had managed to penetrate his phlegmatic emotional interior.

Wiping the spit from his mouth, he stumbled up the embankment and fell against the side of the Bronco, its dark green metal burning his skin. He let it, hoping it would scorch straight through to the bone. They could leave his carcass to brown and rot and become part of the land, part of the nothingness.

His dad stuck his head out the window.

"Alex, are you okay now? We really need to be moving on . . ."

His parents decided to stop for the night at a Best Western in Hays, Kansas. He locked himself in the bathroom to get ready for bed, nervous but suddenly determined to attempt self-gratification, an activity he had been unsuccessful in performing since released from the hospital months ago. His mother and sister had taken a separate room, and his father had fallen asleep watching late night television with the volume turned high. That noise, coupled with the bathroom fan, would cover any action of his. Nobody ever suspected anything anyway, he thought to himself.

Yet tonight, even as he went to the bathroom, he felt something wasn't right. He touched himself and tried to relax, but immediately a burning sensation formed in his privates. Irritated, he drew a hot bath, hoping the water would relax the tension and make him feel better. He settled back against the cold, smooth porcelain and let his body slowly submerge under water. After a few minutes, he again gingerly touched himself before beginning the process of attempting an erection. The burning sensation had passed, and he proceeded.

When nothing happened, he mentally placed himself in a fictitious scenario with a young woman whose features were a blend of cover models and media personalities. Her white blouse was unbuttoned to reveal partially exposed breasts. He began kissing her, his hands clutching at her skin. He stroked himself faster as his body pressed against hers.

A large slap sounded as his palms hit the water. He nearly choked; the abrupt pain was so intense—sharp and searing through his lower stomach. He sat up with a jerk, holding himself tightly, kneading his fingers into his stomach muscle, hoping to push the pain out—to grab it and stop it. He felt his back tooth slice into a piece of his tongue as he clamped his mouth shut to suppress a yell. It would pass, he said to himself. It would have to pass.

That night, he lay awake in the second double bed, listening to the highway noises, uncomfortable on the stiff hotel mattress. He thought about the dream he had earlier that afternoon but soon blocked it out, afraid it would reveal a past he was too frightened to face. After falling asleep, he dreamed again. This time, he was in his old house, running from room to room, frantically throwing open doors and groping in closets. He couldn't find his shoes. They couldn't leave without his shoes.

He awoke to the sound of a semi-truck pulling out of the parking lot.

When they reached Topeka, he resigned himself to the fact that they were going to live in Kansas. There would be no turning around, no second thoughts. He would spend his last two years of high school in a Kansas suburb. If he wanted to hike, it would be at a local park. If he wanted to ski, it would be on slopes of manmade snow.

"The first thing I'm going to do when we get there is go shopping on The Plaza—they have a Saks Fifth Avenue. A *Saks Fifth Avenue*! Can you believe it?" His sister hit him on the arm, snorting with delight over the Kansas City travel brochures strewn around the car seat.

He rolled his eyes and looked out the window. Yellow and brown fields of wheat and grass stretched for miles, with a few clumps of grayish-green trees scattered in-between. At least the land was hilly in spots, and he had seen a few hawks during the last hour, perched on telephone poles and fence posts.

In Montana, they had lived just north of Missoula, in the Flathead Valley near Flathead Lake. Their house was a two-story log cabin on 14 acres of land surrounded by forest, a few miles outside the nearest town center. To the south and east sat the Mission Mountains. He rarely heard the sound of cars, and only an occasional small airplane flew overhead. It was peaceful and beautiful. It was home to him for most of his life.

He closed his eyes and sighed as he remembered the faint smell of Douglas fir in the cool mountain air while horseback riding through fields and forests or hiking up mountain paths, or the feel of the blinding white sun on his face and rush of adrenaline while skiing down the steep snowy slopes.

Opening his eyes, he saw nothing but dark green leather and noticed that his hands were clenched in a silent rage. This emotional awakening surprised him, even scared him, and he tried to push all thoughts and memories out of his conscience. The dull pain started in his stomach again, and he slouched down in the seat, praying it wouldn't turn into nausea. Then he began to wonder why they were moving to a new city in the first place. Nobody had really discussed the move with him, and his parents never even asked his opinion. When he had inquired about it, they simply said his father had gotten a great job at a medical center and would make more money. But he sensed there was something else, some other reason they were withholding—

A loud bang sounded. He jolted forward, grabbing his stomach protectively.

Trisha laughed. "Scared you, huh?"

A truck in the next lane had backfired.

He sat back in the seat, wiping his face with his hand. His father asked if he was alright. His mother offered him a pill. Trisha grunted. He stared blankly ahead, afraid to take his thoughts any further. He had tried not to think about the dream either, instinctively realizing that this new pain and his new emotional state had arrived with the dream. And now he had heard what sounded like a shot, and the pain was returning full force.

How long . . . How long until they got there? To that godforsaken city with the imitation fountains and plastic parks. He found the idea of cold concrete and neatly mowed yards awaiting him at their fashionable suburban home unbearable. Dying, at this point, seemed far more appealing. Toying with the idea of throwing the car door open and letting his body be hurled to the ground, run over by a passing semi and eaten away by vultures, he drifted off into a restless sleep.

He spent his first week in Kansas wandering around his new neighborhood, camera in hand, trying to capture some semblance of the sublime. Beautiful or ugly, it didn't matter, only that something was there beneath the surface, alive and beckoning.

The neighborhood was older and established, lined with tall trees, well-kept emerald lawns and stately houses. His own house was a traditional cape cod, yellow with a brick façade and light blue shutters and trim.

Soon bored with the immediate neighborhood, he borrowed the Bronco and ventured into the city the following weekend. He took Main Street north, guessing it would take him far enough into downtown to find places of interest. His initial curiosity turned to concern when he penetrated deeper into the city and no crowds appeared. Even the streets were relatively deserted of cars. He drove cautiously up and down the empty city streets, studying the barren stone and glass structures from his windshield, half expecting a tumble weed to come blowing around the next corner. But nothing appeared, and no one appeared, except for an occasional poorly dressed straggler.

Bored and growing increasingly depressed, he headed south a couple of miles outside of the downtown area. As he neared a district called the The Country Club Plaza, cars and crowds materialized once more and were even highly congested in some areas. Red trolleys transporting sightseers slowed traffic, and horse-driven carriages rambled nonchalantly among the speeding cars and buses. Here was the true heart of the city, he decided, sapping the lifeblood from downtown like a bloated tick, a miniature Spanish city in the middle of the prairie.

Resolving to discover what the hype was, he parked on the roof of a department store and began to explore. After a ten-minute walk, he concluded that the buildings, despite their white-washed stucco facades, Spanish fountains and terra cotta tiled roofs, were little more than pricey clothing stores in disguise. And he soon found himself the object of a number of odd glances from pedestrians.

He felt his neck burn and self-consciously began to sneak looks at his reflection in store windows and to dart into restaurant bathrooms to make sure his nose wasn't running or his fly wasn't unzipped. What were they looking at? His khaki shorts were standard, and he was wearing a light blue denim shirt. It must be his hair, he finally decided. It hung just below his shoulders in loose, messy curls, small sections of it haphazardly braided with beads.

It could be his size too, he pondered, quickly heading back to the car. At sixteen, he was just over six feet tall and weighed close to 200 pounds. In certain crowds he felt hulking. Among women he felt hulking. Today he felt hulking and left The Plaza in dismay.

At his next opportunity to borrow the car, he headed for the outskirts of the suburbs to one of the largest malls in the area. The mall was a world of its own, complete with trees and large skylights to give the sensation of being outdoors. Joggers brushed past him as they made their rounds from one end of the mall to the other. Quite a few women were walking with strollers.

Strongly encouraged by his mother to buy clothes for school, he wandered in and out of a few stores that looked interesting from the outside. But he was soon bored, and, with some of the money she gave him, grabbed a bite to eat at the food court and went back to the car.

He still had the entire afternoon to continue his exploration of the area before the car had to be returned at four-thirty. Reviewing the city map, he noticed an illustration of a large park just beyond the edge of the suburbs and set off to find it, a vague feeling of hope in his heart. He longed for nature, for the woods—any woods.

The park was not hard to find. He pulled into the entrance and drove up and down its winding, hilly road. Patches of trees dotted fields, with small ponds interspersed between the trees and hills. In one field, a couple of teenagers were flying kites. In another area, a family was picnicking. By a pond, parents and children sat fishing.

Following the main road, he soon reached a larger body of water and parked near the docks. The day was hot, and groups of people swarmed the shore, many sunning. Boats glided lazily on the sparkling water. He walked along the shoreline, heading for woods on the other side. As he walked, he pondered his obscured past and odd dreams, instinctively knowing they were connected. Perhaps if he concentrated enough, he would find the answer, and the dreams and pain would stop. Still, he was afraid to open a door those around him refused even to approach.

He was also nervous about the start of the school year. He would have to make new friends. Have to become involved in activities. Have to do homework. Have to deal with people. Have to deal with women.

At this thought, a sharp pain seared through his stomach but quickly subsided. He held his breath in anticipation, breathing easily again only when the pain did not return after a few minutes. Noticing a sign for a three-mile walking trail, he soon forgot his discomfort, quickly striding through the trail entrance, anticipating a much-needed mental vacation amidst nature.

His enthusiasm was short-lived, as groups of people kept assaulting his private stroll. First it was a bunch of grade school-aged boy scouts, running and hooting like wild animals. Next it was a large group of senior citizens that he thought he would never shake off. And he was just getting into identifying species of trees and collecting some interesting specimens when three horseback riders nearly mowed him down by accident. Enraged, he left the path in search of an isolated and quiet area.

After his bare legs began to bleed from the thorny underbrush, he climbed down a steep pathway that led to a secluded, marshy section near the lake. Sitting down, he rested his back against a large rock, half-shaded by overhanging maples and birches. Though he could still hear shouting and merriment in the distance, he was confident no one would come trampling through this area. He closed his eyes, feeling the sun brush his face with warmth as it shined through the fluttering leaves.

Within twenty minutes, he had fallen asleep. He awakened an hour later to the sound of rustling brush and sat up with a start.

A man was approaching him, heading down the steep incline through the trees. He immediately feared it was the park ranger, there to reprimand him for going off the trail. He could see the red coloring of a long-sleeve plaid work shirt and the dark blue denim of jeans as the figure made his way towards him through the brush. He looked at the face, but the man did not appear to have one—

You don't belong here. You don't belong here. You know you don't belong here. Wake up.

Over and over again the man's gruff voice repeated these lines. Soon they filled his mind, getting louder, seemingly bouncing off the trees and echoing into a jumbled yet deafening din.

Alex felt his heart stop. He rubbed his eyes in disbelief and soon found himself holding his ears, trying to block out the voice. He had to be dreaming again, he thought, and mentally struggled to wake himself. He wanted to wake up. He kept shaking his head, soon hitting it lightly against the stone. He then hunched over, burying his head in his lap, hoping that when he looked up, it would be over. He had to wake up—

He sat frozen in a crouched position for what seemed like an eternity. Every muscle in his body remained tense until he noticed the voices beginning to fade. He then relaxed a bit, trying to get his breathing back to normal.

After another minute, the voices were gone. Silence returned, and he could again hear the soft chirping of birds and distant peals of laughter from the lake and trail above.

Slowly, he loosened his arms, sat forward and raised his head to look around.

The man stood five feet away, pointing the barrel directly at him. And the cold nothingness of the masked face stared him straight in the eyes. He again gasped for air in utter terror and anticipation of what would happen next. The awful thunderous sound. The impact. The searing pain that would rip through his side. The darkness—

He heard the trigger click and, instantly following, the resounding clap of ignited powder. His body was blown against the rock, and he lay clutching his side in agony, the blood streaming down his hands and collecting into small pools next to him. He blacked out.

When he came to, the sun was still shining brightly, though it had changed position. Surely somebody would find him and take him to the hospital, he thought, touching his stomach gingerly.

Upon feeling no wetness, he sat up with a start and stared down at his shirt and shorts. No blood spotted his clothing, and he could now feel only a dull throbbing in his stomach. He looked wildly around, nervously pushing his sweat drenched locks away from his face. He glanced down at his watch. It was four o'clock, and he was a good mile from either end of the trail. The car had to be returned by four-thirty, because his sister had a hair appointment.

Standing up shakily, he brushed himself off and quickly began his ascent towards the trail, pondering his dream and viewing the coming days and nights with dread.

∞

It was a hot Sunday August afternoon, the sun bathing everything in a blinding white glow. Danielle was fanning herself inside the manor house, physically and mentally preparing for the final piece of an outdoor benefit concert. Dvorak's *Ninth-The New World*. Twenty minutes—or over thirty? She asked herself, calculating the movements and corresponding time she would be spending in the sweltering heat.

A young man snapped his fingers in front of her eyes, jarring her out of her inner mental state, and winked knowingly, motioning for her to follow him. It was time to go, time to play.

Though he was her boyfriend, the sight of him made her heart heavy. She became acutely aware of the weight of her black dress as it clung in places to her sweat-drenched body. And suddenly her whole being felt heavy - the mammoth idiocy of the concert, her relationship and her lifestyle crushing her very being. What was she even doing there?

She reluctantly picked up her violin and bow, shuffling outside to take her seat. *New World*, she thought bitterly. *Take me there—show me a new world*, she cried to herself, looking up at the bright white sky.

The next morning, Danielle thought she heard violins in the distance. Very soft yet intense—allegro, as in Vivaldi's *L'inverno*—moments before the crescendos. Then it became more desperate—angry. Maybe Tchaikovsky?

The strings' tones quickly culminated into an annoying buzz. She buried her head further beneath the pillow, wanting to remain enveloped in the comfort of sleep and darkness.

But the buzzing persisted, followed by pings. She thought she heard the blinds lightly banging against the windowpane. Her thoughts soon surfaced to reality. The buzzing turned to sputtering then stopped. After a minute, it resumed with a music-like quality—Rimsky Korsikav, this time. But it soon became sickly, accompanied by pinging metal.

A fly, she concluded wearily, disturbed that it would disrupt her sleep with its swan song. But then she realized that she had never heard such music from an insect before, even cicadas, which she thought obnoxious. It began buzzing again, this time another Vivaldi allegro. Next, a soft Faure before sputtering in its fight for life. When would the poison finally consume it? She considered putting it out of its misery but wondered if that wouldn't be just as painful. She thought about herself in such a situation, choking for breath, gripping her stomach in agony, throwing herself against a glass imprisonment, against the unreachable sun, wind and fresh air. Then, exploding into hundreds of microscopic pieces as a huge, unknown object came bearing down upon her fragile body, every cell screaming in pain as it was destroyed. But the pain would only last a second, wouldn't it?

As the fly launched into a momentary Mozart, her thoughts flew from the plight of the fly to the plight of millions of unwanted cats and dogs euthanized each year, to the millions of cows, pigs and chickens consumed each year, to the dying chimps, birds and jaguars in the raped and pillaged rain forests. Images of the violated, blank-staring women in Bosnia, of starving children in Somalia and bloodied corpses from all over the world that graced the weekly covers and center spreads of her parents' magazines soon replaced the animal images. Pictures of rapists, murderers, torturers and scenes of racial violence then marched across her consciousness in a series of gory, film-like scenarios until she became so horrified she couldn't breathe and half hoped death would envelop her in a peaceful escape from the madness.

The fly quieted down for a while, and she lay staring at the dull, gray ceiling. Her alarm would go off in a half-hour, and the sun's rays were not yet bright enough to streak her walls and ceilings through the blinds. She didn't want to wake up. Her day would have an uncertain ending. Possibly, an unpleasant ending. Her life was becoming increasingly nightmarish, and she found herself preferring the dream world to the waking world. The waking world seemed so violent and angry. Her parents' marriage deteriorating daily. Her brother's hate for her increasing daily. Her relationship with Tate strained and tense. She feared if she did not give in to his physical advances soon, he would snap and use force.

Suddenly annoyed with her imagination and overwhelming sense of paranoia, she threw a pillow towards the now droning fly and was out of bed before the alarm ever sounded.

Once into the day's activities, however, her thoughts fluctuated between terrible angst and feeble hope. The morning was sunny, clear and warm, and she had a perfect view of the rustling, variegated treetops from her seat at symphony practice. They were working on Tchaikovsksy's *Romeo & Juliet*, which she found personally ironic, especially considering her boyfriend, the senior cellist, was seated across the room and had no idea of her intent to break up with him that evening. His close proximity unnerved her, and she tried to avoid eye contact and focus on the piece.

Halfway into the second movement, however, she heard a dull buzzing above her. Looking up and around, she noticed a wasp circling the room, at times diving to just above the students' heads. He then landed on the window, scaling it for an open crack. Frustrated after colliding with the glass a few times, he resumed his manic flight.

As she watched it, the early morning's dark thoughts flooded her mind, and she was again anticipating the evening's impending gloom. She shuddered and was soon so distracted that she fell off time. Being first chair for strings, her error was quickly noticed, and the entire symphony fell quiet. Her face burned in embarrassment.

The conductor, a middle-aged man who taught music at a local university, looked at her over his brown, plastic-rimmed glasses. Before he could comment dryly, she burst out testily, "I can't concentrate with that bee flying around in here!"

After a moment's silence, the entire room burst into commotion, all heads looking up and around for the errant insect. Soon, her boyfriend caught sight of it and snorted that it was a wasp, not a bee. He and a few other male musicians chased it around the room and eventually crushed it with a book, the sound making her flinch. Somehow, she felt responsible for its death. The director just shook his head, and she heard him mumble something about her temperament. She played the remainder of the piece flawlessly but was still shaken by the incident.

"That was quite a ruckus you caused in there," her boyfriend said sarcastically, as they walked down the hallway. His name was Tate Foley, and they had been dating for nearly three years.

"Yes . . . sorry. I just—I just hate stinging things."

"Well, I killed it for you. *Saved the day*," he said, winking at her.

She smiled weakly and turned away.

"Want to grab some lunch?"

"Oh—I'm meeting Brooke for lunch, but thank you. I'll see you tonight, though."

He rolled his eyes in disgust. "Brooke . . . Okay, whatever. Pick you up at six."

She watched him walk down the hall, studying his person intently. He was tall with an athletic build and skin that was tanned from the summer sun. His dark brown hair was naturally curly, but he kept it cropped so short it was hard to tell. A meticulous dresser, even today, when most teenagers were dressed casually for the extreme heat—in jean cut-offs and t-shirts or tank tops—he wore pressed khaki shorts that fell just above his knee, a neatly pressed pink oxford rolled at the sleeves and boat shoes—a poster child for Ralph Lauren.

As she headed to The Plaza to meet her friend, Brooke, for lunch, she again pondered her decision to break up with him, wavering but still determined to do it. Though he was considered extremely attractive—hot, even—by any and every girl who set eyes on him, Danielle didn't see it. She didn't feel it, either, and was growing increasingly repulsed by his sexual advances, at times feeling dirty after having made out with him. She had stopped trying to figure out why, for it made no sense. All she could conclude was that she didn't trust him. Though outwardly polite, there was an underlying meanness he kept well-hidden that revealed itself in given situations.

They decided to eat at the German cafe with an outside patio even though Danielle insisted it was too hot to eat outdoors, the temperature over ninety degrees. Both ordered salads and bottled water.

Danielle considered very few people friends, but Brooke was her best. She had met her freshman year of high school. Acquaintances often commented that they looked like sisters, though Brooke was taller and lighter complexioned than Danielle. Her near-black hair was cut short in the latest pixie style, framing prominent dark eyes and delicate facial features. She dressed chic, today wearing a trendy camisole and short skirt reminiscent of the sixties, and was constantly trying to convince Danielle to modernize her own preppy wardrobe. Danielle felt she was the plainer of the two, wearing her long, thick dark brown hair straight and using very little make-up. And she felt her own features awkward, her brown almond-shaped eyes large, her lips full, her teeth and smile huge and her cheekbones too pronounced. Brooke insisted she looked exotic, but she disagreed.

"So, how has your day been?" Brooke asked, before sipping on her water through a straw.

Danielle said nothing for a moment, her head tilted up to catch a small breeze that slightly lifted her hair from her shoulders and provided a brief relief from the oppressive heat. "I'm—I'm drowning, you know . . . I—I feel so smothered."

Brooke frowned a moment, then nodded in understanding. "Yes . . . But that will all change after tonight, don't you think?"

"I don't know . . . I really don't know. Because you see, it's not just him. I mean, he's part of the whole oppressive picture, you know? I mean, for the past couple years . . . What am I saying—*for my entire life*, actually, I have done nothing but what I've been expected to do . . . I've gotten straight As, I've been involved in student council, I've been involved with the symphony, I've competed, I've done charity, I've done social events, and I—I—" Her mind groped to put thoughts and feelings into words.

"You what?" Brooke asked after a minute.

"I'm not happy. I should be so happy, but I'm not. I feel trapped, somehow. Like something isn't right, you know? I mean—why is it that I'm rich and have a good education and good health and a good family and yet most of the world is suffering? And dying? And, and even me—doing everything I am supposed to do, it—it doesn't equal happiness, you know?" She shook her head, dumbstruck with a sudden realization. "Jesus—nobody is happy. My parents hate each other. Dennis and I hate each other. Shit—Tate and I can't stand each other, which is why it's fucking ludicrous we're still dating. What am I saying—the entire world is miserable. Nobody's happy. Are you happy?"

Brooke was staring off into the distance.

"Brooke—are you happy? I'm serious—tell me. Are you happy?"

She looked at Danielle, shaking her head. "I don't know. I guess. I don't really think of it in those terms, you know? Does it matter?"

"Yeah . . . I think it does. I think we should be happy. I think that's what I want. I want to be happy so much, I could explode. I'm ready to burst with something inside. I don't know—passion, a creative drive, something. I want something to happen, you know?" She sighed, playing with her straw. "My life is a textbook, and I want it to be a novel—a romance . . . Well, at least, a meaningful story."

Brooke burst out laughing. "You poor baby! Always looking for romance. Always looking out for Romeo—or, no—who's the guy in that story you love so much? Rochester. Guess Tate's no Rochester, huh?"

Danielle snorted in amusement. "Hardly."

"So, you're still going through with it tonight, aren't you?"

"I suppose."

The food came, and after a few bites, Danielle spoke again. "I've had the strangest morning."

"Yes?"

"Well, I don't know . . . My life has this *bug* theme going on in it, and I . . . I can't figure it out. I don't know what it means."

"Bug theme," Brooke echoed, shaking her head.

"Yeah . . . there was a dying fly in my bedroom and a wasp in the symphony practice room that Tate *killed*, thanks to me." She shuddered. "Do you think it's an omen?"

Brooke raised an eyebrow. "Do you know what *I think*? I think you're just totally stressed out about tonight, that's what," Brooke interrupted. "That's why I wanted to do lunch. You're a wreck. I figured I could bolster your nerve."

Both sat silently for the next couple of minutes, eating and people-watching. Danielle picked at her own food, waving away a persistent fly.

"So," Brooke started after taking a gulp of water. "How are you going to do it? Do you want to practice?"

She smirked at the suggestion. "I don't know . . . I've been writing the script in my head all day and night, but it always ends the same. Badly. He's going to shit. I just hope that's all he does."

"God, Dan, men are beginning to bore me."

"Hmmm . . ." Danielle mused. "I am more comfortable around women than men. The men I know are so—so domineering. So abusive. I keep thinking I'm going to find a nice guy that actually turns me on, but . . . And I know that sounds vulgar, but you know what I mean . . . Right now, I just want to be free of men. I'm not attracted to any of them."

"You know, I'm really surprised that you never felt anything for Tate. I have to admit, he is pretty hot."

Danielle shook her head in confused agreement. "I know—it's crazy, isn't it? I've never felt that way for him. I've never even *seen* a guy I could feel anything for that way . . . Well, you know what I mean."

"I'm surprised Tate's never sensed anything. What an idiot. He's got to know. I mean—three years, and you haven't had sex yet. Duh . . . Jesus, he's even cheated on you. I just don't get it. Frankly, I'm surprised he hasn't broken up with you first. I would have if I were he—no offense."

"I think it's an ego thing . . . He's tried hard to get me to sleep with him, and I won't. That's a lot of time to put in for nothing. I mean—I'm sure he's not used to that, since so many girls would practically *pay* to sleep with him, you know?"

"God, you're right. And isn't that just *sick*? They're all sick. And we love them anyway." She then leaned across the table and grabbed Danielle's hand. "I'm here for you, you know. I'll be at home all night, so just call me if you need to—I mean it. And I want to hear about everything tomorrow if you don't!"

A sudden breeze blew the napkins off the table, and Danielle felt as if the wind carried with it a premonition of her future. There was something about the air, the smell, an underlying vibe. She left a few dollars by her plate, disrupting the fly, and the two of them departed for their respective homes.

The salad was limp and saturated in dressing. Her tongue burned from the onslaught of vinegar and pepper. Clumps of feta cheese dotted the plate, stuck to the soggy lettuce. The tomato slice was too big to eat in one forkful, and she lacked the energy to cut it. The waiter had forgotten her bread.

His words were lost in the din of clinking dinnerware, surrounding table conversation, feet patter on the sidewalk and grumbling engines on the street. Exhaust fumes made her stomach lurch and eyes water. She pushed the lettuce and cheese around her plate with a fork, making patterns, unable to look up except to swat away a persistent fly. Tate had insisted they eat on the open terrace in spite of the heat.

When she did venture to look up, he was looking down at his own plate, stabbing at a spiral noodle, his mouth still moving at an incredible rate as he droned on about his day at football practice. If she concentrated, she could smell his cologne from across the table. She pondered her resolution, her heart already pounding as she anticipated dropping the bomb on him, somewhat angry that he hadn't already broken things off with her and that he continued to ignore her tension and unresponsiveness to his romantic advances.

The thought sent a shiver through her nervous system, and her fork slipped from her hands, falling to the floor with a dull clank. Both instinctively and simultaneously reached to grab it, and her hand brushed against the skin of his arm. His skin was a rusty brown from the summer months, and when he smiled, the white of his teeth was startling against his tanned complexion. He had deep-set, narrow eyes and rugged facial lines.

" . . . Anniversary."

Her eyes shot up from the plate. "What?" she murmured.

He grinned. "Space cadet. I said in a few months, we celebrate our three-year anniversary."

"Oh . . ."

"I'll never forget that first date," he continued, ignorant of her lack of participation in the evening's conversation. "That Halloween party. You came as a Goth punker. That was just so weird. So entirely out of character."

"And who were you again?" she murmured, thinking out loud.

He thought a moment. "A vampire," he stated matter-of-factly. "I came as Count Dracula . . . So, how do we plan to amuse ourselves this Halloween?" He asked, kicking her shin suggestively.

She forced a smile and choked down a sip of water. A fly landed on her salad plate and began scaling the cheese. "Tate . . . Have you ever thought about why we're dating?"

He swallowed his bite of food and looked at her, puzzled.

"I mean, why do you like me? Have you thought about it?"

"No, I haven't," he responded irritably. "Why are you asking? I hate it when you get this way."

"What way?"

"When you get all—all deep and philosophical about things. It's stupid, okay? I like you because you're pretty and we have all sorts of things in common, okay? So why do you like me, huh? *Or do you anymore?*"

She looked at him, startled, not expecting to be placed in such a perfect position to end everything and not ready to end it yet, either. "I like you, Tate," she said, swallowing hard. "We just—we just don't seem to connect lately—"

"And whose fault is that?" he spat.

She sat quietly as he continued to eat. After a few minutes, she pushed her plate aside and retrieved a cigarette and lighter from her purse. Brooke had given her a half-empty pack for good luck. Hands shaking slightly, she carefully lit the end and inhaled lightly.

Tate looked up. "You know I hate that. It's a nasty habit you picked up from that bitchy friend of yours. You look stupid—put it out."

She thought about a retort but instead took another smoke and looked away, staring out into the street at the passing people, wishing she were one of them.

"What do you hang out with that lesbian bitch for anyway?" he asked bitingly, after a few minutes of uncomfortable silence.

"*What?*" she burst indignantly. "Shut-up—she's not a lesbian. Trust me."

He snorted. "She looks like one."

"Fuck you," she snapped, then blew a puff of smoke his direction.

Before she could take another drag, he reached over and roughly slapped the cigarette from her hand, grabbed it and smashed it into one of the side plates.

"What the fuck—" she started.

He grabbed her arm and pulled her close to him, whispering in her ear. "Watch the language. You look like a slut with that thing, and I don't date sluts."

Her face reddened, and she felt so enraged, it took every ounce of energy not to walk away from him then and there. Instead, she pulled her arm from his grasp and looked away.

He sighed and pushed his chair away from the table.

"Look, I don't want to argue with you, okay? I hate it when we fight, and that's all we seem to do. Let's go try to salvage this evening, okay?"

She nodded absently.

It wasn't until later, with the flat of her back pressed hard against the cold, clammy leather passenger seat of his oversized car, that she knew the time had finally come to expose the illusion.

Her shirt was unbuttoned, exposing her bra. He felt heavy, and her legs and thighs ached from having him bear down upon her, his erect penis thrusting at her through his cotton shorts. She stared up at the gray ceiling of the car, holding her breath, waiting for him to grow tired. She found it hard to participate with any kind of enthusiasm. His cologne, this close, was overpowering. His heavy breathing made her tense. And his breath, with a mixed residue of dinner, alcohol and mints, made her stomach lurch. She tried to remember when it had not been this way between them but could think of nothing. When his hand groped her inner thigh, she grabbed it instinctively, gasping sharply.

He tried again.

She tried to bodily push him away.

He groaned, annoyed. After a moment, he sat up.

"What is your problem?" he asked wearily.

She started buttoning her blouse, her hands shaking slightly. "I think we need to talk—"

"About what?" he asked, turning to her sharply. "We've been dating for almost three years—what do we have left to talk about? You're being totally priggish about this entire matter, and it's just stupid—I don't get it," he said heatedly, running his fingers nervously through his hair. "I mean—what are you afraid of? What are you waiting for? Marriage? Your attitude towards sex is totally—totally unsophisticated—"

She sat in silence for a moment, arms crossed, before crawling into the front seat. Sighing irritably, he awkwardly maneuvered after her before continuing to rant.

"I mean, I have been totally patient and understanding with you. For two years, I have been the perfect gentleman—the perfect date," he continued, cutting the air with his hand. "You know, most guys in my position wouldn't be so patient—they would have taken off a long time ago—"

"Then why don't you?" she interrupted hotly, staring through the windshield, wanting to be outside.

"What? Why don't I what?"

"Why don't you *take off*."

"Excuse me—excuse me? Is that—do I hear you right? Are you telling me to go?" he asked loudly.

His voice seemed to reverberate against the chrome, glass and metal of the inner car. She desperately needed air and wanted to talk outside.

"Yes," she said finally.

"Well that's just great," he replied bitterly, shaking his head. "That's just fucking great—you want me to go. You want to break up—may I ask why? Huh? Why—now—you suddenly want to break up? Did I do something?"

She felt him staring her down and turned away after a moment, looking at her lap, only hearing the chirping of evening crickets and his heavy breathing.

"Goddammit—what is it?" he yelled, his hand hitting the dashboard. "Is it another guy?" he asked arrogantly.

She said nothing, a sick feeling germinating in the pit of her stomach. She felt a trickle of sweat break out on her neck.

"Is it Brooke—did she put this stupid idea into your head? I know she hates me—"

At this, she spun around and faced his glare. "No—it's not another guy or Brooke—it's not even *me*! It's *you*—I *hate* you—you repulse me, and you don't even like me. You have no respect for me—telling me I'm unsophisticated just because I'm not stupid enough to fall for your advances and have sex with you. Did it ever occur to you that maybe I'm not attracted to you in that way? *Did it*? That maybe I've just been dating you out of convenience—and that, that maybe you're just still dating me because you think I owe you something. Well, I don't owe you *anything*."

For a full five seconds, the car fell completely silent. She heard no breathing, no movement. The tension, the heat, the energy were momentarily suspended so that she could almost breathe again.

She didn't know what hit her.

The next moment, her head knocked against the dash, and a searing pain shot through her lower cheek and mouth. Before she could even reach up to feel the wetness forming around her jowl, another pain ripped through her upper left cheek. Her hands instinctively groped the door handle and lock, pulling and pushing for freedom—

"You bitch—you fucking self-righteous bitch—"

Once out, she stumbled towards the concrete path leading from the parking lot into a dark mass of trees. Just beyond was a main street with lights and houses. As she ran, she heard him yelling then laughing.

"You really think that you're *free*? Have I got news for you—"

That night, as she pulled her blinds down to get ready for bed, a small black object plummeted to the floor from the windowsill. She looked down and noticed it was a dead fly.

She shuddered and hours later fell into a restless sleep.

CHAPTER TWO

Newspaper crumpled under his desk chair, and the air was heavy with the smell of turpentine. Simon and Garfunkel played on the stereo. His arms and shoulders ached from working near the ceiling. They would feel better as he made his way down the wall.

Painting temporarily took his mind off a growing concern for his own mental health. He had begun football practice this week but was put on junior varsity and told he would be benched most of the season due to his injuries, spending most of practice tossing the ball back and forth with the least talented on the team. *Charity case*, he had heard one of the coaches say, and he winced at the thought, having been first string quarter back and captain of the varsity team in Montana.

Still, it offered some semblance of normalcy. School started next week, and things were sure to improve, he told himself. The dreams would end, the past would be buried forever and the nausea would go away. He would start going out to parties and possibly dating. And when he started dating, his growing sexual problem would correct itself.

His hand started to shake as he thought about it. The idea of going to his parents was mortifying. He had never had a problem before. This was bound to go away. It was a bad dream.

The door to his room flew open with a bang, catching him off-guard. His heart jumped. His foot slipped from the chair. He grabbed the wall to stop from falling, and his hand smeared the fresh black line. He swore under his breath.

"So, whatch'ya doin?"

He slowly turned around. His sister stood at the door to his room, her arms full of packages from shopping, cracking her gum in a series of three snaps. He winced.

It took her a moment to notice, but she soon dropped the packages at the threshold and made her way towards the center of his bedroom. "Geez . . . Look at these walls . . . They—they look like a prison! God—do mom and dad know about this? Did you *ask* them first?"

He said nothing, wiping his blackened hand on an old T-shirt.

"I know you've been depressed, but—but this—this is pretty intense. I mean, god—bricks? Are you going to paint bricks on all four walls?"

He stood still on the chair, clenching the paint brush and trying to control an incredible urge to hurl it at her and watch her squeal like a pig, black paint splattering her make-up perfect pasty white face, marring her blond hair.

"Well, are you just going to stand there and stare at me all day or what? Geez. I just came in to give you some things we bought you. God, you can be such a jerk," she sputtered, shaking her head and walking back to the door to pick up the packages.

"Yes," he said finally.

She turned around, arms full again. "Yes what?"

"Yes," he said sharply. "I'm going to paint bricks on all four walls."

She shrugged, walking over to his bed and dumping the bags on top of it. "Have it your way . . . I'll have you know, it was a real bitch shopping for you, but I don't suppose we'll be receiving any thanks."

He crossed his arms, letting the brush fall to the papers below, splattering the print. "Thank you," he said between his teeth.

"God—you are such a jerk! You know, you're not the only one who's been affected by this move. I'm not exactly thrilled either, but at least I'm trying to deal with it—not lock myself in a room and brick myself up—god . . . I mean, I did have friends I left behind. I *was* the most popular girl at school, and *had* a chance at being Homecoming Queen this year, not that

that would seem important to *you*. And, I did have a boyfriend I left behind that I dated for three years—*three* years—"

Her voice became shrill, and he feared tears would soon follow. Shaking his head, he jumped down from the chair. It was obvious she had no intention of leaving him alone, and he might as well be comfortable through the ordeal, he thought to himself, plunking onto the floor, his back against the dresser.

" . . . We even talked about going to college and getting married. And guess what? Not that you give a care about anyone else, but for your information, he's already dating somebody else—some stupid slut who waitresses at *the diner*. Two weeks out of sight, trying to pick up the pieces of my broken life, and he's just rolling right along . . . Men are such jerks," she said, putting her head in her hands and starting to bawl.

Rolling his eyes, he reached over, grabbed a box of Kleenex and threw it at her. It bounced off her shoulder and made her wail louder.

"Oh, geez—what am I talking to you for? What do you care?" she cried, starting to walk out of the room and kicking his possessions in the process. "You've never dated anyone *worthwhile* in your whole life, and you don't care about anyone but yourself!" She stood glaring at him, shaking with anger. "You're a jerk, Alex Fahlstrom, and you know, these stupid brick walls just fit you perfectly. You have to be one of the most insensitive people I have ever met! Cold as stone—as bricks!" She waved her hands dramatically.

He picked up an issue of *Rolling Stone* lying on the floor and began to flip casually through the pages. The worst was over.

"In fact, you men are all alike! You probably see nothing wrong with breaking up after three years and dating someone else twenty-four hours later—and you know what? I feel sorry for anyone who ever dates you—or any male!"

She slammed the door behind her, a whirlwind of female rage that blew in, disturbing his tranquility for but a few tense moments, then blew on. The walls and curtains shuddered in the aftermath. He breathed a sigh of relief. Once again he had survived the elements. And this was a mild clash, a mere gale to the usual hurricanes. As was typical, she wound up hurling insults at him without his saying hardly a word.

He started to stand up when a searing pain shot through his stomach, knocking him back to the ground. He gasped, trying to drag himself to the bed. This time it was her fault. Maybe it was all her fault. She represented everything he hated, the worst in women and the worst in society.

Pig.

The image suddenly appeared in his mind. She reminded him of a pig with that pink rouged skin and those black beady eyes. She even squealed like a pig when she laughed and wailed like a pig when she cried. People thought she was so cute. And she had always been very popular, a regular *Susie Cheerleader* complete with a head full of air.

He thought about her old boyfriend. He thought about any guy who would date his sister or someone like her and what they would do on a date. Intelligent conversation would be out of the picture, and he doubted she would put out much. He had visions of guys making out with her and coming up for air with make-up smeared faces. The thought made his stomach lurch. He reached for the empty utility pail. Grabbing it, he dragged himself and the bucket to bed.

After sweeping away the packages, he laid down on the pillows, partly elated. The more he thought of his sister, the sicker he felt. She had to be a reason behind all this anguish.

But the echoes of her crass comments reverberated against his mental walls, taking his thoughts a different direction. *You've never dated anyone worthwhile in your whole life.*

He had dated girls, but they never held his interest for very long. A few had been blonds, now that he thought about it. But he didn't like blonds. He didn't trust them.

And he had cared for someone last year. He had met her while doing summer work on the cattle ranch, and they were friends before dating seriously. Her name was Jennifer, and she had long curly brown hair, freckles and pale blue eyes.

An image of her smiling coyly at him flashed before his eyes. And then she was gone.

He wondered why he hadn't thought about her much over the past weeks and realized that while he thought of her now, tears were streaming down his face. It still hurt to think about it, any of it. He tried to push the thoughts out of his mind, but the harder he tried, the stronger they flooded in, drowning him.

A wave of nausea swept through his system as the pictures swept through his mind. Instinctively, he bent over the pail and vomited. He then lay back on his bed exhausted, depressed and scared. Something was wrong, and before he could take this thought further, he slammed a mental door on the onslaught of memories and blacked out.

When he came to, his mother was bent over him, pressing a damp cloth to his forehead. His sister was in the background, crying and apologizing, and his dad stood at the threshold of his room.

Everyone seemed to breathe a sigh of relief when he opened his eyes and attempted to sit up. Trisha launched into a stream of babble—

"I'm so sorry—it's all my fault—I can't believe what I said—he's okay, right? I can't believe I was so insensitive—I was just so angry—I'm sorry—"

"Sorry for what?" he mumbled, wishing they all would leave. He would be fine, he said. It was just the paint smell combined with lack of good food.

But over dinner that evening, his parents again brought up the fact that he didn't seem well, and if the stomach trouble did not stop, he would be seeing a doctor. They then insisted he take a walk with them around the neighborhood and to a nearby park.

On the way to the park, his dad pointed out trees and discussed work. His mom asked him about the clothes she bought and if he felt ready for school next week. Both asked questions about football practice.

They eventually turned a corner and a block further came to a few park benches. His parents sat down in one near an occupied tennis court. He stood for a minute, taking in the surroundings.

"Is this *it*?" he asked finally.

"What?" his mother responded.

"The park—is *this* the park?"

She and his dad looked around uncomfortably, unsure how to answer. "Well, yes it is," they said, shrugging.

He put his head in his hand. The *park* was located on a corner lot facing a busy thoroughfare and crammed between two residential streets. A large tennis court left but a small space for a few scattered trees and a cluttered playground. All this sat in the shadow of the city's enormous sky blue water tower. He thought of *Planet of the Apes* and collapsed on the bench beside his parents, depressed.

His parents left him to sit in silence a few minutes before tentatively voicing their concerns.

"You know, Alex," his mother started, clearing her throat. "We're a bit concerned about your attitude—or, rather, *reaction* to the move . . . I know it's not been easy for you. It's not been easy on any of us, but we did feel it was for the best. You do know why, don't you?"

"Why what?" he asked absently, staring at a group of little boys who were chasing a lone boy with blond curly hair. The lone boy stopped and began hurling wood chips at his pursuers.

"Why we moved."

"Yeah—yeah sure. I know why. You've told me all of this."

"What have we told you, Alex?" his dad asked quietly.

He answered slowly, becoming lost in the playground drama. "Uh—job . . . More money and opportunity."

"Is that all?" his mother asked delicately.

"Yeah—that's what you've told me." He turned to them for a moment then quickly shifted his eyes back to the children. His parents were looking at him as if they knew something he didn't. He didn't want to know.

His mother cleared her throat uneasily. "We thought the change of scenery best for you after what happened this winter. We were hoping it could be a new start for all of us."

"What happened this winter . . ." he echoed questioningly.

"Alex," his dad started, "you went through quite an ordeal, and I'm not sure that we've really dealt with it effectively . . . I'm not even sure this move was the right thing to do. And the fact that you haven't talked about the move or the incident or anything since you were released from the hospital disturbs me. The counselors said give it time, but . . . We need to talk this out and work through this as a family."

The playground chase had turned into a wood chip war, and as he watched, the scene seemed to freeze for a split second, as if his mind had captured it as a still-life. And when it moved again, it was in slow motion. "I don't know . . ." he whispered hoarsely.

"You don't know what?" his father replied.

"What happened . . . I don't know what happened—I don't remember."

"What do you mean you don't remember?" his mother burst shrilly. "How could you not remember—you—you were shot three times. You—you almost died—"

At that moment, he saw him—across the park—standing still for the moment. His dad calmed his mother down and continued to talk, but he could no longer focus on the conversation. The words were soon drowned out by another voice—a loud, angry voice—

You don't belong here. Wake up.

And then, it charged at him. The figure in the same dirty jeans and plaid work shirt. The masked face—the faceless face—coming at him with a rifle, charging through the group of children as if they weren't even there.

He sat paralyzed for a moment, praying his parents would see it and say something to make it go away. But his mind told him they wouldn't see it, that nobody could see it but he, and he couldn't allow anything to happen in front of them.

He stood up quickly. "I have to go—I just remembered, I need to go do something," he said, breathless, before tearing out of the park, around the corner and down his own street.

As he ran, he tried to look around but was terrified he would actually see the man following him. At one point, with his house just up ahead, he did slow down and turn fully to look behind him. The figure was there, gun in hand, lifting the barrel up to shoot. He raced across his front yard, almost tripping over a tree root. Reaching his front door, he turned the knob and, realizing it was locked, began to pound furiously, looking anxiously behind. The man was charging through his yard.

"Trish—Trisha—open up, goddammit—open up—" he yelled, ringing the doorbell.

The man stopped a few feet behind him and aimed the barrel.

He heard the trigger click. The door opened, and he fell inside, slamming it to the deafening explosion. He collapsed against the closed door, sweat pouring down his face, his entire body shaking in fear and exhaustion.

Trisha stood above him, soda in hand, looking dumbfounded.

Alex walked to school lost in thought and trying to calm his nerves. The morning had been a nightmare. Thank god they had two bathrooms in the new house, he thought to himself, as Trisha had locked herself in one of them, having a tantrum over her hair and a zit. And then she had a tantrum over his hair. He had put it into a thick braid, a style he wore often back home.

"Your new home is here," she screamed, "and people are going to laugh at you. They'll think you're a fag. And why are you wearing that stupid shirt and those stupid shoes—"

He had walked out the door before she could bitch any further, but the whole scene had thrown his mind in a whirl. He looked down at his shoes as he walked. They were his favorite pair, these hardy working shoes, handmade by a local rancher. He was an old guy, Native American, and Alex used to help around his cattle ranch during the summer. The shoes were made from one of his favorite old steers that had passed away. The man had made himself a pair, too. He had loved that steer like a pet and wanted to preserve a piece of him.

And his shirt was from Mexico, hand-woven and bone-colored with brightly hued stripes. A friend had brought it back for him from a family vacation. The other day he had seen a guy at the mall wearing a similar shirt. There was nothing wrong with the shirt. His sister had to be nuts.

The school grounds loomed ahead. Though he was a good half-hour early, the parking lots were lined with cars and the grounds lined with students. Alex had never seen so many students in one place and all clustered in groups. Nobody even noticed him.

Outside, the school hadn't looked very imposing. Once inside, however, he found his heart racing. Confronting him were mobs of people and a maze of hallways. He stood still for a minute, trying to calm himself and remember the paths he had attempted to learn during Orientation Day.

Orientation Day had been at its best cheesy and at its worst depressing. Because they had arrived so late in the summer, he and his mom had spent most of the morning with a counselor putting together a class schedule. They had gotten down to electives, and Alex was adamant about a photography class of some kind.

"Photography's full. You'll have to catch it next semester," the counselor, a middle-aged man with brown plastic-rimmed glasses, said wearily. "Why don't you try art, or even art history."

"But I hate art," he said, feeling a sudden urge to run out of the room. It was a small office with one heavily blinded window and one sickly-looking, potted dieffenbachia. The walls seemed to be closing in on him.

His mother suggested newspaper or yearbook, but the counselor only scanned Alex's paperwork, wincing, shaking his head. He then reminded them that they were keeping his eleven-thirty appointment waiting. Alex reluctantly signed up for Art Foundations. He and his mother were then forced to spend an hour eating a bland lunch in the cafeteria while several administrators boasted about what a great school Shawnee Mission East was. They had spent the rest of the afternoon trying to convince the assistant football coach to give him a chance on the junior varsity team, even though Alex was good enough to play varsity back home. But he had missed most of the summer practice, and his fellow teammates had taken little notice of him the past two weeks. Six weeks in Kansas, and he remained friendless. All of these thoughts and fears replayed in his mind as he walked through the school halls that morning.

As he sat through his morning classes, he found himself studying the students around him, searching for an interesting face, a potential friend.

But most of the students just talked around him or stared straight ahead. If they did look at him, they looked through him with half-closed eyes and expressions of boredom. After scanning the room uncomfortably, he resumed clock-watching. The hands moved with painful slowness.

Finally, in biology, something happened. A guy walked through the door and quickly caught his attention. He was slim and of medium height, with long, dark hair that hung down his shoulders in loose curls. His rust-toned features were sharp, and his eyes small, beady and black. Alex couldn't tell what nationality he was, but he looked as if he had just stepped out of an Italian Renaissance painting. All that was missing was the red velvet beret.

He noticed Alex watching him and nodded a polite hello before making his way towards the back of the class. A few of his friends joined him shortly afterwards. They all wore ripped jeans and oversized concert shirts. One wore combat boots and had a red bandanna on his head, Axl Rose style.

Once or twice in class, he turned around to catch a glimpse of the guy. Each time, the guy looked straight at him—no, straight into him, his black eyes piercing like a hawk's. After class, Alex hoped the guy would say something to him, invite him to lunch or just introduce himself. He seemed like someone Alex would like. But instead, the guy and his friends just sauntered down the hall ignoring him.

Right before lunch, in English, someone actually spoke to him before class and halfway during. In fact, the guy never shut up, and Alex feared an embarrassing reprimand from the teacher. His name was Carl, and he was a large guy with a crew cut. He played on varsity football and insisted Alex was the new player on the team, which Alex denied, embarrassed to say he was on junior varsity. He barely got out where he was from and a few of his hobbies when the guy would start in, making fun of the instructor, talking to others around him, talking to Alex.

Lunch provided Alex an opportunity to get to his locker and collect his wits. He dreaded eating in the cafeteria and found himself scoping the halls and lunchroom for the guy in his biology class. Then again, he thought to himself, the guy probably didn't eat in the cafeteria. He probably sneaked out like most of the cool people with any sense. God knows, he would escape if he had a car. He'd be outside, off the school grounds, eating in some suburban park.

Excuse me, someone said, roughly pushing past him and jerking him back to reality.

He was standing in line in a crowded, noisy cafeteria. Bodies were pushed up against one another. There was no visible place to sit. He'd probably end up eating in the hall. When he finally reached the food counter, nothing looked or smelled appealing. He grabbed a plate of fries and an apple and got a soda from the machine. He then found himself in the middle of a mob with a tray of food and still no place to sit. He made his way towards the exit.

"Hey, you—"

He turned and saw the guy from his English class waving at him, motioning for him to join his group. He made his way towards their table. The guy's name was Carl something, that he remembered.

"Hey—what's your name again?" the Carl guy greeted him.

"Alex."

"Yeah—Alex, eh. Guys—this is Alex. He's from up North. Wyoming or something—"

"Montana."

"Yeah—Montana. Great skiing, I bet. Sit down and join us, Alex. What a lunch, eh—fries and an apple. I'm on my second burger. So—where'd you get that shirt? You been to Padre Island? I got me one of those shirts in Padre. Never wear it, but it was cheap. Man—you should see the chicks in Padre. Gorgeous, absolutely gorgeous. And willing to fuck? You bet they were willing to fuck. As the saying goes, a lay a day keeps the blue balls away."

"Actually, this is from Mexico—"

But the guy had jumped into a conversation his friends were carrying, something about the football season. They were all huge, had short hair and wore athletic garb with some rendition of the *East* lancer mascot. Carl was his name, Carl something or other. He couldn't remember. The guy was definitely a talker.

The conversation eventually changed from football practice to local parties and girls, girls obviously being Carl's favorite subject. Alex only half-listened.

Carl grabbed his arm. "Everybody—everybody—this guy plays guitar. And you know he's good! Like, we're going to get together and form a rock band. We got our guitarist," he said, pulling up Alex's arm. "And we got our bassist here, Ron," he said, grabbing the arm of the guy sitting next to him. "And with me on drums, we're going to kick some ass!"

They laughed and pounded on the table.

"Yeah, Weiss—you've only been getting that band of yours together for two years now," somebody said.

Carl Weiss. That was his name.

"Well, we're going to do it, and you just watch us! Aren't we, old buddy?" He punched Alex in the arm. "Aren't we, Ron?" He said, slapping the back of the guy sitting next to him.

"Sounds great," Alex choked. He then wondered why he had even mentioned to the guy that he played guitar, for it was more of a personal hobby. He had studied all styles of acoustic since grade shcool. At some point, his parents bought him an electric. Though he enjoyed listening to rock music, it was not a style he played as often.

"And gentleman—gentleman—doesn't this man look like he belongs on our glorious football team?"

He didn't realize Carl was still making a spectacle of him.

"You certainly played football back in Wyoming, now—right? Varsity even? Eh—right? Right?"

Alex winced, rubbing his forehead. Before he could answer, the warning bell rang, and students began herding themselves towards the door. Alex sat still, waiting for the crowd to pass.

"Hey," Carl called to him. "I'll catch you later. We need to set up a time for band practice."

By the last class, Art Foundations, Alex was exhausted. He found a table in the back of the room and plunked himself down in the chair. He wanted to be in the back in case he fell asleep.

To his surprise, the strange guy from biology came striding into the room. He scanned the area and, seeing Alex, headed towards him.

"Is this seat taken?" he asked Alex.

Alex shook his head.

The guy threw himself into the chair next to Alex's and set his feet up on the table.

"You're in my biology class," the guy said, taking a wad of gum out of his mouth and sticking it under the table's edge.

Alex just watched him quietly.

The guy eyed him curiously. "Are you an exchange student or something?"

"No," Alex answered.

"Well, what's your name then?"

"Alex. Alex Fahlstrom."

"Dennis. Dennis Sumners." He stuck out his hand for Alex to shake.

Alex just stared at it.

"*Where* are you from?" Dennis asked him, half exasperated and pulling his hand back.

"Montana—it's up north," he added quickly.

"No shit . . ." Dennis took his feet off the table and twiddled his thumbs impatiently. "So—you like art?"

"I hate art."

"So what are you doin' in art class, then? This *is* an art class, you know—"

"No shit."

Dennis drew back, surprised. He then gave Alex a knowing smile and pointed a finger at him. "You're a strange one—but I like you, I do like you . . . So really, why are you in here?"

Alex sighed. "I can't get into photography class. It's full."

Dennis slammed his hand down on the table, drawing a number of glances from around the room. "Bullshit! That's what this school is—bullshit. A regular commie institution. A guy wants photography—he should have photography. I mean—what are we paying taxes for? Where does the money go? Is this not the wealthiest school district in the state? Do we not have one chance to get a good education before being pushed out into the ugly, real world? Huh? You want photography? I can get you photography. I got special connections—"

Alex raised an eyebrow skeptically.

"Well—it's not photography *exactly*—but it's close. I know someone on the newspaper staff. Actually, she's an *editor*."

"Newspaper . . ." Alex echoed dully, remembering the counselor's objectionable expressions.

"Well, now—let's not be picky. I mean, I don't even know you, and I'm offering you this favor, here . . . You take pictures for Newspaper, so photography's *involved*—"

Alex sighed. "I don't think you can do anything."

"Look—you just meet me at the main office Wednesday after school. I'll handle everything. I'll get you on the paper and out of this class. Deal?"

"In exchange for what?" Alex asked warily.

The guy laughed. "Oh, I'll think of something."

The teacher began passing out supply lists. After a minute, the guy turned to him.

"So—what's with the braid? You part Indian or something?" He then faced forward, snickering.

Alex smiled to himself and then strained to look out the window. He thought he saw mountains, but it was just a line of clouds far off in the horizon.

∞

"He hit me."

"He *what?*"

"He *hit* me . . . In the face. I have a bruise—I have two bruises," Danielle said matter-of-factly, lying face up on her bed, the phone cord stretched to its limit, staring at the shadows on the ceiling.

"He hit you *twice?*"

"Well, he hit me once, hard, and my head fell against the dashboard, and I hit my mouth—well, the area by my mouth. And then he slapped me again on the cheek."

"You came home beaten and bloody and you didn't *call me?* How could you! I just can't believe it . . . And Tate of all people. I just can't—I just can't believe it—"

"Well—I thought about calling you, but . . . Well, I was just kind of freaked out and wanted to be alone and go to sleep, you know?"

"Oh my god—OH MY GOD—I just can't believe it . . . Jesus—did he say anything? I mean—did he even apologize?"

Her fat, gray cat jumped onto the bed and started rubbing against her. The sheets were smooth and cool against her skin, and she found herself wanting to be enveloped in them indefinitely. The air conditioner whirred gently through the vent above her, and its steady hum comforted her. As long as she was here, safe within these walls, she felt nothing bad could happen. The cat curled up within the curve of her shoulder.

"No," Danielle said absently, almost forgetting that she was on the phone. "He didn't. I left before he could."

"Would he have?" Brooke persisted.

"I don't know . . ." she sighed, quickly tiring of the conversation. She knew she had to tell Brooke what happened, but once out, she wanted to forget it, shove it into a black abyss in the back of her consciousness with all the other unpleasant memories she had ever experienced. Life would go on. And on. And on . . .

"Dan—I'm so sorry. I wish—I just wish I could say something to make you feel better, but I can't. It was a rotten thing—and he's a rotten person . . . I'll never speak to him again. I'll never look at him—"

Danielle lay quietly for a moment, enjoying the cat's rhythmic purring against her neck. "Actually," she mused, "it was almost *liberating.*" She paused. "Really, Brooke—it *was* my fault. I have to admit, I sort of freaked out on him, and . . . Well, I started yelling at him and said hurtful things. He probably just got so angry and hurt he couldn't control himself. We can't totally blame him. I was part of the cause."

"Bullshit. I still think the guy's a creep, and it was a creepy, bastardly thing to do—"

"At least I'm free, Brooke. That's all I care about."

"Yeah," Brooke sighed sadly. "You're free—but are you happy?"

Danielle froze a moment, her mind whirling. Happy? Happiness continued to elude her. Freedom from Tate had not brought any additional happiness. "No," she choked. "I'm not happy."

"Shit . . ."

"But," Danielle added, trying to change the tone of the conversation, "It *is* the first big step to cleaning out my life. Next, it's the symphony, which I'm through with after Christmas. Then all those stupid high society clubs my father made me join. And then . . ." She mused. "I don't know. Maybe if I clean hard enough, I'll find happiness, you know? Maybe once everything is gone, I'll find something."

"Or nothing. Maybe you'll realize that there's really nothing there."

"Yeah . . . Maybe. Sounds a bit scary."

"Well, I don't have as much *cleaning* to do as you. But I do wish you'd clean out your damn ugly closet. You *promised* me I could help you achieve a new look."

They made plans to go shopping and to a movie one last time before school started, and Danielle got off the phone feeling horribly depressed for some unknown reason.

She lay in bed for another fifteen minutes, thinking about the past and wondering about the new school year. Her cat had fallen asleep, and she felt guilty waking him up. But she soon grew hungry and bored and afraid that she would never want to get up to face the world and quickly sprang from the bed, rudely waking the cat in the process.

He padded after her as she wandered into the bathroom to inspect her wounds. She could put off explanations to her parents until tonight, as they were at social events all morning and afternoon. Really, she thought, if she could avoid seeing anyone until tomorrow, the minor swelling would go down, and she could hide the discoloring with foundation. Having solved the issue, she headed downstairs and into the kitchen for some lunch.

She was in the process of making a salad when the front door slammed and footsteps loudly thudded across the marble and wood floors, through the hallway and living room and towards the kitchen. Her brother Dennis was home, no doubt from being out all night, she mused. Then she frowned upon realizing her car was not in the driveway last night when she got home. She continued to chop tomatoes, ignoring him.

Something metal loudly hit the counter and slid, stopping near the cutting board. She looked over and noticed it was her keys.

"Thanks for the car," a gruff voice sounded.

"I never said you could borrow it," she said hotly, feeling her face turn red in indignation.

"I never ask," he said on his way to the refrigerator. "And I never will."

He was her twin, though she strained to find any resemblance between the two of them, physical or mental. They both had dark-toned skin and almost black hair, but hers was straight, and his hung in loose curls. She had large eyes while his were small and beady. Her nose was small and nondescript while his was shaped like a Roman statue. She worked hard and was successful in school, popular and content with her social status. He refused to work at all, did poorly in school, hung out with an irreputable crowd and constantly criticized the family's wealth, neighborhood and home. He especially criticized her.

"Make me one, will you?" he asked offhandedly, grabbing a soda out of the refrigerator and opening the snack cupboard.

"Make your own—" she snapped, turning to him in anger and immediately regretting the action.

He stepped back. "Well, well, well—what have we here?" He reached out to touch her face.

She slapped his hand away.

"Vicious . . . So Biff and Jane aren't afraid to get their hands dirty. What'd you do, accidentally chip the paint off his car?" He snickered.

She felt the rage building up inside her and resumed her salad-making. She knew she should remain silent, let him mock and snarl and then, hopefully, leave her alone. She knew if she entered into any discussion with him, he would turn her own words against her, leaving her trampled and humiliated and somehow ashamed of whom she was. But the urge to counter—to explain—to dismiss—was too great.

"I broke up with him," she said abruptly, chopping with more vehemence.

Setting down his drink and snacks, he leaned against the counter, his arms crossed. An odor of smoke, alcohol and sweat from the evening's activities still lingered within the fibers of his clothes and assaulted her nose. "Well isn't this interesting . . . You expect me to believe that you broke up with him—and he was so impassioned over the impending loss of your presence that he *struck* you—and risked breaking a nail in the process?"

She breathed deeply, "He slammed on the brakes suddenly, and I flew forward—"

"—And you flew forward my ass. Where do you get your excuses—*90210*? Jesus, you are pathetic. No—you *are 90210*. *Mission Hills – 66208*, the new saga. The pathetic story of a group of privileged teenagers whose lives are so empty and mundane they have to stage love spats to give themselves a sense of purpose."

She said nothing, silenced by his cutting sarcasm. He hated her, and he made no pretenses about hating her. He tormented her cat, trashed her car and would take things from her room and never return them. He would swear at her and criticize every aspect of her being, from her hair to her voice to the clothes she wore. Because Brooke was her best friend, he was even cruel to Brooke, calling her a bitch to her face, among other things. The only thing he did not and could not criticize was her violin playing.

The only reason she didn't have a breakdown was because she was the favored child. Because she worked hard and did everything her parents asked, she got a car, a trip to Europe and a larger allowance.

He continued his assault. "And what did mom and dad say? I can't imagine . . . *Oh, you children are so nuts about each other – just be sure to make up before BOTAR – I certainly hope that heals by the Cotillion. Let's be sure to schedule you with Charles for a make-over.* Or did you tell them you flew forward and hit the dash? After all, they wouldn't believe the *truth*—he is the *son* of Dad's best friend and business buddy." He dangled a potato chip in front of the cat.

She silently scraped the ingredients off the cutting board and into a bowl.

"Where are mom and dad, anyway?"

"Church—then some event," she said quietly, getting a glass of water and slice of bread to complete the meal.

He snorted. "Why am I not *surprised*. Only in *Mission Hills 66208* can a sixteen-year old spend an entire night in drunken, drug-filled revelry—waltz in at one o'clock the following afternoon—and receive no reprimand. No attention—no thought whatsoever. I could be lying dead somewhere, but that would never be discovered until after church and brunch at the club. Heaven forbid I interrupt the Sumners' social schedule."

She left the kitchen before hearing the end of it and locked herself in her bedroom for the remainder of the day and evening.

It wasn't until the next morning when she headed off for practice that she noticed the surprise her brother had left her. Someone had puked all over the back seat of her car, and he hadn't bothered to clean it up.

Danielle greeted the first day of the fall semester like any other day. She crawled out of bed, showered and threw on the regulation plaid skirt, a short-sleeved white blouse, white socks and penny loafers. She picked up Brooke at seven, and they both discussed the inevitable new semester rituals. Nothing would really be taught today because everyone would be too busy catching up with each other, which was really the only thing they dreaded. Neither had discussed Danielle's break-up with anyone, and both knew that at some point the truth would come out, and the reaction would be overwhelming. The two had been a popular item, an institution among couples.

As they made their way down the halls, they had to stop every few seconds to hug someone they hadn't seen since the end of last semester or just chat with those with whom they had kept in contact. Danielle had managed to get three classes with Brooke, one in the morning and two in the afternoon. They parted after first hour, and she did not see Brooke again until lunch.

Brooke was waiting by her locker, looking irritated.

"What's wrong? Are you sick—" Danielle started.

Brooke grabbed her arm, pulled her close and began whispering. "You haven't heard *anything*, have you?"

"Heard *what*?"

"Any odd gossip—has everything been okay? You know, normal?"

Danielle stared at her puzzled. "Yes, it's been great. Everyone seems very happy. No one's told me anything—"

"No one's acted funny?"

Danielle pondered this. She had sensed from a few closer friends that they knew something about her and Tate but wanted her to speak first. People probed, but then everyone was probing. She shook her head. "Not really. I mean—some people obviously know, and they're just being *polite*. It'll be blown open today or tomorrow during lunch. It's okay—I'm prepared."

Brooke just shook her head, rolling her eyes. "Dan—we need to talk. Alone. I want to be the first to tell you. Let's eat in the car."

"Tell me what?" Danielle asked, growing concerned.

But Brooke would not say a word until they were seated in Danielle's car in the parking lot, windows rolled down due to the lingering odor from her brother's disaster.

Before starting, Brooke took out a cigarette and lit up. "Did you talk to Tate about me?"

"What do you mean?"

"Well, it appears Tate's started a rumor with everyone saying that the reason you broke up with him was because you really don't care for men." She took a smoke and exhaled deeply. "In fact—you and I are more than we appear to be." She looked at Danielle tensely.

"I don't—I don't understand—"

"What did you tell him?"

"I didn't tell him anything—"

"Did you tell him you were *into* me?"

Danielle sat there a moment, stunned, letting the full reality of the situation sink in for a moment. "That prick . . ." she breathed.

"Did you?" Brooke pressed.

"No—No," Danielle said, shaking her head. "He—he was complaining about you again. He called you a lesbian, and I—I defended you. I told him to fuck off."

Brooke rolled her eyes, took another deep smoke and looked out the car window. "I don't know what to say. I'm—I'm flattered." She looked at Danielle oddly.

Then, the two simultaneously burst out laughing.

"So, you're not mad at me—"

"Dan—" Brooke burst. Then she laid her cigarette in the tray and leaned over to give Danielle a hug.

"He's such a dick . . . Do you think people believe it?"

"Oh, they'll want to—you know that. This'll be the hot news for weeks," Brooke said, picking up her cigarette and taking a drag.

"Yes. You're right about that . . . unfortunately. Well, they can all just go to hell. Everyone can go to hell."

Suddenly, people seemed a burden, and the whole social prospect—the dances, the organizational activities, the social events that came with the school year—seemed overwhelming. She longed to run and hide somewhere, to escape the scene and her role in it. In some ways her brother was right: her life was a television episode with a lame plot and no theme.

Brooke continued to smoke in silence for a few minutes. "Well, Dan, you've certainly cleaned out our lives of dates for the next few months." She eyed her friend, and the two burst out laughing again.

Danielle went to bed that night exhausted and depressed. For what seemed like an hour, she lay staring at the pattern of light on the ceiling from the street and house lights and contemplating the endless noise. Though the windows were closed tight, she could hear cars driving by every couple of minutes. Sirens could be heard in the distance. Even cricket songs seeped into the room. Through the vents, she could hear mumblings of music from Dennis's room.

She pulled the sheets over her head and tried to count sheep. This activity often worked. She would envision live sheep, the kind she saw in England on her two-week trip last summer. They were large sheep with black faces and yellow eyes that held expressions of almost vindictive amusement. These would jump over a wooden fence repeatedly until she lost count and her thoughts drifted to new places and dimensions.

Her mind took her back to De Sion, through the school halls. She was greeting everyone all over again, hearing the gossip all over again. Then she was in the car with Brooke. Then she was in the car with Tate. He was hovering on top of her, looking sick to his stomach, and she kept screaming at him to get off and let her out. Outside, her brother stood, laughing. She ran through woods that turned into a city she had never seen before. The trees melted into bushes with bright red, orange and magenta flowers on them. The buildings were white-washed stucco, reminiscent of The Plaza. Suddenly, she came upon the symphony. They were all seated in a terrace surrounded by the flowering bushes. They were yelling, telling her she was late and the audience was waiting. She panicked as she realized she did not have her performance dress on. She was in jeans. But someone shoved a violin in her hand and told her to start playing.

She then realized she had no sheet music. But the symphony had started, and she improvised. Dvorak—*Symphony Number 9*. She kept looking for the audience, but there was no audience, just a boy running down an alley, away from her.

The symphony melted away into blackness. She was still on the terrace, but she was not alone. Someone was with her, and she was afraid. It was a male presence, but she did not know who it was. He was talking to her through the darkness, angry. She sprang up to run away but was grabbed and hurled to the rough pavement.

She could feel his breath against her cheek, his face so near her own. A clammy, sweaty hand touched her breast and moved slowly up her neck and to her face, then began to caress it. She wanted to scream for help, but nothing would come out. She couldn't talk. She could hardly breathe. The presence took her own hand and made her caress his cheek.

All she remembered next was struggling—ultimately being pinned down until the full realization hit her—she was not human. She was a fly, choking to get out of the poisoned room, then feeling her body ripped open and splattered into a million pieces—

She sat up in bed, holding her stomach.

It was three in the morning.

She lay awake until sunrise, unable to get back to sleep, trembling, trying to shake off the dream's effects. But even counting sheep could not get her back to sleep.

All she could do was to clutch her cat and remember that her parents were sleeping just down the hall if she needed them.

CHAPTER THREE

Dennis kept his promise.

On Wednesday afternoon at three o'clock, Alex waited by the front office. After a few minutes, he appeared through the crowd, motioning for Alex to follow him. Alex did, and they descended into the bowels of the building where the journalism room was located.

"You wait here for a minute," Dennis said, opening the door. Out flooded a chorus of chaos that stopped when he shut the door behind him.

For the next five minutes, Alex paced the hallway, small photography portfolio in hand, wondering what he was doing there in the first place and whether or not Dennis would really be able to do anything. He then wondered why Dennis wanted to help him at all, when he had known the guy a total of three hours.

Every couple of paces, he would stop in front of the door and try to peer through the long, slim window to no avail. He couldn't imagine what was taking so long. He would either be able to switch classes or not. What was there to discuss? He began to feel nervous and stupid.

After another trip to the window, he heard voices and quickly stood against the wall around the corner. The knob rattled, but the door didn't open for another half minute. He could hear from within—

". . . probably some red-neck cowboy. What does someone from a small town in the middle of nowhere know about a newspaper? You owe me big time—"

The door opened.

Alex tried to curb the burning embarrassment and annoyance over the comments he heard and was about to abruptly depart and have nothing to do with the school paper, when a girl stopped short in front of him, narrowly avoiding a collision.

"Oh—you must be Alex," she said slowly, looking him up and down. "Aren't you in my history class?"

She was of medium height with blue eyes and blond hair that cascaded about her shoulders in a mass of tight ringlets. While he did not remember her from history class, there was something strikingly familiar about her appearance.

He cleared his throat. "Yes—and you are—"

"Kelly," she said, abruptly sticking out her hand to shake. "Kelly Kurtz. I understand you're interested in becoming a part of the newspaper team."

"Yeah," he mumbled, fumbling with the portfolio to free a hand and accept her shake.

"You brought samples," she said, abruptly retracting the hand. "That's just *great*—why don't you come in."

He turned to look at Dennis before being swept inside. Dennis just rolled his eyes.

The room was large and full of students, desks, worktables and massive, unorganized piles of paper. Somewhere, a radio blared. People were laughing, talking and yelling. He was led to a small table in the corner of the room. Clearing the table with a few sweeps of her arm, Kelly sat down, and he took a chair directly across from her. She squirmed a moment, looking uncomfortable.

"Um," she started, "I'm afraid Dennis has put me in an awkward position. You see—first of all, we just don't open up newspaper for anyone—I mean, we can't just open it up—I'm not really sure why. I think it has to do with grades."

He stared at the table, counting the seconds until he could leave.

"Second of all, I can't do anything about getting you in the class anyway. I mean—I'm like, a *student*, not the *instructor*. I'm really sorry—I mean, if it makes you feel better, a lot of people want to join and can't. It's kind of competitive and—"

"Look," he said, interrupting. "I didn't really think that Dennis *could* do anything, because the counselors couldn't—or *wouldn't*—do anything. And I certainly don't want to waste another minute of anyone's time. So, why don't we just sit here for a few more seconds so it looks like we *attempted* to do something and not hurt the guy's feelings."

"Dennis doesn't have any feelings," she said caustically, and then quickly explained, "I'm really not a friend of his—I'm a friend of his sister's."

"Oh," he said dully. "He has a sister?"

"Yeah—a *twin* sister. Her name is Danielle. I've known her since, since . . ." Her expression changed to one of sadness, and she gazed blankly at the table for a moment. "It doesn't matter. A long time. I've known her for a long time."

"Oh . . . Does she go here? To school here?"

"No—she goes to a private school."

He nodded absently, part of his mind curious as to why the other part of his mind had a sudden interest in the sister. After a moment of silence, he rose to leave.

She reached out to stop him, her hand touching his in the process. He winced at the contact, and she pulled it away, reddening.

"Look, I'm sorry again. I—I didn't mean to be rude."

"No problem—no apology necessary," he said, turning to leave.

"Wait," she said, standing up. "Um—you're new in town, right?"

He nodded.

"Well, how would you like to go to a party this Friday night? My friend Michelle and I are going. Well, actually—Michelle has a date, and I don't. And—"

"Excuse me?" Alex stopped her abruptly. "Did you say *date*?"

"Well, no—I mean, yes—but just a party date, you know?" she explained with nervous exasperation. "It doesn't have to be a *date* date. We can go as friends."

He remained speechless, frozen with uncertainty. Part of his mind was eager for the introduction into this high school's society, part of his mind was mildly intrigued with the girl and yet another part was overwhelmed with apprehension and foreboding.

"Look—just forget it. I'm sorry. There I go being forward again."

"No—wait . . . I'll—I'll go. Just—just let me know a time. We can make arrangements in class or something. Okay?"

She smiled coyly. "Okay. That sounds good. See you tomorrow, then."

He nodded and made his way out of the classroom, his mind a swirl of mixed feelings. Outside the room, Dennis lay on a hall bench, napping. He hit him on the head with his portfolio.

"What-what—" Dennis sat up with a start. "Oh—you're done . . . Already?"

Alex stood reflecting a moment. "Well . . . I was unsuccessful in getting into the class. However, I did manage to get a date for Friday night."

"No shit? With who?"

"What do you mean with who? Your friend—Kelly."

"No, no, no . . ." Dennis groaned, covering his face with his hands. "Tell me it isn't so—tell me NO."

Alex frowned, puzzled. "Why—what's wrong with that? I thought you said you were friends—"

"I never said that. You surely misheard me. I hate her. She's good friends with my sister—another primo bitch."

"Oh. Sorry."

Dennis just shook his head in dismay. "Fahlstrom—that is your name, right? Fahlstrom? Fahlstrom—you're something else. But you know, I like you. You appear to hate school. You appear to hate grades. You like dangerous women. You look like a hippie. We need more fine young men like you at East." He stood up, stretching and yawning. "Be at my party Friday night."

"Your party?"

"Yeah, my *School Sucks* party. It's an annual event."

"Well, actually, that's when the date is . . ."

Dennis stopped short, just before the exit. "Exactly!" he exclaimed, spinning around. "It's going to be a long night. See my party as the proverbial light at the end of a long, dark tunnel."

"Well—can I bring my date?"

Dennis rolled his eyes and, without responding, pushed open the school doors and sauntered off into the distance. Alex headed for football practice, his unease overtaking any enthusiasm about the coming weekend.

Carl Weiss's sapphire blue Camaro pulled into Alex's drive a little after seven on Friday night. In the small world of high school, Carl had turned out to be Michelle's date, and Alex would be Kelly's. He watched from his bedroom window as Carl walked up to the front door and rang the bell. While he quickly finished getting ready, he could hear Carl politely greet his parents.

Alex tried to calm his growing apprehension about the arranged date. He hadn't dated anyone since Jennifer. Earlier that day, Carl kept talking about a *game plan* and scoring big. Alex wasn't sure exactly what the *game plan* entailed, but he had an inkling, and it made him sweat to think of it. What if he couldn't? What if she wouldn't? What if she would . . .

"Boy, she's a hot one, Kelly is—and hot for you too," Carl whispered, breaking his train of thought. "A complete animal."

Trying to ignore this last comment, Alex slid into the back seat next to Kelly, forcing a smile and a polite hello. She smiled and greeted him in return.

"Alex—" Carl practically shouted as he started driving down the road, blaring the radio to the local heavy metal station. "Alex—this is Michelle. Michelle meet Alex."

Carl's date turned around and flashed a smile, winking at Kelly. Kelly giggled in return. Alex rolled his eyes and leaned over the front seat so as not to have to yell.

"Where are we going?" he asked Carl.

Carl smiled, "To get some beer and then to Ron's party. You know Ron. He's cool. He plays bass guitar and knows some other guys that you and I will want to meet for the band, and SHIT!" He slammed on the brakes, which sent Alex flying backwards and the girls screaming. "I forgot to ask you," Carl continued, oblivious to the chaos he had caused and ignoring the curses of his passengers. "Can we go back and get your guitar? Me and my friends really want to hear you play—"

Alex groaned and held his head in his hands, not answering for a full minute. Carl in the meantime pulled into a driveway to turn around.

"Well? We can go back and get it, right?" he pressed.

Alex shook his head in disbelief.

"Aw—come on, man, you have to. People are counting on you—the girls are counting on you—*I'm* counting on you for Christ's sake. Be a pal, huh? Be a sport—"

After the girls joined in with high-pitched whines, and Kelly had the nerve to grab his arm and shake it, he threw his hands up and conceded. The Camaro was soon in his driveway and he back inside the house, picking up his classical guitar and placing it in its worn black case. Before exiting, he surveyed his room a quick minute, feeling the comfort of the brick walls, their claustrophobic effect instead giving him a sense of security, barricading him from the pervading strangeness, horror and pain. His mind raced for an excuse to keep him inside, but he instead clenched the case handle and headed out the door and to the car once again. He was welcomed by loud exclamations of enthusiasm that soon died into the wind and blaring music as the car sped onto the main street and then the freeway. The night was beautiful, cool and clear with a purple and rose streaked horizon, the twilight stars just beginning to visibly glimmer. The air had a familiar smell to it, a smell that took him back to his home state.

The city loomed in the distance, but Carl turned off the highway and entered a seedy-looking neighborhood near some railroad tracks. The buildings were run down, some boarded up completely. A few worn-out looking men with darker skin, baggy jeans and work boots eyed them warily from the street corners. As they drove on, they saw more people and a few neon-lighted buildings.

"Is this a bad neighborhood?" Michelle blurted after some men in a rusty, pale yellow Monte Carlo in the next lane whistled at her through the open windows.

"Nah," Carl replied, grinning widely. "I mean, it's not the *best* neighborhood—but they sell me beer—no questions. Besides, you got us to protect you," he said, turning around and winking at Alex. Alex just rolled his eyes.

They soon pulled up to a small liquor store off the main drag, wedged between a Laundromat and a gray, boarded-up house. Carl and Alex went inside, leaving the girls alone in the car, much to the girls' annoyance.

Except for the clerk, an older Hispanic man who was watching a baseball game on television, the store was empty of customers.

"Now, you know the game plan, don't you?" Carl asked while pricing and grabbing various six-packs of beer.

Alex shook his head, eyeing Carl warily.

"Okay—it's almost eight o'clock now. By the time we reach the party, it will be eight-thirty. The girls have midnight curfews. That leaves us a little over two hours to get these fine girls drunk and out of their senses and to some remote area—which leaves us plenty of time to do the old in and out!" Carl made a lewd gyration with his pelvis, laughing out loud and drawing an agitated stare from the clerk. He then reached for a fifth pack of beer when Alex stopped him, convincing him that four packs were enough to get *five* small blond girls plastered. Carl finally agreed, and they went to the counter and paid for the goods, soon back in the car and on the road.

Alex once again settled into the back seat and tried to enjoy the beautiful evening. He even casually put his arm around Kelly. His thoughts turned to the *game plan* when Kelly scooted closer to him, and he could feel her leg brush against his—could feel wisps of her hair lightly touch his face—could smell her perfume. He had never asked Carl how often the game worked or if it worked. The whole idea was ludicrous, and he refused to believe these girls would willingly be led into such a plot. Then again . . .

Knowing that Carl expected him to play along, he mentally toyed with the idea, stirred by the close physical presence of a female. In that moment, he didn't even care that she was blond and they had just met. The power he could have, the thrill he could experience giving her beer after beer, innocently drinking them with her. And then he and Carl driving them into the woods and parking the car. They would pair off, each taking a walk and finding their own private clearing. It would start with a make-out session, and could end there unless he wanted to go on. If he wanted to go on, he could. She would be in no position to protest. And if she did, she would be in no position to stop him. She wouldn't want to stop him. She probably wouldn't know exactly what was going on—

An overpowering sexual longing stirred within him, and he felt his loin muscles tense. Kelly casually laid her hand on his leg, and he felt a jolting sensation that shot into his penis. For a brief second, he held his breath in anticipation that his problem might have passed—that he was feeling sexually stimulated—that he would actually get an erection—

But what should have been a jolt of ecstasy immediately turned into a jolt of agonizing pain—so intense, that he fell forward, gasping for breath.

Nobody noticed, however, for as he flew forward, so did everyone else, as Carl came to a jarring stop to avoid hitting a stalled car in the middle of the street. He then almost hit a car in the next lane while messing with the volume when his favorite Metallica song came on the radio. At the next light, he told everyone to shut up and listen to it, even though no one had been talking because the radio was already too loud to hear anyone speak. So Alex sat with his head between his knees trying to make the pain and growing nausea subside without bursting out in agony. The guitar was nice, but the words pounded on and on, the reverberating beats of the drum and bass soon coinciding with his throbs.

Carl was so into his song that he failed to notice the light had changed and cars were honking at him to move. After a minute of blowing off this chaos, Alex sat up with a start—

"Jesus Christ—will you drive!"

At this impassioned outburst, everyone in the car froze. The song seemed to pause. Carl eyed him strangely through the rearview mirror, then shrugged and drove on, just as the light turned yellow, much to the irritation of the drivers behind him.

No one said a word until they reached Ron's house. As he and Carl were unloading the beer and guitar from the trunk, Carl put a hand on his shoulder.

"Are you okay, bud? You seemed a bit stressed there. Everything's cool, right?"

Alex nodded impatiently. "Yeah—sure—everything's great. I'm just not used to people stopping in the middle of a road."

"Oh—so it wasn't the song?"

"The song? No—no, I like the song. What's it called again?" he asked, wincing. The pain had subsided but still throbbed in spurts.

"Yeah!" Carl exclaimed, slapping him on the back and ignoring his question. "That's my man—he likes Metallica. Awesome, dude—now we can learn to play it and make our own noise!"

Quite a few cars lined the driveway and street, and the house was noisy when they entered. Alex was immediately ushered into the kitchen where Ron and some other guys he had met at school were hanging out. The girls went off to chat with their friends. Carl re-introduced him to everyone. After perching his guitar in the corner of the kitchen, Alex, Carl and Ron each grabbed a beer and struck up a conversation about music. Of the three, Carl was the most into heavy metal, his playlist consisting of songs by Metallica, AC/DC, Iron Maiden and Van Halen. Ron and Alex shared a much broader interest that ranged from alternative rock to folk and classical. Soon bored with their banter about bands in which he had no interest, Carl pulled Alex aside telling him it was time to find their dates and get them drinking.

After finding Kelly, Alex offered her a beer, almost hoping she would refuse and ask for a soda instead. But she took it willingly, and when Carl made the two sign from across the room, meaning two hours, she smiled and made the peace sign back to him. Alex talked to her a bit about school, and she then took him around and introduced him to the people she knew.

The party quickly became loud and overcrowded. Ron offered an abundance of alcohol and very little food and rarely did a group of people stay together long enough to hold anything that could be construed as a conversation. Two or three drinking games remained in constant play, and *Reservoir Dogs* was showing on the VCR in the basement, a movie that Alex had already seen. After an hour of wandering around and saying the same things to the same types of people, he walked through the kitchen and out onto the deck to look at the stars and calm his still aching stomach.

He was soon joined by Ron, who, the more Alex talked to him, began to remind him of Keanu Reeves in *Bill & Ted's Excellent Adventure* due to his mop of dark brown hair and thick, slightly parted bangs that nearly covered his eyes. He offered Alex a smoke, which Alex gladly accepted, and they continued their previous conversation about music, ultimately deciding to jam to a few tunes together. After retrieving his bass and Alex's guitar, Ron led Alex back out onto the deck, where Alex first warmed up with one of his favorite Nick Drake tunes, "Road." Ron strummed along towards the end of the song, and when finished, suggested they try Blind Faith's "Can't Find My Way Home."

Alex had a decent singing voice, deep yet smooth. He vaguely remembered playing rhythm guitar and singing back-up with a local basement band in Montana. Though the two of them played low key, halfway through the song a small crowd gathered on the deck to listen, including his date and a few of her friends. When they finished, Kelly begged them to play something else, so he and Ron decided to mess with an acoustic version of "Don't Fear the Reaper." Soon people began requesting songs and singing along, and all that was missing was a big campfire, he thought to himself. This went on for forty minutes, until Carl pushed his way through the crowd and demanded a beer break for the musicians.

The three talked for a few minutes about setting up band practice, and then Carl drew Alex aside. "It's getting late, dude—we gotta get moving soon. Man—and did you see Kelly eyeing you? She's gone—melted—a snap. You have her—"

As Carl went on, Alex felt a growing sense of uneasiness, and the nausea returned full force. "Carl—CARL—"

He interrupted him, and Carl stopped speaking.

"Can we wait a little longer? I need another beer." And with that, Alex sauntered into the kitchen and grabbed a beer, hoping to delay *the game* as long as he could. Within the next half hour, he downed three more beers and retreated to the bathroom whenever Carl came looking for him. At ten thirty, however, Carl finally caught up with him and physically dragged him to the door.

"Fahlstrom—you idiot! Let's get going—the girls are getting restless."

"My guitar—I forgot my guitar—"

"I already put it in the trunk, you fuck—now let's go—"

Alex was soon seated in the back seat next to his date. Though enveloped by the night air coming through the open windows and sunroof, the smell of alcohol from the amount of beer consumed between the two of them was very potent. He looked at her for a moment, trying to read her expressions and feelings but was met with a tired, glossy stare and a weary smile. He could no longer distinguish her perfume from the smoke and other odors picked up at the party.

As they headed down the street, Alex decided to make a move.

"Oh, Jesus—I just remembered—" he burst out loud. "I promised Dennis Sumners I would stop by his party tonight. Does anyone know where that is?"

Carl immediately slammed on the breaks and turned around to glare at him, but Alex was rescued by the girls, who suddenly came back to life and began chattering about Dennis and his annual party. Kelly, being Dennis's sister's good friend, knew the exact location of the Sumners' house. Carl then brought up curfews to which the girls said they could get extensions—they wanted to go to Dennis' party.

When they pulled up to the driveway, Alex couldn't believe it was the right one. The house—surely the party house, as the drive and street were lined with cars, and there was an actual sign staked in the front lawn—was enormous. It was well-lit, and he could see it was the width of three of his own homes. Situated on a corner, it sprawled out in a v-shape, and the backyard was encased in a tall, wrought iron fence. Along one angle of the front was a walkway with five pillared arches. The front door was attached to a huge turret, which formed the central point of the structure. Windows lined the second angle, which ended in a terrace complete with a fountain. He could hear the dribbling water as they walked up the long, curved driveway.

Upon reaching the imposing front door, they could hear loud music and talking—even shouting—coming from within. Carl moved to press the doorbell, when the door flew open and two people practically fell out, stumbling onto the front lawn. Alex strained to see who they were but couldn't tell. In the meantime, Kelly impatiently pushed them across the threshold, declaring she knew the residents and could even take them on a tour if they wished.

As they stood in the front hall, gaping at the green marble flooring and enormous chandelier, the front door banged shut behind them. Alex turned around to see Dennis quickly bolting it. He thought he heard yelling on the other side.

Dennis turned around.

"Alex—" he burst, almost startled. "I didn't know you were here—welcome to my humble abode. Carl—hi—and Kelly. Always a *pleasure*," he said, his expression saturated with sarcasm.

She tossed her head and gave him a fake smile.

"Well," Dennis continued. "Please feel free to walk around. Help yourself to anything in the kitchen—mingle with the guests. My castle is your home."

Carl and his date soon went to find people they knew. Alex was more interested in exploring the house and convinced Kelly to show him around. Surprisingly, many of the rooms seemed fairly empty of furnishings, though upon closer inspection he could tell much of the furniture had been moved against the walls and covered in plastic. Nails and hooks stuck out of the walls where he supposed pictures hung. Huge rugs were rolled up and set in corners, leaving an expanse of hard wood flooring that made some of the rooms look like ballrooms.

Groups of people were gathered throughout the house, a different crowd than at the previous party. A lot of the people were dressed in Goth attire or hippie-type clothing and had odd colored hair. Alternative music played on one stereo. In another room and on a different stereo, a group was listening to the Dead and getting high. The action seemed wilder upstairs, where people were dancing and necking on the upper landing. As they wandered around and headed back downstairs, Kelly grew increasingly flirtatious, which made Alex uneasy. Casual touches on the arm soon turned into fleeting hugs. When Alex talked, she smiled and laughed coyly at what seemed each pause in speech. Annoyed, he began directing questions to her until they eventually came upon a large game room in the basement, where Alex met up with Dennis. Dennis was playing pool and invited Alex to join him in a game of cutthroat, temporarily relieving him of Kelly.

He enjoyed two rounds when, during the third, just as he had made a critical shot, Carl tapped him on the shoulder and said enough was enough. They were leaving—he was ready.

Reluctantly, Alex pulled out of the game and said good-bye to Dennis. As he turned to go, Dennis grabbed his shoulder and whispered a warning in his ear. "Watch out for her. I mean it."

Alex sighed heavily and then pulled his date from one of the three pinball machines. Again, all four piled into the car. And again, Carl cranked his stereo. And soon, they were on a dark road heading for what looked like the edge of nowhere, the landscape becoming flat, remote and dark. Alex tried to enjoy the night air and focus on the stars, which were becoming increasingly bright as they headed further away from the city. But he felt his heart rate increase and a pang in the pit of his stomach. As the car slowed down and pulled into a dead-end gravel road, he broke into a cold sweat. Then, the car was off, everyone silent and all he could hear was a symphony of crickets.

"Well, here we are!" Carl finally burst, jovially. "My favorite place to come look at the stars on a beautiful summer night . . . I've got blankets in the trunk. Why don't we just go find a nice spot to sit down and enjoy the evening—whad'ya say?"

No one answered, so Carl opened the door and got out. Everyone soon followed. Out of sheer nervousness, Alex leaned against the car and began to talk to Kelly about constellations, ignoring whether or not she was paying any attention. He went on until Carl threw a red blanket at him, from which fell a small object wrapped in plastic. Carl and his date then headed through the field a little ways from the car. Alex stopped talking to pick up the object.

His face burned in embarrassment upon realizing it was a condom, and he fumbled to stuff it into his jean pocket. Kelly snorted, her arms crossed, her eyes following Carl and her friend. Alex knew she had seen the object, and he was at a total loss as to what to do next. His stomach was throbbing.

"So . . . What do we do now? Go find our own little haystack to roll in?" she asked caustically.

He laughed nervously, shaking his head. "It—that wasn't my idea. I—I had no plans. Actually, I'd like to just go home, myself. I'm really, really tired."

Looking down, she didn't reply immediately, and he worried he had offended her. But after a few more seconds of uneasy silence, she yawned widely, stretching her arms above her head, and agreed that she, too, was very tired. She then suggested they take a stroll to walk off the alcohol, to which Alex conceded.

"So, how long have you known Carl?" he asked.

"Oh . . . Since grade school."

"And Michelle?"

She shrugged. "We've been hanging out since last year."

"And, how long have they been dating?"

"Who?"

"Carl and Michelle."

She eyed him oddly. "Whatever . . . They're not dating. I mean, this is their first date, if you can call it that."

"Oh . . . I just thought—you know—"

She stopped abruptly, turning on him. "Oh, please—don't even start with that bullshit. That whole *sex only when you're going steady* shit. Or is everyone in your hometown so pristine? Only nice girls in Montana?"

He reddened, turning away uncomfortably.

"Don't you know we're in the whore click? You mean—nobody's told you about me? You've been at this school for a week, and you don't know? And yet you have a *condom* stuffed into your left pocket. I *can't imagine*—"

"I told you—it wasn't my idea. I'm sorry. Look—let's just go back to the car and—"

"And what?" she asked, her expression saddening. "*Talk?*"

He swallowed hard, pursing his lips. "Yeah—sure. If that's what you'd like to do."

She shook her head before throwing her hands up in the air. "Talk . . . Sure! Why not? Let' see—what would you like to *talk* about? School gossip? Who's who? Who's dating who? Who's fucking who? Or, maybe we could talk about our *hobbies*. Or our families," she spat. "I come from a wealthy family. My dad's a judge. My mom's a lawyer. My brother goes to Yale. I should be in a private school, along with my friend Danielle, but I chose not to go. Do you want to know why?"

He shrugged wearily, walking slowly back towards the car.

"Because I like guys, and my friend doesn't. She goes to an all-girls prep school. I could think of nothing more wretched than going to a school for women. I mean—it's like the dark ages, you know? Like Victorian England. And yet, somehow—in this fucked up city—being beautiful and liking guys makes one automatically a whore."

He raised an eyebrow but before he could say anything, she plopped herself on the ground, buried her head in her arms and began sobbing.

"Oh, what am I saying . . . I fucked it all up for myself . . ." She looked up at him, her eyes reddened with tears. "Do you think I'm beautiful? You don't have to answer . . . I know I am. All my life, I've been considered pretty. I was in pageants . . . did local modeling . . . had admirers since I could remember. And my best friend for most of my life was a plain Jane. Yep—that's Danielle. I always got the good looking guys, and she always got the nerds. And you know what? I like the power. I like the power I have in manipulating guys. You all think with your dicks. It's so easy."

She sniffled before continuing. He remained silent, standing a few feet from where she sat, completely baffled by the outburst and telling himself it was alcohol-induced.

"Anyway—I liked having her for a friend. It made me feel better about myself. It was like a contest that I always won, you know? And then, in seventh grade, she had this crush on Brian McDermott, and . . . and I knew she did. And I knew I could win him, too. And, I did. I won him, alright. And we started going steady. And that—that's when we started drifting apart."

"Why are you telling me this?" he asked hoarsely, his voice barely audible.

She looked up at him, her eyes penetrating. "Because I can. Because you're nothing. Because you're—you're not from here. And you can't hurt me." She burst out sobbing again.

Suddenly overcome with a sense of compassion, he knelt down on the ground, remaining a short distance from her. "Hey—it's okay. Of course I won't hurt you—I won't say anything."

"You don't know the worst part . . . I—I hooked up with her boyfriend. We, like, were all at a party, and he and I were really drunk . . . And, like, I knew—I knew he was attracted to me. And I knew I could . . . and I did. And she found out. But she said nothing. To either of us. And that was months ago. And now they've broken up, and you'd think—you'd think I'd be happy. But I'm not. I hate her. I hate him. I hate everyone."

At this outburst, he stood up, running his hand through his hair in disbelief. "Well—I gotta tell you. If this is the biggest problem in your life—this competitive jealousy thing with your friend—consider yourself lucky. There are people on this planet with much greater problems than you. There are people *dying*. There are people dead . . ." His thoughts drifted off to the past.

"We're all dying."

"Yeah . . . I suppose we are."

She stood up and stumbled shakily towards him. Eyeing him oddly, she reached out and touched his hair. Tonight it hung in messy strands, some braided, some naturally hanging in limp curls, some just matted.

"I like your hair."

He jerked back nervously.

"I do," she continued, grabbing a strand. "I've never seen hair like this on a guy . . . It's sexy."

He pushed her hand away, and she began to giggle, almost uncontrollably.

"What's so funny?" he asked.

"*You*," she said, her bloodshot eyes widening. She stepped closer, and he took a step back.

"Oh—are we playing hard to get now?" she said coyly.

He tried to step out of her way, but she stumbled on a rock, falling forward, and he had no choice but to break her fall by grabbing her arms. She took full and quick advantage of the situation, and as soon as their eyes met, lunged her face towards his, her lips greedily seeking his own.

Helplessness, repulsion and curiosity arose simultaneously, his mind spinning at the impact. Curiosity prevailed, and they locked in a heated embrace, each moment giving rise to a sense of relief that his problem had passed. She pressed her body against his, and he put an arm around her waist, pulling her tight against his pelvis.

He felt a jolt of intense pleasure that peaked but just as instantaneously transformed into unbearable pain, so excruciating that he pushed her violently away, gasping for breath and clutching at his stomach. Heaving, he fell to his knees.

She gasped, startled, quickly assailing his ears with shrill outbursts and questions.

"It's okay . . . It's okay . . ." he managed to mumble, putting a hand up in protest. "It's just a cramp—"

"A cramp? Are you sure—shit—you act like you're dying or something. Shit—a cramp?"

His mind raced. "I have an ulcer . . . It's just an ulcer . . . It gets bad when I drink . . ."

"Jesus-god—are you serious? You get like this every time you drink? Shit—"

He shook his head, collapsing to a seated position and then lying flat on his back. "Not every time . . ." he croaked, looking up at the star-lit night. "Only sometimes. It gets very bad sometimes. I'm sorry."

She plunked down next to him. "God—it's okay. I'm just really freaked out, you know? I mean—here we're, you know. And next thing I know you're, like, freaking out . . . shit."

As he stared absently at the night sky, he focused on his breathing, trying to calm it, trying to control it. The pain subsided as his breathing slowed.

"So—what do we do now?" she asked.

"Nothing," he said quietly. "We do nothing."

She sat silently next to him for a few minutes, but he could tell her nervousness was increasing with each speechless moment, her body continually shifting, her hands tearing at the grass before picking up pebbles and throwing them across the road. Eventually, she could no longer remain quiet and began talking. First about school. Then about movies. Then about her college and career goals. He only half listened, her prattle mixing with the sound of crickets and distant highway traffic, all of it reduced to a dull din, like that of a television station that had signed off its programming for the night.

When Carl and Michelle pulled up a half hour later, he breathed a sigh of relief. But she seemed reluctant to go.

"You know, you're still pretty cool. Maybe we can go out again sometime, you know? Like, when we're both not so wasted."

Alex didn't reply as they climbed back into the Camaro and embarked on the long drive home.

∞

Danielle recognized the voice on the other end of the phone and held her breath, trying to subdue a sudden, sharp pain in her stomach. Lying down on the bed, she stared at the ceiling and manufactured a sincere tone in her voice. "Hi, Kelly. How are you?"

Brooke, who was seated on a floor cushion flipping through fashion magazines, made a loud gagging noise.

"Just great. I called to see how your first day of school went," Kelly said.

"Oh, just fine," Danielle replied absently. "It was the usual thing. We all compared tans, and I lost . . . How was *your* day?"

"Great—great. I like my schedule. Newspaper's going to be a gas this semester." She talked briefly about her classes and activities. "I don't know," she continued after a loud sigh. "I really just called to say hi. We never see each other anymore . . ."

Danielle remained silent. She and Kelly had been best friends since first grade, until she decided to go to a private high school and Kelly chose to remain in the public school. Kelly had never really forgiven her for leaving and was quite jealous of the friendship Danielle had formed with Brooke. In the beginning, the three of them had gotten along. But the relationship had strained during the past year, and now Kelly and Brooke equally hated each other, leaving Danielle to struggle with keeping the peace.

"So, Kel, what's new with you? Any new men in your life?"

"No," Kelly sighed over the phone. "No men, and not much is new. But what about *you*? Do you have any *news* to tell me?"

Danielle sensed she was finally getting to the point of her call. "*Should* I have?"

"Well, I know *you* haven't said anything to me, but I've certainly *heard* some odd things."

"I can't imagine."

"Come on, Danielle," Kelly replied, her tone revealing her annoyance. "I've heard some pretty wild things, and I'm just shocked you haven't called and told me yourself. We are still friends, aren't we?"

"Of course—sure—I just—just—well . . . Why don't you tell me what you've heard, and I'll tell you if it's true—deal?"

"Well, Tate for one. Is it really over? I mean—did you guys break up?"

Danielle sighed. "Yes, I'm afraid that's true." And, now he is legally yours, she thought to herself but refrained from saying aloud.

"Dan!" Kelly exclaimed. "I'm totally shocked—you guys have been going out for three years—"

"Not quite."

"You were perfect for each other—what happened? Or—I mean—did something happen? Is it—is—are—" she fumbled to get out the next question.

Danielle closed her eyes, wincing, trying to control a surge of angry emotion at her friend's continued deceit. She considered tearing into her as she did Tate but remembered the disastrous outcome of her previous indiscretion and physically kept her lips pursed. Anger accomplished nothing and only seemed to lead to more anger. After another moment's silence, she mustered the strength to speak. "Why did we break up? Well, I don't know. I suppose we weren't really right for each other. We both decided it was time to move on."

"Tate's pretty upset about it, though."

"*Really*? You talked to him?"

"Yeah. Just for a little bit. He called me to ask what you had told me about it. And I, of course, didn't know a thing about it, which kind of shocked him. Shocked me, too, considering we've been friends since first grade, and I'm the *last* to know—"

"I'm sorry, Kelly," Danielle interrupted. "I haven't wanted to talk about it—with anyone."

"Except Brooke, I'm sure."

Danielle said nothing.

"Do you know what he said about you and Brooke?"

"Yes."

"Do you *care*?"

"Not really."

"Is it true?"

"Do you think it's true, Kel? Do you *really* think it's true?"

"No," Kelly said flatly.

"Then why are you even asking?"

"Because I feel so out of touch with you—because we don't talk or even do things together anymore. And you and Brooke are always together anyway, so for all I know, it is true."

Danielle closed her eyes, trying to block out the voice on the phone and immerse herself in silence. But she realized there was no silence. Air pumped from the vents above with a whirring sound. Her cat lay purring next to her. She could hear Brooke's breathing and an occasional flap as she paged through a magazine. Through the window, she heard the steady hum of a lawnmower.

She hated conflict. She hated when people were angry with her, and lately she felt everyone was angry with her for something. In her mind she was screaming apologies to Kelly just to appease her. On the phone she was making excuses as to why she didn't tell her of the break-up. It was a sudden affair. It was a messy affair. She had let the rumors fly out of sheer exhaustion. She was sorry she had hurt Kelly's feelings. Did Kelly want to go dancing with them on Friday night to make up for it?

Kelly groaned. "You know I hate that scene—I hate dancing. And there are no good men at those clubs—just fags and artsy nerds."

"Why do we need men?" Danielle burst. "We aren't going to meet men— we're just going to go out and have fun. Brooke, me, Cherise and Susan—just girls. Surely you can give up men for one night."

Brooke snorted in the background.

"I don't know," Kelly said. "I'm feeling damn horny lately. I want me a real man—one with a body and brains. I've had a long dry spell. Let's go double dating sometime—"

Suddenly, the bedroom door banged open. Danielle jerked nervously, and Brooke looked up from her magazine.

Her brother strode into the room. "Is that Kelly on the phone?" he asked abruptly, grabbing for the receiver before even reaching the bedside. "I need to talk to her—"

Danielle sat up and clutched the phone possessively, "You didn't knock— you don't have permission to be here—"

He glared and roughly snatched the phone from her. "Kelly—this is Dennis. . . I have a favor to ask of you . . . I'm trying to help this guy out at school . . . Yeah, he's from up north—a northern state, I forgot. Anyway—he wants on the paper. He can't get on the paper—"

Danielle rolled her eyes and listened absently as Dennis elaborated about this new guy at school. He must be a freaker, she thought. The guy probably had drugs. Her brother never did anything nice for anyone unless he wanted something in return. He certainly never did anything nice for her. He just took, took, took.

She found herself getting angry as she thought of his recent acts of vandalism. She got even angrier at the thought of his upcoming party. Why her parents always vacationed this week, knowing full well what havoc he would wreck while they were gone, baffled her.

He handed her the phone, and she motioned for him to wait a moment.

"Your brother is insane," Kelly blurted. "He's also an asshole. I can't do anything for this *new* guy—"

"Kelly—I have to go—I'll call you later this week—"

"Yeah, we need to get together soon. Maybe do lunch and go shopping, huh? And just let me know when you're feeling up to dating—I can arrange all that."

"Sure thing—bye." She hung up the receiver and turned to her brother. "Before waltzing out of here like the arrogant pig that you are—tell me one thing, because I admit—I want to clear the air." She made a sweeping gesture with her arm. "Since I'm cleaning out my life, I might as well clear the air with you."

He stood with his arms crossed, looking bored and preoccupied.

"Why do you hate me?"

He rolled his eyes. Brooke stared up from the magazine.

"I mean it, Dennis—you hate me—you despise me—and you never let me forget it. You even hate things *associated* with me, like my car—my cat—"

He turned to leave.

"Don't you leave without answering me—you at least owe me an answer—a chance to straighten things out—because I certainly don't hate you like you hate me, even though I should—and I'm fucking floored as to why—*how*—you could know someone from Montana for one day and want to give him the world—"

Dennis jerked suddenly, startled out of his annoyance.

"How you could be *nice* to some *stranger*—while you can't even give me the courtesy of cleaning up the vomit you left in my car—which I was kind enough to let you *borrow*—" she continued.

He gazed at her in wonder. "How did you know that?"

"Know what?" she snapped, agitated, feeling her confidence and momentum build.

"He *is* from Montana—that's where he's from. I couldn't remember, but now that you said it . . ."

"What is so *special* about this guy?" she asked, exasperated.

"There's probably a lot of pot in Montana," Brooke interrupted dryly.

Dennis shrugged. "I don't know. Maybe I'm just being nice—did you ever think of that?"

"No, Dennis—I didn't. You're never nice."

"Jesus Christ—what do you want me to say? Because he's rich? Because he's famous? Deals?"

"Because you're a closet homosexual," Brooke piped.

"You shut-up, you lesbian bitch—"

Brooke stuck her tongue out at him.

"Fine—" he burst, turning on his sister. "I'll tell you why I hate you—why I hate you were born . . . You're fucking shallow—that's why. You just sit here in your Mission Hills frilly bedroom, in your Mission Hills frilly house—so smug and self-absorbed. You parade around in your plaid skirts, waltzing around The Plaza and spending money like water—and have no concept of the world—of pain—of life—of anything outside your sheltered, rich bitch bubble. You look like a prima-donna, you act like a prima-donna," he spat. "And the only thing I can remotely stand about you is your violin playing, because it touches art—which is the world—which is pain—which is real life. Of course, you can only *play* what other people have created and would never consider creating your own." He ran his fingers through his hair madly, as if he could burst a vein just standing there. "Lemme ask you something, Miss Self-Righteous—what do you live for?"

She stared at him, numb. His words stung, and her mind raced to sort out his accusations and examine them for truth. "What?"

"What do you live for, huh? Is it money—is that it? Dances—boyfriends— shopping—what? To get married to that fucking traitor someday and create your own little suburban hellhole? What?"

She was shaking her head.

"What?" he pressed, he shouted. "What then?"

"To be happy—" she cried.

He looked at her in silence.

"To be happy," she repeated, almost breathless. "I just want to be happy."

"That's it? That's *it*? That's your answer?"

"Yes," she burst. "I want to be happy. And I want everyone to be happy. But we're not. We're all miserable. And I think *you're* cruel and shallow to think that just because I don't outwardly whine and complain about my misery . . . Just because I realize how lucky I am to be privileged—to have a good home—and talent—and—and I try to *do* something with it—unlike you, who's just hateful and does *nothing* with what you have but spit on it. That you think because I try to be happy and do something with my life that I don't think—or feel pain or anguish over the world—"

She was choking back the sobs and felt her eyes burn as she tried to hold back the tears.

"I feel quite enough *pain*—thank you—and longing and desire—and confusion over life and the universe—maybe *almost* as much as you seem to—and if you *bothered* to talk to me like a decent human being—like your *sister*—you'd find out." She looked down, brushing the tears from her eyes with her hand.

Her brother remained standing, speechless.

"You ask him," she continued, looking up at him again. "You ask this new guy what you asked me—since he's so special to you. I want to know how a *real* person answers such a question."

But he just shook his head grimly before walking out of the room and slamming the door behind him.

Brooke sighed loudly after he left. "You guys redefine the phrase *sibling rivalry.*"

On Friday night, she stood in front of the long mirror in Brooke's bedroom, examining her figure. Part of her liked what she saw, and part of her disapproved. She had found the dress in the back of her mother's closet. It was tight at the top, a shirred halter with spaghetti straps and meant to fit like a body glove, flaring in chiffon tiers below the waistline that cascaded to just above the knee. But the neckline looked nice, and the baby blue shade complemented her olive skin tone. Still—

"I don't know, Brooke," she mumbled. "Is this me? It's awfully, awfully revealing—"

Brooke sat at her vanity applying eyeliner. Her bedroom was strewn with clothes they had worn earlier and clothes they were deciding on wearing to the club. 4 Non Blondes played in the background, and a strong, fruit-smelling incense burned to cover Brooke's cigarette smoke. "You look great—keep it on."

"It's so tight—" Danielle protested.

"So. It's supposed to be. You have a nice figure—enjoy it while you have it."

Danielle decided to wear it, reminding herself that she was not going to attract a guy, and the man of her dreams wouldn't be found at the Club, anyway. Still, dressing up made her feel better about herself, she thought, fluffing her long hair and arranging her bangs.

"Are you ready to go?" Brooke asked finally. We were supposed to be at Susan's by ten-thirty, and we're already late." She wanted to get there when it opens at eleven."

"Yeah. I just need to stop at the house and get some money and my earrings."

"I have money, and I have earrings—"

"I want to check on my cat, too—"

Brooke rolled her eyes impatiently.

"Dennis is having that stupid party, and I'm worried about my cat and property—I really want to check on things—"

"I thought you were going to lock the cat in your bedroom."

"I did—but that tactic hasn't stopped people from getting into my room and letting the cat out in the past—"

"Fine."

A short time later, their friend's car sat running in Danielle's driveway, while she and Brooke proceeded inside to retrieve money and earrings and to check on the cat. She and Brooke made their way to the back of the house, through small, lingering mobs of people. While Brooke stayed in the kitchen to steal something to drink, Danielle made her way up to her room. She pulled a key from her purse to unlock the door, but to her surprise, it fell open at her touch. The room was dark, but she immediately heard giggling, moaning and creaking from her bedsprings. She angrily flipped on the light.

A young couple she did not recognize lay entwined and half undressed on her bed. Her pillows and books were strewn on the floor, and the covers were pushed to the side. They blinked uncomprehendingly while she stood, shaking in rage.

"Get out—" she barely heard herself gasp, the tone hardly audible. "Get out of my room—now—"

"Who are you?" The guy asked gruffly, rubbing his eyes, his tousled hair almost standing on end.

Before Danielle even considered answering, she charged the bed, shrieking, her sole purpose to chase them out, tear off the covers and throw everything on the bed into the washer for sterilization. Before she could reach the couple, her brother burst into the room and grabbed her while she kicked and screamed.

"I saw you coming, and I knew there'd be trouble—" he said through teeth.

"How dare you—you promised—you dick—you fucking asshole—and where's my cat? You dick—" she clawed at his arms, trying to pry herself free. He was stronger than she, and both were soon in the hallway and moving towards the landing and steps that led down to the front door. Ignoring the wry stares and occasional dry remarks from her brother's guests, she continued to screech accusations and attempt to kick herself free. When her brother's friend Mick joined his cause, she knew the situation was hopeless. After helping Dennis get her to the entrance hall, Mick stepped aside as the two tumbled out of the front door, through a group of people standing on the front steps, and onto the front lawn.

"Why don't you just go to wherever you were planning on going—and leave me the fuck alone! Goddammit . . ." He stood up and brushed himself off.

Brooke appeared with two wine coolers.

"That's a very good idea, Brooke—maybe she'll chill out some," Dennis remarked dryly, then headed to the door.

Danielle jumped up to follow him, but he outran her and slammed the door in her face. She hollered and pounded until Brooke came up, tapped her on the shoulder and reminded her of their plans. Their two friends were still waiting in the car.

Upon climbing into the vehicle, one of them asked what took so long.

"There were two people getting it on in my bed!" she burst. "My *bed*— can you believe it? And I *locked* the door—which means butthead unlocked it. God, I hate him sometimes."

"Yeah, well at least you didn't walk in on your own brother getting it on. I've done that before, and it's weird. Sick kind of," one of the two friends commented.

Brooke unscrewed the lid to a cooler and handed it to her. "Dan just has a problem with copulation in general."

"I do not! I just don't see why people have to do it, that's all."

Her friends snorted.

"Do it *all the time*," she clarified.

"Drink—please. Drink up—loosen up. We're going to have a good time tonight, okay?" Brooke patted her shoulder.

Danielle nursed her drink during the twenty-minute drive to the club. Coolers usually knocked her out, and the last thing she wanted to be was chemically tired and depressed as she was already naturally tired and depressed. All she could think of was her cat and her bed. The newly cleaned, crisp sheets would now have to be re-washed. And what if someone let out her cat, and he got hit by a car? She shuddered and tried to concentrate on the nice evening and music and dancing that would soon greet them.

Club Piranha was the only under twenty-one alternative dance club. Tonight was their second visit. The crowd was comprised of bizarre people from all over the city and surrounding area. A number of college students drove in from Lawrence, which made it seem less like a high school dance. The entire facility was dark, with the main light source coming from the dance floor, and that was spotty at best. Except for two pool tables and a few small high tops with bar stools in the back, the place was a dance floor and too loud to carry on any lengthy, intense conversation. But Danielle and her friends didn't go there to talk.

Music was the only thing that could take Danielle away from her daily angst, and after she began to dance, she quickly forgot the evening's previous worries. Of the four, only their friend Cherise could dance with any talent and grace. But in the dark, packed club, nobody cared how people danced or how they looked when they danced. The lights, when flashing a certain way, seemed to freeze-frame everyone, as in a fast reeling, black and white film. And the music incessantly pounded in a rhythm that soon permeated her body and mind like a manic mantra, putting her into another state of being.

By the time "Head Like a Hole" was played, the group was dancing in a frenzy. They all liked Nine Inch Nails, and even though it was a dance version of the song, arms waved, bodies twirled, hair flew and mouths screamed the lyrics. Danielle could feel the sweat forming and streaming from her brow, strands of her hair plastered against her face until she shook them loose. Her heart pounded, and her ears rang numb, but each frantic moment also brought with it an intense high.

It was only when the song wound down that a strange feeling swept over her, and she stopped. Her physical rush was replaced by a chill, a tingling sensation down her neck, and she had an eerie sense that someone was watching.

She spun around.

All she could see were the oscillating limbs of the surrounding dancers, each in his or her own world, none paying any attention to her.

She tried to get back into the dance but found herself breathing heavily, almost laboriously. She then began to cough and decided to sit out for a while. Brooke followed, and after settling her down with a Sprite, went back to the dance floor. Danielle sat alone at a table, her ears still ringing and her head now spinning.

She sensed a presence near her and turned to look.

Tate was leaning against a pillar, unsmiling, his arms crossed.

She immediately turned away.

"So why aren't you dancing?" he asked loudly, competing with the music, suddenly leaning over the table.

She looked down at her drink, unsure of what to think, her mind racing to plan an escape.

"Can we talk?"

She remained frozen, gripping the cup tighter.

He slid into the stool in front of her. "Come on, Dan . . . We need to talk. I need an explanation. At least give me that."

Sighing, she finally garnered the courage to look at him. He was wearing sunglasses, and she could not read his expression clearly.

After hesitating another moment, she threw her hands up. "Sure . . . Let me go tell Brooke . . ." she mumbled.

Five minutes later she was walking briskly out of the club with Tate, once again wondering if she were in a dreaming or waking state. Both stopped abruptly halfway into the parking lot. She shivered slightly in the brisk air.

"It's a little chilly to be out here like that," Tate said, taking off his shades and eyeing her body. "Do you want to sit in my car for awhile?"

"No—" she burst, then controlled herself. "No. I'm fine." She turned from him, praying he would say his piece and leave.

"Look—can we, can we just go some place and talk? I just want to talk," he said.

She spun around, suddenly feeling uneasy with him standing behind her at such close proximity. "About what? I thought we were done talking—I thought we had nothing left to say to each other."

"Come on, Danielle . . . I need to know."

"What?"

"Why?"

"Why *what*?"

"Why you broke up with me, shit . . . I just want to know why. What—you think I'm ugly, I smell, I'm, I'm a bad kisser? You think I'm stupid—shallow? I mean, it just doesn't make any sense. I'm not bragging, but other women don't share your opinion of me. I mean—how fucking ironic that every girl I know thinks I'm awesome *except* my own girlfriend of three years. *She* thinks I'm repulsive."

Wincing at his choice of words, she stopped him. "No—no, I don't think you're repulsive. Not at all. You're—you're . . ." She scanned his person for a moment. Tonight he was dressed in Levis and a pale yellow Ralph Lauren oxford. He was tall and had a nice build, having worked out regularly since middle school. "You're very handsome. I—I was wrong to say what I did, and I'm sorry."

"You know, if you told me you were a lesbian, I'd actually be relieved. I'd actually be fucking happy to hear that. That—that you're frigid and don't like men. Tell me you're fucking frigid and hate men."

She pursed her lips. "Would that make you happy? Really?"

"Yeah—it might help."

"Fine. I'm a lesbian and hate men. Happy now?"

"Goddammit, Danielle . . ." He turned away from her in frustration, arms crossed.

"Tate . . . you can have any girl you want. Why do you care? Why do you even care that we stay together? I'm not even pretty."

"Who says you're not pretty?"

"Nobody needs to say anything—I just have to look in a mirror. Come on, Tate—why not just go out with Kelly. You know she's been nuts about you for years. You know you like her, too. Let's just cut the façade and do what we want. You go date Kelly, and I'll climb back up into my attic."

He turned around, eyeing her wearily. "You don't *date* girls like Kelly, Dan. You fuck girls like Kelly. You date girls like you. You bring girls like you home to mom and dad and take girls like you to the dance. You marry girls like you. Girls who are intelligent and *pretty* and who don't climb into bed with every guy on the football team . . . And besides, we can't break up. Our parents will be crushed. Shit . . . it's like a divorce. It'll make the fucking *Star* social column. I don't even want to think about it. Besides—we're going to Homecoming together. I got a big party planned at the Embassy Suites. Hotel rooms and all. My parents will never allow it without you. They trust you. Shit—I trust you. I don't want to go with any other girl. Honestly."

She stared at him, her mouth slightly open in speechless astonishment.

"I mean—have you told your *dad* about our break-up?"

She shook her head, still recovering from the shock of what was coming out his mouth.

"He'll shit. He may even ground you, you know that. Let's face it—I'm the only boy good enough for you, and you're the only girl good enough for me. That's the way it is, Dan. That's our reality. Funny thing is, I'm fine with it. I don't feel trapped by it, you know. Because, I like you. I really like being with you. If I get too horny, I'll find some stupid skank and deal with it. But you gotta understand, I have no feelings for them. It means nothing to me. They mean nothing to me. It's like getting high or dropping a hit. It's like jacking off to *Playboy*. Who cares."

She laughed out loud, overwhelmed by the absurdity of what she was hearing. "Oh, my god—oh, my god—Tate. Do you hear what you're *saying*?" She stared wildly around the parking lot for a moment, wishing there was a witness, thinking nobody would even believe the exchange if she were to share it with them. "Are you *serious*? You can't be serious—did you hear what you just said? Am I dreaming? Oh my god, wake me up—now."

He rolled his eyes. "What's wrong with what I just said? What—are you naive? Look around, Dan. Look at your own parents—my parents, Brooke's parents. Open your history book sometime and really read it. It's the way things are. It's the way things have always been. There are women you fuck and women you love and marry—period. What's wrong with that? It's reality."

"*Your* reality, maybe—"

"No—our reality. Come on, Dan. Everybody knows about your dad. Everybody knows about my dad. They have women on the side—"

"Brooke's dad *married* his woman on the side—"

He shrugged.

She took a deep breath and exhaled longer than usual before making her next point. "Tate . . . I don't want to have sex with you. Ever. Yet you keep making advances, so—I just don't think this arrangement you proposed is going to work."

He rolled his eyes and waved his hands in frustration, "You're missing the point. Of course I *want* to have sex with you. I'm fucking seventeen years old—I'd like to have sex every day. But, obviously you don't want to have sex with me, so I let others take care of those needs. If we ever had sex, it would be meaningful. The point is, the sex I have with other girls is not meaningful. It's just a screw. With us, it would be making love, you know. It would be highly meaningful . . . But goddammit, you couldn't get pregnant. Shit—can you imagine your father? Shit . . . That man scares me. He scares me more than my own father . . . So, it's best we don't have sex, anyway. I mean, I'm happy just playing around in the back seat of the car, you know? Just let me go screw off every once in awhile, and I'm very happy."

"That would make you happy?" she echoed.

"Yes . . . that would make me really happy. Going out with you makes me very happy. Occasionally screwing a skank makes me very happy. Dating a skank—now that's a nightmare. Breaking up with you—another big downer. I'm really quite happy just the way things are. Can't you be happy, too? I mean—that's my point. If I'm not taking care of some need you have, just let me know. You know, if you want to make out with some other guy one night, go ahead. But why would you want to date anyone else? You gotta get to know them, learn their history all over, deal with their baggage and their parents . . ." He shook his head in dismay.

"Tate . . ." She approached him cautiously, not wanting to hurt him with what she had to say but knowing it had to be said. "Tate, I don't love you. I'm not in love with you, and I . . ." She gently touched his arm. "I don't want to hang out with you. I don't want to hang out with anyone right now. I think I just want to be alone."

He sighed, shaking his head in protest. "No—look, just stick with me through Homecoming. Please. There are a lot of people counting on me to have this party. I need you. I need you with me. And, I'm telling you—our parents are not going to allow this break-up. You watch. Go home and tell your father."

She shuddered.

"Yeah . . . You know what I'm saying is true. A part of you knows it's even logical. You're stuck with me, Dan. But, shit—if you want space, I'll give you space. We can both pretend. Keep the peace and appearances. It's easier that way. It's easier than the alternative right now."

She stared into the black, pocked pavement, the cracks seemingly widening as they stood there, threatening to engulf them both in darkness and chaos. Suddenly a wave of emotion jolted through her with such force that she was unable to stop the onslaught of tears. "I want to go home—" she burst, sobbing.

Tate sighed deeply. "Okay—I'll, I'll take you home. Come on," he said gently, reaching out to guide her.

"I can't go home," she cried, looking up at him, laughing through the tears. "Dennis is having that party . . . I can't go home. I can't . . ."

"Oh . . . Well, you could come stay at my house—"

She shook her head. "Just take me to Brooke's house. My stuff is there. I'll be fine."

He nodded, and the night ended without further incident or exchange.

CHAPTER FOUR

He had seen the girl before.

She looked so familiar, he thought, sitting face to face with her. They were seated on a wall overlooking a vast brick terrace enclosed by trees. Odd statues haphazardly interrupted the terrace space, the slim feminine figures erupting like barren trunks from the brick floor, armless.

He knew her well, he decided, casually sitting on the stone wall, his legs hung over one side. Her long, curly brown hair cascaded over her broad shoulders. She was smiling at him, and he felt warm inside. He could feel the sun shining upon them, though he could see nothing but a bright haze. There seemed to be neither sky nor anything beyond this stone hideaway, though he sensed the mountains loomed in the mist, just beyond the wall. She had a few freckles on her face and a large dimple on the right cheek that deepened when she smiled.

His eyes moved from her to the statues. They seemed invasive, their long necks and blank eyes twisting towards him, almost accusingly. Their stone hair, initially pulled tightly up on the crowns of their heads, began to crack, shaping into coral-like strands that fell around their shoulders, covering the armless stumps. He turned to share this observation with the girl seated next to him. Her name was Jennifer.

She laid a hand on his leg and leaned close to him. *Silly*, she said laughing, though he never saw her lips move. *This is just a dream. There are no statues. There's no me. There's no you.*

A wind picked up, blowing fallen leaves against the wall. Jennifer's hair lifted gently off her shoulders in the breeze, revealing smooth, ivory toned skin, almost the same as the statues surrounding them. Then the moaning began. At first he thought it was the wind through the trees, but it had a distinctly feminine voice. He could barely make out words, painful, almost screaming, the piercing tone muffled as if coming from the far end of a long tunnel.

It was the statues, he realized, again looking towards the still sprouting human shaped columns. He could see fingers trying to claw their way through the pale, polished stone, scratching and scraping until streaks of blood appeared like aging veins.

He turned again to Jennifer. Her face was close to his now, and he wanted to kiss her. They had kissed before, and it was always pleasant. She smelled sweet, her breath minty, and there was a scent of baby powder around her, that perfume she wore. He closed his eyes, letting his body and mouth naturally respond to hers, trying to block out the increasingly deafening moans, feeling guilty to be experiencing pleasure in the midst of such a nightmare of pain.

As they kissed more intensely, he felt his cheek and chin getting wet and wondered if it had begun to rain. He gently pulled away, blinking, immediately looking up at the sky and seeing nothing but the bright haze, not even a point of light or a cloud. He looked down at her and lurched in horror.

Blood streamed down her face, running over her lips and chin and dripping onto her clothes. It poured from a gaping wound in her forehead. And as he tried to read an answer in her gaze, her eyes rolled back, the whites solidifying. He practically fell off the wall, stumbling to his feet. *What's happening*—he heard himself yell, though his mouth spoke no words. His mind screamed it over and again as he watched her facial features melt into the running blood and her physical structure twist and distort into another form, a much larger and shapeless mass.

He started to walk backwards, glancing behind for an exit off the terrace and staring wildly around at the crumbling stone figures, the fleshy hands and limbs reaching out from within.

He turned to the wall and found himself staring at the barrel of a rifle. A man sat in her place, a large male with no face, no head, just a slightly overweight body dressed in a red plaid work shirt, dirty jeans and work boots. He stood up and aimed the gun at Alex.

Alex spun around and began to run, heading for the other end of the terrace, pushing away the groping fingers of the disintegrating statues. He found himself stumbling as he ran, and each time he looked over his shoulder, he saw the figure charging after him, rifle poised, but just far enough away that he felt he could make it if only he could find his way off the terrace and through the forest.

As he cleared the threshold, dead leaves crunched under his steps. It was fall, and the trees were barren. He could barely make out a path leading to some unseen point in the distance. But he heard water, and as he kept running, the sound of rushing water became louder. As he ran, he found his mind became clearer, and he realized she was right. He was dreaming again. This was all just a dream, and if he could find some way to wake himself up, he wouldn't have to experience the dreaded end again.

He came to a river but had to slide down the steep, muddy embankment to reach the rocky shore.

I can shoot you from here, boy.

He felt his muscles weaken from sheer nervousness and fright. Shaking violently, he plunged into the icy, raging water, letting it engulf him. He woke up as the water filled his lungs but before he could gasp his last breath.

The dream had left him with a fear of his past and a foreboding for the future. After the episode with Kelly, he began to avoid girls altogether, though it was difficult. Homecoming was fast-approaching, and a number of girls had asked him to the dance. He politely declined all of them and was relieved when they found other dates.

A depression settled in, and he found himself wanting to avoid all social contact, retreating further and further inwards. He studied hard at school, compelled to get better grades, if nothing else to please his parents, and put the rest of his energy into football. It wasn't long before he had impressed the coaches and was off the bench and starting for the JV team.

Trisha was struggling to fit in at East, and though outwardly polite, he knew inwardly she blamed him for ruining her life. His parents kept threatening to take him to a shrink. His new acquaintances called daily, insisting he get out more. Dennis pestered him more than once to party after school, but he sensed there would be drugs and alcohol. Carl invited him to jam, and to appease him he promised he would soon—right after Homecoming—even though he had lost interest in playing music.

It did not occur to him that people would have an opinion of his lifestyle choices, but the rude awakening occurred a week and half before the big dance.

"What the hell is wrong with you, Fahlstrom?" Carl asked him after class one morning. "You don't do nothin' anymore, man. You got something goin' on I should know about?"

Alex eyed him tiredly as he headed to the drinking fountain. "No. Just busy. I'm trying to improve my grade point average."

"Okay—whatever—but what's up with you and girls, man? I mean—if you don't watch it, you're going to get a reputation, and it won't be good. Either you're a fag, which is completely fucked up, or you're full of yourself and too good for Kansas women."

Alex nearly spat out the water. "*What did you say?*" he asked, choking and wiping his mouth with his sleeve.

"I said you're either a fag or a dick the way you're acting lately."

Alex just sighed, shaking his head. He was too astounded to reply.

"Look, man—I like you. I'm just watching your back. People talk, and I know what they're saying. You need to, like, get out more. Find a girl. Hang out and act normal, or people are just going to start avoiding you."

"Yeah . . . Alright. I'll—I'll do that."

"Good idea. So how about catching a movie with us Saturday night? There's a group of us going—the usual gang."

Alex nodded. "Yeah—that sounds good."

"You do that," Carl pointed his finger at him like a gun.

He shuddered inwardly and shuffled to his next class alone, only vaguely aware he was surrounded by a swarm of students. They did not seem real. Or, maybe, he did not seem real. He felt like a ghost walking amongst the living, visible to a few but connected to none. For a moment, he wondered if he hadn't really died with Jennifer and was in some kind of denial. Maybe living was the dream and death the reality.

Saturday night, he sat on the edge of his bed, waiting for Carl to pick him up, staring at the brick walls. He did not see them as a prison. He saw them as a fortress, shutting out the rest of the world. The last thing he wanted to do was to see a movie, especially one by Quentin Tarantino.

But he would have to act interested. Have to laugh and joke and pretend he was having a good time. Have to be just like everyone else. Perception was everything. It was better than the alternative. Imagining himself an actor, he closed his eyes to get into the part until the doorbell rang.

There were three carloads of people, all headed to the theater and afterwards to a huge party at some girl's house. Alex groaned inwardly. It would be a long night, and he did not feel like getting trashed or hanging out with chemically altered people. As he stood in line, two girls began flirting outright with him, physically clinging to him and verbally giving him endless grief for being a recluse. They all talked incessantly about Homecoming and teased him for not having asked anyone to the dance. In the midst of defending himself and gently prying people off his person, he looked up and noticed a girl staring at him through the crowd. He paused mid-sentence, captured by her appearance.

He didn't even notice her features immediately, just her presence. She wore a bright white sweater, a glowing star in the midst of a dark crowd. She turned away, but he continued to study her, ignoring his friends' jabs and eventual nosiness as to what he was staring at. She was beautiful in an exotic way, he decided, with long, dark-brown hair and olive-toned skin.

Her eyes rested on him again, and he immediately caught her stare. She had large, expressive eyes, full lips and pronounced cheek bones. Her body seemed mature, and he wondered if she was older than he. Nobody stood with her, and he scanned the area to see if she was attached to anyone else.

She looked down, then up again, and he smiled at her, hoping to make a connection, but unsure why he felt compelled to do so. There was something familiar about her, as if he had recognized someone in a crowd whom he had not seen in years, or lifetimes. A person in their group then figured out the object of his interest and began to make a loud issue out of it. Ignoring the comments, he flung himself over the rope and headed towards the girl with the eagerness of Pygmalion. She didn't see him approach, her face buried in her hands, and his own hand shook as he reached out and tapped her shoulder.

"Hi," he said, grinning at her surprised look and trying to hide his own nervousness.

Her face flushed as she mumbled an apology and tried to avoid looking at him. "I'm—I'm terribly sorry—I—I didn't mean to be staring—"

"That's okay. What were you staring at?" he asked, suddenly self-conscious and fearing he had misinterpreted her gestures.

Her glance immediately averted to his hair.

"This?" he confirmed, grabbing a beaded strand. His heart sank, and he frowned sadly. "So . . . Do you like it?" he asked, swearing to himself to have it shorn tomorrow. His hair, his hair—that's all women ever talked about was his cool hair. He could never tell if the attraction was for him or his hair.

"I—I don't know—" she responded nervously, eyebrows furrowed.

"Really?" he asked, trying to cover his disappointment by staying cheerful. "Why?" he pressed curiously.

"Well—I don't know—I don't know you . . . Does it matter? If I like your hair, I mean—"

He shrugged, breathing a sigh of relief. "No—it shouldn't." This was a good sign.

"So—why did you come over here?" she asked, looking up at him again.

He smiled, his mind searching for the right words before speaking, wanting to relay to her the significance of this moment and the sincerity of his advance. "Well . . . Here I am . . . standing in line, surrounded by a sea of black coats and dark denim. I mean—look around . . . Everyone is wearing black or blue. And then I look up—and there you are," he said, reaching out to touch her sweater. "This blaze of white . . . Like a—like a puff—"

She rolled her eyes, and he mentally slapped himself in the head.

"I mean—I mean a puff of light—a star, or something . . ." he started, reddening, feeling he'd blown everything. "Do I know you from somewhere? There's something . . . something familiar about you."

She shrugged, obviously trying to suppress her annoyance. "I don't believe so, no. You don't look familiar to me."

He shook his head, "Sorry. So—are you seeing a movie?" he asked quickly, changing the subject.

She raised an eyebrow.

His face burned in embarrassment, and he was irritated by his sudden clumsiness. Had he always been this awkward with girls? He could not remember.

"I—I meant, are you seeing a movie by yourself? Or, are you—are you with somebody?"

"I'm alone," she said simply, peering over his shoulder. She then waved, grinning sarcastically.

He turned to see at whom she was waving and saw his friends motioning excitedly, then heard them hooting obnoxiously.

"Sorry," he said quietly, aware that she may think he was toying with her and setting her up for some prank. "I—I really just noticed you through the crowd and . . . Well, I thought you looked interesting." He sighed loudly. "No—I thought you looked beautiful. You're very beautiful, and I'm sorry. I'm sorry I embarrassed you in front of my friends. Please enjoy your evening." He turned to go, his heart sinking.

"Hey," the girl called softly, her voice stopping him. "It's okay. I *was* staring at you. Actually, I was staring at you first."

He smiled.

"My name is Danielle," she said, extending her hand.

Reaching to shake, he paused briefly. "Danielle . . ." he echoed before taking her extended hand. "I'm Alex. Alex Fahlstrom."

"Danielle Sumners," she said, releasing her grip.

"Sumners?" he burst. "Are you Dennis' sister?"

"Uh—yes. Yes, I am—you know Dennis?" she asked, caught off guard. But then her eyes grew wide. "*Alex*—you're the new guy. From Montana, right?"

"Yeah—yes, I am."

"Well," she laughed, "It's very nice to finally meet you. What a strange coincidence. Your name comes up often, and—well, it's just odd meeting you here of all places, you know?"

He nodded in agreement, speechless for the moment.

She smiled then stared at the floor.

"So—what movie are you seeing? Maybe you could join us," he offered.

"Oh—I doubt you're seeing what I'm seeing."

"*True Romance?*"

'Uh—no. I'm seeing a romance, but . . . *Age of Innocence*—with Wynona Ryder," she said, nodding nervously.

He couldn't help but wrinkle his nose in response. The mere idea of sitting through a Victorian romance, let alone one with Wynona Ryder in it, seemed tediously boring.

"I know, I know," she protested. "Now you see why I'm *alone*. I couldn't even get my best friend to go with me."

"Well—just don't go. Why do you have to go at all? Is this for English class or something—"

She laughed, shaking her head. "As absurd as this may sound, I *want* to go. I really want to see this movie, actually."

He rolled his eyes and was about to retort when a girl from his group interrupted them, waving a movie ticket in his face and physically pulling him away from Danielle.

"It's okay—I'm sure I'll see you around," Danielle said, smiling warmly.

Alex waved, wishing the moment hadn't ended so abruptly. By the time he rejoined his friends, he wished it hadn't ended at all, as they were merciless. Upon discovering the girl was Dennis' sister, a few guys exclaimed she had gotten better looking since grade school and where had Dennis been hiding her. The girls snorted, insisting she was a rich private school bitch whom Alex should avoid like the plague. Most thought her boyfriend was in the bathroom and Alex shameless to pull such a stunt in the first place. And since he remained dateless for Homecoming, they considered his mission a failure. Then the redneck Mountain Man jokes started and did not cease until the previews began rolling.

His mind still on Danielle, he barely paid attention to the chatter. There was something very comforting about her, and he longed to see her again. Fifteen minutes into the movie, he realized he wasn't paying attention to the storyline. Overcome with an emotion he could not define, he jumped from his seat and began to crawl over his friends to get to the aisle.

"Fahlstrom—where you going?" Carl whispered loudly. "Get me a Coke—"

He shook his head. "I'm not going there. I don't know where I'm going. If I don't come back—go to the party without me."

Carl began protesting, but he walked up the aisle and out of the dark theater, his eyes wincing to adjust to the light. For the next ten minutes, he searched the foyer and concession stand line, but she was nowhere to be seen.

∞

Saturday morning, Danielle sat up with a start. Forgetting where she was, she began to grope for her cat. Every morning, she awoke to the calm purring of her cat, who usually lay curled up next to her head or stomach. He was especially comforting after nightmares.

Though she did not remember having a nightmare, she had not slept well. Not having packed an alarm clock, she woke up every hour or so, afraid of being late for practice. And now she had awakened again, this time to the sun streaming through Brooke's guest bedroom window. She glanced anxiously at the clock, but it was only seven in the morning.

As the others were still asleep, having gotten back long after she went to bed, she carefully and quietly collected her things, showered and dressed in the guest bathroom and headed to the UMKC campus for her violin practice, feeling tired and depressed.

She neither felt like playing nor going home. The house would be a wreck and smell of party residue, and her room would be trashed. Yet outside of studying at a library or home, she could think of no other retreat. No activity appealed to her—not movies, shopping, coffee houses or socializing. Curling up with a good nineteenth-century romance seemed the best option, but that could only happen after hours of cleaning.

Morose, she finally headed home in the early afternoon, after hanging out at the university library for a few hours. There were still a few cars parked in the driveway, and she prayed they were the clean-up crew and not stragglers from the previous night. She sat in her car for a few moments, unable to find the effort to undo her seat belt, staring absently at the looming brick and stone structure, the massive well-manicured lawn, the eight foot wrought iron fence that enclosed much of their property, the imposing turret. For some reason, the house felt cold and unwelcoming. Or was it the sky, she asked herself, peering out the windshield at the darkening hues, dampening her spirits while the rain still remained miles away.

Something was not right, but what was wrong she could not identify. Daily, she experienced a growing sense of uneasiness, and her dreams were increasingly disturbing. She was always traveling in her dreams but not on a holiday or vacation. Instead it was across a large, barren desert. She was lost and often without any provisions, including food, shelter, water or even clothing. The sun was hot and blinding, blistering her skin, and the wind whipped sand into terrifying shapes with shrieks that pervaded space.

The house did not look real to her. Nothing seemed real anymore. Her entire existence was absorbing into absurdity, and she dreaded more absurdity awaited her the minute she crossed the threshold.

Before the rain started, she ventured inside, surprised to find it eerily quiet and in relative order. While the furnishings needed to be adjusted, any signs of a party had been swept up and put into a number of trash bags stacked in the front hall. Wanting to avoid any social interaction whatsoever, she trod softly up the huge, winding staircase, down the hall and towards her room. Before opening the door, she took a deep breath and closed her eyes, mentally preparing herself for the chaos.

To her utter shock, her room looked untouched. She was so surprised, that she closed the door and re-opened it. To make triple sure she wasn't dreaming, she wandered throughout the room physically touching her bed and furniture, smelling the sheets for fresh detergent, ensuring everything was just as she had left it.

Had she dreamed there was a couple in her bed last night? Did that even happen?

Convinced the room was as it appeared, she then began to look for her cat, who was to be strictly confined to her and Dennis' wing of the house.

Her parents even had a special litter closet built next to the bathroom. When the cat was nowhere to be found after a twenty minute in-depth search and a continuous mantra of *Here, Mr. Kitty*, she headed downstairs in search of her brother.

"Dennis," she said, finding him and a few of his friends in the kitchen, the room still in disarray.

Donned in a stocking cap and dark sunglasses, he looked up and then immediately away. "Yeah . . . What do you want?"

"Well—first I want to thank you and everyone for cleaning my room. That was really, really nice of you. I'm—I'm . . . I can't tell you how nice that was."

He grunted and continued to clean and rearrange the furnishings, acting as if she wasn't there.

"Um—but I was wondering. Have you seen Mr. Kitty?"

"Nope," he said, tying a trash bag.

"Oh . . . Well—you don't think he got outside do you? It's about to storm."

Dennis said nothing, brushing by her as he carried another trash bag into the hall.

"Do you need some help?" she called after him and then turned to his friends. "Do you all need some help? What's left to do?"

"Downstairs," Mick mumbled. "It's fucking trashed."

She nodded and then headed down the stairs to the finished basement, gasping in horror at the site. Trashed was an understatement. Not only did cans, bottles and food litter the floor, the reek of cigarette smoke, pot and stale beer hit her before she reached the last step. She began by opening the basement windows and turning on the ceiling fans. Grabbing a trash bag from the downstairs supply closet, she began picking up what litter could be gathered without a vacuum.

"What are you doing?"

His tone harshly breaking the silence, she jumped back, startled.

Her brother bounded down the stairs. "Give me that," he said, yanking the trash bag from her.

"What—I'm helping. I want to help—"

"No!" he yelled. "This isn't your mess to clean—it's mine. I mean it—get out of here. Go to a movie or something."

"But, I don't want to go to a movie. I want to help," She protested, trying to take back the bag.

"Fuck no—get out of here. Go order a pizza, go read a book—go do something nice . . . Take a bubble bath or something . . . We cleaned the upstairs first."

She wanted desperately to read him, baffled at his sudden generosity towards her, but could see nothing behind the dark shades. Afraid of angering him, she released her grip on the bag and slowly sauntered out of the basement.

A loud clap of thunder sounded as she set foot on the first level, and she immediately thought of her cat. Rather than retiring to her room, she spent the next hour searching every room and closet in the entire house. Failing to find him, she then ventured outside in the rain between lightening storms, calling his name. Since it was too dark to see him, she focused on listening for his cries. When this half hour search yielded nothing, she decided to call animal control and report her cat lost, a sick feeling in the pit of her stomach.

Cold, wet and stressed, she had no choice but to take her brother's advice and draw a hot bath to warm her bones and calm her nerves. Donning sweats, she tried to curl up on her bed and lose herself in Edith Wharton's *Age of Innocence*, but her mind was too distracted to care about Newland's budding and illicit romance with the Countess. In fact, she detested all of the characters, finding their problems trivial in light of her cat's potential suffering.

Feeling tears well up, she tossed the book to the floor and grabbed her remote. Failing to find any decent movies on cable, she settled on a sitcom hoping it would have the power to make her laugh.

Two *Full House* episodes later, a knock sounded on her door. Before she could respond, the door opened.

"Dan—" her brother peered in, still donned in sunglasses.

"Hey, Dennis," she said, sitting up in her bed. "Still hungover, huh? Must be a bad one for you to still be in shades this late."

"Uh . . . I need to talk to you."

"Okay—sure," she said, her heart sinking. She knew what he was about to say and prayed she was wrong.

He slowly ambled towards her bed, eventually plopping himself heavily onto the end of it, a good arm's length from her. Sighing, he looked up and removed his shades.

"It's about Mr. Kitty, isn't it?" she whispered, her throat swelling.

He nodded grimly, his bloodshot eyes moistening.

"He's dead . . . he's dead, isn't he?" she burst, unable to contain her emotion.

He nodded. "I'm sorry . . ."

She cried uncontrollably for the next couple of minutes, waiting for him to leave. At one point, he did get up, but it was to retrieve a box of Kleenex for her.

"How'd he die?" she asked between the sobs.

"Car. He got out last night and must have gotten hit."

"Where?"

"Driveway. He was dead when we found him. I don't think he suffered. I don't think he knew what hit him," Dennis offered.

"So where is he?"

"In the garage. In a bag in the garage . . . Do you want to see him?"

She shook her head violently. "No—no . . . I don't want to see him like that. Mr. Kitty, Mr. Kitty . . . my poor kitty," she cried, again sobbing uncontrollably.

This time, her brother actually put an arm around her. "I'm sorry, Dan . . . It's my fault. You told me to keep your room locked—and I thought I did, but somebody must have gotten in there through the bathroom and unlocked the door. I don't know what happened. I'm sorry—I really am."

"It's not your fault," she said between sniffles. "I had a feeling . . . I knew something like this could happen. But it's not your fault . . . I just wish he didn't have to die alone, you know? Scared and alone. That's what's so horrible."

"But we all die alone, Dan."

"No—there are people who die peacefully—in their beds with their families around them. Pets, too . . . I wish I could have held him and comforted him."

"But he still has to head to his next life without you."

"Next life . . ." she echoed. "I'd like to think heaven. I'd like to think he's in heaven."

"Okay. Sure."

That night, she dreamed she was outside, looking for her cat amongst the bushes. Rounding a hedge, she saw large, gray stone urns filled with magenta roses. They sat upon a low, gray stone wall that surrounded an expansive terrace. Numerous statues of Romanesque-looking females cluttered the terrace, and she thought she saw her cat darting in-between the statues. She began to follow him, and as she approached the far end of the terrace, she noticed a stone platform.

Atop the platform was what appeared to be a stone coffin. A large bouquet of the same magenta colored roses showered the coffin, spilling off the sides. As she surveyed the area around her, she noticed the flowers provided the only color in her view, the terrace being gray, the sky being gray and even the leaves on surrounding trees having a dull brownish tone to them. She felt as if she were walking through a black and white film.

When she turned back to the coffin, the lid had been removed and now lay in two cracked pieces at the base of the platform. She stopped, her heart beating, wondering if she should look inside. Supporting herself on the platform, she stood tiptoed and peered in.

She froze in horror for a moment before jumping back, covering her eyes.

The person lying inside appeared to be herself, clothed in a white dress, the features immaculate except for a large black hole in the center of her forehead.

She shook her head. It couldn't be—It couldn't be—I'm dreaming—she told herself.

You're not dreaming.

A figure spoke clearly from within the coffin.

She raised her head to see a girl sit up and immediately noticed it was not herself. The girl was dressed in white and held a small bouquet of magenta roses in her hands. Her light brown hair spilled over her shoulders in perfect ringlets, and her clear blue eyes bore into Danielle intensely before turning black. Within seconds, Danielle found herself staring into two black pits. A trickle of blood streamed down the girl's face and onto the white dress. The trickle turned into a stream, and the girl's entire upper body began to shake violently.

"Who are you?" Danielle screamed in horror.

Loud, cracking sounds reverberated throughout the terrace, and Danielle held her ears, looking wildly about her as the statues began to crumble.

"Where am I?" she yelled, turning back to the girl.

Welcome to hell.

The girl smiled widely as blood covered her person. The streams of red turned black, and her entire body and clothing turned gray, hardening before shattering into a thousand pieces.

And as she split apart, the entire area exploded into violent motion. Dark black clouds rolled low in the sky in smoky billows. The wind bent the trees sideways and whipped her hair, stinging her face. From amongst the crumbling statues she could see human limbs—arms and hands—clawing, and the air resounded with high-pitched screams.

She thought she was going to die—that perhaps she had already died—when a white-robed figure emerged from amongst the debris. He walked slowly, and as he neared her, she could make out his long, brown wavy hair, his beard, his calm expression. He held a wooden cross in his right hands.

"*Jesus*—" she breathed, wanting to believe.

The figure stopped abruptly, not eight feet away, his left hand outstretched and his right holding the cross upright towards her.

She remained frozen, staring in wide-eyed awe.

A shadow passed over his features. He smiled widely, then laughed out loud. And as he laughed, his physical person transformed, and she found herself looking into the face of a slightly overweight, unkempt young man in dirty jeans, heavy work boots and a red plaid work shirt, unbuttoned enough to reveal a white t-shirt marred with black grease stains. He had dark hair, wild eyes and a heavy five o'clock shadow. The wooden cross blackened and crumpled, taking the shape of a rifle.

Are you a believer girl?

She shook her head—in protest, fear and disbelief.

That's too bad.

The last thing she remembered was the loud crack of the gun through the wind and a burning sensation of lead ripping through her flesh.

She sat up in bed, gasping for breath, the shot still ringing in her ears.

It was a full minute before she realized it was her telephone that was ringing. She groped for the phone, trying to read the clock at the same time. What day was it? What time was it? Had she overslept?

"Hello?" she tried to answer in a calm tone.

It was her father reminding her to go to Mass. They would be home in a few hours. The house had better be spotless.

After hanging up, she fell back into the bed and pulled the covers over her head, wanting to hide from both the dreaming and waking world and feeling her bed was the only place of refuge. She must have drifted off to sleep again, for the next thing she knew her brother was pulling the covers off her and asking her to get up.

She opened her eyes to a burst of magenta colored flowers and had to refrain from screaming in horror.

"Like em?" her brother asked. "They're for Mr. Kitty. I got him a little statue, too, see?" He produced a small, gray stone statue of an angel. "Get up. It's late—Mom and Dad will be home soon, and we need to bury him before they get here. I already dug the hole and everything."

An hour later she was standing in the wet grass holding a large umbrella over herself and Dennis as he planted what turned out to be an azalea over the grave and put the angel statue in place.

"Well—do you have anything to say?" he asked, wiping the dirt from his hands onto his ripped jeans.

She shook her head, trying to refrain from another round of tears, her eyes still swollen and burning from the night before.

"Okay . . . Well, I will then." He reached into his pocket and pulled out a ripped piece of notebook paper. "*The One remains, the many change and pass; Heaven's light forever shines, Earth's shadows fly; Life, like a dome of many colored glass, stains the white radiance of Eternity, Until Death tramples it to fragments* . . . Percy Bysshe Shelley."

Tears streamed effortlessly down her face, but this time not over her cat. "That's beautiful, Dennis. Thank you."

He put his arm around her and they stood, huddled together under the umbrella in the pouring rain, until a large crack of thunder sent them seeking shelter indoors.

A few days later, as she worked quietly one evening on her algebra, the intercom in her bedroom buzzed. "Danielle—"

Her heart jumped at hearing her father's voice.

"Danielle—"

"Yes—" she called, springing from the bed.

"Can I see you in my study?"

"Sure . . ."

The intercom clicked off, and she breathed deeply. Her father only called her into the study when he was displeased with something. Her mind raced through the past couple of days to discover the possible source of his irritation. The party? Did he find out about the party? Her cat . . . Did they finally realize the cat was gone? Did they notice the extra bush in the enormous garden that only landscapers touched?

Straightening her shirt, she slowly strode down the hall, entering the study from its second-story doorway, pacing her tread down the small spiral staircase that led to her father's workplace below.

He looked up from a pile of forms.

"Oh . . . Sit down. Please," he said, motioning to a chair with a nod.

Removing a reference book from the seat, she silently obeyed, waiting patiently for him to begin, which he did after making notes to a few documents. She studied him a moment, almost in awe. How did one get to be like her father, she wondered. He was a workaholic obsessed with perfection, from his house, to his lawn to the perfectly starched collars on his custom-made shirts. His hair, though naturally curly, was combed so neatly it looked fake, with the exception of the gray streaks. Tonight, he wore a pink, tailored shirt with silver cufflinks, but the color was hardly emasculating due to his large build and perpetually intense expression. She was suddenly struck by how closely he resembled Tate, and the realization sent a chill through her body.

As if he could sense her staring at him, he abruptly stopped writing, and she quickly looked at the floor.

"Do you have something to tell me?" he asked knowingly.

Her stomach jolted.

"No."

"Really? Well, that's odd . . . It's been awhile since we've talked . . . You're into the school year. Homecoming is a few weeks away. There's nothing of significance you want to share with me?"

Her eyes met his, and she shook her head before quickly averting them to the Oriental rug.

"Well then," he drawled, sitting back in his chair. "Why don't you tell me about your Homecoming plans with Tate. I do need to approve them, after all."

She blinked her eyes rapidly to ward off a spell of mild dizziness. "Um . . . I don't have any. I'm—I'm not going to Homecoming this year."

"Really?" he said caustically. "And why is that?"

"Um . . . Well . . . Tate and I aren't seeing each other anymore," she whispered.

"I'm sorry—what was that? I can't hear you. Why don't you look at me when you speak."

She looked up at his glowering, deep-set, dark eyes. "I broke up with Tate. We're not going to Homecoming."

"Did you, now? May I ask why?"

She shrugged. "I don't want to go out with him anymore. We don't really have anything in common."

"Nothing in common . . ." he echoed. "Now, let's see. You both attend private Catholic schools, play in the junior symphony, come from wealthy, upstanding families in the community. Your fathers golf together. Your mothers are in Junior League together. In fact, your parents are best friends with the Foleys and just got back from a Labor Day Weekend resort outing with them. And, if that's not enough, Tate's father just happens to be *your* father's biggest client. Would you like to rethink your statement, Danielle?"

She shuddered, knowing the beginning of his lawyer speak meant she was on trial and on the defensive. She also knew she would lose.

"I have nothing in common with him emotionally or intellectually. I don't like him as a boyfriend," she said dully.

"Ah . . . I see. And why does that matter? You're sixteen years old and only a junior in high school. I would like to think you didn't have anything *emotionally* in common with him. That was the point of our getting you two together in the first place."

She looked up at him in shock.

"Yes—we arranged this. What do you think? Or do you? You know, I'm beginning to think I can't count on you anymore, Danielle. I thought you understood. I placed my faith and hopes in you, having lost both in Dennis years ago. But, you . . . Did you think this action through? Did you think of what this could do to our family? Your reputation? Our family's reputation? My business?"

She shook her head in protest, "It shouldn't do anything—"

"You broke up with Tate Foley without warning, Danielle. And at the beginning of the school year—before Homecoming. Were you aware of the parties they had planned? The arrangements? The special festivities—all planned for the two of you, Danielle?"

His tone grew louder and sharper, and she shrunk deeper into the chair.

"And to not even tell me, Danielle. For me and your mother to hear it over dinner one night. The Foleys are devastated. They're shocked by your cold heartedness and had to ask us—over drinks—if you weren't having some sort of emotional problems. If you weren't on drugs."

Her face reddened.

"You should be embarrassed. You should be mortified over your selfish behavior . . . The good news is that I have, as usual, taken care of everything. Cleaned up yet another mess that one of my children made . . . I simply told them you were on allergy medications that were impacting your mind. I told them you had no intention of breaking up with their son and would, of course, be going to Homecoming with im. They're letting him have a large party at the Embassy Suites, you know. You need to be there to ensure it stays under control. We all trust you, Danielle. That's your role. All the great women from the finest families in history understand this. Eleanor was the rock that supported FDR. Jackie was the one who held Camelot together.

They understood the importance of appearance. Perception is everything. Perception is control. It is even more important than wealth. More important than wealth is control. Without control, you are a slave. I did not raise my daughter to be a slave—to other people or to her own silly emotions."

She sat, speechless.

"Now, you will call Tate immediately and apologize to him for your behavior. You will then ask to speak to his parents and apologize to them. You will do this from this phone, on this desk and in my presence. You will then confirm with Tate and his parents that you will be participating in his Homecoming festivities. Thereafter, you will continue as a couple and attend as a couple any socially significant events. What you do outside of those events is between you and Tate. I can imagine this exchange has damaged his opinion of you, but thank god he has the integrity to stand by you and our family in the face of it."

The nervousness turned into a mild nausea, and she wrapped her arms protectively around her stomach.

He then pushed the phone towards her, picking up the receiver and handing it to her. The next fifteen minutes were the most mortifying she had ever experienced. One apology was not enough. Tate and his parents berated her to an extent that her apologies became a mantra, and she was convinced if this took place centuries earlier, they would have placed her in the stocks.

By the time she hung up the phone, the nausea had intensified to such an extent she feared she would throw up in front of him. She got up to leave, but he stopped her with his voice.

"We're not finished young lady . . . Is there anything else you wish to tell me?"

Her lower lip trembled, from fear or the unbearable pain in her stomach, she was unsure. She shook her head.

"Did anything happen while we were away this past weekend? We did put you in charge of the house, you know. Your car and allowance privileges come with a price. That price is ensuring that things stay under control, and if things go out of control that you report such incidents to me . . . Do you have anything to report?"

He knew about the party. Though the house was spotless, and Dennis's friends had actually hauled the trash bags away themselves, he had found some piece of evidence. But she could not bring herself to tell on her brother.

"No. I spent the night at Brooke's on Friday, and I was at the library on Saturday."

"And, your brother?"

She shrugged. "You'll have to ask him. We don't really talk much anymore."

"I'm not asking Dennis, I'm asking you. Now do you have something to report or not?"

After a brief mental debate, she replied that she did not and turned to leave.

"Danielle, I know everything," he said coldly, stopping her in her tracks just as she reached the threshold. "I know everything that goes on, and there is nothing you can hide from me. What you need to know is that I will not tolerate another fuck-up from you, do you understand?"

A wave of pain shot through her stomach upon hearing her father use such a curse word.

"I don't want any problems from you through the end of this school year, do you understand? Not one incident—not one phone call—not one problem, do you hear me? And if anything happens before or during Homecoming—"

He stopped abruptly but did not have to finish his sentence. She mentally finished it for him and shuddered, wondering if all of her dreams were pointing to a family tragedy.

"And don't even think about bringing another pet into this house. You're dismissed."

She lay in bed that night wanting to cry, but no tears would form.

Over the next few weeks, she retreated further and further inward, spending any spare time she had alone in her room with a gothic romance. In particular, she had taken to the Brontë sisters, relating more to the authors than to the characters. As she poured over *Wuthering Heights* and *Jane Eyre*, she felt she knew what both authors were thinking when they wrote the novels. Why they wrote the novels. And why they created Heathcliff and Rochester. Surrounded by sickness, death and suffering, they had written as a means of refuge. They created a world in their minds where they could retreat. And since the real world was absent of true lovers and heroes, they created their own soul mates.

She often wondered if she wasn't a reincarnation of one of them. If she wasn't living a gothic romance of her own, living in this huge castle-like home with an emotionally and sometimes physically abusive father, an alcoholic mother and a resentful brother. Forced to date someone she did not love or find attractive. Surrounded by images of the world's suffering and dreaming nightly of her impending death and doom.

After being shot by Jesus, she had stopped praying, feeling God had abandoned her. She was quite sure there was no God, and if there was, he was as psychopathic as the world he created. Instead of reading the Bible, she read Dickinson and Whitman. Instead of praying, she daydreamed and mentally began constructing her own perfect world and lover. She lived in a Mediterranean-style home by a lake in the mountains, and her lover had a mane of golden hair, the face of Johnny Depp and the body of an American football player. To maintain control, she drank coffee morning and night to stay awake and avoid dreaming, sleeping only when her body physically shut down, and she immersed herself in all of her obligatory activities not only to ensure each was accomplished perfectly but also to avoid having to think.

Outside of her brother, everyone she knew had lost their minds. Even her close friends were suddenly obsessed with dating and Homecoming. Brooke had met a guy from a high school across town and was rarely to be seen anymore. All conversations with Danielle's peers disintegrated into gossip and Homecoming. She felt if she heard the word *Homecoming* again, she would either puke or punch the person who mouthed it. Her brother found the entire affair equally ludicrous, and they would make fun of it together, pondering its meaning and ultimately deciding it meant nothing. She did not have the heart to share with him the awful truth of her impending Homecoming doom. He would find out soon enough.

At least Tate had kept his word and left her alone. They had a mutual understanding that their relationship was for show, and they would show it when required. Of course, the show was only for adults. Tate's trysts with other girls were well-rumored amongst her peers, and her girlfriends were compelled to give her play-by-plays of his antics at weekend parties that she herself refused to attend. She wondered if her all-knowing father was aware, but then came to the eerie realization that he not only knew but preferred it that way. Better Tate get some other girl pregnant. It was all part of the game plan.

The weekend before Homecoming, she decided to treat herself. She had always wanted to go to a movie alone but never had the courage or the time. *Age of Innocence* was playing, and she could find nobody to see the movie with her. What better time to see a movie alone and what better movie, she thought as she changed into jeans. Searching for a clean, warm top, she settled on a bright white v-neck sweater and white and silver striped scarf. White was symbolic of her twentieth-century Emily Dickinsonian act of going on a date with herself. Since the movie did not start until seven thirty, she treated herself to dinner at the Chili's across the street from the theater.

The only thing remotely disturbing was that she felt like a prisoner on death row, enjoying a final, favorite meal before facing his doom. She was convinced that Homecoming was just that—her coming to rest in the ultimate home of all creatures, a six-foot hole in the ground. Though she did not know what would happen, her dreams led her to believe there would be drinking, drugs and guns and that things would get completely out of control.

Though the theater was packed, as she stood in line to purchase her ticket, she felt very alone. Her brother was right. Everyone died alone. She was stranded on an island and saw nothing but other islands, each with its own castaway, as far as the eye could see. She looked around, wanting desperately to make a connection with someone—anyone. To feel she was really there and hadn't already turned into a hungry spirit.

There were a number of families with children, but they were preoccupied. She tried to catch the attention of a toddler two groups up, making faces and waving, but the child stared through her and then turned away, his attention drawn to a toy. There were numerous couples holding hands and whispering things to each other. Even some of the adult couples, parents and elderly, seemed quite engaged with each other. She searched out other girls her age, suddenly desperate to find somebody she knew, but she recognized no one.

The line moved slowly, and she stared at the carpet, trying not to see hideous faces in its garish red and gold floret patterns. Horrified, she once again turned her attention to people-watching, her gaze settling on a male figure two lines down. He had the most unusual hair. It was long and blond and quite messy, strands of it braided with unusual beads. He had a rather large and athletic build, too, but his face was not handsome, with rugged angles, a slightly protruding jaw and narrow, deep-set eyes. He was laughing and gesturing with a rather large group of males and females. At one point he was talking intently to them.

Then he looked at her, and for a moment she didn't even realize she had been staring at him until their eyes locked. When she realized how rude she was being, she immediately looked down, turning red. She tried to keep her eyes glued to the slithering carpet but found herself wanting to catch another glimpse of him. Something about him had stirred her. As nonchalantly as possible, she raised her head and deliberately looked the opposite direction of where he was standing, then slowly turned towards him, trying to act like she was just scanning the place, taking in the whole view—

Her eyes rested on him again, and he immediately caught her stare.

She looked down. Then up again—and he was smiling at her. One of his friends turned around to see what he was looking at, to which she completely turned herself the other direction, hiding her face in her hands. She had never been more embarrassed in her life. How could she be so obvious?

She felt a tap on her shoulder and looked up, nearly choking.

"Hi," he said, grinning.

It was he. Her face flushed as she mumbled an apology, trying to avoid looking at him.

"What were you staring at?" he asked.

She looked up at him fearfully, her glance immediately averting to his hair.

"This?" he confirmed, grabbing a beaded strand. Then he frowned sadly. "So . . . Do you like it?"

"I—I don't know—" she responded nervously, eyebrows furrowed.

"Really?" he said, his countenance cheerful again. "Why?"

"Well—I don't know—I don't know you . . . Does it matter? If I like your hair, I mean-"

He shrugged. "No—it shouldn't."

He had a pleasant scent about him, not cologne, but one of freshly laundered clothes. And he was even larger in person, standing at least six feet and very well built. Her heart beat faster as she spoke.

"So—why did you come over here?" she asked, looking up at him again.

He grinned, then stared off in the distance a moment before speaking. "Well . . . Here I am . . . standing in line, surrounded by a sea of black coats and dark denim. I mean, look around . . . Everyone is wearing black or blue. And then I look up—and there you are," he said, reaching out to touch her sweater. "This blaze of white . . . Like a—like a puff—"

At this she found herself choking to suppress a fit of hysterics. Puff? Puff of what—smoke? The entire scene was too surreal, and for a moment she wondered if she weren't dreaming again.

"I mean—I mean a puff of light—a star, or something—" he started, reddening. "Do I know you from somewhere? There's something . . . something familiar about you."

She stared at him again, trying not to giggle, in disbelief that he would even think she could take him seriously from this point forward and wondering what other cliché pick-up lines he would attempt to use. "I don't believe so, no. You don't look familiar to me."

He shook his head, "Sorry. So—are you seeing a movie?"

She caustically raised an eyebrow, her guard rising in anticipation of the impending prank, especially since she could see his friends laughing at her and making lewd gestures in the background.

"I—I meant, are you seeing a movie by yourself? Or, are you—are you with somebody?"

"I'm alone," she said, waving knowingly at them in response, refusing to be an unsuspecting butt of their joke. If she was to be humiliated in public, she would at least go down with some dignity.

To her surprise, he apologized and then attempted to compliment her, but her heart burned in shame. Part of her desperately wanted to believe him and part of her retreated hopelessly against the deceit. As he turned to leave, she had a vision of a rescue boat pulling away from her deserted island.

"Hey," she called after him instinctively. "It's okay. I *was* staring at you. Actually, I was staring at you first," she admitted, ready to accept defeat, knowing he would either throw her a lifeline or toss her into the cold depths.

He smiled.

"My name is Danielle," she said, extending her hand.

Reaching to shake, he paused briefly. "Danielle . . ." he echoed before taking her extended hand. "I'm Alex. Alex Fahlstrom."

"Danielle Sumners," she said, releasing her grip.

At the mention of her last name, the tone of the entire conversation changed. In an utterly bizarre twist of fate, he burst out that he knew her brother Dennis. In fact, he was *the* Alex of whom Dennis had talked so often and so fondly. After a few more exchanges, he invited her to join his group, but she politely declined, still fearful that he and his friends had truly intended to humiliate her until he discovered that she was his friend's sister.

"Oh—I doubt you're seeing what I'm seeing," she protested.

"*True Romance?*"

"Uh—no. I'm seeing a romance, but . . . *Age of Innocence*—with Wynona Ryder," she said, wincing at his obvious reaction of disgust.

"Well—just don't go. Why do you have to go at all? Is this for English class or something—"

She laughed in response. "As absurd as this may sound, I want to go. I really want to see this movie, actually."

He was about to say something when a girl from his group interrupted them, waving a movie ticket in his face and physically pulling him away.

"It's okay—I'm sure I'll see you around," Danielle called after him, feeling chilled as he dissolved into his group and eventually completely out of her sight.

She chose a seat against the wall, halfway down the aisle, in the row least populated by other viewers. Though she had purchased a Sprite, she was not thirsty, and placed it in the armrest cup holder. She then counted the minutes to the movie's start, anxious for the lights to dim and the darkness to envelop her and hide that she was crying. Crying over the cruel irony of life. Wondering if the Brontës were crying with her. Just when she had resigned herself to being alone, enjoying being alone and ultimately dying alone, he had to literally waltz into her world, shattering its fragile glass walls. Why did he have to be blond? Why did he have to be built like that? And, why did he have to torment her so—as if he knew he was the first male to stir her physically. Had she not suffered enough these past few months? God was such a bastard.

As she wiped a tear away, another would follow in rapid succession, and she eventually had to use her drink napkin to stop the flow. Even though there were five seats between her and the people next to her, she could feel them staring at her, hear them whispering. She was about to jump up and run out of the theater, when the lights dimmed and the previews began to roll. Distracted by the images, her mind calmed down, and she decided to stay and watch the movie.

Engrossed in the beautiful costumes and settings, not to mention the characters and their impending angst, she did not notice the comings and goings of the people next to her until something bumped her arm.

Puzzled, she turned to look and then sat back, startled.

"So—what'd I miss?" he asked, leaning against her after settling in, his right arm casually slung over the back of her seat.

She stared into the screen, frozen in shock before mildly shaking with a nervous joy. Collecting herself, she mumbled the plot to him, still looking at the screen yet keenly aware of his physical presence and every movement, every breath.

Alex settled back in his seat, unaware of her nervousness and simply relieved to have found her. After a few more minutes of quiet questioning, he pieced together the characters and events and began to watch the movie in earnest, trying to see what the girl next to him was seeing. He soon found himself caught up in the protagonist's dilemma. Ultimately, he was baffled as to why the man didn't just run off with the Michelle Pfeiffer character, if not at least have a fling with her on the side.

"Societal constraints," Danielle explained later, as they walked out of the theater. "It wasn't like today. Today people can screw around and nobody really cares, but it wasn't like that then. Impropriety could ruin one's life—particularly a woman's. And society was smaller then. Not like today when one can just pick up and start over anonymously in another large city."

"But people had affairs back then—men had mistresses. They could have been discreet."

"Are you saying he should have married May and kept the Countess as a mistress?" she asked, eyes narrowing.

"Ideally—no," Alex said.

"Ideally, *what*?"

"Ideally, they'd have just run off together."

"Even though it wasn't proper?" Danielle countered.

"Screw propriety," he laughed. "Life is short. You never know how long you have, and you need to make every minute count . . . Besides, he wasn't in love with Wynona."

"But he *was*. He was in love with her first—"

Alex shook his head. "No, he *wasn't*. If he was in love with Wynona—really in love with her—the Countess couldn't have done what she did. He wouldn't have bit. He—he wouldn't have even noticed."

She mused, comforted by his statement, then stopped in the lobby, looking around. "Where are your friends?" she asked, eyeing him squarely for the first time since their last parting.

He shrugged. "I don't know. I ditched them. They probably left."

"Oh . . ." she swallowed hard, gazing at the carpet, its chaotic pattern now having little impact on her mind, which raced elsewhere. "So—do you need a ride home?"

"Yes, actually—I *do* need a ride home . . . What time is it?" he asked, feeling the night was still young and hoping he could extend their time together.

She glanced at her watch, "Quarter to ten."

"Oh . . . Well, it's still pretty early. Do you want to go hang out somewhere?"

Her heart raced, and she feared her face was reddening as she mumbled a *sure*.

"Where would you like to go? Is there a place to grab coffee?" he suggested nonchalantly.

"There's a Tippins on the way home," she choked. "They're open late and serve pie and coffee."

He grinned. "Great—let's go there."

She nodded silently before turning quickly and heading for her car. He had to increase his pace to keep up with her. Before unlocking the passenger side, she nervously cleaned off her front seat, started the car and rolled down the automatic windows, embarrassed of the lingering unpleasant odors that, in her mind, no amount of bleach and air fresheners had been able to eradicate. After a minute of this bustle, she unlocked the passenger door so he could get in.

"I'm sorry," she said quickly. "My car smells. My brother's friends partied in it too hard one night."

Alex laughed, unable to smell anything but vanilla air freshener, which was a bit overpowering. "Yeah—I can imagine. So—do you and Dennis share the car?"

"Well—it's technically *my* car, but he uses it."

Alex nodded. "So—do you guys get along?" he ventured as she pulled out of the parking space.

She shrugged. "We hadn't been, but it's getting better lately, I think . . . You can listen to the radio if you wish," she offered, trying to concentrate on driving safely but completely distracted by his presence, still wondering why he had joined her and questioning his intentions. She desperately wanted to believe he was attracted to her, but her mind refuted the possibility. He was likely a football player and very popular with the girls. He probably already had a girlfriend—or at least a Homecoming date—and was simply toying with her on the side. It then occurred to her that from one perspective, she was toying with him also. It would be best for both of them if she promptly ended the evening after a quick cup of coffee.

Alex felt completely relaxed in her company. She was nothing like her brother, and there was something very sweet about her. But he sensed she did not want to talk and feared she mistrusted him, so he spent the remainder of the drive pondering how to convince her he was being sincere. When they pulled into the parking lot of the restaurant, he made his move.

She put the car in park and quickly turned to open the door.

He gently grabbed her arm. "Wait—"

She turned and looked down at his hand on her arm, unable to look at his face.

"I know what you're thinking."

"Do you," she whispered.

"Yes . . . You don't trust me. You think I'm just messing with you. You may even think that I just mess around, period—with lots of girls. But, I don't . . . In fact, I haven't wanted to be with anyone since moving here. I'm not even going to *Homecoming*," he said with mild sarcasm.

At that, she looked up at him sadly. "Well, I am—going to Homecoming . . . So now who's messing with whom?"

He released her arm, his spirits sinking. "Oh—I'm sorry. I—I didn't know you had a boyfriend—"

"I don't," she said quickly, staring out the windshield, her hands gripping the steering wheel in anger. "I mean—I'm not in a romantic relationship with anyone. It's just an arrangement for show. Kind of like a trophy wife . . . but I'm a trophy date."

He eyed her curiously, trying to read her expression. "So—how do you feel about this—this arrangement?"

"I was coping with it . . . until tonight," she said, yanking open the car door, climbing out and briskly heading towards the restaurant.

He climbed out after her, suddenly perturbed, sensing a drama was about to unfold and wondering if his stomach or psyche could handle it. Then wondering if a girl existed who did not have such baggage. Perhaps it was just his fate to keep encountering them.

She held the restaurant door open for him, still avoiding eye contact.

He approached the hostess stand and requested a table for two. The restaurant was busy, but they were seated quickly at a small two-person booth where they were forced to sit across from each other at close range.

Once settled, she finally mustered the courage to look at him. "I'm sorry," she said sincerely. "I believe what you said, and . . . well . . . if you really were interested in getting to know me, I thought you should know upfront that I am in an odd situation. Not unlike the movie, actually . . . You wonder why I like such movies and novels. It's because I am living one. My father arranged a relationship for me with the son of his biggest client. It's a high society thing. I'm expected to attend "big" events with him—like Homecoming—even though I want absolutely nothing to do with him. I'm sorry."

Alex's mind raced, trying to process what she was saying, the absurdity of it almost shocking. "But—what about Dennis?"

"What about Dennis?" she echoed dully.

"Does he have an *arrangement*, too?"

She rolled her eyes. "No . . . Dennis is considered a lost cause. My father has stopped disciplining him or, really, having anything to do with him for years now. It's as if Dennis doesn't exist," she said sadly.

Alex felt a chill, as if her revelation opened a doorway into his past and unleashed the ghosts in his own attic. He slammed it close, determined to press ahead.

A server approached their table to take their orders. Danielle ordered a half coffee, half cream and Alex ordered a black coffee. Both declined pie.

"So, why don't you tell me about your life, Alex. Montana sounds like a pretty cool place. I've never been—what's it like?" she asked, smiling warmly at him, feeling somewhat emotionally liberated having aired her dirty laundry but wanting to change the subject nonetheless.

She had a wide, radiant smile that was contagious and immediately set him at ease again. He smiled in return. "Well—Montana is . . . it is a *pretty cool* place," he said, sighing. After more prodding by Danielle, he launched into a half hour of story-telling, from describing the landscape and scenery to entertaining her with stories of his various adventures in nature. She then asked about his family, and he told another fifteen minutes of stories about his father's adventures as a doctor and what he had learned from his dad, including his dad having to give him stitches in the wild when he had slashed open his leg on a weekend scouting event.

"So—why did you move out here?" she asked sipping on her now cold coffee, so engrossed in his stories that she had forgotten the drink was there.

His mind froze suddenly as if it had hit a wall, his smile quickly fading as he stared into the distance. "I—I don't know. I don't know why we moved."

"Well—did you have a lot of friends? Were you really involved in your high school?"

He continued to stare into the distance, suddenly aware that he could not remember the past three years of his life. He had described events up through seventh grade, but he could remember nothing of his high school years. "Maybe . . ."

"Did you have a girlfriend?" Danielle asked playfully, already knowing the answer but wanting details.

He shuddered. "Yes . . . I did."

"So—do you miss her?"

"She died," he said dully, staring into his cup of coffee.

Her face burned in embarrassment. "I'm so sorry," she said quickly, mortified. "I didn't mean to pry—"

"No—it's alright," he said, looking at her. "I haven't been able to talk about it. Actually, I don't remember what happened. There was an accident of some kind. In—in February, I think. I was in the hospital for a couple of months, but I don't remember anything. Before it happened, either—I don't remember anything for the past three years. But, we moved . . . I think we moved because of it. Nobody will tell me . . . Nobody wants to talk about it."

She remained quiet, her mind trying to piece together what could have happened. A car accident, she guessed. His girlfriend must have died in a car accident.

"Anyway—I've told you everything I know about my life. At least, anything of interest that I remember. What about you? Tell me about your family."

After tearing apart her napkin for a minute, she hesitantly relayed an overview of the Sumners' family life. While describing her childhood and early years with her family, she couldn't help but smile. They had been a very close family, and her parents had been deeply in love. Her mother, who was full-blooded Italian, used to have a passionately fun air about her, constantly cooking up treats, planning excursions and parties, infusing the household with flowers, food and music. It was she who encouraged Danielle to play the violin at such an early age.

But then her father got promoted to a junior partner at a prestigious law firm. They moved from their small cape in Prairie Village to their mansion in Mission Hills, and she rarely had anything to do with her parents. She could not bring herself to share with Alex her mother's increasing addiction to alcohol in reaction to her father's affair, or her father's psychological and sometimes physical abuse that was primarily directed at herself. Her father desperately wanted a divorce but feared the social, financial and familial consequences. Her mother came from a wealthy and powerful family that had distant but distinct ties to the mafia. Danielle closely resembled her mother and, because of this, believed her father took his frustrations with her mother out on her.

"Then we moved into this humongous castle that was supposed to be my mother's dream home. She told us it would be like living in a fairy tale—as we were quite sad about leaving our old home."

"Yeah—I saw your house," Alex interrupted excitedly. "It's huge! I heard you have servants and everything—"

She blushed. "Well—we have a maid, a cook and a gardener. But they are part-time."

He asked her about her hobbies and violin-playing, and she explained she had been playing since grade school. She was in the Junior Symphony, competed in regional competitions and was quite accomplished though growing tired of it. The fun had gone out of that activity and down the same black hole that sucked the joy out of every other aspect of her life, she thought, but did not say aloud.

"And this arrangement?" he ventured, wanting her to explain further. So far, she had not shared anything about her family that was too terribly odd.

The Sumners were obviously very wealthy and likely had eccentric tendencies typical of such prominent families. He was curious as to how eccentric this arrangement was.

"Oh . . ." she raised an eyebrow and pursed her lips. "Well—I dated Tate, that's his name, for almost three years. Like I said, his parents and my parents are best friends and belong to the same country club, go traveling together, yada yada. What complicates matters is that his dad is my dad's biggest client. So—both families are thrilled we're dating and wanted to strangle me when I broke things off a few weeks back."

"So—you broke up with him."

"Yes. Well—I tried. But, nobody—including my friends, oddly enough—accepted it. So, as far as I'm concerned, I'm free and independent, but to the rest of the world, I belong to Tate. And, since Tate planned some huge bash at the Embassy Suites, I'm expected to attend and ensure things don't get out of control."

Sipping his coffee, Alex nearly choked in amusement. "So—they basically want you to *babysit* Tate—"

"Babysit . . ." she mused. "Hmm . . . I hadn't thought of it that way, but yes. That's exactly what I am. I'm a babysitter for the evening."

He chuckled sadly. "Shit . . . As twisted as it is—and it *is* twisted—I think I actually see what's going on . . . Sure—they're just comfortable with you dating him because he's—he's a known factor. Any other guy is a mystery—an unknown—and, therefore, dangerous to you and your reputation."

"I *suppose*," she said dryly.

"Well—you and I make a perfect pair."

She raised an eyebrow, her eyes venturing to meet his.

"We're both trapped," he said sadly, pushing his near empty mug to the side. "I'm trapped by my amnesia—haunted by some dark past I know nothing about, and you're trapped in a social matrix."

"Sometimes . . . Sometimes I feel as if I am in a dream. As if none of this is real, and I am waiting to wake up from it," she responded quietly. "Do you ever feel like this is just a dream? That maybe life is not what it seems?"

He shrugged. "I don't know . . . I've been having strange dreams lately."

"So have I," she burst. "Horrible dreams—nightmares. I—I don't even want to go to sleep at night. I don't know which is worse—the dreaming state or the waking state . . . I don't know where to hide anymore. Where to go for refuge. There's no peace."

He watched as her gaze drifted to a point in the distance, beyond him, and he felt an overwhelming urge to protect her.

"Sorry," she said suddenly, embarrassed over her morose behavior. "This has been a bummer of an evening for you, I'm sure. I should take you home now—"

He shook his head in protest. "No—No—why do you say that?"

She shrugged. "Well—you spent two hours watching a movie you had no interest in seeing, and then spent the next . . ." she paused, looking at her watch, ". . . two hours talking with someone whose life is as lame as that movie."

He smiled sadly, shaking his head. "Danielle . . ."

"You can call me Dan. My friends do."

"*Dan*—I really just needed someone to talk to. I mean, even the girls I've hung out with, they—they just want to drink and get it on or something. Everybody's always doing . . . Actually, what am I saying—everybody's talking too, but nobody's listening. Yeah . . . I just really needed somebody to listen. Thanks for doing that."

She smiled widely. "No—thank *you*. I've had a really nice time tonight, actually. Perhaps we can listen to each other again sometime."

He smiled. "Yeah—after your Homecoming. I'll have a lot of listening to do after *that*," he said, whistling.

She laughed and went to leave money on the table, but he stopped her, pulling a five and some change from his pocket.

They drove to his house in relative silence, listening to a classic Smiths song on the radio. He only lived ten minutes from her house. She pulled into his driveway, suddenly nervous. Unsure of whether or not to turn off the car, she put it into park and turned to him. "You have a very nice house."

He shrugged. "It's okay." Their eyes met, and his mind raced to decide whether or not it was appropriate to kiss her. He wanted to kiss her, but he didn't want to distress or complicate her life further. Perhaps he should wait until after Homecoming . . . He leaned towards her slightly to see how she would react. To his surprise, she leaned towards him. This was a positive sign.

He grinned and leaned closer.

She smiled nervously and looked down, her heart racing so fast she feared he could hear it pounding. She closed her eyes as their lips touched, soft at first, then firmly, their kiss eager but—oddly—as if a kiss goodbye.

They parted moments later, satisfied with their seal of affection yet both apprehensive for some unknown reason.

"Call me after Homecoming," he said softly.

She nodded. "It'll be late, though . . . I'll call you sometime on Sunday. Maybe we can go out Sunday afternoon or evening."

"Maybe I'll just have to crash that party," he said, winking. "Embassy Suites, did you say?"

She nodded again. "Yes—a monstrous pink hotel on The Plaza. You can't miss it."

They kissed quickly again, and then he got out of the car and walked towards the back door, stopping to wave twice before disappearing behind the house.

Danielle sat in the driveway a minute before backing out, suddenly stunned by the evening's events and once again feeling as if she were not fully awake. Despite how amazing he was and the depth of her physical attraction for him, she knew it would not last. Like everything else, it was only a matter of time before the joyless plague contaminated what she hoped was the first budding romance of her life. Still, for the first time in weeks, she was able to sleep through the night, comforted by the fact that he might be there next week to assist her and, perhaps, prevent what she felt was her impending doom.

CHAPTER FIVE

He sat in the back row of history class, lost in thoughts about the girl he had just met. There were still five minutes before the bell, and even though the room bustled with students coming and going, they were transparent to him. It wasn't until he felt a slug on his arm that he turned, startled, to find Kelly had slid into the desk next to him.

"Space cadet . . . What are you daydreaming about?"

He shrugged.

"I think I know," she said slyly. "Which is why I wanted to talk to you before class. I hear you're still dateless for Homecoming."

He crossed his arms and turned away, shifting uncomfortably in his seat. Not that again.

"Now, now—before you go getting all defensive on me, hear me out. I'm dateless, too, if you can believe it. But I've been invited to this awesome post-Homecoming party at the Embassy Suites. The party's for a different school—but who cares. We can go to our Homecoming and then to another school's party."

Alex sighed loudly. "So, why don't you just go to the party and skip Homecoming?"

"You mean, why don't *we* just go to the party," she said giggling.

"*No*, I mean why don't *you* just go to the party. Why would I want to go? I don't even want to go to Homecoming."

"Because of *who's* going to be at the party. A certain someone I heard through the grapevine you have taken a sudden interest in."

A chill ran through him, followed by anger. How did she know? How did anyone know? He had told no one, and Danielle hardly seemed the gossip type.

"Oh, come on. I heard it from Michelle who was at the movies and witnessed the whole thing. What you don't know is that I am buddy-buddy with Danielle's boyfriend, Tate, who's hosting the party. Danielle doesn't even know I know. She would be mortified if she knew anyone knew what everyone now knows, because she's just like that. Anyway . . ."

His head span as she prattled on and on, drawing mind boggling connections and concocting outrageous plans for Saturday night. He looked at the clock, wondering when the bell would ring, then scanned the room for the teacher, who was nowhere in sight, praying something would end this sudden disruption of what little peace and comfort he thought he gained over the weekend.

". . . what you don't know," she continued, "is that her boyfriend and I have been having a little fun on the side, if you know what I mean."

He rolled his eyes. "You told me," he murmured.

"I did?"

Alex said nothing, enjoying the brief moment of silence.

"When?" she pressed.

"The night of Dennis' party."

"Oh, well—I was totally wasted that night. Anyway—that's my point. Don't you see? Danielle doesn't really like Tate. I do really like Tate. You really like Danielle. So—let's go and do a swap."

"*What*?" he choked incredulously.

She giggled, winking at him. "It'll be fun—I promise. Besides, Carl wants us to go to Homecoming with his group. With this plan, everyone will be happy. I'm so brilliant, I amaze myself. I really should make a business out of this."

The bell rang. It didn't matter that he had never formally agreed to doing anything with Kelly. By end of day, word had spread that he finally had a date and was going to Homecoming. After practice that evening, he left another message with Danielle, this one more urgent. He had to get to her before Kelly did. But by eleven, she had still not called.

That night he dreamed again, this time of Danielle. She was sitting alone on a stone bench in a terrace. The sky was bright, enveloping everything in a white haze. He anxiously crossed the terrace to join her. As he neared, she didn't seem to notice him, her eyes gazing into the distance with an expression of deep sadness.

"Dan—"

A slight breeze gently lifted her long hair from her slender shoulders. He sat down next to her, but she did not seem to notice his presence, her eyes still fixed at some distant point. He sighed and stared at the surrounding wall of trees and half-decayed statues of female figures that seemed to sprout from the ground.

"Are you okay?'

She lifted her head sharply and stared at him directly, her eyes penetrating. *Why did you bring me here?*

He blinked, puzzled. "What do you mean?"

Here—to this place—to this nightmare—

He looked at his surroundings nervously. Surely she was mistaken, he thought. He had nothing to do with her being there. Their meeting was entirely coincidental. He gently touched her shoulder, eager to explain.

You're contaminating me, she said sadly, although her lips never moved.

He stared at her, puzzled, his hand now lightly stroking her upper arm. She made no move to brush him off, but his touch made her wince. The wind picked up, and her hair rippled in its force, actually changing texture and shape. As the wind began to shriek and leaves spiraled around them, her hair began to twist and kink, the naturally straight strands curling, thickening. Her olive complexion lost all color, becoming almost translucent.

He felt a sharp sting and then intense pressure in his hand. A snake had bitten him, and he withdrew his hand in horror as its mouth stayed open, hissing, revealing short yet sharp fangs. It was hanging over Danielle's shoulder, and he yelled for her to watch out, moving to brush the creature off of her. But as he reached out to hit it, another appeared and then another until at least six or seven were slithering around her neck and over her arms. Then he noticed that her entire upper body was being covered in snakes, her beautiful hair having been transformed—

You better leave—

As he jumped up to retreat, he felt something brush against his neck. He turned but saw no one standing behind him. He then felt it slide beneath his shirt collar. Rubbing his neck and feeling the long, thick strand, he began to pull at it. He again felt something sharp sting his hand and, panicking, began to pull harder—with both hands, now—wanting to get it off of his person. But as the snake fell to the ground and began slithering away, he felt another brush against his neck, another across his shoulders, and another down his collar until there were too many to pull off. And the more frantically he fought them, the harder they bit, until his hands were covered in blood and pock marks.

She held out her hand for him to take.

He reached out for it, but as their fingers clasped, her features completely transformed, and he was now gazing into Jennifer's eyes, her dimpled smile mocking him.

He heard a loud click behind him, like that of a gun. Dropping her hand, he spun around and found himself staring at the familiar faceless face, the unkempt clothes and the barrel of the rifle.

The figure laughed. *Caught you in the act, boy.*

Alex turned to Jennifer, reaching out for her hand, but his fingers brushed against gray rock, and in Jennifer's place stood a tall, stone wall that stretched from either end of the terrace. He groped at the wall, eyes closed, shivering in fear of his impending doom. He refused to turn around.

He woke up just as the bullets ripped through his spine.

The clock radio read five thirty in the morning. As he moved to wipe the sleep from his eyes, he felt something run down his neck. Stifling a scream, he frantically grabbed at his t-shirt collar until realizing it was just a drop of sweat trickling down his neck, the pillow, sheets and his entire torso drenched.

His hair bothered him the rest of the day, the long, curly strands scraping against his neck and shoulders. At one point during English he thought he felt something run down the entire length of his back and practically jumped out of his seat, causing the students around him to snicker.

Carl leaned over and whispered, "Are you okay, Fahlstrom?"

"Is there something on my neck?"

Carl eyed him curiously then shook his head.

"Are you sure?" Alex asked, pulling his hair up.

"Fahlstrom—there ain't nothin' on your neck, you crazy freak."

But Alex could not stop from rubbing his neck and pulling at his collar throughout the entire class, running straight to the bathroom before the next hour to ensure nothing unusual was crawling on him. Later, he beseeched any girl he knew to lend him a hair band, hoping that having it pulled back would stop the sensation. It didn't.

By the time he reached home, he was so unnerved that he locked himself in the bathroom with a large pair of scissors and slowly began to chop off his locks, clump by clump, until the haphazard spiral strands hung either at or above his chin in uneven lengths.

"Alex," his mother's voice called from below. "Are you home?"

Her voice startled him, and he quickly began to sweep the large piles of hair off the counter, into his hand and ultimately into the wastebasket. The rest he rinsed off the sides of the sink and down the drain.

Warily, he opened the door of the bathroom and stepped into the hall.

"Alex, is that you?" His mother called from the bottom of the steps. "We need to talk about—"

Upon seeing him, she stopped, a stunned look replacing her initial expression of annoyance.

"Yeah?" he said, trying to avoid her gaze.

"What—what have you done to your hair?" she burst, in shock more than anger.

He shrugged.

"Come here and let me see . . . I mean it, come down here—"

Rolling his eyes, he sauntered down the stairs. She stepped back, scanning his person from all angles. "Honey—why did you do that?" she asked finally.

He shrugged, absently placing his hands in his pockets.

"I—I don't know what to say," she murmured, circling him, her fingers sporadically ruffling through his locks. "I—Why didn't you tell me you wanted a haircut? I could have arranged that for you—"

"I didn't know I wanted it cut until today," he replied, stretching.

"Well, I wish you would have asked me . . . I have to be honest with you, it looks terrible . . . The sides are all uneven . . . It looks like you took a hedge clipper to it."

He rolled his eyes and broke away from her, heading towards the family room.

"Alex—don't walk away from me like that. I wanted to talk to you," she protested, following him. "We need to get a corsage for your date—"

At the mention of date, he winced. In order to borrow the car Saturday night, he had told his parents about his Homecoming date. They were ecstatic and had not stopped pestering him about it or Kelly, wanting to know everything about her, her family and her grades.

To appease his mom and prevent her from setting up an emergency appointment with the shrink, he conceded to have his damaged hair professionally trimmed that evening so he didn't look so *silly*. The term *silly* depressed him, and he found himself growing irritable over the coming weekend and aching to see Danielle again. Danielle wouldn't think it silly, he thought, as he surveyed himself in the mirror at the local strip mall salon. Though the stylist had cut it short, she had left it long enough at the top and sides for the blond wavy curls to sprout from his darker roots. He honestly doubted Danielle would care one way or the other, which pleased him.

That evening he left a message for her to call him, but the phone had not rung when he finally fell asleep a little past midnight.

His family's reaction to the haircut was mild compared to the reaction he received from his classmates the next day, which ranged from dull shock to outright anger. As he passed people in the hall that morning, he put up with jokes and whistling from his male acquaintances and wailing and dismay from his female acquaintances. In biology, Dennis and his gang just eyed him queerly, shaking their heads. Kelly rolled her eyes, reminding him that he was going to a party not a funeral. After ensuring that Alex's parents were not behind it, Carl was the only one who had anything positive to say, expressing his pride that Alex had finally decided to look like a real man. He then jokingly put him in a head lock, knuckled his hair and insisted he go to dinner and Homecoming with his group.

"Am I a bad person?"

The words came apparently out of nowhere, and he could tell they surprised his mother. It was Wednesday evening, and they were in the car on the way to the mall to buy clothes for the dance.

He looked at his mom as she gracefully maneuvered the steering wheel, smiling, turning to him at times, her short, grayish-blond hair groomed to neat perfection. Despite the calm his mother attempted to exude, he sensed her expression was strained. From this sense grew the realization that behind her calm facade - and his father's cool facade - and his sister's forced facade - was the answer to all his problems, and this sudden consciousness shook him into a slight state of paranoia. Here were three people he lived with, his own family, who knew something drastic about him that he didn't, and who never once in the past few months offered to tell him, instead going out of their way to avoid the subject.

He sat, arms crossed, staring out the window at the passing cars.

His mother didn't respond right away, frowning first, then cautiously asking him what made him think such a thing. Of course he wasn't a bad person.

"Why can't I remember anything about what happened? Huh? And be-fore that—I can't remember anything about most of the school year before this—or any of high school, for that matter. Not my friends—or classes—events—anything. It's—it's all this big, vague blur—"

She sighed.

"I mean, I'm having some pretty horrific dreams, and it's become quite clear that the whole reason we moved here was because of me."

She remained silent, looking out the windshield. "Alex, I'm not going to lie to you . . . We did think a change of scene best," she admitted cautiously.

They pulled into the parking lot, and she began to look for a space closest to the entrance.

"Well, then tell me this—did I do something wrong? Did I do something bad?"

"No," she said adamantly, almost angrily. "You did absolutely nothing wrong. You're a wonderful person, and I'm proud of you to this day. It was just all a big mistake—a senseless tragedy. You'll see."

"When? When will I come to see?" he pressed. "This afternoon? At a shrink appointment? Is he going to magically hypnotize me? Give me a drug? Or will it be months? A year? Am I just going to wake up someday and poof—there it is all laid out before me?"

"Possibly," she said quietly, pulling into an empty space and turning off the engine.

"Jesus," he said under his breath.

She sat still for a moment, and he could tell she was mentally forming her speech to him. "Alex," she started finally, tapping the steering wheel as she spoke. "I don't believe—and neither does your father—that simply blurting to you the events that transpired earlier this year is going to do anything to help you. We've consulted psychologists and counselors. You know what happened. It's all right up here, and right in here," she turned and touched his forehead and chest. "Your mind simply can't handle it right now. You're in denial—you've blocked it out as a defense mechanism. You'll remember when you're ready to remember."

"Counselors don't know shit—what's the point?" he burst angrily. "God—why can't you and Dad just help me? Why don't you just tell me yourself? This is ridiculous."

"Please, Alex . . . You don't understand . . . We can't just talk about it with you. It's too painful for us. And, to be honest, we're scared to tell you. We're scared of how you'll react," she said sadly, brushing his hair from his forehead.

His instinct was to push her hand away, but he sat silently, glaring out the windshield at the darkening sky.

"Tell me one thing," he said, turning to her. "Did it involve a girl? My—my girlfriend?" He winced at the word, picturing Danielle and feeling guilty for it. Was it right to have fallen for someone so shortly after losing someone else? Even though he couldn't remember what he really lost?

She sighed and reached down to grab her purse from the car floor. "Yes, Alex, it involved your girlfriend."

"That's all I want to know right now," he said gruffly, yanking the handle to open the car door and then slamming it shut behind him.

His parents had given him use of the Bronco for Homecoming, and as he drove to pick up Kelly, he tried, physically and mentally, to prepare himself for the evening.

For the dance, he and his mom had decided on the khaki and navy look, and the only item he enjoyed purchasing was a colorful tie featuring abstract jazz musicians. Having no knowledge of corsages, he let his mom and sister take care of that, and they picked out a red rose. It wasn't until later in the evening that he realized how much it clashed with Kelly's red dress. Another sign of the disaster to come, he thought.

As he stood in her hallway, politely greeting her family members and posing for pictures, he conceded to himself that she looked nice in the dress. It was rather low cut, short and tight-fitting, accentuating her curves. She had left her hair long. He wondered what Danielle would be wearing.

After the visit with her family, they headed to The Plaza to meet Carl and friends at Houston's. The restaurant had pushed several tables together to accommodate the eight couples. He and Kelly sat in the middle. Shortly into the dinner, Kelly struck up a loud conversation with the couple to her left, the three of them dwelling on current social and political issues and trying to dazzle the others with their knowledge, names and data, obviously drawn from the pages of *Time* and *Newsweek*.

Alex was bored and soon found his eyes and mind wandering. He first examined the others at the table, wondering if their smiles and laughter were sincere or just a ruse. Wondering if anyone was as truly miserable and conflicted as he. Wondering if he had been this way since grade school. He gazed out the window at the passing shoppers and sight-seers and found himself thinking of Danielle. Just a few more hours, and he could be with her.

"Alex's father is a doctor—ask *him* what he thinks of Clinton's plan," Kelly said.

A number of eyes turned on him as he was mentally seated on a sofa, dressed in sweats and a T-shirt, miles from this fu-fu dinner.

"Alex—are you with us?" Kelly asked, bemused.

He glanced around the table, his face slightly reddening, and said nothing, having been totally oblivious to the previous dialogue.

She laughed. "Are we boring you, Alex? Would you rather we discuss outdoor sports or the environment?"

"You're sure as hell boring me," Carl interrupted loudly, rescuing Alex. "How 'bout them Chiefs?"

At this, half the table broke into laughter, and the conversation abruptly turned to football, partying and lewd Carl jokes.

After dinner, they made their way to the actual dance, which was being held in East's gymnasium. Once there, Kelly flatly refused to dance, insisting her only reason for attending the dumb thing was to ensure her appointed newspaper photographers weren't shirking their duties. They stood in the hall outside the reverberating gymnasium, leaning against a bulletin board tacked with torn posters and pamphlets. Kelly crossed her arms and rolled her eyes impatiently.

Alex laughed at her expression. "If you don't want to be here, why are we wasting our time?"

She eyed him slyly. "We're not wasting our time—just biding it. The real fun starts later," she winked, then excused herself to use the restroom.

Instead of waiting for her, Alex found Carl and the other couples from dinner and joined them in slam dancing to the Spin Doctors. Soon a huge group began whirling around, doing the traditional floor moves to "Shout" and starting a massive train to some other rumba-sounding pop song. At one point he even met up with his sister, Trisha, and she and her date joined in the crowd.

When the DJ announced a string of slow songs, some people groaned and others set out to find their dates. Alex found his standing against the back wall of the gym, near the door.

"Well aren't you the crazed maniac," Kelly laughed. "Ready to head out?"

He shrugged nonchalantly, even though he was anxious to leave as she was. "Sure."

The drive to the hotel was silent with the exception of a few comments on the dance and a song on the radio. Located just off The Plaza, the hotel was a garish pink stucco that looked like it belonged on the Florida coast. Inside was a barrage of activity and plastic scenery that made his nerves tense. As they walked through the lobby, he silently watched people strolling and drinking amidst massive potted palms and various exotic flora. Invisible speakers blared bland contemporary music. There were a number of Homecoming couples drifting amongst the glass, greenery and spraying fountains, moving in and out of the confusing scenery like figures in an Escher painting.

He and Kelly merged into the imagery themselves, heading for an upper level in one of the glass elevators, stopping on the sixth floor. As they walked down the hallway, he heard music, R.E.M. Before they reached the rooms, people Kelly knew were milling about the hall, casually drinking and talking in groups. He found himself scanning the area for Danielle but did not see her. Three adjoining suites had open doors revealing communal activity. They entered the middle one, from which "Drive" was pumping loudly, though still not loud enough to mask the din.

Kelly greeted a number of people without introducing him. Once in the suite, she disappeared into a back bedroom, and he wandered around looking for Danielle and something to drink. A number of partiers were passing through the bathroom, which remained brightly lit and perpetually open, and when he peeked inside he noticed why. The tub had been converted into an ice chest, loaded with beer and wine coolers. He swiped a Budweiser and headed back to the dimly lit chaos to continue his search.

Lurking around, he began to feel like a masked Montague. After making the rounds twice, he was about to leave the first suite for the third time when he suddenly felt very hot, then nauseous. Undoing his tie and stuffing it in his jacket pocket, he stumbled towards the balcony in one of the bedrooms. To his dismay, a small group of people was clustered around the sliding glass door, blocking his way.

Frustrated, he decided to head back into the main hall and down the elevator to the lobby, where there was fresher air and fewer people.

"There you are," Kelly burst testily, grabbing his arm just as he had finally made it through the jam-packed hallway and into open space. "Where do you think you're going?"

"To get some fresh air and look for Danielle. I've been through all these suites twice, now, and can't find her. Have you seen her?"

She shook her head. "Well, let's go find Tate. She's probably with him."

He winced inwardly at the mention of the boyfriend's name and at the idea of re-entering the dark, densely packed rooms, for a moment wondering what he was even doing there. He didn't belong there. It was too much baggage—too much drama.

Kelly dragged him through the hallway crowd towards the corner party suite. Of the three, this suite was the darkest. Red strobe lights had been set up in place of the hotel-furnished lamps, casting a hellish glow. His nausea returned full force, and he considered retreating to the hallway for air, but Kelly pulled him onward. Parting through a final layer of people, they stopped just short of hitting a glass sofa table.

A figure sat comfortably sprawled on the sofa, dressed in khaki pants and a navy jacket, his white dress shirt tie-less and unbuttoned at the top. His arms were outstretched to encompass a girl on either side, and one leg rested on the other knee. He smiled cunningly at them, as if he had been expecting their arrival, and Alex felt as if he had stumbled upon the heart of darkness in the suburban jungle.

The guy stood up, shaking off the girls in the process, and slowly made his way around the coffee table toward Alex and Kelly.

"Kelly," he said extending a hand and smiling, revealing perfectly lined white teeth that almost seemed to glow against his complexion, made darker by the environment. "Glad you could make it. And this is?" he asked, turning to Alex.

"Tate, this is Alex Fahlstrom."

The guy stuck out a hand to shake, staring Alex squarely in the eye. He was exactly Alex's height and practically his same build, which Alex found more than disconcerting. Even worse, when he shook Tate's hand it was as if he secured a channel into the guy's thoughts, which were as hellish as the room itself. The negative energy transmitted through the touch was almost electric with rage and ill will. Alex quickly pulled his hand back.

"Where's Danielle?" Kelly asked, glancing around.

"I don't know," Tate replied, his eyes locked on Alex. "She disappeared a few hours ago." Turning abruptly to Kelly, he added, "Perhaps she's in one of the private suites we reserved. In fact," he said, jabbing his hand into his jacket pocket, "here is a key to your own private suite." He handed a small plastic card to Kelly.

"Cool—thanks! Do you have a second key?"

He shook his head. "Unfortunately, Dan has all of the spare keys. Maybe you should go look for her."

Kelly shrugged and turned to leave. Alex went to follow, when the guy grabbed his arm.

"Let me know if you find her. We have some unfinished business."

Alex roughly pulled away, fighting an urge to haul off and punch him, suddenly worried for Danielle's safety. He hoped she had disappeared—fled, gone home. But instinct told him that was a pipe dream.

"Do you mind if we go to the room so I can lock up my purse? I need a bathroom . . ." Kelly said.

Their private suite held a familiar hotel smell, a mixture of air conditioner Freon and cleansing chemicals. She flicked on the lights. After removing his jacket, Alex immediately walked to the television and grabbed the remote, soon plopping onto the sofa and surfing for an interesting program. Kelly disappeared into the bathroom, returning a few minutes later.

"Ready to go back out there?" she asked.

"Actually—I need to use the bathroom, too. I'll just find you in a few minutes. Go on ahead."

She shrugged and left.

Though he eventually used the bathroom, it wasn't for another twenty minutes. And when he did use it, he felt suddenly uneasy—as if he were not alone, which was ridiculous. The bathroom was small, housing only the toilet, a sink and a small tub. As he washed his hands, he stared at the tub. The shower curtain had been pulled across, hiding the inside. He dried his hands, staring at the curtain, almost expecting it to move. But nothing moved. Part of his mind wanted him to pull the curtain aside, but the rational part grossly objected. It was absurd paranoia.

Draping the wet towel on the sink bowl, he wandered back into the main part of the suite and once again stared into the television screen, at a complete loss. He dreaded leaving the room. Dreaded the noise and chaos, loud echoes of which could still be heard through the doors and walls. Something told him Danielle wasn't out there anyway.

His mind carefully retraced the message she had left him, searching for a clue he might have missed. She had finally called him back on Thursday night. She would find him at the party, she had told Trisha, sometime after nine. But, he had searched every party suite. Could she be hiding out in the lobby? Maybe he should search there . . .

He sighed loudly, throwing his head back. The night had been a complete waste, and he was utterly exhausted. This was stupid. The whole thing was stupid. What was he doing here . . .

Mindlessly channel surfing, he landed on a late-night broadcast of a college football game and eventually nodded off to sleep.

When he opened his eyes, she was walking towards him, blouse unbuttoned, barely revealing her breasts, her brown curly hair cascading around her shoulders. She smiled seductively, revealing a small dimple in her right cheek. Upon nearing him, she dropped to her knees, her hands grabbing and stroking his legs, moving slowly up towards his knees and inner thighs. *Jennifer* . . . He sighed heavily, settling back in the sofa, aroused, enjoying his pulsating erection. It had been so long . . .

She unzipped his pants slowly, her hands massaging his pelvis. They moved up to his chest, and she began unbuttoning his shirt. He could feel her hair against his chest as she kissed him lightly on his neck, her lips moving down to his stomach. He touched her hair, letting his hands get lost in the brown ringlets, pulling her closer to himself, unable to contain a moan of satisfaction as she stroked him with her hands and then her lips. She was about to go down on him completely when he heard a click—

It was an odd click. A familiar click of metal against metal. He forced himself to open his eyes, then stared wide in horror.

Standing directly in front of them, less than ten feet away, was the man. He barely made out the glowing head and plaid work shirt before the gunpowder ignited, and he was blown back into the sofa. Lurching in horror at the gaping hole in his side, his initial moan of pleasure turned into an anguished cry. He looked down at the girl, only instead of seeing brown hair, his stomach was covered by a mass of blond ringlets.

The room came into sharp focus again, the faceless man replaced by the hotel television, now broadcasting an infomercial. His shirt was unbuttoned, still revealing the wound, and he cupped his left hand to catch the streaming blood, his right hand pushing her head away. She groaned, resisting him, becoming more aggressive.

He began to dry-heave and thought he would be sick. Panicking, he thrust her away and bolted into the bathroom, locking the door, barely falling in front of the toilet before losing the contents of his stomach. He slumped against the toilet, hugging the seat, panting and still shaking violently from the incident. What a nightmare . . . When would they end? Was this going to happen to him for the rest of his life? Would it happen with Danielle?

A faint tap sounded at the door. "Alex—"

He flushed the toilet, drowning out the weak voice. He then zipped his pants and, soaking a hand towel, wiped the bloody sweat from his stomach before buttoning his shirt and splashing cold water on his face and neck. The knocking persisted, this time with more vehemence.

"Come on, Alex . . . *Please* . . . I'm a little fucked up myself, you know—"

Sighing to himself, he reluctantly opened the door to find her on the floor, just beyond the threshold, slumped against the wall. She looked up wearily, and then her bloodshot eyes grew wide.

"Oh, my god—" she gasped. "What happened to your shirt?"

He glanced down and winced at the coaster-sized red stain.

"Oh, my god, you're bleeding—" she gasped, attempting to stand up. "You're bleeding all over the place—"

He clutched at his shirt in disbelief, hoping to rub it away. He couldn't be bleeding. It was only a dream. She was surely drunk—wasted—out of her mind—

Stumbling to an upright position, Kelly pushed by him, her hand flying to her mouth. "I'm going to be sick," she started, slamming the door shut behind her.

He winced at the sound of her heaves and after all was quiet for a minute, tapped on the door. "Kelly, are you okay?"

He heard a moan but no verbal answer.

"Come on, Kelly—"

"Jesus god, I'm so fucked up . . . You're fucking bleeding all over yourself—"

Looking down at his stained shirt, he laughed nervously in reply. "No—nah—I'm not. You're just—you're just hallucinating. I'm fine—really. Come out and look for yourself."

He shifted nervously in place during another few minutes of silence, then heard the sound of running water and a minute later, shuffling. The door swung open.

Her stare immediately fell upon his stomach, and she winced as if in pain. "Jesus—I'm tripping. Oh, my god, I'm having a bad trip," she wailed, rubbing her eyes and pulling at her hair. "Somebody must have spiked my drink . . . Jesus Christ, I'm having a bad trip—"

He held out an arm to steady her, but she immediately began shaking and crying hysterically. "I'm scared—I'm freaking out—" she sobbed over and again.

Putting an arm around her shoulder, he guided her to the bed, pulled aside the covers and forced her to lay down. "You're fine—you'll be be just fine . . . Just lie down and try to get some rest . . . Sleeping it off is the best thing for . . . for this kind of thing. Really . . ."

He pulled the covers up, and she buried her head beneath the pillows. "Maybe you're right," she mumbled.

Backing away from the bed, he tried to alleviate his own panic and curb an increasing wave of nausea. Instinctively, he turned the lights down, continuing to calm Kelly in the process, and returned to the bathroom to collect his wits and try to wash the blood stain out of his shirt. But once in the tiny room, which now reeked of alcohol induced vomit, he began feeling nauseous again and slumped to the floor, his back against the closed bathroom door, staring blankly ahead.

Unable to comprehend what had just happened, his mind still in shock and his entire torso still trembling with pain, he sat for awhile with his eyes closed, hoping to open them and see he had been dreaming. But when he opened them ten minutes later, he saw the same white toilet and off-white tile floor. The same off-white sink and the same plastic shower curtain with a monotonous pattern of cream, beige and tan blocks. Having nothing else of interest to look at, he absently focused his attention on the curtain. It seemed to breathe. He continued to stare intently at it, his heart rate accelerating. Yes—it moved again, slightly. Resisting the urge to jump up and tear it aside, he remained frozen, his breathing quickening, fear trumping curiosity.

It was only when he heard a human gasp that he sat upright. The curtain shook violently from within, followed by another desperate gasp for air, as if someone were drowning. He darted towards the tub and flung the curtain aside without another moment's hesitation, fearful of what he would find but determined to help.

It was a girl—obviously from the Homecoming party—dressed in a baby blue dress. But not just any girl. He gasped.

She grabbed his arm, still struggling to find her breath.

"Danielle—"

"I can't breathe—I can't—" Her right hand gripped his arm in a tight panic.

"It's okay—calm down. You're okay."

She shook her head.

"What are you doing in here?" he asked incredulously.

Taking two more deep breaths, she replied.

"*Hiding.*"

∞

She was relieved when Brooke called and invited her over the next day. She had seen little of her best friend since Brooke had found a new guy and made preparations for his Homecoming, which had been the night before.

Danielle was anxious to hear how the dance went and to share her movie evening with the only person on the planet she trusted.

Brooke was on an unusually high cloud and had the love glow. Over coffee, she shared with Danielle all of the details of not only Homecoming but the past few weeks. His name was Steve, and he attended Shawnee Mission South. He played piano, was artistic, read a lot of books, ran track—Mr. Perfect. Homecoming was perfect. Everything was perfect, and Brooke hated spending time away from him, which is why she hadn't had much time for Danielle.

"You slept with him, didn't you?" Danielle asked finally.

Brooke tossed her head, "Really, Dan—"

"You did. I know you did—last night, didn't you?"

"Well, maybe . . . It was *awesome* –" She burst, and then went on to describe the evening in more detail than Danielle cared to hear. "Dan, you have got to find yourself a lover so we can share notes. I mean, I love talking to you, but—I don't know, when it comes to this stuff, I feel I'm just . . . You're just . . ."

"Naïve."

"No," she said vehemently. "Missing out. Watching from the outside. Unable to relate, you know?"

Danielle nodded absently, worried for her friend. Brooke's boyfriend of two years had broken up with her early in the summer, before he left for college, convinced a long-distance relationship wouldn't work and wanting a fresh start. She was devastated and hesitant to date again until meeting Steve at a debate tournament. Danielle hoped Steve, a senior, wasn't just looking for a Homecoming date and a little fun on the side until he, too, left for college.

"Anyway, what's been going on with you? Everyone's buzzing about Tate's Homecoming party. I'm thinking of crashing it," Brook continued.

"Oh, would you? That would be wonderful," Danielle said, relieved. "I think it's going to be a disaster. I think something horrible's going to happen," she started, sharing with Brooke the events, dreams and fears of the past few weeks. She then told her about Alex.

When she finished, Brooke got giddy. "Oh, my god. Oh, my god! That's so romantic. That's, like, movie romantic. Oh, my god—do you think he'll show up at the party?"

"I hope so. God, I hope so."

On Tuesday afternoon, Brooke's room was strewn with clothes. As Danielle could find nothing in her own closet that seemed to please Brooke, they had gone over to Brooke's house to look for a suitable dress for Homecoming. Now that Danielle's new man may be crashing the party, Danielle must look stunning, Brooke had insisted.

"I don't know, Brooke," Danielle said as she held up a tight-fitting, strapless red satin dress. "What if Alex doesn't show up? I mean, the last thing I want to do is to send the wrong message to Tate, you know? If I look all sexy for the dance, he's going to think it's for *him*. He has no idea. And frankly, I want to keep it that way . . . I'll just wear that Laura Ashley dress—the navy one—"

"Oh, vomit! You will not! Over my dead body will you wear that matronly dress."

"What's wrong with Laura Ashley?" Danielle asked.

The phone rang.

"Curtains and tablecloths," Brooke said, reaching over from her seat on the bed and swiping the receiver from its stand. "Hello? Oh—hi, Kelly." She turned to Danielle and made a puking gesture. "You're what? Oh—you're invited to Homecoming—how *special*. Yes, Dan's here—and we're both so happy for you—here, let me hand you to her—"

Danielle took the phone as Brooke began playing an air violin and dancing around the room. "Hi, Kelly."

Kelly squealed, "God, Dan—you won't believe it! Guess who I'm going to Homecoming with?"

"Um—did you just call *Brooke* to talk to me?"

"Uh, yeah - duh. I figured if you weren't at home you were probably at Brooke's. God. Anyway—take a guess—"

Danielle's head span, and she wandered back to the bed to sit down. "I have no idea."

"Alex," Kelly said flatly.

Danielle's heart plummeted.

After seconds of silence, Kelly repeated herself. "Alex—you know. Alex Fahlstrom. Isn't that just perfect?"

Danielle was speechless and felt her eyes welling up with tears. Brooke noticed the change in tone and ran over to her.

"Um, I—I don't understand," she said, trying to stay calm.

Kelly grunted. "Jesus Christ, Dan—don't act *so naïve*. Everyone knows you and Tate are just staying together for show. Everyone knows Tate's playing around on the side. And, now, everyone knows that Alex and you got together Saturday night—"

"*How*?" Danielle gasped, mortified.

"Jesus, Dan—he was out with a group of his friends, Michelle being one of them. He, like, ditched everyone to go hang out with you. *Hello*."

"So, *why did you ask him to Homecoming*?"

"So you could be together at the after party, and I could hook up with Tate guilt-free for once. Isn't that brilliant?"

Danielle remained silent.

"Um—I'm waiting for the *Thank you, Kelly – you're the best friend a girl could ask for. Wow*."

Still stunned, Danielle could not bring herself to talk, or even breathe.

"Dan? Hello?"

"Tate doesn't know, does he?" Danielle finally asked.

"What difference does that make?"

"A lot," Danielle said, suddenly panicking. "Please tell me he doesn't know about any of this—please tell me you didn't say anything to him—"

"Okay, fine. I didn't say anything to him. Jesus, Dan. What's your problem?"

But Danielle knew she was lying.

"Nothing . . . I'm sorry—I'm sorry, Kelly. Thank you—for looking out for me."

"Sure, babe. It'll be fun. Catch you Saturday night, then. Ciao."

The phone clicked, and Danielle let the receiver fall to the bed. For some utterly unknown reason, a wave of depression momentarily enveloped her. She could almost swear the room went dark, the sun hidden behind clouds. "Brooke," she choked, eyes wide.

"What the hell?" Brooke asked.

Danielle quickly gave her the run down before bursting into tears.

On Thursday night, her father requested her presence in his office. Though nervous, her mother was home that evening, so he wouldn't harm her. He never acted harshly when her mother was home. Still, she shuddered before opening the door to his study.

"Who is Alex Fahlstrom?" he asked abruptly, not looking up.

She had just crossed the threshold and stopped cold in her tracks, her heart pounding.

"Who—what?"

"Alex Fahlstrom. 642-2903," he said, reciting the phone number. "Do you know this person?"

"Yes, but why—"

"He left a couple of messages for you."

"Oh, well . . ." Her mind raced for a reasonable answer. "Maybe it's about Homecoming."

"Explain."

"He's Kelly's date. Tate invited Kelly and him to the party. He probably just wants directions or something."

"Ah. That makes sense. Very well," he flipped a piece of paper at her. "You may call him back then."

She slowly walked to his desk to pick up the note. "Is that all?"

"Yes. You are dismissed," he said, continuing to read his documents without making any eye contact.

She did not call Alex right away. Instead she sat on her bed, hugging a pillow, regretting what she saw as the loss of something special. She had quietly wanted to get to know Alex, but that was not to be. She had hoped for privacy, but everything had not only blown open but blown out of their control. He had fallen victim to her circumstances, an unwitting spectator now plunged into a stage drama with no say in the action. She was embarrassed and feared his patience for the tumult of her social life would wane quickly.

Hesitantly, she dialed his number. A girl answered.

"Hello—is Alex there?"

"I don't know. Just a minute."

Though muffled, Danielle could hear the girl calling his name.

"I don't think he's here. Can I take a message?"

"Um, sure. This is Danielle. Just tell him I called back and that I'll see him at the party Saturday night. Anytime after nine."

"Oh, okay . . . Are you his date?"

"No, no—he's taking my friend. But there's a big Homecoming after-party, and they wanted to go. They know where it is."

"Sounds fun . . . Can I come with my date?" the girl joked.

Danielle laughed. "Sure, why not. Ask Alex for the details."

"I'm just kidding. So does he have your number to call you back?"

"He doesn't need to call me back," Danielle said flatly, and after polite good-byes, clicked off to get started on a long night of homework.

Her mother surprised her the morning of Homecoming. Danielle had been curled up on the bed in sweats, engrossed in *Heart of Darkness*, required reading for her Honors English, trying to keep her mind off of the time, when there was a knock on the door. Before she could respond, the door opened.

"Good morning, Daniella," her mother piped in her thick Italian accent, which added an extra syllable to many words, including her name. "What are you doing still in bed on your big day?"

"Oh, I'm up. I'm just reading."

Her mother strolled in, looking about as if she had never been in the room before. She wore a trim, stylish sweat suit, the top zippered just low enough to show off her full-figured, olive-toned bosom. Her long, dark brown mane of hair spilled past her shoulders in loose waves. People said she looked just like her mother, but Danielle did not believe them. Her mother was stunningly beautiful, vivacious and social. She looked far younger than her age, and even Dennis' friends would gape longingly at her. Her mother's looks made her father's affair all the more shocking and depressing to Danielle. If her mother couldn't find true love, who could?

The affair had taken its toll on the family, driving her mother to drinking, partying and, so they heard, having her own affairs in retaliation to her husband's. Danielle rarely saw her mother, and it had been months since she'd confided in her or sought advice for the day-to-day social trauma that was high school, turning instead to Brooke.

"This is not what you're wearing to the dance, no?" she asked, gliding towards the navy Laura Ashley dress that hung outside the closet door.

"Yep. I'm all set."

"This old thing? Daniella—you cannot wear this dress. I won't allow it."

"The dress is fine, Mom, really."

"Fine for a funeral maybe, but not a dance. Surely you have something else in your closet," she said, throwing open the French doors to Danielle's wardrobe and beginning to rifle through her garments, ignoring the loud, abrasive squeaks of wire hangers scraping against the metal rod.

Danielle tried to turn her attention to her reading again when the noise abruptly stopped, accompanied by a gasp. She looked up to see her mother slowly pulling out the baby blue dress she had worn to the Club a few weeks ago.

"My dress . . . What is it doing here?"

Danielle's face burned in embarrassment and shame. "I'm—I'm sorry, Mom. I—I borrowed it a few weeks ago for a dance party. I should have asked you . . ."

But to her relief, her mother only smiled widely, gazing tenderly at the garment, gently caressing the material. "I met your father in this dress. We were at a dance party. He said I was the prettiest girl in the room—and the best dancer . . . This dress is very special to me."

Danielle gazed down at her open book.

"Which is why you should wear it tonight—to the dance!" she exclaimed.

Danielle shook her head, "No—I, I can't. Tate . . .Well, he's already seen me in it, for one—"

Her mother shook her head vehemently before launching into an Italian rebuttal. *Impossibile*, she started. If he had seen her in the dress, he would have fallen over himself - ravished her. He was either an *idiota* or *cieco*, and since he was neither, Danielle had not worn it properly. She must have had the wrong shoes. Perhaps her hair and make-up were too plain. Had Danielle made an appointment with Charles today? No? Horrors—her mother would get her in that afternoon no matter what amount of money it took to bribe the stylists. And they would get her new shoes. It was meant to be worn with silver-toned, strappy high heeled sandals—not black bulky pumps. They would have her nails done, too.

Shopping with her mother actually made her feel better about things. She had forgotten how much fun her mother could be and hoped today was the beginning of a closer relationship. Maybe the drinking was slowing. Maybe her mom was healing. After finding the shoes, they stopped for a bite to eat.

"Daniella, what's wrong with you? Something's not right. You are not happy about tonight, I can tell."

Danielle reddened, looking down at her plate. "I'm okay. I just—I just don't care about Homecoming, that's all."

"You don't care about Homecoming, or you don't care about Tate?"

Danielle smiled sheepishly.

"Why do you go out with the boy if you do not like him?" her mother asked bluntly, biting into her sandwich, having no problem with eating and talking at the same time. "There are many boys out there. Maybe you should branch out a little."

"But I thought you wanted me to be with him. Dad said it was important to both of you—to the family—that I date him—"

Her mother grunted in disgust, throwing down her sandwich and swearing in Italian. "Your father doesn't know what's important to me, *figlio di puttana*. He has room to talk. Important to the family—what's important to the family is that a husband remains faithful to his wife, that's what's important to the family. You date who you want to date."

"But, what about Dad—he got so angry with me, he—"

"You tell the son of a bitch I said you could date who you want. *Testa di cazzo*," she muttered. "So, are we still going to see Charles or do you want to just skip it? You don't have to go to the dance."

Danielle sat quietly a moment, amazed at the sudden presentation of options. She mentally ran through the scenario of not going to the dance, which began with calling Tate. *Tate, I'm not going to the dance with you. But why? We have a limo and everything – everything is all set. Because my mother said I don't have to . . .* Ugh. That sounded awful. *Tate, I'm not going to the dance with you. But why? Because you're a bastardo, and my mother says vaffanculo.*

She sighed. Tate was a bastard, but he had been nothing but nice to her all week. Cheerful, joking, gracious and even complimentary. No, she would not bail on him tonight. But definitely tomorrow. Tomorrow, it would all be over. "I want to go. It's the right thing to do."

Her mother shrugged, and they spent the rest of their lunch catching up on people they knew within the family social circle.

Danielle was stunned when she stepped out of the salon dressing room and looked into the mirror at the finished product that was her coiffed hair, made-up face and body wrapped up in the baby blue dress. Per her mother's instructions, Charles had gone all out. She barely recognized herself.

"She looks just like you, Gabrielle," Charles fawned over her while her mother squealed in delight.

Tate was also speechless when he came to retrieve her.

"Wow . . . . I've never seen you look like this before. I've never seen you try so hard. Is this all for me?" he asked.

She smirked, thinking of her mother's keen insight, then eyed him curiously, his dark expression—a mixture of hurt and rage—coupled with the exceedingly soft-spoken manner of speech, giving her pause.

"It's for the *show*. I can be convincing when I want to be."

"Ah, the *show*. Well, I'll have to be sure to stay in *character*," he said with a twinge of cynicism.

And upon entering the limo, to Danielle's utter dismay, the curtains rose.

He did not keep his hands off, pawing at her, grabbing her inappropriately and planting obnoxious kisses at the smallest sign of an audience. She could barely eat her dinner and, halfway through, lost her appetite entirely. When she had a chance to think, which was rare, her mind plotted how to avoid him during the dance. She would find a girl's bathroom and stay there the entire evening. She might even sneak out of the bathroom, out of the school and call a cab . . . .

But she would not get the chance. When the limo pulled up to the Rockhurst High School gymnasium, everyone was allowed to exit except Danielle.

"You're staying with me," Tate said, grabbing her arm.

"Why? Where are we going?"

"To the hotel—to set up."

"But I thought you set everything up this afternoon—what more is there to do?"

"Yeah—the stuff was delivered today, but it wasn't set up. I need your help."

"But what about them?" she asked, motioning to the disappearing couples. "How are they going to get to the party?"

"I'm sending the limo back to pick them up . . . Jesus," he breathed, looking at her like she was an idiot.

Once the limo door had shut, he changed gears entirely, scooting far away from her and remaining silent, staring morosely out the window. The fifteen minute ride felt like an hour, and Danielle was relieved when they finally reached the hotel. As they walked through the lobby, she scoped out her surroundings, her mind once again plotting a hideout until Alex arrived. She would use the bathroom excuse but retreat to the lobby and hide until . . . .

She asked Tate for the time. It was only seven o'clock.

"I don't see why we couldn't have gone to the dance," she started. "How can it take us two hours to put beers in the tub? I'm assuming that's all we have to do, right?"

He said nothing, hitting the button for the sixth floor. But when the elevator doors opened, he grabbed her arm to ensure she exited with him and did not let go until they reached the end of the hall. He stopped and reached into his inside coat pocket, taking out a stack of small envelopes.

"These are the keys . . . . We have these seven suites—four on the left and three on the right. All of the party suites need to be on the right. We can't have people hanging off the inside balconies." He separated the keys into two stacks. "Here—keep these for now," he instructed, giving her the four keys to the suites on the left.

The ice, drinks and alcohol had been delivered to the middle room. They spent the next half hour making a cooler out of the bathtub and rearranging the suite furniture in all three rooms for maximum capacity. When finished, Danielle sat down on a sofa to rest.

"Do you want something to drink?" Tate offered.

She shook her head.

"Not even a Sprite?"

She smirked. "We don't have any Sprite."

"I'll get one at the lobby bar."

She thanked him, completely baffled by his demeanor. While he was away, she picked up the remote and began absently surfing the television for something interesting to watch, eventually settling on an episode of *Mad About You*.

Ten minutes later, he returned with her drink and sat down on the sofa next to her.

"Thank you," she said again, taking a hearty sip.

He watched her intently.

"Is it good?"

She shrugged. "It's Sprite. I like it, thank you. . . . So what do we do now?"

"Do you have the other keys?"

She retrieved them from her tiny, beaded handbag, only big enough to fit her driver's license, emergency money and lip gloss in addition to the keys.

"These," he said, taking out two small envelopes that contained the keys, "are ours. 628—remember that. You can keep your purse in there." He took a pen from his pocket and wrote *our room* on one of the envelopes. "The rest are for our friends," he stated, splitting up the rest and writing corresponding numbers onto her envelopes. "I'll decide who gets what, and you keep the extras."

She nodded absently, yawning. The work had made her tired.

"You look tired."

"I am tired," she said, taking another drink. "I don't know why. I slept in today . . . ."

He eyed her intently.

She shifted uncomfortably. "What time is it?" she asked again.

"Going on eight."

"I thought people weren't showing up until nine or later."

"That's right."

"So—why don't we go back to the dance?"

"Because you're too tired to dance."

"I'm not," she insisted, standing up. As she did, the room spun for a moment, and she faltered, dizzy. "Jesus—"

Tate didn't move, still eyeing her intently. "Maybe you should have another drink of Sprite," he said, his mouth curling into a slight smile.

Her stare moved from the glass to his expression and back to the glass.

"Or maybe you should go rest . . . Room 628."

Her mind shouted one word. *Run.*

"Yes—maybe I should," she said, groping for her bag.

He handed it to her. "628."

She walked out of the room slowly, trying to act nonchalant, like she didn't know, and praying he wouldn't follow her. Closing the door behind her, she glanced down the hallway. It was not a long hallway, but her head was spinning faster and her breathing becoming labored. She felt slightly nauseous and feared she would not make it to the elevator.

Room 628 was right across the hall.

She walked past it, counting doors, until she got to the fourth. Opening her bag, she struggled to read the numbers. 622—she needed. But her vision was getting spotty, and she had to continuously blink away the black patches. Shaking, she opened the door and stumbled into the room, trying to scan it for a place to hide. Sweating and nauseous from vertigo, she made her way into the bathroom.

Hide.

He would find her. She had to hide. Where could she hide?

Switching off the light, she groped her way to the bathtub and crawled in, pulling the curtains across. She then curled up in a ball on the opposite end of the faucet until blackness overtook her completely.

She dreamed she was trying to clear her throat but couldn't. The more she tried, the more she gagged. And then she couldn't breathe. The awful sensation of suffocating hurled her into consciousness, and she opened her eyes, gasping for air.

It took a minute or two for her vision to come into focus, for her waking thoughts to return, along with her memory of where she was and how she got there. Someone was present, assisting her, but it took her another minute to recognize him. She panicked at first, unable to see clearly, thinking it was Tate. But then she saw the blond curls, or what was left of them, the lighter skin, the look of concern and recognized Alex.

"What are you hiding from?" he continued.

Her breathing slowed a bit, and her eyes darted nervously around the bathroom and then down to her person. She put a hand to her hair trying to ascertain how disheveled she was. Reluctantly, she gazed down at her dress and legs, but nothing appeared out of order.

"Am I a mess?" she breathed.

He shook his head, frowning. "No. Not at all. I mean, you look like you just woke up, but you—you look amazing."

She struggled to get out of the tub and eventually did with his help. Her head still felt heavy, her mouth dry and pasty, and she had a severe cramp in her groin. Leaning over the bathroom sink, she gazed into the mirror. Amazingly, most of her hair had stayed in place. The sides had been swept up into tiny pin curls, which must have been sprayed with adhesive, she thought caustically, and the remainder spilled down over her shoulders. She did not see any bruises or odd marks on her face or neck. Could she have possibly escaped scot-free?

"Dan," Alex started quietly. "Are you okay?"

She turned to look at him and immediately noticed the red-stained towel on the floor and his similarly stained clothing. Any concern for herself momentarily vanished. "What happened to you?" she gasped, reaching out to touch his shirt.

"It's nothing," he said, gently grabbing her hand and pushing it away. "Just—just a scratch. I got jabbed with a broken beer bottle."

"Well, are you okay? Do you need stitches or anything?"

"No," he burst, unbuttoning his shirt at the bottom to prove to her there was no wound. "See? I'm fine."

She blinked in confusion before sitting down on the closed toilet seat, suddenly taken aback by his physique. She had forgotten how tall and well-built he was. It pained her.

"You still haven't told me how you got here," he pressed.

She looked down, feeling flushed and trying to stem a surge of fear, loathing and sadness that had suddenly surfaced. "Well . . . I, um . . . He put something in my drink," she whispered, her voice barely audible. "He drugged me . . . I had to hide. I tried to hide, but I don't know—I don't remember anything from the last few hours."

The sobs began before she could even finish her sentence, violent heaving sobs. Alex sighed heavily, sitting next to her on the edge of the tub, taking one of her hands in his. "It's alright. Nothing happened—you're okay now."

"How do you know? How do you know nothing happened?"

"Because I've been here—I've been in this room since, since ten—and when we came in, it was untouched. I fell asleep in front of the TV . . . I looked for you. We both did. We looked all over for you, but when we couldn't find you, we just . . ." His voice trailed off.

She nodded, sniffing and wiping the tears away with the back of her free hand. "I know, I know—I'm sorry. This was a bad idea. You should have never come . . . I should have never come. I should have had more of a spine . . ."

"You have nothing to be sorry for," he said, incredulously. "Life just gets fucked up sometimes. And we don't even need to do much to make it happen. Sometimes, just being in the wrong place at the wrong time, you know?"

She nodded. "So, where's Kelly?"

He grunted, nodding towards the door. "Passed out on the bed."

"Okay," she said, then began shaking nervously.

"Here, come here . . ." he said, moving back to the floor. He patted the spot next to him. "Let's just sit here for awhile, okay?"

She slipped down next to him, and he put an arm around her to try to calm her down. They sat lost in thought, her mind racing between angst over the two hours prior to Alex finding the room and the horror over his finding her in the state she was in. There was no way he would ever want to see her again.

For him, anger and disgust competed with curious confusion as he sorted through what she told him had happened. He was aware of such drugs and had heard of such things, but the use of them was baffling. He wanted sex as much as any guy, but what was the point of fucking someone who was unconscious? It would be like fucking a corpse or a blow-up doll, both equally ludicrous in his mind. A barrage of flashbacks fluttered through his consciousness, too quick for him to hold onto, but they brought him back to his own debacle that evening with Kelly.

He whistled, breaking the silence. "Oh, what a fine pair we make."

She looked up at him quizzically.

"This is definitely the most bizarre date I ever remember having—not that that's saying much." He smirked, and it drew a smile out of her. "Let's get you home," he continued, standing up.

"What about Kelly?"

He helped her to stand up. "I'll come back in the morning for Kelly. Or, she can just find a ride home with someone. She's fine here."

After reassuring themselves that Kelly was alive and sleeping, they quietly slipped out of the room and out of the suite altogether. The halls were eerily empty, all of the open doors to the party suites having been closed. Though quiet, they could still hear reverberating thuds of music coming through some of the walls. "What time is it?" he whispered, but Danielle shrugged. They said nothing during the elevator ride. Upon exiting, she suggested they look at the lobby clock. It was 2:30 a.m.

"Shit . . . I was supposed to be home by twelve-thirty," he mumbled.

Silent, they walked through the empty lobby and out the front doors into the parking lot. Upon finding and entering the Bronco, Alex threw his head back and stared at the ceiling of the car in disbelief. Danielle quietly fumbled with the seat buckle before staring sadly out the front windshield. The night was cool and clear, the city's lights lost in the overpowering moonshine. A breeze rustled through the trees and whipped up tiny swirls of leaves and street trash.

While she studied the scenery, he studied her. For all she had been through, she still looked amazingly beautiful, her long hair cascading over her exposed shoulders, her eyes glistening and her skin almost glowing in the moonlit car.

He reached out to touch her face. She jumped slightly, startled.

"You look so beautiful tonight. I wish it would have worked out for us."

She looked down, embarrassed. "I do, too . . . It was all for you, you know," she said, gesturing to her appearance.

"I know . . . Are you doing anything tomorrow afternoon?"

She looked up at him, surprised. "Tomorrow? No—why?"

He shrugged. "I don't know. I think we should try this again. I'd—I'd like to try this again. Minus the drama, maybe." He grinned.

She smiled. "Yeah, alright. A movie?"

"How about a walk in the park."

During the ride home, they listened to the radio and talked absently about current events. Since Alex was so late, Danielle offered to jump out of the car without his having to even pull into the driveway, but he insisted on parking and walking her to the door. She assumed her parents were home and, not wanting to disturb them, led him to the back door.

The moon was so bright that he could clearly see the statuesque outlines of trees, shrubs and flowers in the well-manicured estate lawn. In the eerie light, everything looked frozen in time.

"Wait," he said, stopping her as she unlocked the door.

She turned, and he stepped towards her, taking her arm and pulling her close to him as he did. He bent down and kissed her gently. When he paused, to his mild surprise, she pulled him back and kissed him harder. He cupped her face in his hands, enjoying the smooth, cool touch of skin, then let his hands caress her exposed neck, shoulders and arms. His lips moved from hers, to her neck, down her chest. She smelled of flowers and soap, and her body felt like home, each kiss a step along a favorite path rather than a venture into dangerous, unexplored territory.

When they finally parted, minutes later, he felt as if he were saying goodbye to an old lover.

"I should go—I don't want to be grounded tomorrow," he joked.

She smiled. "Okay—I'll see you then . . . Oh, and don't forget to pick up Kelly."

He gave her a mock salute and made his way across the terrace, out of the moonlight and into the shadowy lawn.

She spun around and entered the house with such a feeling of joyous exuberance that she had to stop herself from either giggling or screaming. Being with him transported her out of the mundane and into an exotic, colorful and untapped world of sensation and perception. Maybe there was a god. Maybe somebody out there heard her constant cries of anguish and decided to toss her a crumb of hope.

But the euphoria would not last. As she got ready for bed and used the bathroom, she found blood on her panties and inner thighs. The fear that followed was quiet, dull—like a sheet being drawn over a body that had just been drained of its spirit. The panic of dying in one's sleep—completely helpless yet calm in the face of the ensuing catastrophe because of the remote possibility that one might wake up. That maybe it's just a dream, or it's all over, and regardless, there is nothing that can be done to change it.

There was a possibility she had merely gotten her period.

After more than an hour of staring blankly into the ceiling as her mind projected onto it a marathon of drive-in quality horror film scenarios, she finally fell into a restless sleep.

CHAPTER SIX

Alex slept well, his mind absent of nightmares for the five hours of sleep he had. Even though he got home past his curfew, his mother was surprisingly understanding—even believing his stained shirt came from a run-in with the punch bowl. She acted relieved to see him out with friends.

So cheerful was he about the pleasant end to his evening and upcoming date with Danielle that he almost forgot about Kelly. He had just poured himself a bowl of cereal when he remembered.

"Shit . . ." he breathed, looking nervously at the microwave clock. It was quarter to ten.

It took him another ten minutes to find his mother, make up a story of where he would be all day with the car again and then find the keys. At least he had showered before attempting to eat breakfast.

The hotel looked different in the day, its cotton candy pink exterior appearing even more garish and out of place. He nearly ran through the lobby to reach the elevator, and the ride was painfully slow, the car stopping at every level to retrieve departing guests. There were still party-goers lingering on the sixth floor—he could tell by their attire. When he reached Room 622, the door was open, and he held his breath, cautiously crossing the threshold.

"Kelly?" he called, walking into the center of the room.

A maid came out of the bathroom, her hand holding a red-stained towel.

"Can I help you?" she asked.

"Oh, no—sorry," he mumbled, backing out of the room.

Before leaving, he waited in a small line that had formed at the lobby desk. After confirming that Room 622 had officially returned the key and checked out, he shrugged to himself and decided to head to Danielle's. The bizarre dream that was Homecoming was officially over, and he could now get on with his real life.

Pulling into the Sumners' driveway, he noticed somebody standing outside the front door. After getting out of the car and walking towards the entry, he saw it was a girl he did not recognize. She was tall and slim with a shock of cropped black hair. Ignoring him, she rung the doorbell three more times and pounded furiously on the door.

"Goddammit, open up—open up! Wake up—I know somebody's home . . . Shit." She spun around. "Who the fuck are you?"

She was dressed in a close-fitting striped sweater and tight, dark jeans, which made her legs look ridiculously long and skinny, and her eyes were hidden behind large, black sunglasses.

"I'm Alex. And who the fuck are you?" he asked in his most polite tone.

"O-mi-god. You're Alex? *The* Alex?"

"I'm *an* Alex . . . One of many."

She smiled, revealing perfectly straight, white teeth. "I'm Brooke—Dan's friend. Are you here to see Dan?"

"Yeah—but it appears no one's home."

"Oh, *they're* home . . . *somebody's* home," she snapped, ringing the bell angrily a few more times. "I went around the back and looked through the windows—the TV is on. I have a key to the place, but I left it on my dresser . . . goddammit."

"Well, maybe we should come back later—"

At that moment, the front door flew open with a loud creak.

"What the fuck?" Dennis burst, then peered queerly at both of them, his eyes darting from one person to the other more than once. "What the fuck . . ." he repeated, this time more confused than angry.

Brooke and Alex stepped back in surprise but said nothing. His appearance only complemented the outburst, dressed in ripped jeans and a worn concert shirt, his long black hair hanging in wild, wet ringlets that shook when he yelled.

"Jesus Christ—it's fucking Sunday morning. I was fucking taking a shower—why are you here? Oh, wait—I know why you're here," he said caustically, turning to Brooke. "You practically live here. But *you*—" He turned to Alex, his black, beady eyes narrowing, like a bird of prey about to pounce. "What the hell are you doing here? Is there some after fucking Homecoming party nobody told me about? Should I be expecting more guests?"

Brooke just snorted and stepped onto the threshold, pushing roughly by him. Alex did not feel so bold or entitled and waited patiently for Dennis to invite him inside. "Well, come in," Dennis said finally, stepping aside.

Brooke had wandered well into the house, but Alex could hear her calling Danielle's name.

"She's not here!" Dennis yelled at the top of his lungs, causing Alex to wince. "Jesus Christ . . . What do *you* want?" he asked Alex again.

"I was actually looking for Dan, too."

"Are you fucking kidding me? Do you even fucking know my sister? *How* do you even fucking know my sister?"

"Where is she?" Brooke snapped, running down the front stairs.

"I don't know—I'm not her fucking keeper. Didn't she go to some stupid Homecoming dance and party last night? Maybe she never came home."

"No, she came home. I dropped her off," Alex offered, growing suddenly concerned.

Dennis looked at him dumbfounded.

Brooke stopped at the bottom step and sat down abruptly, burying her face in her arms. Alex and Dennis exchanged curious looks and then watched her, waiting to see what would happen next. After a full minute, she had still not looked up, but Alex could tell her body was shaking a bit. He wondered if she was crying.

"Is she okay?" he whispered to Dennis.

"No," he whispered back. "She's completely insane. They're *all* completely insane." He started shuffling out the room. "Coffee anyone?" he asked loudly.

"Sure," Alex said.

Brooke remained silent and unmoving. When Dennis left, Alex walked over to her, kneeling down but keeping a safe distance. "Are you okay?"

She shook her head.

"Can I help? Is there something I can do until Dan gets here?" he asked cautiously.

"Yes," she burst finally, causing Alex to lean back a bit. "There is. Explain to me why all you men are such dicks!"

He stared blankly at her a moment, his mind spinning. *Danger – Danger, Will Robinson.* The Robot's image and deadpan voice flashed through his mind, and he leaned back on his heels. "Right . . . Um—I think I'll go help Dennis with the coffee and, maybe we can talk later . . . Right."

Within seconds, he was stumbling quickly through the Sumners' house looking for the kitchen. He found Dennis standing in front of a huge marble counter, staring at a coffee machine.

"I don't know how to use this," he said, turning to Alex.

Alex leaned towards him. "We got trouble," he mumbled.

Dennis rolled his eyes.

"I think she's pissed off at her boyfriend or something. She hates men."

"Fuck," Dennis breathed, staring at the ceiling. "Where the hell is Dan when you need her? Jesus. Do you know how to use this? What the hell are all these buttons for? I just want to make a pot of fucking coffee. Christ."

Alex looked at the machine, which was three times the size of a Mr. Coffee and with five times more buttons and gadgets. He frowned, opening the lid and peering inside. "I think—I think the filter goes in here," he suggested.

Ten minutes later, they had a pot brewing and had begun talking about music when Brooke shuffled into the kitchen, sunglasses still covering her eyes. Alex froze mid-sentence.

"Is the coffee ready?" she sniffled.

"Not yet . . . Why don't you go hang out in the living room, and I'll bring it to you," Dennis offered.

But she plunked herself down at the kitchen table, within earshot of their conversation.

"I think I'll start breakfast," Dennis announced suddenly. "Go talk to her," he whispered to Alex, nudging him.

Alex shook his head.

"Do it—"

"No—"

"Do it—"

"You do it—"

They started pushing each other.

"What the fuck are you morons doing?" Brooke asked. "Why isn't the coffee ready? Didn't you start it, like, ten minutes ago? Jesus, it's like *Beavis and Butthead* around here."

Both of them looked at each other and spent a few minutes doing *Beavis and Butthead* impressions, thinking it may chase her out of the room. She stayed, the scene having temporarily chased away her anger. Once she began laughing, Alex ventured over to the table. Dennis had decided to make pancakes. He had some special recipe and didn't want Alex to watch—a family secret or something.

"This kitchen is like the size of the entire downstairs of my house," Alex said, trying to keep the subject neutral.

Brooke shrugged. "Have you been here before?"

"I was at his party a few weeks ago. How big is this place, anyway?"

"I don't know . . . Probably five or six bedrooms. Want to take a tour? Dan won't mind."

"Yeah, but I might," Dennis called, eavesdropping.

She stuck her tongue out at him and got up, motioning for Alex to follow her. "Let's go count the bedrooms—"

"There are six—" Dennis yelled after them.

As they meandered through the downstairs level, Brooke talked about the house, the furnishings and what she knew of the Sumners' history, some of which Alex had already learned from Danielle. But he just listened, gawking at the lavish décor, which was completely absent at the party, and losing count of the number of fireplaces and staircases.

They eventually entered a large, long room with a cathedral style antique wooden ceiling, the kind one would find in an old church or grand hall of an English castle. The room must have been closed off for the party, for he did not remember it. Two enormous crystal chandeliers hung from the beams. After taking in the breathtaking scope of the room, Alex's attention was drawn to the wall across from the white marble fireplace, which displayed a collection of framed photographs of the Sumners' family. In the center of the collage hung two large, painted portraits of what he assumed to be Mr. and Mrs. Sumners.

"That's Danielle's mother?" he suggested, staring intently at a painting of a beautiful young woman in an enticing baby blue dress, her long dark hair spilling over bare shoulders, her black eyes inviting but fiery, her full lips slightly upturned in what could be construed as either a smile or a cruel smirk. She looked just like Danielle but more sexual, voluptuous, experienced. And the dress was strikingly similar to the one Danielle wore last evening.

Brooke confirmed. "Yes, and I know what you're thinking . . . Get your mind out the gutter," she snapped, hitting his arm.

"Ow . . . What are you talking about?"

"Oh, please—look at her. She looks like a Victoria's Secret model for god's sake. And that painting doesn't even do her justice. You should see her in person."

"So—what is she doing with *him*?" he asked, nodding to the other painting, this one of a middle-aged man with meticulously groomed hair, rugged facial features and dark, deep-set eyes. He wore a pale pink dress shirt with silver cuff links. On his left hand was a huge gold ring with some kind of insignia. He was smiling slightly, like someone who gets amusement from tearing wings off bugs. While he wasn't ugly, he didn't seem attractive enough to win the wife he had.

"I know," Brooke burst. "And can you believe he had an affair on her? I mean, Jesus. What hope do Dan and I have, right? What hope do any of us have . . ."

Alex raised an eyebrow. "Um . . ."

"Oh, that marriage is over. It's been over for awhile—I just wish they'd kill it for their kids' sake. It's got to be hell living here, I know. My dad did the same thing to us a few years ago."

He frowned then turned back to the other photos on the wall, ones of happier times, like the black and white photo of the same man and woman, arm in arm, smiling. She didn't look so vampy, dressed in a jean jacket with her hair blowing, standing in front of a mountain range that rose above masses of tall, thin columnar pines and a clear lake. She looked just like Danielle in that photo, to the extent he wondered if it was Danielle, standing next to Tate, but he quickly dismissed the thought.

"That's Montana—" he burst.

Brooke joined him in his scrutiny of the photo. "How do you know?"

"I grew up near there—that's Glacier Lake."

She snorted. "I doubt it—it's probably somewhere in Italy. They met in Italy, and that was obviously taken when they were dating or just married."

Alex shrugged, internally convinced it was Montana and making a mental note to ask Danielle about it. He then noticed another photo, this one of Danielle and Dennis when they were small, in grade school—maybe first grade. They were on the grass sitting cross-legged and making silly faces, at the left end of a semi-circle, but the photo cut off the rest of the circle, revealing only the knee of whomever was in the middle. Something about the photo looked familiar to Alex, but he couldn't place why.

A few minutes later, Dennis called to them from the kitchen. The first batch of pancakes was ready. They hadn't even made it to the second floor.

∞

She had been in a deep and dreamless sleep, and it was a full minute before she realized her phone was ringing. "Hello," she mumbled, looking at the clock. It was a little after eight in the morning.

"Dan?" a quivering voice on the other end responded. "Dan—"

"Yes. Who is this?"

"Dan it's me—" the voice burst. "Something terrible's happened—"

She tried to distinguish the voice between the sobs. Her heart pounded in anticipation, fearing the caller was Brooke.

"Who is this? Brooke?" she asked, anxiously.

"No—it's me. Kelly . . . You're the only person I felt I could call . . . Would you come get me?" she asked, choking on sobs.

Danielle swallowed hard, the chill returning. "Of—of course . . . Where are you?"

"I'm at the hotel . . . Where the hell are you? We looked all over for you last night—"

"Yeah, I'm sorry. I—um—sure . . . I need to get dressed, but . . . I'll be there in a half hour or so."

Kelly sobbed in relief and, after giving Danielle the room number, hung up the phone.

Danielle groaned, wishing Alex would have gotten to her first. But it was early, and he was probably exhausted and still sleeping. After showering and throwing on sweats, she headed out, her hair still wet, her face scrubbed but absent of make-up.

The hotel loomed ahead, its massive pink façade hideously out of place amongst the classic colors and timeless styles of the surrounding buildings. She pulled into visitor parking and reluctantly made her way into the building. The lobby was relatively absent of patrons, and the huge interior atrium was quiet except for the sound of cascading water coming from an unseen fountain buried beneath the flora. Walking hastily to the elevator, she pushed the button impatiently. Just being here gave rise to unpleasant memories and unnamed fears. It occurred to her that she still had spare keys to the four suites in her tiny beaded bag. It also occurred to her that her driver's license was in the bag and not in the purse she carried now. She swore under her breath.

Upon reaching Kelly's door, she knocked softly, listening for sound or movement. She thought she heard the television. Moments later, Kelly yanked open the door, retreating back to the room so quickly, Danielle barely saw her face to see if she had stopped crying. When she finally turned around, Danielle noticed her nose was puffy and her eyes were red and swollen. She was wearing a red dress, the fabric reduced to a wrinkled mess, a large run in her hose.

"Thank you for coming," she whispered hoarsely.

"Of course—" Danielle started.

"I think something terrible happened," Kelly continued, pacing the room. Danielle took a seat on the sofa, waiting patiently for her to continue.

"I think . . ." she put a hand to her face, trying to push back the tears. "I think I did something to Alex . . . I think I might have . . . have hurt him!"

"*What?*" Danielle asked, trying to behave as if she had no idea what was going on.

"I know what I saw . . . He was bleeding last night . . . and this morning . . . This morning—I found a bloody towel in the bathroom," she said dramatically, disappearing into the bathroom and returning with the item.

"Kelly—" Danielle started, wincing.

"I feel so stupid! I feel so *sick*—I know my drink was spiked. I think someone put acid in it—"

"Kelly—stop a minute—*please*," Danielle pleaded, putting a hand up. "Alex is fine. I saw him last night," she stated bluntly, her mind rushing to concoct a plausible story.

"What?" Kelly asked dully. "Wait—why? How? We couldn't even fucking find you last night—"

"I know, I know—I'm sorry. I was hanging out in the lobby much of the night. They had some nice entertainment—classical music, you know." She was amazed at how smoothly the lies flowed from her brain to her mouth.

"So—what was he doing?"

"Wandering around wasted and looking for you. He hardly recognized me. And, yes—he was a mess. But it wasn't blood. Somebody spilled punch or grenadine on him or something. I don't know. Look—it's my fault he's not here. I drove him home in his Bronco and then took a cab home, myself." She winced inwardly, hoping Kelly wouldn't ask *how* she called for a cab from

Alex's house. How she possibly got by Alex's parents. Hoping Kelly wouldn't ask anything and just accept her story.

Kelly sniffled, dropping the towel onto the floor. "So he didn't completely ditch me?"

"Of course not. I didn't ditch you, either. I—I didn't even know you were here."

"Oh, thank god," Kelly sighed dramatically, throwing herself backwards on the bed. "I feel like hell—I look like hell. I just want to go home, but I'm almost too tired to get up . . ." she garbled while yawning.

Kelly didn't say much until she had checked out and they were in Danielle's car. She began by asking how the dance went, how Tate was and more details about Danielle's evening. Danielle was as truthful as she could be without telling Kelly anything, which, unfortunately, kept her responses terse and left uncomfortable moments of silence.

"Son of a bitch," Kelly burst after of those moments.

Danielle looked at her askance.

"I just remembered something else . . . Jesus, I can't believe I'm here . . . I can't believe you are driving me home—the morning after my own Homecoming . . . I've been totally and literally screwed. Screwed!"

Danielle raised an eyebrow.

"I mean—I know I was drunk and you *say* he was drunk, but . . . I just feel so used," she sighed loudly, fluffing her hair. "I mean—I did invite him to the dance—took him to a nice a nice restaurant—"

"Didn't he pay for it?"

"Of course he paid for it—that's not where I'm going with this! Jesus Christ . . ." She impatiently waved away Danielle's question. "Anyway, where was I going?. . . *My point is*, that I invited him to the dance, invited him to the group dinner and then invited him to *our* exclusive party with *our* mutually exclusive and wealthy friends, and this—this is the clincher—this is where I'm going with all this. I invite him so that he could actually see *you*, and I could see your ex, and what happens?"

Silence.

"Guess what happens," she pressed Danielle.

"What?"

"He gets it on with me."

Danielle blinked her eyes in rapid confusion. "Who gets it on with you?"

"Who do you think?"

"I would like to think my ex got it on with you—"

"Yeah—that's what you would think. But no—not your ex. Your Alex, that's who."

"*What*?" Danielle burst.

"I know, I know . . . It's awful. It really is. I can't believe it myself."

"*What* did you say?"

"You *know* what I said. I messed around with him. I blew him. *Blew him.* Off—literally. Unlike the figurative blowing off he did me in the middle of the night."

Danielle bit the back of her tongue while clamping her mouth shut to suppress a yelp. Tears formed, from either the pain in her mouth or the pain in her heart, she knew not which. Only that she wanted the ride to be over, and she hit the gas to arrive at Kelly's house quickly.

"God, they're all the same. Every single one of them thinks with their dick."

Danielle remained icily silent, clenching the steering wheel. Liar, she told herself, wanting to scream it at Kelly. She had to be lying or just vindictive. After all, there hadn't been a guy Danielle liked—either up close or from afar—that Kelly hadn't gotten her claws on at some point. Why not Alex? She couldn't let him break her record.

Kelly rambled on a bit more before Danielle finally pulled into her driveway, mumbling an insincere good-bye.

She barely drove a block before bursting into tears, soon heaving uncontrollable sobs. Within minutes she pulled off the road into a filling station, trying to get a grip on her emotions and determine what to do next. Part of her wanted to run away, part of her wanted to die. Neither part could face going home yet. She was torn between wanting to believe the best or writing him off as another life-changing learning experience. Her heart said Kelly was a vamp whose word couldn't be trusted completely, and her logic concluded it was a possibility, the same logic that concluded her being date raped was a possibility, while her heart and every fiber of her being prayed it was just her period.

Twenty minutes into her emotional meltdown, she decided to seek refuge and headed for her church. She would reach the second half of the nine-thirty Mass and be able to stay afterwards to pray privately and light a candle.

Located in downtown, the Cathedral of the Immaculate Conception was one of the more architecturally grand churches in the Kansas City area, with large stained-glass windows and a Gothic façade. Inside was no less grand, the rib vaulting and flying buttresses giving the church a majestic feel. She took a seat in one of the dark, polished wood pews near the back, trying to avoid any stares from the parishioners. Lateness was generally frowned upon, especially by the elderly population, and not only was she late but also inappropriately dressed. Her tear-stained face no doubt raised additional eyebrows, she thought to herself, keeping her head bowed during the sermon.

The priest droned on about stewardship, whatever that meant, and serving the right master, and she let the words flow through her mind without paying much attention. At this stage in her life, she didn't attend church regularly and hardly accepted all of its tenets. It served as more of a retreat, and she anxiously awaited the end of the Mass, when the population would leave and she could enjoy the awe-inspiring atmosphere in relative peace. Even as she went through the motions of the Mass, her mind struggled with the extreme events of the past twenty four hours. She sensed a connection that bordered on supernatural, and her goal this morning was to attempt to discover the significance and proper course of action. Above all, she wanted to ensure she did the right thing.

As she watched the communion procession, she pondered the biblical passage discussing false prophets. Was it a part of the gospel, she wondered, casually picking up the missal. *Beware of false prophets, who come to you in sheep's clothing but inwardly are ravenous wolves. You will know them by their fruits.* This certainly applied to her current situation.

She sighed in annoyance. Men had one fruit on their mind—the forbidden one. There was no such thing as a Prince Charming. No Mr. Right. No perfect relationship. And even if she found someone—married someone—it would likely end in affairs or divorce and eventually death. There was no hope. There was no point.

The tears flowed again, and she became completely oblivious to the comings and goings of those around her, so introspective with grief, that she didn't notice the Kleenex being held out to her until it lightly touched her hand, startling her. She looked up and into the face of a priest she had never seen before. He was middle-aged, not handsome, but kindly-looking, the pronounced lines around his mouth and eyes making it seem as if he were always smiling. His dark brown hair was severely receded, barely visible around his olive-toned broad face.

"You look like you could use one of these," he said, his voice thick with an Italian accent.

She sniffed and silently accepted the offer.

"Would you like an ear?" he asked.

"What?"

"An ear—to talk to."

"Oh . . . Alright," she said absently.

They sat in silence for a few minutes, she waiting for him to begin, but he never did. When the first Kleenex was nearly in shreds, he passed her a fresh one. From where it came, she did not see.

"I—I don't know where to start, really . . . I, I think I was raped last night, but I don't know . . . I think my boyfriend . . . I mean, I think this new boy I like has already cheated on me, but I don't know . . . I think my parents are getting a divorce . . ." For the next five minutes she poured out traumatic highlights from the past few years. "But I don't know," she concluded. "I don't know anything anymore. I think God hates me . . . which is why I'm here, because I—I just don't know where else to go. Everything's so . . . so upside down. Scary. Unreal . . ."

"Why do you think God hates you?"

She sniffed, shaking her head. "I think he hates us all. I mean—look at the world. It's horrible. It's a terrible place, really. I'm one of the lucky ones, and I'm . . . I'm miserable, frightened. And I'm not even starving or at war or horribly sick with cancer or some other disease. It's full of death. We're just surrounded by death . . . and hate . . . Conflict, constant conflict . . ."

"And what does God have to do with this?"

"He created it," she burst. "He created everything—and if he created it, that means he *is* it. Logically, if he created both good and evil, that means he is both good and evil, which means . . . Which means he's a psychopath." She shook her head and inhaled deeply, trying to keep her nose from running. "Sorry . . . I probably shouldn't say that about God."

But he seemed nonplussed. "Yes, that would be the logical conclusion. Logically, how could a perfect being such as God create a seemingly imperfect world without being imperfect, himself, yes?"

She nodded in agreement.

"Yes, yes . . . What if I were to tell you God didn't create the world."

Her whirling thoughts and emotions came to an abrupt halt.

"What if I were to tell you that this was just a dream. Merely a thought—or, rather, strings of thoughts, playing out like a movie. But no more real than a movie or a stage play."

All sound ceased except for the priest's voice.

"God is formless. Thought is formless. The universe is actually formless, empty space. It feels real because we have put our belief in it. We've created our own make-belief world and have forgotten that it's just that—make-belief . . . God's world is perfect—it doesn't contain death, sickness, fighting . . . Our make-belief world does, but that world is not real. It's just a crazy thought. We're perfect, too, see."

She exhaled deeply when he finished, somewhat confused yet oddly reassured, as if what he was saying were simply reminders of things she knew deep down but had forgotten.

"Is—is this in the Bible?" she asked cautiously.

The priest pursed his lips then smiled. "Maybe if you read between the lines. Did you come here for *Bible* study?" he asked, winking at her knowingly.

"No," she said, shaking her head, smirking.

"Exactly."

"So, if this is just a dream, how do we wake up from it? I mean—what if I don't like this dream anymore—can I just close my eyes and change it? Because I *need* to change it . . . Something has to change, or I'm going to . . . I don't know. So, what do I do now?" she asked, sighing loudly.

The priest leaned back in the pew, not responding right away and instead waving at a few parishioners who had drifted in early for the next Mass. "That, Danielle," he said finally, "is the purpose of your life. To find your way out of the dream. I could not possibly tell you how to do so in the next year, let alone the next few minutes, but I can leave you with some pointers to set you on your way."

She wished she had a pen.

"First, you need to understand that the world is not happening *to* you, you are projecting the world. So if you do not like what you see, you need to go into the projector—your mind—and fix it. Your body is simply an empty machine. It is your mind that is the real Wizard—the real Oz behind the curtain, putting up a bunch of smoke and mirrors. Know thyself—become an observer of the play that is your life, not a participant. Watch your mind and emotions. Watch the events. Don't react right away. Watch and observe first, and delay the reaction."

She nodded, and he continued.

"Next, change your reading habits. What do you think those Gothic romances are doing to your mind? Think about what you are feeding your mind—images, thoughts. That's what's going to play itself out."

Her eyes grew wide, and she tried to interrupt him to ask how he could possibly know what she read, but he ignored her, waved at another parishioner and continued.

" . . . And all romance is merely a symbol of our true desire to find

God. We think finding a partner, having sex, making babies and families is so important, but that is all carrots dangling. Distractions from our true purpose. Now, that doesn't mean we don't fall in love and have families and work. That's not what I am saying at all. I am saying don't look for meaning in that. That's all part of the dream, and the more you believe there is meaning in that, the deeper into the dream you go. I would suggest you study some philosophy, quantum physics. Maybe take a yoga or meditation class."

She sat gaping, and he continued.

"And about this boy, Alex—"

At the mention of Alex's name she gasped, now motioning to interrupt him. She had never mentioned Alex's name to the priest and now began to wonder if the priest had some kind of psychic ability or odd connection to the Fahlstrom family, but he ignored her and kept talking.

"That's why you really came here. You wanted to know what to do about Alex. He, too, is part of the dream. Lost in the dream. You need him as much as he needs you. We need each other to get out—all of us. Even those who seem to harm us. You merely dream harm to yourself, Danielle, but all harm is coming from deep within the mind and being projected outside in an endless drama. You're just projecting yourself harming yourself via another body. But there is no body. We're all just thoughts."

She sat in silence for a moment, her head still spinning over the apparent level of detail he knew about her life and now reeling over the outrageous ideas that just spilled from his mouth. His *advice* left her with far more questions than answers, but she knew he would depart soon to prepare for the next Mass. As he moved to go, she stopped him with the one most pressing to her of late. "So . . . if this is just a dream, what happens when we die?"

"Ahh, yes . . . We don't die, Danielle. We simply move on to another story—another dream. We only dream birth, life and death. We dream in-between lives. We never stop dreaming until we wake up. And when we wake up, we wake up in perfect peace and happiness, because we realize it was all just a crazy dream. None of it happened. And, now—my time is up. I must go. Kleenex?"

A Kleenex manifested, from where she did not see, maybe from up his sleeve. She took it reluctantly.

"But how—how do you even know my name? How do you know anything about me? I've never even met you before—I've never *seen* you here before—"

"How indeed," he said with mock indignation, standing up. "Maybe you dreamed me into existence," he concluded, winking at her before making his way out of the pew and disappearing into the oncoming sea of parishioners.

Even though the church was quickly filling with bodies and abuzz with the noise of hushed conversation and an organ tuning, Danielle heard none of it. For the next several minutes, a cocoon of silence enveloped her as she pondered what just happened.

She did not remember walking out of the church or even the drive home, amazed she made it into her driveway without incident. Turning off the car, she sat awhile, feeling the warm inner peace and tranquility slip away with each passing moment, like a morning fog lifting. Sighing, she slowly made her way to the back door of the house, not really wanting to enter. Unsure of what she would find and bracing herself for the worst. Closing her eyes before turning the knob, she told herself repeatedly—*It's just a dream. It's just a dream. I'm only dreaming*—

And opened it to a chorus of hysterical laughter coming from the kitchen, laughter so infectious she couldn't help but smile and eagerly made her way inside after closing the door behind her.

The kitchen was a mess, and around the table sat her brother, Alex and Brooke, in the middle of a breakfast of pancakes, laughing incessantly.

"Dan!" they all cried with the enthusiasm of a holiday homecoming.

"Oh my god—where the hell have you been?" Brooke burst.

"Um," she pondered a moment. Not wanting to break the spell, she decided not to tell them about Kelly. "Church—I went to church."

The laughter immediately stopped, and they all stared glumly at her, as if they did not understand or did not want to understand what she had just said.

"Did you say *church*?" Alex asked. He hated organized religion.

"She's a Jesus Freak," Dennis said dryly. "You should find these things out before dating."

"I am not!" she burst. "I don't even pray to Jesus—"

"But you do *pray* –" Dennis insisted.

"So?" she protested.

"So—it's stupid. It's an act of sheep. Isn't that what the Bible says—that you're a bunch of sheep, and Jesus is the shepherd . . . Sheep are dumb animals," Dennis said.

She reddened, but Brooke and Alex started giggling, and soon the entire table was laughing.

"Have some pancakes," Alex offered, handing her his plate on which sat a half-eaten flapjack. "They're delicious," he burst, barely able to speak coherently.

"Yeah, I'll go make more. I have some batter left," Dennis said, jumping up from the table and knocking a chair down in the process, which brought down the house again.

Danielle studied the room, now suspicious. "What is going on with you guys—are you *high*?"

More giggles.

"No, we're not *high*," Alex said dramatically. "We're just—we're just family. You guys—you guys are the *best*. I feel I've known you forever."

"Back at you, man," Dennis said.

Brooke nodded and then roughly yanked Danielle down into the chair next to her. "You have to have some. Dennis is a great cook. *Who knew?* Alex—pass me your plate. And the syrup."

Danielle looked down at the large robin egg blue stoneware plate, watching the syrup seep off the sides of the pancake and form pools. She picked up a fork and started swirling the syrup with it. The fork felt real.

"Awww—you look *so sad*," Brooke said, making a pouty face. "Eat—eat up. You need your nutrition."

"Yeah, *have some pancakes little girl, heh, heh, heh*," Alex added, impersonating some voice she vaguely recognized from a movie or comedy show.

She looked up at him, baffled. He winked at her, and whatever emotion she had in the prior moment was immediately replaced with a sexual longing so intense she dropped the fork into the syrup. This caused another round of giggles. Annoyed, she grabbed a spoon and began shoveling pancake into her mouth, hoping to curb the growing hunger. They were surprisingly tasty, sweet with a hint of spices.

"These are great Dennis," she said, taking the last bite. "Is there cinnamon in here?"

"Sure," he said. "I'll have more ready in just a minute."

This caused another round of inexplicable laughter and *Beavis and Butthead* impersonations. Danielle couldn't help but laugh with them even though she felt quite outside the joke. Her brother soon placed a plateful of coaster-sized steaming pancakes in front of her.

"Want some coffee?" he asked.

"Sure—half and half, though. Half coffee, half milk."

"*Want some coffee little girl,*" Alex started the impersonation again.

She just shook her head and began cutting into the food, trying to contain her own urge to laugh while eating. Soon, the three of them were seated and just staring at her as she ate. Disconcerted, she stopped.

"What? . . . . What is going on? Why—why are you all even here?"

They looked at each other blankly.

"Why *are* we here?" Alex said. "I forgot . . ."

"To see Dan, you idiot," Brooke burst. "I came here looking for my friend in my hour of dire need, and where the hell was she? *Gone*. At fucking church of all places."

"Oh, yeah . . . I think we had a date," Alex said simply. "I came to pick you up."

"At ten in the morning—after Homecoming. *Right . . .*" Danielle responded, rolling her eyes. "So what's your dire need?"

Brooke sighed dramatically, "Oh, it doesn't matter now. These fine young gentlemen were here for me. I don't need you anymore. I'm fine."

"Well, what happened?"

"Her boyfriend dumped her after Homecoming," Dennis stated simply.

Danielle's heart fell and she turned to her friend. "Oh, my god—Brooke, I'm so sorry—"

But Brooke waved her away. "Stop—I don't want your sympathy. Besides, I have now been trained in the art of male psychology, and I will not be making the same mistake again."

"And that would be . . ."

"Well, sleeping with a guy before knowing what his intentions are for one," Dennis said.

"Yeah, you see, Dan," Brooke started. "All guys want sex, but some guys want sex and no relationship. And some guys want sex and a relationship. And some guys want sex and aren't sure if they want a relationship or not until after the sex. And, if I want a relationship, I should just get that right in the open from the get-go—before the sex. Because after the sex, it's a crap shoot."

"You call that *advice*? How is that advice?" Danielle asked incredulously.

"It makes perfect sense to me," Brooke said emphatically.

"You haven't eaten enough pancakes for it to make sense," Alex added, smirking. "Finish that plate, there, and it'll all be clear as crystal."

She had just swallowed another bite when it hit her what had happened.

"What did you put in here? Dennis—" she snapped.

He shrugged. "Just some herbs and spices."

"Herbs? You put *herbs* in the pancakes?"

At this, the rest of the table burst into uncontrollable giggles. Danielle stared down at her plate. She had started on her second pancake, and there were four remaining. Oh, what the hell, she thought to herself. If it's just a dream, it doesn't matter, anyway.

For the next hour and a half, the four of them drank coffee, told jokes, laughed and took multiple trips to the bathroom. It was early afternoon, when Brooke and Dennis decided to battle each other in a video game, leaving the two of them alone. Alex turned to Danielle to ask her if she wanted to go for a hike at Shawnee Mission Park. The hysteria was beginning to wear off a bit, and he did not want the day to get away from them without spending time alone with her.

While she wasn't thrilled at the prospect of a hike, she wanted to be with him and agreed to go. Before leaving, she changed from sweats into jeans, a cami and a button-down blouse and grabbed a jacket. Though late October, the weather could still get unseasonably warm in the afternoons before plunging by evening, and layers were prudent.

"Do you have any old blankets?" Alex suggested. "It could be muddy."

Her thoughts raced at the suggestion, but she quickly cast them aside.

After finding some unused throws and two bottled waters, they headed out, talking about school, sports and music for the duration of the drive. When they reached the park, she exited the car, stretching and enjoying the fresh air.

"God—it's been ages since I've been here," she said. "I forgot how pretty this park is. In the summer, people boat out here."

He nodded, locking the car and leading her towards the trail entrance. "This is a long trail—I'm not sure you want to walk the whole thing—"

She shrugged. "I don't care. It's just past two—we have plenty of time."

As the path was wider at the entrance, they walked hand-in-hand for some time, he carrying the blankets under one arm, and she carrying the bottled waters under hers, until it narrowed to the point they reverted to single file. They kept the conversation light. He found himself thinking about her mother's portrait and wondering if she had the same fiery passion under her rather reserved exterior. She struggled with whether or not to bring up the previous night, afraid it would ruin the day.

"So . . ." Danielle started, gingerly making her way around a large, muddy spot. "About last night . . . I, I wasn't just at church today, actually. Kelly called me this morning."

Alex's stimulating thoughts came to an abrupt halt, and he mentally braced himself.

"She was kind of freaked out, but I—I covered for us."

"Yeah, I—I'm sorry. I actually went to pick her up this morning, but she had already checked out . . . Um—there's a nice spot to sit just up ahead a bit, slightly off the path."

She nodded, not wanting to push the subject and wondering if he would come clean.

He led her down to the same spot where, only two months ago, he had encountered the faceless man. Today he hoped to erase all traces of the previous event—to prove to himself it was merely a dream, just like last night. It didn't really happen. He could be with a girl he liked and everything would be normal. It only happened with blond girls—or loose girls with whom he did not have a special relationship.

The large rock was still there, and he arranged one of the throw blankets on the ground in front of it. After sitting down, he motioned for Danielle to sit beside him, the rock large enough for more than two to use as a seat back. She complied.

He sighed, not wanting to say what he was about to say but also knowing any hope of intimacy between the two of them would be strained if it wasn't addressed. "She told you, didn't she?"

Danielle's silence was an affirmative.

"Of course she did . . ." he said.

"I'm—I'm sorry, Alex. I shouldn't have even brought it up. It—it doesn't matter, anyway. It was . . . I mean—obviously, it wasn't invited by you . . . Right?"

He shook his head, shrugging nonchalantly, his face reddening. "No . . . I had a beer and was kind of half asleep watching TV, and the next thing I know. . . I don't even know what happened . . . Nothing really did once I realized what was happening, and, you know . . . stopped it."

After pondering his explanation for a minute, Danielle continued the discussion. "So, I'm just curious . . . when that happens to a guy, does . . . does the guy feel bad? I mean, do you feel, like, used or violated? Or is that just a girl thing?"

He pondered the question for a moment, actually relieved by it, as the conversation could have gone a much different direction. "No . . . I didn't feel like that at all. A bit—a bit disgusted. And very annoyed. I guess more pissed off than anything."

She nodded in understanding. "So . . . do you mind if I ask you something else?"

"I don't know yet," he said, then winked at her reassuringly.

She smiled and then reddened at the sudden erotic jolt that went through her. "Um . . . I think I just forgot what I was going to ask."

"Was it about last night?" he asked.

"Um, sort of . . . . Okay, yes," she said, collecting her emotions. "So, why do guys do what Tate tried to do? Like, why is that appealing? I mean—I, I don't want to dwell on it or anything, but . . . I just don't get the whole drug thing."

"Honestly . . . I don't know. I don't really get it myself. But then, I don't understand those sex dolls, either. To me, there's something similar, I mean—if you're screwing someone who's unconscious, how is that any different than screwing a blow up doll . . ."

"So—it's not, like, an *in* or *cool* thing to do?"

He made a face, wincing, "If it is, I wouldn't know. I've never had anything to do with it, and I don't think my friends ever have." But as the words left his mouth, a barrage of images flashed through his mind, like a movie played at the maximum fast forward speed, so fast he could not make them out, but they made him uneasy.

"Okay . . . thanks. That makes me feel better." She smiled and lightly laid her hand on his knee.

He placed his on top of hers and looked at her, studying her features and mentally comparing them to the woman in the portrait. He pictured her in the same dress as her mother, with her hair spilling down onto her bare shoulders and voluptuous chest. He imagined her speaking Italian to him. Then he remembered.

"Have your parents ever been to Montana?"

She frowned, shaking her head. "No—why?"

"I don't know—Brooke took me on a tour of your house and showed me this portrait room. I could swear they were at Glacier Lake in this one photo."

She shrugged, so he described the photo in more detail.

"Oh—that photo. They were very young in that picture, and I—I have no idea where that was taken. My mother's from Italy, and that's where they met."

"Yeah, Brooke tells me you speak Italian, too."

She blushed, turning away.

"You do, don't you," he teased. "I want to hear it—"

She shook her head, still looking away.

"Come on," he said, gently turning her head back towards him so they were face to face and quite close. "Say something—anything."

"Tu sei il ragazzo più bello che abbia mai visto."

He grinned and leaned closer to her. "What does that mean?"

"What does it matter? You just said you wanted to hear me say something."

Their eyes met, and the tension between them heightened. On instinct, he leaned in and kissed her, lightly at first to see if she would respond. She moved to kiss him as eagerly as he did her and within minutes was on her back, her body enveloped by his. He kissed her more forcefully than previously, his hands roughly groping over every part of her body, maneuvering her thighs tighter around himself and pressing his waist so tightly against hers she could barely move her lower torso. Though his movements were aggressive, they neither repulsed nor scared her, instead sending an electrified quiver through the entire length of her body.

To Alex, the moment was an explosive relief of sexual tension and anxiety that had been building for weeks. He felt uninhibited and extremely potent, relieved to experience a full-fledged erection and intent on making the most of his recovery. Her skin was soft, and her hair smelled fresh and flowery. He pushed it to the side, letting his fingers sift through the silky strands momentarily before moving down to her shoulders and chest.

He kissed her neck, starting near her ear and moving down to her throat. As he kissed her, he unbuttoned her blouse and pushed up her camisole, exposing her stomach. She instinctively grabbed his wrist, her heart pounding and her mind waging a battle between desire and propriety.

"*Do you trust me?*" he whispered, his hand resting lightly on her breast.

Inhaling deeply, she froze for a moment, freezing time and action with her, hearing nothing but the soft rustle of fall leaves and the pounding of her own heart. Yet in that millisecond, she was able to analyze the question, the person and her own emotions and arrive at a decision to let go.

She sighed deeply, pulling his lips to hers in reply.

He pushed the camisole up further, and his lips moved from her stomach to her exposed chest. He caressed her breasts and back with one hand, the other wrapped around her waist. Consciously, she knew she was still clothed. Yet at some point, she became acutely aware of an odd sensation in her groin, unlike any she had ever experienced during her time with Tate. His pelvis was pressed so tightly against hers, that it almost hurt—feeling hard and sharp. But at the slightest movement on his part, the sharpness changed to more of a tingling sensation, which intensified as he thrust rhythmically against her. Her legs became weak, and she felt herself growing wetter, the sensation heightening to such an extent that she vaguely wondered if there really was anything between them—if she hadn't allowed herself to be taken by a person she hardly knew—

When she peaked, the jolt rippled through her entire lower body. She clutched his arm, pushing him away, gasping for breath, her head spinning as she tried to comprehend what had just happened.

He un-entwined himself from her, satisfied at her reaction and his ability to cause it. Her body felt tense, and he pulled her close to himself, gently kissing her lips and chin and stroking her cheek. "Are you okay?" he whispered.

She turned her head from him, suddenly embarrassed. "I don't know. . . I don't know what just happened . . ." she breathed, moving to adjust her shirt, ensuring she was still intact.

"Nothing happened," he said reassuringly, helping her. He then rolled over on his back, gazing up through the thinning trees, still resplendent with fall color. She nervously lay down next to him, and he pulled her against him, letting her head rest on his chest. "Did you like it?" he asked hesitantly.

She shrugged in response, though in her heart she knew she had enjoyed it. The enjoyment scared her.

"You've never done that before, have you?"

"No," she said quietly.

They lay quietly for a few minutes, she trying to calm a whirlwind of thought and emotion and he enjoying the view of the trees, while contemplating their next tryst. He had not climaxed yet and intended to get relief before the date's end.

"So . . . would now be the time to ask whether or not you want a relationship?" she asked jokingly.

He laughed. "If I didn't, I would have just gone all the way with you."

"Seriously?" she asked, raising her head up.

"Absolutely . . . Guys are dicks, Dan. I don't think we mean to be, we just are. Stupid and horny."

"Have you, you know . . . had a lot of girlfriends?" she asked.

He grinned at first, until a barrage images flashed through is mind, causing a sudden sense of panic and unease. "I don't know . . . I don't remember . . . Probably a few."

She mused a minute, absently pulling at one of the buttons on his blue plaid flannel shirt. "Have you ever wondered why we are more attracted to some people than others? I mean . . . just last night, you and I were completely disgusted at the prospect of doing this with other people . . . And they aren't unattractive people, either. Why do you think that is?"

His glance moved from the trees to her eyes. She had incredibly large, almond shaped eyes, dark brown with hints of green—and he noticed her right eye was larger than her left, a trait he had never noticed on anyone else. Her dark brown hair spilled onto his shoulders, and he touched it playfully.

"I have no idea," he said. "I know I don't like blonds. They scare me . . . It's probably because my sister's blond, and she's drives me nuts."

Danielle laughed. "But you're blond! It's a good thing I don't feel the same way you do . . . I like the haircut, by the way . . . your hair's curly. When it was long and matted, I really couldn't tell," she said, gently running her fingers through a strand on his forehead.

"I'm not entirely blond. My roots are brown. It just blonds out at the ends for some reason . . . So maybe you have a phobia of dark-haired guys."

She shrugged. "I just think I have a phobia of assholes, and I don't agree with you that *all* guys are dicks."

A large gust blew a shower of leaves down from the trees, and Danielle shivered, the heat of their moment having worn off and her jacket inadvertently left in the car. He sat up and grabbed the second blanket.

She took it hesitantly. "Do you think we should head back?"

He frowned, "Why? It can't be much past three."

"I don't know . . . I just think we should," she said, looking about them, sensing a presence.

"There's nobody here," he assured her. "There were only two other cars in the lot, and this is off the path, anyway . . ."

She nodded, but continued looking around, suspiciously.

Disconcerted but determined not to let the afternoon go to waste or ruin, he pulled her down next to him and rolled on top of her. "You just need me to warm you up again," he said, grinning.

She smiled, but before she could reply, his lips pressed against hers, and he pulled her body against his, caressing her hair, her neck, her breasts. She welcomed the envelopment, her hands pressed against his chest, which felt warm to the touch. This exchange was even more passionate and heated than the last, and at some point she sensed herself being undressed below, sensed him doing the same. He gently led her hand to his crotch, and she could feel something large and firm and wet through the thin cotton underwear. Her mind whirled, but she was in no position to protest.

Alex's sole intention was to come, as all the times he had done so or attempted to do so since his incident had been disastrous. The sexual tension was nearly unbearable, and if he didn't care for her, he could have and would have happily taken the full plunge. Instead, he helped her to participate in the next best and safest thing. He was getting very close to climax when his eyes caught something in one of the brief moments he actually had them open. Or maybe he just sensed a presence and felt the urge to look up. But by the time he realized what it was, it was too late.

At the moment of ejaculation came a horrible burst of pain, so intense he bit his lip stifling the scream. He had to stop himself from collapsing on top of her with his full weight.

She jerked up, sensing something had gone horribly wrong. Seeing the blood, she knew that something had, her shirt and camisole saturated with it.

"Alex . . . what happened . . ." she asked in a hoarse whisper, turning to him. He was lying on his side, clutching his stomach and writhing in agony. She put her arms around him protectively. "Alex—what's wrong? What can I do? Do I need to go get help . . ."

"No," he said gasping, "There's nothing you can do . . . just give me some time."

"Okay . . . Okay . . ." She tried to calm herself down and focus her thoughts on his well-being, still holding him tight, caressing his upper arm and chest. "I'm so sorry . . ."

"It's not you . . . you had nothing to do with it."

"I'm still so sorry . . . . I wish I could help you."

They lay there for what seemed a very long time to Danielle and an even longer time to Alex, who was experiencing his worst bout yet, the prior attacks mere tremors to this earthquake. When he began shaking, it was Danielle covering him with a blanket, but he was too ill to be mortified. He just wanted it to stop. She held him close to herself until it finally did.

"We need to go," he whispered finally.

"When you're ready . . . there's no rush."

He struggled to sit up. "Do we still have that water?"

It was just out of reach, and she scrambled quickly to get it, but as she held it out to him, his eyes grew wide and he began to shake again.

It was the blood, which had caked and dried on her hands and covered her entire stomach. He looked down and saw his hands, too, were stained, though his clothes were not as coated as hers. "Jesus Christ," he burst. "Fucking hell . . . what the fuck? Fucking Christ . . ."

She could see he was about to spiral and tried to calm him down. "Alex—it's okay. Calm down, please . . . Here." Her hand shook as she held the water out to him.

But he shook his head and sat back in horror. "Why is this happening to me? Why the fuck? What did I do . . . What have I done? I don't remember . . . But it won't stop."

She set the water down and moved towards him. But as she got closer, he inched away. She then closed her eyes, trying to bring back the peace she had received from that mysterious priest. Saying a silent prayer to him help in this moment. Imploring him to tell her, again, how to rewrite a scene in a dream that had just turned nightmarish.

"I'm sorry," he said finally, staring blankly ahead. "I just don't know what to do."

"Does this happen often?"

He shrugged. "Only when . . ."

"Is this what really happened last night?" she asked gingerly.

His silence affirmed her sudden insight.

"What happened to you, Alex? Something horrible's haunting you."

He nodded, but continued to stare off at nothing.

"You still don't remember anything?"

He shook his head. "I—I was shot three times . . . that's all I remember," he offered, trying to blink away the fresh barrage of mental flashbacks.

"Was it—was it a robbery? Were you just—just caught in the crossfire?"

He shook his head, shrugging. "I don't know—I just want to live a normal life . . . I just want to move on, but . . . but I can't, because I don't even know what I'm moving on from. This is just unreal . . ."

"Yeah . . . Maybe we're just dreaming all this. Maybe it *isn't* real."

He looked at her with sad fatigue.

"Do you really believe that?" he asked.

She smiled sadly, her eyes tearing. "Yes. It can't be real. How sad if it's real. All the death and pain and suffering."

"But then all the good things wouldn't be real, either. The things and people we love wouldn't be real."

She turned away, thoughtful.

"We should go," he said, standing up and moving to gather their things. She helped him, and they headed back to the car, walking in single-filed silence. Once inside the car, he put his head on the steering wheel, utterly spent and depressed.

She put a hand on his shoulder. "Please don't shut me out, Alex . . . Please."

He sat up and looked at her incredulously, "Why would you want in? What do I possibly have to give you?"

"Your . . . your friendship. Your, your companionship. You don't have to give me anything—I just want to be with you."

"Why? I'm a complete fuck-up . . . You don't even know me. We've known each other for, what—a week?"

"I feel I've known you longer . . . I don't know why, but—I just want to be with you. Does it matter why? I just do. I like you . . . I don't know why I like you, I just do."

He stared out the windshield. "You're just high," he said bitterly. "Tomorrow, it's gonna have worn off, and you're going to freak."

"Do you not want to see me again?" she asked quietly, trying not to let her voice break.

The question hung there like a prison door in an ancient dungeon, its spikes and springs poised to slam downwards, keeping him locked away with his ghosts and torturers.

"I do . . . I do want to see you again . . ." he said hoarsely.

"Okay . . . So we'll be friends first, alright? We'll be friends first and lovers second, okay? For now, at least."

"Yeah . . . okay. Friends first."

She took his hand and squeezed it tightly.

They found a nearby fast food establishment and used the bathrooms to wash up. Danielle threw her shirt and camisole away, covering herself up with the jacket. As they drove home, they talked about lighter subjects. Alex suggested they jam together sometime soon, classical guitar and violin being a fun combo, and he wanted to hear her play.

They had pulled into her driveway and she started to exit, when he stopped her.

"Tell me again everything will be okay," he whispered.

"Of course it will."

"What . . . What's going to happen when I finally open that door to my past?"

"I don't know . . . We'll find out together," she said, smiling sadly.

CHAPTER SEVEN

Alex got home just in time for a rare family dinner, but he hardly felt hungry and begged to retreat to his bedroom. His parents would hear nothing of it and pumped him for information for the next ten minutes.

"For god's sake, Alex, you were out nearly all night and practically all day, and you're behaving as if somebody died," his mother burst in response to his lethargy.

"He's probably hung over," his sister said under her breath.

He glared at her.

"Why don't you ask Trisha about her evening," he suggested.

"We already heard all about Trisha's evening. Yours is the big mystery."

"Are you hung over, Alex?" his dad asked, looking at him curiously.

"No . . . I'm just tired. I barely got any sleep last night."

"Well, whose fault is that?" his mother snapped. "Here I make a nice dinner and we're together as a family for the first time in weeks, and you're behaving miserably . . ."

She nagged him a bit more before his father changed the conversation, thankfully, sharing stories about his patients. Alex just moved the food around on his plate, unable to eat anything. He then stared around the table at his family, comparing them to the Sumners. His mother was decent looking but looked like a mom, with her short, frosted hair and matronly clothes. She usually wore pants and some type of long-sleeve patterned blouse or decorative sweater. His father looked more haggard than usual, his blond hair graying and receding, his jowl lines becoming more pronounced. And his sister . . . He failed to see any resemblance between himself and his sister. In fact, she didn't even look like she belonged to their family. Maybe she was adopted, he secretly hoped, repulsed by her heavy use of make-up and self-righteous attitude.

His thoughts then turned to Danielle's mother and wavered between Danielle and her mother. He wondered what the mother was like, if she made chicken dinners. Remembering that Danielle had said they had a cook, he doubted she had anything to do with the kitchen, or house cleaning, or carpooling. She didn't even look like a mom. She looked like she could be Danielle's twin sister.

He thought about Danielle and felt nauseous. His parents finally excused him when he said he had a lot of homework, which he did but blew off, instead retreating to bed, anxious to fall asleep but tossing and turning, his mind still obsessed with the Sumners family photos. His body still tense with sexual frustration, craving Danielle's touch, while his logic told him she would probably have nothing to do with him again. More than an hour passed before he finally fell into a restless sleep.

He dreamed of the Sumners, the parents seated on two huge armchairs in front of a marble fireplace, regal, as if on thrones. Danielle was introducing him, but he barely noticed her, captured by her mother's penetrating stare, a look so full of lust that it gave him an erection. She wore a baby blue camisole dress that hugged her waist and breasts before flowing to her knees in chiffon waves . . .

So, Alex, I understand you're not from around here. Mr. Sumners spoke.

The voice thundered through his thoughts jerking him from his reverie with the mother, and he turned to the man, a sudden shudder bolting through him. He was well-groomed, his hair meticulously combed in place, no wrinkles in his pants or shirt, which were obviously of the most expensive quality. Their stares locked momentarily, and Alex noticed he had deep-set, narrow eyes.

Alex is from Montana. He moved here over the summer. Danielle spoke.

So—what brought you and your family to Kansas City? That's quite a move. Though Danielle's mother spoke in Italian, he understood every word.

"I—I don't know. I don't remember . . ."

She stood up and walked slowly towards him, suggestively pointing her finger at him. *"You've been a very naughty boy, Alex."*

As the words slipped from her tongue, he felt dizzy, a loud rushing sound pounding in his ears and images bombarding his mind. Leaves, trees. He felt breathless and panicked, as if he were running from something. The landscape changed, living room melting into forest, the fireplace a clearing in the forest. He heard nervous laughter, steps trailing behind his, a hand grabbing his sleeve. Then a thunderous crack that peeled through the twilight.

I'm gonna kill you, boy. I get my hands on you, I'm gonna kill you both.

Shit. . . Come on—let's get off the trail.

But there's poison oak in there—I'm allergic to it.

I don't give a shit—let's go, he whispered loudly, grabbing her arm and pulling her into the woods.

He's drunk off his ass—he couldn't see us if we were standing in front of him.

He has a loaded gun.

And he has poor aim when he's drunk.

I don't care . . .

They retreated deeper into the woods, treading as lightly as possible on the needle and twig strewn forest floor, eventually taking refuge behind a group of large pines.

Jennifer—you goddamn wench—

He heard the click of the trigger before another thunderous clap resonated through the trees.

He awoke to the sound of thunder. It was just after midnight, and with the violent storm, it would be another few hours before he could fall sleep again.

School was unbearable. His friends buzzed with Homecoming stories, but Homecoming felt like ancient history, as if he had lived and died two lifetimes since the dance. He looked forward to football practice, which he usually found boring. Though initially second string quarterback, he had made a name for himself when the first string got injured early in the season, and he led the team to three consecutive victories. They now had a better record than the varsity team.

Practice took his mind off his problems, and the exercise invigorated him. When he got home, he was determined to get his life back together, even if it meant avoiding women for awhile. Even if it meant avoiding Danielle.

He had just settled down at the kitchen table to catch up on his home-work when the phone rang.

He let it ring, ignoring his sister's screams for him to pick it up. It might be her new boyfriend.

She bounded into the room, calling him a jerk and grabbing it on the last ring.

"Hello," she said with breathless anticipation, her smile quickly fading into an annoyed frown. "Yeah, he's here . . ." She handed him the phone. "I'm waiting for a call, so I'd appreciate your not being on it all night," she snapped.

Bracing himself, he spoke into the receiver, "Hello?"

"Alex . . ."

He winced. Though he recognized her voice, he said nothing.

"It's Dan."

He remained icily silent.

"How are you feeling?"

"Uh . . . fine. I'm okay. And you?"

"I'm alright . . . I thought maybe we could get together and jam this week, you know. Like you said . . . jam to some classical music."

"Oh, yeah . . ." he mumbled before falling silent again for an uncom-fortable minute. "Um, I don't know. I'm, I'm kind of busy," he said hoarsely, overcome with a sudden nervousness.

"Oh, I see . . . Okay. . . . Well, I guess that's it, then?" she asked quietly.

Though he couldn't physically see her, he could feel her emotions, see her expression in his mind's eye. Saying yes would be like slamming a door in her face, an act of selfishness and cruelty he had not thought himself capable of until this moment. But now she was forever entangled in the morass that was his past, and whatever pristine connection they shared had been contaminated by his sins, lustful thoughts and degenerate nightmares. He had to walk away from all of it.

"Yes . . ." he whispered.

Though he couldn't hear it, he felt her gasp in pain.

"Okay . . . I understand. Well, take care of yourself. Good-bye."

He could tell she struggled to keep her voice steady, and before he could respond with a farewell, he heard the phone click.

He sat for a few minutes, shaking, still holding the receiver, ignoring its protestant tones at being left off the hook and relieved at the eventual silence. What had he just done? Why had he just done that? Part of him wasn't sure and certainly did not agree with the part that just completely dismissed a girl who had been through hell with him.

Exhaustion overcame him, and he rushed through the rest of his homework, anxious to sleep things off, hoping to feel more clear-headed about things in the morning.

As he brushed his teeth, he wondered if the damage was irreparable, fearing if he changed his mind, it would be too late. He had not only lost a girlfriend but the one friend he had in this city willing to help him.

Looking up into the mirror, he nearly choked. A figure stood directly behind him, leaning against the wall, arms crossed, looking smug.

He spun around, but the apparition vanished.

Shaking it off as frayed nerves, he turned back to the sink to rinse. As he toweled off his face, he looked up. This time the figure leaned over his shoulder, looking directly into the mirror with him. He wore a pressed, pink oxford and belted khaki pants.

The resemblance is amazing, isn't it?

It spoke, placing an arm on his shoulder. Alex jerked away from the touch.

We could be twins. Look at us.

Alex forced himself to look into the mirror again, but he already knew what the figure said was true. Meeting Tate at the party was like looking at a mirror image of himself, only with darker hair and a tan.

But she chose you over me. Why?

"Because I'm nothing like you—"

Really? Oh, I think we're a lot more alike than you're willing to admit.

Bristling, Alex spun around to deck the guy and nearly hit the wall with his fist.

By the time his head hit the pillow, he had made up his mind to call her tomorrow and apologize for his complete idiocy. To undo whatever chaos he had just unleashed in the universe.

His dreams took him back to the brick terrace, its floor scattered with dead leaves, leaves blowing in the wind and raining in a steady stream onto the ground. Seated on a low stone wall, he looked about him, the white Romanesque statues making him uneasy. He looked up at the sky but saw nothing but gray haze, no clouds or sun.

A girl in a white camisole dress of thin, flowing material lay in the center of the enclosed terrace. He could not tell if she was asleep or dead, nor could he tell who she was, her face turned away from him and partially hidden by her long, dark hair.

Ever fuck a virgin, Alex?

The voice appeared out of nowhere, and he turned, startled, coming face to face with a young man of his height, build and general appearance. Except for the clothing, hair and skin tone, he could have been looking in the mirror.

I'll toss you for her. Heads or tails?

Alex looked down at the guy's extended palm, in the center of which glistened a large, gold coin. His gaze slowly moved from the coin to the girl, who lay lifeless in the center of the terrace.

She's not dead. Only sleeping.

He backed away from him, shaking his head.

Oh, that's right. You want yours awake. Otherwise, it's like fucking a doll—or a pillow.

The young man snapped his fingers, and the girl stirred. But even before she sat up, Alex knew who she was and was overcome with dread. He immediately moved to jump from the wall but was held back, by what he could not tell, only that he couldn't move.

Heads or tails?

Heads, he breathed. Or maybe just thought it.

The young man winced, holding out his palm. Tails.

Tough luck, this time. But you can have her when I'm done.

Alex's stomach dropped but his anger heightened, and he moved to jump the guy. Something pinned his arms. *Tate, You son of a bitch . . .* he screamed. And he tried to tell Danielle to run, tried to scream some kind of warning. Or maybe just thought it, as his screams seemed to dissipate before leaving his mouth.

Frantic, he struggled to see what was pinning him down. It was the female statues.

One of them leaned down and whispered in his ear.

Watch.

He shook his head. No—he couldn't watch. He wouldn't watch. He could hear her screaming his name, begging him to make it stop.

It physically turned his head.

He kept his eyes shut, refusing to look until all fell silent, until he was sure it was over.

Silence.

Slowly, he opened his eyes.

She lay, her eyes closed, seemingly unconscious. Blood covered her stomach. But the figure on top of her wasn't Tate. It was himself.

He woke up in a cold sweat, sobbing.

The dream had challenged his perception of himself, and he arose the next morning with a fierce determination to remember his sexual past. Instinctively, he knew he had been with more than one girl, but he couldn't remember his first time. Other than grade school crushes, he had been unable to remember any of his girlfriends since middle school.

But he was nothing like Tate, he told himself. He never used girls for sex. He had had a relationship with Jennifer, one that ended in tragedy, but the tragedy was not his doing. At heart, he was a gentleman. Cool and caring. Unselfish . . .

The mental movie that was his sexual past began rolling during first period, Algebra II, when the room darkened and the school walls melted away, replaced by wood paneling covered with old license plates and other antique oddities. When the teacher sat on a stool and started smoking her chalk, eyeing him periodically. When the room broke into a sudden cacophony as the students chanted.

Alex. . .Alex. . .Alex

Hey, Alex—it looks like you've caught the attention of Wild Wanda. You know what that means.

A buddy's arm around his shoulder. Another mug of beer shoved in his hand. The teacher gets off her stool and saunters toward him, skin tight, electric blue leather pants. Fringed, white leather Western jacket, speckled with silver and gold appliqué. Blond hair teased high on her head. Eye shadow as electric as the pants.

The next beer's on me, boys.

More beer. Country music on the jukebox. He feels a buzz. His buddy and others are dancing with various local women. Wanda is making the moves on him. Pulling him next to her by his belt loops, pressing her electric blue pelvis against him.

Let's go upstairs.

Head spinning. Bony hands briskly moving to unbutton his shirt, the long red nails occasionally scratching his skin, stinging. This close, he could smell her breath, a mixture of smoke and beer. He could see the yellowed stains on her teeth. Could see the white streaks beneath the blond dye. The wrinkles beneath the heavy black liner. The veins on the back of her bony hands that were groping his body.

He stood frozen, part in shock, unable to move, his one hand still holding the mug of beer, two-thirds gone. His face and neck burning over his growing erection. Afraid of her seeing it. Afraid of seeing it in front of her. Wanting to push her away, but remaining frozen as his pants are unzipped and pulled down around him.

At that point he must have closed his eyes because the next sight was her bouncing on top of him, moaning gratingly, cackling like a witch, continuing to thrust herself on him well past ejaculation, his semen spreading across his stomach. His stomach turning over and again with each bounce. The beer, the smell, the rhythmic pounding, the sight making the contents of his stomach hurl back through his system—

He raised his hand, begging to be excused and barely made it to the bathroom before throwing up the contents of his breakfast.

His first encounter had been with a hooker when he had just turned fifteen.

As disgusted as he was with the memory, he had not been an innocent boy when the incident happened. At the time, he had been a heavy drinker and marijuana user, hanging out with an older high school crowd to get more kicks. Still, he felt victimized.

He was still recovering by the time he saw Dennis in biology and dreaded a potentially unpleasant exchange. But Dennis acted as if nothing had happened, and Alex realized his fears had been completely unwarranted. Of course Danielle wouldn't drag her brother into her personal affairs. At least not yet . . .

His next memory didn't hit until lunch, when the cafeteria table turned into a picnic table, and trees burst through the lunch room windows, grass through the dirty tile floors and daylight turned into dusk. She had long, curly blond hair and yelped with each thrust, at times squealing his name. She wore a red flowered blouse, completely unbuttoned, and no bra, her small, white breasts nearly glowing in the twilight. It was summer, and her shorts had been pulled down to her ankles. Alex fucked her furiously, almost angrily. Remembering it gave him an erection, and it wasn't until Carl hit him on the side of the head that he snapped out of his absorption with the past.

"Dude, are you even listening? Are you even here?"

Alex turned bright red.

"What the fuck?" Carl burst, then followed his gaze across the room and concluded he was staring at a girl. He made a dirty joke about it, causing the table to break out in raucous laughter. Once everyone had calmed down, Carl repeated his exciting news. He had booked their basement band for a New Year's Eve party at some girl's house and was insisting they start regular band practice.

As annoying as the prospect of playing with a bad band was, Alex welcomed the reprieve from his mental fuck show.

In art class, his next tryst paraded through his mind, this one not as violent. They were studying the Impressionist period, a metaphor for that phase of his sex life. This girl was a dirty blond and wore her hair shoulder-length straight, decorated with flowered head bands. She dressed in long, colorful skirts and low cut T-shirts. She was a college student willing to teach Alex the moves, among other things. She had felt safe with Alex, he remembered her saying, and he smiled smugly at the memory.

Their sessions were soft and dreamy, often to rock music, and always topped off with a bong. She had also been into fine arts, culture, poetry. She forced him to start looking beyond Polson, showed him that there was more to life than Polson pizza, Polson beer, Polson women. When she left for Italy six months later, he was heartbroken. He never heard from her again.

Fingers snapped in front of his eyes.

He blinked, and once his vision focused, found himself face to face with a grinning Dennis.

"Dude, the bell rang, like five minutes ago."

"Really?"

Dennis smirked, nodding.

"So, why didn't you tell me?"

"I'm telling you now."

"Yeah, but why didn't you tell me sooner?"

"I wanted to see how long it would take you to figure it out. Must be some daydream you got going on there," he said, shaking his head as if he knew.

With a rival game this Friday, football practice was grueling. That, coupled with his lack of a good night's sleep, left him exhausted by the time he got home at six. Unable to wait another minute, he picked up the phone and dialed her number, his hands shaking.

Voicemail.

He tried an hour later.

Voicemail.

By eight, he was too exhausted to stay awake. After the sound of the beep, he took a deep breath and spoke into the receiver.

"Dan—it's, it's Alex. I—I don't know how to say this, and—and I hate saying this on a machine, but—I made a terrible mistake yesterday. I—I didn't mean what I said. I'm—I'm sorry. I'm really sorry. I hope you . . . I hope you

. . . I hope we can see each other again. This weekend, maybe. okay? I'm sorry. You don't have to call me back, but . . . I would like it if you did. Okay?"

His mind raced to put his thoughts into words, but he stumbled on until he ran out of time and then realized he hadn't even said good-bye. The machine had cut him off.

But he went to bed feeling he had done the right thing and had a much needed dreamless night of sleep.

Dennis was not at school the next day. While this did not concern him, his absence oddly made Alex even more anxious to get home to see if Danielle had returned his call. The day seemed to stretch into an eternity, and he burst through the front door of his house, up the stairs and into his sister's room, breathlessly asking her if she had taken any messages for him.

Trisha rolled her eyes and shook her head. "Nope."

Though exhausted from another tiring practice, he stayed up until ten, jumping any time the phone rang. But Danielle had not called by the time he finally turned in for the night.

When Dennis did not show up for school the following day, his nervous anxiety turned into genuine concern. His mother picked him up from football practice around six o'clock, as usual. On the way home, he asked if they could stop by Dennis' house for a moment, expressing concern for his friend.

She protested at first, saying he probably had the flu and suggesting Alex call him, but finally acquiesced upon learning the house was less than ten minutes from their own. When she pulled into the driveway, she was nearly speechless. Before she could say anything, he got out of the car and trotted up to the front door. He rang the bell and could hear the deep chimes sound within.

In less than a minute, it was answered by an older, foreign-looking woman.

"Hi . . . Is Dennis home?"

"No speak English."

He sighed, fearing she was Italian but thinking he remembered something about the help being Spanish. "Dónde está Señor Dennis?" he asked, wincing at his horrible pronunciation and complete lack of accent.

The woman shook her head, then motioned for him to wait. It was at least two minutes before she returned holding a small slip of paper in her hand, which she handed to Alex. On it was scrawled a phone number in painstaking penmanship, so shaky he could barely make out the characters.

"Gracias," he breathed before heading back to the car.

As he slid into the front seat, his mother burst into a torrent of questions regarding the *young man* who lived at the *residence*. How did Alex know him? What did his father do for a living? How good of friends were he and Alex? Was he on the football team? Was that a maid at the door? His mother's tone held a mixture of curiosity and underlying resentment at such an obvious display of wealth. The onslaught continued until they pulled into their own driveway.

He quickly retreated upstairs to use the hall phone.

A girl's voice answered, and he asked for Dennis. To his relief, he was told to wait a minute.

"Hello?"

"Dennis?" Alex asked, confirming.

"Yeah—who's this?" Dennis responded gruffly.

"Alex."

"Alex—" Dennis exclaimed incredulously. "What are you—how did you know—where did you get this number?"

"I stopped by your house, and your maid gave it to me."

"You what? Why?"

"I don't know . . . You haven't been in school, and I . . . I don't know, I just figured I would stop by after football practice to make sure you're okay."

"That's so weird."

"Sorry . . ." Alex mumbled, his face reddening.

"No, man . . . it's cool. It's just . . . I'm, I'm not okay, actually."

Alex heard a slight crack in his friend's voice and frowned. "What's wrong?"

"I can't . . . I can't talk about it on the phone, man. Look—just, thanks for calling. I'm fine. I'll be fine."

"Dennis, do you need anything? Do you want me to, I don't know—stop by? Where are you?"

"I'm at Brooke's."

"*Brooke's*? Is Danielle with you?"

Silence.

"Dennis, what's going on?"

Silence.

"I'll be at school on Monday," Dennis said finally.

"Okay . . . Are you sick? Is somebody sick?"

"No."

Alex was speechless for a minute, wanting to press his friend but fearing he had already hit the dead end. "Okay . . . well, if Danielle's there, can I talk to her?"

"I don't . . . I don't think that's a good idea."

Alex felt his face flush as his mind raced. Dear god, she had told her brother . . . "Why?"

"Because . . . look, we've had a rough week, Alex. I can't . . . I can't talk about it over the phone."

"Well, can you talk about it in person?"

Silence.

"Okay—how about over alcohol and a bowl of weed?" Alex offered, jokingly.

Dennis let out a nervous laugh. "Yeah . . . that sounds really good right now."

"Well, I don't have any weed, but I could probably lift some JD from my dad's stash."

"Are you serious?"

"Yeah."

"You would seriously bring me liquor?"

"Yeah—whatever you need, I mean—within reason. I wish I knew why you needed it, but . . . Whatever."

"That's really cool of you, man . . . But I really just need a smoke. And to let off some steam. Pick me up?"

Alex agreed and got the address from Dennis. He then had to convince his mother to allow him to borrow the car, only after shoveling down some dinner, promising he would be home at a decent time and ensuring her he had very little homework. On the way, he stopped at a 7-11 to purchase two packs of Marlboro Reds and a lighter.

Oddly, the home was on the same street as Danielle's, just down the way. It was equally as large, an enormous brick Tudor-style complete with a turret and set back on a stately front yard. Dennis was waiting for him as he pulled up next to the front door. He climbed into the car and, after slamming the door shut, leaned back into the seat, closing his eyes and sighing as if in huge relief.

Alex threw him the pack of smokes.

"Thanks . . . ." he murmured, but did not yet move to open it.

"Where to?"

Dennis shook his head absently. "I don't care . . . A park. A parking lot . . . I don't care."

Alex decided to head to the park with the large blue water tower. Nearing seven, it was already dark, and he doubted they would have too much company. Dennis was silent the entire ride, and Alex turned up the radio.

Dennis's silence continued even after they had pulled into the park and turned off the car. Alex decided to have a smoke, himself, and opened one of the packs. Upon Alex lighting his, Dennis motioned that he wanted one, too. Alex handed him the pack and the lighter but noticed his friend's hands shaking as he tapped the cigarette out of the pack and tried to light it. As nonchalantly as possible, he took the lighter from his friend and lit the cigarette for him.

Alex turned the ignition enough to roll down the windows, and they smoked for awhile in silence.

"My mother left us," Dennis said finally.

Alex turned to him questioningly.

"Yeah . . . We found out Tuesday afternoon when we came home from school . . . Took half the money in the bank and fled the country for Italy."

Immediately, the seductive woman in the portrait popped into Alex's mind.

"Jesus, Dennis . . ."

"Yeah . . . and that's not the half of it. My father . . ." He swallowed hard before continuing. "My father didn't take it too well, obviously . . . He got drunk that evening, and . . . Well, my sister . . . My sister looks like mom, and . . ."

He stopped, shaking his head, unable to continue.

"And what?" Alex asked hoarsely.

"It's too fucked up, man . . . It's way too fucked up." He took a long drag and turned away from Alex, staring out the window.

"What happened to your sister?"

Dennis shook his head. "He . . . he tried to kill her. That's why we left, man . . . He tried to . . ."

Alex's heart raced, his mind barely able to keep up with the sudden surge of emotions, from outrage to nauseating fear. "Is she alright?"

Dennis nodded. "She's a little . . ." He made a motion with his hand towards his face. "You know . . . a little . . ."

"What?"

"Banged up . . . She's a little banged up but fine. We're both fine, we just . . . We don't know what to do, man."

"Don't—don't you have family? You know—other family?"

Dennis shrugged. "My dad's family is in New York. But, like we'd call them. . . . My mom has family here, but," he shook his head vehemently. "I want nothing to do with them. And the rest are in Italy."

"What's wrong with the family here?"

"You know . . . they're in Little Italy."

"So?"

"Well, I'm not goin' there, okay—neither of us are, okay?" Dennis said, giving him a look as if he should be able to read between the lines. But Alex had no idea what he was talking about.

"Anyway," Dennis continued, "we fled that night and haven't been back since . . . You say you stopped by my house today?"

Alex nodded, trying to calm his racing mind and sudden nausea.

"Was the house okay? Did . . . did you notice anything?"

He shook his head. "No . . . Nothing."

"No broken windows or anything?"

Alex sighed, trying to mentally travel back in time and remember what he saw. The large front door and the maid. Nothing out of the ordinary.

"Was my dad home?"

Alex shrugged. There were no other cars in the driveway that he remembered.

"Do you . . . do you think we could stop by? I—we need our stuff. We need to get some stuff, but I ain't goin' back alone."

"Have you thought about calling the police?" Alex offered, bristling at the idea of a possible run-in with Mr. Sumners.

"Fuck no," Dennis burst angrily. "Would you? If it were your dad, would you call the fucking police?"

Alex's mind whirled as he contemplated the idea.

"Look—you don't have to go in with me. Just—can we just drive by and, and if he's not there, can you just keep watch?"

Alex agreed, and they were soon on their way to the Sumners' house, Dennis offering more bits and pieces of the ordeal on the way, with Alex trying to listen calmly. When they pulled into the Sumners' drive, he could sense his friend's fear.

"Let's not park here," Dennis said flatly. "Let's park on the street—down a ways . . . We can use the back door . . ."

After finally turning off the car, Alex moved to get out. Dennis stopped him.

"What are you doing? You can stay here—"

"No way," Alex insisted, climbing out of the car. "You're not doing this alone . . . Besides, I've had somebody try to kill me before, so I can relate." He then shared with Dennis the one minute summary of his ordeal, which was all he could remember about it, anyway.

With the exception of the drive and porch lights, the entire house was completely dark. They walked around the back, and after fumbling with the key a moment, Dennis opened the door and switched on the kitchen light. Alex gasped.

Though the glass had been swept into piles, the kitchen looked like a bomb had gone off in it—pieces of ceiling hanging, glass blown out of every cabinet, glass blown out of the two windows, the large iron hanger full of brass pots and pans somehow pulled from the ceiling and lying on the counter.

"Fuck . . ." Dennis breathed, treading lightly across the floor.

Alex followed. As they made their way through the house and upstairs to the bedrooms, he noticed some rooms were completely untouched and others demolished. Dennis's room was unscathed, but Danielle's . . . .

Alex felt chilled as they scanned what was left of it, everything glass having been shattered, everything material having been violently ripped, anything hanging on the walls torn down and anything on a shelf lying in pieces and strewn across the floor.

"I guess Rosalie didn't make her way up here, yet . . ." Dennis murmured.

"Has Danielle—"

"No."

Suddenly, Dennis began to shake, his eyes reddening, welling with moisture. Alex put a hand on his shoulder, trying to lead him out of the room. "Come on—"

"She needs her stuff—"

"I'll get her stuff. You . . . you just pack your stuff. And, and—maybe find us something to carry it in. You know—get some suitcases or boxes or something, okay?" He gently pushed him back into the hallway.

But as he re-entered Danielle's room, he began to shake, himself, and wished he had brought the cigarettes inside. The violence was overwhelming, and he tried to comprehend its origin—its trigger—what could possibly drive someone to hate his own daughter. Picking through the debris, disturbing images rapidly flashed through his mind, and he couldn't tell if they were a response to the present chaos or a horrific memory.

There were two doors, one leading to a bathroom and one to a clothes closet. To his relief, both rooms were unharmed, and he began in the bathroom, absently looking for toiletries, trying to think of what he would pack for a trip and trying hard to block out momentarily for whom he was packing and why. Toothbrush, shampoo, deodorant . . . .

Dennis joined him in the bathroom, a suitcase and backpack in hand.

"Here . . . I just talked to her. She needs her uniform, some jeans and some sweats. But she's most concerned she get her uniform and school books. Oh, and her violin."

Alex nodded absently, starting to dump the objects he had collected into the back-pack. The bathroom was impeccably organized, and he was able to clean out the sink and vanity drawers and still have room in the back-pack. The clothing was harder for him, and after a few minutes, he grew too upset to continue and asked for Dennis to help, offering instead to look for the books and violin. But after ten minutes of searching, he came up with neither.

Dennis guessed she left both where she practiced. He and Alex decided to pack the car with what they had and come back to find the rest. To Alex's surprise, Danielle's practice room was the portrait hall where he had spent so much time with Brooke just a few days prior, mesmerized by a family that was only growing increasingly mysterious and sinister. To his equal dismay, all the framed photos had been smashed and laid in broken pieces on the floor, both portraits ripped and the word *whore* handwritten across the mother's breast in a dark substance that Alex later deduced was blood. Their maid had obviously avoided this area, as well, as tiny shards of glass crackled under their feet.

Utterly dumbfounded, Dennis stood in front of his mother's picture, and Alex sensed what little composure he had managed to gather quickly dissipating, his bones sagging under an invisible burden.

"That's my mother," he breathed. "She's my mother."

Alex remained respectfully silent.

"She doesn't deserve this . . . It doesn't matter what she did, she doesn't . . ." he stepped back and seemed to totter a moment before quickly turning his back and collapsing in one of the arm chairs facing the unlit fireplace.

Alex could hear the quiet sobs and remained frozen in silence for what seemed an eternity. At this point, there was nothing he could do, no comfort to provide, no words that would do any justice to the situation, which invited only the reverent silence of a funeral. After collecting his own wits, he began to scan the room for the necessary objects, hoping their discovery would lead to a quick departure. To his relief, he spotted the book bag on the floor, under the second arm chair. He also spotted an overturned music stand and assumed the papers scattered around the ornately patterned rug were sheet music.

The violin nowhere in sight, he slowly and quietly turned his position so he could study the other half of the room, which was shaped far more like a grand hall than a living room, complete with two huge chandeliers, one which hung precariously close to where he was standing and directly over Dennis' head and one that hung in the second half of the room. It could have just as easily been made into a dining room but instead was turned into a library-conservatory, the second half of the room housing a baby grand piano and wall-to-ceiling bookcases stocked with beautifully bound books and antiques.

The room was divided by a sofa that faced the piano and French doors but also partially blocked his view of the other side. After maneuvering around the sofa, he found what he was seeking. The violin case lay open on the floor by the French doors, as if it had been thrown there, and the violin lay cracked in half under the piano. Picking it up, he cradled the fragile instrument in his hands like a swaddled baby, knowing the damage was beyond repair but still carrying it to the case and packing it carefully. He had not seen the bow nor even thought to look for it.

After setting the case next to the book bag, he began picking up the scattered pages of music.

"Is that everything?" Dennis asked.

"Yeah, I think so . . . Does she have more sheet music stored somewhere?"

Dennis shrugged, and Alex continued to work in silence.

"I just don't get it," Dennis burst. "I mean—people get divorced all the time. Jesus—most of my friend's parents are divorced, but they didn't . . . Why the drama? Why did mine have to turn it into some—some stage production. Some—*King Lear* or *Macbeth* of divorces? Look at this . . . It's so pointless."

Alex shoved the gathered sheet music into the book bag.

"Why even bother . . . with relationships. I mean—is this it? Is this our future? What's the point? What's the point of even having a relationship or getting married at all, if this is where it all ends—in, in hate and destruction. Why even have a family . . ."

Alex shrugged picking up the case and the book bag. "My folks are still together . . . I can't tell if they love each other, but . . . They seem to get along okay."

Dennis just shook his head despondently. "She can't come back here . . . It's not safe for her. I can, but she can't."

"Why is it safe for you?"

"Because I don't look like my mother . . . Danielle looks just like her. It's almost eerie. People say they look like twin sisters . . . it's unnatural, I think."

Alex gazed in the direction of the ripped portrait and, as if drawn by some invisible magnetic force, slowly began walking towards it, oblivious to the glass pulverizing under foot. He stared at the woman, stirred by her presence, haunted by her gaze which became more complex as he studied it, a mixture of seduction, sadness or bitter rage depending upon the perceiver.

"What's her name? Your mother."

"Gabrielle."

"Gabrielle . . ." he echoed, reaching out to touch the woman's face. "I don't see it," he said finally.

"Don't see what?"

"How they can be twins. She's not Danielle."

"Well, you've never met her in person, and you've only just met my sister. They look identical, trust me," he said, finally getting up from the chair. "Do you have everything?" he asked, stretching.

Alex nodded, but stayed glued to the spot, unable to turn away.

"Well, we probably should go . . . I really don't want to be here when my dad gets home. Not that he'll come home . . . He has some apartment on the side for him and his, whatever . . . so I've been told."

Alex's gaze fell to the shattered mess surrounding him, broken glass and cracked wooden frames, photos strewn about, some face up. He knelt on one knee and began delicately picking through the shards.

"What are you doing?" Dennis asked.

Alex ignored him, carefully turning over the photos until he found the two for which he was searching.

"Come on, Fahlstrom—let's go."

He ignored the obvious irritation in his friend's voice and began the process of extracting two photos from their broken frames, pricking his fingers more than once and having to lick away the tiny specks of blood to keep it from smudging the photos.

"Alex—you're gonna get cut messing with that. Just leave it for Rosalie—"

But Alex ignored him until he had succeeded in salvaging the two pictures, one of Dennis's parents, still seemingly in love and taken in front of the Montana mountain range, and one of him and his sister sitting in the semi-circle. As he studied the one of Dennis and Danielle, he noticed they were making silly faces, Danielle sticking out her tongue and Dennis trying to make eye glasses with his fingers.

"Here," he said, holding them out to Dennis.

Reluctantly, Dennis took them but refused to look at them.

"They were happier times. You should hold onto them," Alex said simply.

Dennis nodded, then insisted he needed another smoke. By the time they made it back to Brooke's, it was past nine. He and Dennis were greeted by Brooke, and the three of them carried the clothing and various articles into the house, which was as grand as the Sumners' but different in décor, the dark wooden floors and paneling, rich tapestries, ornate rugs and low lighting making Alex feel as if he had stepped through time and into an old British manor house.

When they were finished, he pulled Brooke aside. "Is Danielle here?"

She nodded.

"Can I see her?"

She crossed her arms, sighing loudly, her brow furrowed. "I don't know . . . I don't know if that's a good idea. She's…she's really not doing very well right now. I think she might need more time, you know?"

"Can I try?" he pushed, not wanting to leave without seeing her, growing increasingly tormented at the idea that his little act of undeserved cruelty the other night was merely an overture to a personal tragedy that made his pale in comparison.

Brooke nodded absently and led him up a large staircase and down a hallway to the left, stopping abruptly midway. "It's this one," she said, turning to him before leaving the way they came.

Alex stood facing the dark paneled door, his heart racing. Finally, he took a deep breath, and knocked. When, after calling her name and knocking a few more times he heard no answer, he turned the handle.

After Alex dropped her off at home Sunday evening, Danielle spent the next twenty four hours in a dreamy state of confused angst, marked by conflicting emotions and warring logic. On one level, a part of her felt that she should be totally horrified by the weekend's events, up to and including her fervid interlude with Alex, that inner voice wanting to overanalyze the situation and flee in disgust, a victim in an increasingly terrifying and unstable dream. A voice that insisted the logical and sane next step would be to slow or even cease contact with him until she learned more about his person and his past.

But the other and more overpowering emotion was one of intrigue and desire, regardless of the cost. Alex stirred physical sensations she had never before felt, and they stayed with her when she showered that night, the steaming water cascading upon her body and stimulating memories of his touch. Enveloped her when she fell into bed late that night, the touch

of sheets and clothing triggering a longing so intense that she began plotting the next time they could be together. Lingered the next day like the
scent of honeysuckle on a summer afternoon, completely distracting her
from class work and social conversation to the point her friends asked if
she had the flu or a fever.

Logic be damned, she concluded, completely unconcerned with whatever
baggage he was carrying, convinced they could work through it. Wanting to
be the one to help him work through it—whatever it took—happily willing
to sacrifice her virginity and whatever else was needed in the process.

By the time she got home from after school activities and violin practice,
the fog had only lifted slightly, but enough to reveal the other side of yesterday's
exchange, Alex's pain and feelings. She wondered what he had been thinking
today, and it vaguely occurred to her that he might be embarrassed or ashamed.
He had not, after all, called her yet or left any messages. Perhaps she should
be proactive. Maybe she had not been reassuring enough.

The decision to call him first was swift and unhindered by doubt.

Still, her hand shook slightly as she dialed his number and her breathing quickened. A girl answered, taking her completely off-guard, until she
remembered he had a sister.

"Is—is Alex there?" she asked.

"Yeah, he's here . . ."

Danielle could hear disgust in the girl's voice, and her confidence wavered.

"Hello?"

His tone was no less annoyed than his sister's. "Alex . . . It's Dan," she
said pensively.

The silence was deafening.

"How are you feeling?" she asked finally, after eight tortuous seconds.

"Uh . . . fine. I'm okay. And you?"

At that moment, she could have dropped the phone into the gaping
black hole that began swallowing her entire universe and whatever precari-
ous joy she had begun writing into it. "I'm alright . . . I thought maybe we
could get together and jam this week, you know. Like you said . . . jam to
some classical music."

She kept talking out of sheer nervousness and wanted to kick herself for
inviting him to do anything when she already knew the answer. He wanted
nothing to do with her—ever. Whatever they had shared had been shattered
in a moment of passion gone horribly awry, and whatever positive feelings
she had gleaned from it he obviously did not share.

"Oh, yeah . . ." His voice trailed off unenthusiastically, leaving an uncomfortable silent void. "Um, I don't know. I'm, I'm kind of busy," he said gruffly.

"Oh, I see . . . Okay. . . . Well, I guess that's it, then?" she asked quietly, trying to keep her voice from cracking, her eyes brimming with tears.

"Yes . . ." he whispered.

"Okay . . . I understand. Well, take care of yourself. Good-bye."

Unable to hold back the impending sobbing, she hastily placed the phone on the receiver and buried her head in her pillows, crying so hard she could barely breathe and wondering if she might suffocate herself in the process, a scenario not entirely unwelcome at that moment. The pain in her heart was so unbearable, she welcomed death, wished for it, her previous feelings of anxiety and fear over impending doom replaced by an intense desire to be rendered oblivious.

If this was a dream, she wanted out. And the more she considered herself in a dream, the more trapped she felt and the harder she cried. The harder she cried, the more suffocated she felt, as if she were drowning in the middle of an ocean with no life preserver, having forgotten to write a preserver into the dream and unable to do so in the moment of desperate need.

Somehow, a few hours later, she pulled herself out of the misery and got ready for bed, unable to do homework, which was now back-piling after days of neglect. Staring at the ceiling, she was about to start screaming prayers at God, when she remembered He had nothing to do with what was happening and was, therefore, unable to really fix something that neither existed nor was broken, except from her limited perspective. So she instead mentally called to the priest for help, not believing him to be a priest at all but rather some alien being, an angel maybe, and in a horribly agitated state eventually fell asleep.

She awoke the next morning feeling unusually calm, so calm that in reviewing the events of the previous evening, she had to strain to evoke any emotion, let alone the tumultuous ones she had felt just hours before. She was completely spent, in a state of comfortable numbness, Pink Floyd's lyrics aptly describing her present state of mind.

Not wanting to be lost in any thoughts whatsoever, she attacked the day with a vengeance, catching up on her studies over her lunch break and during any free time throughout the day, focusing on her upcoming recital with a relish and passion her instructor commented had been missing the past few weeks. She also made a note to research yoga and meditation classes and even considered picking up a third language. Something difficult, like Chinese—anything to fill her days and nights with tedious activity.

When she got home that afternoon, the house was quiet as usual, her parents rarely home anymore. It smelled of fresh furniture polish, though, and she knew their maid had worked that day. She considered calling out that she was home but decided against it, figuring her brother was the only one there, and he could care less. Walking into the great room, as her mother called it, she threw her bag onto the floor and set her violin case down on one of the arm chairs, intending to practice after having a bite to eat.

Absorbed in her plans, she did not notice her brother enter the room and jumped back, startled, upon seeing him. After seeing the expression on his face, her surprise changed to concern. It looked as if he had been crying, something she hadn't remembered him doing since grade school.

"Dennis—what's wrong?"

He shook his head, unable to speak.

She instinctively reached out to him, but he stepped back.

"She's gone," he burst in a loud whisper.

"What?" Danielle asked, unable to understand.

"She's *gone*—left us."

"Who?"

"Mom," he burst again, collapsing onto the floor.

Danielle froze, unable to move or speak until she fully comprehended what he said, and upon comprehension, unable to believe it.

"What—that's impossible. You're wrong—she wouldn't do that."

"I know," he said, barely audible, his head buried in his arms.

"Dennis, you're wrong . . . How do you know? Who told you?"

"Dad . . . Dad told me. He was here when I got home from school."

Danielle turned to leave the room, and Dennis jumped up, grabbing her arm. "You can't ask him," he insisted. "Don't bother him right now—"

"Why? I want to know—I want to hear it from him," she burst.

"Because he's drunk . . . and you know how he gets," he whispered gruffly. "He was drinking before I even got here."

"I don't believe you—she would never just leave—"

"Well, she did . . . Fled the country and took half the money with her."

"You're lying," Danielle gasped, her eyes starting to well with tears. "Tell me you're lying."

He shook his head and, to her surprise, walked up to her and gave her a hug. They held onto each other for a few moments.

"What do we do?" she whispered.

"Lay low . . . really low."

Having lost her appetite, she quietly followed her brother upstairs to the bedrooms, away from her father's office which was on the first level, adjacent to their family room. His binges typically kept him contained there, and they simply had to ride the night out without causing a disruption.

Sitting on her bed, she stared absently at the blinking red light on her answering machine. Three messages, at least, but she hadn't the energy to push the button.

Nor did she have the energy to cry, though the tears perched precariously on the edge of her lower lids, threatening to spill over. Sadness, fear, anger, rage, confusion, regret—the emotions paraded through her mind like a film-strip, but all she could do was watch them, abstractions made into pictures. For some reason, she couldn't feel them, overcome by a chilling numbness. Shivering, she changed out of her school uniform into sweats and attempted to work on her studies, an act of futility she decided an hour later, having re-read a chemistry chapter three times and retained nothing.

Frustrated and feeling lightheaded from not eating since Noon, she went across the hall and knocked on her brother's door.

"Yeah," he called from within.

She opened it slightly and found him sitting in front of his television playing a video game. "I'm going downstairs to make a salad. Do you want anything?"

"Sure . . . How about a grilled cheese."

Sighing loudly, she reluctantly agreed, disappointed he had wanted some-thing that actually involved cooking. As she quietly rummaged through the kitchen, she couldn't help but think of her mother. There wasn't an item in the house, a color on a wall or tile on the floor that hadn't been hand-picked by her mother, much of it imported from Italy and other parts of western Europe. Her mother had been so delighted with the house—it was her fantasy castle, and she promised to make every day a fairy tale, with fresh flowers and herbs from their garden, delicious stews, pastas and baked goods from her gourmet kitchen, lavish parties with important guests to entertain her children and support her husband's career.

That was six years ago, when they were still in grade school. What had happened, she mused sadly, waiting for the bread to brown in the pan. What came first—the money or the affair? It wasn't long after they moved in when her mother stopped cooking and hired a personal chef. Within months of that, she lost interest in her gardens and hired a caretaker. Once the place was furnished, she disappeared altogether, spending her days and nights out with various social clubs and volunteer groups.

Her father's affair came to light not quite two years ago, she calculated, laying two pieces of cheese on the slowly frying bread slice. At first, her mother was oddly contained about it, saying nothing, acting as if it never happened. There was some threat of counseling, but that never came to fruition to her knowledge. Instead she lashed out in her own way, by flirting openly with any and every man with whom she came into contact, regardless of their age. There was more than one inappropriate exchange between her mother and Tate, and Dennis eventually flat out refused to bring his friends around when she was home.

People said she and her mother could be twin sisters, a comment that made Danielle extremely uncomfortable, not because her mother wasn't beautiful and it wasn't the highest compliment she could be paid from a purely physical standpoint, but because she was nothing like her mother. Gabrielle was a vivacious extrovert with a colorful imagination and dreams that could barely be contained, while her daughter was an introvert, mechanical in her thinking and approach to life, managing emotional chaos by overachievement and creating endless tasks for herself. Danielle felt herself a mere firefly to her mother's scorching sunbeam.

So lost in memories was Danielle that she failed to notice her bread had turned from brown to black and had begun to smoke. She gasped, quickly turning off the burner and removing the pan from the stove, but it was too late. The smoke hit the sensors, and a deafening buzz reverberated from the kitchen smoke alarm. She quickly turned on the oven fan and grabbed a kitchen chair. Finding a dish towel and placing the chair under the alarm, she climbed onto its sturdy wooden seat and smothered the alarm until the ear-shattering noise stopped, fearing she had lost her hearing in the process.

It wasn't until the ringing had stopped that she heard another deafening noise, the angry roar of her father's voice as he stormed out of his office, cursing.

She nervously stepped down from the chair, almost falling off in the process. He entered the eating area, a bottle in one hand and, to her horror, a gun in the other. Still taken aback by the gun, she didn't hear half the things he was saying. She had no idea they even owned a gun, her mother completely against having firearms in the house, instead compromising by allowing an antique sword collection.

You have a lot of nerve coming back here, Gabrielle.

Upon hearing her mother's name, her gaze moved from the gun to her father's face. Somehow, even in a state of utter rage, he had not a hair out of place, his face clean-shaven, his tailored pants and navy striped dress shirt looking somewhat pressed, the sleeves rolled slightly. She had never noticed, but her father had deep-set brown eyes. Just like Tate. Just like Alex—

Her thoughts mislead her once again, and she was unaware of what happened until her head hit the tile floor and she felt a warm rivulet of moisture form just under her right nostril. Much of what happened thereafter was reduced to a blur of noise and color, scattered pieces of a puzzle she had no desire to put together. The physical abuse had not stopped until her brother burst into the room and tried to physically pry her father off of her.

Dad—what are you doing—Stop it—

She doesn't deserve to live after what's she's done—Look at her—

She vaguely remembered feeling her head pulled back and the touch of metal against her cheek, but at that moment she was too stunned and dizzy to comprehend the danger.

Give me one reason I should let this whore live—

Dad - that's not mom—it's Danielle—

Whatever gripped her suddenly let go, and she steadied herself to keep from falling face down.

There is no Danielle. There's only Gabrielle—everywhere I look, everything I see—I only see her. She haunts me. I hate her. With all my being, I hate her. Maybe it's best she's gone. Maybe I can finally have peace.

As he turned to depart, her brother ran to her side. But it wasn't ten seconds later when the footsteps stopped at the threshold and the room resounded with a guttural cry and explosive blasts as what bullets were in the gun either splintered through wood, wall and glass or pelted through metal.

It was a few minutes before they could let go of each other and raise their heads to review the damage. All was quiet except for the occasional rain of debris from some damaged part of the kitchen.

"We have to leave," her brother said finally. "We can't stay here—"

She nodded absently, wiping her nose with her sleeve and saturating it with blood in the process. "Fuck," she breathed.

"Where are your keys?"

"I don't know . . ."

"Dan, we need your keys. Where did you leave them?"

She continued to dab her wounds with her sleeve, praying the damage didn't look as bad as it felt. "I don't know . . . my, my book bag. It's . . . it's probably in my bedroom. I think I keep it there . . . or the great room."

Suddenly, they heard more yelling and another round of explosive claps and shattering glass from a distant room of the house.

"Shit . . . We have to go—now."

He helped her to stand and led her to the back door.

"Where are we going?"

"I don't know—we'll figure it out. A neighbor . . . A friend's . . ." He pulled her over the threshold and across the terrace.

"Brooke . . . We can go to Brooke's. She's just down the block a bit."

He nodded grimly and did not let go of her hand until they had made it to Brooke Trahan's front door. Nor did he leave her side, despite the fact that Brooke's house had seven bedrooms, until Alex called for him two days later, on Thursday evening.

The Trahans were more than accommodating and supportive of Danielle and Dennis, Brooke's mom, Barbara, having been close friends with Danielle's mother. They also did not overly pressure Danielle or her brother to call the authorities over what took place in their household, willing to wait patiently a few more days for one of the Sumners to come looking for their children. To ensure they could be found, Dennis phoned home Thursday morning to convey to their maid, Rosalie, what had transpired and where they were. Having taken Spanish in high school, he was the only one in the household that really could talk to her.

She slept through the greater part of Wednesday and much of Thursday, absently watching television with her brother in-between long naps. They had been placed in the largest guest suite, a brightly lit room with two large windows, white embroidered curtains, pale yellow walls and a huge colorful floral area rug. The room had its own bathroom, a fireplace, a television and two large arm chairs, one with an ottoman. It also contained a huge walnut wardrobe that Brooke stocked with clothes she leant to Danielle and even a few items for Dennis, borrowed from her older brother, Nate, who was away at college. It only contained one large, four-poster double bed, which Dennis insisted his sister have, he opting to sleep on the chair and ottoman.

The two rarely spoke with the exception of pondering their next move. Neither wanted to go to school the rest of the week. Both somehow wanted to get back into their house, if nothing else for some of their belongings. Though neither was surprised they had not heard from their father, both were confused and hurt over hearing nothing from their mother.

Neither really wanted to leave the room, either, and Mrs. Trahan kindly brought food and drink up to them throughout the day. Danielle thought she looked sort of like Cher with much shorter hair but kept the observation to herself, feeling sorry for Brooke's mom, who had been abandoned by Brooke's father for a much younger woman. Brooke's stepfather was very wealthy but also very old, constantly being mistaken for her grandfather.

Danielle pondered this bizarre relationship, along with all the others she had witnessed over the past few days, weeks and even years. There wasn't a happy ending among them, she concluded, remembering what the priest had said and finding her own experiences in complete support of his hypothesis.

But no amount of logical reasoning and profound insight could eradicate the occasional and horrible pain she felt, a pain catalyzed by thought and emotion, but manifested physically as a severe stomach cramp or sharp grip in her chest. A pain that generated a well of tears she refused to spill, sobs she choked down and a horrible sensation of loss and longing she, at times, feared would never leave, even though it eventually would within minutes, sometimes hours.

His name evoked such pain, and Danielle was relieved when her brother finally left her alone to hang out with his friend, Alex, allowing her to freely deal with her pent-up grief. She had been lying on the bed crying when there was a knock on the door. Unable to answer, she heard the door open and Brooke's voice.

"Danielle—it's your mother."

Jumping up and turning towards the door, she saw Brooke extending her the receiver.

"It's your mom—she wants to talk to you."

Danielle quickly wiped her eyes and grabbed the receiver. "Mom?" she burst. "Where are you?"

But instead of the comfort she sought, she was met with cold disdain and curt orders. Her mother was in Italy and would send for them when her affairs were in order. Had she taken them with her, she would have been charged with kidnapping and extradited. She had already made arrangements with the Trahans for her and her brother to remain there until the end of the school year and would be wiring plenty of money to ensure they were well provided for.

"But, but we don't need money—we need you," Danielle protested.

"Really, Daniella, you're a young woman now and need to start acting like one. You don't need me, and frankly, I have absolutely nothing to offer you anymore except for a share in my wealth and a bit of worldly advice. Don't for a moment think you can survive in this world without money. And for the love of God and all that's holy, don't ever marry for love. A marriage is a business relationship and should be treated as such if there's any chance of it surviving. My mother tried to tell me this years ago, and I didn't listen to her. I hope to spare you from my mistakes."

She then asked to speak with Dennis, and Danielle could hear the disappointment in her mother's sigh upon hearing he was out. Reluctantly, she left them a number at which she could be reached, but also made Danielle swear not to abuse it and to only call when absolutely necessary.

When the conversation had ended, Danielle sat at the edge of her bed looking out one of the windows. The sky had already grown dark, but because her room was unlit, she could make out the shapes of trees and rooftops. It was quiet except for the occasional whistle of wind that blew through the old window frames. She sat still for the next half hour, at moments considering getting up and turning on a light or the television. Hearing the wind, she contemplated crawling under the covers for warmth. But she didn't stir until the phone's piercing ring startled her out of her melancholy reverie. She looked down, surprised to see the receiver still clutched in her left hand.

"Trahan residence," she answered hesitantly.

"Danielle?"

It was her brother, asking her what she wanted brought from home. Her father was not there, and Alex was helping him to pack. What did she need?

Her face burned at the mention of his name and the shame of what he now knew. Collecting herself, she rattled off a list of items before hastily hanging up the phone, feeling the surge of yet another tearful onslaught.

Please don't, she pleaded with herself as if it were a separate entity. *Please stop crying – please stop feeling this way. Please just calm down.* At times, she felt she were multiple people, siding with one and fighting with the others, often losing.

Finally standing up, she walked across the room and turned on a small lamp before beginning to pace nervously, arguing with her inner-self. She wished her cat were still alive, as he was always a comfort during distraught times, but should he have lived, she doubted he would have survived the other night.

It occurred to her she may actually have to encounter Alex, and that thought temporarily shot her out of depression and into a small panic. Striding into the bathroom, she surveyed her face and hair in dismay. While the wounds were ugly, it was the crying that had done far more damage—swelling her face and creating puffy circles under her eyes. She vigorously washed her face, brushed her teeth, brushed her hair and then washed her face, again. She even set the blow dryer to her face, hoping the heat would somehow magically melt away any signs of sadness.

Considering asking Brooke for some make-up, she stared into the mirror at her black left eye and cut and bruised right lip and cheek and sighed dolefully. Only stage make-up could help the face that stared back at her.

Retreating back to the bed, she sat on its edge, once again staring out into the darkness, hoping they would just leave everything downstairs for now. Hoping they would at least leave her alone. But a half hour later, there was a knock on the door, and her heart jumped. She heard her name called and recognized his voice. *Please don't come in, please don't come in* . . .

The handle turned, and she froze, holding her breath, still seated at the edge of the bed, her back to the door.

"Can I see you?" he asked, and she could tell he crossed the threshold by the creak of his footsteps on the wood flooring.

She said nothing.

"Did you get my message?"

"*No*," she said, though no sound followed the thought.

She heard the door close, but he had not left. Instead, he walked around the bed and sat down next to her. The mattress sunk under the sudden increase in weight, his jacket lightly brushed against her arm, and in that moment, she wished she could die rather than face whatever he was about to say.

Because the light in the room was so dim, the lamp being across the room from where they sat, he could see only a soft outline of her profile, unable to make out details of the wounds. Her long dark hair hung in a perfect stream down her back, exposing her neck as she kept her head slightly turned away from him.

"You didn't get my message, did you?"

She shook her head, still unable to speak or even look at him.

He sighed and leaned closer to her, their arms touching. He smelled of mints and cigarette smoke.

"I made a mistake. The other night, on the phone with you. I didn't mean what I said. I—I don't even know why I said it . . ."

Instinctively, she turned to look at him, to see if he was telling the truth. When she did, he could see the damage and winced. Ashamed, she turned away again, shifting away from him in the process.

"I'm . . . I'm sorry about what happened to you. I am."

After a minute of silence, she spoke. "Why are you here?"

"I don't know . . . There was something you said the other day that, that stuck with me . . . You said, we should be friends first. We should be friends first, and lovers second . . . Isn't this what a friend would do?"

She had said that, but now, she was not sure she even agreed with her own words for they did not reflect how she felt inside. Friends, yes—but lovers also, and the idea of losing him as a lover was so unbearable, she feared she could not be just his friend, that she would have to leave him entirely if that is what he was requesting.

"I mean, I've been thinking about relationships," he continued. "Ours, other people's, our parents, ones I've had in the past . . . Without a friendship, they're . . . they're nothing. They're—they're meaningless activity. Just sex or fighting . . . Or sex and fighting. Or just fighting."

"Were you friends with your girlfriend . . . the one who died?" she asked quietly.

"I don't know . . . I don't remember . . . I wasn't friends with any of the others that I do remember."

"Were there many others?"

He shook his head.

"My parents hate each other," she said. "They hate each other so much, they would hurt each other."

Alex nodded, sighing. "Yeah . . . well, love and hate are just two extremes of the same emotion. I'm not even sure what that emotion is. It's like a raging desire that you can't control. A desire either to—to fuck the other person or kill them. Either one is completely out of control . . . I've seen it . . . I've seen it in myself. I know what it can do . . . There's—there's almost a sick high to being cruel. To doing bad things. Destructive things . . . I saw it the other night . . . when I treated you the way I did . . . On some—some deep level I wanted to hurt you . . . I did . . . until I stepped outside of myself and saw what it looked like. Saw what I looked like. What I became in that moment. Everything I ever hated in others."

She looked at him, so taken aback by his words that she forgot her previous insecurity.

"Why did you want to hurt me?" she whispered hoarsely.

He looked at her sadly. "I don't know . . . Because I could. Sometimes, we don't need reasons to be cruel. We just are."

She swallowed hard, staring at the floor, trying to process his words, searching her memory banks for evidence of this in herself, for times she had done the same thing—been intentionally hurtful and cruel to others.

"I'm sorry," he said, gently touching her shoulder.

His touch stirred her, and she closed her eyes, wishing she didn't desire him so and baffled as to why she still did. Never in her life had she felt this way about a person, so ready to throw all caution and sense of propriety out the window. So ready to forgive even the most unimaginable offenses. So willing to be abused all over again in exchange for one more kiss, one more passionate embrace.

"Do you still want to hurt me?" she asked.

"No," he said, stroking her cheek.

She grabbed his hand and pressed it harder against her skin, slowly moving it to her lips, kissing his fingers.

Her response startled him, as he had braced himself for an entirely different scene, one full of tears, hugs and endless apologies. She looked up at him, and for a moment he saw the woman from which she had sprung, and it both frightened and intrigued him.

It also triggered a sense of lust so overpowering that he pulled her head towards his and kissed her, forcefully, greedily, and she responded in kind. She was less pensive this time, her hands exploring the lower parts of his body, her lips exploring his ear, his neck. Lying on his back, he watched as she gently unbuttoned his shirt and kissed his chest, his stomach, the feel of her hair on that part of his body, of her lips touching him at the edge of his jeans making him hard.

Unbuttoning and unzipping his jeans, he guided her hand lower, inside his jeans, gently placing it on his privates. With his other hand, he pulled her face towards his, kissing her deeply and hungrily. They soon changed positions, he now on top of her, pushing down her sweats, her underwear, pulling down his own, pressing his groin tightly against hers, his fingers soon exploring her soft parts. He would have entered her then had the inevitable not happened, a bolt of searing pain so intense that he felt as if he were suffocating.

Unable to catch his breath, he nearly collapsed on top of her, but she wasn't startled, having been through it before, only concerned for him and distraught that she could do nothing to stop it, to help him, other than hold his body close to hers until the tremors stopped.

"It's a curse . . ." he breathed later, as he lay in her arms, the pain pacified but the pent up lust lingering. "For all the cruel things I've done."

"What things," she said, gently running her fingers through the curls on his forehead.

"I don't know . . . But just because I don't remember them doesn't mean I haven't done them."

"We've all done cruel things."

"But this is a punishment . . . I know it."

"God doesn't punish us . . . We punish ourselves."

"I don't believe in God."

She remained thoughtfully silent, lightly stroking his arm, at times kissing him gently.

"I see no use for God . . . He's just another thing to blame for our problems . . . He's just an excuse," Alex continued.

"Maybe . . . Maybe this is just a dream, and you need to rewrite it."

He groaned.

"Rewrite us."

"I wouldn't change a thing about us," he said, kissing her. "*Us* is the best part of this dream."

CHAPTER EIGHT

While the next few weeks would bring good times and a sense of normalcy for Alex, he saw, with growing dismay, that it was merely the calm before a catastrophic storm, one that would literally rip his universe apart.

The Sumners' separation had its benefits. Not only had it brought him and Danielle closer but also, oddly, her brother and Brooke. When the couples weren't off on their own, the four of them spent time together, be it going to parties, going to movies or hanging out in their favorite Westport coffee house. Danielle, Brooke and Dennis even attending Alex's final home and away football games to cheer him on.

Danielle being kicked out of the house also had its advantages. The Trahans were hardly disciplinarians, so she enjoyed a freedom she would not have had under the scrutinizing eye of Mr. Sumners. With a seven-bedroom house, Brooke's parents were able to give each of the Sumners' children their own room and private bath, and for Alex and Danielle, her room was more like an apartment. She could lock it, and nobody asked what went on behind closed doors.

But their romantic trysts were leading to a growing chasm in Alex's mind.

When he didn't try to have sex with her, he experienced a pleasant world, one enjoyed by an average teenager who attended high school, played football, had an attractive girlfriend, went on typical dates, enjoyed parties and jammed to rock and roll with his friends. Their quiet times were spent listening to music, playing their instruments, watching television and casually making out.

Danielle had been able to purchase a new violin with the money her mother had wired. She was amazingly talented, and Alex found himself looking forward to her recital in December. He would visit her in the evenings, after football, just to listen to her practice. When she finished, they would play together—pieces by Vivaldi, Bach and Paganini, to name a few. Though both shared a passion for classical music, Danielle knew little about folk or bluegrass, and Alex shared his collection, pleased at her growing appreciation for Nick Drake, a musician he admired. "Know" being Danielle's favorite, he often played it for her. For him, she wrote a version of it for violin, and together they worked on a collaboration for both instruments.

But there were other times, when she gave him a look or struck a certain pose—probably one of which she was completely unaware—that triggered such an overwhelming feeling of covetousness, he was unable to contain it. Those were the times when he did not see her but, instead, the woman in the portrait. And because he could not see his friend, the lust inspired was violent, angry and completely devoid of love. During these times, his brightly lit suburban world seemed to melt into a barren landscape populated by stone walls, treeless mountains, blood-streaked skies and creeping shadows, a world completely absent of music or culture, where the only sport was feeding an insatiable hunger for sex and rage.

Unable to bear his painful impotence, which he feared was fueling the encroaching nightmare, he had talked his parents into letting him see a doctor under the guise of painful urination. But after a few weeks of various and often humiliating tests, even the specialists could find nothing physically wrong with him. And when the lust presented itself, he gave into it anyway, knowing full well the agony and degradation that would follow. Up until the Thanksgiving holiday, these episodes had been infrequent and contained to the bedroom, where he and Danielle could deal with the after-effects in private. But that weekend, the darkness would follow him mercilessly, triggered by disturbing flashbacks and painful memories.

For reasons he had yet to deduce, he had wanted to keep his relationship with Danielle hidden from his family, especially his mother. But on the Sunday before Thanksgiving, he realized he had failed. He and his family were seated around the dining room table for a rare dinner together. His mother being a good cook, he was relishing her hearty meal of roast beef and homemade gravy, carrots and mashed potatoes, and was just poised to enjoy another mouthful when she seemingly asked out of the blue.

"So when are we going to get to meet your new girlfriend?"

He choked, dropping his fork in the process. All eyes turned on him expectantly.

"Girlfriend?" he repeated, trying to act naive but failing at that, too.

"Oh, really, Alex. Did you think we were born yesterday? We know you have a girlfriend. What's her name?" she asked with slight irritation.

Alex turned red, and Trisha snorted at his obvious discomfort.

"Danielle," he mumbled.

"Danielle what?"

"Danielle Sumners."

"Oh," his mother replied, and he hoped that had settled things. But a minute later she continued. "Is she related to your friend—Dennis? I thought that was Dennis's last name."

'Yeah," he said, swallowing hard. "She's his sister."

"Well, now we know why you've been spending so much time with Dennis," his father commented jovially, winking at him.

He smiled weakly in return, having suddenly lost his appetite.

"So, when can we meet her?" his mother asked.

"Meet her," he repeated dully.

"Yes, meet her—your girlfriend," his mother said, looking him squarely in the eye.

He looked down at his plate, shrugging. "I don't know . . . Why do you want to meet her?"

"For god's sake, Alex, why wouldn't we want to meet her," his mother burst, her slightly hysterical tone causing him to shift uncomfortably in his chair. "Is there a reason we shouldn't meet her?"

"Yeah—is she as slutty as the last one?" his sister cracked.

"Trisha—" his mother snapped.

"Well it's true," Trisha burst. "When are you going to stop sheltering him about his past? When are you going to tell him what happened—what he did?"

Alex watched his mother's face redden and her eyes well with tears. His father just buried his head in his hands and sighed in exhaustion.

"She's not a slut," he said finally. "She's—she's from a wealthy family. Her—her father's a partner in a law firm. Her mother's a—a socialite . . .

She attends private school. Plays violin. Speaks fluent Italian. You saw their house," Alex said, turning to his mom. "It's hardly a trailer home."

"Hmm—well at least you remember something about Jennifer," Trisha mumbled caustically.

"Yes, I did see the house," his mother said softly. "She sounds lovely. Why don't you invite her over for Thanksgiving dinner."

"I'm sure she has plans that night," Alex countered. "Actually, *we* have plans that night. She wants me to see some Plaza lighting ceremony."

"I thought you told me Dennis's parents were getting divorced," his mother said suddenly.

"What does that have to do with it?"

"Well, maybe she won't have plans for dinner. Maybe being invited here will relieve her of having to make a choice between two households."

Alex rolled his eyes, relieved he hadn't told his parents everything.

"Fine. I'll ask her to Thanksgiving dinner," he said grimly.

∞

For Danielle, the next few weeks were spent trying to adjust to a new life, one of an independence she did not expect to have until graduating college. Her mother had made a monetary arrangement with the Trahans to provide boarding for her and Dennis through the end of the school year. While they had house rules she and Dennis were expected to follow, they granted both of them privacy, and the rules neglected to outline behavior with the opposite sex, concerned more with drugs, alcohol and destruction of property. Mrs. Sumners had also set up bank accounts for each of them which she kept well-funded, from which Danielle and her brother were to manage their day-today needs such as fuel, clothing and school or activity fees.

While her mother had provided for them, her father had not attempted to make contact. When two weeks had passed, Dennis reached out to their dad and eventually began regular visits. But according to her brother, he never asked about Danielle. It was as if she had ceased to exist.

As time passed, her mother grew equally distant, and Danielle noticed she spent the majority of her phone conversations with Dennis. She later learned from Brooke that her mother often called the Trahans after school, when Dennis was home but Danielle was away at practice or other activities.

"Why does mom only want to talk to you?" Danielle asked her brother one evening, after learning from Brooke she had missed yet another phone conversation that took place between her brother and mom earlier in the day.

"What are you talking about?"

"She only talks to you—she doesn't even want to talk to me anymore. Why? Have I done something? I mean—does she talk about me?"

"Yeah," he burst incredulously, "She talks about how much she loves us and misses us."

"Us—you mean, *you*. She loves and misses *you*."

"She means *us*. In fact, we may be spending the summer in Europe. Sounds kind of cool, actually. She said Brooke could come."

"Did she say *I* could come? Or just Brooke?" Danielle said with pained sarcasm.

Dennis rolled his eyes. "Mom loves you. You know that . . . You're the *favored* child, remember?" he said, eyeing her intently, and she couldn't tell if his intent was to hurt or console, for she saw both cruelty and sadness in his eyes.

To keep herself from the ensuing paranoia, jealousy, anger and other negative emotions smoldering just beneath her outwardly composed exterior, she stayed busy with school and enrolled in both a yoga and meditation class, which were to begin in early December.

Her relationship with Alex, while providing a welcome distraction, at times also seemed to make her already unreal existence even more nightmarish. It was as if the two of them skirted completely different worlds—one reminiscent of the typical high school dating scene and one a mental hell, where all people and surroundings seemed to melt away, leaving only them and their legions of inner demons.

While she cherished time alone with him, she was relieved when there were others around, especially Dennis and Brooke, whose previous hatred of each other had mysteriously turned into attraction, seemingly overnight. With their love of The Comedy Channel, grunge, cinema and video games, Brooke and Dennis provided much needed comic relief to the over-the-top drama she and Alex staged when left to their own devices.

What Danielle feared most about her relationship with Alex was utterly losing control of herself, both physically and emotionally. Her physical attraction to him was becoming so intense that she would do anything to satisfy it—anything he asked—regardless of the fallout. When she was with him, she didn't care about consequences. All time seemed to cease, and all cause and effect with it. She was also painfully aware that their tryst was most likely a temporary one and he would soon tire of her and their inability to fulfill their collective sexual appetites. He had already left her once, so it was not inconceivable that he would walk away again, but the pain she felt upon just imagining his absence was unbearable. She hoped the yoga and meditation would help her to quench a burning desire and hurt that often threatened to consume what shreds of logic, peace and humanity she had managed to salvage from her shattered world.

When Alex invited her to his house for Thanksgiving dinner to meet his family, she could barely contain her enthusiasm and felt a huge sense of relief. She had often asked about his family and commented more than once that she would like to meet them, but he would merely grunt, wince or change the subject. His reluctance hurt her, and she spent more than a few nights pondering what about her shamed or scared him. Was it her parents' messy affair? Or the fact that they had abandoned her—that she had become a pariah to them? Or something completely unrelated to her—perhaps his having entered a relationship too soon after his girlfriend's death? Or something worse. A fear his parents—his mother especially—would pick up on their intense sexual attraction for each other. That somehow, Alex feared his parents would see her as loathsome, dirty even—a threat to their son. At times, the way he looked at her, she wondered if he, himself, saw her this way, and it scared her.

The invitation helped to dispel these darker suspicions, and she was determined to make a positive impression on them. She remembered that her mother would bring gifts to dinner parties they attended, so the evening school let out for the holiday, Danielle headed to The Plaza to put together a gift basket, carefully selecting a variety of gourmet breads, jams and chocolates from the various specialty shops and including four hand-painted Italian wine glasses as a special touch. She and Alex had made plans throughout the four-day weekend, and she went to bed optimistic, enjoying an unusually restful night of sleep.

∞

Alex wished he could share Danielle's enthusiasm about meeting his parents and wished he had a reasonable explanation for her as to why he didn't want her to meet his parents, but he didn't. Because of The Plaza lighting ceremony, which his family now also wanted to attend after hearing about it, his mother set dinner for late afternoon instead of evening.

Nervous did not begin to describe the surge of conflicting emotions Alex felt waiting for Danielle's arrival. He tried to sit calmly in the living room with his dad, watching the endless football bowls, but soon found himself in the kitchen with his mother and sister, watching them scurry from the oven to the counter.

"Do you need any help?" he offered.

"Oh, that's okay, sweetie—we have things under control—" his mother said breathlessly, turning knobs on the stove and opening the oven door, allowing a cloud of smoke to escape, cursing under her breath.

He nodded absently, about to walk out of the room when a sudden crash startled him. His mother had dropped a wine glass onto the ceramic tile floor. Without thinking, he went to the pantry to retrieve a broom and dustpan, ignoring his mom's protests and mild curses. As Trisha tried to calm her down, he silently swept up the tiny pieces, his thoughts drifting to another time.

The table had been set, and the food was now re-heating in the oven.

"Where is she?" his mother asked. "I thought you said six o'clock—it's now a little after seven."

"I don't know. . . I called her house, but no one answered."

"Did she forget? Maybe we should go ahead and start eating," his father suggested.

No, she knew it was tonight. His sister stood up, sighing impatiently, and headed for the television room when an obnoxious knock sounded on the door. Alex jumped up from his seat to answer it. He opened the door to find her standing on the porch, laughing and barely able to stand, obviously drunk. She had a swollen lip and a bruised cheek. He was afraid to ask how she had found transportation to his house.

"I'm sorry I'm late," she giggled, before bursting into tears.

The sound of glass pieces shattering against the tile startled him momentarily. She had broken one of his mother's wine glasses. The tension, the icy silence, Jennifer's tear-stained cheeks as she knelt on the kitchen floor, cutting her fingers as she desperately tried to pick up the glass and fit the pieces back together.

He shut the pantry door and looked at his mother, who was now stirring something in a pan, while his sister began setting the table. His mother had taken care to make the dinner special, buying fresh flowers for the centerpiece, making everyone—including himself—dress nicely for the occasion, despite his protests that the fanfare was hardly necessary. Today, she had pulled her short hair back into a stubby ponytail, exposing all the gray, making her look old and tired. He suddenly felt sorry for her and for whatever pain he had caused her, whatever shame.

Walking over to her, he lightly touched her shoulder. "Everything looks really great, Mom . . . Thank you."

She smiled sadly. "Well—she sounds pretty important . . . We want to make a good impression on her."

Squeezing her shoulder reassuringly, he headed into the television room to continue watching football games until Danielle arrived a half hour later and on time, to his relief.

He opened the door, smiling widely.

She smiled back, stepping over the threshold, her arms loaded with an ornately ribboned basket that she handed him as she removed her coat. His mother quickly joined them, taking her coat and hanging it in the hall closet. Danielle studied his mother, looking for a resemblance but not finding too much of one outside of the very light freckling she and her son seemed to share, scattered here and there on the bridge of her nose, cheeks and forehead. She had very blond hair, almost white, and light blue eyes that drooped at the edges. She looked old and tired, her matronly attire—brown slacks with a fall-themed sweater, marked by embroidered and ornately beaded gold, rust and brown leaves—only burying her figure and accentuating her lifeless features.

"What's all this?" Alex asked, holding up the basket.

"Oh—that's my contribution," she said, shifting uncomfortably in place as Alex's mother scrutinized her person. She had dressed conservatively, wearing a gray, fitted v-neck sweater, pearl necklace and a black skirt, tights and boots, the skirt hanging just above the knee.

"That was totally unnecessary but very kind," his mother said graciously, taking the basket from Alex. "We're just happy to meet you finally."

Danielle blushed, shifting nervously as two other family members joined the group. First, his father, who was a very tall, muscular man with rugged facial features and dark, deep-set eyes. He was taller than Alex, and more hulking, but the resemblance was striking. Next it was his sister, but Danielle could find no resemblance between her and Alex—or even her and the parents. She had straight blond hair, the hair color being the only thing she shared with her mother and brother. They did not share the same nose or eyes—or even mouth shape. And, Danielle could tell she had no freckles in spite of the heavy make-up she wore.

At dinner, his mother seated her across from Alex and next to Trisha, which she felt was comforting, the two creating a natural buffer from continued parental scrutiny. After fifteen minutes of being grilled by Alex's mother on all aspects of her family background and hobbies, Alex's father jokingly suggested that they *let the poor girl eat.*

While Danielle was struggling with nerves, Alex was internally confident in her ability to charm his family. Her manners were impeccable, her composure elegant, and even in her nondescript clothing, she looked radiantly beautiful. He stared at her throughout the dinner, at times forgetting to eat, his fork poised midair, his eyes often falling to her exposed chest, graced only by the strand of pearls.

Near the end of the meal, the conversation had turned to football and sports in general when his mother decided to brag about the few sporting accomplishments he had prior to the move.

"Did you play football in Montana?" Danielle asked.

"A little bit—"

"He was actually an accomplished football player before the accident," his mother interrupted, then gasped.

A fork dropped to a plate. His father cleared his throat. Trisha sighed dramatically.

Danielle eyed Alex, who shrugged in response. Neither understood the sudden tension.

"I mean—you know, the—the *car* accident I'm sure Alex told you about," she said hastily.

"Car accident?" Danielle burst. "What car accident?"

Alex rolled his eyes at his mother's panicked attempt to smooth over a statement Danielle hadn't even noticed.

"When did this happen?" Danielle asked, turning to his mother.

"Well—this past winter."

Alex kicked her under the table. She looked at him wide-eyed, trying to read his gesture. "You didn't tell me this," she said softly. "Was this before or after the shooting?"

Trisha choked on her water. His father put his head in his hands. Alex leaned over and whispered to his mother. "It's okay. She knows."

Danielle peered around the table, trying to hide her sudden agitation and fear she had offended someone.

"She knows. . ." his mother echoed uncomprehendingly, turning to Danielle. "You know about what happened?"

Danielle swallowed hard before responding, glancing at Alex for nonverbal clues. He just shook his head impatiently, averting his eyes. "Well—yes. I. . . I know as much as Alex can remember."

"Well that ain't a hell of a lot," his father burst dryly, causing Danielle and Alex to smirk and Trisha to suppress a laugh. He then excused himself to resume watching football until dessert was served.

"You told her about *Jennifer*," Trisha asked in a hushed voice, leaning over the table.

"Sort of."

"And, none of this bothers you?" Alex's mother asked incredulously, turning to Danielle.

Danielle clutched nervously at her faux pearls. "Well, no—not really. Should it?"

His mother suddenly excused herself from the table, exiting the room and heading upstairs. Danielle looked at Alex with concern. He nodded, then got up to follow her, relieved to hear his sister changing the subject to the latest Hollywood gossip.

As he walked up the steps and entered the landing, a barrage of images and voices flashed through his mind.

"How could you. How could you bring that—that whore into this family." His *mother was on her knees next to the bed, sobbing. "Do you know her reputation at school? Do you know her family's reputation in town?"*

"She's not what you think—"

"Then what is she—"

"She's a victim."

"That family is low-class, and I want no part of them."

Stopping in front of the door to their room, he listened before turning the handle. Silence.

He knocked softly. "Mom?"

No answer.

"Can I come in?" he asked, turning the handle. He opened the door.

She was seated on the bed, her back turned to him.

"Are you okay?"

She nodded, turning to him and attempting to smile, her face tear-stained.

"What's wrong?" he asked timidly.

She shook her head. "Nothing, nothing—I just. . . I guess I'm just a little overwhelmed. She—she seems so accepting, and I . . . I wasn't expecting that. After the past year, it just frightens me. . ."

"Why?"

"Because, Alex . . . Because the last girl you fell for, you got pregnant. And I don't want to live through that again . . . I don't want our family to live through that again. And I especially . . . . I especially don't want *her* family to go through something like that. With their social stature, the embarrassment to them would be . . . . Would be unbearable—I know."

Her words stunned him, and he stepped back, momentarily losing all sense of balance.

"What? Jennifer was *pregnant*?"

She nodded, wringing her tissue.

"I . . . I had no idea . . . I still don't remember . . ."

"I know," she said bitterly. "But I felt it important you remember that part of it. You can go, now. I'll be down shortly."

He slowly backed out of the room, its vertical flowered wallpaper making his head spin, momentarily grabbing the edge of their dresser to steady himself. As he did, his eyes fell upon an old photo his mother had framed, not of their wedding day but taken around the same time. His parents looked so young and happy. She, especially, looked youthful—and even beautiful, with long, golden brown hair that spilled down her shoulders in ripples. And she was smiling, laughing maybe, she and his father hugging on a lakeshore, their backdrop a white-capped mountain range. There was something familiar about the photo—recent, even—but he blinked away the ensuing confusion and quickly headed out of the room. When he reached the dining table, he couldn't look at Danielle, not just yet, and was relieved his sister was such an avid talker.

His mother rejoined them shortly thereafter, apologizing for her lapse, and the afternoon proceeded without drama.

After dinner, Danielle took him aside, "What's wrong?"

"Nothing . . ."

"That's not true—you're completely pale. You look miserable. Are you not feeling well?"

"Not really."

"Do you want to skip tonight?"

"No," he replied vehemently, grabbing her arm like a life ring. "I need to get out of here. In fact, the sooner the better."

"Sure—okay. We can go."

"I just need to get my wallet and jacket."

"Can I come with you?" she asked.

"Why?"

She shrugged, smiling, "Just curious—what your room looks like."

"It's nothing to look at—" he protested.

"I don't care. It's you. It's a part of you—"

"It's a mess. . . I haven't cleaned it in weeks—"

"So. You saw mine after a bomb supposedly went off in it."

He sighed, reluctantly escorting her upstairs, wincing.

"Let's go to your room," she said, eyeing him lustily.

"Why?"

"So we can have privacy, silly. We don't have privacy—"

"But my parents are outside on the porch—"

"So? I'm feeling damn horny."

From the corner of his eye, he caught his mother eyeing them suspiciously.

Throwing open the door, he switched on the light.

Danielle blinked, adjusting her eyes, at first taking in the whole room and seeing nothing extraordinary—a wooden dresser, old wooden desk and a twin bed with a dark blue plaid comforter. But she blinked again after noticing the walls and realizing they weren't wallpapered. They were painted—oddly. Painted like bricks. Gray bricks with black mortar, much of the surface covered by posters and photographs. Impulsively, she walked towards the far wall and, upon reaching it, gingerly touched the surface, as if to test her vision.

Alex sighed in irritation at himself for not having painted over the bizarre façade. Leaning against his closet door, he waited for her to comment.

"My god," she breathed. "You've imprisoned yourself."

"You think?" he replied caustically.

"Why?"

He shook his head. He didn't know, but he was beginning to guess. "We need to go. My mother won't like this," he said gruffly, opening his closet to grab his lined, flannel jacket.

"Your mother doesn't like me, does she?"

"Why do you say that?" he asked, surprised.

"I can tell . . . I can feel it."

"She doesn't like anyone," he mumbled, leading her out of his room.

"You mean she doesn't like anyone *with you.*"

Alex shrugged, not wanting to pursue the topic. He then hastily said good-bye to his family, promising to be home before midnight.

Once in her car, he threw his head back and let out a deep sigh. "Please—get us out of here."

"Alright . . . where do you want to go? We still have more than an hour before the ceremony."

"I don't care . . . I can't breathe here. Just—just find us a parking space, and we can walk around or something. Or just sit in the car. I don't really care."

Cars had already filled all of the shopping district's parking lots, and they ended up parking on a residential street a few blocks away.

"Do you want to talk about it?" she asked quietly, taking the key out of the ignition.

"Not really," he answered, his arms crossed defensively.

His anger unsettled her.

"Is it—is it something I did?"

"No . . . you did nothing . . . It's me."

They sat in uncomfortable silence for a few minutes.

"What do you see in me, Danielle?" he asked, staring through the windshield, his arms still crossed.

She stared at him in bewilderment. "What do you mean, what do I see in you—"

"I mean what I asked. Just answer the fucking question," he snapped angrily.

She bit her lip, trying to stop a sudden spasm. "Well, *Tu sei il ragazzo più bello che abbia mai visto.*"

"In English . . . For god's sake, I'm being serious."

"I said, because you're the most beautiful boy I've ever seen," she burst. "The most beautiful person, I've ever looked upon. And, and the fact that . . . that you have more than half a brain, and—and play music, enjoy culture and—and can converse about just about anything, from I don't know—history to politics to crazy questions about the meaning of life. That . . . that just makes you all the more attractive."

"What if all that's a lie," he murmured bitterly. "What if I'm just a crazy, lower-class loser fuck? Who fucks other low-class losers? Who fucks just about anything that moves?"

As his voice grew louder, Danielle shrank further away from him, and he mercilessly continued his assault, almost fueled by her horror. She had never seen him like this before.

"What if I fucked a whore—who had fucked every other guy in the school—who had been fucked by her father? And what if I actually got her pregnant? What then? What if I told you I was prepared to be the child's daddy—to get a job at the local gas station and raise a family? What if that's what I was doing, right now—instead of sitting here—in your fancy fucking Volvo at some fucking fancy shopping mall? And what if you just happened to be driving through Polson—though god knows fucking why—and you drove through my gas station, and I pumped your fucking gas. Would you even notice me? Would you even notice I exist? Would you fucking even let me lay a hand on you, let alone kiss you—have sex with you?"

She just stared at him in wide-eyed shock, trying to paint the picture he was describing in her mind so she could honestly respond to his question but being utterly unable to do so.

"Of course you wouldn't . . . I know that. But what you don't know is that's exactly what I'd be doing had Jennifer lived. And we'd probably have another one on the way," he added spitefully.

"But—but she's not. And you're not—" Danielle burst in protest.

He looked at her with a disdain meant to sting, and he felt a small sense of satisfaction when he saw it had.

She felt it manifest as a physical pang in her chest.

"I don't care, okay? I don't care what you did, or—or who you *fucked*. What difference does it make? It never happened that way—so it doesn't matter . . . I love you. I love you so much, I feel my heart could burst sometimes, it hurts so badly," she said, her voice lowering to a whisper as she brushed tears from her eyes. "And, don't even ask me why . . . I don't know why I love you. I don't know why you can continue to tell me horrible things about yourself—your past—and I just don't care. I still love you. I'd, I'd still make love to you . . . if we could. But we can't . . . and that doesn't matter, either. I'd love you till the end of this life, whether we can ever do it or not."

She turned away from him, but he continued to stare at her, not wanting to believe her, wanting her to see him for the disgusting creature he was. Wanting her to hate him—to walk out on him so he could move on with his pathetic existence in private.

"What if I killed someone?" he continued, this time scooting towards her.

"You didn't," she mumbled, continuing to stare out the driver's side window, ignoring his advancing presence.

"I might have. I might have cold-heartedly blown a man's head right off his body," he whispered in her ear, and as the words left his mouth, he saw a vision play out before him, a shrapnel of memory.

He wasn't sure what possessed him. Some crazed instinct. Some internal, lethal rage that jolted through his person. Yelling wildly, he pushed himself up from the wall, stumbling towards the gun. Picking it up, he charged through the doorway and started down the hall, stopping suddenly as the figure loomed just a few feet ahead of him. Brushing the blood from his eyes, Alex raised the shotgun.

"You son of a bitch—" he cried, releasing the trigger.

The figure fell backwards. Alex stood breathless, shaking violently. Suddenly feeling the searing pain of his wounds, and a chill. A cold chill.

"I don't care," she answered defiantly, continuing to stare out the window.

He gently pushed the hair from her ear, "What if I raped someone?"

This caused a slight gasp, and he smiled bitterly to himself, feeling her shudder.

"You wouldn't," she breathed, turning towards him slightly.

"You don't know that," he said, caressing her neck.

"I don't care. There's nothing you can say—I don't care what vile things you say . . . I love you."

He leaned into her, his lips barely brushing her ear. "What if I raped you?"

He felt her tense under his touch.

"You can't . . ." she said quietly. "Even if you wanted to, you can't. But you don't want to."

"I don't need a dick to rape you," he said with an air of finality, waiting for the cause he intended to effect and utterly surprised at what happened next.

"Then do it," she rasped, turning on him. "Do it . . . take me to some, some back alley and rape me with a beer bottle . . . I don't care. There's an alley not too far from here. I'll drive us there, and you can do what you want with me . . . and when I wake up—if I wake up at all—if you don't kill me in the process—ask me if I still love you."

He stared intently, her words transforming into images that surged through his mind, unleashing an intense, violent desire to release his pent-up sexual frustration at any cost, even if it meant harming her, and he wasn't sure what was more frightening, the realization that he could hurt her or the sudden erection he got thinking about it. He pulled away, dizzy, and as he did a new onslaught of images assaulted him, memories this time. He was no longer in a car.

He walked towards a small crowd that had gathered on the pier. It was a late summer evening, and the sky was brightly lit with stars. The lake house had grown crowded with party-goers, and he had stepped out to get some fresh air. As he neared, he recognized his teammates. They were watching something, and he wanted to see what it was.

Pushing his way to the front, he stopped short.

A young girl lay on the rough, wooden boards of the dock. A familiar girl. Her eyes were closed, but she would let out an occasional moan and turn her head to the side.

Jennifer. Her name was Jennifer Hicks, and she was his girlfriend.

A guy from his football team was writhing on top of her, he was—

His heart pounded and his stomach turned as the gross reality of the situation became clear.

Hey, Alex, they encouraged after his teammate had crawled off her person. Why don't you have a go at it? Yeah, Alex—your turn.

Somebody roughly pushed him forwar, and he tripped on the uneven piering, falling to his knees, his hand grabbing her knee to break the fall. She moaned, turning her head towards him, her eyes starting to flutter open.

What the fuck . . . What the fuck are you people doing? She's my girlfriend—What are you thinking? What are you fucking thinking?

Your girlfriend's a fucking slut.

Overcome with a sudden, overwhelming rage, he turned around and decked the guy who had said it. Then he started screaming at the others, arms swinging punches, blocking return hits. Upon realizing he wouldn't be calmed down, the group overcame him.

He felt arms envelop him and moments later realized why. He had broken down and was sobbing uncontrollably.

"How can you love me . . . how . . . when I don't even know if I love you? When I don't even know what love is . . ."

But she said nothing, responding only by pulling him closer to herself, kissing him gently and telling him everything would be fine, though not sure, herself, if it ever would. If they could really ever be together in the world he had created for himself. His mood swings scared her, and while she did not want to become the victim of a dysfunctional, abusive relationship, she also saw how easy it would be to do so.

By the time he calmed down, they had missed the ceremony but were able to stroll through the streets and enjoy the lights. Most of the stores were open, and they browsed through a few shops. Danielle insisted they stop in a bookstore so she could try to find a palatable book on quantum theory—one for dummies—but after scanning the titles and back covers, they left the store empty-handed.

"What's this recent interest in quantum physics?" he asked, grabbing her hand and holding it as they walked.

She shrugged. She never completely shared with him her exchange in the church and did not feel compelled to do so now. "I don't know . . . I heard a teacher talking about some interesting ideas one day that were supposedly based on quantum physics . . . you know, the nature of reality—of the universe. Why we're here, that sort of thing."

"Why are we here?"

"I have no idea . . . But supposedly, our life's purpose should be to find out."

"Life's purpose . . ." he echoed, his mind spiraling into an uncomfortable place, a black hole devoid of his usual thoughts and emotions. An empty silence.

"I know—it's heavy. Hey—let's go up to one of the rooftop parking lots so we can see the lights from above." she said, quickly changing the subject upon seeing dark shadows cast upon his previously optimistic demeanor.

They walked two blocks to a multi-story garage above a Japanese steakhouse and headed up an enclosed stairway to its roof. While the lot was jammed with cars, it was relatively absent of people, and they found a corner spot to themselves.

Alex looked out at the sea of lighted buildings and crowded streets. The crisp air was filled with the noise of cars, holiday bells and pockets of merriment. Nothing could be more romantic, and no one was more beautiful to him than the girl standing at his side, yet he felt . . . cold. Restless. Agitated. Even angry, the brightness of the multi-colored lights taunting him with an invitation to a world in which he could not participate. A world where everything was beautiful, and everyone was kind and people fell in love and stayed in love until death parted them and angels took them away on some fucking chariot. It was a world he did not believe in nor did he want to, because he felt it was a lie. That underneath all the glitter and tinsel was the real world of death and destruction.

Hell wasn't a separate place, he realized. It was the fire that burned within, fed by the quenchless hunger and ensuing rage at never being able to attain complete and perfect satisfaction due to a complete inability to understand what was to be attained. In his mind, every bulb on every strand of every building in the entire Plaza district suddenly shattered into a million pieces, plunging their entire little world into darkness.

He looked at Danielle, who was leaning on the ledge, staring off into the distance, completely oblivious to the danger she was in.

And then he felt it. He felt the presence like one feels lightening before it strikes—a tingling sensation down the spine, the hairs of the neck and head standing on end. He slowly turned his head to look behind them.

Across the parking lot stood the man, the faceless man in the red plaid shirt.

Alex choked and faced forward again.

"Danielle . . . Is there anyone in the parking lot with us?"

She raised an eyebrow slyly, then fully turned her body around to look. "Yes, there is. Too bad," she sighed.

"What does he look like?"

"He's wearing a red plaid shirt and jeans," she said, suddenly smiling and waving.

"What are you doing," he whispered harshly, pulling her arm down and close to his person, hunkered against the wall. "He's got a gun."

"*What?*"

"We have to get out of here—let's go—" he said, roughly pulling her towards the door.

But she stopped midway, shaking him off. "Look—he's gone already. And, I didn't see a gun. He waved at me with one hand, and the other hand was in his jean pocket."

"Did he have a face?"

"Yes, he had a face," she burst. "Alex, what is wrong with you tonight?"

"You shouldn't have been able to see him," he said quietly.

"What? What are you talking about?"

"Because he doesn't exist," he interrupted angrily. Turning away from her, he walked back to the ledge and sat down on the ground, facing the cars, his back against the low wall overlooking the street below.

"Are you saying . . ." she started to speak, her mind racing to comprehend. "Does he appear often?"

He nodded.

"In public?"

He nodded.

"And . . . and nobody else can see him—"

He shook his head.

"Does he . . . does he always have a gun?"

"Yes . . . And he always tries to shoot me."

"Oh," she said quietly, joining him, tucking her skirt around her legs as she sat down next to him. "That's so strange . . . He didn't seem threatening to me. He waved as if he knew me."

"I'm a terrible person, Danielle . . . You have no idea the thoughts I have."

She sighed but said nothing.

"If it wasn't as bright as daylight up here, do you have any idea what I would do to you?"

Blushing, she turned away. "Don't talk like that . . ."

"Why? Does it make you *uncomfortable*? Do I make you *uncomfortable*?" he whispered, placing a hand on her leg and leaning into her.

She sighed deeply, shuddering. "No . . . you make me hot. You make me ache. Goddamit, Alex . . . You think this is just hard for you . . ." she whispered back, grabbing the hand on her knee and moving it up to her breast.

He looked at her incredulously. "You're telling me that if I—I threw you against that wall, there, and fucked your brains out, that actually turns you on. You'd like that - because that's exactly what I want to do right now and fucking would if I could."

She stared at the wall. "Yes . . . If the lights were off, that would be pretty hot."

"Why? I thought—I thought you were into romance and relationships and—and all that bullshit."

"I told you why—but you're not listening. Because I love you—because I don't care what you do to me. You breathe on me, and I—I just die inside, I'm so turned on."

"But I don't love you. Look at me—" he turned her head towards his so they were staring eye-to-eye, mere inches apart. "*I don't love you.* At all." He pulled away from her. "I don't even like the word love. I hate it. I think it's bullshit."

She looked at him keenly, hearing what he was saying but feeling completely unaffected by it for a reason she could not herself fathom. It was as if she were listening to an adult from a *Peanuts* episode. *Wa wa wa.* The only thing even remotely disturbing was that he had pulled away from her and now sat, arms crossed, staring forward.

"So, why are you with me?" she asked finally.

"Because you're hot, and I want to fuck you."

"Okay . . . So, let's pretend—just for the hell of it—that—that we could do what you want to do. In fact, let's pretend we just did. We're sitting here against this wall utterly exhausted and sweaty and barely breathing because, you know . . . What next? Like, in your fantasy—what do we do next?"

He mused a moment, arms still crossed. "Go back to your place. Your room . . . and do it again."

"Hmmm . . . . And after that? Tomorrow, say—since, you're supposed to be home by midnight tonight."

His arms loosened a bit. "Tomorrow . . . I would pick you up, and we'd have breakfast together . . . go to the coffee shop or something. And then . . . I don't know, hang out until we got horny again."

"Okay—this sounds like a nice weekend so far. So, on Monday—when we go back to school. What then?"

"What do you mean?"

"Well, like—how far down the road are we taking this fantasy of yours. Do we just have a weekend fling, and then that's it. We move on. Find other partners to fling with. Like, by Christmas—maybe there's some hot girl you've been eying in your math class. And—and maybe there's this guy I met on the symphony that I find intriguing. And, now that I am experienced at this, maybe I just want to, I don't know—go fuck him and compare notes. And, who knows, maybe if you're better than he is, we can have a spin on New Year's for old time's sake. How does that sound?"

"There's a hot guy in the symphony?"

She raised her eyebrow suggestively. "More than one, actually. And, I don't know—now that I'm no longer a virgin. Now that you've—you've opened me up to the world of sexual intercourse and desire, I—I just can't look at men the same again. They are all so intriguing now—and on such a different level than they were before."

He laughed, shaking his head. "You're full of shit. You're still a virgin."

"No . . . I don't know about that . . . I think Tate got to me first, actually," she said quietly.

For a moment, all movement and sound ceased and even the lights seemed to blackout as the air between them became still as death.

He exploded.

"What are you talking about?" He jumped from his seated position and faced her, roughly holding both of her arms. "That's impossible. I was there—I got to you first—"

Though she expected a reaction—intentionally eliciting one—his anger surprised her, and she stared at him wide-eyed.

"Don't lie to me, Danielle—and don't even joke with me about such things," he said bitterly, releasing her as quickly as he had grabbed her.

"Why does that even bother you? If you don't love me and I'm just another fuck—in obviously—a long line of fucks, why does it even bother you?"

"I don't want to talk about it," he said, crossing his arms again.

"No—we *need* to talk about it."

"It would have been against your will . . . it's wrong to—to do that . . . to do it against someone's will—"

She waited a moment before speaking, aware that what she was about to say might evoke another violent response. "But that's exactly what you were ready to do with me, isn't it? Here—tonight? And earlier—in the car. You, at the time—you didn't know how I'd feel about—about being fucked in an alley or in a parking lot. You didn't know. Worse—you thought you did, and that I'd—I'd hate it and, and somehow that—that turned you on. So . . . what are we talking about here? What's really going on?"

He sat in icy silence for a few minutes before responding. "You're right . . . It's what I said a few minutes ago . . . I'm a really bad person. I am."

"No—you're not. You're just—you're just human . . . Tell me something . . . tell me about the girls you've, you know—you dated in the past."

"I didn't *date* half of them . . . I just slept with them. They were all whores."

"All of them?" she echoed dully.

He shrugged in irritation. "Yes—in fact one was a *whore*, a *paid hooker*. The other one was a one night stand and . . . there was the horny artist and . . . and Jennifer."

"You're telling me that Jennifer was a whore—the girl you got pregnant was a whore," she said in disbelief.

"Yes . . ." he whispered sadly, staring into the distance. "The worst kind." As a wind gusted through the parking lot, he no longer saw cars or the occasional people coming and going from the lot.

The wind was blowing furiously, spinning snow particles from existing drifts into massive, almost blinding clouds. A snow storm was forecast. He knocked on her door, shaking but firm in his resolve.

Her mother answered, looking haggard as usual, greasy, graying strands of hair falling from a loose bun on the base of her neck, nearly tripping on the ties to her worn, sea foam green house robe as she shuffled across the worn carpet.

"You shouldn't be out on a night like tonight. And not with her father due home any minute. You know how he feels about you. Jennifer's in her room. Make it quick. I don't need any trouble around here tonight."

He nodded, heading down the hall, which reeked of cigarette smoke.

After knocking on the door once, he turned the handle and went inside. She looked up from her desk where she was working, smiling widely. "Alex—I didn't hear you come in."

"I—I can't stay long. Your father'll be home soon. But I—we need to talk." "About what?" she asked.

He took a seat on the edge of her bed. "I've . . . I've been doing a lot of thinking, lately. About us and all, and . . . I'm not sure about us anymore."

His hands shook as he watched her entire countenance fall.

"What do you mean?" she asked.

"I—I can't live like this anymore, Jen . . . I mean—I love you. You know I love you, but . . . I can't continue to live like this—"

"Like what?"

"Watching you stand by and get hurt. Watching you drink yourself to oblivion every weekend—throw yourself on other guys because you're too fucking drunk to remember you have a boyfriend. Do crazy things just to get attention—and almost get yourself killed. And, I know why you do it. I know what goes on around here—in this house. I'm not fucking blind. What do you think? I don't see how he looks at you—how he looks at me. I don't know where your bruises come from?

She shook her head vehemently. "You don't understand my father—nobody understands him. He cares about me deeply, that's his problem. He cares about me too deeply—"

"But that's bullshit—" he burst, standing up, pacing the room. "You're acting as if his behavior is normal—it isn't. Normal fathers don't beat their daughters. And they certainly don't sleep with them," he added spitefully, immediately regretting the words and the obvious pain they caused her.

"Fuck you . . ." she breathed. "What do you know about my life, my family—my feelings?"

He swallowed hard, wincing at the venom in her voice. "I'm—I'm sorry. Maybe you're right—maybe I don't understand. Look, I—I think we need a break, Jen . . . I came to tell you I think we need a break. I know I do."

She looked up, eyeing him cruelly. "Really?" she whispered.

He nodded.

She turned away from him slowly, saying nothing, putting her head in her hands. He thought he heard her start to cry as he began to leave.

"I'm pregnant—" she burst.

He froze in his tracks, his head spinning.

"I was going to tell you when we out for Valentine's . . . I'm sorry."

"How do you know?" he whispered loudly, his throat drying.

"I—I skipped my period—"

"So?" he burst, turning around, refusing to believe the news. "It could be a fluke—"

She shook her head. "I've been nauseous in the mornings . . . Sometimes even sick."

"How? How?"

She eyed him bitterly.

"But you said you were using protection—you said you were on the pill—"

"I lied."

Walking over to the bed, he collapsed into a seated position, speechless, burying his head in his arms. "Jesus, Jen . . . Jesus."

"Yeah, I tried him . . . He can't help us now."

After letting him sit quietly a moment, lost in his thoughts, Danielle turned to him, laying a hand lightly on his leg. "How am I different than any of them? You were obviously closest to Jennifer—how am I different from her?"

"You're nothing like her," he said, swallowing hard. "Nothing."

"Alex . . . I think I know what's wrong. And I don't think it has anything to do with your ability to remember the past. I think you remember the past quite well—whether you want to or not . . . I don't even think it has anything to do with your being shot. That was just an unfortunate side act. But it has everything to do with how you judge it. How you judge your past—your girlfriends, your friends, your actions, your—your town. And especially yourself. I mean, when you think of all those girls as whores—what are you really doing? What is it saying about you—you, who were somehow attracted to them. You—who, who wanted to be with them, date them, make love to them. Don't you see? Your calling them whores and thinking ill of them doesn't hurt them. But it's *killing* you. You think you did something wrong making love to them—you, you feel guilty, dirty—I don't know. And now, you can't make love to anyone. You see sex as an act of aggression, meanness. You see love as a sham. On some level, you saw them as harming you, and maybe they did. Maybe Jennifer really hurt you—betrayed you even. Maybe you don't even know if it was yours. She might have even lied about the pregnancy—girls do that sometimes. I don't know . . . But you've got to let it go. You're dragging your memories around with you like a ball and chain. For god's sake—you're manifesting ghosts, that—that even I can see now. Men in plaid shirts that want to kill you. Why?"

"I don't know how to stop it," he said suddenly. "It's too late . . . he's here, and he's going to kill me, I know it . . . and I don't know how to stop it."

She pulled one of his arms down from its crossed position and held his hand. "There's something I want to share with you about that morning after Homecoming . . . I haven't told anyone about it . . . I haven't really wanted to, but . . . but maybe it will help you. I met a strange priest at church, and he said . . . he said this is all just a dream. That we're all just dreaming our lives, our births and even our deaths. That none of this is real, even though we think it is because we can feel something with our hands or see something with our eyes. In reality, it's all being projected from our minds. We're, like, creating it. And we're believing the stories that we're spinning and making them real for ourselves. But because we're creating it, we can uncreate it. We can—we can just look at the world differently and—and it will then appear differently. You need to do that with your past, you know? Don't—don't look at Jennifer like that. Don't label her something—something so negative—and then freeze her in time."

"What about you—and your father . . . how do you rethink that? How do you change what that was?"

She sighed, shaking her head. "I don't know . . . I can't change what it was. I can't change what happened. For one, it's still happening. My father hates me. My—my mother doesn't like me much, either, I'm finding out. It's ironic, really . . . You don't know this, but—but Dennis and I didn't get along at all until just recently. He hated me—openly hated me. Told me he hated me—to my face. And I know why . . . I was horribly cruel to him at his worst time. When he was at his lowest point, I took advantage of the situation. Consciously, too. I shudder to look back on how completely selfish I was—how I had no regard for him or his feelings. Wasn't even thinking about that."

"What happened?"

"Something at school. I don't remember the details because—well, I just didn't care about my brother. He used to go to a private school, too, and was great friends with Tate, actually. He was an awesome baseball player, but I hated going to his games because they bored me, even though he came to my recitals. Anyway, he and Tate and their gang of cronies were, you know, troublemakers. Kind of like the cool kids at the school—popular, smart, good at sports but also good at getting into trouble. Well, I guess they pulled some stunt that was bad enough to get them expelled, but . . . but only Dennis got expelled. Tate let him take the fall for everyone . . . He tried to tell us he was framed, but . . . but we didn't really listen. I didn't even care. I just saw it as an opportunity to kiss my parents' asses and look even better in their eyes. To—to become the *favored* child . . . All I ever wanted was for them to think of me as number one. I lived for their approval. I did anything for it—even dating the enemy of my brother. Didn't give him a thought, really . . . And when it all came falling down—literally—around me, who was there? Who's still there . . . . My brother." She threw her hands up. "I mean—it's unreal. It's so unreal, it's almost laughable. I'm laughing. When I'm not crying, I'm laughing."

He smiled sadly, stroking her arm. "So—how are you? . . . What do you do now? How do you deal with it?"

She shrugged. "It's completely beyond my control—there's nothing I can do but wait. Just wait for them to change their minds again and—and remember they love me. They've obviously *forgotten* that I'm their *favorite* child," she said sarcastically.

He smiled sadly, and they sat quietly for a few minutes, watching as more cars began to clear out of the spaces.

"We should go," he said finally. "All this talk has completely shattered my sex drive. I just want to go to bed."

She punched him in the arm, only half jokingly.

"Ow . . . I can't help it, it has. I want nothing to do with women right now. Not you or any one. You're all exhausting."

She stuck her tongue out at him. "You're an asshole."

He giggled as she punched him again. "Ow—stop it."

She hit him again.

"Stop it—or I'm going to punch you back."

She hit him again, harder.

"I mean it, Danielle—that hurts. Cut it out—"

"You're such a dick," she burst, hitting him again, even harder.

He hit her arm in retaliation, just enough to make a statement.

She looked at him with a wide-eyed fury, a part of her angry but an even greater part truly hurt by his words and hoping he had been joking but fearing he had not.

He smirked, staring at her intently, satisfied he had finally touched a nerve. While the talk had exhausted him, what he didn't admit nor wanted to admit was that it made him feel better, at least for the moment. She was kneeling in front of him, poised as if she might haul off and swing again. Though chilly, it wasn't frigid, and her gray wool coat was unbuttoned, revealing the v-neck sweater and necklace of pearls.

"That is the ugliest necklace on you," he breathed.

As she swung furiously, he grabbed her arm and twisted it behind her back, pulling her body close with his other. "Stop," he whispered in her ear, and when she finally relaxed, he released her arm, pushed her hair away from her neck and unclasped the pearls. They slid down her sweater and into her lap.

Their eyes met briefly before he lunged, kissing her roughly and she responding with equal vehemence, both completely oblivious to their surroundings until the loud, grating sound of a car horn and cat calls from its passengers startled them.

Blushing and laughing, they helped each other up and headed down to the streets and shops below. He spent the remainder of the evening at her place, watching football games until his curfew, avoiding any intense physical contact other than a casual kiss.

That night, Alex dreamed he was in a hospital room, surrounded by people. The room was bright, and his vision was blurry. Jennifer . . . A tall man with a mustache whom he didn't recognize . . . A beautiful woman with long, wavy, golden-brown hair. Her face bent down to his, so close that he could now clearly see her face. She had petite features, bright blue eyes and a warm, sweet smile. She whispered in his ear.

Wake up.

He opened his eyes and sat up in bed, startled, breathing heavily, staring wildly at his surroundings and calming down once his eyesight adjusted to the dim light, and he saw the painted brick walls, desk chair and articles of clothing scattered about his floor.

CHAPTER NINE

The dream left him agitated and brought new meaning to the term Black Friday. Danielle had wanted to go shopping that morning, but he was intolerant of large crowds, which were unavoidable. They had finally retreated to their favorite coffee shop to meet Brooke and Dennis before heading to a movie, another act of futility, Alex thought, as the theaters were sure to be crowded. Danielle was displeased with her brother and Brooke's choice, *Mrs. Doubtfire*, instead wanting to see *The Piano*. Alex would have rather gone back to Danielle's place to watch football or make-out or even play music. Something about being in public unnerved him. He feared he could dissolve into the masses and simply vanish.

He sat with his arms crossed, tapping his leg nervously on the floor, his mind shifting consistently from the dream to the movie dilemma to Danielle's outfit. She had taken to wearing skirts lately, which he found arousing, but today she was wearing a short black skirt and thigh high stockings with a lacy, low-cut blouse underneath her unbuttoned wool coat. He had not even realized they were thigh highs until he had casually placed his hand on her leg and, expecting tights, felt skin. Though he quickly retracted his hand, it did little to stop the near instant hard-on it had created.

Completely oblivious to the sexual anxiety she had caused, Danielle assumed his irritation was in response to Brooke and Dennis now being more than twenty minutes late. The table at which they were seated was tiny, and while their bodies were not quite touching, they were close enough to each other for her to feel his tension.

"We can go without them," she said suddenly.

He shrugged.

"We don't have to go at all if you don't want to."

He mumbled something and looked away from her.

"Alex, what do you want to do? We don't have to see a movie. I know you're not excited about anything playing, anyway—"

He turned towards her, staring at her intently. *I want to fuck your brains out right now*, he thought but refrained from saying it aloud.

But she recognized the look and turned away, her face flushed. This was neither the time nor the place, she thought to herself. "Why don't we go back to my place and just—just hang out?"

He said nothing.

She changed the subject. "Isn't your birthday coming up?"

He said nothing.

"I thought you said it was in December sometime—"

"December fourth."

"Oh . . . that's next week."

"And you better the fuck not make a deal out of it . . . No gifts. I think it's completely retarded when people buy each other cheesy, schmaltzy gifts. So don't get me some fucking *meaningful* gift. Pack of smokes would be fine."

She blushed, feeling a mixture of mortification and anger at his response and fear over his souring mood. "Fine," she snapped back. "I won't be around on your birthday, anyway. My meditation and yoga classes start on December fourth. *How convenient.*"

He stared at her blankly.

"I'm kind of excited about them, actually," she said quickly, suddenly worried she had hurt his feelings. "You could come with me . . ."

"No," he responded vehemently.

She sighed, rolling her eyes. "Must you be so hasty in your judgment? It might be kind of interesting, you know. Something different—"

"I can think of nothing more miserable than sitting in a room staring at a wall for an hour."

"That's not all they do—"

"Yes it is. That's what meditation is—sitting cross legged for hours and hours . . . Forget it."

"It's supposed to help your concentration—and help you to relax."

"It sounds gay."

"What about the yoga?"

"What the hell *is* yoga?"

She blushed. "Um—it's kind of an exercise class. But it's supposed to help your mind and spirit, too. Kind of like a mind-body balance thing . . . People who take yoga supposedly also have better sex," she threw in playfully.

He eyed her darkly, smirking.

She reddened, turning away.

He leaned into her, whispering in her ear. "If they're not going to show, I say we go make our own movie."

A shudder shot through her lower body, as it always did at his touch. Just the feel of his breath against her skin, the light brush of his arm against hers, triggered every nerve in her being. She closed her eyes, sighing. "Alright . . . We can go back to my place."

"Maybe I can't wait that long," he said, gently taking her hand and moving it to his crotch.

"Jesus, Alex," she whispered.

"Let's do it here."

"You're crazy," she gasped, trying to suppress a nervous laugh. "We can't—it's a public place."

"Bathroom's not public . . ."

"I'm not doing it in a bathroom—" she whispered hoarsely, slapping him. "That's disgusting. The floors are disgusting. That's just . . ."

"Against the wall."

She burst out laughing. "Right—I've never even done it lying down, and you expect me to do it against a wall? I don't even know how that works—"

"I do."

She stared at him incredulously, "You've done it standing up—against a wall."

He sat back, musing in mock contemplation. "I don't know, actually. Maybe . . . Maybe not."

"You're crazy. You're completely insane."

He suddenly jumped up from his seat and held his hand out for her to take. "Try me."

She remained seated, shaking her head in utter disbelief but knowing she would do it. She would do anything he asked, and he was soon pulling her towards the rear of the coffee house, where there were two restrooms.

"We'll use the women's," he said, smirking, trying to ignore what he saw from the corner of his eye. A flash of red and white, accompanied by an overwhelming sense of dread.

The bathroom was occupied. She spent the next minute trying to keep her stimulation heightened and herself from laughing hysterically. He spent the minute in anxious anticipation, trying to avoid looking into the crowd, making a firm determination that he would defy the odds this time, as if overcoming his inability to perform had become a matter of life and death.

A middle-aged woman finally emerged, and when she had walked past them, Alex shoved Danielle in, following her, closing and locking the door behind him.

The bathroom was clean but small, painted garnet red with black and white tiled flooring. Had the tiles been zigzag-shaped instead of square, Danielle would have imagined they had entered Lynch's black lodge. To her relief, the light switch also activated an extremely loud fan, which would completely drown out any noise they might make.

Alex pushed her against one small portion of wall absent of décor or appliances, his lips hungrily meeting hers before moving down her neck to her breasts, his hands caressing, undressing and exploring previously uncharted territory.

And while she responded with equal passion, a part of her felt like a bystander, an observer staring dumbfounded at a scene that could possibly have been filmed for a B-rated movie, or worse. Wondering what had happened to her sense of propriety, her vision of romance, all the nights she had spent fantasizing about the man of her dreams. Their outings together always cultural—art shows, theater, symphony. Their make-out sessions sensual and in beautiful surroundings—well-furnished bedrooms or living rooms, gazebos in moonlit gardens, the soft sound of crickets in the distance, the air saturated with the scent of summer-blooming honeysuckle.

Never in her most unchecked dreams would she have conceived of a blood-red bathroom, stinking of piss and cleanser, with a fan so loud it made it nearly impossible to think, not that she wanted to at that moment. She was a participant in Alex's dream now, and she feared it would end the way they always ended—in pain, humiliation and confusion. Only when it was over—his hunger and rage satiated—could she gently lead him back to her realm, where they would watch television, discuss books and ideas, enjoy music and culture and just appreciate each other's company.

Alex noticed nothing of his surroundings, completely taken by her scent, the feel of her skin, especially her thighs, which he wrapped around his own, directing all his energy and focus towards taking her, entering her and losing himself within her body, and in doing so leaving behind whatever sludge he had been dragging with him from his past. Her body was a refuge, and while he tried to be gentle, sensuous, there were moments his hands probed in desperation, clawing their way to sanctuary. Though he could feel her jerk slightly at the discomfort, he could not stop—there was no time. He didn't brace himself for the pain of entry, fearing even a millisecond of hesitation would thwart his success. He had actually succeeded, pushing deep, deeper into her until the pain became so unbearable he simply slipped out, his body collapsing to the floor, utterly deflated.

Alex was so consumed with his own mental and physical pain, he didn't notice Danielle, didn't hear her own gasp of anguish at the moment of consummation, when she experienced a spasm so agonizing she struggled to catch her breath. Horrified, shaking, she was barely able to pull her panties up and her shirt closed before collapsing next to him. The spasms only intensified, and upon coughing up blood, her head began to spin and she feared she might faint, if not over the pain over the images that now flashed in her mind.

"Jesus, Dan—" Alex burst, momentarily forgetting his discomfort upon seeing her own. "Are you alright?"

She shook her head, coughing up another spatter of blood.

Without hesitating, he jumped up and went to the sink, hurriedly grabbing some paper towels, wetting a few of them before kneeling down next to her.

"Here . . . "

Shaking, she wiped her mouth and tried not to cry.

He put an arm around her. "I'm . . . I'm sorry," he said nervously, completely at a loss for words or even thoughts. "I- I don't know what happened . . . I don't understand . . ."

She groped around her for her purse, which had fallen to the floor in the tumult. "Can you . . . can you drive me home?"

He stared at the small black bag that she held out to him, her hands still trembling, her eyes refusing to meet his.

"What—are the keys in there?"

She nodded, her head still turned away.

He took it, reluctantly, and fumbled through it for a moment until he retrieved her key set. She was now using the wad of paper towels to stem a well of tears, and he knew they had little time to get themselves out of the public eye and to the car, which was at least a five minute walk. "Come on," he said, helping her up. Picking up her coat, which had at some point fallen to the floor, he helped her put it on and buttoned it. He then slipped the purse strap over her shoulder, took her hand and led her out of the room, ignoring the small line that had formed outside.

Though sunny, the day was bitter cold and windy, and they walked in a gray silence, her mind still reeling from the experience and his racing to figure out what happened. Did he have a disease? Did he somehow hurt her? Did she have a condition? The paranoia intensified as they approached the car and she was still avoiding his gaze.

As he adjusted the driver's seat, she completely broke down sobbing. He sighed loudly, burying his head in the steering wheel.

"I'm so sorry," she burst after a minute. "I'm so sorry for you . . . It's so awful."

He stared at her incredulously. "*What*?"

"The pain—your pain . . . that you go through, you know. Every time . . . I don't know how you can take it . . . it's so awful . . . it's so unfair."

"What are you talking about?"

She sniffed, dabbing her eyes with the now saturated paper towels, trying to collect herself before continuing. "Did you . . . did you have it this time? . . . I—I know you did. You don't have to answer."

"Have what?" he asked, exasperated.

"Your attack—did you have your attack?"

"Of course I had my attack—isn't that what always happens? It's—it's fucking inevitable."

"Well . . . I had it, too, this time. I felt it . . . I felt what you feel. . . And, I . . ." she stopped.

He shook his head protest. "That's impossible. That's—that's fucking impossible. Don't even talk like that . . ."

"I did," she countered vehemently. "Impossible or not—I felt it. I saw it. I—I—feel so bad for you . . . All this time, all these weeks . . . Here we're messing around, and—and you're just being tortured. I'm—I'm fine. Clueless . . . Well, not totally—but I had no idea they were that bad. If I'd have known . . ."

"What?"

But she just shook her head and ripped at the brown paper in her hands.

"Does it only happen with me?" she asked after a moment's silence.

He shook his head. "No . . . not just you."

"And the doctors said there's nothing wrong with you . . ."

"No . . . There's nothing wrong with me."

"But you told them the truth—right? You told them what was going on—"

"Yes, I told them. I didn't tell my parents the real reason, but . . ." He sighed, running his hand through his hair nervously. "Danielle, I . . . I would never hurt you . . . I never meant to hurt you, I swear," he said finally. "I don't understand—"

She gently laid a hand on his arm, finally looking at him. "Alex . . . I know. I'm not mad at you. I'm so, so sorry . . . I would do anything to stop this—anything for you. I would—I would leave you if it would help." She had barely gotten the words out before another onslaught of tears.

"Jesus, Dan . . . That's not going to do anything . . . Look, I—I don't even care about these attacks. I'm just—I'm just very sexually frustrated right now. The pent up frustration is far worse than the two or five minute attack, because it *fucking never ends*. I can't—I can't get any relief. And, I haven't had sex in . . . shit, I don't even really know . . . Since I got shot. And I probably didn't get much before then, either, not from what I remember . . . Other guys did, but not me . . ." he added bitterly.

Just then, he saw Dennis and Brooke through the passenger window, waving wildly and headed across the street, towards their car. "Shit . . ." he mumbled.

But before Danielle could figure out what was happening, Brooke was pounding on the window. Alex turned the key in the ignition, and Danielle reluctantly rolled it down.

"We are *so* sorry!" Brooke burst. "The traffic was a bitch," she started until noticing her friend's tear-streaked face. "What happened?"

"She saw a cat get hit by a car," Alex said quickly, unsure of where the thought even came from.

"Oh, dear god—that's not good. That is so not good—Jesus, where?" Brooke burst.

Alex gave her a look.

"*Right*—" she said quickly before spinning around and telling Dennis.

"Mother fuck," Dennis burst, sticking his head through the window. "Jesus Christ, Dan—are you okay? Of all the fucking things . . ."

"Maybe a comedy would be good for you—" Brooke offered.

But Danielle had buried her head in her hands, the lie touching a sore spot and making her feel even worse than she already did.

"No—Alex is screwed. You might as well just take her home and call it a day, dude. You have no idea . . ." Dennis said, walking around to the driver's side and motioning for Alex to roll down the window. "Say—I have a bag in my sock drawer, if you know what I mean. It's actually in a sock . . ." he whispered.

Alex sighed. "Excellent."

"Sure thing, dude."

When they had left, Danielle burst into a new fit of tears.

"What's wrong now?"

"Why did you say that?"

"What?" he asked, exasperated.

"About the cat . . . how did you know?"

"Know what? It just popped in my head—Jesus, what did you want me to tell them? The truth?"

"But my cat did get hit by a car," she cried. "Just a few months ago . . . Mr. Kitty," she sobbed.

Alex sighed, burying his head in the steering wheel again. He had never seen Danielle so emotional, and it unnerved him. He tried to think of a time when this had happened before but came up with nothing. His sister was the only female that continually tormented him with tears and ranting, and with her he found distance and silence to be the best remedy. Deciding on that tactic, he started the car and maneuvered out of their parallel parking space, a few minutes later turning on the radio.

She had calmed down by the time they reached the Trahan's house. Taking the key out of the ignition, he was about to get out of the car when she stopped him.

"Wait, I . . . I just want to be alone, if that's okay. You can have my car. You know . . . You can have it today. I won't be going anywhere . . ."

"What's wrong?" he asked, concerned. She had never wanted him to leave before.

She shrugged. "I don't know . . . I'm not really feeling very well right now. I'm sorry . . . I ruined our day."

"This isn't about the cat, is it?"

She laughed softly, "No, it's not about the cat . . ."

"Jesus . . . I swear I had no idea—you never told me about your cat."

"I know. It's okay—really. I'm okay, I just—I just want to take a nap."

"Alright . . . So, maybe I can stop by later tonight?"

She shrugged. "I don't know . . . Maybe. If I'm feeling better, maybe we can go out or something . . . How about just call me later, okay? Like, after dinner."

He leaned over and kissed her on the cheek, then watched her leave the car, his eyes following her to the door and lingering even after it had closed behind her. Feeling empty and restless, he drove around aimlessly, dreading going home. After stopping for more cigarettes, he decided to hang out at the park with the sky blue water tower and try to clear his head, which was spinning with a barrage of images and emotions.

It was late afternoon and there were only a few people at the tiny park, a mother with two bundled up toddlers and an elderly man walking a golden retriever. The park looked even more desolate with its near-barren trees. Alex stood outside the car, sitting casually on the hood of Danielle's silver Volvo coupe, smoking and taking in his surroundings, wondering how he had gotten to this strange point in his life, to this strange park and with a car that he had no business driving.

By the third cigarette, his nerves had calmed and he was able to reflect on the day, which from any outsider's perspective would be considered a complete train wreck, but for he and Danielle could be considered life as usual. What bothered him now was not even what transpired in the bathroom but what had happened afterward and what was continuing to happen, even as he stood smoking and trying to blink it from his mind.

Upon learning she had somehow shared his experience, instead of being mortified, which would have been a far more comfortable reaction, having grown accustomed to the shame he felt for much of the past year, he found himself almost obsessively thinking about it from her perspective. Trying to understand why she wasn't angry or mortified, herself, which was how he would have reacted had the experience been reversed. He doubted he would even stay with her, had their roles been reversed, which is why he didn't understand why she stayed with him. It was absolutely baffling and only became more so when he mentally switched roles.

Don't switch them.

The thought just manifested, as clear as if someone had been standing behind him and spoken them aloud. So clear, that he physically turned around to scan the park and ensure there wasn't anyone present.

"Yeah, right . . ." he mumbled, exhaling, then pondering what that meant. On his fifth cigarette, while walking through the vast forest of his mind, he stumbled upon a rough path of thoughts. By merely switching bodies and situations, he was still seeing things from his perspective, through his mental filter. He could switch bodies all day long, and it would change nothing. It was like *Freaky Friday*, when the parent and child simply switched bodies but kept everything else—their own thoughts, fears, wants, mental baggage—so that even though the parent became the child and the child the parent, nothing really changed, regardless of whatever sentimental message the movie tried to beat into the viewer.

Danielle saw the world completely differently than he did. Everything they experienced together was seen differently. Other than attempting to share each other's bodies, they shared nothing. Such was the lonely way of the world. At least, his world, he thought sadly.

An hour had passed, but the day was still too young to give up on it and head home. Suddenly, every part of his being wanted to do the opposite of what she had asked.

Crushing the cigarette butt with his shoe, he climbed back into the car and headed back to her place.

∞

As Danielle walked from the car to the house, she struggled to keep from crying, fearful she would encounter an adult Trahan prior to making it to her room, one who would ask her what was wrong and pump her for information until she spilled—no less vomited—her guts all over the antique Persian rugs that graced their hall floors.

By the time she hit the shower, the sobs had started, uncontrollable heaving sobs that left her gasping for air. She had hoped the steaming water would help to wash away not only the physical impurities which had streamed down and caked to her inner thighs and legs but also the psychological stains of her first time being so completely absent of privacy, warmth and any sense of intimacy, let alone love, a word she was beginning to loathe as much as Alex apparently did.

She wasn't even sure which was worse, her shame at feeling used or her overwhelming sense of sadness and desperation at having had a glimpse of his world, of having seen what he had forgotten as clearly as if she were watching it on screen, larger than life. The tiny cramped store, its shelves stocked with outdated items, smelling of smoke and fuel. The blond, dimpled girl at the counter, who bore a striking resemblance to Kelly, giggling. The jingling of the bell as it opened, and the chaos that ensued moments later.

Watching the bullets strike him, almost in slow motion, and then seeing him lay bleeding and half-dead on the floor was by far more horrifying than anything that had transpired that day, it was so vivid. It felt so real, as did the accompanying pain—not just his but her own at the idea that she could have lost him, that he could be gone.

After quickly washing her hair and skin, she sat on the shower floor, huddled in a ball, until the hot water turned tepid and she was forced to leave the protective box, clammy and shivering. After combing the wet knots from her long hair, she put on some sweats and headed straight to bed, pulling the down comforter over her head, hoping it would, like a final curtain, stop the raging mental stage show. It didn't, but she was out of tears and now could only lay in a fetal position, shaking and unable to find warmth or comfort, wondering if he would even call her later that evening, or tomorrow or ever. Wondering why she had sent him away when she needed him now more than ever.

She had finally started to fall into a fitful sleep when the knob to her room turned. At the sound, her eyes fluttered open, and her body jerked nervously. She prayed whoever it was would see she was sleeping and leave her alone.

The door closed, but the person remained in the room. She could hear the footsteps and sense their presence. Though the sounds were muffled, it sounded as if they were rifling through something, and all she could imagine was her brother had snuck in needing cash, having already spent his allowance. Annoyed at this possibility, her ensuing thoughts so distracted her that she was completely unprepared for what happened next and didn't notice him until the covers were momentarily yanked skyward as his body bounded next to hers, slowly drifting back down as she was pulled next to him.

"Jesus, you're an ice cube . . ." he breathed.

She embraced him as swiftly as he did her, so relieved was she to see him, to feel his living body. "You came back," she whispered. "Why?"

He sighed, lying on his back and holding her close to his chest. "I don't know . . . The thought just popped into my head . . . that's been happening a lot today," he said, grinning.

"I'm so glad you did."

When they awoke, it was dark outside, and Danielle groped for the clock radio, which read seven thirty.

"No wonder I'm starving . . . Do you have anything to eat around here?" he asked, sitting up and stretching.

"I don't know . . . We can go out."

He groaned. "Do we have to?"

"We can go to the Thai restaurant . . . You know, the one in Mission."

"Yeah, we and a hundred other people. I honestly can't wait that long."

"That place is never *that* crowded."

"Tonight it will be," he said adamantly, pulling on his jeans. "I promise you. Tonight, there will be at least an hour wait."

She shook her head. "It's a holiday . . ."

"Exactly. Jesus, Dan—there were more people at the mall today than the entire town of Polson . . . I can't do it . . . I can't handle these crowds. I'm just not used to it. I need food *now*."

She sighed dramatically. "It's not my house."

"What?"

"It's not my house, Alex—and I don't feel comfortable scrounging around for food, okay?"

"But you *live* here. How do you eat?" he asked, incredulously.

"When I'm invited, I eat dinner with them, otherwise . . . ."

"Otherwise *what*?"

She threw her hands up impatiently. "I don't know—I store some snacks up here but usually just go out and get myself some food."

"Well do you have any snacks up here now?"

She shook her head. "Dennis took them. He does that. He doesn't . . . he doesn't entirely feel comfortable here, either. It's hard—I can't explain. I just—I just feel like a house guest, you know? I'm—I'm embarrassed to go into their kitchen and get food as if it's my kitchen because it's not. They're not my family."

He sat on the edge of the bed, shaking his head. "No—I don't get it. I mean—you see this room as yours, so—how come the kitchen can't be an extension of that."

"I'm paying for the room. I mean . . . my mother's paying for the room, so . . . I feel. . . I feel okay with the room, I guess."

"Well, I'm going to pass out if I don't eat something," he said finally.

"Oh, my god—fine! I will go downstairs and find something to tie you over until we get to the restaurant."

He grinned, and as annoyed as she was and wanted him to think she was, she had a soft spot for his smiles and couldn't help but smirk back, sticking her tongue out at him in the process. The adult Trahans were in the family room watching television, far enough away from the kitchen for her to tiptoe in, grab an apple and two slices of bread, and leave unnoticed.

She presented the goods to Alex, who looked displeased. "This is the best you could do?"

"What did you want?" she asked, exasperated.

"Something to drink, for one . . . and—and it's the fucking day after Thanksgiving, and all you could find was an apple and two slices of white bread? With nothing on it? No—no peanut butter. Or, hell—just butter would be fine."

"Are you, like, being an asshole on purpose?"

"No—I'm not. I'm being fucking serious. This is not what I had in mind."

"Oh my god . . . I can't believe you."

"I want to eat here. I don't want to go out," he said firmly, crossing his arms and giving her an intently serious look.

She sighed, momentarily disarmed, trying to decide which was more painful—the thought of going out into the bitter cold to fight a potentially crowded restaurant or going downstairs and asking Mrs. Trahan for some Thanksgiving leftovers.

"Fine," she said, dropping the goods in his lap and leaving the room.

With nervous trepidation, she crept back downstairs to the family room, holding her breath before crossing the threshold. Mr. Trahan was in a large brown leather recliner, watching football, and Mrs. Trahan was seated on the matching leather sofa, flipping through a catalogue. She looked up as Danielle entered the room and smiled widely.

"Well, Miss Danielle, what a nice surprise! We thought you were out running around with your brother and our daughter. What brings you home so early?"

She shrugged, nervously, "I'm not feeling so hot. I mean, we're not—Alex and I. We just want to hang out and watch football upstairs, if that's okay. In fact, I was wondering if I could maybe make a sandwich or something. If you had any leftovers . . ."

At this, Mrs. Trahan burst into a steady stream of talk, expressing her incredulousness over Danielle having to ask permission to get food all the way into the kitchen and halfway into helping her prepare the food. Danielle was family and didn't have to ask for anything, let alone food. She could use the kitchen whenever she wanted and was then given a small tour of where everything in the kitchen was located.

"Danielle, you're like another daughter to me, and now that your brother is moving out next week, maybe we should start planning some girl's nights or something—just you, Brooke and me," she prattled, assembling plates and drinks on a tray for Danielle to bring up to the room.

The statement left a mental blow that stopped Danielle mid-gesture, the flatware she was about to place on the tray hovering slightly above it.

"Moving out," she repeated dully.

"Why, yes—next weekend. I thought—I thought you knew. He didn't tell you?"

She shook her head. "Where?" she asked hoarsely, bracing herself for the answer.

"Well, back with your father. It's probably for the best, you know."

Danielle breathed a sigh of relief. "Yeah . . . Right—sure. So . . . So not with mom?"

"Oh, no . . . your mother needs time to get back on her feet, you know. She's asked that you stay indefinitely—possibly through the end of high school, which is absolutely fine with us."

"What about the summer?"

"Of course you're staying here in the summer," Mrs. Trahan responded, misunderstanding the implication. "Danielle," she said, stopping what she was doing and facing Danielle directly. "This is your home, now, and we want you to feel a part of it. I mean that. I know it's not been easy on you. In fact, I'm—I'm amazed at your poise throughout this entire incident, but I'm also worried. It's not natural for people—especially ones as young as you—to be so calm and controlled. I guess what I'm trying to say is . . . Well, Mr. Trahan and I are here for you if you need us, okay? And not just for food," she said, winking. "We're here for you as parents. Think of us as adopted parents. At least try."

Danielle nodded, swallowing hard, unsure of what to say in response.

"Good girl . . . Would you like some help with that?"

Danielle shook her head, lifting the tray from the counter as Mrs. Trahan headed out of the room.

"Mrs. Trahan," she called after her. "Thank you. For—for everything."

She waved Danielle off with a smile and a mutter.

When she got back to the room, Alex was seated in the arm chair, watching football, and a fire was burning in the fireplace for the first time since she had inhabited the room.

"How did you do that?" she asked quizzically.

"Do what?" he asked, jumping up to help her.

"That," she said, pointing to the fireplace.

"It's fake . . . There's a switch on the wall . . . Really backbreaking getting it going," he said, winking and taking the tray from her. Using the ottoman as a dining table, they both sat on the floor and ate in silence, letting the football commentators fill the void.

When they had finished and during a commercial break, Danielle felt the need to talk.

"Dennis is moving out next week," she said flatly. They were seated side-by-side on the rug, now using the ottoman as a chair-back.

Alex looked at her.

"Mrs. Trahan told me earlier . . . He's moving back in with our dad."

"*What*?"

"Yeah—it's okay, though. I knew they had been talking—visiting, even. I'm okay with it, really . . . I'm relieved, actually, if you can believe it."

Alex shook his head, confused.

"Yeah . . . I am. I know this sounds strange, but . . . but if he had been moving in with mom, I would be devastated. But since it's with dad, I . . . I don't care."

"Where *is* your mother, anyway?"

"Still in Italy . . . The good news is I'm going to be here for awhile. Through the end of high school, actually. According to Mrs. Trahan . . . According to Mrs. Trahan, this is my home now. This is my family."

"What about spending the summer in Italy?"

She shook her head, staring blankly at the moving images on the television screen.

"I thought you wanted to spend the summer in Italy—"

"It doesn't matter what I want," she burst angrily, then regretted it. "Sorry . . . I'm sorry. I just . . . I just don't understand why my mother left us. Left me. She left *me*, okay? She doesn't—she doesn't love me, anymore, and I don't know what I did . . . I didn't do anything . . . and I'm just . . . .I'm relieved because if she had asked for Dennis to live with her and not me, I . . . I don't know. I'd have had a real hard time with that. Harder than I am now, and I don't know why . . ."

Alex sighed, wanting to provide Danielle with an explanation but not wanting to hurt her with it. "It's not that your mother doesn't love you . . . I'm sure she does," he added, not because he believed it but only to soften the blow. "It's because she's in competition with you."

Danielle looked at him curiously.

"You . . ." he started, searching the for the right words. "You're competition to her. She's—she's looking for another man to start a life with, and . . . She doesn't want you around. I mean, you're a younger version of herself."

Danielle drew back, frowning. "That's—that's crazy. That's insane. What are you talking about? She's my mother."

"You asked," he said, turning back to the television.

"How do you know? You've never even met my mother," she said.

"I don't need to meet her . . . I've been with enough women in my life to just know these things . . . Once she meets her guy, she'll call you and be all mother-mother again . . ." But looking at Danielle he realized that even then, Danielle would be a threat. Perhaps a bigger one.

Danielle's countenance fell as she wrapped her head around the implication. "No, she won't . . . If what you say is true, she'll never be my mother again. Why would she? How could you say such a thing? How can you think it? That's a horrible thing to say . . ."

"But it's the truth."

Danielle buried her head in her knees, and Alex feared she would start crying. To his great relief, she didn't, but instead launched into a ten minute incessant chatter about the precariousness of her future, a direction Alex did not seeing coming at all, only confirming the gulf between their respective worlds. Somehow, instead of convincing Danielle that her mother loved her but was subconsciously jealous and self-serving, he had triggered a fear that she would be abandoned not only physically but also financially, homeless and on the streets, having to scrape her way through college if she even made it there.

As if talking to herself, she not only planned the next six months of her life, starting with looking for a job tomorrow, but also the next six years, including changing her college major from music and French to something practical, like business or law. By the time she had gotten to worrying about his future, he had tuned her out and resumed watching the game.

"I'm serious, Alex," she continued, grabbing his arm.

"What?"

"What are you going to do with your life?"

He stared at her in disbelief. "*Are you kidding me?*"

"No, I'm not . . . I mean, we've never talked about this. We've never talked about the future—ever. I don't even know what you want to do career-wise."

"Neither do I—which is why we never talk about it."

"Well—you're going to go to college, right? I mean—we're juniors. Haven't you put together your list? I put mine together over the summer, but now I have to rethink the entire thing. Oh, my god."

He rolled his eyes.

"So—where are you going? Maybe I can get some ideas."

"I'm probably not even going to college, Danielle . . . I'm too stupid. Trisha's the smart one."

"What are you talking about? You're not stupid—"

"Do you know my grade point average, Danielle? Do you? Did you ever bother to ask?"

She stared at him with wide-eyed anticipation.

He leaned towards her. "2.1."

Her brows immediately furrowed.

"Yeah . . . Now you're getting the picture. Now you see why I don't talk about the future . . . I don't have one."

She slunk into silence, afraid she had offended him and fearful she would only dig herself into a deeper hole, but even more fearful of the implications of his comment, especially after her vision that afternoon.

"I'm sorry . . ." she whispered after a few minutes of tense silence. "But I don't believe you . . . You have a future. Everyone does."

"Maybe . . . But I don't like to think about it, okay? In fact, I prefer not to think *at all* half the time. It gives me a headache. I don't know how you do it."

"What?"

"Go on and on and on . . . Your mind, it's just . . . It's exhausting. I'm exhausted . . . I slept half the day, and I'm suddenly ready for another nap. The game's not even over," he said, gesturing at the television.

"Sorry . . . Do you need an aspirin?"

"Not yet," he said, glaring at her.

She knew the look and shrunk away from him. While he enjoyed casual conversation, he preferred activity, and lengthy diatribes often put him in a foul mood. After a few minutes of quiet and once the tension between them waned, she quietly picked up the plates and cups and brought the tray downstairs. During the tour of the kitchen, she had noticed two pumpkin pies in the refrigerator and, after putting the dishes in the washer, decided to apologize to Alex with more gifts of food.

It worked, though he teasingly hinted at wanting a cup of coffee to go with the pie, which she promptly ignored.

"Well then, I may just have to go buy some coffee myself. I'm sure the convenience store has a pot brewing . . . twenty-four seven," he moved to get up.

"No," she burst. "Don't go—I'll go," she said, grabbing him.

He frowned, taken aback by the panic. "I'm just—I'm just kidding."

"Really?"

"Yes—Jesus, what's wrong with you?"

"If you want coffee—I'll go get it. Just let me do it, okay? Let me go get it."

"I don't want it *that* badly . . . I was just joking around with you . . . I was just going to go downstairs and get some milk. Okay? Do you want anything?"

She shook her head but then stopped him. "Don't—I'll get it for you."

"No you won't," he said, grabbing her by the shoulders and physically moving her to the chair. "You're a mess," he said, pushing her to a seated position. "Just—just sit down and calm down and, and . . . . I don't know, enjoy the fire. Quite frankly, the last thing you need is coffee . . . Jesus, you're spastic enough tonight . . . I'm going to get some milk . . ." he said, heading out the door. "I might even warm yours in the microwave."

Alex had spent enough time at the Trahan house the past few weeks to feel comfortable getting a drink from the tap or refrigerator. As he headed downstairs, his mind was split between accomplishing the task at hand and worrying about Danielle. Once again, he tried to put himself in her shoes, this time in an attempt to understand her family drama, which he felt was the reason behind her sudden mood swing. And this time, as he consciously ventured into her world, he caught a glimpse of what she saw and felt and was devastated.

When he returned to the room a few minutes later, glasses in hand, she was seated exactly where he had left her, at the edge of the arm chair, staring blankly into the fire, not looking up as he crossed the threshold. He studied her a moment, taken by her beauty which almost pained him at times, as in his mind he had still never met someone as intensely stunning as her, who even tonight, in sweats and no make-up, made him ache with desire. He deliberately averted his eyes as they traveled down her long tresses that tonight spilled over her shoulders in loose waves, down to her exposed chest and to the thin, low-cut white camisole that clung to her skin, perfectly outlining her breasts and causing the beginnings of a hard-on.

Normally, he would have pursued this initial desire, not thinking twice about pulling her down from the chair and to the floor, in front of the fire, undressing her, hungrily exploring every inch of her body with his mouth and hands and once again attempting to take her, for more than anything, that was what he wanted to do. But he knew it would end in disaster and even more, he knew that was not what she wanted or needed right now.

He handed her the glass of milk, but she shook her head, motioning for him to set it aside.

"I'm not thirsty, thank you."

Setting both drinks down, he quietly picked up the remote and turned off the television. Positioning the ottoman in front of the fireplace, he grabbed a blanket and made a spot for them in front of the fire. Sitting down, he motioned for her to join him, and they were soon seated next to each other against the ottoman, the blanket draped lightly across their laps, staring into the fake flames.

She rested her head on his shoulder.

"I know you want to talk," he said finally.

"But you don't want to listen," she replied quietly. "I don't blame you . . . I annoy myself, even."

He sighed, putting an arm around her.

"Danielle, this weekend has been a complete and utter disaster," he said softly. "And I haven't been there for you—at all. I've been a terrible boyfriend . . . and an even worse friend. I'm sorry."

She frowned, looking at him in disbelief, completely caught off guard. Before she could protest, he stopped her.

"Don't—don't talk right now. You can talk in a minute. In fact, you can talk for the next two hours, but let me say this . . . It's Thanksgiving weekend, and I haven't once—not once—thought about what this weekend might be like for you. How you might feel not being with your family for the first time. Being with strangers. I haven't thought about your feelings at all . . . Because I've been way too consumed with my own. All I think about is what I want. And all I seem to want is your body . . . That's what I think about most of the time . . . Sex—with you. . . Food. Football. Rock 'n roll . . . And pretty much in that order . . . It's awful, but it's the truth . . . It's who I am . . . And I'm not—I'm not sitting here telling you I'm going to change. I don't even think it's possible—that I *can* change. I'm just—we just . . . We made a promise to be friends first, so . . . For once, I'm . . . . I'm going to try to be your friend and—and do what *you* want. And, I think tonight you want to talk. You need to talk, and you need a friend to listen. So that's what I'm going to do."

She smiled sadly. "I think a lot about it, too, you know . . . Sex. . . I want it as badly as you do, actually, but . . . We can't. It's horrible . . . It's cruel . . . And I can't help but think it's me. That somehow, it's me—and, and—if you were with someone else, it wouldn't be happening."

"Dan, I can't even *masturbate*. Okay? I can't—I can't do anything. And it started before I ever met you . . . The question is, would *you* be better off with someone else. Maybe that's what we should start talking about."

She turned to him, almost angry, "No. Absolutely not. You're the only person . . . You're the only person I want to be with. That—that I have been with . . . I think . . . Even if it was only for a few seconds . . . We'll just have to wait and see. We can wait and . . . and try again in a few weeks. Or something."

He rolled his eyes. "You're willing to try again?"

She nodded. "But—but in my bedroom this time. Just in case . . . you know?"

He sighed. Even casually thinking about trying it again—and in that very room—gave him a hard on, and he shifted is body to compensate.

"There is something I want to talk to you about," she said after a few moments. "But I . . . I don't think you'll like it . . . That you'll want to talk about it . . . You haven't before."

He mentally braced himself after verbally giving her the okay, along with a promise he wouldn't get angry.

"I—I saw something today . . . when we were, you know . . . physically together for . . . however long that was . . . a few seconds. Before . . . before the pain and all, I saw—I saw what happened to you. You know, this past winter . . . the, the incident. But . . . but it doesn't match what you say happened."

He groaned, burying his head in his knees. "Yes, well," he said finally, "It doesn't match, because you weren't there. You saw nothing—"

"No, I did—I saw it. The—the store—it was an old store, everything old and kind of worn. And, and the girl at the counter—Jennifer—it was on her nametag. And, and the man in the plaid shirt. I saw him—I saw his face. And the gun—and, and you."

"Did you see it as a participant or a bystander?" Alex asked wryly, pretending to play along.

"Both, I think . . . Mostly as a bystander, but not all . . ." she mumbled, remembering being a participant while talking to the girl, which is why she could see the nametag so clearly, but an observer of the violence. "You never told me what happened . . . I know you don't want to talk about it, but . . . do you even remember?"

"Oh my god, I need a cigarette," he said, throwing his head back.

She sighed, and he could hear the disappointment.

"Seriously, Danielle—I'll fucking talk about it, but I need a cigarette. Or alcohol. Something, for god's sake . . . A cigarette. Get me a smoke," he said, motioning to his coat, which was hanging on one of the bed posts.

"We can't smoke in here—house rules."

"Jesus . . ." He ran his hand nervously through his hair.

"I can . . . I can go find you a drink. I—I know where they're at," she moved to get up, but he stopped her, pulling her back down next to him.

"No . . . No, I'll . . . I'll be fine. Jesus . . . Let me just sit here a minute . . . Christ . . . I don't even know where to start. Where do you want me to start?"

"Where it happened . . ." she suggested meekly.

"At her house, okay?" he burst. "It happened at her house . . . Jesus Christ. . ."

"I need to talk to you about something. Something important." He walked out of the kitchen to find his coat and retrieve the papers. "I want to go over these with you. I mean, you can't – you can't exactly sign these now, because a social worker and an attorney need to be present, but . . . I want you to promise me you will. Monday morning."

She giggled, rolling her eyes. "Papers schmapers . . . I thought we were going to spend an evening together—"

"We are, I just—I just want your word, okay? You're going to start showing soon, and . . . And I don't want your father going postal, that's all . . . You need to get out of here, you know this."

She threw her hands in the air. "I suppose. I still don't understand all this fuss. I don't even think I'm pregnant anymore," she said, a twinkle in her eye.

He stopped, trying to curb a sudden feeling of elation that his intellect told him was premature. "How—what—what do you mean?"

"I think it's gone . . . I started having periods again."

"You—you what? You've been bleeding and you didn't call the doctor? Jennifer—there could be something wrong with you—that's not normal—"

She shrugged. "You can still show me the papers, though . . . Why don't we go to my room where it's more—private," she said suggestively, approaching him, placing her hands on his chest.

He sighed, overcome with conflicting emotions, a part of him wishing desperately that what she said was true. Wanting desperately to have his life back. He wanted to have fun again.

Sitting on the edge of the bed, he sorted through the papers, trying to remember his mom's instructions. When he looked up to start talking to her about them, his mouth dropped open. She had removed her clothes and stood before him in a black, lacy teddy.

"How do I look?" she whispered, walking towards him.

He swallowed hard, clearing his throat. She looked stunning, her stomach still relatively flat. He had forgotten how attractive she was. He had forgotten how beautiful her body was. "Um—you look, you look beautiful . . ." he whispered, physically stirred by her vision.

"Don't you want to make love to me?" she asked, walking up to him, into his outstretched arms.

He stood up, pressing her body against his. They began to kiss. She began unbuttoning his shirt.

The sound of a car pulling up to the drive made him jump back, startled. "What was that?"

She groaned, pulling him back to her, kissing his ear, his neck. "It's nothing . . ."

Heart pounding, he found it hard to concentrate on her. It sounded like a car. He could have sworn he heard a car—

Upon hearing a loud rattling noise and then a slam as the front door swung open against the wall, both jumped back from each other.

"Jenny . . . Jennifer, goddam you little whore . . . Where is he—I told you I never wanted to see that son of a bitch again, goddamit . . . Jenny—"

The loud voice bellowed through the halls and vents. Alex began to panic. "Jesus—get dressed. Hurry, shit . . ." he breathed, buttoning his shirt as she frantically began pulling her jeans up.

"Sweet Jesus . . ." she whispered. "I'll sign the papers—I'll sign them tomorrow, baby or no baby—"

Footsteps thudded down the hall. He ran over to her just as she zipped her pants, throwing her blouse around her bare shoulders. Loud banging sounded on her bedroom door, shaking the walls.

"Jenny—open up, goddamit. I know he's in there. I know what you're doing, you devil's wench—"

She had just pulled her arms through her shirt when the door swung open. Alex wrapped his arm protectively around her, pulling her next to him—

He would never forget what happened next, time having frozen, the entire scene moving forward in slow motion. Even the echoes of voices and screams sounded sluggish, like a warped tape recording.

His figure loomed in the doorway, reeking of alcohol and smoke that could be sensed from across the room, screaming obscenities at them before raising the rifle barrel and pointing it straight at them. Neither could move, though he remembered raising his arm to protect her as the trigger clicked, covering her chest, turning his body to shield hers—

He winced as blood splattered across his face, the first bullet having ripped through her forehead, her body slipping through his arms, slumping lifeless to the floor. No—he screamed, maybe just in his mind. His mind was screaming. He spun around just as a bullet tore through his side. He clutched his side, stumbling against the wall. Within milliseconds, another seared through his upper chest. A third through his left shoulder.

Almost pinned against the wall, his hands tried to cover the wounds, tried to catch the pools of blood that began streaming from his person.

The gun fell to the floor with a thud. The man turned and started to walk down the hall.

He wasn't sure what possessed him. Some crazed instinct. Some internal, lethal rage that jolted through his person. Yelling wildly, he pushed himself up from the wall, stumbling towards the gun. Picking it up, he charged through the doorway and started down the hall, stopping suddenly as the figure loomed just a few feet ahead of him. Brushing the blood from his eyes, Alex raised the rifle.

"You son of a bitch—" he cried, releasing the trigger.

The figure fell backwards. Alex stood breathless, shaking violently. Suddenly feeling the searing pain of his wounds, and a chill. A cold chill . . . The room began to spin, and he knew he had little time . . . Jennifer . . . He must get to Jennifer—

But she was dead. He knew this, even if his heart and soul refused to accept it. And he would soon be joining her . . .

That was the movie he watched in his mind and tried to describe dispassionately and without detail. Just the facts, enough to explain to Danielle what had happened and prove her own vision wrong. When he had finished, she sat, having moved apart from him during the discourse, her arms wrapped protectively around her knees, her body shuddering.

"I'm . . . I'm so sorry . . . I don't understand," she said.

"That's because there's nothing *to* understand . . . Don't even try. Just forget it."

"But . . . but why did I see something different?"

"Because *you weren't there*," he said vehemently. "You saw nothing . . . Or maybe the future," he laughed bitterly. "Yeah—maybe you saw my future. Maybe I didn't really kill the bastard, and he's out there waiting to hunt me down."

"Don't say such a thing," she burst, before bursting into tears. "It's horrible . . . It's worse than death, losing you . . . I don't want to lose you . . . not like that . . . not like that."

"Oh, for god's sake," he mumbled, pulling her close to him and trying to calm her down. "I'm, I'm sorry . . . I was just . . . I was just being, I don't know . . . Stupid . . . He's dead. I promise."

"I know he is," she said quietly. "But you didn't kill him . . . Somebody else did . . . You think you did, but you didn't . . . There was another man there . . . Tall . . . with a mustache. It had to be him . . . There was nobody else in the store."

He was about to protest but stopped, realizing that contradicting her was an act of futility. She would believe what she wanted to believe, regardless of how utterly delusional it was.

"Did you love her?" she asked after a few moments of silence.

He sighed irritably. "No . . . I mean, I tried . . . Maybe, I did. . . I don't know. Why? Is that important to you? Is that what you want to *talk* about now?"

She shook her head. "Not really . . . I'm just curious . . . I don't think she's dead."

"*What?*"

"Only you got shot . . . I saw it . . . You got shot and then somebody shot the guy in the plaid shirt . . . Probably the man with the mustache."

"Danielle, *are you high?*" he burst, pulling away from her. "Seriously—I know your brother stashes weed here. Did he, like, spike your Cheerios today?"

But she just looked at him oddly, as if she didn't even really see him, as if she were seeing through him. "What if she's alive? What if it didn't happen the way you remember it? Do you still love her? Would you?"

He looked away, unnerved by her stare but even more so at the suggestion that triggered a disruptive stream of thoughts. "I don't know . . . No," he said finally. "No—I don't. I don't love her. I—I love you," he said, immediately regretting it, wincing as the words left his mind and became heard.

She stared at him curiously. "Really?"

"No . . . I don't. You know what I mean. I fucking hate that word. I mean, I *like* you. I want to be with you, not her. I don't . . . I don't want to go back there."

"How did you even meet her?" she pressed.

"God, Danielle—this is torture. This is actually worse than my attacks, if you can believe it . . . I'm not kidding. I can't—I can't do this. Please stop. Please."

She looked down at the floor, pursing her lips. "Tell me how you met her . . . how you came to love her . . . and I'll stop," she said quietly. "I promise . . . I won't bring it up again."

"Yeah . . . Right . . . Okay, well . . . I met her at a party. I had . . ." He abruptly halted, settling back against the ottoman, closing his eyes and trying to calm his nerves and organize his fractured thoughts. At the moment he had started speaking, he realized he did not remember clearly. He could not remember the story and had to piece it together, from the beginning. There was a reason he and Jennifer connected that had started before Jennifer.

"I—I think I told you—about my past . . . the girls I dated in my past. Well, didn't date, actually. The girls I *fucked* in my past . . . starting with the hooker . . . Look, I—I lost my virginity with a hooker, okay? I was like . . . fifteen. It was my birthday . . . Anyway, after that, I just slept around with girls, you know? I didn't want a relationship . . . I just wanted to fuck. And, that summer, I—I hooked up with a college girl from Missoula, and, you know . . . we basically smoked pot and had sex. She liked me because I was younger and . . . what'd she say . . . I was *safe*. She thought I was *safe*. She was a hippy artist type just hanging out and waiting to go to Europe. Italy, ironically. She wanted to live in Italy and was working that summer to make enough money to travel there for a semester. And after she left, she sent me one postcard from Venice, and I never heard from her again. And I . . . I missed her. I missed what we had . . . as empty and shallow as it was, it was stable. Like, it was a routine. We had a routine together. And after that I didn't want to just go fuck around anymore with just anyone, you know. I wanted to find a routine with someone . . . So, school had just started and, I don't know . . . I was at some big back-to-school party and, had a bit too much to drink and . . . hooked up with Jennifer . . . Jennifer Hicks . . . We just, connected . . . I don't know—we just did on, on some level. And I . . . I asked her on a date. My first proper date. To the movies . . . My first proper date was with Jennifer. We saw *The Unforgiven*. And . . . and started having sex a week later."

"That was last year?"

He nodded.

"But, but how's that possible. You were shot on New Year's Eve—"

He raised an eyebrow. "*No* . . . I was shot in February . . . late February. Can I finish? Or would you like to tell me what happens next."

She blushed and fell quiet.

"Okay, so you were asking how I came to love her. Right? Isn't that how this whole agonizing conversation got started? Well, I came to love her trying to be a proper boyfriend, okay? You know—doing what we're doing now. Talking . . . getting to know each other . . . meeting the family. I mean, you think your family's messed up . . . Jesus, the Hicks . . . She was . . . She was physically and sexually abused by her father, who was a drunk . . . And her mother . . . She was . . . She was a religious freak, you know? God, I'm so glad my parents aren't religious . . . Jesus . . . Anyway, I digress . . . of course, I discover this weeks into the relationship and in the process of trying to find out why my girlfriend, who I was completely committed to, was behaving like such a slut. I mean, people—my friends, I guess, I don't really remember all that clearly—were telling me she was wild and dangerous and sleeping around on the side, even, but . . . I—I didn't believe them. I didn't want to believe them until she—she started getting wild with me, you know? Like—wanting to have sex in crazy places."

Danielle tried to suppress a smirk, but he caught it.

"Laugh all you want—today was nothing. We were in a locked room. She didn't like locks—she wanted to do it in a stall, whether or not there was a door on the stall, let alone a lock. In cars—in my parents' bed—in, in her parents' bed—and with her fucking crazy father in the next room . . . She was completely out of control."

He stopped for a few moments, staring into the fire, imagining himself throwing each memory he voiced into the flames, hoping to incinerate them and the corresponding emotional nausea for good.

"And what I'm not telling you is the other side of Jennifer . . . the one that was a good student . . . an avid book reader . . . She dreamed of leaving Polson . . . leaving her family, her father . . . but, like I said—when I . . . I realized she was beyond help when I—I went to a party one night . . . and saw her gang banging a bunch of guys. And that . . . Well, let's just say I tried to break up with her the next day and was informed I couldn't . . . She was pregnant. Of course, it didn't occur to me at the time that it might not be mine . . . I just—I just accepted what she said and . . . and tried to do the right thing. And it was . . . it was for nothing. She's dead . . . The baby's dead . . . Her father's dead . . . and, I'm here. Sometimes wondering if I'm not dead, too. If this is all, like you say, a dream. Maybe I died, too, and this is just a dream."

He stopped speaking, and Danielle sat quietly, inches away, wanting to reach out and hold him but waiting, knowing the time was not quite right. Knowing that he would have to make the first move.

"Was she blond? . . . Did she have blond hair?"

Alex shook his head. "Nope . . . She had brown hair. Curly—very curly. Kind of like my hair gets, actually . . . And blue eyes. And—she had freckles. Very light, but . . . you could see them up close. She was . . . She was very pretty. Not beautiful but . . . but pretty. In a . . . in a twinkly sort of way. Like—like a fairy or sprite . . . Like what I would imagine those Shakespeare fairies would be like."

Danielle nodded and looked into the small fire, the rigid consistency of its flickering flames and lack of errant sparks hinting at its inauthenticity.

"Anything else?" he asked quietly.

She shook her head.

"Are we done?"

She turned to him, her eyes suddenly tearing. "I don't know . . . Are we?"

He turned away, not realizing the implication of his question until she had responded. He had not meant to imply what she perceived.

"No," he said suddenly, moving to her so their bodies were nearly touching, placing a hand lightly on her leg. "There's something else. There is something else *I* want to say and, and do."

She looked at him with sad curiosity.

"I—I want us to start over."

Seeing her brows furrow, he followed up quickly.

"Listen to me—it's not what you're thinking, so don't let your mind go there. Wherever it's going—don't. I—I want to start over with you and do it right this time, okay? I mean—even you have to admit, it's—it's been a complete wreck. I mean, after our coffee night, you know—at that pie place, it's been nothing but one crisis after another. Tate, your parents, my wretched past, my—my attacks, my—my complete inability to make love to you or, or even, well, love you. I mean, yeah—we've—we've had some fun times now and then, but . . . Jesus, Dan. You've got to admit. This is . . . Frankly, I don't know how we've made it this long. Under these conditions . . . It's . . . I just don't."

She nodded, trying to curb the swelling nausea, wanting to be optimistic but not able to completely understand his thought process.

"Okay, so . . . What do you propose?" she asked with forced hopefulness.

"Well . . . First, I just . . . I just want to bury the past. All of it. Yours, mine . . . what you think is mine. Everything. Gone. Like, let's just—throw it into the fire," he said, making a gesture towards the flame.

She nodded. "Okay . . . I can do that . . . Happily."

"Okay . . . So now," he said standing up, stretching in the process, his legs and back aching from being seated in a cramped position for so long. "I'm going to walk out that door—"

She thought she would vomit.

"And come back in and ask you on a proper date. And you're going to pretend that you've never been on a date with me and . . . Well, we'll go from there. We're going to rewrite this story, you know? Throw all the other drafts into that . . . that tiny fire."

Danielle watched him stand pensively for a moment before promptly exiting the room. Though he was gone for mere seconds, it felt like years and she had, in that tiny fraction of time, convinced herself she would never see him again. But before the welled-up tears could spill over her lower lids, the door opened, and he walked across the room.

Standing over her, he extended her a hand, as if to shake or help her up, she wasn't sure.

"Hello, my name is Alex. Alex Michael Fahlstrom. I don't mean to be forward, but I saw you from across the room and . . . Well, I thought you were the most beautiful girl I have ever seen and . . . and I would like to get to know you better."

Upon finally catching his drift, she laughed, sniffing in the tears and sorrow. Happy to play along, now, she took his hand, and he helped her off the floor. After stretching her legs and back, she extended hers. "Hello, *Alex Michael.*"

"So, are you alone this evening? Are you . . . available? Or, dating anyone?"

"Well," she started wryly."I was dating this redneck from Polson, but . . ." then stopped, feigning remorse. "I'm *so sorry*, let me hit the rewind button . . ."

He grinned as she pretended to collect herself.

"*Well*, I was dating this self-centered asshole from Kansas City, but . . . I broke up with him for good and am completely free now."

"And, may I have the pleasure of your name?" he said with exaggerated politeness.

She chuckled, blushing, "Yes, of course—*how rude of me.* My name is Danielle Gabrielle Francesca Sumners."

At that, he burst out laughing. "Jesus—are you kidding me? That's your name?"

"No, I'm not—and *yes it is my name.*"

He started counting on his fingers. "I'm sorry, I've—I've lost count of the syllables. I can't—I can't even count them on one hand."

She put her hands on her hips, trying to act annoyed.

"Christ—what's Dennis's name?"

"Dennis Sebastian George."

"*Sebastian?*"

"Don't tell him I told you . . ."

"Oh, I'm not going to let him live it down. Are you kidding? . . . So, seriously, what is with the three names?"

She shrugged. "The third's our confirmation name—it's a *Catholic* thing."

"Oh . . . okay. Well, I don't go to church," he said, crossing his arms. "My parents aren't religious."

"I don't either anymore."

"Except to think . . . right?" he said with a quiet gleam.

She smiled and stepped towards him, placing her hands on his shoulders. "Yes . . . that's right."

His arms remained crossed. "Aren't we being a little forward for a first date?"

She reached up and pulled his head down to hers, her kiss soft but infused with an emotional intensity that demanded he respond, which he did by pulling her close to himself, completely enveloping her in his arms in the process. He experienced a feeling of closeness so potent that, even though it ended when they eventually pulled away from each other, it was ingrained in his memory for nights to come.

CHAPTER TEN

On the morning of his birthday, Alex went outside to retrieve the newspaper for his mother and found a small gift bag on the porch. Smiling, he picked it up and brought it inside. Handing the paper to his mother, he headed out of the kitchen, gift in hand, when she stopped him. She wanted to know what he had and, after seeing it, wanted him to open it in front of her.

He reddened and then protested to no avail. His mother stood her ground, coffee mug in hand, threatening to ground him if he didn't show her what was in the bag.

"It's from Danielle—why do you care? What do you think it is?"

"Well, judging from the size of it, I wouldn't think *wine glasses*," she said dryly.

His mother looked particularly old and worn today, he thought, in her oversized plaid work shirt and brown slacks.

"When were you born?" he asked suddenly, unsure, himself, from where the question came. It had just popped into his head.

"Alex—don't try that with me."

"What?"

"Changing the subject."

"Oh . . . No, I'm serious. When is your birthday?"

"April 1. I was an April Fool's joke, my mother used to say."

He chuckled. "That's harsh . . . So, when? I mean—what year?"

"1932."

"Geez . . . . That's a long time ago."

"Yes it is."

"How old were you when you had me? How—how is that possible?"

"What's in the bag, Alex?"

He sighed loudly, accepting defeat. Rifling through the tissue, he began to retrieve the objects but stopped, trying to suppress a grin. "Um . . . It's a pack of gum."

She raised an eyebrow. "All that for a pack of gum? May I ask what brand?"

He pulled it out, careful to leave the cigarettes and lighter at the bottom of the bag. "Dentyne," he said, flashing it at her. "Want a piece?"

She laughed. "Well, I'll be . . . Why don't you invite her over for cake tonight?"

He paled. While they had not made specific plans, bringing Danielle home to spend an evening with his mother was the last thing he wanted on his birthday.

"Oh, come on, Alex. You've been dating how long now?"

He shrugged. "A couple months."

"Yes, and we've met her *once*. You should bring her by more often. She needs to become part of the family."

"*Are you kidding?*" he burst incredulously.

"No—I'm not. Family's important. Remember that. If she's that important to you, then she should become family."

She gave him a list of small chores and left to do a load of laundry. He focused on the tasks at hand and, by afternoon's band practice, had forgotten the incident entirely. Since the football season had ended, Carl set up band practice every weekend and even some weeknights to prepare for the New Year's Eve basement concert. While Alex and Ron were serious about the music, Carl and the other band members, a singer and a keyboardist, were more into the party aspect of rock n 'roll, and their practices often turned into screaming, axe grinding, binge-drinking sessions.

Carl was a reckless drummer, excruciatingly off-beat with a zealous affection for the cymbals. The keyboardist was hardly better, immediately challenged when having to play a song outside of the keys of C or A minor, a fault barely obscured by chorus and string presets on his Korg synthesizer. And the singer, some senior from the varsity soccer team, was off-key, with no sense or rhythm or melody. Alex was convinced Carl had chosen him solely for his ability to attract women and to execute 360 karate kicks on stage. The band's screaming set list, which included classics from AC/DC, Metallica, Van Halen and Poison and two grinding numbers from Nirvana's *Nevermind*, only served to satisfy the egos of its least talented members and hide flaws from the audience.

Though supremely annoyed by the end of most band sessions, today was his birthday, and Alex was feeling unusually relaxed, happy even. He headed home for dinner, slightly buzzed and optimistic about the evening and his future.

His optimism had not waned by the time Danielle arrived later that evening. He had spent a quiet dinner with his mother and sister, his father having to work a late weekend shift again, and Danielle joined them for cake and ice cream. She had a glow about her tonight, Alex thought, admiring her across the table. Though dressed in jeans, her attire was conservative, the long-sleeve blouse barely unbuttoned enough to reveal the camisole beneath. And her hair was in a ponytail, making her look more mature and sophisticated.

"I made Alex's favorite cake," his mother said proudly, carefully carrying it to the dining room table. "Homemade Devil's Food."

Danielle smirked, and Alex kicked her under the table.

The three women then sang a mortifyingly lame version of "Happy Birthday" before breaking into mindless chatter. Alex was grateful at Danielle's ability to converse, allowing him to tune all of it out and enjoy his dessert in the quiet of his own mind.

"You know what I thought would be fun?" his mother announced suddenly, disrupting his eating reverie. "How 'bout we look through Alex's photo album? I'm sure Danielle would love to see it," she said, clapping her hands in delight.

"*What*? How 'bout we don't—" Alex burst, reddening.

But his mother had already jumped from the table.

"Why—*I'd love to*, Mrs. Fahlstrom," Danielle said, grinning and giving him a wink.

He then watched his mother take Danielle by the hand and physically pull her to a sofa in the living room. "How 'bout we don't? How 'bout we do what Alex wants on Alex's birthday and seriously not do that," he protested.

His sister snorted in delight over his discomfort, making immature comments about his nude baby photos. Utterly disgusted, he began clearing the dishes, hoping that by the time he was finished, they would be done looking through the album, and he and Danielle could escape the growing madness.

But when he ventured into the living room fifteen minutes later, they were still there, on the garish overstuffed loveseat, their bodies lost in the gargantuan magenta flowers and even larger turf green leaves. He stepped back, leaning against the door frame, arms crossed, listening to his mother's incessant chatter, which was a likely culprit for the delay.

"Are you done yet?"

"We've made it to grade school," Danielle said solemnly, but Alex could see the amusement in her eyes.

"Yes," his mother expressed joyfully. "I was telling Danielle how you wanted to be sheriff. You often played sheriff when you were little."

"Really?" he said dryly. "I don't remember."

"Here—look," his mother motioned for him to join them even though there was no room left for him to sit.

Reluctantly, he walked over and stood next to his mother, looking down at the album in her lap. She pointed to a picture

The photo was in color but a bit yellowed. There he sat, cross-legged, in what was obviously a ring of children, though the children on either side of him had been cut off, only their knees visible. He was probably only seven or eight, his hair a mess of blond curls, wearing jeans, tennis shoes and a long-sleeve shirt. Alex didn't know what was more disturbing, the fake sheriff badge clearly pinned to his front shirt pocket or the fact that he had cocked one eye, made a gun out of his right hand and was shooting the photographer.

"Where are the rest of them?" he asked suddenly.

"The rest of who, dear?"

"The children . . . Look—I'm in a circle. You can see their knees, but . . . do you have the full picture?"

His mother blinked her eyes in confusion.

"It's so . . . so weird," he continued. "I feel like I've seen this photo somewhere . . ."

"Why don't you sit here with us, Alex," his mother pressed, motioning for Danielle to move over and make room.

But Alex stopped her. "No . . . I'll just sit over here and watch. You can tell me when you find anything interesting," he said, plopping himself in the matching, overstuffed arm chair, his mind still struggling to remember where he had seen the photo, it looked so familiar to him.

He noticed Danielle trying to hurry his mother along, as if sensing his discomfort. They were nearing the end of the album when the conversation changed. Walking back to the loveseat, he discovered it was because his mother had made the end of the album a collection of photos he took while in Montana. As Danielle started to look at them and ask questions, his mother got up and motioned for him to take her place. He should be the one to answer her questions. She would finish cleaning up.

Alone at last, they kissed a minute before breaking into laughter, which neither of them had to explain. "Ready to cruise this joint?" he asked, leaning into her and whispering in her ear.

"In a minute . . . I'm actually enjoying this," she said playfully.

He groaned, throwing his head back.

"Seriously . . . I want to look at your photos. You told me you liked photography, but . . . I don't know—you don't talk about it much. Do you still take photos?"

He shrugged. "I haven't in awhile. I did when we first moved here . . . Actually, I've been considering shooting those lights. You know—The Plaza ones. There could be some cool shots there. Especially if it snows."

"Tell me about these," she said, turning to a page filled with pictures of a cattle ranch, some landscape photos, some close-ups of the cattle, some images of work hands.

He smiled, letting his mind flood with memories of happier times, and he could think of few memories more pleasant than his summers spent working on the cattle ranch. The ranch was owned by an elderly Native American and friend of the family. Alex had started working summers during middle school and was taught many aspects of ranching, from haying, tacking and general care of the horses and cattle, to fencing, equipment maintenance and roundups.

Danielle seemed fascinated, having had no exposure to ranch life and thinking it had become a thing of the past, cowboys and Indians only living in the movies. She assumed big business had taken over almost all aspects of farming and agriculture, including raising cattle. For the next fifteen minutes, they sat discussing the photos and life in Polson, a town located on an Indian reservation and populated with *cowboys and Indians*, Alex joked.

"You know, there are plenty of cattle farmers in Kansas, too. I would venture to say within an hour of here," he said tauntingly.

She nodded, "I know—I know. I've just, I don't know—grown up here in the city and suburbs. Even when we travel, we spend our time in cities. The only time I ever spend in the mountains is skiing in Colorado."

"Yeah, well . . . now you know why I'm so *simple* . . . I'm not a city boy."

"You're not *simple*. I don't think you're stupid, either, regardless of your GPA . . . I just don't think you care about grades or school. If you tried, you could probably get straight As."

He shrugged.

"Do you miss it?"

"What?"

"Polson . . . Do you miss living there?"

He took a long, deep breath, pondering her question. "I don't know . . . Yeah, I miss parts of it. Like the ranch work . . . I think I miss the quiet most of all. It's—it's so quiet, you know. And, there's a rhythm—a routine there, not like here. It's steadier. More grounded. Maybe it's the mountains, I don't know."

"Well, maybe you'll go back some day. Maybe that's what you can do for a career—own a ranch."

He laughed. "Yeah, right . . . You mean be a ranch hand. I'll never *own* anything. I'm just not ambitious enough for that."

"Well then maybe I will," she said defiantly. "Maybe I'll major in business and buy a ranch. We can start a business together."

He shook his head, still laughing. "Uh-uh . . . No way that's happening."

"Why?" she asked, sounding slightly offended. "We can do whatever we put our minds to—whatever we visualize—"

"Yeah—that's just it. I can't visualize *you* on a ranch. Sorry—but you don't belong in that picture. You just don't. You're—you're a city girl. You said it yourself. You belong in New York or, or LA. Or Milan, Paris. Something like that. Some place with lots of art and culture and activity—coffee houses . . . But that does give me another thought," he mused. "I could become a vet."

"A vet," she said dully. "You don't even own a pet."

"I did. If you were paying attention to the photos and my mother's endless chatter, you would have noticed the golden retriever in the background of my baby pictures."

Danielle started flipping backwards, but he took the album from her and slammed it shut.

"I wanted to see—" she protested. "What happened to him?"

"Trisha's allergies, that's what. Haven't had a pet since then."

"I had a pet, once" she said sadly. "I had a cat."

"I know," he said wryly, standing up. "Mr. Kitty."

She stood up, too, stretching and looking morose.

"Fucking dumbest name for a cat I've ever heard."

At this, she punched him hard in the arm, staring at him in a wide-eyed fury that caused him to giggle uncontrollably and contagiously until she, too, began laughing. After calming down, he insisted they leave, and after saying good-byes to his mother and sister, they headed out for the evening. Though unsure of what to do, their lack of plans did not concern them, and they discussed just hanging out in Danielle's room.

"Your mother was so pretty when she was younger," Danielle mentioned later in the evening.

"Yeah," Alex mumbled absently in response.

"Is she okay?" Danielle asked with concern.

"I think so—why?"

"I don't know . . . She just looks so tired. Older and tired, you know? Not much like the lady in the photos . . ."

"I guess," he said.

That evening he dreamed of his birthday party. He was seated at a circular table, with Dennis and Danielle to his right and Carl and some other guy he didn't recognize to his left. A pretty woman with long, golden-brown wavy hair and petite features approached the table, carrying a birthday cake loaded with seventeen candles.

I baked your favorite, she said, her spritely eyes twinkling. *Homemade lemon cake with butter cream frosting.*

He frowned as the cake was placed in front of him.

But my favorite is Devil's Food . . .

Now, honey, you know you can't have that. You're allergic to chocolate.

No, I'm not.

She insisted he blow out the candles and then asked everyone to pose for a photo.

Now open your gift.

A large red and white striped box suddenly appeared where the cake had been. Though topped with a bow, it was unwrapped, and he could easily remove the lid. Inside was a gray cat.

Curious, he gingerly reached into the box and retrieved the cat, expecting it to react and possibly claw him in the process. But it didn't move.

He held up the cat and looked at the woman in confusion.

What is this?

It's Mr. Kitty, she said.

He stared down in horror at the lifeless creature he now held in his hands. *But he's dead—*

I know. And if you don't come home, you'll end up in a box – just like him, she said sweetly, her eyes still sparkling.

Alex looked down into what had become a tiny casket and immediately woke up in a cold sweat.

While the dream had unnerved him, he did not speak of it to Danielle and worked hard the coming days to ignore it, convincing himself it was a mere remnant of the past—a test of his will to completely bury his former life and move on. Determined not to give in, he consciously worked on remaining optimistic during the weeks leading up to Christmas. Danielle's recital was the kick-off to their holiday school break. He was excited to see her play in public and intent on doing nothing to distract or distress her.

They had settled into a comfortable routine, careful to avoid overheating their passionate interludes and learning to enjoy doing very little, sometimes nothing more than drinking coffee and people-watching. Since starting her yoga and meditation classes, Alex noticed she had already become slightly less conversational, at times able to sit more than five minutes without feeling moved to fill the space with verbal thought.

He had not seen the faceless man in plaid, either, concluding he, too, had disappeared into the flaming void from where he had come.

Really, Alex thought as he dressed for Danielle's big day the Sunday before Christmas, his life had completely turned around since Thanksgiving. He was getting decent grades and working out in the off-season with the varsity football team, having been told he would be moved up in the fall. Hanging out with Carl more often had increased his circle of friends and social requests. His parents had even talked about getting him a car next year.

The only adversity he foresaw was being separated from Danielle for a week. The Trahans spent each Christmas in Aspen, and they had invited—insisted—Danielle go with them, as it was a family tradition, and she was now a part of their family, a comment he knew unnerved her. She would be returning on the thirtieth, just in time for New Year's Eve and the big basement concert, which he began to dread less.

Danielle's symphony concert was in the afternoon, and she had received four tickets for family members and given two to Alex and two to Brooke and Dennis. Alex invited his mother, who was ecstatic, but Brooke and Dennis declined, the show conflicting with some comic book convention they wanted to attend.

Alex bounded down the steps in his usual attire of jeans and a flannel plaid shirt layered over a concert tee and was promptly sent back upstairs by his mother to change into something more appropriate. He was surprised to see her dressed so stylish, herself, having lost the usual oversized and overly garish cardigan for a fitted white turtleneck, which gave her a bit of a glow and made her look less tired. Changing from jeans to khakis but keeping the rest of his look, he went back downstairs, and they headed to the concert, which was being held at a performing arts hall on the campus of the University of Missouri–Kansas City.

They had excellent seats, center and only a few rows back from the stage. As they waited for the show to begin, his mother earnestly read nearly every page of the program flier, fussing over Danielle's photo and write-up, feeling the need to read it aloud, even though Alex had his own copy. She then began to read the write-ups of other highlighted performers, which Alex ignored until he heard the name *Tate Foley*.

The mere name made his neck hairs bristle, and he grabbed the flier from his mother's hands, momentarily forgetting he had his own. Staring out from the page was a familiar face—too familiar, Alex thought angrily, reddening and throwing it back in his mother's lap. He didn't remember Danielle mentioning Tate being in the symphony, and the thought agitated him. All these weeks . . .

Before his mother could ask questions, the symphony director walked onstage to introduce the program, and the curtains rose shortly thereafter.

After finding both Danielle and Tate in the orchestra and seeing they were on opposite sides of the stage, Alex felt slightly more at ease and was able to enjoy the show. The music alternated from group-wide performances of Dvorak, Grieg and Tchaikovsky to works that catered to the instruments of the individual performers. Tate played a movement from Walton's cello concerto, and Alex, unfortunately, could find no fault in it. Danielle played Sarasate, *Fantasia on Themes from Carmen*, also executed flawlessly.

He and his mother lingered in the lobby after the show with the other audience members, mostly family and friends of the Symphony students, who were waiting for the performers to enter and mingle. When Danielle finally emerged, she did not see him and was greeted and congratulated by a number of people whom he did not know, the last being a stylishly dressed couple whose demeanor exuded wealth. The lady looked somewhat familiar, with golden-brown wavy hair pulled into a loose bun, delicate features and a spritely expression. With them was Tate, and he could only assume they were his parents.

Alex watched as Danielle smiled at the adult couple, giving both of them hugs. She then faced Tate, and while he could sense the tension, he also saw something else transpire. An exchange of words that turned into a short conversation, smiles and then an embrace. And as much as Alex felt like he ought to be angry at the unfolding scene, he was not. For the embrace held no hint of passion, only forgiveness.

After they said their good-byes, Danielle began looking for Alex, and upon seeing him and his mother, smiled widely, waving and hurrying towards them. She gave them both hugs and then immediately launched into a conversation with his mother, who had begun prattling, lavishing praises and launching questions. As he scanned Danielle's figure, her hair piled up with a few strands spilling onto her bare shoulders and chest, her body draped in a low-cut, tailored, silk black dress that flowed from the waist down, he felt a rising sexual tension. She could have just as easily been dressed for a portrait sitting as a concert, and his feelings competed between fierce lust and reserved admiration.

To his surprise, his mother offered to take them out to dinner at Houston's to celebrate, and Danielle accepted on their behalf. She then disappeared to change into street clothes, planning to meet them at the restaurant. When he saw her again, a half hour later, his raging feelings had abated. Gone was the Italian temptress, having transformed once again into his beautiful and benevolent companion, and he was able to enjoy the rest of the evening and look forward to their few days of vacation together before she left for the holidays with the Trahans.

On the morning of Alex's birthday, Danielle was anxious to start her yoga and meditation classes, hoping to find some semblance of inner peace for her increasingly troubled mind. The intense exchanges with Alex over the Thanksgiving weekend left physical and psychological scars, and though she would never tell him, she truly believed their ill-fated sexual union had mentally bound them in some capacity that was beyond earthly explanation.

Both classes were held at a local Buddhist center that had just opened that year in a renovated downtown church and, being new, had sparse attendance. Yoga began Saturday morning, and Danielle found herself one of a handful of individuals that included two elderly women, two college students and a middle-aged man. The group was in a corner of a huge room that used to be the church nave but had been stripped of pews, altars and any sort of religious décor, its bare white walls now hung with a few ornate tapestries of lotus blossoms and strange looking beings, its expanse of polished wood flooring dotted with a few burgundy meditation cushions. For the next hour, Danielle engaged in gentle stretching exercises to strange music and the soothing voice of the instructor. By their last relaxation meditation, as she lay staring up at the wood-beamed ceiling, she felt as if she had taken a plunge into pampered bliss.

The calm stayed with her throughout the day, and any nervousness about spending an evening with Alex's family dissipated. She found herself enjoying the company of Alex's mother and sister, comforted by being a part of a family—any family, at this point—her own having disappeared.

Sitting with his mother in the living room, flipping through the large photo album, their bodies touching, made her melancholy. His mother smelled warm, of bergamot and cedar wood, and she tried to remember what her own mother smelled like, the perfume she wore that used to comfort Danielle when her mother held her. Danielle wondered what had become of their own family albums and of the portraits and photos that hung in their great room, a part of her fearing they had been destroyed. That perhaps all traces of her past had been somehow eradicated.

As she looked through his photo album, she found herself drawn to photos of his parents, for his mother was beautiful in a fairy-tale sort of way, with long, wavy golden-brown hair, elvan features and a sweet smile. Yet the woman seated next to her on the sofa looked so drastically different—a good forty years older than the woman in the photo. So different, that Danielle wondered if she weren't seated next to Alex's grandmother. If perhaps he still had amnesia and forgotten his mother had either left them or died.

She had also been struck by the photographs Alex had taken of the Montana landscape. There was something moving about them, familiar even, especially the ones of a large lake bordered by mountains. There were a number of these, taken at different times of the day and in different seasons, so over the course of six or seven photos, the sky and water reflected nearly every color in the spectrum. Though she didn't say anything, it had wounded her deeply when he said he could not see her in Montana. How could he not see her in such a beautiful place? Such a peaceful place? Why wouldn't he want to bring her there—to the lovely part of his memory, to the safe place in his mind? It hurt her to think that when he looked at her, he only thought of buildings, dirty streets and treeless, smog-ridden horizons. Or of painted landscapes trapped in ornate wooden frames screaming to come alive but destined only to be looked at from a distance, never touched, never entered.

If he wouldn't imagine her there, she would.

In her meditation class the following morning, she found herself visualizing the place in the photos, trying to recreate the images in her mind and actually transport herself there. She envisioned herself sitting on a hillside, overlooking the lake, a body of water so clear and pristine that the snow-capped mountains rising from the opposite shore were perfectly mirrored on the water's surface. She saw the dark green pine trees and tried to smell them in the wind, tried to feel the wind caress her skin and face, tried to experience the absence of noise that Alex had described, to feel what he had felt.

In the days that followed, she found herself hallucinating mountains out of the clouds in the Kansas City sky, especially if her travels took her on the highway, away from the dense suburbs and where the horizon was expansive. And she noticed an increasing number of Montana license plates on either pick-up trucks or Ford Broncos in the parking lots of stores and gas stations. At times, she thought she saw the man in the plaid shirt, the one they had seen on Thanksgiving, once in a gas station and once in the parking lot of a Hy-Vee. Though she stared at him obviously and intently, he never seemed to notice her, his blank expression staring through her, as if she didn't exist. But the reminders of Montana only made her want to escape further into her mental retreat, a place she was building in her mind that became clearer and more real with each meditation class, to the point she failed to hear the instructor at all and wondered if she wouldn't open her eyes one day and see the lake spread out before her, Kansas City having dissipated into a mere memory, a dream.

In this new world, she would walk down from the hilltop to the lakeside and find him standing there, alone and gazing into the distance. And when he turned around and saw her, he would smile—his smirking eyes narrowing as his face broke into that huge mischievous grin, before pulling her close to him and kissing her. And their kisses would become more intense, their embrace fervid as they groped for skin, feverishly undressing each other, their discarded clothing forming a mottled blanket they lay upon, patches of exposed grass brushing against her back. She imagined them as they were in the park that day, weeks ago, only free this time. Free of clothing, free of the past, free of any pain or guilt, shame or fear. She tried to remember his every move and recreate the scene—relive the scene—all the way through to its earth-shattering climax, which she had not forgotten and for which she ached to have again. Only this time, he climaxed with her, intensifying the ensuing rapture. And instead of pain and tears, there would be laughter. They would laugh and hold each other, so entwined she could feel his heart racing, eventually slowing.

You can open your eyes, now.

She barely heard the instructor's voice, her head still on Alex's bare chest, his breathing the only sound outside of the gentle rustle of pine needles and a soft lapping of water against the shore.

Meditation became her favorite activity, one she actively engaged in even outside of the classes. She spent so much time making love to Alex in their mountain retreat that their times together in the waking world began to pale in comparison. The day-to-day routine of school, violin practice and even holiday shopping was becoming tedious, and she longed for kayaking and woodland hikes. Though she had never been horseback riding, she found herself fantasizing about it and made a New Year's resolution to take lessons.

Even conversing had become strenuous, and she became less interested in talking to Alex, preferring to take her mind elsewhere as they sat in their favorite coffee house or watched their favorite television shows. The only thing she wanted to talk about was sex, but she was afraid to even broach the topic, as his appetite for it had seemed to wane, their make-out sessions lacking the fiery, almost angry passion they used to hold. But by the evening of her recital, her resolve to discuss it at some point became more acute.

As much as she and Tate had tried to completely avoid each other since Homecoming, they could not entirely do so at symphony practice. If they did happen to glimpse each other, they would quickly look away, avoiding additional eye contact. And when they practiced his featured piece, Walton's *Cello Concerto*, the *Allegro Appasionato* movement, she would try to imagine Yo-Yo Ma in his place. She often wondered if he did the same with her, mentally replacing her body with some famous violinist—Itzhak Perlman or Sarah Chang—the anger, resentment and embarrassment still too potent to be able to appreciate the real performer.

However, the Music Hall stage that Sunday afternoon made avoidance particularly difficult. The featured musicians were seated center stage and to the right of the conductor, directly in front of the first violins, so she couldn't help but see him and, as his performance was flawless, think of him with admiration. He'd already been accepted to the Juilliard School, a feat she was reluctant to try herself, unsure of a future in the performing arts, especially with the potential loss of family and financial support, and equally unsure of her abilities as a violinist. Though talented, she lacked ambition and found competitions increasingly nerve racking. Or maybe it was just Alex, she mused, his directionless attitude wearing off on her. Regardless, by the end of the show, she felt moved to find Tate and compliment him.

The lobby was crowded, and as she worked her way through it, looking for Tate, she received numerous compliments from fellow symphony members, acquaintances and even a few strangers. So consumed was she to find Tate, that she did not notice a hand gently tapping her until her arm was tugged slightly. She turned around to find a stylishly dressed woman, and it took her a full moment to realize it was Tate's mother, for she didn't remember her looking so youthful and attractive. His mother smiled warmly at her, giving her a hug, and Danielle could smell her perfume, a blend of spice and flowers. She didn't remember his mother having such golden hair, strands of it framing her face in perfect waves. His father, a large, well-built man with a neatly trimmed mustache, completely towered over his petite mother. Though not handsome, he had an imposing presence that was only slightly diminished by the bear hug he gave her.

Danielle stared in awe at the two individuals before her, people who should seem as familiar to her as her own parents yet felt like complete strangers. For years, her parents and the Foleys had been best friends, and the families often hung out together, spent holiday weekends together and occasionally traveled together. But she had never really paid much attention to Tate's parents. Never scrutinized their physical features or even thought much about them until now, as they praised her performance and chatted pleasantly with her, careful to sidestep any mention of her parents and the divorce.

She then turned to Tate, who had been standing off to the side, still avoiding eye contact.

"Tate . . . That was a brilliant performance. Unbelievable—really."

With their awkward silence finally broken, he looked at her, hesitant at first, mumbling a compliment but still avoiding her gaze. As she studied his appearance, she was suddenly struck by his resemblance to Alex, an affinity she had failed to notice until that moment. His hair color was different, much browner and cropped short to hide the curls. His skin tone darker, too, and he lacked the light spattering of freckles Alex had on his cheeks and forehead. But the eyes—the jaw line—even their physical build was identical.

She walked up to him, standing mere inches away, so close she could hear him breathe. "How are you?"

He ventured a look down at her, and she smiled warmly at him.

His body relaxed in relief. "I'm okay," he said, nodding. "How . . . How are you?"

"I'm okay . . . you know, considering."

His expression saddened. "Yeah . . . I'm, I'm really sorry about all that. I can't—I can't believe it. I mean, none of us can. It's—it's just so, well . . . Unexpected. I never . . . I'm sorry. I don't even know what to say. I—I'm just sorry," he mumbled, his face reddening as he struggled to articulate his thoughts.

She put a hand on his arm to calm him. "It's okay . . . There's nothing to say. It happened. It sucks . . . Life goes on."

He stared uncomfortably at the hand on his arm, and she withdrew it.

"You look good," she said with finality, stepping back.

"Really?" he asked, obviously taken aback.

She nodded, smiling. "Tuxedos become you."

He flushed, trying to contain a grin. "Really?"

She nodded.

"Well, you don't look so bad yourself. Beautiful. . . ."

She looked down, slightly embarrassed.

"You still dating that guy?" he asked suddenly.

She nodded. "Alex? Yeah . . . He's here somewhere. How about you?"

He shrugged. "Ah . . . Not really. Still sleeping with Kelly," he joked sadly.

She laughed and reached out to hug him, whatever anger, jealousy or disgust she might have previously felt evaporating, being completely replaced by a feeling of kindness, almost a kinship. He met her embrace, and they held each other for a moment in weary relief.

Over dinner, Danielle could not help but study Alex, who was seated across from her, slightly baffled as to how the person seated in front of her could stir such raging sexual desire, such intense passionate love, while his near twin generated a mere spark of friendship.

"I dreamed about you last night," Alex whispered in her ear later that night, as they lay entwined on her bed watching television.

"Really . . . Did it end well?"

"I fucking came . . ."

She looked at him, barely able to contain her surprise. "Seriously?"

He grinned, nodding.

"Oh, my god—well, what are we waiting for?" she asked, jumping up and sitting seductively on top of him. "Let's—let's do it."

He laughed. "Jesus, Dan—aren't we being a little vampish tonight."

She smirked. "Maybe . . . But I'm serious," she said, running her hand down his chest, down his stomach and to his groin.

He shook his head sadly, stopping her hand and taking it in his own. "Uh-uh—not yet. Things have been going too well. I don't—I don't want to jinx anything . . . Not before Christmas. Not before your trip."

She flopped on the bed next to him, sighing loudly in mock frustration.

"Tell you what," he said, rolling over and kissing her lips, cheek and ear. "Why don't we ring in the New Year together . . . You know, after the concert. Shit, with only six songs, we'll be done before eleven."

She mused a moment, his breath on her ear causing a shiver that coursed achingly through her loins. Though only ten days away, New Year's Eve might as well have been ten eons away, such was the agony she felt at having to wait.

"Okay," she said finally. "Maybe we can, like, time it so we both *come* at Midnight . . . That would be so cool . . ."

He laughed. "Jesus, you're a horn ball . . . I thought I was bad. What's gotten into you, anyway?"

"*You* happened to me," she whispered playfully, knowing she could retreat to the happy place she had constructed in her mind and make love to him whenever she wanted between now and then.

Her holiday with the Trahans was enjoyable and so packed with activity that the days passed quickly. They owned a second home in Aspen, a two-story log cabin that they rented out the majority of the year for extra income. Danielle and Brooke shared a large room on the ground level with its own bath. Brooke's older brother Nate flew in from New York, where he was studying at Syracuse, and took a room down the hall from them, and Brooke's parents took the master suite, which was the entire second story of the house.

Because Mr. and Mrs. Trahan treated Danielle as if she were their own child, there were moments Danielle could forget her own family and shake off the melancholy of their absence. They made her an integral part of the Trahan tree trimming party, an annual tradition, letting her top the towering fir with a gold angel, a feat accomplished by climbing a six-foot step ladder. She was also invited to be in the family photo, taken in front of the finished tree by a local professional photographer. And while Danielle had gotten small but tasteful gifts for each of them, she was lavished with gifts by the Trahan parents—receiving almost as many as Brooke and Nate.

Even Brooke's older brother, Nate, was affectionate towards her—actually going out of his way to talk to Danielle and hang out with her and Brooke—which was a complete turnaround from his behavior a few years back, when they were in ninth grade and Danielle had a crush on him that he obviously didn't notice, treating both of them with arrogant disdain. Though he was good looking in a Victorian hero sort of way, with brooding eyes and shoulder length black hair that framed his chiseled face perfectly, Danielle could not even remotely stir up whatever physical attraction she had previously felt for him.

During their days together, he had complimented Danielle more than once on her appearance, commenting repeatedly on how much she had grown up, how striking she looked now, how mature. But it wasn't until the three of them went skiing together three days after Christmas that Danielle wondered if something else wasn't going on. They had been clowning around on one of the Snowmass intermediate trails, racing each other to the finish, at times getting dangerously close to each other, so close at one point, that Danielle jerked to avoid being mowed down by Nate and lost her balance, tumbling a ways down a hill. As she sat brushing the snow out of her mouth and off her person, he trudged up the hill towards her.

"Sorry . . ." he called breathlessly. "Are you okay?"

"I'm fine," she said reddening, unhurt but highly annoyed, expecting such an antic from her own brother but not Brooke's.

He held out his hand for her to take, but she refused it, attempting to stand up on her own, an action that met with no success.

Laughing he walked behind her, and putting his arms under hers, pulled her up, catching her as she faltered while regaining her balance on the skis and continuing to hold her moments after, his face lingering precariously close to hers, so close she could feel his breath against her cheek. Unnerved, she pulled away from him, nervously laughing it off and soon tearing back down the hill, avoiding him as much as possible the remainder of the day and evening, retreating deep into her mind before falling asleep, letting Alex's touch eradicate all traces of pain and confusion the waking world continued to wreak upon her person and experiencing the most intense mental orgasm she had felt yet.

She awoke feeling peaceful and fulfilled, her mood made even lighter upon realizing Nate was leaving that morning, feeling nothing but a sad sense of sibling kinship as she gave him an awkward hug good-bye.

That afternoon, the last before heading back to Kansas City the following morning, she and Brooke sipped hot cocoa at an Aspen cafe with an outside patio, even though Danielle insisted it was too cold to sit outdoors, the temperature below freezing. But they were bundled in their ski attire and two space heaters whirred laboriously on the terrace floor, providing some relief.

The two talked aimlessly for awhile, reminiscing over the week, discussing the merits and flaws of movies they had watched together, sharing school gossip. Then fell quiet, observing the town's comings and goings.

"You look really happy today," Brooke said suddenly.

"Really?" Danielle said, taken aback. "Hmmm . . . I am happy," she declared, smiling dreamily and settling back in her chair, her mind turning to last night's dream, her body quivering in memory of it. "Very happy." She gingerly took a sip of cocoa, wishing it would cool faster.

"Did you fuck my brother?"

At this, Danielle choked and nearly spilled her cup, jerking upright in her chair, a stream of hot brown liquid scalding her hand in the process. She swore under her breath, reaching for one of the two tiny beverage napkins.

Brooke burst out laughing.

"Jesus, Brooke . . ." Danielle said, reddening. "What the hell?"

"I had to ask . . . You have the glow."

"What glow?"

"You know—the glow. The happy glow. The *sex glow* . . . In fact, this is the first time I've ever seen you with it."

"I have the *sex glow*?"

"Well, yeah . . . Wish I had one . . . Haven't had it this week with my man left behind."

Danielle closed her eyes, inhaling deeply. "No," she said vehemently. "I most certainly did not have sex with Nate. Oh, my god. I can't believe you even asked. Oh, my god . . . He's your *brother*. He's practically my brother, now. I mean, Jesus, Brooke."

Brooke made a face at her. "Oh, please. I'm fucking *your* brother. Why wouldn't you fuck mine? And, he's been pining away for you since he got here. Asking me all kinds of questions about you. About your love life. Jesus—he's been all over you. Didn't you notice? *Hello* . . ."

"Eew. And—no, I didn't notice," Danielle said, feeling slightly guilty about lying to her friend. "Not really," she added quietly.

"Okay, okay . . . So, where'd it come from then?" Brooke asked skeptically.

"Where did what come from?"

"*The happy glow.*"

Danielle shrugged, sucking the burn spot on her hand.

"Oh, my god," Brooke burst suddenly. "You found some townie, didn't you? The other night—at the skating rink—that guy who was flirting with us. You hooked up with him, didn't you? And right under our noses!"

Danielle rolled her eyes, shaking her head. "I don't know what you're talking about," she said finally. "I don't even remember anyone flirting with us. I don't even know why we're having this conversation . . ."

"Because I'm fucking horny, that's why, and you're sitting there looking all happy and smug—glowing as if some hot guy fucked your brains out all night. It's entirely unfair. And it's just plain mean for you not to tell me, either. Jesus, we're practically sisters."

Danielle sighed in exasperation. "Brooke—did you forget I'm dating Alex? *Hello*—I have a boyfriend. He's my only boyfriend. I'm completely and entirely in love with him. Like, painfully in love with him. There's nobody else. I swear."

"Hmm . . ." Brooke mused, taking a sip of cocoa. "Well, then I'm just jealous."

"*Why?*"

"Well, I'm in love . . . I love Dennis and, well—we've had some hot times together and . . . I'm not happy being away from him. But I'm not glowing. I'm rather miserable right now—no offense."

Danielle winced, wanting to wipe all traces of Brooke's comments from her mind while at the same time wanting to support her friend. "Brooke," she said finally. "You know, just because you're not physically with Dennis doesn't mean you have to be apart from him. I mean, I . . . I daydream. You know? I think about Alex and us . . . and I just, you know, put myself there. Mentally."

Brooke gasped, grabbing the table violently, causing another spill of cocoa. "You masturbated!"

Danielle flushed, staring at her friend in wide-eyed horror, utterly mortified by the word.

"You . . . You sneaky vixen, you. Danielle Sumners—who'd have thought. And in my bedroom—that's so . . . that's so bold of you."

"Shut-up," Danielle whispered harshly. "I did not. That's disgusting."

"Oh, please . . . there's nothing disgusting at all about it. I should have thought of it myself, but, you know . . . We're, like, sharing a room."

"*I didn't do that.* My god, I've never done that. That's—that's disgusting. And, I don't—I don't even have to do that. I can just think about it."

"*Oh, please.*"

"I can—and I do. In my meditation classes. It's awesome. I can just—just create this place in my mind and go there. It's like it's real. It feels real."

Brooke snorted, pulling a lighter and cigarette case from her fanny pack. She held the case out to Danielle, who declined.

"Why don't you believe me? Why would I lie?" Danielle asked, slightly hurt.

Brooke lit up and exhaled a plume of smoke to her left side. "It just . . . . It seems impossible. I mean, without touching yourself. I don't know . . . So, do you come?"

"What?"

"When you *think* about it . . . Do you come? You know—*orgasm*."

Danielle turned red, her gaze falling to the contents of her cup.

"Oh, my god . . ." Brooke breathed. "What kind of meditation class is this?"

Danielle remained silent, still avoiding her gaze, feeling horribly exposed.

"I want to go with you. Jesus—do they teach you this? They actually teach you how to visualize sex?"

"I don't know what they teach," Danielle burst. "I don't even care. I don't even hear the instructor. I, I—just go to my place. It's my place. I created it. I go there. I live there half the time. Because it's—it's sometimes so much nicer than this one."

"Isn't it in some Buddhist temple downtown?"

"I guess . . . It's in an old church they renovated."

Brooke took another smoke and then began giggling uncontrollably.

"That's just so wrong . . . . Oh, my god . . . So—so tell me this, young Jedi . . . Which sex is better? The mental or the physical?"

Danielle reddened, wanting to remain in control, even wanting to be angry with her friend's mocking behavior, but feeling the pull of her laughter.

"I'm serious—it's a valid question."

Danielle remained speechless, trying to contain a smile.

"I mean—you've got the glow, but the physical Alex is a couple hundred miles away from here," Brooke pressed. "What's up with that?"

"Brooke—there's no dream Alex without the real Alex. I mean, I didn't just make this world up out of nowhere. He provided the inspiration for it."

"Yeah, well . . . Maybe without dream Alex, there's no Alex at all," Brooke said quietly.

She leaned across the table and grabbed Danielle's wounded hand.

"I'm here for you, you know. We're practically sisters, now . . . We may as well be sisters."

Danielle nodded absently. "Yes . . . Thank you. You know, Dennis didn't even call me this week. Not even to wish me Merry Christmas."

"Well—did you call him?"

"No," she replied, suddenly ashamed at her momentary pity party.

"You two don't look anything alike, you know," Brooke said cheerfully, as if the observation should somehow void Danielle's pangs of loss and separation.

"We're fraternal twins . . . We're not supposed to look alike."

"Yeah, but you don't even look like brother and sister."

Danielle was about to retort but stopped, knowing Brooke was right. Knowing that for years, she herself had failed to see a resemblance with her brother.

"Shit . . . you look more like Nate than you do Dennis . . . Isn't that ironic?"

"Yes . . . I guess it is," Danielle replied dully, feeling slightly dizzy.

That night, she dreamed she was standing with a large group of people, all dressed in their Sunday best. All dressed in black. The sky was gray and cloudless, and a cold, bitter wind blew skirts and coat tails. She and Alex stood near the back of the crowd, hand-in-hand, listening to what turned out to be a sermon.

The One remains, the many change and pass; Heaven's light forever shines, Earth's shadows fly; Life, like a dome of many colored glass, stains the white radiance of Eternity, Until Death tramples it to fragments.[1]

Some people were crying, but she could not see their faces until they slowly began turning around and walking away, one-by-one, and she saw a parade of people she had met throughout her life, both recently and from years past. Dennis. Brooke. Nate. The Trahan parents. Her girlfriends from high school. Her grandparents. Her aunts and uncles. Classmates from grade school. People she knew from symphony. The small crowd turned into almost a wave of people that surged through and past the two of them until they were left alone, staring into an expanse of field, cattle grazing in the distance, and in front of the barbed fencing two freshly dug graves. As she glanced across the field, she thought she saw a mountain range but wondered if she weren't hallucinating. If they weren't just clouds.

She looked at Alex, but he was staring ahead.

Letting go of his hand, she walked towards the plots to study the tombstones.

One read, *Danielle Grabrielle Francesca Sumners, June 4, 1976 – December 31, 1993*

---

1   Percy Bysshe Shelley, *Adonais*

The other read, *Alexander Michael Fahlstrom, December 4, 1976 – December 31, 1993*

Horrified, she spun around to find Alex, but he had vanished.

She sat up in bed, gasping for breath, wildly scanning the room. Brooke lay peacefully asleep in the bed across from her. The clock read three in the morning.

Her anxiety over the dream was slightly curbed by seeing Alex in person the next evening, when he picked her up to take her to dinner, having borrowed the family Bronco. Once inside the car, they spent a good five minutes kissing before heading to their favorite Thai restaurant.

After dinner, they spent the rest of the evening in her room, making out and watching television, at times their interludes become dangerously intense, and Danielle paid attention to every physical detail, storing them away in her memory bank. The feel of his flannel shirt, especially the collar, just at his neckline. The feel of his close-shaven cheek and jaw, so soft with only an occasional hint of bristle where he had missed shaving. His thick blond hair, thinly streaked with a hint of brown, some strands spiraled into a perfect curl and others matted masses, as it framed his face and graced his ear. The feel of his biceps as he held her close. The feel of her cheek against his chest, against his stomach. And his smell, a light blend of mountain spring soap and fabric softener from his clothes, as he didn't wear cologne.

She didn't want to wait until New Year's, fearful of the dream's foreboding symbolism, and when he began to pull away from her, she would physically try to persuade him to continue, even becoming slightly aggressive. But his will being stronger than hers, he would slow it down and eventually direct their attention back to the television or even mindless conversation.

As it neared midnight, he maneuvered himself out of her arms, out of the bed and began getting ready to leave.

"Don't go," she said quietly.

"I know . . . I don't want to."

"So don't."

He shook his head, buckling his jeans. "I can't . . . My mom's been a hawk lately, and I don't want to get grounded. Not before New Year's."

"Do we have to go tomorrow?" she asked, lying on her side, one arm propping her head.

"Well—yeah. I'm looking forward to it—aren't you?"

She shrugged.

"Come on—it'll be fun. I'm playing in a *rock band*," he joked, making an air guitar gesture.

She smiled sadly. "Yeah . . . I want to see that."

"Look," he said, walking back to the bed and sitting on its edge. "We're on at ten, and we're only playing, like, six songs. I mean—we can be back here before midnight, if you want. We'll celebrate New Year's however you want—and wherever you want. Here, The Plaza, making out in a car somewhere . . . Whatever you find most romantic."

"I love you," she said, her voice dropping to a whisper, her eyes suddenly tearing.

He flushed, turning away from her. "I know. You've told me . . . Have you suddenly figured out what that means?"

She shook her head. "Not really. It's just a feeling, I guess."

"What does it feel like?"

"It hurts," she said, bursting into tears. "It hurts my chest . . . It feels horrible . . ."

"Exactly," he said quietly. "And now you know why I hate it and don't believe in it. How can anything so fucking painful be a good thing?"

Not wanting to be late, he kissed her on the top of her head, which was now buried in a pillow, and left the room, closing the door behind him.

She spent the next morning having a late breakfast with Brooke at the coffee shop. Alex, Dennis, Carl and their growing group of friends had made plans to have band practice and hang out all day until the party. It was a guy thing, he had told her on the phone. She could meet him at the party later that night.

The two of them sat at her and Alex's usual table next to the window, staring at the passer-bys on the sidewalk and the stragglers who had wandered inside to warm themselves. Every few minutes, Brooke tapped her foot anxiously on the floor, and Danielle could tell she was agitated. She would then reach into her bag for a cigarette but stop, remembering smoking wasn't allowed inside. This would be followed up by dramatic sighing and rolling of her eyes, each time concluding with a sip of coffee.

"I take it your evening was about as exciting as mine," Danielle said morosely.

"Jesus Christ—are you kidding me? Please tell me you are."

Danielle shook her head sadly.

"Yeah, what the fuck is up with them . . . Jesus. I mean, we've been apart for an entire week, and all he wants to do is watch the football game. He doesn't even play football."

"He does now . . ." Danielle mumbled, her head resting on her hand.

"Shit . . . I think there was some serious male bonding going on while we were away," Brooke said, nodding her head. "Yep . . . That's what happened."

Danielle waited expectantly for her to continue with her psychological hypothesis.

"They're all closet homosexuals. Every fucking one of them . . . They're all a bunch of women at heart, I swear . . . I swear we have fucking more balls than any one of them. We do . . ."

"I don't understand," Danielle said after a few minutes. "I don't understand what happened."

"They all fucking got together, drank beer and smoked weed all week, that's what. And they listened to their rock and roll and pretended to be the shit at music . . . and at the bowling alley. And at—at the pool hall. And on the fucking football field. And told their blond jokes and their fart jokes and basically had a group jerk off. And they got so exhausted getting high and jerking each other off, that they don't have anything left for us."

"Um . . . you're speaking metaphorically, right? You don't mean literally—"

But Brooke continued her rant.

"Nothing like a bag of weed to kill a sex drive . . . Jesus. Completely takes the edge off it. And you know they'll be tokin today . . . Probably already high, the fuckers . . ." Brooke tapped her foot anxiously before taking a sip of coffee and continuing. "I say we bag that party. Why are we even going? To watch our boyfriends get wasted and act like idiots? I don't need to see that, you know? I really don't . . . I see him act like that, and . . ." She stopped speaking, sniffing.

Danielle frowned, surprised to see her friend's eyes well up.

"What?" she asked quietly.

Brooke shook her head, brushing a tear away from her eye. "I don't want to see him like that, okay? I just don't . . . If we're going to have a future, I can't see him like that. Or . . . or there just might not be one . . . I don't need that bullshit in my life right now, Danielle . . . And quite frankly, neither do you. We both deserve better than that."

Danielle sat up, concerned for Brooke and somewhat taken aback by her fear and anger.

"Brooke—it's okay . . ." she said, reaching across the table and lightly touching the top of her friend's hand. "It's—it's just a stupid party. I mean, so what if they get drunk and play bad music. Everyone else will be drunk, too. Nobody will even remember the next day."

Brooke looked at her darkly. "You have no idea what goes on at these parties, do you? *Do you*? Why do you think they don't want us showing up until—like—ten o'clock. I'm surprised they asked us to show up at all . . ." she said bitterly.

"Well, probably so they can practice. I thought—I thought it was so they could, you know, look good for us."

"Dennis isn't even in the band, Danielle," Brooke burst. "God, you're naïve. You're so fucking naïve, and it . . . I'm sorry. I wish—I wish to God I could be as, I don't know—simple-minded as you. As innocent . . . Jesus, you don't even masturbate, how the fuck would you know what goes on? Your mind has no frame of reference . . . Look, I don't mean to burst your little Alex bubble, but I'll tell you what's going on. They'll start drinking in . . ." She glanced at her watch. "An hour. The weed will follow and after that there'll be girls and lines . . . coke lines—and I don't mean soda pop, okay? And sure, they'll practice their music and listen to music and crack jokes and get a fuck on in-between. And by the time we see them tonight, they'll be so fucking wasted, they won't even remember what happened and will convince themselves the next day that *nothing did happen*. That it was all just a dream—a weird drug trip. And they'll believe this, because they'll have to in order to lie to us. In order for us to believe it, too."

Danielle stared numbly out the window, the tombstones from her dream taking on an entirely new meaning. She had automatically assumed they meant bodily harm—bodily death. It had never occurred to her they could signify the death of a relationship. The death of trust. The death of love.

"Well," she said finally. "I'm going anyway . . . What you say may be true. It may even happen, but . . . I'm going to see it to the end. I have to. I can't—I can't give up yet, Brooke. I don't . . . I don't want to."

Brooke nodded absently. "Yeah, yeah . . . you go. I'm calling Cherise and Susan and seeing what they're up to."

"Do you even know where this party is?"

"Yeah . . . Dennis gave me the address. It's in Leawood somewhere. I'll give it to you when we get home."

∞

Alex and his friends spent the morning and early afternoon of New

Year's Eve at Carl's, drinking beer and jamming together. It was a Friday, and both Carl's parents were at work. He lived in a modest split level, each of the rooms decorated in variations on a theme of pewter blue and mauve. The living room had pewter blue carpet and mauve sofas, while the dining room had pewter blue carpet and mauve striped walls and curtains. The kitchen was all maple and mauve. Carl had never invited anyone to his bedroom, and Alex didn't ask to see it, the overall décor already so out of line with Carl's personality, that Alex had to stop himself from laughing out loud. Instead, Carl kept his friends to the living room and kitchen.

By three in the afternoon, the group had moved to the party site, a monstrous new home in a neighborhood called Leawood. Alex was half trashed when they arrived to set-up and barely paid attention to his surroundings, only noticing how white the entire house was. The carpet white, the walls and ceilings white, the sofas and chairs white and the tables glass. Even the wall furnishings were shades of light gray and white, and he felt as if he had stepped into Willy Wonka's television studio.

The girl's parents were in Europe for a holiday vacation, and she had the house to herself. She directed them to a first floor great room in front of a stone fireplace that stretched to the top of a cathedral-style ceiling. When they arrived, the house was already swarming with students, most of whom Alex didn't recognize as they attended a different high school than he, and it just got more crowded and rowdy with each passing hour. After setting up and testing the equipment, they headed downstairs to an enormous finished basement that was the size of Alex's house and contained a separate kitchen, two bathrooms, two bedrooms and a fitness room in addition to the large gaming room and bar that not only had a pool table but also two card tables, foosball, three pinball machines and two pachinko machines.

By four in the afternoon, Dennis had broken out the weed. Alex smoked two joints on his own and continued to drink heavily, keeping up with the pace of his friends and thoroughly enjoying the feeling of being completely carefree. Of making a joke out of everything. Of seeing life as a big game with no consequences for losing, both winners and losers celebrating over another beer, another smoke, another rock song.

The band members were constantly being hit on by girls, even Dennis, who posed as the band manager, and by five Alex found himself hanging out with a girl who had been lurking around since they arrived. She was attractive, with shoulder length dirty brown hair, bangs, blue eyes and a tan. Though thin, she had chubby cheeks and a pearly smile, which she flashed constantly in her attempts to coerce him into playing songs for her on his guitar. He had refused, instead heading downstairs to play poker and pool with his buddies, still firm in his belief that real musicians did not play to get girls and believing he would compromise himself and his music by doing so.

But the girl followed him and began physically hanging onto him, standing behind him with her arms around his neck during a card game and later with her arms around his waist as he waited for his turn at pool. By six o'clock, completely wasted, he found himself making out with her in a corner. When people asked who she was, he introduced her as Jennifer. By seven o'clock, she was his girlfriend Jennifer, and they wandered through the house, joined at the hip, looking for a more private place to make out, eventually ambling into one of the basement bedrooms.

Though dark, it was not private, and there were at least two other couples engaged in some phase of fornication. Leading him to a corner farthest from the others, she began aggressively making out with him, and he followed her lead as he had followed everyone's lead that day, riding the current wherever it took him, refusing the helm. There was a thrill to letting fate take over, to completely abandoning responsibility. There was a defiance in doing the opposite of what was expected or prudent, in breaking all rules society had set, his parents had set or even those he had set for himself. The girl meant nothing to him, but as he pushed his tongue further into her mouth and his pants further down his legs, he felt as if he were giving the universe the finger.

At some point, she went down on him, and he let her, participating with vehemence, roughly pushing her head against his groin, refusing to let her extract herself until he had come, and coming as deep into her mouth as he possibly could.

While he didn't feel pain, he felt no release, either. He felt nothing. An explosive build up of sexual tension and then nothing. Emptiness.

He pushed her away and after dressing himself collapsed on the floor against the wall. She eventually left the room, he assumed to find a bathroom. Part of him hoped she would disappear into the void from where she came, but it was not to be. She returned sometime later with a beer and a cigarette.

"What time is it?" he asked absently.

"I don't know. Going on eight, I think."

He groaned, standing up. "I can't drink this . . ." he said, handing the beer back to her, his head suddenly spinning. "I need something to eat . . . I need some water. I . . . I need to get my shit together before ten."

"I'll find you something to eat. Come with me," she offered, taking his hand and leading him out of the room and into the bright fluorescent lighting of the downstairs hall. The house had grown more crowded, and Alex began to see people he recognized from his own school.

As they neared the kitchen, Ron appeared and pulled him aside.

"Jesus, Fahlstrom—where have you been?"

Alex shrugged. "Downstairs . . . Where have you been?"

"You need to stop drinking, man—we're on in less than two hours . . . Look, Weiss has got a line for you if you need it. It'll help—trust me."

Alex waved him off, uninterested. While he had crossed many lines that day, doing cocaine was way over the edge for him. "I'll be fine, man. I just need some food."

"Okay . . . cool. Let's go get some—"

"Jennifer's getting it," he said, gesturing towards the kitchen into which the girl had disappeared.

Ron rolled his eyes. "Jesus, dude—you need to stay away from that chick, man. You gotta girlfriend, remember? Danielle. Isn't she coming?"

At the mention of Danielle's name, the gently rolling filmstrip in his mind came to a screeching halt. His environment fell eerily quiet but felt charged, like the atmosphere before a summer thunderstorm.

"Danielle . . ." he echoed.

"Look—we're getting out of here for awhile. Let's go grab a bite to eat, okay?" he said, pushing Alex the opposite direction of the kitchen and eventually out the front door. Though they had left their jackets in the house, the bitter cold air felt good, momentarily refreshing, and Alex began to feel clearer-headed by the time they got to Ron's car.

"Where are the rest of us?" Alex asked absently.

Ron shrugged. "Everyone's back there . . . We stopped partying about the time you disappeared with your little groupie . . ."

Alex winced. "She's not my groupie . . . I don't even know who she is."

"You said her name was Jennifer."

"Yeah, maybe . . . I don't know. I don't even care, anymore. Fuck . . . is everyone as wasted as I am? How are you even driving right now. I don't . . . . I don't even know where Burger King is. I couldn't even get us there . . ."

"Shit . . . I know Sumners and I smoked more weed than you, man, but you can drink us all under the table, dude. You drank Weiss under the table, man, and that's no small feat."

"Where is Weiss?"

"Probly banging some girl . . . He told me his goal was to bang one an hour until Midnight," Ron started laughing.

Ten minutes later, they were parked at the Burger King and eating whoppers in the car, listening to mixed tapes on Ron's stereo. While the food made Alex feel physically better, the gentle current of his thoughts and emotions had turned into a raging maelstrom as he relived scenes from earlier in the day, scenes with the girl whom he called Jennifer, wondering if they were real or hallucinations brought on by the overabundance of drugs and alcohol.

Before nine, they finally headed back but had to park a block away due to the additional carloads that had arrived while they were out. Alex looked for Danielle's Volvo, suddenly apprehensive, but couldn't find it. He hoped she was not there. A part of him hoped she wouldn't show up at all.

Any physical improvement provided by the food and fresh air quickly dissipated as Alex entered the house, the smoke and putrid smell of beer, weed and sweat making his stomach turn. He didn't get far before an arm grabbed his shoulder. He turned around to see Dennis.

"Where the fuck have you been?" Dennis asked loudly.

"Ron and I grabbed a bite to eat," Alex practically shouted back. They were in a hallway between the living room and kitchen trying to talk as people shoved by them, between them, around them.

"Shit—why didn't you take me with you?"

"Couldn't find you . . . This place is getting crazy—"

"No shit—let's go outside."

Alex nodded, happy to comply, following his friend out to the driveway.

"Have any smokes?" Dennis asked.

Alex groped in his back jean pocket and pulled out a smashed pack of Marlboro Reds. There was one left. Dennis said he felt bad taking his last one, but Alex insisted. It was the least he could do in exchange for all the joints Dennis had generously supplied him over the past week.

"Jesus Christ . . ." Dennis breathed, exhaling smoke. "Danielle's here, you know."

Alex reddened.

"Don't worry . . . I won't say anything . . . But Carl, man . . . That boy's all over her. You better watch him, man. I didn't want to leave her alone with him. Seriously."

"Isn't Brooke with her?"

Dennis shook his head, sniffing and taking another drag. "Nope . . . In fact, I, uh . . . I can't stay, dude. Sorry."

Alex frowned.

"I guess Brooke's not too happy with me right now. Thinks I love my weed more than her," he said jokingly. "Danielle told me she wasn't coming. Was going to see a movie with her friends."

"A *movie*?" Alex burst. "It's fucking New Year's Eve . . ."

"I know, I know . . . Which is why, I'm . . . I'm going to spend it with her, you know? It'll be cool. We'll play some Mortal Kombat and watch the ball drop on TV."

"Whatever, dude. It's cool. It's really cool of you, actually."

"Yeah, well—you better get back in there. I mean—she is my sister, and . . . Well, I just trust you more than Carl, that's all. That boy is seriously out of control today."

They said their good-byes, and Alex made his way back into the house, trying to curb his growing anger by convincing himself that Dennis was exaggerating. Carl would never move in on Danielle. They were friends, and that was crossing the line.

Since it was nearing show time, he pushed his way into the great room, where the band was set up. As he did, he saw Danielle seated on one of the two large, white leather sofas. A girl he did not recognize sat on one side of her, and on the other sat Carl, his arm casually around her shoulder. She smiled upon seeing him and moved to stand up, but Carl held her waist, pulling her back down next to him. Alex felt his face flush as he strode over to where they sat.

Before he reached them, an arm wrapped around his own waist, and he stopped, startled, even more unnerved when the girl kissed him on the cheek.

"There you are," she said, giggling, wrapping herself around him and giving him a hug. "I've been looking for you for the past hour. I went and found you some pizza, but you were gone."

"Hey, bud," Carl called from the sofa. "Glad you and your friend decided to join us. You ready to play, dude?"

Alex said nothing, all noise a dull roar in his head, as if it were coming from deep within a seashell. He wanted to look at Danielle but didn't. He wanted to think she did not see what had just transpired but couldn't.

"You know Danielle, don't you?" Carl said with mock joviality. "She's been keeping me company . . . My girl of the hour."

At this, Alex looked at Danielle, who looked down, whether out of hurt or shame, he could not tell, her long dark hair hiding her face and expression. She was dressed seductively, in a low-cut, silky, blue sleeveless blouse and black mini skirt, tights and boots. She looked more like her mother than herself, tonight, so it wasn't hard for him to assume she could behave like her mother. Dressed as she was, her long mane of hair tousling about her shoulders, it was highly possible she made out with Carl, and the picture infuriated him. Since she wouldn't look at him, he deduced the worst about her, more angry with her than Carl.

"Danielle, so nice to see you. What a fine pair you and Carl make," Alex said caustically. "This is Jennifer. *My girl of the hour.*"

The girl stepped towards them, holding out her hand. "My name's not Jennifer," she said giggling. "I don't know why he keeps calling me that. It's Jamie."

Danielle finally looked up to greet the girl, and Alex immediately knew he had made a horrible mistake. Through the forced smile, he could see the devastation, her eyes welling with tears that she was struggling hard to contain.

"Nice to meet you, Jennifer," she said, her voice barely audible.

Carl pulled her closer to him, wrapping his arms around her protectively, kissing her forehead. He was whispering something in Danielle's ear, but Alex had no idea what.

As if sensing the potential meltdown, Ron and the band's singer jumped in and insisted on starting the show early. Alex unencumbered himself from the girl while closely watching every move Carl made as he left the sofa. But nothing happened. The girl hosting the party appeared and asked everyone to help move the furniture, including the sofas, from the center of the room to the sides so there could be more space for people to watch. Somewhere in the confusion, Danielle had left the room.

As shaken as he was by the exchange, Alex was relieved she was gone, somewhat able to focus on the music. They opened up with AC/DC's "Back in Black," and by the middle of the song, more people spilled into the room to politely listen. By the end, the room was filled to capacity, and people were singing and cheering along. By the second song, Poison's version of "Rock and Roll All Nite," things became a little rowdier. With all the screaming, hooting and slam dancing that ensued, Alex had no idea how he made it through the entire set, having been physically bumped into numerous times. When a beer bottled whizzed by his head and smashed against the stone fireplace, he motioned to Carl and Ron that they needed to wrap it up fast.

They finished with Nirvana's "Breed" moments before a fight broke out in the audience, sending some guy hurtling into Carl's drums. Carl then began beating the crap out of the guy, Alex and Ron having to pull him off.

Ron and the other two band members offered to pack up the equipment, as Alex led Carl out of the room, trying to calm him down, having—in that moment of camaraderie—completely forgotten what had transpired between him and Danielle earlier.

"Jesus—that guy was a fucking dick. Did you see that guy?" Carl continued his tirade down the hall. "Fucking asshole. They should have taken that shit outside, man. Those drums aren't cheap . . . Fucking assholes."

Alex patted him on the shoulder. "Yeah, I know . . . It's okay. The drums are fine—nobody got hurt. Everything's fine."

"That guy got hurt, man. I fucked him up okay. Did you see that? Did you see it? I fucked him up."

Alex nodded, praising Carl for his brutality, as they wandered towards the opposite end of the house, where fewer and fewer people appeared, finally retreating to a small, enclosed patio near the garage. It was a cold room, sparsely furnished with a wicker sofa and matching chair. Carl sat on the sofa, and Alex took the chair. Both of them wanted to smoke, but neither had any.

"Where's Danielle?" Carl asked finally.

Alex shrugged. "I don't know . . . I don't think she even watched the show."

"Yeah . . . I'm sorry about that, dude. I wasn't going to say anything, but then your girl showed up outta nowhere."

"She's not my girl," Alex said bitterly. "She was just a . . . a nothing. She was nothing."

Carl remained quiet, staring blankly ahead.

"Did you make out with her?" Alex asked finally.

"Shit . . ."

"Did you? I'm not angry at you, I just . . . I need to know."

Carl nodded. "I wanted to . . . I did. I tried, actually. I mean—look at her, dude. Danielle is hot, man. She walked in looking like that . . . I didn't even recognize her. I just thought, *man I want me a piece of that*, you know? Jesus Christ . . . Talk about fuckable. No offense, but I got a hard on just introducing myself to her. And she just started laughing . . . She's got a nice smile, too. She's a sweet girl, Alex . . . Kept me at bay all night. Wanted nothing of it."

"So . . . if she would have at all been flirty back, you would have . . ."

"Abso-fuckinglutely . . . Are you kidding me? Look, the way I see it, if you're gonna go messing around on your girl, she's open game, dude. There's no commitment there."

"Right . . . You're a fucking liar, Weiss," Alex said, laughing bitterly. "My messing around had nothing to do with it. You'd have still gone after Danielle. I know it, you fuck."

Carl mused a moment "Yeah . . . Yeah . . . Alright, so I have no moral backbone whatsoever. We're cool, right?"

Alex groaned, rubbing his forehead, which had begun to throb. "Yeah, sure . . . We're cool."

"By the way—what the fuck happened to our band manager? Where the fuck is Sumners?" Carl suddenly burst.

Alex groaned again. "Home . . . with his girl. Watching the ball drop on television."

"Pussy."

"I think I'm going to need a ride home," Alex said finally, wanting to leave and escape into the oblivion of sleep.

They grabbed their jackets from the corner of the great room and did one more check to ensure Ron had gotten all of the equipment and wiring. Finding nothing, they left the house and were about to walk across the front lawn, when Carl stopped, grabbing Alex in the process. He pointed towards the driveway at a figure leaning against the garage door, her back to them.

"You still have a ride home," Carl said quietly.

Alex stood frozen in place.

"Dude, she ain't waiting for me." He then hit Alex on the arm and headed off without him.

Alex approached her warily, dreading her reaction, fearing tears and sobbing hysteria, already unable to cope with it. Another part of him felt it was pointless to even talk to her, that whatever had existed between them had died that night and was beyond resuscitation.

"Hey," he said quietly, standing behind her.

She turned, smiling sadly. "Oh . . . there you are. Are you ready to go?"

He nodded, and they walked in silence, side by side, so close his hand brushed the fabric of her coat a few times. More than once, he considered grabbing her hand but refrained.

She unlocked the doors, then threw him the keys. "You can drive . . ."

Surprised but not wanting to press her, he accepted. Since Thanksgiving, he drove the car more than she did, and she had let him borrow it while she was in Aspen. He was about to start the car after adjusting the seat and mirrors but stopped.

"I can't do this," he said finally.

"What . . . Drive?" she said, jokingly.

He smiled weakly. "No . . . Pretend like nothing happened."

"Did anything happen?" she asked quietly.

"Yes . . ." he said, his voice barely a whisper.

She sighed. "Let me guess . . . You got completely wasted and messed around with some girl you didn't even know . . . I would even venture to guess you didn't seek her out. She found you, and you just . . . just let it happen. Went with it."

He frowned, puzzled at her accurate summary. "Did Ron tell you?"

She laughed bitterly. "No . . . He didn't have to tell me . . . Nobody told me. Nobody had to. I saw it. I saw it for myself . . . You called her Jennifer. That's not even her name. But . . . That's how you saw her. That's who you saw."

He remained silent.

"Who am I, Alex? When you're totally wasted, who do you see when you look at me? Do I have another name? Or do I even exist?"

"You have another name . . ." he whispered.

"What? What is it? Who is she?"

He shook his head. Even as her mother's name and image filled his mind, he wouldn't tell her. He would never tell her. Not to his grave.

"Fine . . . alright . . . So—so tell me, Alex, how we move forward from here. How we get away from Jennifer—because she keeps coming up. Like a ghost—a, a poltergeist—she keeps haunting us. You keep repeating history— over and over and over. And you know what? I can't help you anymore. I just can't. I never really could, actually . . . You are the only person who can stop this. You're the only person who can rewrite this story . . . But I don't think you want to. I don't think you want to see yourself other than how you do—and, and I don't think you want to see yourself with anyone outside of Jennifer, because you can't."

He shook his head silently in protest.

"No—it's true. There's—there's some part of you that doesn't think you *deserve* to be with me. That you deserve to be happy. That—that we deserve each other, I don't know. I just know you keep trying to sabotage us, and I don't know why . . . It's like you want something to tear us apart so you can feel vindicated somehow. Or maybe you're just a martyr . . . A victim . . . But you're not. And I wish you'd stop acting like one. Or pretending as if you have nothing to do with what happens to you, when you have everything to do with it . . . The world doesn't just happen to us, Alex. We're participants in it. Co-creators . . . Co-conspirators . . . Co-producers of this fucked up universal drama."

He held his breath, waiting for her to finish, his head now pounding with a severe headache. While what she said may be true, he couldn't focus on it. His nerves frayed, his body had begun to shake and he needed a cigarette, a glass of water, something to calm him down.

Minutes passed in tense silence.

"Do you . . . you don't have a smoke on you, do you?"

She looked at him wide-eyed but after seeing he was in obvious pain refrained from whatever retort she had been formulating, her expression turning to concern. "Sorry—no. Are you okay?"

He shrugged. "I'm fine . . . I just . . . I just have a bad headache. I need a smoke . . . My nerves are shot," he said, gripping the steering wheel to stop the shaking.

"Do you want me to drive?" she asked, placing a hand on his arm.

He shook his head. "No, but . . . Can we get going? Please?"

"Yes . . . Of course, I'm sorry . . ."

He turned on the car, and they pulled into the street, eventually heading north on Mission Road. There was a Shell convenience store up ahead, and Alex asked if he could stop and get some cigarettes and aspirin. Looking at her watch, Danielle reluctantly agreed. It was eleven forty.

There was a blue Camaro at one of the pumps, and Alex laughed out loud, motioning to the car. "Look, Weiss is here."

But as they drove past it to park in front of the store, Danielle saw a Montana license plate and pointed that discrepancy out to Alex, who shrugged absently before pulling into a space next to a dark green Ford Bronco, also parked in front of the store. Alex got out, promising to return in a minute.

Danielle reminded him to get a bottled water, too, and waited restlessly in the car, her head suddenly throbbing from the onslaught of tears she had struggled all night to contain. After seeing him with the girl he called Jennifer, she had spent the rest of the evening wandering aimlessly through the house, wringing her heart and mind, wanting so badly to hate him and just leave him there but being unable to do so. Though she refused to watch the concert, she stayed in the strange house, nursing a can of Pepsi that had become lukewarm, burning her throat without providing any refreshment, keeping to back rooms that had the least amount of people, piecing together a likely story of what had happened to Alex and then convincing herself it was palatable.

In the end, she had decided to forgive him. She would forgive him and see where it went, knowing it might lead to the end of their relationship, that she might actually leave him, but also knowing the pain of hate and resentment was far worse than the pain she would feel parting as friends. That if they stayed friends, there was still a future between them, still hope.

As these thoughts and emotions clamored around her mind, she found herself staring out the passenger window, absently reading the decal on the side of the Ford Bronco. It read SHERIFF in bright yellow lettering, with the words *Lake County* in a banner underneath. All this was above an imperfect rectangle that housed a colorful illustration of snow-capped mountains, a bright blue lake and dark green pines. Below this were the words *Big Sky Country 15*.

Her first thought was relief that a sheriff was there, that somehow law enforcement presence would protect them from New Year's mischief and drunken party-goers looking for trouble. But they were in Johnson County, not Lake County, and she didn't remember there even being a Lake County in Kansas, or mountains for that matter. As she studied the illustration closer, a white Ford pick-up pulled into the space next to the driver's side. To her surprise, it was driven by the man with the plaid shirt, who looked extremely agitated. As he rummaged through the front seat, she could almost make out the curse words spewing from his mouth. But when she could also make out the shape of a rifle, her bemusement turned to terror. He then abruptly got out of the truck, slamming the door loudly behind him, but he did not yet enter the store. Instead, he stood next to the truck, loading his gun.

Shit . . . Shit . . . Fucking shit . . . Danielle's mind screamed its own chorus of profanity. Hands shaking, she fumbled with the door handle until it swung open. She then stumbled to the front door of the convenience store, barely closing the car door behind her and nearly tripping on the curb in the process. Her hand was on the large, rectangular metal door handle when she was grabbed roughly from behind. She nearly vomited in her mouth.

"I wouldn't go in there right now if I were you, little lady."

His unshaven face was inches away from hers, and she could smell the alcohol.

"P-pl . . . please," she stammered. "My boyfriend's in there. Please. Please don't. Please let me get him first. Please—I promise we'll leave."

"There ain't nobody in there you know . . . You ain't even from around here," he said, looking her up and down. "Go back to where you came from, *city girl*."

He roughly shoved her aside and yanked open the glass door.

It was in that instant that time stalled and everything moved as if in slow motion. Seconds felt like minutes, and even though what happened next took less than fifteen seconds to transpire, she had time enough to think through each of her actions and their possible consequences.

When she walked through the door behind him, she knew she would never leave. She could tell by the décor of the store that she was no longer in the Prairie Village Shell station, a place she had frequented often in the past, often enough to remember what it looked like inside—small but clean, the metal shelves painted white, the floor tile white. She could tell when a bell jingled above the door as it closed, and the door was no longer glass and metal but glass and wood, and the floor no longer white but dark green with specks. And while the shelves were tidy, there were twice the number of them, along with a postcard turnstile full of photos, photos of snow capped mountains and a crystal blue lake.

She saw Alex standing at the counter in the back of the store, talking to the clerk, a girl with blond hair who bore a striking resemblance to Kelly. A few shelves back, she saw another man, tall, with a thick but neatly trimmed mustache who bore a striking resemblance to Tate's father. And just within arm's reach was the gunman, so close that she could reach out and touch him, that she could feel the cotton wrap around her fingertips as she pulled at his shirt, grabbing it enough to slow him down so she could pass him, so she could warn Alex.

The man abruptly stopped and spun around, and their bodies momentarily collided, but when she looked at his face, she no longer saw the dark haired unshaven man in a plaid shirt. Instead, she saw a clean-shaven young man with blondish hair, cut short with just a hint of curls, dark deep-set eyes and a rugged jaw line, his skin tone fair, with a light brush of freckles across his forehead and cheeks. Gone was the plaid shirt and worn jeans, having been replaced with a pressed light pink oxford and khaki pants. His eyes narrowed at her in hate, lifted the rifle and fired off three rounds. The first bullet ripped through her left lower left side, the force jolting her backwards, but she kept her balance and remained upright until another ripped into her upper chest and a third tore through her left shoulder.

Someone called her name, and she looked up to see Alex hurrying towards her, fearlessly brushing past the gunman as if he didn't notice him.

She looked at them curiously for a moment, the two young men identical twins except for their clothes, before her legs buckled under her and she collapsed onto the floor, her hands still clutching at the wounds as she instinctively tried to stop the flow of blood, which began pooling onto her clothing. He caught her before she hit the floor, helping her lay down, screaming for somebody to call 911, to get help, unaware that there was nobody there.

She tugged at his flannel shirt, "Alex . . ." she coughed. "Look at me."

But he continued to call for help, tears streaming down his face.

"Alex, they can't hear you . . . They're not there."

He looked down at her, shakily taking off his jacket, trying to cover her wounds and stop the bleeding, his mind reeling in horror at the sight that was unfolding, a sight so completely unexpected it seemed unreal. His mind racing through the last five minutes, trying to sort out what had happened. Time slowed, allowing him to examine each action, from the moment he slammed the car door shut and walked up to the convenience store door. Opening it, he strode to the counter, surprised to see Kelly Kurtz. He greeted her warmly and called her Kelly, insisting she was Kelly even when the girl denied it, pointing at her badge, which said *Jennifer*. She flirted with him playfully, as if she knew him, asking if he had made a special trip in just to wish her a Happy New Year. *No*, he had said. *I just need cigarettes and aspirin. Marlboro Reds, please*. But she giggled, grabbing his hand and kissing it. *Putting on an act for your father, I see*, she said, motioning to the man a few aisles behind him. He stared at her in blank confusion until she dropped his hand in frustration. *Fine, I'll play along*, she said, setting a pack of Reds on the counter in front of him. *And some aspirin*. She rolled her eyes, pointing behind him. *Same aisle as your dad. Maybe that's what he's looking at, silly*. She winked at him, and the door burst open. He turned at the sound of the jingle. He turned and saw the man with a plaid shirt holding a rifle, but he still saw no face, only a void. Danielle was behind the man, grabbing at him. And then something happened that he couldn't explain. He couldn't explain it because it seemed so unreal, so completely senseless.

"Alex . . . This isn't real. This isn't happening. It's a dream," Danielle said, trying to smile.

He shook his head, taking one of her hands in his, sobbing.

"It's okay . . . Trust me, it isn't real."

"It feels real . . . it feels so real . . ." he said, shaking, his hands covered in blood.

"Look at the gunman, Alex . . . He has a face . . . He has a name. Look at him, and you'll see. You'll know . . ."

He shook his head, having forgotten there was a gunman, he was now too terrified to turn around, the hairs on his neck bristling, like the charge of lightning before it strikes.

Slowly, he turned his head, and who he saw first chilled him, the preppy attire, the arrogant smirk. Consumed with rage, he jumped up and flew at him, knocking him against a back-wall shelf, cans and boxes loudly tumbling to the floor.

"You son of a bitch," he screamed, grabbing him by the shirt collar and slamming the back of his head repeatedly against the shelf, each contact causing his own head to throb.

The young man laughed, staring him squarely in the eye. "Kick me . . . Punch me . . . Go ahead and beat the crap out of me . . . You'll only hurt yourself."

Furious at his smugness, Alex punched him violently in the gut before knocking him in the face, surprised at his sudden nausea and the trickle of blood streaming down his own face. The guy hadn't even touched him.

"Who do you think I am?" the young man asked, bowled over in pain but still smirking.

"I know who you fucking are, you mother fucking bastard," Alex screamed, flying at him again, hurling both of their bodies into another section of shelving. He then began pounding him in the face and head.

Tate, you mother fucking bastard . . . Why'd you do it . . . you mother fucker. She didn't do anything to you. She forgave you, you fucking shit. You didn't have to hurt her. You fucking shit.

He beat him until he could no longer see clearly due to the blood that streamed from his own brow and forehead, stinging his eyes.

"Tate?" the young man said with mild hysteria, staggering away from Alex. "You think I'm Tate? You think Tate did this?" He laughed, holding his stomach. "Of course you do . . . I forgot, you're a victim. A poor, helpless victim. This has nothing to do with *you*. Her death has nothing to do with *you*."

As Alex struggled to stay upright, his vision blurred and head spinning, the young man grabbed him, dragging him down the aisle and behind the counter, violently knocking away a rack of cigarettes to expose a mirrored sign.

"Look at us," he said, grabbing Alex's hair and pulling his head next to his. "Look at me now, and tell me who you see."

Hands trembling, Alex moved to push away the strands of hair that were plastered to his face by blood. Blinking repeatedly to clear his vision, he looked in the mirror and saw double. Though his eyes saw a twin, his mind rejected it, replacing recognition with anger and hate, an abhorrence so deep he shoved the young man aside and strode around the counter for the gun. It was a hunting gun, a Winchester 30-30, and the polished wood felt familiar in his hands.

"You're only shooting yourself," the young man said, holding his hands up in surrender.

Alex narrowed his eyes in hate, lifted the rifle and fired off three rounds. The first bullet ripped through his left side, the force jolting him backwards, but he kept his balance and remained upright until another ripped into his upper chest and a third tore through his left shoulder.

The young man collapsed behind the counter, and Alex staggered towards Danielle, collapsing to the floor before he could reach her and having to crawl the remainder of the way. He feared she was already dead, her skin ghostly pale, her hair spilling around her, flowing into the pools of darkened blood. Though her chest was bare, his jacket draped across her waist, there was blood spattered on it that almost made a pattern, a pattern of letters that spelled a word, a very ugly word. And the word made him weep, for he didn't believe it. He didn't see her that way. She was not a whore.

"You're not . . . you're not," he sobbed, holding her close to himself. "I love you, Danielle . . . Please come back. Please don't go. I need you. I need you in my dream. I want you here. Please."

Alex, wake up.

"No . . . I won't leave you," he said, feeling the blood pour from his own wounds, feeling the cold numbness slowly begin to surge through his system. "I love you . . . I lied when I said I didn't . . . I do . . . Don't leave me, please." He lay down next to her, his armed wrapped around her waist, his head on her chest, as he would do if they were in her room, in her bed, after watching television or making out.

"I've never left you, Alex . . . You just don't recognize me," she whispered. "Maybe you will next time," she said.

Seconds later, her breathing stopped. He could tell, but kept his head on her chest and his arms around her until minutes later his own vision faded into a clear light.

CHAPTER ELEVEN

When Alex awoke, he was relieved to feel the touch of sheets beneath his fingertips and to see a white ceiling above his head. As his vision adjusted to the dim light, he could make out other shapes—a curtained window, a television, a furnishing he did not recognize. Every cell in his body cried out in relief that his nightmare was over and it was just that—a nightmare. A dream, just as Danielle had said. He wanted to turn on his side, to reach out and see if she was there, lying in bed with him, but he was too weak to move, barely able to claw at the sheets with his fingers. His breathing was labored, still recollecting the horrific scenes, and he lay still for the next few minutes, trying to calm himself down, telling himself repeatedly it was just a dream.

At some point he heard voices, dull and muffled at first but gaining in clarity, along with his vision and other senses, his mouth feeling chalky and tasting acrid, as if laced with aspirin, his stomach nearly lurching at the smell of ammonia and urine. As he completely came to, he realized he was not alone and he was not at home. He was in a strange bed surrounded by a woman, a girl, a nurse and a law enforcement officer. He recognized no one, but the girl looked like Jennifer Hicks.

As he tried to move, the voices got louder—more excited. He heard his name called but could not respond. The woman sat down on the bed next to him, grabbing his hand. She looked familiar, her long, golden-brown, wavy hair lightly brushing his arm, her bright eyes, made more spritely by tears, staring at him intently. She smiled and brushed a strand of hair from his forehead.

"*Alex, honey . . . You're awake.*"

Her voice was light and sweet, like a song, and he thought he smiled at her.

"Who are you?" he thought he asked.

"*Honey . . . It's your mother. I'm here, and I'm so glad you've come back to us,*" she said, bursting into tears of relief. "*We love you so much. We've missed you so much.*"

He swallowed hard, his stomach churning at the foul taste in his mouth and the sudden realization that he was still dreaming.

"No you're not," he thought he said, chuckling to himself before closing his eyes again and drifting off to sleep.

When Alex awoke, he was relieved to feel the touch of sheets beneath his fingertips and to see a white ceiling above his head. His senses adjusted quickly, and to ensure he was fully awake this time, he attempted to move his right hand from his side, where it rested, grab the sheet as it lay across his chest and fling it off. But he could barely lift his arm. He then tried to sit up in bed, but his body felt heavy and limp, almost lifeless.

He looked around the room, straining to turn his head from side to side, confused by the unfamiliar shapes in the dim light. A curtained window, a television, a furnishing he did not recognize. It was eerily quiet, except for the hum of a machine. His mouth and throat felt parched, and he could barely swallow. The air smelled stale. He thought he heard someone say his name, but it sounded as if it were coming from the inside of a seashell.

Concluding he was still dreaming, he drifted back into sleep.

Each time Alex thought he woke up, he saw the same strange furnishings, heard the same steady humming of a machine, smelled the same pungent odor of chemicals masking bodily waste. Sometimes he heard people talking, sometimes he even felt someone touching him, grabbing him, jostling him. If his eyes adjusted properly to the light, he could make out faces or clothing. There were people in white, white coats, white pants and white shirts. There was often a police officer. But the person he saw the most was the pretty lady with the long, wavy golden-brown hair, blue eyes and sing-song voice. Because he did not believe in God and had little exposure to religion, he did not believe in angels. To him, she could have been an elf from Middle Earth. Or a fairy. He vaguely wondered if Dennis's weed had been laced with hallucinogens.

And each time he realized he had not woken up in an environment he recognized, he went back to sleep.

How long he slept, he was unsure, for he felt groggy and disoriented the moments he thought he was awake. But with the passing of time, the room became brighter, the furnishings more defined and the noise clearly audible to the point he realized the woman with the long golden hair was actually conversing with him, providing a steady stream of information about people he knew. His father, Danielle, Carl, Trisha, Ron and someone or something named Genghis. The Trahans came up quite often, along with someone named Barb. He even thought he heard the name Gabrielle but didn't remember hearing *Sumners* with it. She also spoke often about Pirates sports, which confused him, Kansas City the home of the Royals or Chiefs and no one in his family having ties to Pittsburgh. Polson came up often, and there were times he could swear she was reading a Montana newspaper to him, including the obituaries. At other times she read what he assumed was the Bible or even prayed out loud, and after listening to entire mantras of *Jesus*, or *Our Lord Jesus Christ*, he concluded she was not from Rivendell.

But there were just as many moments when he lay awake completely alone in the room, which, much to his dismay, he began to realize was located within a hospital. Everything in the entire room was beige or white, with the exception of some partially deflated silver and blue balloons that bobbed on a table in the far corner. There was a small curtained window barely to his front left through which he yearned to look but could never quite get the strength to turn his head far enough. And one day, when he did, the curtains were pulled shut.

At some point in time, he grew agitated over his half-sleeping, half-waking state and formed a determination in his mind to fully wake himself up and stay that way, regardless of what he saw or thought he saw. He was tired of lying down and wanted to physically move.

He had been lying for some time with his eyes open, staring at the white tiled squares on the ceiling, and began collecting his thoughts and memories. If he was in a hospital, how did he get there? His last memory was bleeding out in a convenience store with Danielle, who had also, seemingly, bled out. But she had said they were dreaming. It wasn't real. Did his mind continue to play out the dream, sending himself to a hospital to recuperate? If so, did hers do the same? Or did something happen at the party . . . He remembered objects whizzing through the air during their raucous concert. He remembered the fight breaking out. And even though he clearly remembered talking to Carl afterwards and Danielle after that, maybe those conversations never happened. Maybe he got knocked out during the concert, and he was recuperating in a Kansas City hospital.

With a steady stream of thoughts and questions, mysteries and musings, he could lay awake for hours, now, content to stare at the ceiling and watch the comings and goings of nurses, doctors and the occasional visitor without losing his mind from boredom. He felt his strength returning ever so slowly, soon able to lift his hands and arms. Soon able to completely turn his head in either direction. To move his feet and legs under the covers. To grab and release the sheet with his fingers.

Many times, he tried to talk, but it sounded so odd, guttural. Embarrassed at the inhuman sounds he first made, he would only practice when nobody was in the room. Mentally hearing and seeing the words, he would try to mouth them, to say them, but often couldn't—or did and only heard gurgling, as if from an infant. So, he practiced sentences he wanted to voice. *Hello, my name is Alex. Who are you? Where am I? What happened to me? How did I get here? Where is Danielle? How is she? Where are my parents? Where is my father? He is a doctor. I miss them. I need them. I'm thirsty. Please give me some water. Please open the curtains. What the fuck . . .*

One afternoon, it actually worked. A nurse came by to check on things, and as she was leaning over his chest, he grabbed her sleeve. Meaning to say, *please give me some water*, it barely came out *water*—was barely audible at all—but she heard him, and her eyes grew wide.

"Water, Alex? Did you say *water*?"

He nodded.

"Oh, dear Lord, praise be!" she burst, all smiles, then trotted out of the room, returning momentarily with a cup, another nurse, and a doctor. Though he could not hold the cup himself, after helping him sit up, one of the nurses put the paper cup to his lips and he felt the cold water touch his tongue and stream down his throat, offering such invigorating relief that he didn't care that half of it dribbled out of his mouth, spilling down his chin and onto his chest.

The event caused a ruckus and a steady stream of nurses and doctors followed, administering bodily tests and proddings and asking questions to which he had only the energy to nod or shake his head. As physically exhausting as it was, he was mentally awake and could not fall asleep. To his relief, one of the nurses asked him if he would like to watch television, to which he eagerly nodded. She turned on a local station, and he spent the remainder of the afternoon watching sitcom reruns and talk shows.

At some point, a group of visitors arrived. Though he had seen all of them before, their presence unnerved him. The law enforcement officer, the pretty golden-haired lady and the girl who looked like Jennifer Hicks. The lady held an old teddy bear dressed in a University of Montana Grizzlies T-shirt and a bouquet of red, heart-shaped helium balloons. She immediately came to his bedside, followed by the law enforcement officer, a tall, well-built man with a thick, neatly trimmed mustache. He stood right behind the lady, his arm on her waist. The girl stayed away, sitting in a chair at the opposite end of the room, looking morose.

"Happy Valentine's Day," she said, all smiles, her eyes shining brightly. She held onto the bear but handed the balloons to the man, motioning for him to put them on the dresser. "We heard we have something to celebrate. That you were able to talk today. Honey, we're so proud of you. That's such wonderful news," and she bent down and gave him a hug, her hair brushing against his face. She smelled of flowers and citrus.

"Look—we brought you some company," she said after pulling away, holding out the worn bear. "Mr. Grizzly . . . Would you like to keep him with you?"

He shook his head, staring at the bear in mild horror.

She nodded cheerfully, but he could see the pain as she walked over to the dresser and set the bear next to the balloon bouquet. While she did this, the law enforcement officer approached and, to Alex's surprise, sat on the edge of the bed, right next to Alex, reached out and gently placed a hand on his own.

"You're looking better every day, Alex. How you feeling, son?"

This close, Alex could see he was no ordinary policeman, the prominent gold, star-shaped badge pinned to his breast indicating he was the Sheriff.

"Danielle, come say hi to your brother," the lady said.

Alex watched the girl wave to him from her chair without making eye contact and began shaking his head in dismay. The Sheriff thought he was responding to his question.

"Not feeling good today?"

He continued to shake his head, his hands starting to tremble.

The lady joined the Sheriff, walking up to Alex and placing her hand on his forehead. "You don't feel warm, honey. You're probably just tired after your very big achievement, today. You know, the doctors say your recovery looks good. They're going to start physical and speech therapy next week. You might be able to come home in March."

At this point, his entire body started to shake slightly as a maelstrom of thoughts surged through his consciousness. He wanted to scream the words but was unable to produce enough force. "Who are you?"

The lady heard them, for she stepped back, a surprised look on her face. She looked curiously at the Sheriff before turning to Alex.

"Alex, I'm . . . I'm your mother."

He shook his head, trying to mouth the word *no*.

She reached out to him, and he tried to shrink away from her touch. Soon, she was trembling, insisting she was his mother, *didn't he remember her? How could he not remember her*, her voice getting higher pitched with each word. The Sheriff then intervened, holding her, trying to calm her down. But she continued.

"Alex, we're your family. I'm your mother . . . This is your father . . . That's your sister, Danielle . . ."

But with each sentence, Alex shook his head more vehemently, screaming *No* in his mind and soon voicing the word, gasping the word and eventually shouting the word audibly enough for the people in the room to hear, to panic. Somehow finding the strength to bellow the word loud enough for nurses to come running into the room. By then his entire person was shaking violently and he began to thrash about hysterically, feeling trapped by his body, his mind, his circumstances. He had no idea how long the attack lasted, at some point feeling a warm numbness pervade his body, starting in his arm, before falling into a deep dreamless sleep.

When he awoke, he heard voices nearby, a conversation. He opened his eyes but could not see them, as they were on the other side of the curtain. He could tell by the melodic tone that one was the voice of the lady with golden wavy hair. The other was a man's voice.

He's my son. I don't understand why they won't let me see him.

Jayne—They need to do some tests. He needs a complete psychiatric evaluation. There's a good chance he's suffering from severe amnesia—

How is this possible? How? He's—he's doing so well. He was watching television. He—he spoke words—

Coma victims, especially ones who take weeks to wake up, like Alex, often suffer from extreme amnesia and delusion. It can take months—years, even, for them to recover fully. At almost four weeks, he's lucky he woke up at all. Consider his progress a miracle, because that's exactly what it is.

He doesn't know me. He doesn't know Bill. He doesn't know any of us.

I know.

Will it come back—his memory?

Hard to say. Maybe but . . . not likely,

This is so hard . . . It's so hard . . . He's right behind that curtain, and I can't . . . I can't see him . . . I can't hold him. I'm his mother, and I can't help him . . .

At that point, she broke into tears, and he could tell she was led out of the room entirely, the room falling silent except for the hum of the feeding tube machine. While he did not like to see people in pain, he was unmoved by her emotions, instead feeling a simmering rage over what he felt was a cruel ruse. Coma . . . Another coma? Hadn't one coma been enough? How could he possibly have survived a second? Or was he still dreaming? He had to be dreaming. There was no way he was going to relive another few months of painful therapy. Of struggling to retrieve his memories. His mind drifted to the last time he woke from his coma, and he tried to remember what it felt like. Had he recognized his parents? His sister? Or did that come later? He couldn't remember much at all about the first few days, let alone the first few hours.

To distract his agitated mind, he groped for the remote, which the nurses had kindly left within his reach, and turned on the television. For the next hour or so he watched game shows, wishing he would fall asleep, until news programming came on. Too lazy to figure out which button on the remote would actually change the station, he watched with disinterest until he started hearing names and phrases that didn't make sense.

This is KECI 13, where Western Montana turns for the latest in news, weather and sports.

Something about a car chase outside Kalispell. A bank robbery in Missoula that ended with a standoff. A feature story about sheep getting pneumonia. But when the weather map clearly revealed the State of Montana and showed temperatures throughout the Mission Valley, he pushed the off button, trying to curb an intense surge of panic. His heart racing wildly, his hands gripping at the sheets, he struggled with a plan of action.

Escape. He had to escape, it was the only way. He had been kidnapped by strange people against his will and brought back to Montana. But when? When did this happen? The convenience store? The party? And more importantly, why? Who on earth would want to kidnap a 17-year old boy? Nothing made sense.

Desperate, he moved his hands to the feeding tube in his stomach and began pulling at it, trying to disconnect it from his person. He then worked on the tube in his arm. When he eventually succeeded, it set off some kind of monitor alert, which sent nurses flying into his room, which sent him into a greater panic. Once again, he started thrashing about wildly, screaming at the top of his lungs, until a warm numbness pervaded his body and he fell into a dreamless sleep.

The next time he woke, his arms were strapped to the bed, completely disabling him, causing him to lay flat on his back and stare at the white ceiling squares in complete terror over the helplessness of his situation. His chest ached from the pounding of his heart, labored breathing and fear that heightened every nerve down to the pit of his stomach.

He had no sense of time and no idea how long he had been lying there before a doctor came in to check on him. She was older, with darker skin, short black hair and silver wire-rimmed glasses that were so thick, it was hard to see her eyes.

"I see we're awake, Mr. Fahlstrom," she said, standing by his bedside. "How are we feeling today?"

He stared at her, seething inside, his mind screaming *I hate you*, but only saying *Hate*.

"Ate? Are you hungry?"

Enraged, he said it louder. *Hate. Hate.*

She stepped back a bit, pursing her lips. "Hate? Is that what you said?"

He nodded, tears starting to form in the corner of his eye.

But she nodded, sadly. "Yes. . . I understand completely. You're very angry. I would be, too, if I were in your situation. I would hate everyone. Strapped to your bed like that. Unable to move about freely. Unable to talk clearly. Unable to do what you want to do."

The tears began welling.

"Do you remember what happened to you?" she asked softly, sitting on the edge of his bed nearer his feet.

He shook his head, jostling a tear from his lower lid, feeling a stream down the side of his face.

"Do you mind if I ask you some questions?"

He didn't move.

"Is your name Alex?"

He nodded.

"Alex Fahlstrom?"

He nodded.

"Good . . . That's good. Are you sixteen years old?"

He shook his head.

"No? Well how old are you then?

He remained silent.

"Are you fifteen?"

He shook his head.

"Seventeen?"

He nodded and noticed she scribbled something on the clipboard of papers she held.

"You like football?"

He nodded.

"Do you remember playing football?"

He nodded.

"Good, good . . . How 'bout your home? Do you remember where your home is?

He nodded.

"The address?"

He nodded.

"Is it 38621 Big Sky Lane?"

He shook his head.

"Is it in Polson, Montana?"

He shook his head, tears now streaming down both sides of his face, causing his skin to itch.

"Is it in Montana?"

He shook his head and with every bit of energy he had voiced *Kansas*.

"Kansas? Did you say *Kansas*?"

He nodded, but his heart sank. Like Dorothy, he'd been blown into some Oz-like hell hole. He could tell by the tone in her voice that he was not supposed to be from Kansas City. Probably never even lived in Kansas City, which seemed to have been a mere delusion.

She kept talking, but he ceased to hear her, the sound of his own inner screaming filling his mind. The tears streamed faster, steadier, followed by heaving sobs, but strapped down, he could do nothing. Only when he began to choke on his own saliva, did the woman call for help, moving to unstrap him, at which point he once again lashed out, swinging at everything and everyone until a warm numbness pervaded his body and he fell into a dreamless sleep.

"You're a very strong young man, Alex. You have amazing strength, will and determination. You focus that on getting well, and you can walk out of here soon. But we've had to sedate you four times in the last 72 hours. That's just going to set you back, honey."

He stared at her with hate, trying to penetrate her thick, silver-rimmed glasses.

"Now, we'd like to start you in therapy. We'd like to move you out of this miserable ICU room and into a more homey, private room with a beautiful view of the mountains. But I can't do that when you try to attack everyone the minute you have a chance, as impressive as it is given your condition."

She sat on the edge of his bed, this time closer to his face.

"And, I want to talk to you about Kansas." She leaned closer to him, taking her glasses off so he could see her eyes, which were rather large and dark brown. "We have a mystery to solve, don't we?"

Surprised, he held his breath for a moment, meeting her stare.

"You have family in Kansas, don't you," she said gently, more as a statement than a question.

He nodded, exhaling in relief.

"Parents?"

He nodded, closing his eyes, their faces coming to mind.

"A sister, maybe? Friends?"

Yes, yes, he thought and tried to voice.

"A girlfriend, maybe?"

At this he stared at her wide-eyed, trying to grab her arm, but unable to do so, still strapped to the bed. Instead, he nodded. "Yes."

"I thought so," she said, nodding, putting her glasses back on. "Well, we're not going to be able to find them without your help. You need to tell us your story. You can't do that doped up and strapped to a bed, now can you? No . . . You get better. You work with me and the other doctors and nurses to get better, and we'll help you find what you think you lost."

He relaxed his body, closing his eyes and picturing Danielle. He wanted to believe this woman. He desperately wanted to believe her.

"Alright . . . We're going to make this official. I'm going to unstrap you, and I want a hand shake on this . . ." She moved to undo his left arm, which was closest to her, then slipped her hand under his.

He grabbed it firmly.

Within a week, he was moved out of the ICU and into a private room.

As promised, he had a picture window with a view of the snow-capped mountains, and they were the only physical aspect of his present existence that brought him any peace, that stopped him from finding a way to kill himself in an attempt to wake up from what he believed to be another bad dream.

Aside from dying again, he decided that telling his story might be the only other chance he had of finding his past, and he set about his various therapies with a fierce determination to recover as quickly as possible, tirelessly doing his exercises, practicing movements well after sessions had ended. Talking aloud to walls for hours on end in order to revive his complete range of vocal mobility, masking the noise he made by the sound of the television.

But his biggest concern was preserving his memories, which he felt he could best do by writing them down. To keep his sanity, he spent every spare waking moment recording and re-recording his life history as he remembered it, reciting it aloud as part of his own speech therapy. But he soon felt compelled to write it down, and began doing so on pharmaceutical tablets of paper donated to him by the nurses. Because he had not re-mastered his handwriting yet, only a few words would take up an entire page of the five by seven sheets of paper, the letters scrawling three to four times larger than he could write them under normal circumstances.

One day, the doctor with the silver-rimmed glasses surprised him with a gift—two large lined note tablets designed especially for student writing exercises, along with a new pack of pens. She was his counselor and visited him for a half hour each afternoon. He enjoyed practicing talking with her, and they usually discussed what he watched on television.

"Thank you," he said smiling. "Thank you so much."

"Oh, these aren't from me. These are from Jayne Fahlstrom. Do you remember Mrs. Fahlstrom?"

He felt his blood chill and looked away.

"She would like to see you, Alex. Do you want to see her?"

"No," he said clearly and audibly.

"Not even to thank her for the gift?"

"No."

"Okay. Alright."

But a few days later, she brought up the subject again, this time after reading through his tablets, which he had already filled to capacity, one with basic facts about himself—who he was, his birth date, his birth place, his family and his parents' occupations, where he went to school, his hobbies, his friends, where he lived down to his current address and telephone number,

Danielle's address and number and those of his closest friends. The other he began diary style, sharing memories of his earliest childhood. Deciding to start at the beginning and be as thorough as possible, he had run out of room well before middle school, still describing grade-school memories in Polson, adventures with his family, antics with his friends, medical stories he had heard or seen with his father.

"What does your mother look like, Alex . . . Do you remember? I mean, you say her name is Laura, and you have interesting stories about her, but what does she look like? Why don't you tell me. Describe her to me."

Alex took a deep breath, trying to bring his mother's memory into focus. She was of medium height with very blond—almost white blond—hair, which she wore straight and cut in a sharp page boy style. She had a fair skin tone and freckles and narrow set, dark blue eyes. Though she was not pretty, she was agreeable and well-groomed, even if her clothing was a bit matronly at times, usually an attire of neatly pressed slacks with a striped blouse or an overly colorful, boxy sweater.

"Good, good . . . Do you remember what your mother looked like when you were a child—when these stories you wrote about took place? Did she look different?"

He closed his eyes, traveling back in time . . . Yes. She looked quite different. Though he couldn't make out her features, she had long hair and wore flowing skirts.

"Do you mind if I show you a few photos?" she asked, undoing her clip board and retrieving a large manilla envelope. "Tell me if any of these look familiar to you," she said, handing him a small assortment of photos, a few wallet sized and some larger.

To his surprise, he recognized all of them. There were a few baby pictures of himself, along with a few photos of him as a toddler with his parents and one with his entire family, including his sister. There was also a photo of his parents when they were younger, one he remembered seeing on his mother's dresser in Kansas City on Thanksgiving. He remembered it clearly because he had been so taken aback by how youthful and beautiful she looked, with long, golden-brown hair that spilled down her shoulders in ripples. And she was smiling, laughing maybe, she and his father hugging on a lakeshore, their backdrop a white-capped mountain range.

"You know that photo, don't you?" the doctor asked quietly.

He nodded.

"Alex," she said, taking off her glasses so he could see her eyes, as if she knew it was important for him to ascertain her sincerity. "Don't you think that Mrs. Fahlstrom, the lady who gave you the tablets, who visited you often a few weeks ago, looks a little like the lady in that photo?"

"Yes," he said flatly, for it was true. She looked just like her, maybe slightly older, but not as old as the woman he remembered being his mother before the coma.

"Is it possible that you're just remembering her being older than she really is?"

"No . . . I know what she looked like before the coma, and it wasn't anything like this . . . I just don't remember the transition, you know? I don't . . . I don't remember how she went from looking like these pictures to what she does now."

"Fair. That's a fair and logical answer. I have another photo for you," she said, digging into the envelope. "What about this one?"

His eyes grew wide as he stared at it, for the lady in the photo was the mother he remembered, with the short, page-boy cut and slacks. She was standing with an older gentleman, and Alex was in-between the two, holding their hands, maybe seven or eight years old.

"That's who you remember, isn't it?"

"Yes . . . Yes—this is my mother. That's her, but . . . I don't understand? Where is she? Why isn't she here?" he asked, getting excited, wishing he could jump out of his wheel chair.

"Well . . . That is your grandmother, Laura Kay Fahlstrom," she said, turning over the photo so Alex could read clearly the names—*Alex with Grandma and Grandpa Fahlstrom* - and date, handwritten in a felt tip pen. "And your grandfather, whose name I don't know. Do you?"

"William," Alex said dully, suddenly feeling dizzy and slightly nauseous.

"Okay . . . I'll take your word for it."

"She's dead, isn't she," he said, feeling chilled, the room beginning to spin. "My grandmother's dead, isn't she?" he demanded.

But before the doctor could respond, he turned to the side and vomited on the floor.

He hadn't needed for the doctor to confirm she had been dead three years for Alex to begin piecing together what was happening. Somehow, he had woken up to a life he did not remember, and the people in this life would begin trying to convince him that his previous life was a mere dream, a delusion he experienced while in a coma. It was as if everything he had experienced and everyone he had ever known or loved had completely ceased to exist except in his mind. But what they wouldn't understand—indeed, what he was sure they couldn't understand—was how devastated he felt over the loss. He would have done anything to get back what he had, at times even praying to a god he did not believe existed, at other times screaming at hell, offering to make whatever bargain necessary with a devil he believed equally nonexistent.

As the days waned on, he increasingly contemplated suicide, and because he was losing interest in life, pushed his body beyond its capacity in his therapy sessions, soon able to move himself in and out of the wheel chair, to eat, bathe and dress on his own. Having come to terms with losing his family, he now focused on memories of his friends, especially Danielle, a part of him still holding on to a shred of hope that he might find them, in what form or capacity, he did not know. He missed her terribly and would spend hours at night either reliving his times with her or actually having conversations with her, as if she existed somewhere and could hear him, repeatedly apologizing for their last night together, for his loathsome behavior. He would close his eyes and try to recall the way she looked, the way her hair and skin felt, her smell—fresh, flowery, what her voice sounded like, which was becoming harder to hear, fading with each passing day.

I've never left you, she had said, but he had no idea what she meant, and it sounded even more cryptic now. She had also said something about not recognizing her, which was equally cryptic and in his present situation, frightening. Still, there was a thought, fleeting at first but growing in its presence and urgency that said *stick around awhile longer—see if you can find her.*

It was this thought that led him, almost two weeks later, to allow a meeting with Jayne Fahlstrom.

On the afternoon of her visit, he found himself extremely nervous, almost nauseous with dread. She had continued to send him gifts even though he had refused to see her in person. Novels to read, along with crossword puzzle and word search books. Notebooks and pens so he could continue his journal writing, along with practical items: a week's supply of sweat pants and shirts that the hospital would keep laundered for him, plus socks, underwear, tennis shoes and slippers. She sent a grooming kit with toiletries that he was allowed to keep except for the razors. Nightly, she would drop off dinner plates and a fresh supply of home-baked cookies, which he came to relish, having tired quickly of hospital fare. Thick homemade stews of beef, carrots and potatoes. Pot pies loaded with steak and vegetables. Roasted chicken and mashed potatoes.

When she arrived, he was seated at the small table in his hospital room, right in front of the picture window, which was open to reveal the Mission

Mountains, today graced by a clear blue sky. She knocked hesitantly before coming in, approaching him with caution. He tried to look up, to greet her, but was too embarrassed, looking out the window instead.

Pulling the chair out from the table, she took a seat across from him. "Hi, Alex," she said quietly.

"Thank you for the food and stuff," he said gruffly, still looking out the window. "That's . . . It's very nice of you to do all that for me."

"Oh, my goodness . . ." she burst in the sing-song tone she had. "Why wouldn't we? We're your family. We love you."

"I don't know you," he said, finally turning to her. "I don't know who you are."

Her bright eyes teared, but she did not cry, instead nodding her head resolutely. "I know. I know you don't. I'm sorry. You can . . . You can call me Jayne if you'd like."

He looked away. "Did you read my diaries . . . I'm sure she showed them to you."

"Who, honey?"

"The doctor. My *shrink*."

She inhaled deeply before responding, and Alex could hear the fear and hesitation. "I'm not angry," he said calmly. "I just want to know if you read them."

"Yes . . . Yes, I read them."

"So, how much of it is true?"

"I'm sorry—" she said, taken aback.

He looked at her. "How much of it is true? Is real? Any of it?"

"Oh, well . . . I—I don't know . . ."

"How can you not know?" he burst angrily. "It either happened that way or not—it's all real or not. Just tell me."

"I—I can't tell you that. It's—it's real for you, so—so how can it not be real? I believed what I read . . . And I'm . . . I'm very sorry for you and what you're going through. Your loss . . . But I . . . I suffered a loss, too. I lost a son. He looks . . . He looks a lot like you. His name was Alex Tate. He was born on June fourth. Right here in Polson . . . Right here in this hospital, actually."

"Did you say Alex *Tate*? My name is *Alex Tate*?" he said, feeling his face flush.

She nodded, brushing an errant tear from her cheek and taking a tissue from her purse, an ugly tan leather bag that was worn on the bottom and frayed at the handles. It looked like something a much older woman would carry. "Yes. After my great grandfather, Tatum Smith."

"My name is Alex Michael," he said icily.

"I know . . . Alexander Michael Fahlstrom. And you were born on December fourth, 1976 in Seattle, Washington. You moved to Polson when you were in kindergarten. Your . . . Your father is a heart specialist, and your mother, Laura, a physical therapist. You have an older sister named Trisha. And you live in Kansas City. And, um, have a girlfriend named Danielle. Danielle Sumners. You talk about her quite a bit."

At the name, he reached across the table, almost instinctively. "Is she real?" he asked.

The lady took his hand. "Danielle?"

He nodded.

"She could be," she said, her eyes brightening. "I mean, the only Danielle we know is your sister, but . . . She's obviously not your sister. Maybe . . . Maybe she has a different name."

He exhaled loudly and deeply as relief flowed through his body. "I have to find her . . . I have to. Will you help me? Please?"

"Of course," the lady said, holding his hand, massaging it soothingly. "Of course I will."

He breathed another sigh of relief before absently pulling his hand away and running it through his hair. "So . . . do I have a girlfriend now?"

The lady nodded, but looked down at her lap.

"What's her name? Could she be my girlfriend now?"

"Oh . . . That's . . . That's not important. She's . . . she's not Danielle."

"How do you know?"

She pursed her lips, "Oh . . . motherly instinct. We mothers just know these things . . . Why don't we talk about something else? Like your hobbies and—and what kind of food you like—"

"No—it is important. This is the most important thing in my life right now. Who is she? Who is my girlfriend? I want to know her name—what she looks like. *Please.*"

The lady sat a moment, staring at some distant point behind Alex, still pursing her lips. For being a mom, she was very pretty in a girly sort of way, and she was unwaveringly nice to him, making him feel increasingly guilty when he behaved cruelly or inappropriately to her. "Alright . . ." she said finally. "Her name is Trisha. Trisha Kurtz."

The blood drained from his face, and the room began to spin.

"You're lying," he said, chuckling weakly. "You're lying."

"No. I'm not."

"You're just fucking with me, right? Because—because that would be a real, sick fucking joke, wouldn't it? Wouldn't it?" he yelled.

She winced but remained calm.

"Ju—what does she look like? Huh? Does she look like my sister, Trisha? Huh? Does she?"

"I don't know, Alex . . ."

"Does she?" he screamed. "Do you have a fucking picture? Do you? Cause let's just settle this now. Let's just settle the fact that I'm a sick fuck whose lost his fucking mind and am never going to get out of this mental hell hole."

The lady bowed her head a moment, closing her eyes and remaining silent. Then she looked up at Alex, smiling, her eyes calm. "I do have a picture with me. And I am willing to show it to you. But I have a question I would like you to answer first."

He stared at her, still wide-eyed with rage, but nodding in compliance.

"If the girl in this picture looks just like your sister Trisha—or *is* your sister Trisha—will you continue to date her?"

"No," he burst, flabbergasted. "No—that's, that's disgusting. I'd—I'd rather shoot myself."

"Then what's the problem, Alex? Hmm?"

He frowned, taken aback by her response, by her complete lack of judgment, by her calm acceptance of what was to him a twisted circumstance of psychotic proportions.

"That's right. There is no problem, Alex. It goes away—poof. Just like that."

She picked up the bag and rummaged through it a moment, taking out an equally worn black wallet. After digging into the wallet, she produced a small photo and slid it across the table towards him. "This is from Homecoming this past October."

Hands trembling, he reached across the table and pulled the photo closer, his stomach lurching at the sight of two well-dressed individuals, both smiling widely at the camera. One looked strikingly like Tate Foley and the other like Trisha Fahlstrom.

Had the light lunch he consumed earlier not already digested, he might have vomited. Instead, he buried his head in his arms and sobbed convulsively as the walls of his precariously built universe came tumbling down around him, threatening to entomb him. The lady was quickly at his side, holding him, comforting him, trying to ease his pain with her melodic voice. He did not push her away this time, and she stayed with him until he had calmed down.

"Miss Jayne," he called as she started to leave, well after it had grown dark outside.

She stopped.

"Will you . . . Will you come back tomorrow?"

"Of course, sweetheart. And I'll bring more cookies."

∞

When Gabrielle Trahan learned that Alex Fahlstrom had woken from his coma, her first thought was to draw a warm bath and slit her wrists, just as she had read in the recently published novel, *Virgin Suicides*. But then she remembered the girl had been saved and began musing the pros and cons of other methods. Hanging seemed like it took too long, and she didn't trust her knot tying skills. A gun would work, but her father kept his hunting rifles well-locked up, and she didn't know where to begin looking for his keys. Pills would be the cleanest way to end everything as long as she took enough and didn't end up simply vomiting her guts out in a hospital, the same hospital where he lay now, no doubt plotting new ways to torment her and all the poor souls who crossed him.

She had been in the stable, grooming her horse, Razor's Edge, when her sister Brooke marched in, eyes flashing.

"Oh, my god. How could you?" she said. "*How could you?*"

Gabrielle stared at her in dumb nervousness, her mind racing for what possible trespass she committed against her sister's property today, as it was a daily affair. Did she leave the curling iron plugged in? Had she left her underwear on the floor on Brooke's side of the room? Had she gotten make-up on one of Brooke's towels? Did she eat the last Pop Tart?

"Don't look at me like you don't know. Oh, you know. *You know.*"

She continued to brush her horse. "I have no idea . . . Go ahead. Let it rip."

"Guess who woke up today?" Brooke asked, her arms crossed, her right foot tapping the ground impatiently.

Gabrielle stopped mid-motion, her bright Saturday morning suddenly turning black, so black she thought she might pass out.

"But you already knew that didn't you. *Didn't you?*"

She stopped brushing her horse, letting the brush fall onto the hay ridden floor and collapsed onto a nearby wooden stool. "No . . . I had no idea. Why would I—"

"Oh, gee—I have no clue. Why would you know? Hmmm . . ." Brooke began with her usual dramatic flair, arms flying while pacing as she spoke. "I mean, it wouldn't be because you're *astrological twins*, born on the same day—in the same hospital—at the same fucking time. It wouldn't be because somehow that bizarre fucking coincidence led to your knowing what the other is thinking or feeling, knowing when each other was sick or, or broke a bone. Going into a fucking seizure and coma the same time he did, even though we were just fucking making Chex Mix and getting ready for our New Year's Eve party. No guns. No fucking crazed robber in our house. You just fucking hit the floor, and I was . . . I was so fucking terrified."

Gabrielle buried her head in her arms, wishing the nightmare away, having really believed it was over when she woke up from her own coma a week ago, feeling completely at peace. For the first time, feeling completely free of the past and ready to move on with her life.

She felt Brooke's arm around her.

"I'm sorry—I'm sorry, Gabs . . . I—I didn't mean to upset you. And—I should've believed you when you said you didn't know. That you didn't remember what happened . . . After all these years, though, it's just hard to believe . . ."

Gabrielle shrugged, keeping her head buried, trying not to cry.

Brooke sighed, sitting down on the ground next to her. "Mom told me I shouldn't discuss it with you right now—that it was too soon. She was right . . . I'm sorry."

"I didn't bring him back, Brooke," Gabrielle said quietly, turning her head to look at her sister. "I didn't even know what happened to him. I still don't—not really . . . Nobody wants to talk to me about it. Mom's even been hiding the newspapers . . . All I've been able to piece together is what I hear from Kelly and Cherise and others at school."

Brooke inhaled sharply, "You haven't told them about *you*, have you? You told them you had pneumonia—right?"

Rolling her eyes, Gabrielle nodded and stood up. Her horse was getting restless, snorting nervously, sensing the anger and tension. She took his rein, leading him to his stall to secure him, trying to calm her growing sense of fear and unease.

"You know it's for the best, don't you? Do you realize what a circus this thing is—do you have any idea what life will be like if *anyone* finds out about the two of you? *Do you*?"

The double-entendre behind Brooke's statement caused Gabrielle to choke on a laugh that could have been a sob. Shaking it off, she closed the stall door and latched it.

"Of course you do . . ." Brooke said quietly. "I'm sorry . . . I'm just so angry right now. You have no idea how angry I am," she said, brushing a tear from her eye. "This is such a gross injustice of—of universal proportions—"

Gabrielle stood frozen, shaken by her sister's tears. While Brooke was a drama queen, her repertoire consisted mostly of sarcasm, shock and rage.

"He should have died—his prognosis was terrible. There is *no reason* he's alive right now—none. And as much as I hated him, I had to pray for him to make it. Because if he didn't make it, neither would you. And it made me sick to do it. And I was so happy when you woke up before him . . . I thought—finally. The curse has been broken. Gabby's free. There is a God—there is justice in the world . . . My sister can move on . . . But now he's back . . . And he'll be treated like some fucking hero . . . Stepped in front of the gunman, my ass . . ."

Feeling dizzy from the onslaught of emotions brought on by the conversation, Gabrielle stumbled towards her sister and plopped onto the ground next to her, lying her head on Brooke's shoulder. Brooke was a year older than she, and they had been very close companions throughout their childhood. Gabrielle thought Brooke the prettier, stronger and smarter of the two of them and wished she could be more like her. She felt ashamed at the trauma she had put them both through during the past year.

"I'm sorry, Brooke."

Brooke snorted. "Why are you sorry? Jesus, Gabby—you're the one who almost died . . . I'm not crying for me right now—I'm crying for *you.*"

Gabrielle smiled to herself. She had died, but it was lovely. "Dying isn't so bad, Brooke. It's really nice, actually."

"*What?*"

"It's—it's really peaceful," she said, lifting her head up and smiling reassuringly. "You just—you just melt into this—this light that's made of love. It's like—a being of light. Like—like falling and being caught by a being of light and—and becoming one with it. Like—like being cradled by your mother, held tightly against her breast, but there's no body. But you know you're being cradled with absolute love."

"What the *eff* are you talking about, Gabby? I thought you didn't remember anything?"

"I don't," Gabrielle protested. "But I do remember dying . . . "

"*How?*" Brooke asked incredulously.

She shrugged. "I don't know . . . I was lying on the ground, and I know I was wounded, but I don't remember how. I think I knew blood was pouring from my body. It didn't hurt, though . . . I mean—it was scary, because my body was getting cold, and I knew I was dying. But the fear came from being afraid of dying—not dying, itself."

"You did bleed," Brooke said dully, staring off into the distance.

"What?"

"You bled . . . When it happened, you actually bled. In three places. There was no real wound, but you bled as if there was one . . . It was the most frightening, god-awful thing I have ever seen. Because—there was no reason for it . . . We were in the kitchen—in our kitchen, in our home—making Chex Mex. And we were having so much fun . . . Well, you and I were having fun—Nate was just annoyed," she joked. "And we were singing "Smells Like Teen Spirit" really loudly and then you stopped singing and just stood there a moment. And your eyes . . . even with all that make-up, Gabs . . . you're eyes got so black and wide . . . and you looked so terrified . . . And you wouldn't talk—wouldn't respond—nothing. I shook your arm, hit your shoulder . . . And then you went down. But your eyes were still open. They stayed open for a few minutes."

"That was my Sex Pistols shirt, wasn't it," Gabrielle said sadly.

Brooke smirked and hit her in the arm.

"Well—I liked that shirt. It sucks . . . The whole thing just sucks."

"I'll get you another fucking shirt. Jesus . . ."

Gabrielle smiled a moment before pursing her lips in thought. "So . . . how did you keep my coma a secret? I mean—*nothing* is a secret in this town. It's like—impossible."

Brooke grunted, rolling her eyes. "No shit . . . The parents took care of that one. It helps that Mr. B. is the sheriff. He kept it all under control. *Nobody* except for immediate family was allowed to see either of you. They put you in the same ICU and had it guarded 24-7."

"*What?*"

Brooke's raised an eyebrow.

"The *same* ICU—we were both in the same room together?"

"Yeah . . . So?" Brooke asked, puzzled.

Gabrielle shook her head and waved her hands in irritation. Of all the things she had heard, this one disturbed her for some reason, made her feel vulnerable. "So—so that's just *wrong*. I should have had my own room. That's just—that's just morbid."

"It was mom's idea. She thought it would, you know—help the connection between you two."

"Eeeww. Really? *Really*?" She stood up abruptly, brushing herself off as if she were crawling with ants.

"You know, Gabs—I have to admit, I really don't understand your reaction to this. I mean—you could care less about bleeding out and going into a coma in our kitchen—but the fact that you were both in the same ICU room is horrifying?"

"Well—he wasn't there when I woke up. I didn't see him. I—I didn't see anyone. I wasn't even hooked up to any machines. I just . . . got up, completely disoriented, in that god-awful hospital gown and started wandering the halls looking for a nurse—*anyone*—to tell me what the hell happened."

Brooke sighed. "That's because that was the *second* time you woke up. You know—mom's going to kill me for telling you all this. You know that, don't you? You can't tell her I told you any of this."

"Fine—I won't say anything. Why would I? I'm not allowed to say anything to anyone, anyway . . . All our parents care about is whether or not I saw Alex in the coma, which I didn't. I don't remember what I dreamed about in my coma . . . I told you—I only remember dying, but I don't even remember how I died."

"Well, we think you were in Italy," Brooke said, standing up and brushing the hay off her back seat.

"*What?*"

"Yeah," Brooke said smirking. "See—the first time you woke up, you were psychotic. Seriously—like screaming, thrashing, babbling in another language. It was pretty freaky. You had no idea where you were or who we were or anything . . . So dad finally gave the okay to give you some serious sedatives and anti-hallucinogens . . . But we were so scared you'd go back to sleep and not wake up, you know? But you did—thank god, and they moved you into a private room, off the machines and stuff."

"So—how do you know it was Italian? I don't know Italian. I barely speak Salish," Gabrielle asked as they walked out of the stable and headed for the house.

Brooke grinned. "Well—there was a phrase you kept repeating, so mom wrote it down and, I don't know—she sent it to the college language department or *somewhere* for an opinion."

"And?"

Brooke laughed out loud.

"What—what was it?" Gabrielle pressed.

"*Testa di cazzo*," Brooke said with her best accent.

"What does that mean?"

"Dickhead," Brooke burst.

The two of them laughed a minute, and Gabrielle enjoyed a brief reprieve from her previous state of angst.

Then Brooke stopped short, looking squarely at Gabrielle, her eyes narrowing with hate. "That dickhead hurts you again, and I will castrate him. I fucking will."

Gabrielle turned away, shuddering inwardly, disheartened at the black thoughts that, in the brief time Alex had been awake, had already begun to invade her life and the people in it.

The news did not undo her resolve to break up with her boyfriend that night, something she had been toying with prior to New Year's Eve and was determined to do once she had awoken from her own coma. It was an ill-fated relationship, a knee-jerk reaction to rejection and fear, founded on loyalty rather than love. She had to be the one to end it and hoped he would be as relieved as she for things to go back to the way they were for the past twelve years—platonic.

Dennis Wiseman had been a friend of Gabrielle's since kindergarten and part of a grade school posse that included herself, Carl O'Malley, Brian McDermott and Alex Fahlstrom, the ring leader. Their parents had been close friends, the mothers brought together through quilting and cooking and the fathers through poker and hunting, so the children had been constantly thrown together, completely left to their own devices and often getting into trouble for inadvertently destroying property or terrorizing other children. While there were occasional fights amongst the five of them, they remained close friends until the sixth grade, when Trisha Kurtz moved into town, entirely changing the dynamic.

Trisha was unlike any girl they had ever seen in a small town populated by hard-working, low to middle income, rugged Caucasians and Native Americans. She was a pageant girl, bright and shiny with long blond locks, always groomed to perfection. Her family being the wealthiest in Polson, she lived in a large, brand new house on the lakeside, with six bedrooms, an equal number of bathrooms, an indoor pool and a yacht-sized boat. She wore exquisite clothes and shoes that always matched and literally sparkled with fancy embroidery or sequins. She had large brown eyes and pearly white teeth, flawless skin and rosy cheeks and lips. And even though Gabrielle could see it was merely face paint and costuming, all the boys fell in love with her.

Then they competed for her, fought for her, until in eighth grade Alex claimed victory over the girl's heart, and the group began to dissipate. With his new girlfriend, Alex wanted nothing to do with Gabrielle, and while he and Carl became best friends, he and Dennis drifted further apart, their relationship bitterly ending in an act of sabotage Sophomore year. Brian had moved to Kansas City in the ninth grade, and while Gabrielle kept up with him for awhile, they stopped writing over a year ago.

Her life-long friendship with Alex had also terminated in an act of brutality and betrayal last summer, and Dennis had been there for her, the only one left, playing the role of friend, brother and eventually lover, something Gabrielle had neither expected nor wanted to happen. But friendly hugs turned into warm embraces. Casual kisses turned into make-out sessions, awkward at first but eventually long and somewhat heated exchanges, as Dennis naturally reacted to surging hormones and Gabrielle tried to erase her past by enacting love scenes with a different actor.

All these thoughts and memories played through her mind as she watched him study the menu at Drifter's, a diner owned by her aunt and uncle that she and Dennis frequented for the excellent food and family discounts. Tonight, they had decided to eat there before seeing a movie, *Body Snatchers,* which had just opened at their theater. Being science fiction buffs, both were looking forward to a good horror flick, possibly one they could make fun of afterwards.

As she studied his features, she wondered why Dennis had never made her feel the same raw attraction that she had for Alex Fahlstrom. Dennis was good looking and, though nowhere near as physically built as Alex, could hold his own in an altercation. Being Native American, of the Salish tribe, he had black hair, which he kept long and allowed to hang past his shoulders in loose, perfectly spiraled curls. His complexion was dark olive, his face statuesque with a prominent, almost Romanesque nose, and his eyes small, black and beady—like a hawk's. He often dressed in black—black jeans, black heavy Doc Marten boots and a black leather jacket layered over plaid flannel shirts and concert tees. Tonight, he wore a red and white bandanna, Axl Rose style, and his normally sharp eyes were red, droopy instead of piercing, and Gabrielle knew he had gotten stoned earlier in the day.

They ordered cheeseburgers, fries and sodas and spent a few minutes discussing movies and the latest school gossip and politics.

"So, Gabby . . . You're looking rather plain Jane today. What's up with that?" he asked, referring to her attire, or lack thereof. "Not feeling well?"

One of the few Goth punkers in the entire school and hard core in her authenticity, Gabrielle rarely left the house without her look, achieved with various black and multi-colored wigs, heavy black eye makeup, black lipstick and nails, outrageous clothing, a spiked choker and multiple piercings to make the casual onlooker shudder in pain. She was also Salish, and tonight, her long black hair hung in two perfectly braided strands. Other than lip gloss, she wore no makeup and was dressed in jeans and a black hooded sweatshirt, the only traces of her usual self a smattering of metal across her façade—a lip ring, a nose stud, a small barbell in her right eyebrow and multiple rings of various sizes on both ears. She had even begun the process of stretching her left lobe, having enlarged it enough for a six gauge ring.

She shrugged. "I don't know . . . I've been thinking of . . . Of losing that look, you know?"

Dennis shook his head, "Don't do that, Gabs . . . You're like the most kick-ass looking girl in the school. Why would you want to look like everyone else?"

"It's not that I want to look like everyone else, it's just . . . Well . . . something happened a few weeks ago, you know? I haven't really, well . . . talked to you much about it. But, well . . . I need to."

He rolled his eyes, shifting uneasily in the booth, and Gabrielle could feel his agitation.

"Dennis, this isn't about him. It's not. I don't—I don't even know what happened to him. I swear—I don't. My family keeps asking me—his family keeps asking me, but I know nothing. I remember absolutely nothing. I—I . . . All I remember is being in the kitchen with Nate and Brooke listening to Nirvana. I remember that clearly, because Brooke was doing her impression of "Smells Like Teen Spirit," and we," Gabrielle smiled remembering. "We both screamed *Here we are now, entertain us* really loud, you know? Just to freak Nate out, which is not hard to do. He hates it when we sing obnoxiously . . . and that's it. I don't remember what happened. I just blacked out, I guess."

"Yeah—for over two fucking weeks. Jesus, Gabby. We all thought you were fucking dead, too."

"I know . . . It was the worst New Year's Eve . . . I feel so bad for my family. Nate didn't even want to go back to college, but they made him. I feel terrible about it."

"So what caused it? Did they say?"

She shrugged, her mind racing to come up with a white lie, knowing Dennis would never believe pneumonia. "They said I had a seizure."

"A seizure," he echoed, staring past her into the distance. "At around the

same time *he whose name shall not be spoken* was getting his guts blown out .
. . Coincidence?" he asked sarcastically. "Or does sharing someone's birthday
means you get to share their death day, too? Jesus . . . That would suck . . ."

She remained silent. While most friends of the families knew of their
shared birth date, time and place, nobody outside of the families were aware
they shared a psychic connection.

"Yeah . . . That is a bit freaky, I guess," she said, playing along. "Actually,
it could have been caused by an allergic reaction to . . . to something I ate
earlier. That's what they said," she continued, only slightly uncomfortable at
the lies. "Anyway—I woke up as if nothing happened. I just woke up, right?
And even though I was a bit freaked out that I was in a hospital bed, I—I
woke up from this most amazing dream, but—but it wasn't a dream I could
see. It was more like a dream I felt."

"Was *he* in it?" he asked dryly.

"No," she burst, trying to contain her frustration. "No—goddammit. Jesus
. . . Alright, you know what? Just forget it. It's—it's nothing. *Nobody* believes
me. Nobody wants to hear about it. All people want to talk about is *him*.
And this had nothing to do with *him*. I didn't wake up thinking about *him*.
I didn't wake up even knowing what had happened to *him*. I fucking found
that out, like, afterwards. A few hours later."

He leaned across the table, "So what is it about, then?"

She shook her head sadly. "Peace . . . Love . . . Freedom. Complete freedom
from . . . from fear. From—from anger and hate. From just the weight of
things. Of living. Of being confused. I woke up feeling so good about myself
. . . and, and so free. I felt so free—for the first time. And, I want it back,
you know? I want to hold onto it, but it's slipping away, day by day. It's, it's
leaving me. And . . . I just want to start over, Dennis. I do. I want to forget
the past—to, to walk away from it and just start over. A new look. A new .
. . perspective. And, I'm thinking . . . I'd like to be on my own for awhile,
you know? I'd like maybe some time to find myself again, if that's okay. You
know, just . . . slow it down a bit."

He suddenly sat upright and crossed his arms, his eyes turning very black
and honing in on her.

"What'd you say?"

She glanced down nervously, ripping a piece of her napkin.

"I said . . . I said I'd like to just, you know . . ."

"What? Be *friends* again?" he said caustically.

Her fingers rolled the paper into a tiny ball. "Maybe . . . But, just for awhile."

He shook his head bitterly. "No, no, no . . . I know what this is about .
. . No—what you're really saying is, you don't want to sleep with me."

"*What?*"

"*What!*" he mimicked, eyes widening.

"I don't know what you're talking about—" she said abruptly, ripping
the napkin in half.

"Oh, really? How 'bout Thursday afternoon . . . There was no reason we
didn't do it on Thursday. We certainly were headed there pretty fast, when
you just put the brakes on."

"We were *high*."

"So? What the fuck does that have to do with anything?"

"I don't want to do it *high*, okay? I mean . . . I just don't."

"That's stupid. That doesn't even make any sense. In fact, that's just a
fucking excuse."

She rolled the entire napkin into a wad.

"Okay. Let's just test this. How bout, we skip the movie and just—just
go someplace private. Hell, I'll even spring for a hotel room."

She shook her head, "You're *high*, Dennis."

"No, I'm not."

"Yes you are—look at your eyes. You're fucking wasted."

"I had a joint like, four hours ago. I'm not high. A little tired, maybe
. . . Fine. Then we'll get a room after the movie. It'll have worn off by
then. Anyway, I'm . . . I'm kind of excited about making out with you
tonight. You know—looking like you do. All natural. No crazy lipstick
and stuff."

She flicked the wad across the table at him. He missed blocking it, and
it fell into his lap.

"Let's just skip the movie," he said, kicking her under the table. "I mean it
. . . You look really pretty tonight. I could get used to this new look, actually."

She smiled sadly at him, and he closed his eyes, wincing.

"Yeah . . . Right . . . and I already forgot the part where you said you
wanted to just be *friends*. To which I said, that's because you don't want to
sleep with me. And, obviously, you still don't."

"That has nothing to do with it—"

"It has *everything* to do with it. But you know what—that's fine. I'm
okay with it."

"No—you're obviously not okay with it," she said, feeling the pain and
anger in every word he iterated, in every gesture of his body.

"I am okay with it—I am okay with it, you know why?" He leaned towards her again, his voice getting low. "Because unlike some people we know, *I won't go raping girls who won't put out for me.*"

The words were a blow that cut deep and hurt far worse than any physical hit.

She felt her face flush before all the blood quickly drained from it. The food arrived at that moment, and the mere smell made her stomach lurch. Her body suddenly felt very hot, and her head began to spin. Excusing herself, she made it to the bathroom stall just in time to empty the contents of her stomach. After crouching in the stall for at least five minutes, her stomach now queasy from the smell of bleach and urine, she exited, washed her hands and face and returned to the table.

Dennis had begun eating, as if nothing had happened.

She slid into the booth and immediately pushed her plate to the edge of the table, as far as she could to lose the scent without hurtling the contents to the floor. "Can I have your water?" she asked, her voice hoarse.

He slid the glass towards her, and they sat in silence a few minutes.

"Sorry I made you puke," he said finally, having finished his sandwich.

She shrugged. "You didn't."

"Well, I'm sorry for what I said. It was mean . . . I meant it to be."

She sighed, staring into her lap, feeling utterly drained.

"I—I'm sorry, but I—I couldn't help it. I'm hurt, Gabrielle. I am. I mean, I'm your friend, and I've been your friend forever, and I'll continue to be your friend, but . . . I'm . . . It hurts me. It hurts me that, that you would give yourself to someone who—who didn't love you. Who *never* loved you. *Ever,*" he said, leaning across the table as he said it, as if to brand it into her soul. "And I—I love you. I would do anything for you, and . . . You won't have me. You don't want me. Not that way, at least."

If there were tears left to cry, she might have started crying them, but those, too, were spent.

"You know, there are so many guys you could go out with. So many guys who think you're cool. Who—who want to date you but . . . you don't see any of them. And it kills me, because I don't think you see yourself how they do. How I do. I mean, you're—you're beautiful. And, you're talented—you play drums, for Christ's sakes—and can sing and act. And, and you've not only seen *Star Wars*, you can *talk Star Wars*. And kick my ass at *Mortal Kombat*, too . . . He didn't see any of that. He didn't appreciate it . . . Why? I gotta know . . . You at least owe me that."

"Why . . ." she echoed dully. "I don't know . . . I've stopped asking myself that question, because there's . . . there's no answer. I just drive myself crazy. All I can say is . . . falling in love with him was the biggest mistake I have ever made in my life, and . . . I just want to stop hating myself for it, you know? That's   that's what I've been trying to tell you. About the dream. That two-week sleep I had. I woke up and—and didn't hate myself anymore. I felt—I felt loved. I felt so loved and . . . and so accepted and not judged . . . and, and I just wanted to share it. I wanted to hold onto it, and share it . . . but it's fading. I can't."

"It's his fault you ever hated yourself," Dennis said bitterly.

"No—it's not. That's just it—it's not his fault. It's not anyone's fault. It doesn't even matter. Look, I just want to forget it, okay? Forgive it and forget it. And, and—maybe you and I will be a couple one day but not like this. I—I don't want us to date like this, you know? I want us to be together because we're celebrating something, not running away from something."

"I wasn't running away from anything—"

"Okay, well I was, okay? I was. I'm sorry. It was unfair to you."

Dennis looked at his watch. "We should head out. Movie's starting soon. You're not going to eat any of that?"

She shook her head.

Digging into his jacket pocket, he pulled out some money, but she stopped him. "I've got it . . . I'll put it on the family tab."

Shrugging, he threw down a tip.

"Dennis . . . As my friend, could you . . . do you think you could forget it, too? Since he is half dead and . . . and may never, well, completely recover . . . Can you just forgive him and move on? Like I am?"

He stared at her intently, eyes narrowing.

"Can you at least try?"

"Fuck no. That fucker comes out of a coma, I'll kick his ass back into one."

CHAPTER TWELVE

It took Jayne Fahlstrom almost another two weeks to convince Alex to let Bill Fahlstrom visit, and Alex would only see him if he were in plain clothes—no uniform. When the man entered the room one Saturday morning, in jeans, a flannel shirt and jacket, minus not only the uniform but also the mustache, Alex believed for a fleeting moment that he had woken from his two and a half month nightmare. There stood a familiar figure, the first living person he recognized, and he actually moved to hug him, which was difficult, as he still needed a walker for balance.

But he didn't have to move far, for the man strode across the room and gave him a huge bear hug, completely enveloping him. Alex tried to feel the warmth, a connection of some kind while at the same time trying to remember what his father had felt like, smelled like. He could not remember. He could not even remember the last time he had been hugged by his father.

Ruffling his hair, the man said he needed a haircut and a shave, then put his arm around him helping him to sit at the table, which had been set by the nurses with two breakfast trays.

Alex studied the man for a few minutes as he talked about the weather and his plans for the weekend, stunned at the physical resemblance, remembering well the large build, square face and jaw carved with rugged grin lines that became more pronounced when he smiled, the narrow, deep set brown eyes. But neither the hospital room nor the mountain range outside the window magically dissipated, and as they began to eat, the conversation soon turned awkward as the man tried to strike up a conversation about topics with which Alex was either unfamiliar or disinterested. For ten minutes he talked about sports, starting with the Super Bowl results and ending with a hockey update, and Alex deduced his predecessor must have been an Edmonton Oilers fan, the way the man went on and on about their miserable season thus far. Having no interest in hockey, all Alex could do was nod and attempt to smile. The man eventually changed the subject.

"Genghis misses you. Caught another rabbit this week. That's his third this month."

"What?"

"Genghis. Genghis Khan."

"Yeah...Who?"

"Your dog, Genghis. Don't you remember your dog?"

Alex shook his head. "I haven't had a dog since I was three. Trisha's allergic to animals."

"Danielle doesn't have allergies."

Alex cleared his throat nervously. "What kind of a dog is he?"

"Golden retriever. Eight years old, now."

They ate awhile in silence.

"Wrestling team missed you this year. Took second in divisional and didn't place well at State, either."

Alex stared at him blankly. He had never wrestled in his life and thought the sport gay.

"You're the best they got, you know."

Alex tried not to choke on his food. As if sensing his growing discomfort with that topic, the man took a drink of coffee and changed the subject.

"Sister's going to New York with the Trahans for Spring Break...Wants to visit her school."

"Oh..." Alex said and assumed the girl Danielle was his sister, Trisha's, age and going to college in the fall. "So, where is she going?"

"You don't remember?" He grunted. "She got accepted to Juilliard."

"Are you kidding me? *Juilliard*?" he burst, dropping his fork. "How? How on earth?" He was surprised anyone from Polson could make it into Juilliard, let alone someone from his family, and someone who looked just like Jennifer Hicks. Obviously, this girl Danielle was no Jennifer Hicks.

"She applied. Tried out and all that. Your mother can tell you more about it...I just pay the bills. And they keep coming," he said with gruff sarcasm.

"Yeah, but—what does she do? Does she play an instrument? Dance? Sing?"

"Don't you know?"

The man who looked like his father eyed him with a mixture of sadness and exasperation, and Alex wondered if he was pretending to be ignorant of his amnesia or willfully challenging Alex. In no mood for a challenge and feeling increasingly nervous, Alex remained silent and pushed his half eaten plate to the side of the table.

"You should finish your breakfast...Need to keep that strength up," the man said quietly.

Alex remained silent, crossing his arms and staring out the window, wishing the man would finish his own breakfast quickly.

"You know, I was thinkin'..." the man continued, "Maybe you and I can take a trip this summer to check out your two schools. Might help you make your decision faster...We've focused so much on Danielle, I...I'd like to make it up to you...There's a law enforcement convention in DC, so... County may pay for some of it. Annapolis is just outside of DC...We spend a day or two in Annapolis, take a tour of the Academy, then rent a car and drive up to New York from there."

Alex stared at him wide-eyed, his mind racing to piece together what colleges were in Annapolis and New York, completely thrown off by the term *academy*. But never having given college a thought, he was at an utter loss.

The man took a big gulp of coffee and looked at him.

"Oh, don't you worry, son...We'll catch you up. You'll get into both institutions, and you can pick which one you like best. But I think it's important you visit them—see them in person. You deserve that opportunity—it's the least we can do after all we've done and spent on your sister and her education and—and lessons. Training and recitals...Your mother and I have already talked to your high school, and they're going to work with you on this semester's grades. In fact, she'll be bringing homework for you to work on so you can start catching up. Teachers are even willing to come in off hours to tutor you."

Alex felt a spasm in his stomach, and his body felt flush.

"Got a commitment from Senator Baucus's office for a recommendation…Saving that girl's life didn't hurt," he said, winking. "See…there's a silver lining in every gray cloud."

The man took a hearty mouthful and another gulp of coffee before looking at Alex again. This time, he shook his head, leaned back in his chair and crossed his arms.

"Son, you have no idea what I'm talking about, do you?'

Alex swallowed hard, the spasms moving from his stomach to his chest and down his arms. He could feel a trickle of sweat on his hairline and was slightly dizzy.

"I thought your mother would have caught you up by now," he said, sighing loudly. "You're a hero, son," he said finally. "You don't remember it, but you saved a life that night, in the convenience store. Gunman came in—drunk, looking to rob the place or shoot his girlfriend—or both, we'll never know…And you stepped in front of him and saved that girl and her unborn child."

The man's eyes welled with tears, and Alex's hands began trembling uncontrollably, along with the rest of his body. He buried them deeper within his crossed arms, trying to stabilize himself and block the flashing images from his mind, images that triggered corresponding pain and emotions. The convenience store bell, jingling innocently. The feel of small indentations as his hands rested on the wooden counter, waiting for his change. The confusion and fear upon hearing the yelling, seeing the gun and then feeling the bullet hit his side. Another his chest. Another his shoulder. Being knocked off balance, maybe falling, he couldn't remember. The pain came later but worse than that the feeling of his blood streaming from his wounds, of his body becoming cold, colder, of his mind trying to comprehend the situation and face the idea of death.

"I'm proud of you, son…Real proud. That took courage—leadership. Everything you need to be a soldier and an officer. It's the reason you got that recommendation so quickly, too. In our sleepy town, it was the big story for weeks…Still is. And, I made sure it got heard where it needed to. With your grades, athletic ability and accomplishments—not to mention school leadership—both academies will take you. Although, I know your little sweetheart would rather see you in white," he said, winking. "You get into the Naval Academy, and you're set for life."

The shaking turned into convulsions. Alex remembered trying to grab the table but knocking off the plate and glassware before completely blacking out.

When he came to, he heard voices. Though still groggy, he recognized them. The lady, Miss. Jayne, the man who looked like his father and his psychologist. His body felt limp, and he could barely move his head. His mind raced, trying simultaneously to remember what had happened while focusing on the conversation taking place across the room.

He's stabilizing. He'll be alright. We believe he had a non-epileptic seizure.

A seizure? How—why—I don't understand—

These type of seizures are often triggered by severe emotional stress. You didn't tell me you were going to visit him today. Did you surprise him?... Bill, I need to know what happened.

Nothing happened. We had a nice breakfast. We talked…About things—his life. His college plans. I caught him up on what's going on.

Honey, I told you to keep it general—to talk about skiing and sports or politics. What's going on in the world—the globe, not our world.

Honey, I tried. The boy doesn't talk much. What was I supposed to do?

Ask him about his life—his memories.

What good is that? His memories are all wrong. If you ask me, we need to stop pandering to the boy and educate him on his real life. What's going to happen when he comes home in a few weeks? You can't hide him from reality forever.

At that point, he closed his eyes and tuned out the conversation, not wanting to hear anymore. Though unsure of the date, he knew it was mid-March, and he was scheduled to be released on April 1. Every night he went to bed praying he would wake up in his old body, in the life he remembered living, and every morning he woke up in the same hospital room, in a broken body, surrounded by unfamiliar people and objects. Supposedly, he had friends practically breaking down the hospital doors to see him, but he wanted nothing to do with them, not even the one named Carl, fearful of who would actually walk through the door and knowing they would likely have nothing in common.

The only two friends he was willing to see were Dennis and Danielle, but his mother had been unable to find them, despite his exhaustive descriptions. Supposedly, there was a Dennis, but he was not a friend of Alex's and he didn't have a twin sister. While his mother knew of twins, none were a brother-sister set. The only Danielle Alex supposedly knew was his sister, and his mother was equally unaware of anyone with a strong Italian heritage, reminding him that they lived on an Indian reservation and asking him if, perhaps, she could be Native American, as Danielle Sumners' long black hair, dark eyes and skin tone described forty percent of the girls in his school.

Alex lay in his hospital bed the remainder of the day and into the next, both restless and depressed, a part of him wanting to jump up and tear out of the hospital, to run and move about again, to breathe the fresh air he saw from his window every day, and another part of him wanting to die, wanting to put an end to an emotional grief so acute, he was beginning to believe death would be the only way to stop it. A grief brought on by a growing belief that his former life and everyone in it, including Danielle, was gone, never to be found, or, if found, never to be as he remembered. The idea that Danielle existed bodily in some capacity but would not recognize him—be a stranger to him—was as unbearable as if she had died.

On Sunday afternoon, he got up and began pacing, first using the walker and then practicing without it, walking next to the wall or bed for support if he needed it. His legs still felt weak and the muscles somewhat disconnected from his brain—his will—as if his mind couldn't get them to behave the way they should. For the next few days, he alternated between focusing on walking and thumbing through the stack of textbooks and homework his mother brought to replace the stack of puzzle books and pop fiction novels with which he had been amusing himself. Half the subject matter seemed familiar and half didn't. He had never taken Calculus and didn't even want to crack open the text, nor had he any interest or knowledge of physics, last struggling with Biology. The idea that his predecessor was more intelligent than he only increased his growing depression and anxiety over the impending discharge.

The following Saturday, both his parents came to visit him and this time brought the dog, Genghis, thinking it would cheer him up. But the dog did not recognize him, barking obnoxiously at Alex as if he were a stranger, at one point growling, and he did not recognize the dog. His mother nervously laughed it off, blaming his longer hair and bearded face, but he knew dogs could care less about physical appearances and saw the entire awkward exchange as an omen of what his life was to be when he was finally discharged and thrown into the real world.

Later that night, after they had left, he sat on the edge of his bed, staring at the outline of the mountain range, all that could be seen in the night sky, contemplating ending his life. While he had considered suicide frequently since waking from the coma, his musings had morphed into a determination. Now, the question was how to do it. The hospital had stripped his room of anything that could be used as a weapon against himself. He had no access to guns, razors, knives or even extra pills. He was only allowed to wear sweats with no strings, and his room was absent of cords, having no phone and a

TV that hung from the ceiling. Even the window curtains were absent of cords, opening with a long glass stick.

If he were going to die, he would have to leave the hospital. If he could make it to the lakeside, he remembered there was a bridge and hoped it would be high enough to kill him once he jumped. After playing out the scene in his head for an hour or so and conquering any lingering fear or hesitation, he stood up and walked to the door of his hospital room. It was going on ten at night, and the halls were nearly empty of staff, only two nurses visible and both engaged in a lively conversation. Taking a deep breath, he quietly walked down the hall and towards the elevator until he remembered that elevators ding and beep, at which point he headed down the stairs.

The ground floor was as deserted as the third floor, the security staff distracted by the lobby television, the hospital receptionist occupied by impatient visitors, and any remaining inhabitants completely oblivious to him, making it easy for him to walk out the front doors and into the night. What he did not expect was the cold gust of air that quickly penetrated his sweat shirt, the temperature just below freezing that time of year.

Dauntless, he headed across the parking lot and to the street, walking north on Main Street, towards the lake. Though he could now walk steadily, his pace was slow, and he underestimated his body's strength, shivering and feeling fatigued after only a few blocks. By Eighth Avenue, he contemplated stopping to rest but feared he would never get up again. Seventh and Main was a busier intersection, and it was there that he formulated a better idea. Seeing the headlights of what looked to be a large truck traveling at a decent clip, he closed his eyes, took a deep breath and stepped out into the middle of the street, bracing for the impact.

When Alex awoke, he was surprised to feel the touch of sheets beneath his fingertips and to see a white ceiling above his head. As his vision adjusted to the dim light, he could make out other shapes—a curtained window, a television, a small table and two chairs. He heard a noise, someone breathing loudly, sighing, maybe crying. A woman sat on the edge of the bed, near his feet. She had long, wavy golden-brown hair, and her head was buried in her hands.

"Fucking Christ…." Alex breathed. "I'm still fucking here. I don't believe this…" He moved to get up but could not and soon realized he had been strapped to the bed.

"Why am I still here?" he asked, loudly. "Why the fuck am I still alive?"

The lady shook her head, wringing an overused Kleenex. "I don't know... I would say it's a miracle, but you don't believe in those. Or God...I guess someone in the universe really wants you to be here....I just wish you felt the same."

"Why would I feel the same? Why the fuck should I want to be here—to, to live some—some other guy's life. To wake up in some other guy's body—to some other guy's parents—to, to some other guy's friends and girlfriend—and, and dog, for Christ's sake. Even the fucking dog doesn't know me...And what kind of a name is Genghis? Jesus Christ..."

"I'm sorry...We shouldn't have brought him to visit. The hospital was a strange environment for him—"

Alex sighed loudly, struggling against the straps. "That's so fucking not the point."

She winced, and he knew it was the language, which she had asked him to refrain from using in the past. But what she wanted ceased to matter to him anymore.

"I know," she said quietly. "And I can't stop you from wishing death...I can't stop death from taking you, which it will at some point, if you want it that badly...I'm even ready to let you go, you know. There's nothing I can do for you...I can't—I can't give you your life back. I can't—I can't change reality and, and magically transport you back to Kansas City. If I could, believe me, I would do it. I would give you up, my own child, to make you happy...if that's what it took."

She looked at him, and he felt his guard drop a bit. Even in great distress, she had a sweet, pretty face, bright eyes and a smiling expression, and he was sorry he had caused her pain, for she had been nothing but kind to him and, even now, he felt no anger, resentment or bitterness from her.

She took his hand and held it. "There is something you should know... Something to think about, maybe...I, I saw her today. Your Danielle. I did... It was the eyes. You said she had one eye slightly bigger than the other," she smiled, looking into the distance. "And that's how I knew."

"You're lying," Alex said, not believing her nor wanting to at this point.

She shook her head. "No...I wouldn't do that. Not now—not with so much at stake."

"Then where is she?" he asked bitterly. "Why didn't you just bring her here?"

"To see you like this? Strapped to a bed—suicidal, mentally and physically incapacitated and hopped up on drugs? She'd be terrified...Besides, you're, you're somewhat strangers to each other...Acquaintances, but...She's not good enough friends with you, right now, to see you like this. Believe me, if I thought any good would have come of it, I would have dragged her here, myself, even kicking and screaming, but…I just couldn't do that. So, you'll either have to believe me or not. It's your choice."

"So, when can I see her, then?"

"Frankly, the best place to see her is at school…Both of them, actually. Your Danielle and your Dennis…I know who they are, but…let's just say you're—you're merely acquaintances. Not friends, really. Might recognize each other in the halls…Frankly, you'll…you'll probably have to build a relationship with them…You don't really have one right now."

He laughed bitterly. "Then what's the point? I might as well not know them at all. It sounds like I *don't* know them at all, so what good is just seeing them as—as strangers? You think that's comforting to me right now? You think that actually makes me feel better? Fucking hell…"

"No…You're right. I'm sorry…I thought that might—might give you some hope—"

"It gives me no hope, okay? I have no hope, okay? I'm just fucked. For the rest of my life, I guess."

She sighed, patting his hand. "I certainly hope not…But, I will say, the doctors are, um - concerned about discharging you…They…They're suggesting maybe transferring you to a mental health institution for awhile. There's a youth facility in Billings, a boys and girls ranch with residences. It's excellent, really. A very nice place—sounds more like a resort than a hospital, you know? They have horseback riding and—and outdoor activities and therapies."

"You're sending me to a loony farm?"

"Alex, please—"

"No—no. You're fucking sending me to a loony farm—just say it. But what are they going to do? Give me shock therapy? Give me a drug that magically makes my entire life's worth of memories just disappear? Poof— I'm no longer Alex Michael, I'm Alex Tate…Shit, maybe I'll come home after months knowing how to fucking wrestle and—and wanting to join the fucking military, like the last son you had. Because that's what this is about, *isn't it*? You want your son back. You want your *fucking precious* son back—the one who—who plays every sport in the school and wants to go to college and—and fucking understands calculus. Well, I'm not him. I'll *never* be him—because *I don't want to be*. So they better have some fucking potent drugs at that—that crazy ranch."

She shook her head, still smiling under another stream of tears. "Alex, honey, they're discharging you in two weeks...You have two choices. Home or Yellowstone Ranch...That's what it's called, Yellowstone...They're both terrible choices for you, I know...Neither will be easy, but...That's what we have. And your father and I will stand behind whatever choice you make and...and we'll suffer right there with you. And, well—hopefully, all of us will come out alive in...in a few months. Or years...whatever it takes."

Alex sighed, closing his eyes, his mind racing, attempting to play out multiple future scenarios based on his decision. "Can I think about it for a day or two?"

On Friday, April 1, Alex was discharged from St. Joseph Medical Center and stared out his hospital window for the last time, bemused by the irony of the date and wondering if his choice would make a fool of him. He was in decent physical condition, having only suffered bruises and a mild concussion from the near head-on collision with a delivery truck, the rest of his bodily faculties completely healed from the injury and ensuing coma.

Hugging the staff good-bye and thanking them for their kindness, he felt deep loss and anxiety over the impending change. As confining and miserable as his time in the hospital had been, it had also been his home, and the staff had become like family. They followed him out, a group of nurses and doctors, his psychologist, waving to him as the dark green Bronco pulled out of the parking space in front of the facility and headed for his new home on Big Sky Lane. In the end, the possibility of seeing Danielle—even if she didn't recognize him—had outweighed the appeal of retreating to a ranch and avoiding his new life for a few additional months.

In less than ten minutes, they were pulling into the driveway of a house Alex did not recognize. It was a light gray split level set back on a large front yard with a huge front wooden deck that doubled as a car port. Once inside, however, Alex was struck by the familiarity of the décor and had to keep from either laughing or screaming in hysterics at the variations on a theme of pewter blue and mauve pink. The furnishings matched what he remembered in Carl Weiss's house, the only difference being wood floors covered with mauve and pewter blue area rugs instead of carpet and a huge picture window with a breathtaking view of the lake and mountains instead of a large brick fireplace. The scenery was so stunning that Alex dropped his back-pack and walked up to the window, staring out in awe.

His momentary reverie was soon broken by barking and the frantic click of dog nails on hardwood as the golden retriever came bounding in to greet him, this time jumping up, licking him and pawing for attention. He kneeled down and pet the dog, soon taking in the rest of his surroundings, which he now noticed included a number of *Welcome Home, Alex* posters and a third person, the girl Danielle, who leaned shyly against the doorway. He turned away, embarrassed, avoiding eye contact, wishing he did not see Jennifer Hicks every time he looked at her.

Ms. Jayne offered to take him on a complete tour of the house, leaving his bedroom last, a grand and bizarre finale that ended in his stepping across the threshold to his own bedroom, the bedroom he remembered from his home in Kansas with the exception of the walls, which were a plain, grayer shade of the pewter blue that ran through the house, minus the black brick mortar he had painted. He wandered around, lightly touching the furnishings as if to test their solidity, their reality, the over-varnished dark wood dresser, old wooden desk with two broken drawers and wooden bookcase, painted black. He sat on the edge of the twin bed, covered in its worn, navy and white plaid bedspread, looking for differences, hoping to find them and eventually seeing unfamiliar objects—framed photos he did not recognize, trophies he did not win and a huge pile of deflated foil balloons, stuffed animals, cards and other items stacked neatly on and around a chair, as if on display. These, along with the plethora of *Welcome Home* posters throughout the house, were get-well gifts from family, friends, teammates, students and a community of well wishers.

"Well…I'll leave you to get settled. Let me know if you need anything," the lady, Ms. Jayne, said cheerfully, before closing the door and leaving him to the privacy of his room and troubled thoughts.

For the rest of that day and the next, Alex spent most of his time alone, retreating to his room and lying on the bed to stare at the ceiling, since his bedroom window only had a view of the backyard, or venturing to the living room to stare out the window at the lake and mountains. He mustered every ounce of energy he had to stem the internal storm he knew was brewing, the overwhelming sense of panic and entrapment that would lead to rage that would lead to a despair that would last for days. He refused to eat dinner with the family, asking to eat in his room, and politely declined the man's invitations to watch hockey on television, not wanting to get too close to these people or their home, not wanting to look too closely at his surroundings, the furnishings, the photos, afraid of what he would see. Avoiding exploring even his bedroom, sticking to the bed, living out of the bag of clothes and belongings he had brought home with him from the hospital.

He thought about Danielle constantly, feeling a sense of camaraderie given his current situation and her past, now empathizing with how she must have felt when she moved in with the Trahans, wishing he would have been more sensitive to what must have been an agonizing ordeal for her, wishing he would have been more understanding over her reluctance to eat their food or drink their water. He felt guilty using the Fahlstroms' toilet, let alone rummaging through their refrigerator for a snack, a guest in a strange family's house. But thinking of her and mentally talking to her only fueled his smoldering grief and confusion.

By Sunday morning, he regretted his decision to move in with the Fahlstroms so quickly, wishing he had opted for the ranch in Billings, knowing it was only a matter of time, mere hours or even minutes, before he would have another explosive meltdown.

He awoke that Sunday as he did every morning, hoping he would open his eyes and be back in Kansas City. Momentarily fooled by his familiar surroundings, his hope was quickly shattered by a knock on his door and the appearance of Ms. Jayne's head.

"Good morning, sweetie. Did you have a nice sleep?"

He closed his eyes again, sighing loudly, saying nothing aloud but cursing inside.

"I was hoping you'd be up," she continued. "We leave for church at nine, and I wanted to be sure you had time to get ready."

His eyes flew open.

"Um…They don't allow sweats, so…Be sure to pick something out that's appropriate, okay. Do you need my help?"

"Did you say *church*?" he burst, sitting up.

"Yes—we go to church every Sunday and then have family breakfast out. I think you'll enjoy it—"

"I'm not going to church," he said flatly. "I don't do church. I don't even remember going to church—my parents were hippies. I—I don't even know how."

She smiled sadly, walking into his room and sitting on the end of his bed. "Alex, honey, it's really important to us that you go to church on Sundays. That's what *our* family does, and you're part of that family now. It's a one-hour worship, followed by fellowship, and then we have a nice breakfast or brunch at Drifter's or the Lodge. You don't have to do anything but just sit. You don't even have to listen."

"Will I see *Danielle* there?" he asked caustically.

He could see it took a brief moment for her to understand his question, and she blushed. "Oh...Um, no—I don't think so. No. She doesn't go to our church."

He rolled his eyes in disgust. "Fine...Tell me what you want me to wear. Better yet—just pick something out. I haven't even looked in my closet yet."

She smiled, patting his leg through the bedspread before standing up and walking to his closet. He watched her retrieve a pair of khaki pants and a light pink, long-sleeve dress shirt, which she draped over the end of his bed before leaving the room, shutting the door behind her.

"Fuck..." he breathed, staring dumbly at the shirt. "You've gotta be fucking kidding me," he mumbled, throwing back the covers and bounding out of bed towards his closet. Opening the closet door, he expected to see his belongings—a jumbled mess of tennis shoes and T-shirts piled on the floor and an array of plaid flannel shirts hanging haphazardly from hangers, along with the few jeans he had decided to hang instead of stuffing into a dresser drawer. He had only owned one pair of khakis, one navy blazer and two dress shirts—and neither shirt was pink.

Instead, he saw an entire row of perfectly pressed, perfectly hung dress shirts in a variety of pastel colors—pink, yellow, light green and pale blue, a few white with pastel stripes and two completely white. Next to these hung five or six pairs of perfectly pressed pants in a variety of shades of taupe and brown, and below these were two pairs of dress shoes and three pairs of tennis shoes, all on a shoe rack.

He felt his face flush with anger, his heart beat accelerate, and he slammed the door to the closet. He then strode to his dresser, violently yanking open each drawer looking for his clothes—his jeans, concert tees and flannel shirts—but instead finding neatly rolled dress and tennis socks, neatly folded boxer shorts, neatly pressed and folded white undershirts, folded sweat pants and shirts and, finally in the very bottom drawer, two pairs of neatly folded jeans.

"Fuck me...Fuck me..."

He felt the trickle of sweat on his brow, a rush of heat through his body and the dizzying sensation that accompanied a rage so black, he had to continually blink to see in front of him and stay conscious as he began tearing through the room, looking for the rest of his belongings—his guitars and amplifier, his camera, his stereo and music collection, even his wallet - it suddenly occurred to him that he had not seen these things the past two days, not that he had thought to look for them.

After a few minutes, he concluded there were no musical instruments.

Where his stereo should have sat was the chair loaded with get-well crap and behind this a boom box. While there was a CD tower, it was filled with popular country and a few top 40 artists. Enraged, he picked the entire thing up and threw it against his bedroom door. Cursing at the mess, he again picked up the tower and after shaking all the CDs onto the floor, threw it against the wall before picking up each individual CD and hurling them against whatever he could—the walls, the windows, the doors. Flinging them with such fury, he barely noticed or cared that the girl, Danielle Fahlstrom, had attempted to open the door to see what was happening and, upon nearly getting hit with a flying plastic case, fled screaming down the hall.

After disposing the CDs, he turned to his dresser and began throwing the trophies, starting with the wrestling ones but soon viewing them all with equal disdain. The desk was next, and after emptying all the drawers of their contents, he took aim at the framed photos—both of Alex Tate with Trisha, though it could have just as easily been Barbie and Ken model look-alikes.

"*I fucking hate you,*" he screamed at the photo, laying it flat on the desk before smashing his fist into it. He felt the glass pierce his skin, the pain fueling his adrenaline. He smashed it again, grinding the pieces deeper into his flesh, stopping only when the frame could no longer hold the shattered glass, which rained upon the desk and floor around him.

He moved onto the next photo, this one much larger, punching his fist through the pane in hopes one of the shards would slash his wrist, determined to smash every photo in the room until his wrist bled out. "*I hate you…I fucking hate you. All of you,*" he screamed at a team wrestling photo before attempting to smash it with his left hand, his right too damaged and throbbing.

So loud was the screaming in his own mind, that he didn't hear the two adults enter the room, didn't hear them attempt to calm him down or their own shouts of panic at his bloodied hand and arm. At some point strong arms grabbed him and forced him to the ground, and he was sitting on the floor of his bedroom, the man firmly pinning Alex's upper arms back with one arm and cradling his head with the other. The lady sat, tears streaming, hands shaking as she began picking glass out of his skin, calling orders to the girl who returned with a medical kit and whatever else the lady asked her to retrieve.

The rush fading, he could now feel the searing pain from his hands and wrists, at times wondering if he would black out, but he stayed conscious, his mind eventually focusing on his injuries and only partly aware of the adults' hushed conversation.

Should we take him to the emergency room—

No—they don't look deep enough. I'll call Lawrence and see if he can make a house call.

I don't know, Bill—I think he needs attention. I—I don't know if I can do this.

Jayne, I'm not taking him back to that hospital. I'm not. I take him back there like this, and he won't come home. They'll send him away—you know they will.

Maybe—maybe that's for the best. Maybe he doesn't belong here. Maybe we made a mistake.

We didn't make a mistake…You know it, and so does he…Don't you, Alex? You know you belong here. This is your home. This is where you belong, son.

I just don't know…I don't know if I can get all the glass out. I'm afraid he'll get an infection-

Do the best you can. Lawrence can look at it later. We just need to stop the bleeding.

Yes…It's slowing.

It was minutes later, after most of the shards had been removed and the blood mopped up with hand towels fetched from the bathroom, that Alex was clear-headed enough to realize the adults were now addressing him, asking him questions.

"What happened, honey…Why'd you do this? Why'd you do this to yourself, Alex?" the lady asked as she tenderly wrapped a clean bandage around his hand and wrist, her eyes still bright with tears.

"That's not me in that picture," he said dully. "It's not me…It's not my room…It's not my stuff," he continued, tears welling, his body starting to shake with the familiar grief.

"Alright…But how is hurting yourself going to change that?"

"I'm not him…I hate him…I was never him…"

"Well then, who are you, Alex? Who are you son?" the man asked, now just hugging him, holding him.

"I'm Alex Michael Fahlstrom," he burst. "I was born on December Fourth, 1976 in Seattle, Washington. We moved here when I was five. My father's a doctor. My mother's a physical therapist. My sister's name is Trisha…. I play football and guitar. I play guitar and like rock music and classical music. I have a girlfriend named Danielle. My address is…sixty-ninth street…It's on sixty-ninth street in Prairie Village, Kansas…I don't remember the zip code. My phone is…913…something…I forgot it. I forgot…" He sobbed convulsively against the man's shoulder.

In his state of utter despondence, Alex had no concept of time passing and had no idea how long he sat on the bedroom floor with the man and woman, crying until his tears were spent, surrounded by the debris of his former life. At some point he was on his bed, slumped against the headboard, his bandaged, smarting hands resting limply in his lap, but soon lying limp and handcuffed, the man taking his own measures to keep Alex from hurting himself while unattended. The lady visited him frequently, offering him food and drink, asking him how he felt and threatening to call a doctor.

Somewhere in time, the girl crept into his room and began rummaging around, followed by the dog. He said nothing, turning away from her and staring at his wall, waiting for her to leave. To his dismay, she approached the bed and stood there for a minute, waiting for him to acknowledge her. The dog then jumped up on the bed, approaching Alex cautiously, tail wagging.

"Alex..." she said after more than a minute of silence.

He continued to ignore her, staring sadly at the dog, who obviously wanted to be pet.

"I...I have something for you."

He turned his head towards her but remained silent. She stood, holding the handle of the boom box in one hand and a large notebook-looking object in another.

"Here," she said, holding out the notecase, her hand trembling.

He remained unmoved, and she ended up dropping it onto the bed, unable to hold its weight with one hand. It fell open, and he noticed it held pages of CDs. She then fumbled around next to his bed, looking for an outlet, before setting the now plugged-in boom box on the bed next to him, close enough for him to reach it with his cuffed hands.

"It's my CD collection...I...I like rock-and-roll, too. And classical. Maybe...Maybe you'll find something you like."

"Do you have any Nirvana?" he asked hoarsely, still avoiding eye contact.

She smiled, flipping through the pages. "Oh, yeah...and Pearl Jam and Hole. Hole, is coming out with a new album, you know. I have *Pretty on the Inside* and some bootlegs from their shows, but, you know...It should be good. Brooke and I will be first in line for that one." Finding the Nivana CD she was looking for, she took it out and placed it in the CD player.

He looked at her. "Brooke? Did you say Brooke?"

She frowned, nodding and backing slightly away after hitting the play button. "Yes...Why?"

"Brooke Trahan?"

She nodded.

As the introductory guitar chords from "Smells Like Teen Spirit" poured from the small speakers, his momentary excitement soon faded. Of course she was friends with Brooke. Danielle was best friends with Brooke, and her name was Danielle. It meant nothing.

"Why?"

He turned away, staring at the gray wall. "Nothing...Tell her I said hi."

"You remember Brooke?" she asked, turning the volume down on the box, her voice excited.

He remained silent.

"Um...Do you...Do you remember me? I mean...Was I someone in your life?"

He said nothing, shifting his entire body away from her.

"Was I mean? Did I hurt you?" she asked quietly. "I—I only ask, because.... Well, because you obviously want nothing to do with me...It's okay, though."

"I could ask you the same thing," he said gruffly.

"I'm sorry? What do you mean?"

"I doubt I was the nicest brother."

"Oh...Well...We had our differences, but...You're still my brother, you know."

He said nothing but heard the volume increase and knew she departed shortly thereafter. The music was comforting, and he was soon lulled to sleep, still handcuffed, *Nevermind* replaying in a continual loop, the dog curled up next to his feet at the end of his bed.

It took a week for word of Alex's awakening to fully circulate, the Fahlstroms having initially kept the news close to themselves and the Trahans, not wanting to publicize anything until they had a better idea of his prognosis. For Gabrielle, his recovery awakened something much deeper and darker, something she thought had been buried for good. But with each passing day, she became more and more aware that what she thought had been destroyed was still very much alive. And strong. And completely intolerant of her desire to replace the black clouds of her past with bright blue skies, her fear and loathing with peace and acceptance. Despite her initial determination to start the year over with a new look, she soon realized she would not be trading in her Goth attire for the Gap anytime soon.

His recovery made it impossible for her to forget about him, even for a day. Alex Fahlstrom was incredibly popular at school, Junior class president and top of his class in grades and athletic honors. While the average high school girl may have fawned over a boy like Alex, these attributes never really impressed Gabrielle due to the small size of their class, the entire four-year high school having just over three hundred and fifty students. And Polson was a happy, peaceful town with a low crime rate that primarily consisted of theft and alcohol-related incidents, violent crimes being practically non-existent and a murder happening every few years at best. The combination of a star student-athlete and such a violent shooting in Polson's most popular gas station and convenience store was almost too much for the residents to bear, and they simply couldn't stop talking about it.

Or get enough, Gabrielle thought sadly, every time she overheard conversations in the classroom, the school cafeteria, drama rehearsal, the diner, the grocery store. Every time she opened up the *Lake County Leader*, she read a news update about the incident or saw an ad taken out by a church or local organization, asking the community to support Alex with prayers and the Fahlstroms with donations. But then Alex had been made a local hero, not a victim of hapless circumstance or his own indiscretions. He had stepped into the line of fire, a line supposedly meant for the girl behind the counter, and saved her life, his father having shot the gunman in the head before he could take anyone else down. That was the story the convenience store girl, Jennifer Hicks, had told the police and media. That was the story Mr. Fahlstrom had told his peers and state law enforcement investigators. That was the story everyone believed.

But Gabrielle knew there was more to the story, and as February marched on and Alex's consciousness strengthened, so did her mental and emotional connection with him, the one they had shared since birth, and the one she had thought was finally severed on New Year's Eve. She knew the only hero that night was his father. She knew Alex had secrets.

To cope with the encroaching despair, Gabrielle threw herself into school, activities and hobbies with an even greater abandonment than usual. She was popular in her own circle, one that consisted of students interested in music, art, drama, speech, debate, yearbook and, basically, every activity in which Alex Fahlstrom had no interest. She was an avid drummer, active in pep band, Native American performing arts and random basement bands.

She could also sing and had made lead in the spring musical the past two years. This spring, however, the musical was *West Side Story*, and she hardly felt up to playing the part of Maria, instead trying out for Anita. To her dismay, she was still selected as Maria, and Brooke got the part of Anita. Unfortunately, Brooke would hear nothing of trading roles with Gabrielle. Brooke usually made lead in the fall plays and fancied herself the better actress of the two, seeing Gabrielle as having a stronger voice and, therefore, more deserving of lead in the spring musical. A senior named Mick, who was not only the most talented theatrically but also a flaming homosexual, got the role of Tony, and Gabrielle could only laugh at the irony that a known fag and a supposed slut were playing the roles of heterosexual Tony and his virginal Maria.

But play practice offered a welcomed distraction, and with the show being two months away, the group began rehearsing four nights a week. It was after practice Thursday evening when Mick stopped Gabrielle on her way out to remind her of his *School Sucks* party that weekend, an annual affair he had hosted for three years now.

"Oh, yeah…It is this weekend, isn't it," she said thoughtfully, then shrugged. "I don't know. Maybe. If I feel up to it—"

"What do you mean if you feel up to it? It's not a party without the Trahan girls, sweetheart, and I expect you and your sister to be there in full style."

She laughed but shook her head. "I don't know…Dennis and I broke up. I'm just not in a partying mood right now."

"Sugar, I'll be your date. It'll be good for you. Take your mind off things. Plus, it's my last one. I'll be in LA this time next year," he said, doing a gyrating dance around her and making her laugh.

The laughter felt good, and she acquiesced. On Saturday night, she found herself in the back seat of her sister's car, headed to the party with Brooke, Brooke's boyfriend, Steve, and Danielle Fahlstrom. She had dressed in full Goth attire, wearing her favorite black and purple wig that she teased up and out, skin tight black acrylic pants, a ripped long-sleeve, low-cut T-shirt, spiked collar and full metal facial regalia. Brooke and Danielle had decided to channel the B-52s, and only Steve was attending the party dressed as himself, though he didn't seem to mind the surrounding theatrics.

Mick's house was a large, two-story, modern log and stone home with a second-story deck that spanned the entire width of the house. Unlike many parties, this one was chaperoned by his parents, whom Gabrielle thought awfully open-minded. While alcohol was not served, it was snuck in and stashed in various places, and while the party was by invitation only, anyone who wanted to show up could and did. Still, the presence of adults kept things under control. Mick always found someone to DJ, and the basement was lined with speakers and cleared for dancing, which is what most attendees did—dance in the basement and snack and socialize upstairs.

Once there, she met up with her two best friends, Kelly and Cherise, and after chatting a bit, the three headed downstairs to lose themselves in the music. The basement was dark and already packed with students, most of them slam dancing, nobody caring how anyone danced or how they looked when they danced, and Gabrielle quickly lost herself in the group vibe. The disco lights, when flashing a certain way, seemed to freeze-frame everyone, as in a fast reeling, black and white film, and the music incessantly pounded in a rhythm that soon permeated her body and mind like a manic mantra, putting her into another state of being.

By the time "Head Like a Hole" played, the group was dancing in a frenzy. They all liked Nine Inch Nails, and even though it was a dance version of the song, arms waved, bodies twirled, hair flew and mouths screamed the lyrics. Gabrielle could feel the sweat forming and streaming from her brow, strands of her wig lying plastered against her face until she shook them loose. Her heart pounded, and her ears rang numb, but each frantic moment also brought with it an intense high.

It was only when the song wound down that a strange feeling swept over her, and she stopped. Her physical rush was replaced by a chill, a tingling sensation down her neck, and she had an eerie sense that someone was watching.

She spun around.

All she could see were the oscillating limbs of the surrounding dancers, each in his or her own world, none paying any attention to her. But as she stood there, observing the room, it changed, morphing ever so slightly, still reverberating with dancers but different dancers with different faces and clothing. Brooke was no longer in a mini dress and go-go boots but black satin pants and a beaded halter. She looked down and noticed her black punked-out attire had been replaced with a baby-blue camisole party dress, one with a tiered chiffon skirt that flared when she twirled.

She looked again and saw him, leaning against a basement support pillar, his arms crossed and a smirk on his face, and she knew she had stepped back in time, to last year's *School Sucks* party, when Alex Fahlstrom had stood in that very spot, quietly watching her dance.

"Alex Fahlstrom," she said, putting her hands on her hips and laughing. "What are you doing here? Crashing the party?"

He shrugged, walking towards her. "Something like that. We wanted to see how the other side lives."

She peered around him, looking for his friends. "So, where's the rest of your posse? No—bigger question, where's your girlfriend?"

"Away at a pageant," he said, looking away from her.

"Oh...Well, this is a peaceful party, you know. We don't want any trouble from you and your *jock homophobes*," she said jokingly.

He put his hands up in surrender. "We're just here checking it out...We got nothing better to do on a Saturday night. Besides, I wasn't aware it was invitation only."

"Well, *it is* but...if anyone asks, I'll speak for you and Carl. Can't speak for the other three, though. They'll have to find their own friends here. Want to join me?"

He shook his head. "I don't dance."

"Well neither does anyone else," she laughed, motioning to the erratically jumping crowd. "Come on," she said, holding out her hand. "Nobody cares what you look like—*really*. Nobody's even paying attention."

"I was," he said, eyeing her intently.

She flushed, completely taken aback. Though she saw Alex daily at school and frequently at joint family functions, they had drifted so far apart that they rarely carried on a conversation beyond the weather and sports standings. Both lived completely separate lives in completely different worlds, their only connection the occasional injury, illness or intense emotional surge that they psychically shared but had forgotten was coming from the other person. For the past three years, they had simply ignored each other.

"You look very nice tonight," he said. "I—I didn't even recognize you at first. You don't usually wear dresses."

"Oh, well...Thanks. I guess I can clean up well, huh?"

He grinned, and she blushed. Unnerved by his behavior, she invited him to dance again and decided to make her way back into the crowd and get lost in the music, regardless of whether or not he followed her. To her surprise, and that of her sister, his sister and nearly everyone else there, Alex did. And after a half hour of dancing, they both took a break to get food and drinks. While Alex was dancing, Carl and friends had discovered some of the hidden alcohol, which they willingly shared with him and Gabrielle. They drank for awhile, and Gabrielle was happy to catch up with her two old friends and become acquainted with their group. They were very amiable, and, after achieving a sufficient buzz, the entire group headed back downstairs to dance, Carl soon becoming the life of the dance floor.

At some point, Alex pulled her aside and asked her if she wanted to take another drinking break with him. She agreed, and they headed back upstairs, but since neither of them knew where the alcohol was stashed, both settled for water. He then suggested they find someplace quiet to just talk and chill out, the heat and noise having given him a headache. She agreed, and they snuck upstairs to find an unoccupied room furthest away from the pounding music and speakers, which could still clearly be heard and felt on the first floor.

Finding what appeared to be a storage bedroom from its sparse furnishings and piles of clutter, they sat on the floor in the only open space in the room and talked, but this time about everything, spending the first hour catching up on each other's lives, like two best friends who hadn't seen each other in years. Spending the next hour sharing their thoughts and interests, dreams and fears. It was then that she got an insight into what Alex had become over the past few years and the façade he was living, as he shared with her his frustrations at home, feeling completely overshadowed by his talented sister, his stress at school and, most agonizing for him, his decaying relationship with Trisha. A relationship in which he had poured his entire heart and soul and received little in the way of love or affection and nothing in the way of sex, the girl having proclaimed herself a virgin until marriage.

And somewhere in that second hour, out of sheer instinct, Gabrielle had moved closer to him, eventually sitting next to him, eventually putting her arm around him as a show of comfort. Like she did when they were children and he had suffered some abuse, setback or punishment. But instead of slapping her away like he would when they were young, saying he didn't need sympathy from a sissy girl, he looked at her intently.

"You look so beautiful tonight...I don't know what it is," he said, lightly touching her hair with his hand. "Did you do something different to your hair?"

She blushed and turned away. "I don't know...I did dress up a bit tonight, I guess...I did curl my hair, which I rarely do."

"I've...I've just never seen you this way. I've—I've never noticed. I don't know why."

She looked at him, searching for sincerity in his expression, her heart pounding and her mind raging with conflicting emotions. Her entire life, she dreamed of a moment like this, alone with him when he would see her as something more than the annoying tomboy she grew up with. She had always found him insanely attractive, even after he cut off his curls in the seventh grade, an act she found personally devastating. But no matter how short he kept his hair, he couldn't hide them entirely. And even in his preppy attire, a light pink-striped Oxford and neatly pressed jeans, he couldn't hide the wild boy that still resided deep within himself. She could see it in his dark, deep-set eyes and the occasional, mischievous smile.

But he had given his heart to someone else, someone whom he still cared for, whom he had spent the last half hour pining over. She knew he was simply lonely that night and looking for momentary companionship and that to let him go down the path he was headed would be a mistake. Nothing good could come from taking advantage of the situation, no matter how much she ached to know what he felt like, what he kissed like. This was neither the time nor place. It could only end badly, like a hackneyed television soap opera.

Her mind was saying this, but her body was saying something quite different, meeting him as he leaned towards her, not turning away as his lips met hers, shyly at first, hesitant until she put an arm around his neck and pulled him closer to herself.

Looking back at that night, she still had no idea what caused such an explosion of physical chemistry between them, attributing it to alcohol and pent-up sexual tension, his from getting nothing from his girlfriend and hers from getting nothing at all, having been dateless since Brian had moved away a year prior. But light kissing quickly turned into French kissing, intense, hungry, and his lips moved to her neck and her chest, his hands moved from her waist to her thigh. She lay down on her back and pulled his body on top of her own, unbuttoning his shirt, his jeans, groping for skin, wanting to feel every part of him. And she didn't stop him from exploring her body, letting him slide the thin dress straps down her shoulders, push the top down to reveal her breasts. She would have given herself to him had he wanted it, but he didn't, content to hold her tightly against himself, pressing and thrusting his pelvis against her through his jeans until he peaked, and they lie together afterwards, slightly apart, staring at the ceiling, laughing in-between labored breaths, asking each other what had just happened.

After helping each other to re-dress and straighten up, they headed back downstairs to the party, which had only grown in attendance while they were away, disappearing into their own crowds of acquaintances and acting as if nothing had happened.

Gabrielle felt the tears stream down her face and quickly headed upstairs to find a bathroom and wipe away the black streaks they would cause from her heavy eye make-up. But as she looked into the mirror at the grotesque image that stared back, she burst into uncontrolled sobs and spent the next half hour locked in the bathroom, ignoring the occasional knocks and inquiries. By the time she had calmed down, she had washed all the make-up from her face and had to reposition the wig to hide her red, swollen eyes.

Venturing out of the bathroom, she quickly made her way to the kitchen to use the phone, trying to hide her face and brush off friends and acquaintances. To her relief, her mother answered and agreed to pick her up. After finding Brooke and feigning a headache, she went outside and waited for her mother on the porch, staring at the clear, star-filled sky with both yearning and remorse.

Her world quickly became haunted by memories, even places where she typically found retreat and comfort, like the stable, contaminated by a past she could no longer keep buried. Grooming her horse the next day, she remembered their next meeting, which had taken place close to where she now stood.

It was a few weeks after the party, and neither had spoken to each other, avoiding even looking at each other in class. Though a day did not pass without her thinking of him, she tried to erase the memory from her mind and to dash all hope of him calling her again. But one Sunday afternoon, he appeared on her door step, asking to speak with her in private, clearly agitated about something. She led him to the stable.

"What's wrong?" she asked with concern.

He crossed his arms, eyes narrowing at her. "What's wrong? I can't get you out of my mind, that's what's wrong. I can't—I can't forget that night. It's driving me crazy."

Her face flushed, and she looked down, embarrassed.

"I don't understand what happened," he continued, his voice an angry hush. "I don't understand what you did."

"What I did?" she burst. "You mean what *we* did—"

"No—I don't. I've never done anything like that before—with anyone. You obviously have."

"I have not," she protested, trying to calm a surge of anger. "I've never done anything like that—I've never even had the opportunity."

"Yeah, right—we hardly know each other."

"*What*? Are you *kidding* me? We've known each other since birth—"

He turned away, glaring. Feeling the first creep of guilt, she reached out first.

"Alex, I'm…I'm sorry. I am. But I swear—I've, I've never done that. I couldn't do that with someone I didn't…I couldn't with just anyone."

His shoulders relaxed and he looked at her, his eyes suddenly melancholy.

"When I look at her, I see you...When I'm with her, you know, *attempting* to make out, I imagine you...But when I see you in class, or just hanging out, I don't...I don't have those feelings. Even now, I'm looking at you, and I...I don't see what I saw. I don't feel what I felt."

Her heart fell. "So why are you here?"

"To see if it was real...To be alone with you and...and see if something happens again." He walked to her, so close she stepped back to create space. He looked down at her, studying her intently, his hand moving towards her hair, which had been pulled into a thick braid. To her surprise, he pulled out the band and undid the braid with his hands, letting her hair spill about her shoulders. After staring at her curiously another moment, he leaned in and kissed her.

Again, her mind told her to push him away, to send him away, to run away—far away, but her body instantly responded, having missed the touch of his skin against her own, the feel of his well-toned arms, his smell, a fresh mixture of detergent and mild aftershave. Moving to a far corner of the stable, they fell into a heated embrace, soon feverishly undressing each other, enough to explore previously uncharted territory, their jeans pushed down enough for him to penetrate her, and, as fumbling and awkward as the entry was, as painful the tear, once he was inside her, she lost herself in the moment, in his climax, her body trembling against his as he fell upon her momentarily, spent.

And again they lie, side by side, staring at the ceiling of a barn, the sound of horses stomping and neighing barely covering their labored breathing and nervous laughter.

"That felt real to me," Alex said, jokingly.

She nodded, unable to speak.

"So, what do we do now?" he asked after a few minutes had passed.

"What do you want to do?"

"I don't know...We can't tell anyone...Jesus," he said, sitting up and sounding panicked. "You can't get pregnant can you?"

She shrugged, momentarily unconcerned. "I don't know. I hadn't thought about it."

"Well, we need to think about it," he said, running his fingers nervously through is hair. "We can't do this again without protection."

"Okay," she said, smiling, her entire body filling with joy at his desire to see her again, to make love to her again. "I can get protection. My dad's a doctor."

"Jesus—you *can't tell* your dad."

She laughed, "I'm not…But Brooke and I know where the drugs are stashed, okay? We might have to wait awhile, though. Maybe a week or two. I don't remember…Brooke knows how it works."

"Well, you can't tell her, either. *Jesus Christ.*"

After she had calmed him down with numerous personal assurances, they dressed themselves and lie down again, shoulders touching and holding hands. Staring at the wood-beamed ceiling, they talked about life in general before he left an hour or so later.

Looking up at the same wood-beamed ceiling a year later, Gabrielle felt her eyes well with tears, and she collapsed on the ground next to her horse, sobbing, gripping the hay-strewn floor, wishing she could somehow turn back time and stop the impending doom while at the same time wishing she was back in that corner, lying next to him, feeling on top of the universe.

Brooke had reluctantly given her the birth control pills but had also hounded her mercilessly to provide details, at a minimum who her new lover was. But she remained firm in her resolve to keep it a secret, only admitting that she was having an affair, thus the need to keep it a secret.

"You're *what?*" her sister burst, hands on her hips and long hair flying.

"You know…I'm kind of, having an affair, I guess."

"What the fuck? How *old* is he?"

"Not *that* kind of affair," Gabrielle burst in defense, making a face. "Jesus—that's disgusting."

"Well, *what* kind, then?"

"You know," she started, staring down, her face completely flushed. They shared a bedroom, though both occasionally retreated into Nate's old room, and she was seated on her bed, picking at the threads in her brightly colored quilt. "He has a girlfriend."

"Oh, for fuck's sake, Gabby…That is a bad idea. That is *so* wrong."

"Well, you should talk—"

"Exactly! And I'm damn well going to, too. Why the *fuck* would you make the same mistake I did? Let me tell you something—they *never* leave their girlfriends. *Ever.* I don't care how good it is, how much chemistry, how much you have in common…It doesn't matter how cold or ugly their existing girlfriend is…Or how little she's putting out…It's all a load of shit. I was strung along for six months. No—shit, it was worse than that. That fucker actually told me he *broke up* with her, and I found out he was still seeing her behind my back."

"I know…And I don't care," she said resolutely.

"You don't care now—but you will. I promise you, you will regret this."

Gabrielle shook her head. "I know he'll never leave his girlfriend. I don't expect him to, and I don't care…I'm just happy to be with him when I can."

"Jesus, you're pathetic…I love you, but you are fucking pathetic. A fucking hopeless romantic. Let me tell you something—there are no heroes out there. No Mr. Rights. No perfect men. It's survival of the fittest, and you gotta find someone you can keep in line, or…Or they'll just fuck you over. And I don't like to be fucked over."

"But you'll still get me the pills, right?"

Brooke cursed, throwing a pillow at her head, but ultimately agreed to the request, and thus began a three month clandestine relationship, one that Gabrielle found personally liberating but would come to see had the opposite effect on Alex. Having finally connected with the one she always had seen as her soul mate, Gabrielle felt rooted, her confidence and esteem increasing daily, along with her zest for living. Colors seemed more intense, the Montana scenery more beautiful than it had ever looked. The air smelled fresher, and music—even songs she had listened to over and again—sounded new and infused with emotion and meaning. Food tasted better, and she found herself trying new dishes at Drifter's Diner, eating slowly, relishing each bite.

Having lost her virginity so recklessly, she felt more daring and inclined to try things socially questionable, like smoking cigarettes and eventually trying pot with her friend, Dennis. Like experimenting with her wardrobe and her hair, playing with streaks of temporary color. Like piercing her belly button, which was the current rage, and eventually getting a small tattoo on her back, just within her right shoulder blade, of an infinity sign, which looked like the number eight on its side. Being into theater and having been chosen lead in the spring musical, *Annie*, she saw the world as her stage and easily embraced the optimism and playfulness of the title character. The musical got rave reviews, which further convinced Gabrielle that all was right with her world, and until May, she didn't believe anything could go wrong.

Polson was beautiful in the spring, the weather warming and flowers coming into bloom. Unlike much of Montana, the Mission Valley enjoyed four seasons, and May brought everyone outside, parks brimming with families, streets with cyclists, trails with hikers and the lake with boats, from Sunfish sailboats to yachts. They had just made love on a blanket on the floor of Alex's garage-workshop, of all places, his refusing to do it in their home or his room. His sister and mother were out of town at a recital, and his father was on duty. It had been an intense session, Alex taking longer than usual to climax, Gabrielle having come awhile before he did. When he finally rolled over on his back, she sat up momentarily, stretching and planning on lying down on his chest, wanting to hold him, but he stopped her.

"You have something on your back," he said, and she felt his hand brush her skin, as if trying to brush something off.

She laughed. "It won't come off that way. Do you like it?"

"What is it?...Is that a *tattoo*?"

"Yeah...I got it a few weeks ago—after the play. I'm surprised you haven't noticed it before," she mused. But they had both been busy with spring activities and unable to sneak away as frequently. Now that she thought about it, their last two meetings had been late at night, on the side of an obscure road in the back seat of his car.

"*What the hell?*"

"It's an infinity sign. You know..."

"Yes, I know what an infinity sign is. What I don't know is why the fuck you would want to get one in the first place."

She shrugged, moving to lie down with him, but he pushed her away, abruptly sitting up.

"What the heck has gotten into you lately, anyway?" he asked angrily.

"What are you talking about?"

"You—your, your look. The crazy stuff you're doing. You're acting like a slut—with your tattoo and that, that awful belly ring. And I see you smoking in the parking lot with that group of losers—"

"What?"

"You're fucking him, aren't you—aren't you?"

"*Who*?" she burst, moving quickly to dress herself, her hands now shaking as her mind raced to process his sudden change of mood.

"You know who...You're with him all the time—I see you together all the time, the pot head. Are you doing drugs with him, too? *Are you*?" he asked, grabbing her arm.

"Are you kidding me? Dennis—*really*? Dennis is one my best friends. He was yours, too, before you got him busted for drugs."

"He got himself busted for drugs. He's a pothead."

"So? What do you care? It never hurt you—he never harmed you—"

"Bullshit—we lost a meet because of him. Showing up all hung over and strung out. He got what he deserved."

"Oh—and you and your friends never go drinking—"

"Not before meets we don't, and we never do drugs. *Ever*. My father's the sheriff for Christ's sake. Do you have any idea what could happen to him if I go anywhere near that shit? Do you have any idea what would happen to my family's reputation? Are you that insensitive?"

"What the *hell* are you talking about? *Insensitive*? Are you kidding me? I've been nothing but sensitive to you and your situation. I've told *no one* about us. I don't bother you—I leave you alone at school and pretend I barely know you. So what the hell do you care what I do when we're not together?"

"I do care—okay? It matters to me who I fuck, and I don't fuck sluts."

"Well, I'm not a slut," she burst, her eyes welling with angry tears. "And who the fuck are you to call me one? You're the one cheating on your girlfriend. I don't even have a boyfriend other than you."

She didn't know what hit her.

A searing pain shot through her upper left cheek and she sat stunned, too shocked to even move, time having frozen, the world having stopped momentarily.

He grabbed her by the shoulders, and she tried to shrink away, tears of shame and rage welling in her eyes.

"You don't get it, do you? *Do you*? You think this is just a game, don't you? That you can just fuck with me on the side and then go—go do what you want, go fuck who you want. Well, it doesn't work that way, do you understand? *Do you*?"

She shook her head, trying to wriggle from his grip, which just got stronger the more she moved, the tears starting to stream down her cheeks.

"Do you know why I will never love you like I do Trisha—*ever*. *Do you*? Why I can never be with you in public—why I *would never want to*. Do you?"

She shook her head. She did not want to know. She did not want to know because she already knew it had to do with his completely different way of looking at the world and the people in it, of his completely different value system, one that placed reputation and perfection in high regard, that had no tolerance for mediocrity or deviation from a black and white moral code, regardless of the inconsistent logic on which it was based. Of his irrational fear of chaos, of losing control, of being perceived as a failure or a loser or inadequate. A fear she had tried to abate during their short time together, after the lovemaking sessions, through conversation, sharing her favorite music, reading him lines of poetry. Through bringing him books of her favorite artists and paintings, trying to show him how beauty and art can come from chaos, confusion and constant questioning, even challenging

God and the universe. How perfection either didn't exist or was all that existed, in everything around them, depending upon one's perception. How she didn't care how he dressed, how he did in school, what trophies he brought home or whether he went to college or became a ranch hand. She loved him regardless and had assumed that he felt the same about her, an assumption she now realized was wrong.

"I love Trisha, and I choose to love Trisha because *she is everything you're not*. Wealthy, beautiful, graceful, poised, talented, disciplined, speaks fluent French, is well-traveled—is respected amongst her peers. Because she's headed for an Ivy League school, while you're headed for god knows where—some art school or community college. Because she and I are going to get out of here and make something of ourselves, while you fuck around in this stupid town, fucking losers and potheads behind my back. Making me look—and feel—like an idiot."

She struggled to pull away, turning her head away from him, wanting to crawl away and hide in utter defeat, but he would not let her go.

"Look at me—goddammit," he said, turning her face towards his, and she was surprised to see his own eyes brimming with tears. "You don't get it, do you? I wanted us to work out—I did. I wanted so badly what we had to be real, but it wasn't. You're not real. You're not who I saw at that party—that beautiful girl in the blue dress, your long black hair spilling about your shoulders…The best dancer in the room. The classiest looking girl in the entire place. You're *nothing* like her. If you were, maybe things could be different. Maybe we could be together. But *you're a lie, a fucking lie*," he said, finally letting her go, turning away from her to wipe away his own tears.

It was a blow more devastating than anything physical, completely shattering the fragile, delusional world she had built for herself. More painful than his words was the realization that she had lost him, probably for the rest of this lifetime, if not for lifetimes after that. She had lost him, because she *had* been insensitive, so confident and enthralled with her own perception of reality that she had failed to accept his, had dismissed his, had the arrogance to try to change his instead of seeing things through his eyes. She had hurt him, however unintentionally, she knew she had wounded him on some level and would have done anything to turn back time, to rewrite the last three months, for none of her antics were worth this. If she had only realized how important it had been to him—the clothes, the hair, the proper persona—she would have happily put on that costume and played that role.

She was not surprised when a few weeks went by without any contact from him and was relieved when school ended and she would not have to see him on a daily basis. What she never expected was for him to show up at her doorstep one Sunday afternoon, wanting to speak to her in private. It was déjà vu, standing with him in the stable, barely able to make eye contact as he mumbled an apology, saying he was sorry for what he had said and that he missed her, missed their time together.

But she shook her head, "No…No you don't."

He stepped close to her, their bodies nearly touching, and she stepped back, trying to create distance. "I do…I miss you, I need you," he said, moving in to kiss her, forcing himself on her as she turned her head the other direction.

She pushed him away. "No you don't…You miss the sex, that's what you miss. But I told you—I'm not a slut. And I won't be your slut, I won't. It was only you, Alex—whether you believe me or not, it was only you. It's always been you—since we were children. So if you want sex, you'll have to get it from Trisha. And since that's not likely to happen, you'll just have to find someone else willing to be your whore. I'm done."

But even as she said the words, her heart broke and it took every ounce of strength not to hold him, comfort him, love him. To feel the touch of his skin against her own, to feel his body pressed against hers. She would miss his grin, the smell of his clothes and the way he looked at her before they made love, the way she held him afterwards.

He glared at her, his eyes narrowing. "So that's it, then. We're over?"

She nodded, "Yes," she said quietly, looking down.

He walked up to her, their bodies nearly touching. "You bitch—you self-righteous bitch…You think your free? Do you? You think you can just walk away—like nothing happened—like it never happened? Do you?"

She remained silent.

He turned away, laughing under his breath. "We'll see…"

The revenge had been swift and brutal, and Gabrielle still shuddered thinking about it, his hate and cruelty utterly taking her by surprise. The only thing he spared her of was the memory of what actually happened, instead leaving her with just enough physical evidence to fuel her own paranoia and complete the details in whatever fashion she wished and as gruesomely as she wished, depending upon her mood. She had seen him at a summer party, another large house, another large celebration but this one absent of adults and teeming with alcohol and drugs. Trisha being on vacation in Florida, he was there with his friends, hanging out on the sidelines, the five of them drinking beer and watching the activity, acting more like bouncers or security than participants.

He was coldly polite but soon warmed up to her, asking if she would like to dance. She declined, but offered to have a drink with him outside, on the shore near the dock, the house situated on the lakeside, hoping to heal things and end the relationship the way it should have ended, with their friendship intact.

He insisted on getting her a drink, and she let him, asking for a Sprite.

The last thing she remembered was having a laid back conversation about their summer jobs and looking up at the clear, starlit sky. She vaguely recalled feeling a bit flushed and dizzy.

The next thing she remembered was waking up the following morning under a tree in the back of her family's 14-acre property, chilled from the morning dew and completely confused as to how she got there but growing increasingly nauseous as she stood up and started to walk, feeling horribly cramped and bruised throughout her stomach and pelvis. It wasn't until she had made it into the bathroom and looked into the mirror that she fully realized what had likely happened, her face and neck bruised, her inner legs bruised and on her chest, above her right breast, a word, written neatly in black ink, small but readable, and almost the same size as her infinity tattoo. *Whore.*

She knew it was Alex and, strangely, hoped it only was him. Somehow, in her mind, if it was just Alex, she could live with it, get over it. But she feared others had participated—Carl, his other friends, his posse. Something about the way they stared at her when she saw them, days and weeks later, around town, or in the school halls that fall. And though she had tried to hide it from her family, feigning the stomach flu, after two days of not eating, drinking or even leaving her bed except to use the bathroom, Brooke surmised something was up, refusing to leave her side until she told her what was wrong, insisting on taking her temperature one evening and seeing the bruises herself.

"Gabrielle…" she breathed. "What happened to you?"

But Gabrielle just retreated further under the blankets, wishing for sleep or even death to overtake her. The ink washed away a few days later, but the shame did not. She never did discuss the incident with Brooke, or anyone else for that matter, leaving those closest to her to surmise the worst. And though she never told anyone of her relationship with Alex and thought she had been discreet—that they both had been discreet—her sister had somehow known. And so did Dennis Wiseman.

By March, her memories were so vividly unforgiving, her grief and despair so acute, that she was finding it hard to focus on her studies and activities, no matter how hard she tried. The unending news of Alex's recovery was grueling to hear, and every time Jayne Fahlstrom stopped by to visit with her mom or Danielle Fahlstrom hung out with her sister, which was almost daily, Gabrielle would retreat to Nate's room or some far corner of the stable with her horses and barn cats. Not even their prospective Spring Break trip to New York to visit Brooke and Danielle's colleges and see a few Broadway plays could cheer her, and she contemplated forgoing the trip altogether, feigning illness. To help out the Fahlstroms and support Danielle, her parents had offered to take Danielle with them on the trip, to spend time at both Juilliard, helping her to finalize paperwork, and Brooke's school of choice, The New York Film Academy. But the prospect of hearing Danielle talk about Alex was unbearable.

On Saturday night, a week before the family was to leave for New York, her mother paid her a visit. Brooke was out partying, and Gabrielle was alone in her room, reading a book by Edith Wharton called *The Age of Innocence*, not even sure why she was reading it, having stumbled upon it in the library looking for Walt Whitman's *Leaves of Grass*.

"Gabrielle, I want to talk to you. I need to talk to you," she said, gently taking the book from her daughter's hands and setting it on the nightstand. "I've let you carry this burden by yourself far too long. It's time you let go of it, and give it to me. Give it to me to send it back to where it came from. I can help you."

She eyed her mother strangely, comforted by her appearance but confused by her words. Barb Trahan was an attractive woman with long black hair that she often wore braided, strong cheekbones and dark, almond-shaped eyes. Both her parents were Native American, but Barb's Salish bloodline was stronger than her husband's, whose father was British Canadian. Her mother had always been a reassuring presence in her life, both her parents completely loving and supportive of her and her siblings, never using harsh discipline or words, relying instead on patience and wisdom, allowing the universe to lead them and acting as mere directional guides along the way.

To Gabrielle's surprise, her mother motioned for her to scoot over and climbed into bed with her, under the covers, the two of them seated with their backs against the headboard, her mother's arm wrapped around her shoulder, pulling her close. She smelled of fresh cedar and flowers.

Her mother sighed. "You and Brooke think you're so clever...Think we don't know what goes on. What antics you're up to. What you do when we're away or at work or *not watching*...But we know. *I know*—and not just because I'm a medicine woman. I know because I'm your mother, and I love you. I know because I am you, and you are me. Because I'm human and have traveled the same road you have, made the same mistakes, in this life and past lives. Time is irrelevant. Bodies are irrelevant, and on some level you know this. You know the world is a stage, to quote the great Bard—you've actually seen this to be true, been willing to flippantly change your masks—your personas—to fit the moment. But when you're on stage, completely immersed in your part, you forget that you're merely *playing* a role and begin to believe you actually *are* the role. Which might be okay if you happen to see yourself in a positive light, as a role model, a mentor or a healer. A helper, a lover of life. But certainly not when you see yourself in a negative way. As a failure, a loser. A victim or even—a *whore*."

She whispered the last word in Gabrielle's ear, and Gabrielle burst into tears, burying her head in her mother's chest.

"*How did you know?*" She cried. How did she know...

"Honey...You think I didn't see that word, small as it was. You think I didn't care for you those two days you were in bed, while you were sleeping. I didn't pray over you. I didn't notice your behavior days later, weeks later, months later—the mask of death you selected for yourself. That you've worn since last fall."

"I didn't write it...I didn't..."

Her mother let her cry until the tears were spent, holding her close in calm silence. "No...You had absolutely nothing to do with it, did you. It just appeared. It all just happened to you, didn't it. You were a victim of hapless circumstance. Just as you had nothing to do with the assault. Nothing to do with the relationship or why it ended. Nothing to do with your birth. Nothing to do with your family, your town, your school...The sun rises and sets as if by magic. The seasons change as if by magic. You grow from a seed in a womb to a child to an adult as if by magic and are blown through your life like a dead leaf in the wind, completely ignorant of the fact that you're not only the leaf but the tree and the roots. The ground and the wind. The sun and the moon. You are either all of it or none of it, but there is no separation between the leaf, the tree, the roots, the earth, the sun or the stars, Gabrielle. There is no separation between us."

Gabrielle remained silent but hugged her mother tighter. After a few minutes of silence, her mother continued.

"Jayne and I are best friends, you know…Closer than sisters. And we shared something very special the day you and Alex were born, almost as special as what you and Alex shared. It's extraordinary, really—your births. At the exact same time—what are the chances, Gabrielle? What are the statistical chances of such a coincidence? In two different towns or even countries, sure. But in the same town—in the same room? It was as if you two came into this life holding hands. That's how we saw it, anyway, Jayne and me. We had such hopes for the two of you. Not that we expected you to necessarily be together the rest of your lives—or to become romantic or any of that. But that you could have such a bond—such a strong friendship to get you through life's challenges."

She felt her mother move her arm to her face and could tell by her voice, her breathing, that she had begun to cry.

"We've watched the two of you suffer enough for your foolish mistakes. We've also watched you throw away this wonderful opportunity, this gift, really, to realize such an important lesson. To realize that whatever you do to yourself, you do to the other, and whatever you do to the other, you do to yourself. To this day, you deny having anything to do with his coming out of a coma, with his surviving. Just as you deny having anything to do with being assaulted, seeing yourself as a mere victim of another's cruelty, forgetting the fact that anything he did to harm you would only harm himself. That he would feel your shame and humiliation as acutely as if it were his own. Forgetting the times when you were children, and while only one of you broke a bone or suffered a fever, the both of you would feel miserable. Forgetting how you would try to comfort the other, as if knowing by doing so, you were helping yourself. Did it ever occur to you that you could also share joy? Share love? Actually make each other's lives even better than you could imagine?"

Gabrielle lie in stunned silence. She had completely forgotten, focusing only on a small segment of the past, a segment she didn't even remember, and blowing it out of proportion when compared to the rest of her life. She had forgotten what she had known most of her life, and the memory of it brought her a glimmer of hope.

"Jayne and I love our children…She grieves deeply for her son, for he doesn't recognize her and won't accept her help. And I grieve deeply with her…I feel her pain as acutely as my own. So I'm doing all I can do…By helping you to heal, helping him to heal…That's how it works, you know."

Gabrielle's eyes welled with tears, her heart once again filling with grief, but this time for him. And with the grief came compassion. And with the compassion a determination to make things better, to reshape their future.

Gabrielle went to New York with her family and Danielle Fahlstrom, consciously working to enjoy every moment of the trip, relishing the sights, sounds and smells of New York City, a place so vastly foreign from her home town, with its manmade, mountainous skyscrapers and giant park, and yet, on some deep quantum level, the same.

Danielle Fahlstrom did not speak much of her brother, wanting to escape into the New York scenery and her college future as badly as Gabrielle had wanted to escape her past. There were times when she wanted to talk, to even break down, and Gabrielle was able to provide some comfort, even if just to listen in calm, loving silence, next to her sister Brooke.

And when they had returned home, met by a grieving Jayne Fahlstrom who had just learned her son had attempted suicide, had somehow left the hospital grounds seeking death, Gabrielle was able to comfort her, too, and, for the first time, be willing to talk to her about her own coma, about the relationship, about Alex.

They sat at the Trahan's kitchen table, over tea and a box of Kleenex, just the two of them. Gabrielle had always thought Mrs. Fahlstrom the most genuinely sweet person she had ever met, the woman never having an unkind word for anyone, regardless of how vile their actions. She was pretty, too, her long hair still golden brown and rippling in soft waves. But Gabrielle could see the gray, could see the dark circles under her normally cheerful eyes, the sad lines around her mouth, and knew the past few months had taken a horrible physical toll on her.

It was amazing to her that Jayne and her mother were best friends, for they were so different. Jayne quiet, conservative, deeply Christian with an unshakable faith in Jesus, and her mother loud, musical, artistic with icons of every major religion represented in the house, from Native American totems to Tibetan Buddhas to statues of the Virgin Mary. They even dressed differently, Jayne in soft pastels, and her mother in brightly patterned skirts or scarves. Today, Jayne looked so pale that Gabrielle could barely see where the sleeve of her white blouse ended and the skin of her arm began.

"I…I know this is painful for you, Gabrielle…I know you haven't wanted to talk to me…to see me. Since last summer, really…I don't know why…I can only guess whatever happened between you and Alex was…was loathsome. But I must know…If you can tell me…do you remember anything about your—your attack on New Year's? Did you dream during that time you were unconscious?"

Gabrielle sighed, shaking her head. She did not remember but knew why Jayne was asking, having heard the story of Alex's strange amnesia from his sister Danielle. Jayne now told it again, providing details Gabrielle did not know and painting a picture of Alex's state of mind that Gabrielle found devastating. She imagined herself in such a situation—waking up to a world where everyone was a stranger, where nothing was as you remembered. The mere thought of it was terrifying to her, and she could understand why he would seek death.

"I...I just don't understand the fascination with Kansas City...I mean, of all places...New York would make more sense, or Los Angeles. Even Seattle or Missoula. But Kansas City? Where on earth did that come from..."

Gabrielle smiled. "You know, Brian McDermott moved to Kansas City a few years ago. He and Alex were good friends."

Jayne's eyes grew wide. "Really? My goodness, I—I completely forgot. I haven't kept up with Sally McDermott. I mean—I send her a Christmas card every year, but I send tons of cards and pay little attention to the addresses anymore. I had no idea."

"Maybe you should call her—see how they're doing," Gabrielle suggested.

Jayne nodded absently, getting a fresh Kleenex.

"Maybe you should ask her about the places Alex talks about. About the addresses in his journal. Maybe they exist. Wouldn't that be interesting."

Jayne's eyes grew wide again and she sat straight, a slight smile appearing on her face. "Yes...It would. It would be very interesting...It might prove he's not completely crazy, if to no one else, at least to himself," she laughed nervously. "Do you think...Do you think Dennis Wiseman has—would...well, you know. Do you think it is possible Dennis might...stop by the hospital one day? You know...Pay him a visit? I know...I know about the falling out. I do, but...Maybe out of some kind of pity. Maybe?"

But Gabrielle shook her head. "No...That's not going to happen. Dennis is still far too bitter and angry...I'm sorry. I hear Alex talks about him a lot."

Jayne nodded. "Yes...*Dennis Sumners*...Dennis Sumners and his twin sister, Danielle. That's all he talks about, sometimes...Those are the only two people he wants to see. I told him I would look for them, you know. But...I can't tell him the truth, I just can't...He's going to have to find that out on his own, and it's...It's hard for me, you know. I just want his suffering to stop...it's so endless...I keep praying...Every day, I pray...It has to end, right?

The Lord will make it end…He will…He didn't perform all these miracles for nothing…"

She began to cry again, and Gabrielle got up and hugged her. "Is there anything I can do?"

Jayne smiled, shaking her head. "Goodness, no…You've done enough." Then she looked up at her, her hand gently brushing Gabrielle's bangs to the side. "Gabrielle, honey, is that a piece of metal in your eyebrow?"

Gabrielle grinned. "Yeah…I kind of went a little crazy last year."

"You know," Jayne said thoughtfully, still studying her face, "If I didn't know any better, I would say you have one eye slightly larger than the other. Have you noticed that?"

Gabrielle snorted, shrugging. "Yeah…Brooke says when I stare a certain way, I look retarded."

Jayne laughed, giving her a hug. "Oh, I doubt that…I know someone who would vehemently disagree with her."

CHAPTER THIRTEEN

On Tuesday afternoon, Jayne Fahlstrom invited Alex down to the kitchen to show him something. She was very excited, and Alex braced himself for the worst. He was still handcuffed, Mr. Fahlstrom only allowing him to be free while showering or eating, the latter being an activity he still did in his room, unable to bear sitting at the dining room table with all of them. But until he would sit at the dinner table or watch television or make even the slightest attempt to become part of the family, Mr. Fahlstrom refused to release him, so they were at an impasse.

Alex slid into one of the black, wooden kitchen chairs, plopping his cuffed hands onto the table as loudly as he could and momentarily taking in his surroundings. It was a bright kitchen with a huge picture window that overlooked their yard, the décor all oak and mauve—with wooden floors, oak cabinetry and oak French doors leading to the living room. The walls were painted mauve, and the dining room table sat on a huge mauve, blue and gray, floral-patterned area rug.

He sighed loudly, rolling his eyes when he saw her enter the room with what looked to be a photo album and a large FedEx envelope.

"I've told you, I don't want to look at *his* photo album," he started, unable to hide the irritation in his voice. She had been trying to get him to look at photo albums of his childhood since he was in the hospital, but after seeing the few the psychologist had shown him, he couldn't stomach the prospect.

"Honey, calm down . . ." she said, sliding into a chair next to him and plopping the album on the table. "This isn't about Alex Tate—it's about Alex Michael, Okay? Starting today, it's all about Alex Michael. So whatever you're thinking, just . . ." She waved her hand as if waving away a pestering fly. "Just don't, okay?"

She smiled, and her eyes were very bright and cheerful, but he remained skeptical and would have crossed his arms if he could. But all he could do was to tap his foot impatiently on the floor.

"Alright…So, I'm really—I'm really going out on a limb, here, honey. I have done a lot of praying to the Lord about this…Yes, roll your eyes, *the Lord*, Alex. Praise Be Jesus Christ. And—and I really think—I really think this will make you happy. But I don't know. Really, well—I just don't know. You'll either be happy or try to kill yourself again. Anyway," she continued, clasping her hands together in excitement. "I've started a new photo album for you."

She slid the album in front of him, its cover a black faux marble design with gold stickered letters neatly aligned at the top center that read *Alex Michael*. He groaned, throwing his head back.

"It's one of those new albums, you know—with the special sleeves that won't turn the photos yellow," she said, opening the cover and showing him. But he could care less.

"There's nothing in it," he said, exasperated, pushing it away from himself with his cuffed hands.

"Not yet," she said, smiling widely, clutching the FedEx envelope. "Are you ready?"

He shrugged absently.

She retrieved a handful of photos from the envelope and neatly stacked them into a pile, placing the stack directly in front of him and within his reach. At the sight of the first photo, he nearly choked in shock, the image taking him by complete surprise.

"Do you recognize that?" she asked quietly.

He could barely respond, his mind raging with emotions, his eyes welling with tears. "That's my house…That's my home. Where did you get this?"

She smiled. "Do you want to see the next one?"

He nodded, capable of turning the photos himself but too stunned to do so.

"Jesus…. That's the Sumners' house—that's the Sumners' house."

"Yes—and quite a house, too. My goodness—how many bedrooms did you say they have?"

"Six—and six bathrooms. Each bedroom had its own fucking bathroom… I mean, bathroom. Sorry."

She continued, nonplussed. "How about this one?"

He smiled. "That's the Trahan's house."

"Really?" she burst. "Well, I'll say…Barb Trahan would be *shocked* to see this. It looks even bigger than the Sumners' house."

"It is—they have *seven* bedrooms."

"What do you do with seven bedrooms?" she asked wistfully. "I can't imagine…I can't. And cleaning it would be a nightmare . . ."

He shrugged. "They have maids and stuff to do that. They're all ridiculously rich."

They continued to look through the pile at photos of his high school, of local grocery stores, of local tourist attractions, including the stadiums, even though Alex had never seen a game in either one. There were numerous photos of *The Plaza*, including a few postcards of the fountains and the lighted buildings during the holiday season. There was even a picture of their Westport coffee shop.

"Where did you get these?" he asked finally.

"Well, it turns out your friend, Brian McDermott—oddly, the only friend you remember from your childhood in Montana—moved to Kansas City a few years ago. I got in touch with his mom, Sally, who I knew quite well, and…Well, I asked if she would be willing to do a photo scavenger hunt."

"This isn't his house, is it?" he asked, frowning, pulling the photo of his home out of the pile.

She shook her head. "No…I'm not really sure whose house that is."

He shook his head, trying to blink away tears—but not tears of sadness. "I don't understand…It's all real. Everything I remember—it, it actually exists…I thought I was crazy. I really did," he said, brushing a tear from his cheek, the cuffs making a clinking sound. "I—I was going to ask you to send me away—to that, that ranch you talked about. I—I was convinced I was schizophrenic or something. But…I guess I'm not completely crazy, huh?" he said, laughing nervously.

She laughed with him. "No…You're not at all, I don't think. You know, strange things happen to people in comas. At least, that's what I've heard. If you talk to Barb, she thinks this has to do with past lives and—and *karma*

and things of which I have no concept or understanding, but that's Barb...
She thinks your mind died, lived another life and ended up coming back
because your body didn't or something...I don't know I don't understand. I
could never keep up with her."

"What do you think?" he asked quietly.

She blushed, shaking her head. "Oh, it doesn't matter what I think. I'm
a simple woman, Alex. With a simple mind."

"It does matter...You're my mother." The words came out in a hoarse
whisper. Though he meant them, he could not look at her when he said them,
but for the first time he wanted it to be true. He wanted her to be his mother.

She moved her chair next to his and held him for awhile. He permitted the
embrace, ready to accept whatever warmth, peace and even prayers she had to
offer. Ready to greet the new world as Alex Michael, suddenly confident that
he could do so and that this world was ready to meet him, at least half way.

That night, he had dinner with his family at the kitchen table, and the
handcuffs came off for good.

The next day, she drove him to Missoula for lunch and an afternoon
of clothes shopping. He had received a significant amount of money from
well-wishers and she took a few hundred dollars out for him to buy a new
wardrobe, too much in his opinion.

"I just need some jeans and flannel shirts," he protested. "Preferably
ripped jeans."

"Yes, that's fine. There's better shopping in Missoula, though. They have
a nice mall and department stores there."

"The Goodwill is fine, too. Why don't we just go there."

"Alex Michael, I am not taking you to the Goodwill. That's—that's ridiculous. We're not broke...Not yet, anyway," she said jokingly.

But on their way to the mall, they passed a Goodwill, and he insisted
they stop in. Though he did not find any jeans, he purchased a week's worth
of flannel shirts and found some interesting vintage concert tees, barely
making a dent in his envelope full of money. His mother acquiesced to the
purchase but insisted on washing everything twice before he wore it. Five
minutes later, they had reached the shopping center and parked outside a
store called Herberger's.

While he disliked malls, walking through Southgate reminded him of
Oak Park Mall in Kansas, and he found the familiarity comforting. He hated
shopping for clothes and saw nothing he wanted to purchase at any of the

specialty clothing stores, instead darting into music stores to scan the latest collections, purchasing a number of CDs he had owned in his former life. Before they left, she insisted he spend some time in Herberger's, refusing to take him home until he found at least three new pairs of jeans and two new shirts, leaving him alone in the men's department while she shopped elsewhere. Ignoring her shirt request, he found the Levis section, bought the jeans and began a five minute search for his mother, eventually finding her in the handbag department, thoughtfully holding a small navy and brown purse.

"You gonna get that," he said, walking up to her.

"Oh," she said, nearly dropping the purse on the counter. "No, heavens no. Did you get your clothes?"

"Yes, I'm done. I'm ready to go, now."

She thanked the lady at the counter, and they headed to the parking lot.

"You didn't get anything?" he asked.

"Oh, no…I don't need anything," she said. "That store's too expensive, anyway."

He stopped suddenly, just before they reached the car, an idea forming in his mind. "You know—I forgot to get the shirts. Here," he handed her the bag of jeans. "I'll be right back. Give me five minutes." She started to follow him, but he picked up his pace and was soon striding through the store to the handbag counter.

After more than two minutes of waiting, he finally got the attention of the clerk, who seemed to be deliberately ignoring him, by actually shouting at her. Reddening, she strutted towards him and sharply asked him what he wanted.

"Yeah—you know that lady that was just in here. She was looking at a purse."

The clerk eyed him suspiciously, scanning his person continuously, from his hair to his clothes.

"Well, can I see it?" he said impatiently.

"See what?" she asked curtly, and Alex felt his face get hot as his rage began to simmer. She was an older woman, her brown hair pulled into a severe knot, with large pores and uneven lipstick.

"*The purse.* Can I see the purse she was looking at?"

"Young man, that's a hundred and seventy five dollar Dooney & Bourke."

"I don't care what it is. I just want the purse."

She remained steadfast. "It's one hundred and seventy-five dollars. Plus tax."

"Yeah, you said that already. Whatever. Here," he said, retrieving a thick stack of twenties from his envelope.

Her eyes grew wide, and she just stared at the money.

"I want the fucking purse," he said, throwing the money on the counter. "Jesus Christ, What is your *fucking problem?*" he asked, leaning over the counter towards her and watching her shrink back in fear, feeling slightly exhilarated by the exchange and the sight of her trembling hands as she handed him his change and his purchase.

As he strode towards the exit doors, bag in hand, he caught a glimpse of himself in one of the many department store mirrors and stopped, suddenly aware of what her problem might have been, seeing himself as the clerk must have. A tall, almost hulking figure with a mass of brown and blond ringlets half hiding his eyes and partially framing a bearded face. He had not shaved in months, and even though his beard was blond, it was wild and untrimmed. His clothes were equally unkempt, having hand-ripped a few tears into one of Alex Tate's jeans, his white T-shirt also torn in places, un-tucked and layered with an old gray sweat jacket. He looked like a poster child for drug and alcohol addiction, he thought, smiling to himself, rather pleased with his appearance and new found ability to frighten people who annoyed or thwarted him, or both.

But he was even more pleased about doing something nice for his new mother, refusing to let her see what he had bought, wanting to wrap it up as a surprise. After they had gotten home and settled, he decided to ask Danielle to find him some wrapping paper. He knocked on the door of her room, but she did not answer. After searching the house, he asked his mother if she was home and was told she was practicing out in the garage. Practicing what, he could not imagine, but sauntered outside to the detached building to find her.

As he approached, he heard violin music, a piece he well-recognized. Opening the side door, he was first surprised to see the disorganized mess that was his family's garage, a large cluttered room that contained a huge table-saw and various woodworking accessories, a riding mower, a snow blower, lawn tools, shelves of storage boxes and stacks of old newspapers—everything but an actual automobile. More shocking was the site of Danielle seated on an old wooden chair in the corner of the room next to a window with a curtain that hadn't been washed in years, her music stand in front of her, furiously working her bow and producing the concert-quality sounds he had heard outside the door.

Seeing him, she abruptly stopped, staring at him wide-eyed.

"What are you doing?" he burst.

She stared at him queerly. "What does it look like I'm doing?"

"Yeah, I know that. What are you doing *out here*? This is the garage. What are you doing playing violin in the fucking garage? How do you even concentrate in here?"

She narrowed her eyes at him. "For your information, I'm in the *fucking* garage, because this is the only place I could practice without you throwing a fit. While you were in the hospital, I actually got to practice in the living room, but now that you're back, I'm back in the *fucking* garage."

He stared at her, dumbfounded. "Let…Let me get this straight. You play violin. You get accepted to *fucking* Juilliard. And you practice in the garage, because…because . . ."

"Because you're an asshole," she burst testily, her face turning red. "There, I said it."

"How am *I* an asshole?"

"Because you're the reason I'm out here. You *hate* my violin playing—you *hate* classical music—you *hate* the fact that I got into Juilliard, and I'm out here to keep the *fucking* peace."

He shook his head vehemently. "No—*he's* an asshole. *I'm* not an asshole. In fact, you can come back into the house now. Please—for the love of god—come back into the house. And for your information, I like classical music. I'm fucking *trained* in classical music."

She laughed, "You don't know Beethoven from Bach."

"Try me."

She stared at him, and he met her glare, suddenly willing to fully look at her features, features he now realized were very similar to his mother's. The hair, though much browner, was long, rippling and wavy, and her blue eyes bright and spritely. She had a mess of freckles across her cheeks, similar to his own but more pronounced. While she looked like the Jennifer Hicks he remembered, she clearly was someone completely different.

"Go ahead—try me. Play something, and I'll tell you what it is. In fact, I'll tell you what you were playing when I walked in."

She rolled her eyes.

"Dvorak—*Ninth Symphony*. First movement—Adagio."

She stared at him, mouth gaping, and he grinned in triumph. But she met his challenge and, for the next ten minutes, played a variety of violin solos, starting with popular riffs from Beethoven and Mozart and moving from Paganini to Vivaldi to Saint-Saëns. He knew every one of them, and when she ceded he was not a musical imbecile but perhaps an idiot savant, she spent the next twenty minutes playing pieces he wanted to hear. He then helped her to carry her musical belongings back to the house, listening to her excited talk about how she got into Juilliard and her plans, so distracted by the conversation he had forgotten why he bought her in the first place.

"Hey," he said, when she had finished her thought. "I need some wrapping paper. Do you know where it's kept?"

"Yes...But why?"

"None of your business—I just need some."

"Did you get me a gift?" she asked slyly.

"No, I didn't get you a gift. I don't even know you."

She snorted but left the living room and returned a few minutes later with a roll of paper, scissors and tape, refusing to give him the items unless he proved to her he really had a gift and was not going to use the scissors to kill himself. Exasperated, he led her up to his bedroom and reluctantly handed her the shopping bag.

She retrieved the purse, her eyes growing wide. "Oh, my god—who is this for?"

"Who do you think? *Dad*?"

"This is a Dooney & Bourke—a *real* Dooney & Bourke. Where did you even get this?"

He shrugged. "Some store. She was looking at it."

"What—did you steal it? You stole it, didn't you—"

"I didn't steal it."

"Alex, this is almost a $200 purse. We can't afford this. Shit, I had to buy a rip-off one in New York. Mine's not even real...She's going to shit, you know. She'll make you take it back."

He shrugged.

"God, this is gorgeous...Let me wrap it for you. You don't know what you're doing...and I, I can't give you these scissors. I just can't," she said, shuddering.

"Suit yourself," he mumbled, sitting on the edge of his bed, watching her absently as she carefully measured out and cut a large sheet of paper from the roll.

"Maybe she'll let me borrow it," she continued. "I can't even see mom with this...It's so extravagant for her."

"No—*you will not*. I bought it for her...Jesus, I'll just buy you your own. For your birthday or something... When is your birthday, anyway?"

"Oh, yeah...About my birthday...For your information, it's December Fourth. And, quite frankly, I would like it back, thank you very much."

"December Fourth is my birthday."

"Technically, no—it's *my* birthday. *Yours* is June fourth."

"June Fourth," he burst. "Are you serious? What does that mean? Does that mean I haven't turned seventeen yet? Because I distinctly remember turning seventeen."

"Yeah, in your head . . ." When she had finished the job, she carefully handed the package to Alex, sighing loudly. "Here…I still don't know how you paid for this. I still can't believe you *did* pay for this."

"Frankly, I can't either. I got most of what I needed at the Goodwill for next to nothing. I have no idea why she gave me all that money to go shopping."

"*What?* Are you *kidding me?* You went to the *Goodwill?* Oh, my god… You really aren't my brother are you? Oh, my god—if my brother is really dead, and I am beginning to believe he *actually is*, he is rolling in a grave somewhere. *Rolling.* I mean, hello—did you *look* at the clothes in your closet? All Ralph Lauren—or, or Izod Lacoste. I mean, you wouldn't settle for anything less than the best," she burst, now kneeling on the floor, picking up the leftover shreds of paper.

He rolled his eyes then leaned towards her, his voice hushed. "Can I ask you something? About your brother . . ."

She looked at him askance. "I guess . . ."

"Was he, you know—a…a closet homosexual or something?"

"*What?*" she burst, inadvertently dropping everything she had picked up. "What did you just say? You're kidding me, right? Please tell me you are—"

"No, I'm not…I'm fucking serious. I mean—that's not a normal closet. Pink is not a normal color for guys. Neither is yellow. And who folds their underwear? Who the fuck?"

She stared at him, dumbfounded. "You really think you're somebody else, don't you?" she asked, but there was sincerity in her voice. "You really have no idea who you were, do you?"

He stared at the floor, growing suddenly disheartened.

She got up and sat on the bed next to him. "Okay…Okay, I accept that…I do. I think I'm beginning to understand. I do…I think I…I think I can even get to like you. I mean, you like my music. You're happy for me and what I've worked my whole life to accomplish. He wasn't…We didn't really get along these last few years, actually. I don't know what happened, but…It doesn't matter now, does it? You don't even remember, anyway. And I don't have to…So, back to your question—*no.* My brother, Alex *Tate*, was not gay. He was preppy and meticulous and obsessive-compulsive and—and a control freak. Very smart and athletic, but a neat freak. A perfectionist. And a complete asshole. But not gay. In fact, he had quite a healthy appetite for sex."

"How do you know?"

"We live in a town of 3500 people. It's hard *not* to know."

"Did he...Did he get anyone pregnant?"

"Jesus—*no*," she burst but then asked slyly. "Did *you*?"

He turned away, his face reddening. She had no idea. Nobody in this world did, those memories stored solely in his mind, his never having committed them to any of his written journals.

She giggled, hitting his arm playfully. "Good thing it was all just a dream, then, isn't it?"

He watched her collect the scissors and other items before bounding out of the room.

Contrary to his sister's concerns, his mother was thrilled with her present, showing no intention of returning the purse, taking a picture of it with her thirty five millimeter Kodak Fun Saver so he could have yet another photo to add to his album. She took an additional photo to put into her own album, and he made a mental note to purchase the family a new camera—a real camera—once he could scrounge up the money, lamenting the loss of his Canon EOS 5QD from his previous life.

For the next week, he was allowed to adjust to his new family life in private, his parents keeping friends and visitors at bay and even allowing him to stay home on Sunday morning, his sister volunteering to babysit him while they attended church. He spent his time walking or playing with his dog, catching up on what homework he could understand, watching television and listening to music, and he would have been quite content to spend the rest of the school year alone, studying at home and at his leisure. But he was due to start school on April 18, and on the Wednesday before, his mother sat him down after breakfast to talk, and he braced himself.

"Honey, you start school on Monday, and...Well, your father and I think it's too soon, but...Well, frankly, I need to go back to work. I just do. We can't afford my taking any more time off. I'm sorry, sweetie...I really am."

He shrugged, staring out the picture window.

"You know, um...You have a lot of friends. You do, actually. And, well—they've been practically breaking the doors down. You have no idea how hard we've had to work to, well...to keep everyone away. I mean, the phone rings all time you know. All day long, it seems."

He stared into the distance, trying to remember hearing the phone ring. If it did, he had ignored it completely, having no interest whatsoever in answering it.

"So, um, I think we need to start letting your friends come over. Don't you think? Don't you think that would be a good idea?"

He crossed his arms, shaking his head. "I don't really want to see anyone. I don't really have any friends…How can I have any friends, if I don't remember them…I mean, I don't see why I can't just start school like an exchange student or something. That's what I am."

"Honey…You're—you're not an exchange student. Technically. And, I really think you need to meet some of the people who, well—who can help you to adjust. Your friends want to help you, Alex. They do. Especially Carl. My goodness, that boy calls here every day—sometimes twice."

"Fine," he said, exasperated. "I'll see Carl. But he has to come here. I'm not going anywhere."

"Okay, wonderful. And Ron?"

"Ron? Ron's in this life, too? Does he play bass?"

"I—I have no idea, honey, he's on the wrestling team and football team . . ."

Alex groaned.

"And Trisha—"

"No," he burst vehemently. "Absolutely not."

"Alex, you have to. She's your girlfriend—she's been your girlfriend for three years. My goodness, your entire world revolved around that girl."

His face flushed in anger. "She's not my girlfriend—never has been, and never will be. You can tell her that."

"I will *not* tell her that. You will be a *man* and tell her that yourself. And, quite frankly, if you're not going to get a haircut or shave before meeting her, I don't think you'll have too much trouble ending it. She was a runner up for Miss Teen Montana, you know. She has a reputation to uphold, and frankly, I'm not sure she's going to know what to make of you now."

"Did you like her?" he asked quietly.

"What do you mean, did *I* like her. *You* liked her. You adored her, and that was enough for me. I'm here to support your choices, Alex, not to make them for you. And what's not to like about her, my goodness. You couldn't have picked a more perfect or popular girl."

"Fine . . ." he said gruffly, after a few minutes of pondering. "Bring them in. Bring them all in."

Carl was the first, showing up that very afternoon, before dinner. Alex

paced the living room in anticipation, his stomach tense, a headache beginning above his left eye. His mother had offered to facilitate the meetings,
greeting the visitors at the front door and remaining in the kitchen in case
he had a panic attack or seizure. When the doorbell finally rang, he thought
he would vomit in fright.

But when Carl O'Malley entered the living room and looked at him,
Alex saw the fear was mutual. Carl stopped short, his eyes widening, his
brow furrowing. "Alex?"

Alex stood in front of the picture window, arms crossed, studying Carl,
relieved that it was the Carl he remembered with the exception of the hair,
which was still cropped very short but now red instead of brown, and the
extreme mess of red freckles on his face. He was dressed in jeans, a T-shirt
and a Polson Pirates letterman's jacket.

Carl remained frozen, barely beyond the threshold of the living room
entry. "Do you...Do you remember me?"

Alex wanted to shake his head no, but he couldn't, not entirely. "Sort
of," he said hoarsely.

Carl nodded, stepping a few short paces forward. "That's good...That's...
That's real good. You know, I...I didn't know what to expect. You know. We
were told you have severe amnesia. That you didn't remember anything. Is
it coming back, then?"

Alex swallowed hard, staring down at the knotted patterns in the wood
flooring. Finally, he shook his head. "No...I don't remember this life at all.
Not the way it happened, at least. I remember something completely different...You were somebody completely different. You weren't even from here,"
he said quietly.

"Well...Was I your friend at least?"

Alex nodded.

"Well...That's all that matters then. Right?" he asked sadly.

Alex shrugged, unable to look up at him, his mind swimming with fond
memories of his times with Carl Weiss and his eyes welling with tears. He
had forgotten what it was like to have friends. He had forgotten what it was
like to have fun, to jam to music, to play football and shoot hoops, to watch
movies and play video games. To drink beer, joke around and talk shit with
the guys. He had forgotten how much he enjoyed hanging out with Carl,
having only held on to the momentary anger he felt towards him at the New
Year's Eve party, an anger that he knew was entirely unjustified but that he
had let color his perception.

Collapsing onto a nearby chair, Alex buried his head in his arms and sobbed, not wanting to do so but unable to cope with his emotions. He was surprised when Carl joined him, kneeling next to the chair, gingerly placing an arm around him, like a coach trying to cheer up a disheartened team member.

"Hey…It's okay, buddy. It's gonna be okay. I promise. We're gonna get through this together. You just need some time, that's all. Time to adjust, you know? But we're here for you, man. We are—all of us. We're gonna get you back on track."

Alex looked up after a few minutes, wiping his face with his sleeve. "Sorry about that."

Carl patted him on the back.

"You don't play drums by any chance…Do you?"

"Drums? Shit…I got no musical talent. I can't even whistle. Neither can you, buddy," he said, laughing and hitting him in the arm.

Alex smiled weakly but remained silent.

"Say, um…I know this whole thing has been, you know, rough on you. I mean, getting shot. A coma. Shit, man…But…Well, you're going to clean up, right?"

Alex sniffed, staring blankly ahead.

"I mean—you're not coming back to school like this, right? You're gonna, you know."

"What?"

"Get a haircut, man. Shave and shit. Jesus, Fahlstrom, I didn't even recognize you. I wouldn't have recognized you if I saw you on the street. It's no wonder you feel terrible."

"What the fuck are you talking about, Weiss? There's nothing wrong with my hair. My *hair* has nothing to do with the way I feel. Are you fucking kidding me? Do you have *any* idea? At all? Any concept of what I have been through? Do you? *Get a haircut?*"

"Why'd you call me Weiss?"

"Cause that's you're fucking name, *Weiss*. Carl *Weiss*."

"No, it's not. It's O'Malley. I'm Carl O'Malley. And let me tell you something, Fahlstrom. Getting a haircut is exactly what you should do, man—and you would have told me to do the same. We're soldiers, man. Athletes, students and soldiers. *Duty. Honor. Country.* Without discipline, we're shit, man. We're just like animals. That's what you always said."

"What? I said *what*?"

"We need you, man. I'm dead serious—we need you back. Wrestling team's in shambles, and we don't have a lot of talent coming up from the middle school. And football team's not much better. This is our last year to shine, man—to make our mark. I can't keep it together without you. I'm completely stressed out."

Alex was speechless.

"And your girl's out of her mind. I've been doing my best to comfort Trisha, but…You gotta clean up. She'll have none of this. I'm not even bringing her here until you do," he said, standing up.

"I think you should bring her here tomorrow," Alex said quietly.

Carl slapped him on the back, "That's my man…Now there's the spirit. Shit we got a lot to do. You coming to practice on Sunday? You should. I'll pick you up. Two o'clock, man—"

But out of seemingly nowhere, he heard his mother interject. He wasn't aware she had enetered the room.

"Now, Carl—I told you, no sports for awhile. Doctor's orders. He's starting school on Monday, and that's to be his sole focus until the end of the semester," she said, leading Carl out of the room and, eventually, out the front door.

But Carl stopped by later that night, this time with three other guys. It took Alex a full five minutes to recognize them, and when he did, he almost fell on the floor, in shock or hysterics, he wasn't sure at that point. All three had very short cropped hair, almost buzz cuts, and all were dressed in some type of sports attire—full sweats, partial sweats, shorts and a football jersey. Their names were Ron, Stewart and Chad, his fellow rock band members.

And all they could talk about was his hair, his beard and his attire, even venturing into other parts of the house to find his parents and convince them to do something about it. They then proceeded to catch him up on the *Polson High School* winter and spring sports seasons, providing him with good news updates regarding their friends and comrades as well as gossip regarding their enemies, most of who were on opposing high school teams, sports being the obvious obsession of this group.

Nobody noticed that Alex wasn't adding to the conversation, wasn't even asking questions and hadn't spoken a word after learning their names. They took over the living room, television and kitchen as if it were their home, even rummaging through the refrigerator for food and drink. They called his mother Miss J and his father Mr. B and proceeded to watch an NBA basketball game, screaming at the television in-between hollering amongst themselves.

Alex sat on the floor, his back against the picture window, clutching his dog to his stomach as if he were a large pillow, petting his fur and mentally counting the strokes to keep from having an anxiety attack.

It was his sister, Danielle, who finally got rid of them an hour later by casually strolling into the room, picking up the remote and changing the channel.

"A new episode of *90210* is on, and—well, you'll all just have to leave now, because I want to watch it."

Somebody actually threw a sofa pillow at her, but she remained standing and resolute, her arms crossed, her eyes burning with female rage. But they eventually collected themselves and sauntered out of the room, promising to be back the next day and with a pair of scissors if Alex didn't get his hair cut, leaving a trail of napkins, half empty glasses of soda and an empty bag of potato chips in their wake.

After wiping crumbs off the seat surface, Danielle threw herself in the recliner, arms crossed, face red and brow still furrowed as she stared at the television. Alex remained frozen on the floor next to the window, still clutching his dog.

"Those are my friends . . ." He said dully.

"Yep."

"Are they really coming back?"

"Yep."

"Can we lock the door?"

At this she smirked, but just shook her head sadly as if there was nothing she could do.

The next afternoon, a Friday, Carl returned, this time bringing Trisha Kurtz. He had left Trisha in the car at first, wanting to give Alex ample time to get ready and make his best appearance. But Alex showed up at the door looking as he did the day before, hair disheveled, beard untouched, this time in gray sweats, a red plaid flannel shirt with a small tear in the collar layered over a vintage concert tee of The Who, the entire ensemble having been purchased at Goodwill.

"Jesus, Fahlstrom—What are you doing?" Carl whispered harshly. "I told you I was bringing Trisha, and I told you I'd come by today. Look at yourself, man. I can't let her see you like this. You had all day, man—all day."

Alex rolled his eyes, looking up at the ceiling. "Yes, and I told you to come by today. I told you to bring her here today."

"But why? Do you want to fuck this up? Do you? Because if you do,

I'm—I'm shocked, man. I'm actually hurt. This is actually personally devastating to me, man. I can't…I can't believe this," he said pacing the front
hall, clearly distraught.

"No—what you *can't* believe is that I have amnesia. You *think* I know
who Trisha is—you *think* I remember her as my girlfriend. What you don't
understand, is that *I don't know her*. I haven't a fucking clue who she is. And
you don't have a fucking clue who I am, because if you did, you'd stop telling
me to cut my fucking hair and change my clothes. Did it ever occur to you
that I like my hair? That I like these clothes? Did it?"

Carl shook his head, his eyes welling with tears. "You really are crazy….
Jesus, Fahlstrom. I thought—I thought you were coming back. I thought you
were going to fight back, man. I thought you would fight for what you had."

Alex closed his eyes, trying to stay calm. "Carl, I don't remember what I
had, okay? I don't know what I had…How can I possibly fight for something
that I don't know I've lost?"

Carl sniffed, nodding. "So…You really don't remember Trisha?"

He shook his head.

"At all? Not at all?"

"No…My mom even showed me pictures. Shit—my room was full of
pictures of her, but…I don't recognize her. Sorry."

"Okay…Well…She's hot, right? You think she's pretty, right?"

Alex nodded absently. "Yeah, yeah…She's okay."

"Well, I mean—if you want to get to know her again, you know. If you,
you think she's hot and want to date her and all…You know, we can make
that happen. I can. I can do that for you. But she can't see you like this. She
won't…She's very particular, you know. She has real high standards. But she has
to, you know. She's going to be Miss Teen Montana. She is. She definitely is."

Alex studied Carl as he stared wistfully in the distance, suddenly curious.
"Do you think she's hot, Carl?"

"Oh, yeah…But who doesn't, right?" he said quickly, laughing nervously.

Alex smiled to himself. "Bring her in," he said finally.

"*What*? No way—I can't."

"Absolutely. Bring her in, and let her meet me. As I am—right now. And
let her make up her own mind. I mean—if she *loves* me, which after—how
many years have we been together?"

"Three," Carl said dully.

"If she loves me, and we've been together for *three* years—have had a
loving, devoted relationship for that long, well…She should just be happy

I'm alive, right? I mean, isn't that what love is all about? She should just throw her arms around me, and kiss my bearded face—right? Unless, I don't know…She *found* someone else while I've been languishing in a hospital all these months," he said caustically. "Or, the relationship wasn't really built on love at all. Just appearances."

Carl looked at him wide-eyed, and the mixture of fear and anger in Carl's expression all but confessed to Alex that his comment had touched on something sensitive.

Five minutes later, Trisha walked into the living room, where Alex was seated calmly on the sofa. She was taller and slimmer than he remembered his sister being, and her makeup, though heavy around the eyes, was less garish. She was meticulously groomed, her long blond hair pulled into a neat ponytail, not a wrinkle in her crisp white blouse or tan capris, her hands clutching a small purse that looked similar to the one he had purchased for his mother, her feet attired in low-heeled pumps that matched the trim on the purse. She could have stepped straight off the cover of a Herberger's catalogue.

Upon seeing him, she put her hand to her mouth and gasped in sheer horror. The tears quickly followed. "Oh, my god…He told me, but I didn't believe it. I just didn't. I couldn't . . ." She shook her head.

"You must be Trisha," he said, standing up to greet her. "I'm Alex."

At this, she burst into tears. "No, you're not…You're not Alex. You can't be. You're not my Alex . . .You're not."

Carl quickly joined her side, putting his arms protectively around her, trying to calm her down, unsuccessfully. After she nearly collapsed, he led her out of the room and eventually out of the house. Alex remained standing, lost in thought long after they had gone, feeling like a corpse at his own funeral, his friends paying him his last respects before they went on with their lives and left him to rot in the ground.

Depressed and exhausted by that afternoon's exchange, he had decided to go to bed early that night, heading up to his room a little after eight. He was alone, his family having gone to see his sister in the high school musical's opening night, his father giving him a rather lengthy lecture on trust and how they were trusting him to be alive and well when they returned later that night.

He was brushing his teeth when the doorbell rang. To his surprise, the entire group was back, this time with pizzas, beer and a rented video, *True Romance*.

"You're bringing beer into my house," he said, flabbergasted.

"Mr. B. don't care as long as we don't drive drunk. And if we're too drunk, we just crash here, man," Carl said, ruffling his hair.

"You remember seeing this movie, Fahlstrom?" Ron asked later, as they watched the opening credits.

"You know, I don't...I think I missed that one."

"You actually did, you crazy fuck...But, anyway—it's by the same guy who did *Reservoir Dogs*, which is completely fucked up. But you don't remember that either, do you Fahlstrom? What do you remember?"

"He forgot how to shave, that's for sure."

Alex laughed, relieved that they were at least bringing him into the conversation and, he admitted to himself later, relieved that they hadn't given up on him yet.

By Saturday afternoon, Alex was tired of company and looking forward to a quiet evening at home, but it wasn't to be. His sister was in the school musical, and the entire family had tickets for the show. After discovering she had a small role, Alex protested, feigning ill, but his parents would hear nothing of it, only compromising by allowing Alex to sit in the back row of the theater in case he needed a quick exit.

As his sister was rushing around the house, getting ready to leave early for that evening's performance, the dog barked, the doorbell rang and Danielle screamed for Alex *to get off his ass and get it.*

Jumping up from the living room recliner, he sauntered to the door, wincing in anticipation before swinging it open.

"Oh, my god," a familiar voice burst.

He stared blankly, then grinned.

"*Alex Fahlstrom?*"

"*Brooke Trahan?*"

"Channeling Charles Manson, are we?"

"Why, yes...And what are we, *Channeling Cher?*" he said, matching her sarcasm. It was Brooke just as he remembered her with the exception of her hair, which was long, black and straight, cut perfectly square with a severe Egyptian style bang. Since he last remembered her with short hair, he wondered if it weren't a wig.

"Oh, my god...and you woke up with a sense of humor. I'm stunned. Truly. Where the fuck is Danielle," she asked, pushing him aside and strolling through the front door. "Danielle—we're late," she yelled up the steps.

"Are you in the play, too?"

"Sure am, big boy. Or should I say, big foot. What the fuck, Alex. Do you smell as bad as you look? Really . . ."

Danielle came bounding down the stairs.

"What the fuck, Danielle?" Brooke continued, motioning to Alex with her head. "You could have warned me, you know. Jesus…You said *idiot savant*, but I didn't think you were serious. I thought you were being sarcastic . . ."

Danielle pursed her lips, "No…I feel a little like Tom Cruise living with the rain man. But he's harmless. Aren't you, Alex," she said, ruffling his hair.

Brooke snorted and breezed out the door behind his sister.

Alex was in no mood for a musical and hardly one like *West Side Story*, a modern day rendition of *Romeo & Juliet*. While his parents sat near the front of the stage, he took a seat in the last row, prepared to stand if he had to, and even more prepared to wait out in the lobby. Because their school was too small for an auditorium, the high school productions were held at the Port Polson Players Theatre down the road. The musical ran three shows, the final being the following afternoon, and his mother was adamant he went to at least one show, going on and on about how talented the students were, the leading actress in particular. He should pay close attention to the female lead, who was an extremely talented singer, having done a bang up job in last year's musical, *Annie*.

Whatever, he sighed, sitting back in his seat and contemplating falling asleep. Except for *Rocky Horror Picture Show*, he thought musicals dumb, written for people who could sing and dance but not act. But he found the opening number to be engaging, the scenery and dancing a bit mod and edgy and not at all what he expected. He then became pre-occupied looking for his sister and Brooke, but he was too far away to see facial features clearly. Eventually, he became engaged in the story, saddened by the story and eventually depressed by the story, walking out of the theatre in a fog of gloom. Why did the lead have to remind him of Danielle, he thought to himself, with her long dark hair spilling over her shoulders. And why did Tony and Maria's first glance at each other have to be so much like his and Danielle's—down to him seeing her in a white dress across a crowded dance floor. And why on earth did Tony have to get shot in the end? Alex shuddered in the car the entire way home, his body physically shaking, trying to convince himself the entire play wasn't a bad omen or a sick joke the universe was playing on him, feeling like Scrooge must have after visiting one of his past lives.

"Did you like it?" his mom asked sweetly as they drove home. "It was excellent, wasn't it?"

He shrugged, unable to speak and unable to get the lead actress out of his mind, whoever she was. He had been too far away to see her features up close—too far to see anyone that clearly, only being able to distinguish Brooke by her black wig-like hair and unsure if he had even found his sister in the mass of dancing bodies on stage.

It wasn't even the actress, he thought to himself, but the role she played. The character Maria reminded him of Danielle, he decided. But the more he obsessed about it over the weekend, the more anxious he became, fearing he would scope the school halls on Monday morning looking for her and, out of desperation, see her face in someone who was not really her.

After the New York trip, Gabrielle decided to put aside her Gothic look for awhile, despite having purchased a number of fantastic pieces, including punked-out kilt skirts, stockings of all shades and stripes, T-shirts and a fitted jacket made of patched black denim, suede and leather. The musical was fast approaching, and she wanted to embrace her role of Maria, in part out of integrity to her artistry and in part to stop her stage counterpart, Mick, from laughing every time they had to do a romantic scene together or bursting into a parody every time she practiced her number, "I Feel Pretty."

*I feel bitchy...Oh, so bitchy...I feel strung out and hung out and gray... And I'll fuck up any guy who crosses me today . . .*He would sing, prancing about the stage in a boa.

By show time, she had discarded her piercings, conditioned her hair to its normal color and consistency and given herself facials to cleanse her pores of the heavy makeup she had been wearing for weeks. People noticed the transformation, some joking about it but others sincerely complimenting her, and she had already received two invitations to prom, one from a fellow classmate, also in the musical, and one from a senior she knew from pep band. Both were attractive, and both were nice, and feeling completely torn, she decided to put off her decision until after the musical.

Initially, the play and her character, Maria, had depressed her, but the more she studied the script, the more closely she observed Natalie Wood's performance in the film and the more she read *Romeo & Juliet*, the more she began seeing the entire exercise as an opportunity to heal the deep wounds from her own tragedy. And the less she was afraid to relive her own first love through Maria, to see his face in Tony's, to feel Maria's joy and confidence from being in love—to really believe, as Maria did, that Tony loved her in return. Even willing to risk everything to follow her heart and face, again, the utter devastation at their love's violent and brutal end.

Because she believed in the story and one of its most famous songs, when she and Mick sang *Somewhere*, they received a standing ovation all three shows.

After the final show on Sunday afternoon and the huge cast party and dinner that followed later that evening, she did not think anything could knock her off her cloud of hope and optimism. Still donned in her white stage dress, hair and make-up intact, she spun around her bedroom, picking up their fat gray housecat and swinging him in the air, like a dance partner.

I feel pretty – Mr. Kitty – I feel pretty and witty and gay...And there's nothing...that can even bring me down today...

Brooke snorted, having entered the room in the middle of her soiree.

"Yeah, well, I hate to burst your bubble, but guess who's coming back from the dead tomorrow."

Gabrielle stopped, the cat poised mid-air above her head.

"If it makes you feel better, I saw him. I actually saw him in person at Danielle's yesterday, and...Shit. I barely recognized him. He's...barely a shell of himself."

Gabrielle gently brought the cat down and set him on the floor, where he began immediately licking his tail. "Why would that make me feel better?" she asked quietly.

Brooke shrugged, sitting down on her bed and brushing out her long hair. "Payback is hell, you know . . ."

"What...you think that makes me feel better? All his suffering—his, his depression and suicide attempts these past few weeks. How does that help? How does that possibly make me feel better?"

"Sorry...I thought you weren't connected like that anymore, you know—physically...I mean, you haven't seemed to be connected to him like that, or you should have been knocked unconscious a couple of times these past months, the idiot."

"I don't think we *physically* are, either, anymore—but that's *so not the point*. I mean, the point is...When somebody you love hates you—hates you so much, they want to hurt you—how does their getting hurt make it better? How does it make the pain go away? Only...Only their loving you again can really make the pain go away. More pain just creates more pain."

"You *loved* him?" Brooke burst. "You actually *loved* him?"

"What do you think? I was just going to fuck somebody I didn't love?"

"Maybe. Quite frankly, I didn't know what to think when I finally figured it out. I still don't. I think you have an inferiority complex and are in serious danger of falling into abusive relationships," she said matter-of-factly.

Gabrielle just stared at her sister, hurt and frustrated at Brooke's inability to at least try to sympathize with her situation, her perception.

Brooke met her stare, narrowing her eyes. "As I said earlier while you were twirling around the room, he's coming back to school tomorrow, and I believe you have some classes together. So the question is, what are you going to wear? Huh? You wanna keep channeling Maria, or do you feel more *Courtney Love*? Is tomorrow the day Tony and Maria find love in their next life, or Sid and Nancy kill each other? Hmmmm?"

Brooke then turned on her stereo, cranking the newly released *Live Through This* CD, turning it specifically to the song "Asking For It."

Gabrielle scooped up her cat and retreated to Nate's bedroom to think. To pray. To cry. As mad as she wanted to be at her sister for destroying her happy mood, for completely dousing the small fires of hope that the weekend's success had brought, she saw the validity in Brooke's taunting questions. For the past few weeks, while aware of Alex and his progress, unable to escape it with Danielle Fahlstrom practically living at their house when things got rough, she had been able to distance herself, to react to it as if it were happening someplace else, in some other time, to someone she didn't really know because she couldn't really see him.

But tomorrow, she would see him, not as a memory, but in person. In the realm of the senses and in a physical body she could see, touch and smell. And it filled her with dread and sorrow, as did the memories of their short time together, which played in her mind like a movie stuck on continual loop.

The next morning, she considered staying home sick but knew that would be a mistake and only serve to prolong the inevitable doom. Instead, she chose to hide behind her old mask, getting up an hour early to re-insert her multiple piercings, secure her favorite black wig and apply her palette of white, gray and black make-up. To honor Sid and Nancy, she donned a British flag T-shirt to wear under her new black patch jacket with her black skinny jeans and black chucks.

She sat in the very back row of home room, next to her friend Kelly, slumped down in her desk, foot tapping nervously on the floor, watching the classroom door in anticipation and wanting to vomit. But nothing could have prepared her for what she saw. She didn't even believe what she saw, the awe completely overshadowing her anxiety.

In walked Danielle Fahlstrom with a tall bearded male, his face half-framed by a mass of wild brown and blonde curls, his eyes partially hidden by errant strands. His jeans were baggy and torn in a few places, and he wore a blue and white plaid flannel shirt, un-tucked, over an old, rust-colored concert shirt, the graphics having peeled and faded. Danielle Fahlstrom, the bearded male and the teacher talked for a moment, then Danielle left and the teacher motioned for the bearded male to find a seat. He scanned the room, his eyes immediately falling on Gabrielle, who slouched deeper into her chair.

Smiling, he made a beeline for her, and she found herself cursing under her breath.

He slid into the open desk next to her.

"Are you an exchange student?" he asked after getting settled, his tone cheerful.

Utterly baffled, she remained quiet, unable to move or even breathe.

"Are you from Britain," he continued, motioning towards her T-shirt.

"Are you retarded?" she burst testily, remembering his sister Danielle's cracks about his mental incapacitation and beginning to wonder if it weren't true.

He shrugged. "Probably...I have amnesia, so I could be. My name's Alex," he said, offering a hand to shake.

She stared at it, arms still tightly crossed. "I know who you are."

"Well, I don't know who you are. What's your name?" he asked, nervously withdrawing his hand.

"Gabrielle."

"Gabriel? Nice to meet you Gabriel."

She rolled her eyes, *dear god*...It was far worse than she expected.

"I don't remember there being any punkers in Polson. This is really cool."

"You have amnesia...Why would you?" she asked caustically.

But he just grinned.

Two of his friends then entered the room and, spotting him, strode to the back of the class.

"What are you doing back here, Fahlstrom? You don't want to be back here," Ron said, practically pulling him out of his seat.

"I'm talking to Gabriel."

"Gabriel?" Ron repeated, looking confused.

Alex motioned to Gabrielle, and Ron looked at her, exchanging glares with her, before bursting out laughing. "Right—*Gabriel*. Well, *Gabriel* is not your friend, Fahlstrom. You don't want to be hanging around *him*. Come on, let's move up front."

But the words stung, and Gabrielle had to brush a tear from her cheek. Her friend Kelly leaned across the small aisle towards her. "What the hell... What the hell happened to *him*?"

Gabrielle shook her head.

"Jesus...I mean, I've kept up with it in the paper and all, but...Jesus. He's our fucking class president. Or, he was...Did he just call you *Gabriel*?"

Gabrielle nodded, and they both burst out laughing.

After first period, Gabrielle did not have to see him again until lunch, so she was somewhat able to focus on her studies, allowing only part of her mind to contemplate the bizarre interaction they had that morning. Intrigue replaced fear, and she found herself anxious to see him again, unable to recognize any part of the Alex Fahlstrom she knew in the person who greeted her today. Surely, he had to be there, buried somewhere under the hair and beard, she mused.

During lunchtime, she almost got the opportunity to study him again. While the high school lunch room wasn't large, it was big enough for students to eat in clusters, and the clusters were comprised of friends or those who at least shared similar interests. Gabrielle typically sat with her girlfriends, Kelly, Cherise and Susan, with Dennis and his friends and with a lot of the students involved in band, theater or yearbook. She had just slid onto the lunch bench next to Dennis, when she heard a familiar voice behind her.

"Dennis?"

Dennis turned to see who was calling his name and immediately turned back, swearing under this breath. Gabrielle did not have to look.

"Dennis Sumners?"

Dennis immediately straightened up, and she could feel his tension, could hear it in his breathing.

"It's me, Alex. Alex Fahlstrom—"

"I know who the fuck you are," Dennis said coldly, staring straight ahead.

Gabrielle gently placed her hand on his arm, leaning close to whisper in his ear. "He has amnesia...He has no idea who we are."

Alex walked up to the table, moving to set his tray down in the open space on the other side of Dennis. "Can I sit here?"

What transpired next unfolded so quickly that Gabrielle was unsure of the exact sequence of events. Dennis jumped up. A tray flew in the air, its contents hurtling to the ground. As Dennis lunged at Alex, Gabrielle jumped out of her spot, fleeing to the other side of the cafeteria, along with everyone else at the table who had no desire to participate in the brawl that had begun, a brawl that eventually involved more than a dozen students and destroyed at least twenty lunches, including her own.

When Alex did not show up for the last two classes of the day, instead of relief, she felt disappointment, looking forward to the following school day, which she hoped would offer the next opportunity to study him.

The opportunity arose the next afternoon. While Alex and everyone else involved in the fight had been sent home the previous day, the school decided not to issue any suspensions, only stern warnings, and all students were allowed back the following morning. Still, the halls were abuzz with gossip, the story continually embellished as it was passed from student to student so that by the time it got back to Gabrielle, it had become an all-out food-fight that involved forty students, destroyed three teachers' outfits, sent someone to the hospital and did a couple hundred dollars worth of damage to the cafeteria, none of which was true.

As the day waned, she noticed Alex's posse of friends were particularly protective of him, and he was never left alone, neither in class nor between classes. It was as if they had created a formal chaperone system amongst themselves. Standing in a short line for the water fountain before last period, she felt a tap on her shoulder and nearly choked upon turning around and seeing him in line behind her, unattended.

"Can I talk to you?" he whispered, leaning close to her, his eyes darting around nervously.

"Okay…About what?"

"*In private*," he whispered, quickly straightening up as Carl exited the bathroom and approached him.

Gabrielle frowned as she leaned her head over the fountain, taking longer than usual to sip the water, her mind working frantically to solve this puzzle. When she was finished and turned to leave, she leaned towards Alex.

"Library…After school," she said quietly, then quickly proceeded to class.

The final period dragged on as Gabrielle found herself unable to focus on anything the teacher said, instead staring into the back of Alex's mane of curls, wondering what he could possibly want to discuss with her.

When the class finally ended, Gabrielle quickly visited her locker and then headed directly to the library and into the stacks, sitting on the floor next to the fiction section, her backpack on the floor next to her, her heart pounding. When ten minutes had passed, she wondered if he was even go- ing to show and was just considering leaving when he rounded the corner, nearly tripping over her.

"Oh, Jesus...Sorry," he said, plopping himself and his backpack down across from her, throwing his head back and sighing loudly before speaking again.

"Um ...Your friends with Dennis, right?" he asked, sounding tired.

"Yes."

"I really need to talk to him."

She rolled her eyes. "That isn't happening."

"It has to happen—Gabe, I need it to happen. Seriously."

"*Gabe?*"

"Yeah, sorry...Isn't that your nickname? Gabe? Maybe . . ."

"No, it's not," she snapped, but relaxed again after seeing his confused expression, finally able to study his face up-close. It was difficult to see the features she had once found so handsome, the rugged jaw, the dark, often melancholy, deep-set eyes, the spray of light freckles across his cheeks and brow. But his hair was striking, and she had to refrain from reaching out to touch one of the coiled blond strands that fell across his eye, it had been so many years since he had let it grow out like that.

"*Gabriel*...I need to see Dennis Sumners."

"You mean Dennis Wiseman."

"Yeah—whatever. I'm serious. I—I don't know what happened between us, but...Well, I want to apologize. I will—I'll do whatever it takes. Please."

"Why is he so important to you?" she asked thoughtfully, placing her chin in her hand.

"He's one of my best friends...Well, he *was*. I—I need...Does he have a sister by any chance?"

She shook her head but knew where the conversation was headed, having heard bits of his confused story from his mother and sister.

He ran his hands through his hair in frustration. "I don't understand...I don't understand why I'm enemies with all the cool people around here... You, Dennis—"

"I'm not your enemy," she interrupted.

"Well, according to my friends you are. You fucking hate me. And I don't even know you. I don't remember knowing a Gabriel or any Goths or punk- ers for that matter. So I guess I should apologize to you, too, for whatever I did...So, sorry."

She shook her head, laughing quietly at the huge practical joke the universe continued to play on her.

"Anyway, I want you to set up a meeting with me and him. Off site somewhere."

"No...I can't. I can't do that."

"Why not? It's just a fucking meeting—"

"Because he'll kick your ass, that's why."

Alex sighed loudly, hanging his head despondently. "Fine," he said finally. "Then he can kick my ass, if that'll make him feel better. I don't care."

"No, you don't understand. He will *kick your ass*. As in *hurt you*. I know him. I know where his mind is right now, and he will show you no mercy."

"I don't care."

"Alex, I don't think you understand. If he's angry enough, he might even kill you."

He tossed his head back, brushing away an errant strand. "Really? Well then I definitely want to meet with him. The sooner, the better."

Gabrielle's heart fell as she stared into his sad, dark eyes and saw that after months of pain and struggle, after weeks of cheating death, Alex Fahlstrom had given up hope.

CHAPTER FOURTEEN

On Thursday afternoon, Alex sat in the library stacks near the fiction section, waiting for Gabriel to take him to get his ass kicked. While Alex's parents had been more than sympathetic about the fight with Dennis, there had been a call from the school, and, during the embarrassing reprimand from the principal, Alex was explicitly instructed stay away from Dennis Wiseman upon pain of expulsion. It seemed that no matter how hard he tried to explain his situation, they could not understand his pain and frustration, dismissing Dennis as a troublemaker and drug user. Knowing that any hope of piecing together the intricate puzzle that had become his life was dependent on communicating with Dennis, and feeling as though the world was carefully conspiring against any prospect of this communication, Alex found himself more depressed by his circumstances than apprehensive of the impending beating.

And where was Danielle, he had asked his mother earlier that morning, before leaving for school. She had promised him he would see her—likely his first day back—but he hadn't. And he had scrutinized nearly every female in the building, including the lunch ladies. It took everything he had not to call his mother a liar, not to scream it to her face, and in his mind he did, watching her shrink back in fear before crying. But it was an ugly scene he had enacted one too many times, a part he was tired of playing, that of the angry young man, fists ever poised to inflict harm on anyone who opposed him, especially the weak or sensitive at heart.

This time, he would just quietly and take his punishment, even if it meant becoming more brain damaged than he already was. He wasn't even sure why he wanted the meeting with Dennis. Now that he thought about it, he wasn't even sure what he would say and attempted to rehearse a possible script in his head. *Dennis, I want to apologize to you for whatever I did...Dennis, I'm sorry if I was an asshole. Can we just move on?...Dennis, where the fuck have you been all these months? My life has been a living hell. I was there for you when you needed me—don't you remember...*

He was so lost in thought that he didn't notice Gabriel had arrived until the guy lightly placed a hand on his shoulder. Alex jumped, startled, unsettled by the touch for some reason and growing increasingly disturbed by the person, himself. There was something effeminate about the Goth punker, and Alex wondered if the hard core metal and make-up was hiding something soft, overcompensating for something lacking in his manhood. And even though he couldn't see the guy's eyes through the mass of black and purple-streaked hair that jetted out and down over his brow, partially covering his eyes, he sensed his stare, unnerved at times by how intently he felt the guy looking at him.

He followed the guy to the parking lot of the school, eventually climbing into a 1988 silver El Camino and scrutinizing the interior, which had distinctly feminine touches, including a leopard print steering wheel cover and Hello Kitty window decal amidst a collage of stickers that featured skulls, the *Eraserhead* icon and various rock and punk bands. And he could have sworn he saw a pair of pink chucks in the back but refused take a closer look.

The car had an excellent sound system, which began pumping angry music the minute it started. Hole, the guy said, their new album. Alex shrugged, in no mood for angry music at all right now, let alone that of an enraged girl band. Nick Drake would have been nice.

They drove in silence, ten minutes later pulling up to an abandoned-looking warehouse on the edge of town, with broken windows and an overgrown parking lot strewn with junk metal.

"He's in back," the guy said, parking in front of the building and stopping the car.

Alex nodded, feeling suddenly nervous.

"Do you want me to come with you?" the guy asked.

"No…No. This is between me and him."

"But he's not alone, you know. He brought his own posse today."

Alex frowned, "What do you mean? I thought it was just going to be the two of us—you know, talking. I didn't bring anyone. Why the fuck would I?"

"I told you—I told you what he was going to do. He's going to beat the shit out of you and likely brought at least two people to pin you down while he does it. Is that what you want? Because we can leave. We can just turn around and go, and—and I'll say it was my fault you didn't show."

"Jesus . . ." Alex breathed, feeling slightly nauseous. "This sucks…This really sucks."

The guy remained silent.

"Can you tell me something?" Alex asked finally, having made the determination to get out of the car but wanting what little ammunition he might be able to muster. "What did I do to him? Why is he so angry with me? At least tell me that, and maybe I can…I don't know. Have some place to start. Sound more sincere when I apologize . . ."

The guy sighed. "Well…you *did* used to be friends. Good friends, actually. Since, like, kindergarten. You and Carl and he—you were all friends until about a year ago. You all played sports together and stuff. But, well… Dennis is a bit of a pothead. He just is. His family grows the shit on their property and has for decades. For medical purposes, they claim and, well, it's a small town. There are things we just roll with—overlook, if you know what I mean. And the truth is, he's not supposed to be using it—he's definitely not supposed to be selling it—and if he did, his family would be toast. Seriously. And he doesn't, thank god. But, well, he started getting into it, I'd say, summer before Sophomore year. And then he started, you know, sharing it with us—not selling it, just sharing it. Which is still legally *wrong*, I *know*—but *whatever*. And, and—you freaked out and told him to keep that shit at home and if you ever saw him with it again, you'd kick his ass. And…honestly, Alex—I don't even know what happened. Supposedly, the team had a terrible showing at some wrestling meet last year, and Dennis wasn't on his game, and you blamed it on the pot and, and—I guess you told the coach you suspected him of drug use. He was tested, and he failed. And he feels you betrayed him, because you didn't give him any warning. Didn't even talk to him about it. You just—you just turned him in. And he hasn't played any sports since. And, well, it…It pretty much destroyed his reputation, as you can imagine. It doesn't take too much to do that in a town this size, you know."

Alex stared out the windshield, trying to process the story and sort through his conflicting thoughts and emotions over his role in the drama, gaining more insight into the person that was Alex Tate, a nemesis he feared would never stop haunting him.

"Jesus," he said finally, shaking his head despondently. "What the fuck am I supposed to do now? He's not going to forgive me…Why would he? I'm not sure *I* would forgive me. What an asshole. I mean—who the fuck am I to turn my friend in for drug use? He wasn't really hurting anybody, was he?"

"Well, you thought he was…You did. You really believed he was hurting the team. He wasn't being a team player. Was—was being selfish and endangering people—"

"Yeah, and I was perfect, right? I never did anything wrong. I had some, some god-given right to be a self-righteous asshole," he said, his voice tinged with sarcasm.

"Well, you didn't do drugs—*ever*. Actually, you were pretty…disciplined. You walked a pretty straight line. Didn't drink much, either. Only beers. Never hard liquor. You never got so drunk you lost control—at least, I never saw it or heard about it. But, you had a reputation to uphold, you know. I mean, you were top of the class, straight A student, star athlete…dating Miss Teen Montana—well, almost. I think she came in second…So, it's kind of a tough call, isn't it…You did what you believed was right at the time."

He shook his head, "No…No, I—I just don't see how that's right. I mean—you're acting as if there were only two choices, A or B. Turn your friend in or not. There's always other options. There just are. This isn't a black and white world, believe me. The world is fucking gray, and getting grayer…every minute it seems."

He sat another moment before yanking the door handle.

"This is bullshit…I'm settling this now. You know, it's going to suck, and…and my parents are gonna kill me, they are…or just send me away to that ranch, but…I gotta say my peace. I gotta at least try. He was my friend—and pothead or not, I would have *never* done that to him. Not like that. I would have talked to him. I would have found some other way. I swear."

Slamming the door shut behind him, he began his walk around the building, a walk that seemed agonizingly long, as if the universe had slowed time simply to prolong the pain of his shattered nerves. As he rounded the corner, he saw them ahead. Three figures, just as Gabriel had said, leaning against the side of a black pick-up truck, smoking. Dennis was dressed as he always had, even in Alex's memories, primarily in black with an imposing pair of Doc Marten boots. As Alex studied him, he clearly saw his Native American bloodline, in the dark olive skin tone, in the shine of his black hair, which he wore in two long braids that framed his face. Alex did not recognize his two friends, trying to avoid eye contact with either of them and keep focused on Dennis. He walked up to within a distance of about twelve feet.

"You came alone?" Dennis asked, taking a final smoke before flicking the cigarette butt to the ground in front of him.

Alex nodded.

"No friends of yours waiting in ambush? Shocking."

"No…I got a ride from that guy, Gabe. Gabriel."

At this, Dennis's eyes narrowed in on Alex, turning beadier and blacker than they already were, like a hawk about to pounce upon his prey, and Alex instinctively stepped backwards as Dennis lunged towards him a few steps.

"That guy *Gabe*, is that what you said? Did I hear you right?"

Alex nodded, gingerly stepping backwards as Dennis crept closer to him, putting his hands up in surrender.

"Yes—I swear. I only came with him, but he's a friend of yours, right? So—we're cool. I didn't bring anybody, you know…to cause trouble for you. I don't want to cause any trouble. I just want to—"

"You don't want to cause *trouble*?" Dennis interrupted before flying at him, knocking him backwards onto the ground.

Alex moved to get up and felt a searing blow to his stomach as Dennis' heavy boot pummeled into him. He grabbed his stomach instinctively, trying to catch his breath.

"It's too late, you fuck…You've already done that, you miserable fuck . . ."

Alex felt another blow to his side, just under his rib cage, and was soon lying on his hands and knees, still trying to catch his breath from the first blow, his mind reeling, searching for escape options, garnering the mental strength to stand up and fight back but unable to do so before a final violent kick sent him flat on his back into the dirt.

Even though time slowed, Alex could not keep track of the next sequence of events, and Dennis's curses and accusations sounded muted, as if coming through a wall. At some point his former friend was on top of him, grabbing his shirt with both hands and pulling him slightly off the ground, screaming in his face. At some point, Alex heard the roar of a fast approaching car, the squeal of its breaks as it skidded to a stop mere feet away from where they were. But before he could turn his head to study the car, Dennis slammed his fist into his upper right cheek. There was a shriek, he distinctly remembered hearing something like a shriek before the next blow, this one to his jaw, then yelling, shrieking yelling, but effeminate, like an angry girl. A third blow hit his nose.

"Dennis, you fucking son of a bitch—"

He felt Dennis being roughly pushed off as another body nearly fell on top of him, and he let his head fall completely back, the ground its rocky cushion, closing his eyes tightly in anticipation of either another blow or something far worse, as two people began a fight over his now disabled person.

"This isn't your fight Gabrielle—"

"Yes it is my fight, you fucking dick. He came here to apologize, and I let him."

More shoving and pushing.

"Get the fuck out of here, Gabrielle, and let me finish this—"

He sensed his assailant roughly push the person who had come to his defense completely out of the way, hearing someone fall to the ground next to him. A fourth blow hit just under his eye. There was another ear piercing *stop it*, and he felt himself enveloped by a person, someone who had thrown themselves on top of him, not to harm him but to shelter him from additional blows, who held onto him despite the repeated attempts of Dennis to pry them off of Alex's person. After a minute, all movement stopped except for the heavy breathing of whoever still lay sprawled on top of Alex.

"Is this how it's going to be then? After what he did to you—did to us—this is your response? To come save his ass...To shelter him."

Alex felt the chest on top of his expand and contract faster, heard the breathing get louder, felt the hand that held onto his shoulder clutch harder.

"He came to apologize to you," the person on top of him said, and even though he could not see the person, he realized it was the Goth punker. *"He wants to be friends with you again—Don't you understand? He has no memory of what he did. No clue. He remembers you as his friend. Why can't you just accept that? Why can't you just forgive him?"*

"Have you? Have you forgiven him?"

"Yes."

Alex felt a drop on his neck and then another. Whether they were from tears or blood, he could not tell, refusing to open his eyes until it had ended.

"You're pathetic...You're as fucking pathetic as he is. And you know what, if this is what you want, you deserve it. You deserve what you get."

Moments later, he heard the sound of car doors opening and closing, the start of an ignition and the sound of an engine as the truck departed. Soon, all was silent except for the labored breathing of himself and the person Gabriel, who had not moved and remained still for a few moments more before gingerly getting up and off of his body.

"Are you okay?" Gabriel asked finally, kneeling next to him and gently pushing his bangs aside from his brow.

The gesture felt feminine, reminded him of what his mother might do, and he slapped the hand away, struggling to sit himself up, dizzy with pain. "Don't touch me . . ." he burst, his voice hoarse and barely audible. "I'm not like that."

"Like what?"

He looked at the guy askance, "I'm not a *fag*," he said, quickly turning his head the other direction.

Something hit him on the side of the head, and he winced, coughing on spit.

"And I am not a guy. Goddammit…You idiot."

He stared at the ground in blank confusion.

"My name is Gabrielle—not *Gabriel*. Fucking moron. Gabrielle Trahan. And I'm a *girl*," she said, standing up and walking to her truck.

For a moment, Alex thought she was going to get in and drive away, leaving him there, which, he mused, she had every right to do. He heard the car door open and, after a few moments, shut again. He expected to hear the sound of an ignition but didn't, hearing her angry footsteps instead as she returned and knelt beside him. He continued to stare at the dirt, the name suddenly troubling him more than the body. *Gabrielle Trahan…*

While his mind pondered, his eyes looked askance, watching as she unzipped her black jacket, taking it off and throwing it to the ground. Alex's eyes grew wide as she then moved to take off her T-shirt.

"What are you doing?" he burst.

"First," she said, pulling it over her head and revealing a black tank-top style bra. "I'm using this to wipe the blood off your face…And second, I'm doing this to prove to you that I am a *girl*. See? I have fucking breasts…You fucking idiot."

To his horror, she took her shirt, a Psychedelic Furs concert tee, and ripped it into three pieces. Uncapping a bottled water, she put some water onto one of the pieces and began dabbing it against his face, the white cloth quickly turning crimson.

"We should get you to the clinic…One of these cuts is pretty bad. This one on your cheek…But I think the beard actually helped you."

As she leaned in close to him, he could smell her exposed skin. It was a familiar smell, that of flowers and soap.

"What did you say your name was?"

"Gabrielle Trahan."

"You're not related to Brooke Trahan, are you?"

"Yep...I'm her sister."

He felt his face flush and his head spin as his mind tried to process the information. "That's impossible . . ." he breathed.

"Come on, get up," she said, pulling at his arm and momentarily out from his mental fog. "The clinic closes soon, and we should just have you looked at, you know? Cleaned up better. I think you'll be okay. He didn't kick you in the head, did he?"

Alex stood up, stumbling as he did, struggling to regain his balance and soon wrapping his hands protectively around his throbbing stomach and side. "No . . ."

She walked him to her car, helping him into the passenger seat. He watched her through the windshield as she collected her jacket, water bottle and bloodied shirt shreds, throwing the last items into the bed of her truck. Before getting into the car, she slipped on the jacket, zipping it up enough to cover most of the tank bra. After sliding in, she checked herself in the rearview mirror, wiping away a few small black streaks that had formed on her cheek during the exchange, re-touching her hair and pursing her lips before starting the ignition.

Alex stared at her dumbly while she drove, relieved that he had been wrong about her sex but also curious as to why he had been wrong, how he could have been so grossly off-mark about the girl, studying her with a mixture of horror and fascination—horror at the extreme mask of multiple piercings, stark make-up, severe hair and rough clothing that so well hid her femininity while at the same time in awe of the female underneath.

Since Hole was still blaring on the stereo, they did not have to talk, and Alex had not felt good enough to do so, as much as he wanted to ask her questions, starting with her family, still finding it impossible that she was related to Brooke and soon looking for similarities between her and Brooke.

Within ten minutes, they had reached the downtown area and were pulling into the parking lot of a clinic close to St. Joseph Medical Center.

"Wait a minute, I can't just walk into a clinic...Don't I need, like...I don't know. My mom or something?"

medical staff and Alex's parents, helping them to navigate the confusing and sometimes seemingly cold-hearted process, trying to ease their pain and fear.

As Alex came to, her father gently sent the nurse out of the room and asked for Gabrielle's assistance in helping him back onto the patient table where he could lay until fully recovered.

"Is he going to be okay?" she whispered.

"He'll be fine…The seizure's stopped. He just needs some time to rest," he said matter-of-factly, turning off the harsh fluorescent office lighting and moving to the window to adjust the blinds and let the late afternoon sun cast a pale glow into the room. "But how about you? How are you holding up?" he asked, giving her a hug and leading her out of the room.

She burst out crying, burying her head into his crisp, white coat, letting him hold her a minute until she had calmed down. After giving her a Kleenex from his pocket, they walked arm in arm to his office, where she settled into one of the two brown leather chairs in front of his desk. He took the second chair, for the next ten minutes patiently listening to her confession of what had transpired and her role in it, up through the moment of the seizure and Alex's baffling comments about Nurse Wanda.

"I don't understand," she said, still sniffing back the tears, her tissue in saturated shreds. "It's like somebody put his brain into a blender and—and poured it back into his head. He's—he's so confused. About everything. He didn't even know I was a girl…It's so stupid…And I feel so stupid."

Her father sighed, leaning forward in his chair, producing a clean tissue from his pocket and handing it to her. Though not handsome, he had kindly features and pronounced lines around his mouth and eyes, making it seem as if he were always smiling. Half Salish, his hair was dark but severely receded, barely visible around his broad, olive-toned face.

"Gabrielle…What you and everyone else in this town needs to understand is that Alex is a changed person. He's not the same as he was before the coma, and it's quite possible that he may never fully recover. Never be the same—mentally or even physically—as you remember him. He has acute amnesia, is prone to seizures like the one you saw today and, well, is also prone to violent outbursts. Violent and even destructive behavior—against himself or others. It can take months—even years—for coma victims to adjust socially to their environment. Some never completely do."

"He doesn't know me at all…Doesn't know who I am or was…It's so weird."

"No, but he does have memories. And he believes those memories are real. They are as real to him as our own, so…We need to be sensitive to that. If he believes someone harmed him—as outrageous as it sounds—in his mind, they did. And, he'll experience and behave as such. Understanding this might help you. If you want to be his friend, that is. You certainly don't have to get involved, you know. Nobody expects you to."

"That's just it…I do care. I do want to. . . I do want to get involved. What is wrong with me? Brooke says I have a complex…That I'm addicted to abusive relationships…But I'm not, I don't think…I'm just addicted to *this* abusive relationship for some…for some reason, I don't know why."

Her father said nothing, smiling kindly at her.

"If…If I try to be his friend, you know. One more time. Will you and mom be mad at me? Will you think I'm—I'm stupid?"

He sighed heavily. "Gabby, he's my best friend's son. And he could be my son. He is on some level. Anger is the furthest thing your mother and I feel over this situation. If you want to reach out and help him, we could only feel pride."

They talked a bit more and then Gabrielle asked if he would call the Fahlstroms and explain what happened, as she was too mortified by it all. But she wanted to take Alex home. To spend some time with him and apologize to him for what happened earlier, for Dennis's behavior, for her not stopping it sooner.

After stepping into a hall restroom to freshen up, completely washing the makeup from her face with the exception of her waterproof eyeliner and mascara, she tidied her hair, manipulating the fake tufts to cover her swollen eyes and headed back to the room to retrieve Alex. Taking a deep breath, she quietly opened the door.

"Alex…Are you awake?"

Unsure of who had entered the room, he said nothing, still lying on the table, but with one leg hanging off and barely touching the floor, one arm under his head, staring up at the pale, pock-marked ceiling tiles.

She closed the door behind her, quietly walking towards his side.

When Alex saw who it was, he sighed despondently, having hoped his memories of that afternoon had been dreams. Clearly, they were not. And as she stood next to him, looking down at him, he remembered her name and frowned.

"Brooke doesn't have any sisters," he said.

Gabrielle stared blankly a moment, completely taken aback by his comment which seemed to come out of nowhere.

"What? Are you okay? I—I came to see if you were feeling okay."

"I'm fine…But you're not a Trahan. Brooke doesn't have any sisters. She has a brother, Nate. That's it."

Gabrielle's mind raced to process the gist of the conversation. Remembering what her father had said, she tried to play along. "Well…um. I understand that…that in *Kansas City*, the Trahans were minus a daughter—"

He sat up abruptly, eyeing her intently. "How do you know about Kansas City?"

"Um…Your mother told me…About Kansas City. And your sister. She told us."

He looked away for a moment. "Gabrielle…You don't look like Gabrielle . . ." he mumbled, agitated at the idea that this extreme looking girl he did not recognize would have Danielle's mother's name but none of her or her daughter's features. But then something clicked, a memory, a sentence he had replayed so often in his mind, that he had even committed it to his journals. *You just don't recognize me. Maybe you will next time.*

He jumped off the table, excitedly. "Who are you?" he asked, bearing down on her.

Startled, she shrunk away, taking a step back.

"I told you—I'm Gabrielle Trahan."

"No, I mean—who are you to me? Who are you in my life? Because I don't remember you. I remember Brooke and Nate and your parents. But, I don't remember you. I mean—they didn't have another daughter. At least, not a biological one. Are you adopted?"

"No!" she said laughing nervously. "I'm quite sure I'm not adopted… You mean, nobody told you about me. About us?"

He shook his head.

"I'm your friend. I've been your friend since, well—since birth. We're birthday twins—born in the same hospital on the same day."

He shook his head, baffled, but took a step closer to her. As he did, she took a step back, unable to read his emotions or intent.

"Let me see you," he said, taking another step towards her.

She took two more steps backward, stopped by the wall. He moved to turn on the office light, blinking a moment to adjust his vision under its harsh glare, before moving up to her, so close their bodies were nearly touching and she tried to shrink into the wall. And when he lifted his hand, she lifted her arm as if to shield herself from a blow.

He grabbed her arm, pulling it down, "I'm not going to hurt you...I just want to see you. I want to see what you look like," he said, holding her arms down with one hand and using his other to physically turn her face up towards his, to roughly push her bangs back

She cried out. "That hurts...It's attached to my head, you know. With pins."

"This isn't your hair?"

She shook her head.

But he soon had both hands on her face, pushing back the bangs with less force, looking into her eyes, physically refusing to let her turn away from him.

"Look at me—why won't you look at me?" he asked, gripping her tighter as she tried to wriggle out, to escape his scrutiny.

"Because I don't want to...I look like hell...I feel like hell...Please—please don't—"

But he was much stronger than she and kept her head turned up, towards his, leaning his own down so closely, he could have been moving in for a kiss.

Her eyes grew wide, met his and he saw that which he had sought, what the make-up could no longer hide. "Oh, my god . . ." he breathed.

His body suddenly relaxed, his arms dropping to his sides momentarily. He even stepped back, to Gabrielle's relief, her nerves still on edge. But before she could recover completely, she suddenly felt herself enveloped by his person, so swiftly and entirely that she could do nothing but remain still, experiencing a feeling of closeness so potent she thought she might have lost herself in his person, unable to tell where she ended and he began.

Alex wrapped his arms around her as though he had been lost at sea and found a piece of driftwood, holding onto her as if his life and any possibility of future happiness depended on it. As if she had been tossed back at him from the depths of the death and despair where he thought he had lost her, and he had no intention of letting go this time. He had no idea how long he stood there holding her, but at some point his emotions overcame him, and he began to weep, a choking mixture of relief and joy. *Where have you been? I can't believe I've found you after all this time. Thank god I've found you again, it has been such a nightmare.* The elated thoughts raced through his mind, but he did not verbalize them, instead holding her tighter, lightly stroking the hair on her head, real or not, it ceased to matter in that moment.

Gabrielle felt as if she could cry with him except she had already spent most of her tears earlier and was too overwhelmed with happy relief, feeling nothing but sincerity in his embrace and believing that her deepest wish had finally come true.

When at last they parted, he just shook his head, staring sadly at her. "I've missed you," he whispered.

"You have?"

"You have no idea . . ." he said, wiping his face with his sleeve. "Can we...Can we just go somewhere?"

She nodded.

"To talk. To catch up. Maybe...Maybe for coffee somewhere. Is there a coffee shop here?"

She pondered a moment. "The Diner sells coffee...We could go there."

"Yeah...Okay, let's do that," he said, nodding and finally smiling.

He took her hand as they left the clinic, and she let him, knowing he saw in her some person he knew from his dream, relieved that the recognition was a positive one and deciding to go with it. To play whatever role he wanted her to play in the moment. When they got to the car, he seemed reluctant to let go of her hand but finally did. She soon was seated in the driver's seat, turned the ignition and was met by a blast of loud angry music.

So offensively jarring was the sound that she slammed her hand onto the button to shut it off. "Jesus . . ."

They both laughed.

"Sorry 'bout that...That is *so* not the mood I'm in right now . . ." She reached into the back storage area, fumbling around for her CD case, eventually retrieving *Pink Moon*. "Here...This is much better."

It only took a few chords for Alex to recognize the song. He smiled widely. "How did you know?" he asked, with a touch of sarcasm.

"Know what."

"How much I love this album...He's one of my favorite artists."

"I didn't, actually...You never understood Nick Drake the few times I tried to play him for you. I guess you've changed your mind since then."

"Not me...I've always loved Nick Drake. You must be talking about Alex Tate."

She frowned a moment, pulling out of the lot and onto the main street. "Alex Tate?"

"Yeah...I'm not him. I'm Alex Michael."

"Oh...Okay. Okay. That's cool. I like that name."

"What's your middle name?"

"Danielle."

He chuckled. "Of course it is."

They listened to the music in silence for the five-minute drive to the diner. While they stood inside, waiting to be seated, Alex caught a glimpse of himself in a mirrored wall and was stunned at what he saw, as if he were seeing himself for the first time. He walked up to the wall, and Gabrielle absently followed him, looking into the mirror with him.

"Jesus...I look like ass."

She shrugged sadly. "I can't say anything."

"Look at us...We don't look like this. What happened to us?"

She shrugged. *Hate happened to us...Fear and loathing happened to us,* she thought to herself but refrained from commenting.

"Christ...No wonder you were fucking scared of me...I'm sorry," he continued.

"It's okay...I wasn't really scared of your looks. Just your temper, you know...And your seizures. They're very scary. I thought you were dying."

"Oh, those . . ." He turned away from the wall and took her hand as they waited to be seated.

She let him but glanced nervously about the diner to ensure nobody from school was there to see it. Because her relatives owned the restaurant and she worked there in the summer, she knew most of the staff, including the waitress who seated them. It was not, however, these people whose observation she was hoping to evade but rather anyone from school, for if any fellow students were to see them holding hands on an apparent date, the repercussions would be drastic. Erring on the side of caution, she requested a booth in the very back and selected the side with her back to the restaurant crowd. To her surprise, he sat next to her instead of across from her.

One of her cousins came to take their order, making a fuss upon finally recognizing Alex, and Gabrielle held her breath, hoping Alex had no ill memories of the waitress. But he was pleasant and ordered a cup of coffee, black. Gabrielle ordered a soda.

"No coffee?" he asked.

She shook her head, making a face. "It tastes disgusting."

"Well, you don't drink it black. I mean—I do, but you don't. You usually put cream and sugar and other crap in it to sweeten it."

"I do . . ."

"Yeah. You want me to show you?"

She bit her lip, wondering how long she would be able to continue to play along like she knew what he was talking about. Wondering if he would even accept the fact that she didn't.

"Okay, sure."

Eventually, they had two empty mugs, a steaming pot of coffee and a bowl of creamers placed in front of them, along with the errant soda. After filling his own cup, Alex meticulously filled her mug half way before experimenting with creams to get it the right color. It was all about the color, he said, then added a number of sugar packets before gingerly placing the mug in front of her. She stared at the beige liquid for a moment before tentatively taking a sip.

While it wasn't bitter, it wasn't pleasant or refreshing, either, but she forced a smile and sat the mug down, soon reaching for her soda to wash out the taste.

"You hate it," he said, grinning sadly.

She shrugged uncomfortably, "I'm just not used to it. It's not bad, though...I'm sorry."

"You don't know who you are, do you . . ." he said quietly, looking askance at her.

"Um...Well...I—I don't know who you think I am. I know who I think I am, but...I don't know. Who am I?"

"It doesn't matter," he said, staring down at his mug, flicking an empty sugar packet. "We have to start over, don't we...As if we're meeting each other for the first time. Don't we?"

"Maybe...Is that such a bad thing? Did I know you well? I mean, how long did I know you—in your world?"

"A couple months, but...We spent a lot of time together, so...You knew me better than most people, I would say."

"A couple months?" she burst. "Only a couple months? Shit...I've known you your whole life...Maybe getting to know each other again won't be as painful as you think," she said, smirking.

"Alright," he said, smiling back. "So where do we start?"

"I say we start with your *couple months*, since I have, like, sixteen years to cover...Why don't you tell me all about you and me and Kansas City and how you got here. And whatever else I should know about you...and whoever I am, or was or am supposed to be."

"Well, I don't know—that's a long, sordid tale that could take awhile."

She rolled her eyes, pushing her sleeve up to look at her watch. "It's only a little after five. We have all evening."

He took a deep breath, settling back in his seat, casually putting an arm across the booth ledge behind her before beginning his narrative, a narrative he was relieved to finally be able to voice in its entirety to someone he could trust, to someone who would listen with no judgment, willing to accept his experience as true, help him to cope with it and help him to move on from it. For the next few hours, Gabrielle listened thoughtfully, engrossed in his world, interrupting him only to ask questions or gain clarification. Amazed at the bleakness of it, the brutality of it, the sorrow that began with one coma and ended with another, that began with death and ended with more death, that began with a shattered relationship and ended with another. The same story, different details. It was a story that felt chillingly familiar, personal.

But in between the harrowing details were glimpses of the person he thought he was, nearly a polar opposite of the person she remembered him being, as if he had drawn a line down the middle of his mind and chosen a side for everything—from music to clothes to hobbies, from politics to religion, from one romantic interest to another. Thus the death of Alex Tate and the birth of Alex Michael.

As it was going on eight, a familiar figure stopped by the booth, sliding into the empty seat in front of them, providing a needed break from the intense conversation.

"Dr. Trahan said I might find you here…You kids eat?" Mr. Fahlstrom asked kindly, donned in his sheriff's uniform.

They had forgotten to eat, and Mr. Fahlstrom refused to leave until they had studied the menu and ordered. After a bit of awkward small talk, both Alex and Gabrielle launched into apologies at the same time but were soon waved to silence. "Lawrence told me what happened…I hate to say it, son, but I can't even tell," he said, leaning across the table to have a closer look at Alex's face. "You look no worse now than you did when you woke up this morning."

Alex grinned sheepishly.

"You know…You can't force forgiveness, Alex. You gotta give it some time…You and Dennis were friends once, and…I think he'll come around, but…It's gotta be on his time. You said your apologies. The ball's in his court."

"Well, technically, *no*—I got knocked out before I actually said I was sorry."

His father shook his head and got up to go, patting him on the back as he left. "Get him home by nine, Gabrielle. You both have school tomorrow."

"He knows you . . ." Alex said thoughtfully, after his father had left them. "Yes."

"I mean he really knows you…Like you're his own kid or something.

That's so…That's so weird…My parents never knew any of my girlfriends. It was always so uncomfortable, you know. I hated introducing them. Even Danielle. It was a nightmare."

She said nothing, still fascinated by his ability to effortlessly shift from one life to the next, from one set of parents to another.

Their food came, and they ate awhile in silence. When they had finished and taken bathroom breaks, he turned to her, again putting his arm on the ledge behind her. "So…Can you tell me about yourself? At least—begin the story, and—maybe we can finish it later on, you know. Another day."

She shrugged. "Okay…But I don't know what to say…I don't really see it as a story. I just kind of hang out day to day, you know. What do you want to know about me?"

He smiled. "Everything…I don't know. Well, I guess here's the big one—do you have a boyfriend?…I've learned not to assume anything."

She shook her head, and he breathed an obvious sigh of relief.

"Alright…What do you like to do? Your hobbies and stuff."

She shared with him her activities, her passion for theater, for singing, for playing the drums. Her love of art history and poetry. Her love of horse-back riding, skiing, the mountains, her home town. She had taken Spanish in school but was not fluent. Her family traveled annually, but she had never been out of the country except to Canada, which she didn't think counted. Since Alex had forgotten Polson was on an Indian Reservation, she provided a brief history of the Salish and Kootenai tribes. Though Salish, she was baptized Catholic, but her parents were lax, her mother a spiritual healer and into a variety of religions and belief systems, so she was never forced to go to church. Her parents, like his own, were comfortable but not wealthy, having worked hard for what they had. She and Brooke worked at the diner over the summer to make extra money.

Alex listened, having to continually prod her to talk, something he had not had to do with Danielle, taken aback by the simplicity of her answers and her life. The same lack of fanfare and drama he had begun to see in his own home, as the days stretched on in a steady flow with the exception of whatever discourse he would cause, momentarily disrupting its tranquil rhythm.

"So, what's with the look?" he said, motioning to her. "It's pretty hard core. I mean—I have never seen anything like it in person. Only in magazines, you know. Even the punkers at my high school weren't this authentic."

She shrugged. "I don't know—it's just a mask…Clothes are just costumes… I often dress to express how I'm feeling. What role I'm playing at the time."

"What role are you playing?" he asked quietly.

"Slutty, angry bitch," she replied after a moment.

He frowned, sensing there was more to her story but apprehensive about digging too deeply just yet. "I doubt that . . ."

"Do you?"

He nodded. "You're not like that."

"How do you know? You don't really know me. You didn't even know I was a girl until this afternoon."

He laughed nervously. "Well, I'd…I'd like to get to know you better. I mean—is there any reason we can't?"

"Can't what."

"You know—be together. Get to know each other, but—as more than friends."

She stared at him intently, trying to read his sincerity.

"Will you go out with me—again. Like, maybe, tomorrow night."

"As in a *date*?"

"Yeah—on a date. I mean, it could be a friends date, if you want."

"Is that what *you* want?"

He shook his head. "No…I want to go out on a date with you. You know—take you out to a movie or something. Get to know you better."

She sat stunned at the request, at once ecstatic and apprehensive, feeling time had collapsed, bringing the past into the present and offering her another opportunity to make a choice.

"Is there a reason we can't do that…Why we haven't done that . . ." he continued cautiously.

"Um, no—I mean, *yes*. I mean—okay. Okay. But we need to keep this to ourselves right now. You can't tell anyone. *Anyone*. And…Well, we'll need to be discreet. Go to Missoula."

He laughed, "Why?"

"Just trust me, okay? Please. You obviously have no memory of this place or this life, so…So let me be your guide, okay? For awhile."

"Alright…But will you tell me more? Will you tell me why?"

She shifted uncomfortably in her seat. "I don't know. Maybe. Someday—not tonight. It doesn't matter, really."

"Okay—so, tomorrow night?"

She shook her head. "I can't—but Saturday. How about Saturday?"

"Yeah—that's, that's great. We can get together earlier, you know. It doesn't have to be evening. Maybe you can come by and watch TV some . . ."

She shook her head, wanting to avoid Alex's sister and, possibly, her own. "I can come by early, but we should head out. But we can swing by Morgenroth's in Missoula, and you can check out the instruments. You know, check out the guitars," she offered, wanting to support his dream hobbies but inwardly skeptical that he had any skills whatsoever.

"Okay…That sounds great," he said, happy but suddenly nervous, feeling awkward, as if he really were going on a first date, which logic told him he was but his heart continued to deny.

He offered to pay for their dinners, but they later found out his father already had, so he left the tip, wanting to hold her hand on the way out, but suddenly shy about it. They drove to his house, letting Drake's "Which Will" fill the silent void. Once in his driveway, she put the car in park, muted the stereo and turned to him.

"Alex…Do you really not remember *anything* about this life? I must know—truthfully."

He shook his head. "I don't—honestly. And any memories I do have are either wrong or incomplete. Some people I do remember from when I was a young child, and others are missing. Or—I don't remember them as they really are in this life…But I don't remember you, Gabrielle—not as you are now at least. I swear."

She nodded, smiling. "And you…You really want to go out with me? On a date?"

"Absolutely," he said, meeting her stare intently.

"Even though I'm not her…I'm not Danielle. Not really."

He reached out and gently stroked her face. "She doesn't exist…Not anymore. And whether she did or didn't doesn't really matter now. Because you're here—and I can see you and touch you and be with you. Talk to you…If we grew up together—were friends since birth, as you say—that must mean something. There must be something there, don't you think? It's at least worth finding out…I think it's worth finding out. It's worth trying."

Instinctively, she grabbed his hand, moved it to her lips and gently kissed it.

"Okay…thank you…But, remember—we can't act like anything is different between us. Tomorrow. Just—just pretend you don't know me."

∞

His mother was waiting for him at the kitchen table, reading her Bible. Upon seeing him, she immediately got up to fuss at him and inspect his wounds, but he was too distracted to care or even focus on her comments and questions.

"Can I borrow the car Saturday night?"

"What? Why? No, you *cannot* borrow the car. We don't even know if you remember how to drive—"

"I *know* how to drive. In fact, let me drive us to school tomorrow. Make Danielle give me the keys."

"Absolutely not. Honey, why on earth would we give you a car? You have been in two fights this week, you nearly got suspended, you're failing two classes—"

"Because I have a date," he interrupted, nodding and grinning widely.

Her eyes grew wide.

"I know—isn't that cool. So, I need the car, because she wants to go to Missoula—"

"No—you're not getting the car, and *who* wants to go to Missoula? Because you're not going to Missoula, either."

"Gabrielle—Gabrielle said we had to go to Missoula."

"*Gabrielle*? You're going on a *date* with Gabrielle? Honey, are you sure about this…I mean, that it's a date, and…Well, she's not just being nice and…Being nice. You know, I think she is . . ." she said quietly, brushing away an errant strand of hair. "I think she's just wanting to be your friend right now…Don't you?"

He sighed, but decided it best not to press the issue. "Okay—yeah. Yes, it's just a friend thing…So, can I have the car?"

"Absolutely not. If Gabrielle wants to take you to Missoula, then she can drive. But frankly, I think it's a terrible idea. My goodness, Alex, you had another seizure today. What if you—you have one there—or, or worse. Have one in the car on the way there. It's over an hour, and there's not much in-between."

He sighed, sauntering over to the kitchen table and collapsing into one of the chairs, petting his dog, who had been patiently waiting for his attention. His mother asked if he wanted anything to eat or drink and then started to ask about his homework and what he had due tomorrow.

"Why didn't you tell me about her?" he asked, changing the subject.

She sighed, joining him at the table after pouring herself a cup of tea.

"Well…There was no reason to talk about her. You had some kind of falling out. You haven't spoken to each other in, I don't know, months. Wouldn't even attend family functions if the other one was going to be there. We don't know what happened, her parents or your father and I. We didn't really want to. We just hoped it would work itself out one day."

"Do we really have the same birthday?"

"The same birth *day*?" she said with mock incredulity. "The same *birth minute*. You were born at the exact same time." And then she proceeded to tell him the story in much greater detail, her eyes sparkling as she relived the time with her friend, Barb.

"Do you have pictures?" Alex asked.

"Of course…Are you ready to see them now?"

He nodded, and she returned a minute later with two large photo albums. For the next hour, they went through the albums, and he studied each photo with a sense of wonder. Some he recognized, even remembered very clearly, but others he had never seen. While he remembered his newborn photo, he did not remember the one of him and Gabrielle, the two of them only distinguishable by the color of their blankets, one pink and one blue. There were a number of baby and toddler photos of her, of him, of their families, even of his sister that he had never seen, and as they got to the second book, the number of unfamiliar photos far outweighed what he remembered.

Except for one—one that the minute he saw it, he nearly gasped.

It was in color but a bit yellowed. Five children sat cross-legged in a semi-circle, making silly faces at the camera, and he sat in the center, his hair a mess of blond curls, wearing jeans, tennis shoes and a long-sleeve shirt with a huge fake sheriff badge pinned to the front pocket, one eye cocked, making a gun out of the fingers of his right hand. He carefully removed the photo from its sleeve to study it more closely.

"What is this one…Tell me about this one."

His mother smiled. "That, I believe, was taken at your second grade graduation picnic. We called you *The Little Posse*…Oh, you were naughty. All of you were, well, very naughty children," she laughed. "And you were at the center of it."

He smiled. "So, who were we? Who are these kids? I mean I recognize myself—"

"Well, here's Gabrielle at the end, sticking her tongue out. And this is Dennis Wiseman next to her…making glasses with his fingers. Then you and Carl, doing who knows what. And Brian McDermott."

"What did we do? I mean—why were we so bad?"

She shook her head, smiling. "Oh, you weren't bad—you were just naughty. There's a difference, I think. The five of you were like a little gang of troublemakers. You did mischievous things. Traumatizing for your parents at the time, but…It seems more harmless now, looking back. You know, getting into messes—always making messes, breaking furniture, breaking toys, destroying property—*gardens*. You tried to mow a *crop circle* in our neighbor's prized herb garden. Oh, and you all flooded the McDermott's cellar trying to dig and make your own swimming pool one summer. Oh, dear…It was awful," she said, laughing. "They had to get a truck to vacuum out all the water."

"So…How long were we friends? How long did the group last?"

She sighed. "Well…You were all friends until, well, maybe a year or so ago. Except for Brian, who moved in ninth grade. But, the rest of you stayed friends, I think. Not as close, though. Definitely not as close as you were when all of these pictures were taken. I'd say, by sixth grade the group started calming down. Changing. Everyone going in different directions."

"Can I have this?" he asked, holding onto the photo.

"Of course. It's yours."

"I just want to…I just want to hold onto it, if that's okay."

She nodded, and when they had finished the second album, she started asking him about his homework again.

He sighed, stretching, "I'll do my homework…But I need to shower first. I feel like hell. Oh, and can I have a razor?"

"*What*? Dear god, why?"

"So I can *shave*…Jeez. I want to shave this thing off. It's killing me," he said, rubbing his beard. "Seriously, it itches. I hate it. I don't know how I've lived like this."

She shook her head thoughtfully but ten minutes later gave him the razor.

Not having a dressing table, Gabrielle sat in front of the rather small lighted make-up mirror on her desk, staring absently at the image, unsure of who it was staring back at her. For the moment, she had the room to herself, Brooke hanging out in some other part of the house, and she relished the solitude and opportunity to quietly sort through the last few hours of her life.

After undoing the wig, she unpinned her hair, shaking it out, eventually brushing it out, relieved at how light her head suddenly felt. She had not realized how non-conducive wigs were to fully embracing another person, not that she had ever been embraced quite like that before, not even after they had made love.

She peered into the mirror, trying to see what he saw, studying her eyes, which she thought large and crooked and her sister accused of being hug-like. Her lips were full, made fuller by dark lipstick, but she felt like a fish. Her nose was the only feature she found proportionate to the rest of her face. She sighed sadly, staring at the various shards of silver and black metal that pierced her skin in places, confused by their presence. The belly piercing had been done with joy, but not the rest. The rest had been done in anger, revenge, with the intent to inflict a bit of pain on her birthday twin, wondering if he felt them as she had, wondering if his tongue ached or his ear throbbed.

She hugged her body, trying to reenact the intense embrace in her mind. Confused by it, scared by it, enthralled by it, ready to once again throw all caution to the wind.

But looking into the mirror, she feared she was a lie through which he would see. Maybe not now, but in a few days. A few weeks. When he realized she was not a beautiful, wealthy Catholic school girl who spoke fluent Italian, played flawless concertos, traveled the world and drank cappuccinos in sidewalk cafes. When he saw she didn't drive a Volvo but an El Camino, when she didn't live in an English manor house but on a horse ranch.

She stared at herself in the mirror, tears running down her cheeks, knowing she could play the part for awhile—it would be so easy to play. She had rehearsed it for the past few months—lit up the stage with it. Long hair, curled and flowing. Soft dresses. Blouses instead of concert tees, chinos instead of jeans, plaid skirts instead of punked-out kilts. Sandals instead of chucks. Delicate pearl stud earrings instead of the garish black stud that sat like a cancerous mole on her lobe.

But he was in love with Danielle, and she was not Danielle, and no amount of paint or costuming could magically transform her into something she was not. He would eventually see through it, as he did before, and hate her for it.

But her body again remembered his embrace, felt it, shuddering in protest at her mind's self-pitying, morbid musings, and she couldn't help but wonder what it would be like to make love to Alex Michael, to make love to someone who could hold her so close, envelop her so completely.

Staring into the mirror again, she made the decision to simply start over. To go back to the last time she was happy and remove whatever metal scars had been inflicted since then, which meant removing everything but the belly piercing and the tattoo, which she could not remove and had no intention of doing so, anyway. The wigs would go, too, as she hadn't begun wearing those until after the fall. And her clothes she would play by ear, as she always had, dressing however she damn well felt depending on her mood.

When she awoke the next morning, she had to remind herself that yesterday had even happened, suddenly unsure, the entire thing feeling like a dream. And since she slept late, not hearing her alarm for some reason, only getting up thanks to Brooke slapping her, she had little time to get ready at all, throwing on some jeans, a skull T-shirt, striped hoodie and chucks while pulling her hair into two ponytails. There was no time for make-up, and she didn't feel like the fuss of it anyway. Applying some mascara and lip gloss, she dashed off to school, both apprehensive and excited, wondering if there would be any acknowledgement of their exchange the day before, even though she had strictly forbade it. If even just a look . . .

Because she was late, he was already seated when she entered the classroom, near the front, next to his friends, and she had to turn away to hide the complete shock and bewilderment she felt upon seeing him, for a moment thinking she had seen a ghost. She spent the next few minutes in a panicked stupor, feeling dizzy, almost nauseous, fearing he had returned, scared to meet his stare or even look at him. Gone was the beard, and his hair was so neatly combed back that she thought he had cut it off. It wasn't until she was fully seated and staring at his back that she saw it had been pulled into a stubby ponytail.

He turned to look at her, the grin and wink momentarily calming her nerves.

But she wasn't entirely convinced until, near the end of class, a wadded ball of notebook paper landed in her lap. She looked up to see from where it had come and then quietly moved to flatten it. Scribbled on it was a smiley face and a message. *You look nice today. Is that your real hair?*

She smiled, blushing, and as she was leaving class, placed the same wadded ball on his desk with a message of her own.

CHAPTER FIFTEEN

He had been so consumed with seeing her again that he barely paid attention to his friends' exclamations of pride and joy at his having shaved his beard and combed his hair. That was the Alex they knew, they said, before harping on his clothes, asking if he had gotten them out of a dumpster, which baffled him, as he had actually worn a pair of Alex Tate's khaki pants but with his usual plaid flannel shirt, which hung buttoned but untucked.

When she walked through the door, his heart nearly stopped, and it took everything he had not to jump out of his chair, grab her, kiss her, hold her, classroom be damned. Everything be damned, for there she was—just as he remembered her, except for the ponytails, which he had never seen on Danielle. But they swung dark, long and full, and he could imagine them loosened. He couldn't help but turn around and look at her, longing for her recognition, some sign, some gesture that he hadn't just imagined their time together the evening before.

When she didn't give him a sign, he sat through class in distracted agitation, finally deciding to scribble a note and toss it to her when the teacher wasn't looking. He had thought about drawing some hearts but kept it friendly instead, remembering it was technically their first date together and not wanting to seem too forward.

To his relief, as he was collecting his books and papers, she walked by his desk, setting the wad down. He smiled, opening it eagerly to the response. A tongue had been drawn on his smiley face's mouth. *Yes it is. Is that your real face?*

He chuckled to himself, musing at her rather sassy sense of humor, then spent the next period plotting another communication. Between classes, his friends grouped by the lockers and began plotting a retaliation against Dennis. Alex frowned, unsure of how word of the event had gotten around that quickly, almost having forgotten that his clean-shaven face only accentuated the injuries and confirmed the rumors that probably started yesterday afternoon.

"How many were there Alex?" somebody asked, either Chad or Stewart. Alex got them confused.

Carl continued the questioning. "Who were all of them, Alex? Do you remember?"

"Yeah—was *Gabriel* involved?" Ron added, snickering.

At this, Alex flew at him, throwing him against the locker. "You leave her out of it. She had nothing to do with it," he said angrily.

Ron stared at him in wide-eyed shock before putting his hands up in surrender. "Okay, sorry, man. I didn't think you even knew who she was."

"Alex," Carl said, putting an arm around him and pulling him away from Ron. "We're just watching your back, man. Okay? That's what we do for each other."

"Well, I don't need you to watch my back," Alex said, shaking him off. "I don't need you to fight my battles for me, okay? And this is my fight—between Dennis and me and nobody else, okay? Just stay out of it…In fact, I'm—I'm putting a veil of protection on both of them. I'll fucking kill anyone who touches either of them, alright? I fucking will."

At this his friends eyed him queerly.

"A *veil of protection*?" one of them repeated. "What the hell is that? What the hell is that?" the guy asked again, turning to Carl.

Carl shook his head, throwing his hands up. "Alright, alright—if you're saying you don't want us to go kick Wiseman's ass, we won't, okay? We'll respect your wish. We just want you to know that we would—happily. Anyway, you're still going bowling with us tonight, right?"

"It's Rock n' Bowl, man—you gotta come," one of them added.

"Yeah—you remember how to bowl, right?" Ron asked, laughing, patting his back.

Alex nodded, smiling at him apologetically.

"You know, I think your girl's coming tonight," one of them continued. "And I'm bringing her friends. It's the look, I ahlstrom. They finally recognize you."

"Yeah—just buy a belt, and we're almost there," someone said.

Alex forced a smile, both confused and suddenly disheartened at the prospect of seeing *his girl*, a girl he thought had fled in horror never to return.

"Hey, did your parents give you your car back yet?" one of them asked as they walked to their next class.

Alex looked at the group, confused and surprised by the question.

"Apparently not." They laughed.

"I have a car? Are you joking?"

"Dude—you have *the car*."

"No shit," another added.

"What do I have?"

They laughed.

"No—seriously. What kind of car do I have?"

"Is he serious? He doesn't know?"

"He doesn't *remember*, you dumb ass. He has amnesia."

"It's a Camaro," Carl said finally. "Nineteen eighty seven Z28…Sapphire blue."

Alex laughed, shaking his head. "Nah…That's not my car, Carl. That's *your car*. You drive a sapphire blue Camaro. I don't drive anything."

"Is that how you remember it?" Carl said, raising an eyebrow.

"Yeah…You had the car and the girls to go with it."

They all laughed and somebody put Carl in a headlock and roughed his hair, saying "O'Malley's the *Man*."

Later, Alex sat at the lunch table, lost in thought, thinking about his car and Gabrielle. Then thinking about driving Gabrielle around in his car, soon scanning the lunch room for her, eventually spotting her at a table across the room, talking to her friends. He sighed, looking at the clock, unsure of how he was going to manage another twenty seven hours without seeing her. His friends had been telling a story about something funny that happened to somebody's brother when the jovial mood suddenly came to an abrupt halt. Alex could feel Carl tense and turned to see what had happened.

Dennis Wiseman stood between Carl and Ron, a hand on each of their shoulders.

"I don't mean to break up this happy little *part-tay*. But since we all know you're itching for it, I thought I'd make it a little easier for you. You can just come and get it. After school. Warehouse off Caffrey. Alex knows where it is. Don't you, Alex?"

Alex watched Carl's face turn as red as his hair, but Carl remained calm.

"That won't be necessary Wiseman," Carl said, roughly brushing Dennis's hand off his shoulder. "We're gonna just forget whatever happened happened, okay? So you can just get your sorry ass out of here."

"But I humiliated your boy. Doesn't that *piss* you off? Kicked his ass—you should have seen it. He obviously doesn't *remember* how to fight back. Won't be much good to you on the wrestling team next year, will he?"

Ron started to get up, but Carl held him back, clearing his throat.

"What happened is between you and Alex. We won't be getting involved. So once again, I invite you to take your sorry ass back to your table."

"Are you kidding me? You're not going to defend his honor?"

"We can't," Carl said between his teeth. "He's put a *veil of protection* on you."

Dennis stepped backwards, completely taken off guard. "What the *fuck*?"

At this, Alex's friends began snickering, and Alex could tell even Carl was having a hard time keeping a straight face.

"What the fuck is that? Is he a fucking moron, or something?"

"Why don't you ask him? He's sitting right here," Carl said.

But it was too late. The tension was broken, and all of his friends burst out laughing simultaneously. Embarrassed and bewildered, Dennis cursed under his breath before sauntering back to his table.

But Alex soon forgot the incident entirely, looking forward to his last two classes of the day and the chance to pass Gabrielle another note. *I'm going to Rock n' Bowl tonight*, he wrote. Minutes later, he felt something hit the back of his head. The ball of paper lay on the ground next to his desk. *Good for you.* He shook his head, turning around to look at her, but her gaze remained steadfast in her textbook. *Maybe you can stop by*, he wrote, hurling it back at her, aiming for her head this time. It hit her in the forehead before dropping into her lap, and he caught a smirk. But the reply didn't come until after class, left on his desk. *Nope.*

Frustrated, he sat further back in the room during his last period, where he could be closer to her desk and continually pelt her if he had to. Instead, he scribbled one word, wadded the sheet into a ball and tossed it back to her. It said *Library?* And landed in her open textbook.

When the class was half over and she still hadn't responded, he turned around in his desk, determined to stare at her until she looked up. He didn't have to stare long. She looked up and smirked, mouthing *okay* and then motioned for him to pay attention to the teacher, a task he found utterly futile.

He waited in the stacks, his heart racing and then jumping when she turned the corner and was standing there, alive and in front of him. "Hi," he said, grinning sheepishly.

She smirked. "Hi...What do you want?"

"To be with you. I can't wait until tomorrow—seriously," he said, taking a step towards her, their bodies nearly touching since she had nowhere to go in the narrow aisle.

She blushed, looking down. "We can't, not here. I told you. And I can't see you tonight, either... But if I could, I would—okay?" she said, her tone softening.

He reached out and touched one of her pony tails. It felt soft. "Okay... Three-thirty tomorrow, right? You'll have to pick me up, though...I'm sorry. My parents won't let me borrow the car."

"It's okay. I was planning on it, actually."

He touched her cheek, but she turned away. "I really have to go—we can't...Tomorrow, okay?" His heart fell, but she smiled at him reassuringly, and he watched her walk away, pony tails swinging.

His friends picked him up after eight thirty, and all of them packed into Carl's beige 1986 Buick. Since Rock 'n Bowl didn't start until ten, they hung out at Sacajawea Park on the shore of the lake, drinking beer and shooting the shit about school, sports, girls, politics and whatever else somebody wanted to talk about. Alex could only listen, unable to participate in any discussions regarding their school or social life, only occasionally able to comment on politics, current events or movies.

"You're awfully quiet, Fahlstrom," somebody said, Chad or Stewart, he forgot which.

Alex shrugged. "Sorry...I just...I can't really talk about things I don't remember."

"Well, why don't you talk about what you do remember," Carl suggested. "Why don't you tell us a bit about this other life?"

"Yeah, the one where O'Malley gets the car and the girls," somebody joked.

"Yeah, Fahlstrom. Why don't you just tell us about O'Malley."

"This oughta be good."

Alex sighed, debating in his mind whether sharing anything with them was a good idea but ultimately deciding it couldn't hurt. The times spent hanging out with them had been among his fonder memories. And for the next half hour, he told them a bit about their band, avoiding any mention of Kansas City, letting them think it could have happened in Polson. The idea that they were all in a rock band had them in hysterics, especially since Alex Tate had despised heavy rock, being into country and pop music, Springsteen and Mellencamp the extent of his tolerance. They all eagerly wanted to know what instruments they played and spent a few minutes joking about that. Finally, somebody asked the band's name.

Alex laughed. "It didn't have a name…But it could have been called Carl's Band. It was his band, anyway. He started it."

Everyone laughed except Carl, who stared at Alex thoughtfully. "Are you serious, man? It was *my* band?"

Alex nodded. "Yeah…It wouldn't have even existed without you. I mean—you pulled everyone together. You even got us our first gig. New Year's Eve."

After amusing them with a few details about the New Year's Eve party, the five decided to head to the bowling alley and claim their lanes, Rock n'Bowl being a popular Friday night activity. It was a large bowling alley with an arcade and restaurant. The group grabbed two lanes in anticipation of being joined by their girl friends and were able to get almost a full game in before the girls actually showed up. When Alex saw Trisha, he immediately felt flushed, then dizzy, and headed to the restroom to try to recover. He was leaning over the sink when Carl joined him.

"Are you okay?" his friend asked, concerned.

Alex shook his head.

"What's wrong?"

"I can't see her, Carl…I can't do this."

"Are you serious?"

Alex nodded.

"But she's…She wants to see you, Alex. She saw you in school today and was so happy. You have no idea how happy you made her. Made all of us, actually. Seriously, man—it meant a lot to us that you finally cleaned up."

"I didn't do it for her . . ." He turned on the water and began splashing it onto his face, trying to cool himself down.

"Well, she doesn't think it's over, Alex. Not officially, that is."

"What are you talking about?" he said, his heart starting to race.

"Trisha…You don't get it, do you—"

At this, Alex turned on his friend. "No, *you* don't get it Weiss. You have no idea who she is to me. Because if you did, you'd stop throwing her at me. Stop pushing us together. You'd be a friend and keep her the hell away from me."

Carl turned red, shaking his head. "Be a *friend*? Are you serious, man? Be a friend and *keep her away* from you? That's…that's really ironic coming from a guy who said he'd kill me if I ever laid a hand on her," he laughed bitterly.

"What are you talking about?"

"Oh, that's right…You don't remember do you? How convenient."

"No, I don't. I have no idea what you're talking about."

"I have been in love with Trisha Kurtz as long as you have. And, yeah, okay—you won her. You won her heart three years ago. But you know what? You *lost* it. You didn't fight hard enough to keep it. Shit, you didn't even appreciate what you had after awhile. But you wouldn't let her go. And you knew I would do anything to be with her…But what did you do? Told me that if I ever dated her, I would be betraying you. *Betraying*. That I would be the lowest form of scum if I ever dated her. And you managed to scare her, too. Scare her into staying with you. And now she feels so fucking guilty, I don't…I don't know. But you're the only one who can release her, man. And you at least owe her that."

Alex studied his friend in pensive silence for a few moments, ignoring the comings and goings of other patrons, remaining frozen in place. He knew there was a bigger story and, since it involved Alex Tate, one that involved senseless pain and drama.

"Did I hurt you, Carl?" he asked quietly.

Carl looked at him, taken aback. "What?"

"Did I hurt you? Did I hurt our friendship?"

Carl turned red, and he shook his head, flustered. "No…I mean. No. You just. You just—"

"I was just an asshole. I have no doubt, I was an asshole."

Carl hung his head despondently.

"Look," Alex continued. "I want to make things right, okay? If I can—I want to make whatever I fucked up right again. But I need your help, man…I don't know how to fix something I don't remember breaking. I need you to tell me what to do, and I'll do it. Whatever it is—I'll do it. okay?" He put a hand on Carl's shoulder and was surprised to see his friend's eyes well with tears.

Carl nodded. "Yeah—thanks, man. You've always been my best friend…You've always been there for me, and…And that's why I've stuck with you. Through all this shit these past ten months. It's been a fucking hell of a year, man."

Alex couldn't imagine. "What do you want, Weiss? You want to go out with Trisha?"

He nodded. "You know I do…And, stop calling me Weiss," he joked, hitting him on the arm.

"Alright…Sorry, *O'Malley*. I'm—I'm ecstatic you want to go out with her, actually. You have no idea how happy I am. Seriously, man. I am seriously happy for you. So—how do we make this happen?"

Carl shook his head, laughing nervously. "I can't believe this…I almost don't believe you."

"*Believe me*," Alex said sincerely. "So, what's the game plan?"

Carl brushed his face with his sleeve and simply requested that Alex sit down with her at some point in the evening, over a soda or something, and formally break up with her. But nicely, he repeated more than twice, nearly begging Alex to be kind to her, for she had shown him nothing but loyalty.

"Alright," Alex burst after his friend's fifth plea. "I'll be nice…I can be nice, you know? I'm not a complete dick."

Somebody had assigned teams while he and Carl were in the restroom, pairing Alex with Trisha, Carl with some other girl and so on. Alex didn't recognize any of the other girls, completely disinterested in their presence. Upon seeing him, Trisha smiled shyly, and he was again taken aback by how perfect she looked, even in jeans, which were so straight, he wondered if she ironed them. Her blond hair was swept back into a clip, not a strand out of place, and her smile revealed perfectly white, straight teeth. He shuddered inwardly, wondering what Alex Tate and Carl saw in her, unable to even fathom making out with someone like that and possibly wrinkling their perfectly pressed blouse.

When it was her turn, she gracefully walked up to the line and stood for a moment, her feet poised as if she were at a pageant, holding the ball like a victory bouquet before awkwardly dropping it with a thud. It wobbled down the lane slowly, eventually landing in the gutter. She shook her hand out, wringing it, and Alex wondered if she had hurt herself.

Instinctively, he walked up to her. "You okay, there?"

She bit her lip, refusing to make eye contact. "I'm not very good at this," she said quietly, still holding her injured hand.

Alex waited with her for the ball to return. He then picked it up for her. "Jesus, Trisha," he said, laughing. "It's no wonder you hurt yourself. This ball is way too heavy for you…Here, let me take your turn for you, okay?"

She nodded, smiling.

The action was met with loud protests, but he waved them off, telling them he was pinch hitting for an injured bowler. "I'll get you a spare," he whispered to her. "Watch this."

Hurling the ball down the lane, he watched in pleasure as all ten pins fell to the ground.

"Booya," he yelled to his booing opponents. "Let's go find you a different ball," he said, leading her away from the lane and toward the ball racks. But she was still wringing her hand.

"Are you sure you're okay?" he asked, concerned.

She shook her head.

"Here—let me see," he reached out, but she held her hand close to herself.

"No—no. It's ugly. I—I broke a nail, and it hurts. I broke two, actually. They look terrible."

He would have laughed out loud if she didn't look so sincerely downcast and in actual physical pain. Instead, he saw this as the opportunity to have the talk and asked her if she would like to sit out and grab a drink at the restaurant. She nodded in relief.

"You look good," she started nervously, once they had been seated at a small table. "Almost like yourself."

"Well, thank you. And you look nice, as well."

She blushed.

They requested two sodas and talked for a few minutes about school, the weather and current events.

"You know...I did a lot of reading about comas while you were...Anyway, they say memory loss is common. But it can come back...Has any of yours come back?" she asked.

He shook his head.

"You still don't know who I am? You don't...You don't remember me at all?"

"No."

She stared down at her lap. "I'm sure you've been told, though...You've heard we were dating. For three years, actually...It's hard...It's still hard for me, you know, to let go. I keep thinking that—that you're going to recover. Any day now...And when you do, when you remember us, you'll...You'll want it back. So I keep waiting . . ."

"Trisha," he said. "Stop waiting. Please. You can go—move on. It's okay. You don't have to stay with me any longer, really. I—I doubt I'm going to ever recover, and...And even if I do, why would I—" he stopped himself.

"Be upset?" she said. "Because you would, you know. You'd be very upset if you remembered."

"Look, I think the best thing we can do is…Well, pretend I died, you know? Pretend that part of me—that part of us—died, unfortunately. And I know that sounds horrible and, and callous, but…But you've got to move on. You do… And, and I need to move on. And, well…Somehow I just. I'm just not sure you'd date a guy like me. Like who I am now."

"*Who* are you now?" she burst. "How have you changed? Really—because, I don't know. I haven't even had a chance to get to know you again."

He sighed. "Alright…Well, let me tell you a bit about myself, then…I like rock and roll. Love it, actually…Play guitar—acoustic and electric…I do play football, but I don't wrestle or run cross country or, or play baseball…I ski…And I fish…But I hate hunting…I hate guns, to be honest with you. I don't even want to see a gun again for awhile . . ."

She laughed sympathetically. "Yes. I can understand that."

"Yeah…So then you can understand why I'm withdrawing my applications to *West Point* and the *Naval Academy*."

"What?" she said, looking at him in shock. "You *what*?"

"I'm not going—I'm not joining the military right now. I'm just not."

"Does Carl know this? Did you tell Carl? He's going to be devastated. That was your dream—both of you…Oh, my god. Why? How could you?"

He shrugged.

"How could you just give up like that? After working so hard. That's all you ever wanted, you said, to become an officer…To become an officer and to marry me, that's what you said," she said quietly, brushing a tear away. "Of course, you don't remember that…I'm sorry. I have no right to be upset. It's not your fault."

"Yeah, well…*Carl* will make an excellent officer, you know. I mean—he's quite a guy. And quite a friend. My best friend, I know. Even though I don't remember, I can just tell. You know, people like Carl who—who have those kind of qualities. Honesty. Integrity. A strong sense of loyalty—to their friends and country. They're rare. Very rare. He's a great guy."

She nodded, refusing to make eye contact.

"It's funny," Alex continued, carefully choosing his words. "When I look at you, and…and I look at Carl. When I think about the two of you, you know…I just—If I didn't know any better, I would have thought you were a couple. Really. You just…You just seem like you belong together. But I guess, I guess that's natural…For me on—on some subconscious level to want my best friend and my, my best girl to be together. It's silly, I know . . ."

She stared at him wide-eyed, as if confirming his sincerity. "Do you mean that?"

"It's crazy, I know…But, yes. Yes, I absolutely mean that. And, you know… If—if this accident somehow brought the two of you closer, you know, and I can understand why it would have…I, I think that's great. I mean…At least something positive came out of it, you know?"

"Nothing happened between us, Alex," she said, suddenly nervous.

"I don't think anything happened between you…I'm just saying . . ."

She stared at him dumbly, waiting apprehensively for him to continue.

"Shit, Trisha," he finally burst, throwing his hands in the air, suddenly losing all patience. "Just go out with Carl. *Please*. He's horribly in love with you—and I don't need a memory or even much of a brain cell to see that. Fucking Christ."

She shrunk back in her chair, wide-eyed.

"I'm serious, okay?" he continued with vehemence, unable to stop himself despite having obviously frightened her with his sudden change in tone and mood. "Please. I want you to go out with him—I mean, if you want to, that is. Actually, even if you don't want to, *please do*—as like a last request from me. A final favor. Shit. I can't take this anymore…This is fucking driving me crazy…This conversation is driving me crazy."

After collecting herself, she straightened her posture and cleared her throat. "You—you want me to go out with Carl? Your best friend—"

"Yes—*for the love of god*, yes. In fact, I'll put it in fucking writing, if you want. I'll even sign it—in blood, since you don't seem to believe me. Jesus."

"Do you always use such foul language," she said, staring down, wringing her hands nervously. "You never used to . . ."

"Fuck yes."

At this, he got her to laugh.

"Alright…I guess I could go out with him. At least once…If you want me to, that is."

"Nothing would make me happier. In fact—you should go to *prom* together," he suggested.

"He has to *ask* me to prom."

"Yeah, well, *I'm* asking you on his behalf, since I have no manners anyway. No sense of propriety whatsoever…Go to prom with him. You'll make his day. His life, maybe."

She blushed, and he left money on the table to cover their drinks and tip. They rejoined their group, and he swapped bowling partners with Carl, winking at him knowingly, hoping he had cleaned up yet another one of Alex Tate's debacles.

Though he had gotten to bed late, he woke up early, unable to sleep, too excited about seeing Gabrielle again. To distract himself, he walked the dog, helped his mother with chores in the morning and begged his father to drag him along on his errands, mostly because he hoped it would afford him an opportunity to practice driving. He then pumped his father for information about his car, asking when he would be able to drive it again, but his father simply grunted.

After Alex kept pressuring him, his father burst *"When we're convinced you won't run it into a wall,"* abruptly ending the conversation.

Alex was showered, dressed and ready by three, selecting his best pair of jeans and the nicest of his plaid flannel shirts, and combing his hair but ultimately letting the curled locks fall where they may. To his relief, Gabrielle showed up a few minutes early and was waiting in the front hallway for him, his mother having greeted her while he checked himself and his wallet before heading down the stairs.

He stopped mid-way down, completely taken aback by her appearance, which was neither Goth nor punker but trendy, even stylish—like someone from a large modern city, like New York. Some of her long dark hair was pulled up into a pony tail on the top of her head, the rest hanging down around her shoulders. She wore a short skirt of denim and plaid—the fitted waist made from a pair of jeans and the bottom pleated wool plaid—black tights and black heels of some sort, it was hard to tell, but they added at least two inches to her height. Her black fitted jacket was partially unzipped, revealing her chest, bare with the exception of a metal studded black band that fit around her neck like a collar. Her face seemed absent of the make-up he had seen earlier in the week—of almost any make-up at all, with the exception of her lips, their dark red shade making them look even fuller than usual.

Feeling the start of an erection, a sensation he hadn't felt in months, he choked on his greeting.

Gabrielle winked at him, and he nearly covered himself, feeling harder.

"Alex, your father and I would like you to be home by eleven, okay?" his mother said, smiling brightly at the two of them. "Okay, Gabrielle? That should give you more than enough time to eat and watch a movie, goodness. In fact, if you get done earlier, you're both welcome to come back here and watch television."

"Okay, Miss Jayne," Gabrielle said, smiling at his mom.

"Gabrielle, honey, can I talk to you a moment," his mother said, before quietly leading her out of the hall and out of earshot. Alex rolled his eyes and sat on the steps, somewhat relieved by their exit, hoping to get his sexual excitement under control.

Gabrielle followed Mrs. Fahlstrom into the living room, trying to hide her nervousness. She had spent the entire day deliberating over what to wear—wanting to present herself to Alex in the most honest way possible, wanting to avoid being who she thought he wanted her to be. If they were to have a future together, it would be decided tonight, in the next eight hours, when she would fully share with him who she was and, if the opportunity warranted, what had transpired between them. He would learn the ugly truth anyway at some point, she thought to herself, deciding it would be best if he heard it from her first.

"Sweetie, I'm a little nervous about tonight," his mother said, folding her arms. "I mean, we appreciate your reaching out to him—we do. *You have no idea.* But, this is his first night out like this. His first date, you know, since the accident. And, well—you're just going so far away. I wish you would stay closer. Maybe see a movie in Rohan instead."

Gabrielle bit her lip. "Well—there's just so much more to do in Missoula. It'll be okay. My dad taught me what to do in case he has a seizure—"

Jayne Fahlstrom stared at the ceiling as if in prayer. "Oh, dear lord, honey. Let's certainly hope that doesn't happen."

"Miss Jayne…. What does the Lord say?" Gabrielle asked, gently laying a hand on her arm.

"What?"

"You know—what does the Lord say? About this. Ask him."

Jayne blushed, staring down at the floor. "Oh, Gabby."

"Really," Gabrielle asked sincerely. "How do you feel—right now?"

"Nervous. And anxious—very anxious…But happy. Also very happy. To see you two together again, you know. Friends again." she said, smiling, taking Gabrielle's hand in her own.

Gabrielle smiled. "Well, we'll go with *that*. See you at eleven, Miss Jayne." And she spun around, bounding out of the room.

But Jayne followed her, then followed both of them to the front door, calling out to Alex as they left the house. "Alex Michael, you be a gentleman. I mean it."

"She calls you Alex Michael?" Gabrielle asked, laughing, as they got into the car.

"Yeah...I told you. That's my name. That's who I am."

She nodded absently, starting the car, handing him the CD case and letting him pick the music. He flipped through the pages, relieved to have something on his lap and deciding to keep it there until his still throbbing erection had calmed.

"You look very nice," he said.

"Thank you," she said simply.

"Even more beautiful than I remember," he mumbled.

She blushed but remained silent, wanting to return the compliment but unable to do so. He selected *Quadrophenia* by The Who. They drove awhile in silence, listening to the music.

"So, how was bowling?" she asked.

"Oh, Jesus...Well, I'm officially a free man, I guess...I officially broke up with Trisha Kurtz," he said. "Now, that is a baffling relationship. Do you have any insight into that?"

She pursed her lips, her stomach nerves tensing.

"Did you know Carl was in love with her?" Alex continued. "I guess he has been...How fucked up is that?...You know, there's something else going on there...There has to be. There's more to that story, I just...I don't have a clue. I don't even know what Alex Tate saw in her. I feel nothing. Nothing at all."

"Well, *you* shouldn't," Gabrielle said wryly. "Not if she was your *sister*."

"Yeah—you're right. You're *so right*. Thank you. Thank you for being the only person in the world who understands all this. But still, if you don't mind my asking...Was Alex Tate in love with her? Do you know?"

"Yes...He was very much in love with her. Since the sixth grade—when she first moved here. Everyone was in love with her, but especially Alex Tate... He spent two years trying to win her over, too."

"Do you think she loved him? You know...back."

Gabrielle nodded. "Oh, yes—definitely. They were quite the couple, you know. An *institution* among couples. Like, the perfect match."

"So, um...I don't know...What do you think the sex was like, there?"

"Alex," Gabrielle burst, laughing. "Jesus . . ."

"Well, it's a natural question to ask. Come on. I mean, if you're with someone for three years, I'd imagine you'd do it at some point, right? And, I just...I'm just not imagining it. That's the thing. I can't even imagine it...I mean, have you seen her?"

"Every day," Gabrielle said dryly.

"Yeah, but—have you seen her clothes? Her—her hair? Her nails? Jesus...

It's like she stepped out of a catalogue…How do you get close to that, you know? I can't . . ."

"You don't," Gabrielle said quietly. "You don't get physically close to that…And, they didn't."

"Didn't what?"

"Have sex."

"How do you know?"

"He told me…But he didn't even have to. Trisha's virginal. She's all but proclaimed it. Very Christian, too, you know—community services oriented. I think it's part of her pageant duties, actually. In charge of S.A.D.D. In the Key Club. Volunteers at some homeless shelter in Missoula. You know, that kind of thing…She's really nice, Alex. She's nice to everyone. And not fake, either, like some people. Like you might expect her to be."

But Alex was still baffled by the absence of sex. "I couldn't do it…I just couldn't."

"Do what?"

"Date someone for three years and not have sex. Shit, I can't even go for three months without losing my mind."

"Is that how long it's been for you?" she asked dryly.

"No—longer. It's been, like, a year. It's been fucking over a year. No wonder I'm crazy . . ."

"How is that possible? Didn't you have sex with Danielle?"

He shifted nervously in his seat, distressed by the topic and the memories of their times together—moments so passionate that just thinking about them made him ache with longing and yet wrought with so much pain and grief. "Well, not…not technically. No. I mean, we tried. It's not like, you know, she didn't want to. We just…We just couldn't."

"I don't understand…Why?"

"I don't either, believe me. I think—no, I know. It was because of my injuries. You know, from the last shooting. The last coma. I mean, the first coma, technically. The first coma."

Gabrielle stared quietly out the windshield, focusing on the highway while remembering what he had told her the other evening about Danielle, now realizing she had assumed many things, possibly in error. But she sensed his discomfort and changed the subject.

"Well, anyway, I don't think their relationship was built on sex. There are many healthy relationships that aren't, you know," she continued.

"Then what was it built on? Friendship?" he said caustically. "Were they *just friends*, because if so, what's the fucking point. Seriously. If you're going to be *just friends*, then why even date? Why the pretense?"

Gabrielle smiled, laughing to herself, having to continually remind herself that she was sitting next to Alex Tate, for he sounded and acted nothing like him. Fearing she was beginning to believe the person next to her really was *Alex Michael*, whoever that was, and wondering if his own mother had done the same thing. If, after living with him these past few weeks, Jayne Fahlstrom had begun to see a completely different person in her son and just accept it.

"Actually, I think their relationship was built on achievement."

Alex stared out the windshield, unable to even comment, so Gabrielle continued.

"You know, Alex Tate was very goal-oriented. He had huge ambitions. I mean, he always wanted to be in charge. Be in control and take the lead. Completely fearless in that regard. But he also wanted to be the *best*—at everything. And he would get horribly frustrated if he wasn't. Would push himself mercilessly. And, well—Trisha's a lot like him. She's going to be Miss Teen Montana, and I have no doubt Miss America one day. Honestly—she's that determined. And they would help each other, you know. He used to go to some of her pageants to support her, and she always went to his games and meets. Well, she's a cheerleader, too, so, that wasn't too hard…They were both straight A students. Both had college goals…and career goals and…I don't know. They were happy for awhile. For a long time, I think."

"But . . ."

"But what?"

"There's a but in there…I heard it," Alex said.

"But *nothing*."

"Yeah, well…I'm not convinced. You've convinced me of nothing except for there being some huge part of this story you're leaving out…This fairy tale romance. Where's the dragon, Gabrielle? You know, there's no such thing as Camelot…So, where's the dark side? The treachery?"

Gabrielle remained quiet.

"Okay…You don't want to talk about it. That's fine…But what about us? My mother said we had a horrible falling out, but she didn't know why. I know you know…You want to tell me about it?"

"Not really," she said quietly. "It doesn't matter to me anymore…I'm over it."

He sighed, his heart heavy, feeling as if there was a wall between them. Wanting so badly to reach across the seat and touch her, to put his arm around her, to connect with her. She was holding something back, he knew it. He feared it, too, sensing its enormity, like a massive black plume of smoke so thick one couldn't see the fire causing it. But he also knew there could be no future with her if she kept the burning secret to herself.

"Alright...Well, will you at least tell me about yourself? You said you would, you know...And I'm not talking about what you like to do or your family or your tribe and Salish culture. I want to know about *you*—who you are on a deeper level. What the family photo albums don't say...What parents don't know...What's not on your high school resume, if you catch my drift."

"There's not much to tell, really...I'm kind of boring."

"*Boring*? Are you kidding me?...Yeah—and you're a terrible liar. You are. For being an actress, you're a horrible liar."

She remained silent, not knowing what to say.

"Gabrielle...I've told you everything about myself. *Everything*. I mean, I have shared with you some of my deepest, darkest secrets...Stuff *nobody* here knows. Nobody but you. I trusted you...I don't know why. Maybe because I trusted you before. You seem...You seem very trustworthy...God, I told you about the fucking hooker. I mean, how mortifying is that? I'm not even sure I shared some of the shit with Danielle that I shared with you...And, Jennifer Hicks...God. I mean...I guess it's amazing you're even here, really... Still willing to go out with me. But...This isn't a one-way street, you know. I mean—you're so quiet. You didn't used to be. Danielle used to talk all the time. I couldn't get her to shut up sometimes...But you...I feel like...I feel like you won't even talk to me. Like, like you're still not speaking to me on some level."

She bit her lip, wanting so badly to just shout out the stupid story, wishing she could concoct a sixty-second version of it, like a commercial, and be done with it. Quickly change the channel. At the same time, she was terrified of what the knowledge would do to him, fearing he would have another seizure, possibly in the car. Wishing she could put it off until they made it to Missoula. Maybe over dinner...But dinner was no place for such a tale. No setting was right for such a tale. Except a desert, maybe. A war zone. Hell, maybe.

"I had an affair," she burst. "Okay? I had an affair with someone."

He sat back, momentarily stunned by her outburst, his mind racing with a million images, none of them pleasant. Turning the stereo volume down, he looked at her. "What did you say?"

"I said I had an affair. Last year."

"Jesus...With a *married man*? Jesus, Gabrielle—how old was he?" he asked, feeling nauseous and enraged simultaneously, hoping to god it wasn't somebody's father.

"He wasn't *married*, you idiot. And he wasn't an older man. That's disgusting."

"*Yeah*, it is…Oh, thank god," he said, throwing his head back and staring at the roof of the car, breathing a sigh of relief. "So…How is this even an affair, then?"

"Because he was in a relationship…He was in a committed relationship, that's how."

"Well, how old was he?"

"He went to Polson High…Jesus, Alex…*You* should talk . . ." She added, not meaning to be cruel to him but irked at his double standard.

"Yeah, you're right…I'm sorry…I am, I'm just…Well, I'm…You know."

"What?" she asked, testily.

Completely in love with you, he wanted to scream but didn't. "An asshole, okay. I'm an asshole. Sorry. Please continue."

"Well, there's not much more to say."

"What do you mean, *there's not much more to say*. You haven't said anything yet. Who is he? How'd it happen? How long did it last? Jesus."

Relieved he had given her a line of questioning to frame her thoughts, she continued. "Well, it happened at a party…He…He was in one of those relationships, you know. Where they've been together for a long time, but she wants to wait until marriage."

"Oh, fuck . . ." he groaned. "Does anybody fucking have sex in this town? Because they sure did the way I remember it. Or, at least *I* did."

She laughed. "Um, anyway…Well, anyway, he was at this party, and, you know—we danced a bit and probably drank a bit too much."

"Where was the girl? Why was he at a party alone? There's a sign right there . . ."

"Oh, she was out of town. On vacation or something, I don't remember… Anyway, we had a bonding session. You know…where you talk and get to know a person really well and feel like…like there's something special there. A connection."

"Like at the diner," he said quietly.

She smiled. "Yes…Like at the diner."

"Okay…So go on."

"Well…That's it."

"What do you mean *that's it*? Did you have sex with him? That night? Is that how you *bonded*?"

She blushed. "No—we didn't have sex that night. We just talked—well... We did make out. It was pretty intense, actually."

"You made out with some guy at a party, and you call that an *affair*? Jesus, you are a drama queen...Literally."

She laughed.

"Keep going."

"Um...Well...I don't know what else to say, I mean...We did keep seeing each other on the side for awhile."

"For how long?"

"A couple months."

"Did you sleep with him?"

She bit her lip.

"You slept with him, didn't you...You had sex with this guy."

"I know, I know—it was a horrible, slutty thing to do. It was . . ."

"It wasn't a slutty thing to . . ." he said quietly.

"Yes it was...It was...I feel so slutty just...just thinking about it. I do."

"Gabrielle, did you love him?"

She remained silent gripping the steering wheel, staring intently at the stretch of road ahead.

"Did you love him, Gabrielle?"

She nodded. "Yes...Very much."

"Then how are you a slut? How can you even think such a thing—let alone say it. That's a horrible thing to say about yourself, and it's...It's not true. Do you want to know what a slut is? Do you?"

She shrugged, her stomach quivering, her hands starting to shake.

"A slut is someone who doesn't really love the person she has sex with, okay. It's someone who just loves sex—but it could be with any guy. Sluts have sex with anyone—they happily change partners, like a flavor of the month. There's no real sense of commitment. But the guy thinks there is, see... The guy who sleeps with a slut, thinks he's special...Thinks he's *the man*... And when he finds out he's not...Well, thus the term. And the reputation. Okay? I know...I've been that guy...I've been the guy thinking he's...he had something special going with a girl who, well...Who didn't think so herself."

"Jennifer Hicks . . ." she said quietly.

He nodded.

"Well...I still feel awful. It feels awful...It was the biggest mistake of my life. And, I'm sorry for it."

"Yeah, well...I can tell you how it ended. He didn't leave his girl, did he?"

Gabrielle sniffed, trying to hold back tears. "No."

"They never do…I should say, we never do. I am, after all, of that species…He break up with you then?"

She shook her head. "No…I ended it."

"Really?" he asked, surprised. "Shit…That probably pissed him off."

"You have no idea."

Something in her tone, the way she tensely held her body, the way she gripped the steering wheel, her knuckles almost white, told him there was more. "What did he do?"

"Got angry…Like you said."

"How angry?"

"Very angry."

"Did he hit you?"

"Something like that . . ."

Alex felt his body flush with heat and his nerves tense. "Did he assault you?"

"Something like that . . ."

"Jesus, Gabrielle—what the fuck. You break up with the guy, and he fucking rapes you?"

She winced upon hearing the word, a word so violent in its implication, she wished it were verboten to speak.

"Who is this guy? Where is this guy?"

"He's gone," she whispered.

"Gone? Gone where…He moved?"

"Something like that . . ."

"Where? Went to college? What?"

"Something like that . . ."

Alex's mind raced, as did his pulse and his heart. His nerves fired frantically, causing all of his muscles to tense simultaneously, as a very ugly picture formed in his mind, a very ugly memory, a horrific scene from a distant dream. The realization hit him with such intensity that he exhaled as if he had been punched in the gut, his body nearly collapsing under the weight of it, burying his head in his hands against the dashboard.

"Alex—are you okay?" Gabrielle cried out nervously, reaching out and placing a hand on his arm, searching for a place to pull over.

"He did it to you, didn't he . . ."

Gabrielle clicked on her turn signal and began slowing the car down, her hands shaking, praying he didn't have another attack.

"The fucking bastard…I hate him…I fucking hate him," he sobbed.

Pulling well onto the shoulder, she turned off the car and turned her attention to Alex, scooting close to him and putting her arms around him. "It's okay...It's over...It is...I promise."

"How could he do that to you? How could he?" he sobbed, his head still buried in his arms. "You were his friend...You grew up together...I saw the pictures . . ."

"I know . . ." she said, holding him tighter, her eyes welling with tears.

"I can't fix this...How can I fix this...How can I possibly . . ."

"You don't need to fix it . . ."

"I do," he said, sitting up, looking at her in agony. "I want to fix it...I'd do anything to fix it...What can I do?"

She smiled through her tears, putting a hand to his face. "Just...Just tell me you love me. That you're sorry...That it was a mistake. Just—a horrible, mistake. You know, something done in a fit of rage—without thinking it through...That's all I ever wanted him to do...That's all he needed to do was . . .Was to just tell me he still loved me. He was still my friend...But he didn't. He never did...He never even spoke to me again. And when he... When he would look at me, it was with hate...And disgust. And it broke my heart, because...I've loved him. I've loved him my whole life...Since we were children...And...He just never saw it. Never felt it, I guess, which is strange...I don't know if anyone told you, but...Alex Tate and I were, kind of psychically connected, you know. We—we shared some of the traits that identical twins have been known to do. Like, feeling each other's pain or knowing how the other is feeling. Our moms think it's because of our births...Being born at the same time. Who knows . . ."

He grabbed her hand, holding it tightly. "What happened to it? The connection . . ."

She shook her head, wiping her face with the back of her free hand. "I don't know...I went into a coma the same time he did, you know...Or, maybe you don't. Most people don't know. I mean, the big story was the shooting... But, anyway—I woke up from mine as if nothing happened. I didn't even know what did happen," she laughed quietly. "I was so disoriented—waking up in a hospital bed. I didn't even know how I got there—or why I was there."

"Have you felt anything since then? You know . . ."

She shook her head. "No...Nothing physical, that is. When I got really depressed a few weeks ago, I thought I might be, but...No. The seizures I should have known about—felt them but didn't. Or your suicide attempts... Nothing. I'm sorry. . ."

He released her hand, sitting back in his seat, sighing. Feeling both completely responsible and yet utterly removed from what had happened. Still having no memory of it, no concept of it. As horrified by it as she was, he wanted nothing more than to be able to wipe away the mess of pain, shame and guilt that now sat like a giant cesspool between them.

"Maybe he broke it," he said finally. "Maybe he broke the connection."

She remained silent, staring at her empty hand.

"Maybe that was his gift to you...His apology. He died...And, you could have died with him, maybe you should have, but...He let you go. Because he loved you and...He didn't want you to suffer with him. You know...He didn't want you to suffer anymore."

She said nothing but smiled at the thought, it was such a lovely thought, one that suddenly seemed to be reflected in the world around them, in the stretch of green, wildflower-strewn fields on either side of the highway. In the majestic skyline of the mountain range ahead. In the beautiful blue of the afternoon sky, dotted with a few white clouds, gliding through the atmosphere on the gentle spring breeze.

"So...Alex Tate dies...And then *you* show up . . ."

"Yep."

She laughed. "*Where* did you come from, Alex Michael? Where on earth?"

He grinned. "Kansas."

She burst out laughing again.

"Dropped here just like Dorothy...And just as fucking confused as she was. This place feels like fucking Oz sometimes, too. I swear . . ."

"So, are you still trying to get home?"

"I fucking was—let me tell you. Why do you think I stepped in front of that truck a few weeks ago? Jesus Christ...It was a nightmare. It's been a fucking nightmare...But, I guess it has been for you, too."

She shrugged. "Yeah...A little bit."

"Gabrielle...Do you want to go back? I mean, really. We don't have to go out—we can turn around."

"No," she said, frowning. "Do you?"

"No...No, I don't but...I mean...I look like him, don't I? Sort of?"

"Sort of...Not really. I mean, I can see a resemblance. Until you open your mouth, that is," she said, laughing.

He smiled but then shook his head sadly. "I...I was really excited about today," he said, staring into his empty lap, the CD case having fallen to the floor of the car.

"So was I…Look—I dressed up and everything."

"Yeah…you did," he said, looking askance at her.

"Do you like it—my outfit? I got it in New York…Over spring break."

"Yeah, it's…it's hot. You look…You look very . . ."

They stared intently at each other, letting their eyes convey what words could not, the air between them, so heavy at first, growing lighter, brighter, as if the car and all its barriers had disappeared, and they were seated outside, in the grass, surrounded by fresh air and infinite possibility.

Blushing, she started the car. "Well, let's move on, then. The music store closes early—before six, I think, and we're not even halfway there."

They spent rest of the drive listening to music and talking about music and other interests, the past becoming more distant with each milepost. The Missoula Morgenroth Music Center was just around the corner from the Goodwill store. Gabrielle's family had purchased all of their instruments there, so she was on close terms with the staff, soon chatting excitedly with them about a candy apple red Pearl Export drum set. While Alex was browsing through the acoustic guitar section, a huge racket broke out and he realized Gabrielle was test driving the set, putting on a show for the entire store.

She was a good drummer, he thought, light years ahead of Carl Weiss, and she even had the stick twirling moves. But it was funny seeing her there, in such a different role. For a moment, he thought longingly of Danielle, remembering their times listening to and playing music together, mostly classical or folk. Trying to imagine such times with Gabrielle, knowing they could happen but would have such a radically different energy.

Upon finishing her solo and receiving a round of applause from the handful of people in the store, she slid off the stool and reluctantly set the sticks down, staring longingly at the drum set before rejoining Alex.

"Those are so *sweet* . . ." she sighed. "So how are you faring? Did you find anything?"

He carefully picked up a used Martin D-35 six-string acoustic and after politely asking a sales assistant if he could play, the two of them settled in the back of the store. While Alex adjusted the tuning and got comfortable with the instrument, Gabrielle sat on her hands, which were starting to shake in nervous anticipation, She did not believe that Alex could possibly know how to play guitar, given that he had never touched one before. And she began to fear that the frustration which would accompany his realization that he could not play might cause another seizure.

"Don't you need a pick . . ." she said.

"Nope," he said, beginning to strum the first chords of a familiar tune, soon humming along to it, grinning at Gabrielle who quickly picked up on the piece, Nick Drake's *Know*. He started softly singing the lyrics, taking the short song to completion.

Gabrielle was stunned, almost too shocked to fully enjoy the song, one of her favorites. But before she could say anything, he launched into *Dust In the Wind*, softly singing a few verses before she interrupted him.

"Oh, my god, Alex...*Oh, my god*...How do you—where did you?"

He grinned widely, "You didn't think I could play, did you?"

"No...Why would I? Where did you even learn?"

"In my *head*, I guess," he said sarcastically, then launched into a riff from Vivaldi's *Lute Concerto in D, Allegro*.

After her shock had worn off, she excitedly put in a few requests of her own, until a staff member approached them saying the store was closing in a few minutes.

"We're not leaving without a guitar," she said, jumping up from her seat and bounding to the front of the store to talk to the manager, who offered them a less expensive model for twenty dollars down and a hand-shake promise that Gabrielle would be back the following weekend with the rest of the money. If she didn't, the manager warned with mock sternness, he would be calling her parents. He then found a used case in the back and offered it to them for free, his gift for all the business the Trahans had sent them.

If Gabrielle had been quiet up to this point, the guitar had opened the channels of talking. Alex laughed to himself as she chatted non-stop during their walk to the car and throughout their five-minute drive to the riverfront, parking close to the theater and deciding to walk the few blocks to The Oxford Saloon, where she wanted to eat. They held hands as they walked, stopping to look in window fronts along the way. But instead of being annoyed, Alex was relieved at her excited chatter, the mood between them so vastly different than just a few hours prior. They were feeling like old friends by the time dinner had ended and they headed back to the theater, this time arm in arm.

It was during dinner that he began to notice the differences between Gabrielle and Danielle, starting with what they ate, Danielle always ordering a salad and Gabrielle having no issue relishing a burger and fries. Gabrielle had a bouncy, playful energy about her and a scathing sense of humor, which reminded him a bit of Brooke. And while she was as beautiful as Danielle, there was something more approachable about her, more open, and she had a mischief in her eyes, in her smirk, that would send a periodic jolt through his groin, one that would only intensify if she followed it by a light touch of her hand, or the brush of her leg against his own.

He thought about all this as they sat in the back of the theater, watching trailers for upcoming films before the main movie, *Serial Mom*, one both were ambivalent about, seeing it merely because it happened to be showing at seven. As he sat back in his seat, putting his arm around her, he was acutely sensitive to the feel of her hair on his hand, the touch of her jacket, the sound of her breathing. At some point after the movie began, he stopped watching the screen and began studying her, the graceful line of her face and neck, his eyes moving to her chest, wondering what she was wearing under the partially unzipped jacket. If she knew he was looking at her, she pretended not to, continuing to stare straight ahead, a slight smirk on her face, a smirk that could have been a dare, he mused. Testing his theory, bent down and kissed her cheek, then her ear, then moved down to her neck.

At that point, she pulled away, and he sat back, startled. But she swiftly moved to undo her studded necklace, shoving it into her purse before sitting back in her seat, scooting closer to him than she was before.

"I didn't want you to hurt yourself on it," she whispered in his ear, smirking.

After recovering, he grinned to himself, soon repeating his actions. At some point, she turned away from the screen, her lips meeting his, and they made out for a short while, until they felt someone kick the back of their seats, at which point they attempted to watch the movie.

She held his hand and a few minutes later, to his surprise, slowly moved it up her skirt until he no longer felt the touch of her cotton tights but skin, just at the thigh level, and he realized she wasn't wearing tights at all but rather those long stockings.

"Jesus . . ." he breathed, trying to calm his throbbing erection.

She leaned over and whispered in his ear. "Do you really care about this movie?"

He just shook his head, barely able to breathe.

"Wanna cruise?"

He nodded, and they both stumbled out of the theater, laughing. Neither remembered the walk to the car, only the moments after they had gotten in and immediately began making out, Gabrielle soon climbing onto his lap, her legs straddling his own, her hands holding his face, her intensity meeting his, at times exceeding it, to his pleasant surprise. As his hands moved up her thighs and she pressed herself closer to him, he actually contemplated having sex with her, right there in the car, it would be so easy, the way she was dressed.

But as he was merely contemplating this, she had already moved a step ahead, unbuttoning and unzipping his jeans, having fallen in love and lust all over again, back at the guitar store, when he played his first song. Completely enthralled with his body, so achingly familiar and yet so excitingly new, longing to kiss him, to feel the skin of his face against her own, to feel the weight of his body against her own.

She gently moved her hand down his pants, and he let her at first, completely lost in the ecstasy of the moment, a rapture that heightened as her fingers gently wrapped around his member, massaging it. An orgasm was imminent, and it was at that point that he panicked, remembering the disastrous outcomes of his prior attempts with Danielle and horrified at the prospect of reliving those with Gabrielle.

He grabbed her hand, "Stop."

She frowned. "Why? You don't like it . . ."

"No, god…I do. God…But I can't…We can't."

"Why?" she whispered, kissing his ear.

"Because I'm…I'm broken," he said sadly, holding her hand tightly.

"You don't feel broken," she said playfully, pulling her hand away and placing it on his groin.

"I am…Trust me…It happens at the end . . ."

She repositioned herself on top of him, pressing her pelvis against his own as tightly as she could without hurting him. "What happens . . ." she whispered, moving rhythmically on top of him, smiling to herself upon hearing his breathing quicken.

"I…don't want to hurt you…Please, Gabby . . ."

But the ejaculation was swift, premature and completely beyond his control. He gasped, in relief and horror. Relieved by the amazing jolt of ecstasy and horrified by the prospect of the pain and blood that he fully expected to follow. Though the pain never manifested, his body began to shake as if it had, and he kept his eyes closed, afraid to look.

She giggled and kissed his ear. "Tell me again how you're broken…Cause I'm not seeing it."

"I'm…I'm bleeding . . ." he gasped, still trembling. "Everywhere…It's everywhere…I'm sorry…I'm so sorry."

Disturbed by his response, she sat back on his lap, moving her skirt aside and looking down, but seeing nothing out of the ordinary.

"Alex…You're fine. You're …You're not bleeding. There's nothing wrong with you," she said quietly, moving to kiss him again.

But he pulled her close to himself, wrapping his arms around her tightly, burying his head in her shoulder, nearly weeping in relief.

Having more than two hours to spare before Alex had to be home, they headed back to Polson, listening to Nick Drake the entire drive, neither wanting or needing to talk, content with letting the songs hold a conversation for them. She drove to a remote area on a hill overlooking the lake, and taking a few blankets from the back of her truck, they spread out on a grassy spot nearby, using one blanket to cover the ground and another to keep them warm, the temperature chilly. The sky was clear, revealing a thick mass of stars, and they spent quite a while staring into the sky, he holding her close to himself to keep her warm.

But he soon found himself distracted by her body, the feel of her arm across his pelvis, the feel of her back under her jacket, the light floral scent of her skin. His mind was absorbed by his recovered manhood, a part of him still in disbelief that he had successfully come, the greater part wanting to try it again, to confirm its reality.

He walked through the scene in his mind first, quickly working himself into an erection, which only became harder as he began kissing her, gently at first but with greater vehemence, positioning himself on top of her, wrapping her legs around his waist, the skin of her thighs driving him crazy. She helped him to undress, helped him to unzip his own pants and push them down, even as he pulled down hers. She even helped guide him inside of her, completely opening herself to him, and once there, he remained tensely still for a moment, before pushing deeper, treating each thrust with a sense of utmost reverence, in sheer awe at the overwhelming joy and love he felt in those moments, as if he were embracing the entire universe and it embraced him in return.

She cried out, peaking slightly before he did, and he clutched her close to himself, kissing her before gasping at his own orgasm, one so explosive he nearly collapsed on her.

They lay entwined for minutes afterwards, unable to move or speak.

"I love you...I love you so much," he whispered, his breathing still heavy.

She remained silent but held him tighter.

"Please tell me this isn't a dream...Please tell me I'm going to wake up tomorrow...And you'll still be here...And we'll still be together...And we can do this again."

She smiled. "Well...It may still be a dream...But it certainly isn't *yours*."

CHAPTER SIXTEEN

When Alex and Gabrielle walked through the front door a few minutes before eleven, both parents and the dog were up and waiting to greet them, and because Alex held an obtrusive black guitar case in his hands, both were invited into the living room for pie and refreshments and grilled mercilessly for the next half hour. Alex was even made to hold a small concert for his parents who, by his fifth song, Blind Faith's "Can't Find My Way Home," finally conceded he was a good guitar player. His mother began to ask where he learned but quickly stopped, blushing and offering to get more refreshments.

They then spent another twenty or so minutes carrying on a conversation with Gabrielle, and once again, Alex was taken aback by the familiarity between her and his parents, the easy flow of talk, how she was treated as an extension of the family. And yet an hour ago, he had made passionate love to this same girl who now sat on their over-stuffed pewter blue sofa, behaving and chatting with the utmost charm as if she were at high tea.

It was after Midnight when he walked her to her car, holding her tightly before she got in, kissing her lips, her forehead, her hair.

"I don't want to let you go . . ."

She smiled to herself but remained silent, enjoying the warm envelopment of his arms.

"When can I see you again?"

She shrugged, pulling away. "Tomorrow, maybe…Tomorrow afternoon. We can go horseback riding," she offered.

He grinned widely. "You have horses?"

She smiled, shaking her head, almost having forgotten he had amnesia. "Yes…I live on a horse ranch. Why don't you come over and meet my parents and…you know…we can go riding. You know how to ride, right?"

"Of course," he said, sounding indignant. "I can rope cattle, too . . ."

She laughed out loud. "You hate cattle."

"No—I don't. He may have, but I don't…I loved working on that ranch. Does it…Does it exist by any chance?"

"What?"

"That…That cattle ranch. It was owned by some old Indian guy."

"You mean my *grandfather*?" she asked wryly.

His face reddened. "Yeah…Sorry," he said grinning sheepishly.

But she kissed him lightly, putting him at ease. "Yes…And, yes, you used to work there summers but hated it…You hated the smell… In fact, you were *so* thrilled to get a job at the convenience store this past summer."

He frowned. "I worked at the convenience store?"

She nodded.

"The same one…."

She nodded, staring at the ground, feeling the sudden tension and sorry she had caused it.

"Well…Do you think I could get my old job back?"

She looked at him, smirking. "I'll see what I can do…I'm sure I could pull some strings . . ." she said, stepping close to him and playing with a button on his shirt.

He pulled her close, embracing her again, engaging in one last kiss before she got into her car and drove into the night.

When he awoke the next morning to the blue plaid comforter, familiar wooden furniture and gray walls, he was momentarily terrified he had woken up in Kansas, finally calming down upon seeing the walls were absent of bricks. That the photo of the five children was still taped to the wall next to his bed, close enough for him to touch it, which he did.

Happy to see his pretty mother pop her head through the door to make sure he was awake and ask if he needed help getting ready for church. While he was unexcited about the prospect of going to a church service, he was relieved to be in the same life he had seemingly been in the night before. Selecting one of Alex Tate's white shirts and khaki pants, he quickly dressed and bounded down the steps with energetic exuberance.

His family attended the First Presbyterian Church of Polson, a pristine white wooden structure, complete with a bell tower. It could have been the subject of an oil painting epitomizing the historic American small-town church. His parents knew everyone, and it took them awhile just to make it from the car to the front steps of the building, and since this was Alex's first time coming to church, he was greeted and hugged or arm-pulled by everyone they knew. Thank god for his mother, he thought, who sheltered him from any extended conversation as much as she could, quickly directing people away from him and to topics not related to himself.

The church interior was more modern, with two rows of pews making up the sanctuary, all facing a small, non-descript table, which he guessed was an altar of some kind, and angled walls with large stained glass windows of religious figures whom he did not recognize. There were two rows of seats behind the table for the important people, Alex guessed, quickly becoming bored with the environment and even more bored with the actual worship, his thoughts soon moving to Gabrielle and their time together. Just thinking about her got him excited, and to stem an erection, he would occasionally grab a prayer book from the pew holder and flip through it, feigning interest. By the time the ceremony was over, he was ready to crawl out of his skin, counting down the minutes to when he could see her again.

But the walk back to the car was even more excruciatingly slow than the walk from the car, every attendant of the church feeling the need to greet him and thank their lord for bringing him back to their spiritual *family*. He shuddered, wanting nothing to do with that particular family, completely disinterested in Jesus, the Lord, God, angels and anything remotely related to those topics. Thankful that Gabrielle likely felt the same way, obviously feeling there was no sin in what they had committed the night before and wondering if she would feel inclined to do the same again, later today.

The idea of making love to her again was so distracting that he could barely concentrate on the family brunch, today at Drifter's diner, ironically, the place only serving to heighten his impatience. He ate quickly hoping to leave quickly, but his family was in no hurry, seeming to savor each bite of pancake or sausage, his dad pouring himself a third cup of coffee.

Near the end of the meal, Alex asked if he could borrow the car that afternoon.

"Where are you going?" his father asked dryly.

"Gabrielle's house...We're going horseback riding."

His sister gasped, nearly snorting her orange juice. "*What?*"

Alex looked at her dumbfounded. "What?"

"Did you say horseback riding—*with Gabrielle?*" she repeated, looking utterly astounded, as if someone had just told her a yeti had been captured right outside of town.

"Am I missing something here?" Alex asked.

His mother cleared her throat, and his father took another gulp of coffee.

"*Yeah...*You two, like, hate each other. Are you sure you aren't dreaming again?" She turned to their mother. "Is he having more amnesia?"

Her mother shook her head, pursing her lips.

"They seem to have patched their differences, Danielle...Went to a movie last night and had a good time together," his father said. "I think it's safe to say they are friends again."

Danielle Fahlstrom sat with her mouth open in mild shock.

"Oh, and, while we're celebrating life's little miracles, your brother plays excellent guitar. He gave us a concert last night, didn't you, Alex?" his mother said sweetly, her eyes wide and sparkly.

Danielle continued to look as if she had stepped into an *X-Files* episode, and Alex turned away in embarrassment, still uncomfortable with the reminder of his predecessor's treatment of Gabrielle and dismayed by his sister's reaction to their being friends again.

"I don't believe it," Danielle finally said flatly.

"What dear?" his mother asked.

"Any of it. Either of it. Any of it. Anything...you just said."

"Well, it's all true, honey, praise be Jesus on this glorious Sunday morning," his mother said with genuine delight in her voice.

But Danielle put her head in her hands.

"I'll let you borrow the car if you promise to be home by dinner time and finish your homework," his father said finally.

"He doesn't even remember where she lives," Danielle burst, exasperated.

Alex said nothing, his momentary elation now hanging by a thread.

"Do you?" his father asked quizzically.

Alex sighed, shaking his head.

"Well, I'll give you directions. She's only ten minutes away. It's not too hard to find."

After changing into jeans and casual shirts, he got the instructions from his father and, borrowing the family's light blue Taurus station wagon, headed to Gabrielle's house. As he pulled into the long drive of the 14-acre property, his heart ached with nostalgia, especially when the two-story log cabin, nestled in the trees, came into view. It was a home and property he remembered as his own, minus the horses grazing in a field near the house, the enormous barn and other structures that dotted the nearby landscape. Minus the large and beautiful flower and vegetable gardens that her family had planted, his own family having been too busy to do much with the property.

As he parked near the house, he wondered if it would look the same inside as he remembered it. The front porch was completely covered by a low hanging roof and appeared to wrap around the entire house. Slightly nervous, he knocked on the door and was met by an attractive middle-aged woman with long black braids, dressed in jeans, a denim shirt and colorful neck scarf.

It took him a moment to recognize her as Mrs. Trahan, but it took her no time to recognize him, and after receiving a welcoming hug, he was ushered into an open living and dining room area, brightly lit with white washed walls and numerous windows, each window adorned with magenta flowered curtains. Dr. Trahan was on an overstuffed brick-red leather sofa, watching the news, but also got up to greet Alex warmly, inspecting his fight wounds as he did and nodding in approval at the progress. Though he did not recognize the man as being part of the Trahan family in Kansas City, he recognized him from the hospital, Dr. Trahan having stopped in to check on him nearly every day during his three-month stay. Since he was one of a number of doctors, Alex had never asked his name but remembered looking forward to his visits, for the man always seemed to be smiling, just as he was today, and Alex felt relaxed in his presence.

The living room furniture was sparse, made of either dark red leather or wood, but the wood floors were covered with colorful rugs, and there were a number of interesting clay pots, statues, decorative wall art and house plants scattered about. Though nothing coordinated, it felt cozy. And since nothing matched, the house ceased to be as he remembered it, both his mother here and his mother in Kansas City being obsessed with color coordination.

Mrs. Trahan called upstairs for Gabrielle, and Dr. Trahan offered Alex a refreshment, which he politely declined. As he engaged in friendly conversation with her parents, Gabrielle appeared, and he smiled in relief. She was dressed in jeans, riding boots and a white blouse, her long hair in a side braid, looking stunningly beautiful but nothing like the girl he saw last night, which almost made him nervous, as if he were introducing himself to her all over again.

After a few more minutes of talk, Gabrielle grabbed her jacket and they left the house, first stopping by the stable to grab two rope halters before heading towards the field to walk two of the horses to the stable and equip them for riding.

"This is a new look," he commented.

She eyed him oddly. "What do you mean?"

He shrugged, grinning but nervous. "You look different every time I see you...I feel like I meet somebody new every time I see you."

"Well, I do consider myself an *actress*, you know," she joked. "Does it bother you?"

He shrugged, unsure if it did or didn't. It was just something he needed to get used to, as Danielle's appearance had remained fairly consistent except near the end, when she began dressing a little racier.

"It's still me," she said quietly, holding out her hand for him to take, which he did.

They walked awhile in silence.

"I see clothes as costumes, you know...And I just dress to reflect my mood or the day or the activity, you know...Today I'm dressed to go horse-back riding. Tomorrow, it's a school day, so who knows. I might feel punker, I might feel city, I might feel preppy—though not likely . . ."

He smiled to himself, musing on her comments. After a few more minutes of silence, he spoke. "You know...I remember this house and property as being my own—from my previous life. In my dream, that is. This is the house from which I moved to Kansas City...I mean, it's not exactly the same. We didn't have horses or—or all those gardens back there," he said, motioning to the distance. "And we had that big detached garage but none of the other buildings. No stables."

"Does it make you sad?"

He shook his head. "No...It's just weird. Confusing, still . . ."

When they neared the horses, she pointed out the one she thought he should ride, a reddish-brown gelding, selecting a gelding of a darker brown for herself.

"What about those horses?" he said, motioning to two jet black stallions in the distance.

She shook her head, laughing. "No way…You need to prove you can ride first."

"You don't believe me? Jesus…I know what I can do…I was right about the guitar, wasn't I?"

"I don't care…That's my horse, over there—Razor's Edge. And the other one's Brooke's. There's no way we're taking them out today…Maybe next weekend."

As they walked the horses back to the stable, discussing breeding, riding and care in general, he began to feel more comfortable with her again, the sense of familiarity returning, along with a sense of awe at his ability to share this experience with her. To his knowledge, Danielle had never even seen a horse in person, much less rode one. Yet here was Gabrielle, acting as if *he* needed training lessons.

Once in the saddle, Alex experienced a joy and exhilaration he had not felt in a long time, and after showing off a bit for Gabrielle, the two settled into a steady pace, with her slightly leading the way. The day was sunny and warm, nearing sixty degrees, offering a crisp view of the still snow-capped mountains in the distance. They wandered through fields and down roads, eventually to a ridge overlooking the lake, where Alex had to stop for a moment, suddenly in utter disbelief at his surroundings and his own happiness. Wondering if he hadn't stepped into another dream and trying to stem a creeping fear that the universe was simply toying with him, cruelly dangling a carrot, waiting for an opportune moment to snatch it away.

Gabrielle rode up next to him. "Are you okay?"

He looked out over the horizon. "Am I dreaming, Gabby? Tell me the truth."

She sighed heavily. "That's…That's such a loaded question, Alex…I mean, on some level we're all dreaming. All our lives are dreamlike…But if you think you're still in the coma—that you haven't quite woken up yet, no. You've woken up from that. There's no going back for you . . ."

"How do you know? How do you know for sure?"

"I just do…You'll have to trust me. I wouldn't lie to you."

"This just seems too perfect," he said, smiling sadly. "I mean look at this—it's…It's like a paradise. How is this even possible I'm here? I…I couldn't even begin to dream a day like today…A night like last night…It's too good to be true."

"Well…Perfection's in the eye of the beholder…Not everyone who lives here is happy here. Not everyone who looks upon this land sees the same paradise you see. Or feels the same way about it you do…You see what you want to see…You could just as easily see hell."

"Is that what he saw . . ."

"I don't know...I know he wasn't happy before he died. I know he felt trapped. That he struggled...I hope he's found peace."

Alex shook his head. "No...No he hasn't...He's still restless...He keeps haunting me. I'm just waiting, you know . . ."

"For what?"

"For him to fuck something up again...Fuck up my happiness."

She eyed him curiously, then leaned towards him. "I'll race you back," she said slyly.

He smirked. "And what does the winner get?"

"Whatever the winner *wants*," she said quietly, winking at him and sending a jolt of desire through his body, straight to his groin and literally spurring him into action.

She was an excellent rider, more skilled than he, and at times he wondered if she didn't deliberately slow down, didn't willingly give him an advantage. There was even a moment when he thought he might win, but she tore ahead, laughing, and he knew she had been toying with him the entire way.

"You're a tease," he said, chuckling as they unsaddled the horses.

"Maybe...Or maybe I'm just better than you."

He shook his head, grinning. "So—what does the *winner want*?"

She shrugged absently. "I don't know...I'll think of something."

He walked up behind her, putting his arms around her and whispering in her ear. "How 'bout a repeat of last night?"

She tossed her head. "I don't know what you're talking about."

"Yes, you do."

"No, I don't...What happened last night?"

He laughed, spinning her around to face him. "You know what happened...How could you forget? Shit...I haven't stopped thinking about it."

She mused a moment before shaking her head. "No...No, I remember nothing out of the ordinary. I mean, if you're implying something inappropriate happened between us, well...You must have dreamt it," she said simply, turning back to her horse.

"You're lying," he whispered in her ear.

"Am not...And I'm shocked you would accuse me of such behavior. I'm not that kind of girl. Good grief—it was our first date. *Please*."

At that he began to panic, starting to wonder if she wasn't being serious, if things hadn't happened like he remembered. If he had imagined the entire exchange—seen what he wanted to see. "Gabrielle," he burst, grabbing her shoulder.

She turned to him and, as if sensing his confused panic, smirked. "If something happened last night, you're going to have to jog my memory…I've suddenly developed amnesia," she said, leading her horse back to the field.

Alex followed with the other gelding, smiling to himself, beginning to understand her sense of humor, her playfulness only making her more intriguing and him more sexually stimulated. After setting the horses free, they headed back to the stable.

"Jog your memory, huh . . ."

"Yep."

He stopped her, leaning down and whispering in her ear. "It started something like this . . ." he said, moving his lips to her neck, kissing her gently.

She sighed pleasantly, and then continued walking. "Is that it . . ."

He stopped her again, this time kissing her passionately on the lips, soon French kissing her, pulling her body close to his so she could feel his hard on before letting her go.

"Is it coming back to you at all?" he asked wryly.

"A little . . ."

She walked into the stable, hanging the halters on a hook, and continued to stroll to a far dim lit corner in the back, away from where the horses were kept, where there was clean hay and hay bales. He followed and, unable to contain himself any longer, grabbed her arm and pulled her close to him, one hand wrapped tightly around her waist and the other cupping her face, kissing her vehemently. Now throbbing, he quickly moved to undo her jeans and, like last time, she helped him, seeming as anxious as he, and once they were undressed enough, he pulled her down onto one of the bales that functioned as a makeshift bed. Maneuvering on top of her, she again helped him to enter, but this time he felt more potent, more lustful, pushing as hard as he could, at times making her cry out, whether in agony or ecstasy, he did not know, but her cries only made him pull her body more tightly against his own and push harder and deeper, climaxing only when he was sure she had already done the same.

They held each other tightly for minutes afterwards, their bodies still shaking, their breathing still heavy, neither of them having the energy to move or speak. As the intensity wore off, he began kissing her, caressing her face and neck.

"God that was painful . . ." she said finally. "That was the most excruciatingly wonderful sex I've ever had . . ."

"Did I hurt you?" he asked, concerned.

"Yes…But…It was worth it in the end. Jesus…I still feel it."

They continued to lay entwined.

"I love you, you know," he whispered, holding her close.

She remained quiet.

"I'd marry you, you know…Would you marry me?"

She smiled, shaking her head. "No…No—that's too far in the future. It's as dangerous dwelling there as in the past…I can't go there with you… I prefer living in the present. In the moment."

"But this moment won't last," he said sadly.

"No…But we can create more…It's best not to worry about it…Not to try to freeze them or capture them…Just experience them and enjoy them… Then let them go."

He sighed, wanting so badly to capture her as his own, feeling she could slip away at any given moment. "Will you at least go to prom with me? Or is that too far in the future . . ."

At this she sat up suddenly. "Shit…I forgot all about prom…I have two invitations to prom, and I completely forgot to respond to either of them."

He grinned. "Well…Now you can tell them both *no*."

She shook her head, starting to dress herself. "Alex, I can't go to prom with you . . ."

"Why not?" he asked, his heart jumping nervously as he pulled up his jeans.

"Because…we can't . . ." She sighed sadly, turning to him, placing her hand on his leg. "People won't understand this…They would never accept this—they just won't. At least, not in the short-term. In a few months, maybe, but…If people knew what we just did—what we're doing, they'd . . ." She shuddered inwardly.

"They'd what?"

"I don't know…I don't even want to think about it . . ."

"But why? I don't understand why—"

"Because—that's what people do. They take single events in time, freeze them—judge them—and turn them into defining moments. And then they believe that that one moment is true for all time—that it can never change… There are people who believe that what happened between us, in the past, is unforgivable. And while we can fix it, we can't…We can't fix it tomorrow. It's just going to take time…for people to forget, you know…And I don't think three weeks is enough time."

"That's fine if we *have time*," he burst. "But what if we don't? What if we don't have three weeks? I'm not going to let what people think stop me from seeing you—I'm just not."

"Of course not," she said quietly. "Of course we can see each other. We just need to be discreet about it, that's all. We can't take this public, that's all…We have to pretend to the outside world that we're—we're acquaintances. And then we can show them we're friends and then, later…lovers."

He shook his head. "I don't like it. I don't like it at all—it's not right."

"Alex—"

"It's not—it's bullshit, and you know it. I'm not lying to the world about this. I'm not going to do what he did and hide you or us or the fact I love you—I'm just not. I'm not *him*. And I don't give a fuck what people think."

She mused thoughtfully a moment. "Alright…alright…If I go to prom with you, will you at least compromise with me?"

He eyed her pensively.

"Can we at least keep quiet about it another week?"

He nodded.

"And…Would you talk to Carl about it? You know, ask him what he thinks of your taking me to prom…He's your best friend. Maybe he can give you some perspective…If Carl accepts it, then the world will accept it…Okay?"

"Yeah…Sure. Okay."

She kissed him, and they sat on the ground against the hay bale, holding each other for awhile, extending the moment as long as they could before Alex had to head home for dinner.

He was lying on his bed attempting to study that night, when he heard the doorbell ring, a part of him hoping one of his friends or even Gabrielle had stopped by to rescue him from his government history textbook. A few minutes later his mother knocked on the bedroom door, soon peeping inside.

"Alex," she said quietly. "Honey, you have a visitor."

He looked up. "Who?"

"Well," she said, opening the door and stepping inside. "It's actually the girl from the convenience store. You know, Jennifer Hicks—the one you saved," she said.

His heart nearly stopped beating, a heated flush surging through his entire body, making him dizzy.

"Honey, she's been asking to see you…She wants to thank you, that's all. And she brought the baby."

"The baby . . ." he echoed numbly, feeling suddenly nauseous.

"Yes…She was pregnant at the time. You know this—we've told you all this," she said, walking towards him and sitting on his bed.

"I don't want to see her . . ." he whispered hoarsely.

"Alex…I know this is hard for you, but . . .Well, she's moving back to Billings next week to be with her family, and…She just wants to see you before she goes."

He shook his head. "No…I don't care. I don't—I don't even remember what happened that night. So, why does it matter? Why is she even here—I don't even know who she is," he protested, his heart racing.

His mother reached out and gently rubbed his arm. "Well…Because it matters to *her*. She knows you don't remember, and she doesn't expect you to—nor want you to, quite frankly. Nobody does. Goodness, in some ways it's a blessing you don't…Come on," she said, prodding him to get up.

"Give me a minute, okay . . ." he said quietly.

She nodded and left the room.

But he remained frozen in horrified expectation of what he would see when he walked down the steps. Of whom he would see. Of what she would say. And he could hear Alex Tate's cruel laughter as the curtain fell on his perfect day, replacing joy with pain and tragedy.

His body was trembling as he moved to get out of the bed, and he tried to shake off the vertigo as he stood up and walked towards the bedroom door, over the threshold and into the hall, stopping to collect himself before moving down the steps.

She was waiting for him in the living room, her back turned, staring out the large picture window. But he could see the blond ringlets and knew who she was before she looked at him. And when she finally did, he saw what he expected. He saw Kelly. A little older, a little sadder and dressed in torn jeans and a worn navy and white ski jacket.

Taking a step forward, she greeted him, smiling coyly at him, but he remained frozen and unsmiling, a good ten feet from her, his arms crossed. Flustered at his lack of response, she blushed.

"You don't remember me, do you?" she asked.

He shook his head.

"Not at all…Not even a little bit?"

He stared at her with blank intensity, trying to contain his loathing.

"Oh…Okay, well…My name is Jennifer. Jennifer Hicks…We…We worked at the convenience store together—last summer, and…Well, we got to be friends . . ." she said, wringing her hands nervously, and in her body language he could read there was more to the story.

"Anyway…That night you…You don't remember, but…Well, we were robbed by my boyfriend, and…you, you took the hit for me and…and my baby…He got to you first, you know."

He continued to stare, completely unmoved by her presence or what she was saying.

"I brought her," she said, motioning to a plastic, basket-looking thing with a handle that sat on the floor next to what he guessed was her purse. It was turned towards the window, and he could not see what lay in it, nor did he want to.

"Would you like to see her?"

He shook his head.

Her face fell. "I—I named her after you. Alexis. Alexis Jessica Hicks."

He felt he could vomit, the shaking becoming worse, and he knew if she didn't leave, it would soon be beyond his control, and he would either puke or pass out, possibly both. "Where's the father," he said between clenched teeth.

"Oh, he's…She doesn't have one…He's dead."

"Are you sure about that?"

She nodded, a darkness falling over her countenance. "Oh, yeah…He's gone…But it's for the best."

A noise came from the plastic basket, and he knew he didn't have much time, his body overtaken by a shaking he couldn't control. "You should go now . . ."

She looked at him, her pale blue eyes reflecting a mixture of fear and sadness. "Are you alright?"

He shook his head, "No…You need to go…And get my mother…please. . ."

But he blacked out before his mother entered the room.

∞

Long after Alex had left, Gabrielle still felt him inside her, the steaming hot shower washing away his scent, their scent and any lovemaking residue but unable to calm the aching throb, its intensity still so sharp that she could do little more than don sweats and fling herself into bed until it stopped, imagining being enveloped by his arms instead of the quilt.

Grabbing a pillow, she held it to tightly her chest, unsure of whether to laugh or cry but wishing, at that moment, they had been a little older. Old enough to have the privacy needed after an experience like that. Old enough to spend the night together, for she needed him next to her, holding her, unable to bear the thought of facing the long dark night alone with the raging aftershocks of an orgasm she could only describe as brutal—brutally painful and brutally blissful.

So she clutched the pillow tighter, pretending it was he, her only comfort being words. His words of love and assurance that he wanted to be with her for a long time. Taking a deep breath, she smiled to herself, starting to relax some of the tension, when the door flew open with a bang.

"Mom wants to know why the dishes aren't done . . ."

Gabrielle groaned, burying her head in the pillow. The cat padded in and jumped onto the bed, his heavy paws kneading into her stomach as he walked over her.

"What the fuck, Gabby? It's nine o'clock—are you sick or something?"

Gabrielle sat up, pushing her cat to the side. "Fine...I'll do the fucking dishes. Jesus. Can't anyone get any *privacy* around here? Can't anyone just take a nap . . ."

Brooke's eyes narrowed intently. "A nap? At nine o'clock at night? Are you kidding me?"

Gabrielle smiled to herself before flinging the cover aside.

"Oh, my god—did you masturbate or something? Is that what you've been doing in here?"

"No!" Gabrielle protested vehemently. "Really, Brooke—*please*. That is so—disgusting. I would never...*Please*."

"No, it's not—it's perfectly normal. But you did something, because you have the *glow*...Did you have sex today?" Brooke burst.

Gabrielle felt her face flush, and she quickly turned away from her sister.

"Oh, my god...you did. You fucking did—with whom? Dennis?"

"I didn't—okay? And not with Dennis—god, I broke up with him two months ago."

"No—you *did*, but the question is with whom . . ."

Brooke began pacing, and Gabrielle quickly jumped out of bed and began looking for her shoes.

Brooke suddenly stopped pacing, and Gabrielle braced herself for the blow she knew was coming.

"Please tell me you didn't . . ." her sister said quietly.

Gabrielle sighed, her shoulders sagging under the weight of Brooke's emotionally charged words.

"Gabby, why? Why? Why the fuck . . ." she asked, plopping herself on her bed and staring at Gabrielle in dismayed confusion.

Gabrielle shook her head, seated on the floor, having found only one flip flop. "I don't know...Because he's—he's not the same person. He's changed..."

"Changed? How do you even know that? Jesus, Gabby—he's, he's not even mentally stable right now. I mean, you've heard dad talk. He has amnesia, he's—he's clinically depressed, he has seizures is—is prone to violent outbursts—"

"Well, that may be—but he's a hell of a lot nicer now than he ever was before, so…What's your point?"

Brooke shook her head in frustration. "My point is…What's going to happen when his memory returns, huh? Because it can—any day, any month—even a year from now. What's going to happen when he wakes up and remembers who he was—and that's *all he remembers*…What the fuck happens then?"

Gabrielle sat back against the side of her bed, dropping the sandal to the floor. The thought had crossed her mind, but she had quickly dismissed it, just as she would senseless predictions about the destruction of the planet. "Yeah… and what if I get killed in a car accident tomorrow—or next month—or next year. Or I get cancer or some other disease. What if? What if? I'm not going to live my life based on what ifs—on, on fears of things that may never come to pass. I don't think he ever will remember his former life—but if he does, some day, what the hell am I supposed to do about it now? Throw away any happiness I have with him now because he might—maybe—someday—wake up thinking he's somebody else? Shit, he thinks he's somebody else right now. It's great, actually. Because I really like the somebody else he thinks he is."

Brooke fell silent a moment, and Gabrielle resumed the search for her other flip flop.

"What did you see in him? Last year, I mean…You never did talk to me about it. You made me piece the entire thing together, not that it was *that* hard, but…I guess I never really understood why you got together with him in the first place."

After retrieving the lost sandal from far under the bed, Gabrielle got up and sat on the side of her bed, across from Brooke. While she wanted more than anything for her sister to understand and accept her decisions, she feared it would be impossible in this case, and the rejection pained her deeply, for she valued Brooke's approval over anyone's, including her parents'. Her sister played many roles in her life, including protector, friend, mentor and judge. And all she could offer her today was the truth.

"I've been in love with Alex Fahlstrom since…like…second grade. I know that sounds stupid, but it's true…And, the truth is, when he…When Trisha Kurtz moved to town and he…he fell so madly in love with her, it… it broke my heart," she said, brushing away the tears that had begun to swell and spill over. "You have no idea…Nobody does. I kept it to myself…I didn't think I could ever love someone like that again…Someone else, that is. And

I tried—I did. I, I got pretty close with Brian, you know. I—I kinda had a crush on him in eighth grade, when Alex and Trish finally became a *couple*, and I had to…I don't know, concede it would never happen. But…By the time Brian noticed it was too late…He had to move."

Brooke reached over to her nightstand for a Kleenex, handing it to Gabrielle.

"Anyway…When Alex and Trisha's relationship started deteriorating last year, you know…It just happened. I—I wasn't looking for it. I—I wasn't even looking for him. I had gone on with life without him—nearly forgotten about him, I swear. He saw me—at Mick's party. He approached *me*—not the other way around. But I—I took advantage of the situation. I did—and I—I paid the price…And so did he. He did…I know he did. We both did—and we're both tired of paying for it, Brooke. We just are. We just want to move on. And now we can't—but not because we, as in he and I, can't—because we already have—but because nobody else wants us to. Everyone else wants us to continue to hate each other. Expects us to.…I don't…Look, if my life were to end tonight, I could honestly say, I got everything I wanted out of it. I have no regrets, and I could die in peace. And that's all I can tell you, Brooke."

"But what do you *see* in him, Gabby? Why do you love him so much?"

Gabrielle shook her head, pursing her lips. "I don't know—I could ask you the same. What do you see in Steve, huh?"

"This isn't about Steve—so don't even try to change the subject—"

"But it *is*—how is it not about Steve? Or any guy you and I like or date or—or screw. I love him because he's fucking hot, okay? He drives me crazy—I, I love his body and the way he looks. I—I love his expressions. I love the way he feels. Okay?"

"Because he's *hot*? You've gone to hell and back for this guy because he's *hot*?"

"Well, *yeah*…What do you think . . ."

"I think you're fucking crazy. Either that or you're a guy—a guy with a vagina. Because you're starting to act like one."

Gabrielle smiled. "Well…He plays guitar, too."

Brooke stared at her blankly.

"He's really good, actually…And he doesn't need a *pick*."

"What the fuck did you just say? Because, I didn't hear you the first time."

"I said he plays guitar—"

"Yeah—in his head."

"No—no, that's my point. Not in his head—in, like, real life. I saw it—I heard it. His parents even saw it—go ask them. Call Miss Jayne now, I swear to god."

"You're shitting me."

"I'm not, Brooke—I swear. He plays acoustic guitar. Electric, too, but—he prefers acoustic, and I could barely afford to buy him that one."

"You *bought* him a guitar?"

Gabrielle grinned sheepishly.

"How are you going to pay for that?"

"Well…I put twenty bucks down and I was going to trade in Nate's saxophone for the rest . . ."

"You are not—" Brooke burst.

"Oh, *I am*—He never plays it anymore, anyway…Shit, it's been lying in the garage for two years now."

"He's gonna kill you."

"Nate? Are you kidding me? Nate's a putz."

Brooke shook her head, the beginnings of a smile on her face.

"Anyway, I'm…I'm thinking of having a jam session Saturday night. You know—inviting some friends and musicians from school and stuff," Gabrielle continued. "Can Alex borrow your electric guitar?"

"*Fuck no.*"

"Oh, come on, Brooke—you're not going to be using it—"

"I'm not even convinced he can play."

"He *can* play…Come watch if you don't believe me. Actually, we were going to get together later this week and jam some. So…can we borrow it then, too?"

Brooke looked at her wide-eyed. "Oh, my god…You're…You're…You're just something else. I got nothing else to say to that. To you. To any of this…Thank god I'm getting out of here this summer, because I can't take any more . . ."

"So—will you set it up for us? In the garage."

"Sure—would you like me to set up a bed in there, too? Or, maybe you should just take over Nate's room, since you seem to have no problem selling off his belongings…Why don't you just fuck in his bed while you're at it."

But Gabrielle had jumped up to give her sister a hug.

"What's the sex like, anyway?" Brooke asked after pushing her away.

"*Brooke*…Jesus . . ." Gabrielle countered, slipping on the flip flops.

"Well…I have to ask since that's all you seem to want to do with him anyway…That's all it's ever seemed to be about."

"I don't ask you such questions—"

"That's because I'm not dating a psychopath. Seriously. I'm dating a *normal* guy. We have normal relations. There's nothing to tell...But *you two*...I mean...Was it different, you know? Having that—that psychic connection? Did you, like, double orgasm or something? Because, frankly, that's the only damn thing I can figure brought you two together . . ."

Gabrielle blushed, her mind traveling back to her times with Alex Tate. "Yeah...well...I can't speak for him, but...I usually came, if that's what you're asking...And since he always came, I...I was always left pretty satisfied."

"So...Who's a better lover? Alex Tate or...Alex...What's his middle name, again?"

"Michael . . ." she said, smiling to herself. She had not wanted to draw a comparison, not yet, but the current conversation forced her to do so. While the sexual experience was vastly different between the two, the sex with Alex Tate always consistently satisfying, there was no question who was a better lover. "Alex Michael—by far."

"Why?"

"Because he actually loves me," she said, skipping out the door of their bedroom to tackle the kitchen mess, her burden made lighter by Brooke's unspoken approval.

Gabrielle did not realize how hard it would be to continue the pretense until she saw him the next day in home room, when their eyes met but they could not hold each other, touch each other or even acknowledge each other. When she had to walk past him as if he wasn't even there.

He would turn around to look at her periodically, but today, instead of pretending she did not see him, she met his gaze and smiled.

When the paper wad hit her on the shoulder last class of the day, she did not have to read it to know what it said and watched the clock hands move with grueling slowness, anxious to see him. He was waiting for her, in the library stacks. They dropped their books and embraced each other for a moment before pulling away.

"This is hell . . ." he breathed.

"I know . . ." she said quietly, staring at the floor. "I had no idea it would be this hard...It wasn't the last time...I'm sorry."

"That's because you had something to hide last time...We don't. We really don't."

"Did you talk to Carl?"

"No, I didn't talk to Carl...I don't really want to right now.... I need—I need to talk to you. I need to see you…today," he said, holding her shoulders, his eyes sad and anxious.

"Okay…I can give you a ride home as soon as, you know…things clear out a bit. Just meet me in the parking lot in fifteen minutes."

She sat in her car listening to Pearl Jam and staring at the gathering clouds through her windshield, wondering if it would rain. Two songs later, the passenger door opened, and he climbed in, throwing his backpack behind the seat.

"Jesus . . ." he burst. "Do you have any smokes?"

She raised an eyebrow. "Cigarettes?"

"Yes," he said impatiently. "I seriously need a fucking smoke right now… Christ, I haven't had one since I got here . . .It's probably why I'm so fucked up and stressed out all the time…"

She rolled her eyes before digging around in the storage area behind the front seat and retrieving a slightly smashed pack of Marlboro Lights.

"I smoke Reds," he snapped irritably.

"*Really*? Well, I don't have those, so these will have to do—"

"*No*—We'll go buy *Reds*, because I'm not smoking some fucking chick cigarettes."

If he wasn't so appealing, she would have hauled off and punched him at that moment. But his hair framed his face in loose, messy curls, and his chest was exposed under his flannel shirt today, his having forgone a T-shirt. "Fine," she said, slightly seething, "We'll go to the convenience store and buy you *Reds*."

"Are you fucking kidding me?" he burst, looking at her incredulously. "The convenience store?"

"Not *that* convenience store…You idiot. Jesus, Alex—what is wrong with you today? You're in a miserable mood."

"Yes—I am. And when I get my cigarettes, I'll tell you why."

"Do you need some Jack Daniels to go with them?" she asked caustically.

"That would be nice, thank you, if you could manage that . . ." he said, staring out the passenger window morosely.

After pulling into a corner gas station a few blocks from school and purchasing the cigarettes and lighter, Gabrielle was instructed to head to Alex's house, since nobody was home there, anyway.

"Can I smoke in your car?" he asked.

She shrugged. "I don't care . . ."

"Want one?" he asked, holding the pack to her.

"No thank you," she said curtly.

"You don't smoke?"

"Not much...When I feel like it, and I'm really not feeling like it right now . . ."

"Well, what *are* you feeling like?"

"Like kicking your goddamn ass . . ."

He sighed and remained quiet a moment. "You like nice today," he ventured sheepishly.

"Oh, please . . ."

"No—you do. You...You...I really don't know what you've got going on there. It's like military meets...military meets . . ."

"What?" she asked wryly, as he studied her camouflage cargo pants and tight-fitting pink hoodie with massive tattoo-like illustrated roses screen-printed to the front.

"It's like guns and roses. That's what you're wearing...I just figured it out. Seriously—did you do that on purpose? Do you even like that band?"

"*Seriously*, Alex—what the fuck is up with you today?"

"I...I think I fathered a child."

"*What*?" she burst, nearly slamming on the breaks.

"Yeah—I know...It's seriously fucked up...And I'm a bit pissed off that you didn't at least warn me."

"*What*? What are you *talking about*?"

"I told you he'd fuck something else up in my life . . ."

"Alex, I don't even know what the hell you're talking about. What do you mean fathered a child—*what* child? *Whose* child?" Her heart was racing, and she could not get to his house fast enough, contemplating pulling over on the side of the road.

"Jennifer Hicks...That fucking Jennifer Hicks—that's who."

"Oh for god's sake . . ." she said, almost laughing in relief, her pulse slightly slowing. "That's not your child. She had a boyfriend...Is that what this is all about?"

"It *is* my child—I know it...I just know it."

"Well—why is it suddenly *your* child? Wouldn't it be *Alex Tate*'s child? What do you have to do with it—you weren't even here."

"Well that's obviously the one thing we both have in common—we both fucking fathered a child with Jennifer Hicks."

"No...You didn't. *Neither* of you fathered a child with Jennifer Hicks... Jesus, Alex—the girl's like twenty-one years old...Not to mention, she's not Alex

Tate's type. I can't even imagine he'd go out with her, let alone have sex with her. God—I mean, he thought *I* was a whore? *Please*…That girl was a known slut…She had a reputation for sleeping with everyone…And her boyfriend was a scumbag, too…He was a lot older than her and had a criminal record and everything. Assault, theft…Drug trafficking. Stuff like that."

"Then why did she name her baby after me?"

"*What*?" At this, Gabrielle pulled off the side of Rocky Point Road. Though close to his house, she felt the conversation was too heated to continue while driving.

"She did—she told me. I saw her—last night. She fucking came to my house so I could see the fucking baby," he said, and she could see he was beginning to shake just talking about it.

"Okay…Okay…Let's just stay calm…Did she tell you it was your baby?"

He shook his head.

"Did you ask her about the father?"

He nodded, taking another smoke.

"And what did she say?"

"She said he was dead.…"

"Well there's your answer, then."

"Yeah—Alex Tate is dead," he burst, his hand trembling.

"She wasn't talking about Alex Tate," she said quietly, leaning over and putting her arm around him. "She was talking about the guy who shot him…The guy your father knocked off. A guy you have absolutely no recollection of, even though—I assure you—everyone in this town does…Really, Alex—if she had named you as the father on the birth certificate, don't you think you or your parents would have gotten a phone call by now? A letter? A—a judgment? But she didn't…'Cause you're not."

"Gabby…something happened between her and Alex Tate. I know it…I saw it in her eyes, her body language…They had something."

She sighed, sitting back in the seat, believing him and suddenly angry. Angry at her former lover's complete hypocrisy if what Alex Michael said was true. "Well, there's only one person who knows…If you want to unravel the mystery that was Alex Tate, there's only one person out there who knows all his secrets. I know you think it's me—but it's not. I know nothing. Less now than I even thought. I saw what I wanted to see, and what I saw was…Well… We weren't friends, Alex. Maybe when we were kids, but not the past few years."

"Who?" he asked quietly.

"Carl…I told you to talk to him…You need to talk to him. You just do.

I can't help you anymore. Not with that, at least. I've told you all I know—or thought I knew."

"Yeah…Okay. Yeah…I'll do that."

"Soon."

He nodded absently, taking another smoke.

"So…what'd she name the baby…Alex Junior?"

He shook his head. "It was a girl…Alexis."

"*Alexis?*" Gabrielle echoed.

He rolled his eyes, and she burst out laughing.

"It's not funny," he said, flicking the cigarette butt out the car window.

But to her, it was, and she continued to laugh so hard she had to hold her stomach.

"Stop it—I'm serious…It is seriously not funny to me. It's going to fuck everything up."

She stopped, wiping a tear from her eye. "How?"

"Look, I…I just want us to be together, okay? I don't want anything to come between us . . ." he said, his eyes dark and brooding as he stared at her.

She smiled sadly at him. "But we are together. And nothing can come between us except *us*…our own fears and insecurities…Frankly, even if it was your baby, I could care less…I mean, do you want to move in with her and raise it?"

"God no."

"Well…then who cares? I don't . . ."

"Speaking of . . ." he said, leaning into her and nearly whispering in her ear. "You are, you know…you have protection, right?"

"No," she burst with feigned incredulousness. "I thought *you* were taking care of it."

He pulled back, staring at her wide-eyed.

"You mean—you weren't wearing a *condom*? What the fuck's *wrong* with you," she continued, seeing how long it would take for him to either blow up in anger or diffuse in a smirk.

"No—*you know* I wasn't—" he protested, still looking nervous.

"Well, that's just irresponsible . . ." she said curtly, tossing her head.

After a tense moment, he sat back, sighing loudly, barely able to contain his smirk.

She started laughing.

"You're getting fucked today…You are," he said, shaking his head. "You're unreal…Guns and roses . . ."

They drove to his house in silence, letting music fill the void. She pulled into the driveway but left the car on, watching him collect his things.

"You're coming in with me, aren't you?" he asked.

"Do you want me to?"

"Of course I want you to—are you kidding? My parents are at work.... We have the house to ourselves until five-thirty...Besides, I'd like to make love to you in a bed for once...My bed, actually."

"Your bed . . ."

"Well, yeah...I mean—that way I can—I can smell you...at night, when I'm alone. You know, feel like a part of you is still there with me. The memory, at least."

She kissed him, once again overwhelmed by a side she had never seen in his predecessor, then followed him into the house.

After greeting and petting the dog for a few minutes, they dropped their bags in the kitchen, got something to drink and headed up to his room. It had been a few years since Gabrielle had seen his room, and she was taken aback by how sparse it had become—completely barren of all the photos, trophies and sports paraphernalia Alex Tate loved to display. The gray walls barren of any posters, mottled by big patches of white dry wall that had yet to be painted. The only décor at all being dirty clothes and school books scattered about on the floor.

After securing the door with the desk chair, he sat on the edge of his unmade bed.

"What happened to your lock?" she asked, eyeing the jimmied chair warily.

He shrugged. "My parents removed it...You know. When I was...you know."

"It looks like a bomb went off in here," she burst. "You don't find this slightly depressing?"

He sighed, surveying his surroundings with apathy. "No...I don't really care."

She walked to the bed and sat on his lap, facing him, her legs straddling his torso, her arms around his shoulders. "This room makes me sad . . ." she said, kissing him. "I don't like the idea of you living in such a sad place."

He smiled. "It's not sad anymore. Not to me, anyway."

They began to make out, eventually completely undressing and covered only by a sheet and the worn plaid comforter, his body on top of hers, poised for entry.

"Can we do something different today," she whispered, as his one hand caressed her entire person, lingering on her inner thigh, his other arm wrapped around her back.

He grinned. "Like what?"

She shrugged, blushing. "I don't know…just different."

"Describe it to me in music . . ." he whispered. "Like a song…What song do you want me to play . . ."

She smiled. "Nick Drake…But not *Pink Moon*…Something from *Five Leaves Left*…Like 'River Man.'"

"Okay . . ." he said, kissing her.

Later, when they lay completely spent, their bodies entwined, he again told her he loved her, and she again remained silent, unable to speak, unable to voice the overpowering love she felt for him, feeling the words would somehow lessen it, cheapen it. Hoping he would just feel it pour through her without needing the assurances.

It was while resting her head on his shoulder that she noticed the old, yellowed photo taped to his wall, right next to his bed. She well-recognized the five children who sat cross-legged in a semi-circle, making silly faces at the camera.

"Where'd you get that photo?" she asked, reaching over to touch it.

"My mom had it in an album."

"It means something to you . . ."

He nodded. "Yeah…I'm not sure what…Except for the guy on the end, the rest of you…Well, you're the most important people in my life next to my family. I just…I want it back, I guess…It was in pieces last time I saw it…I want to put it back together again."

She sat up on one arm, studying his face, his body, running her fingers lightly over his the scars on his chest and shoulder, kissing each one tenderly. "Yes," she said finally.

"Yes what."

"Yes, I'll marry you…In five years. If we still love each other."

"Why wouldn't we?"

She shrugged, lying back down, holding him tightly against herself.

"I could do this every day . . ." he said finally. "A life lived like today is a life well-lived…Who needs anything else."

CHAPTER SEVENTEEN

The highlight of Alex's day was seeing Gabrielle walk through the door of home room, wondering what persona she would be channeling next. Today's look was vastly different from yesterday's, a short red knit shirt dress and striped tights replacing the casual pants and sweatshirt, high-heeled Mary Janes replacing the Chucks, and he couldn't help but wonder if the tights weren't thigh highs, going so far as to wad up a note and ask her. But she only responded with a wink.

By lunchtime, he was still day dreaming about her and getting under the little red dress, when she actually walked by his table, within mere feet of where he, Carl, Ron and the other two were seated, stopped right in front of Alex, and lifted the hem of her dress to pull up what were obviously stockings, not tights. She then tossed her head, the ponytail she had pulled high on her head swinging seductively behind her, and strode to the other side of the lunch room.

Alex stared dumbly at the blank space she had previously occupied, a hand on his lap to cover any signs of his erection. Ron cleared his throat uncomfortably, Carl turned bright red and one of the other two laughed.

"Man...Did you see that?"

"Shit...She's mind-fucking with you, Fahlstrom..."

Alex turned red and looked down at his sandwich, suddenly unable to eat.

"Jesus...When did she get so hot?" somebody said.

"She's always been hot," Ron said. "She's just weird...She's in that weird artsy girl group...Those chicks scare me, man..."

"You think she's hot, Fahlstrom?" either Chad or Stewart asked, winking at him, Alex now convinced he would never be able to distinguish them.

Alex coughed nervously. "Yeah...Yeah, I do...Think she'd go to prom with me?"

At this, the entire group froze in place, eyes wide, food poised mid-air.

"What did you say?" Carl asked, turning to Alex.

"Um...I was thinking of asking her to prom..."

"Yeah—and she'll say no, you dumb ass," Ron burst.

"Whether she says no before or after she cuts off your balls is the question," either Chad or Stewart said.

The other one whistled. "Man...He does have amnesia..."

"Fahlstrom, we told you to stay away from her, and we meant it. No—she will never go to prom with you, and no—you will not ask her," Carl said with quiet intensity. "Jesus Christ..."

"Yeah...She'll pull a *Carrie* on you, man..." one of the two said, laughing.

Alex felt himself flush at the small spark of anger that had just ignited deep within. "What if I already did ask her, and she already accepted? What then?"

At this, everyone stared down at the table, their plates, their lunch bags, shaking their heads.

"That's just fucked up...She's baiting you, man..."

"Then you *un-invite* her, Alex," Carl said. "You *un-invite* her today, and that's the end of it."

"Yeah, Alex, you can't go with her...Seriously, she will mess you up. She just will—there's no way it's not a trap," Ron said. "We'll find you another date to prom. Jamie—one of your bowling partners from Friday night—she likes you."

"Hell, Trisha still likes him," Carl said irritably. "You can always get back with Trisha."

"I told you...I don't remember Trisha...I don't remember anybody. Look—just forget it, okay? I don't give a shit..." Alex snapped, getting up from the table with his uneaten plate.

"Where you goin, man? You haven't even touched your lunch—"

"I'm not hungry," he said, stuffing part of his lunch in his bag and throwing the rest away before heading into the hallway to eat alone and calm his growing rage. But even after he found a relatively quiet stairwell in which to sit, he did not feel like eating, starting to understand why Gabrielle had wanted to keep their relationship quiet.

He did not have much time to think, as Carl joined him a few minutes later. "You okay, bud?"

Alex said nothing, refusing to look at him, angry that the Trisha problem he thought was resolved was still lingering, blaming part of it on Carl.

"Look—Alex, I know you say you don't remember anything—"

"No, I don't just *say* it—I *don't* remember anything, Carl. And I'm fucking sick of you not believing me. But I get it…I get it—he had secrets. He had a history with the people here—and not all of it good. Fine. Whatever."

"Who?"

"Alex Tate."

"*You are Alex Tate,*" Carl said, deliberately enunciating each word. "It's *your* history, Alex. Not somebody else's. And, yes—your history with Gabrielle Trahan is a train wreck, to put it mildly. And I was a witness. And seriously—I can't watch that again. I won't—I just won't."

"So, what happened?" Alex asked, feigning innocence.

Carl smiled sarcastically, shaking his head. "No…No—we're not going there. If you really have amnesia, then good for you. We'll consider it forgotten…In fact, I wish I had amnesia. How convenient."

The hall got busier as students started scurrying between periods, and Carl stood up to avoid getting bumped. Alex remained slumped against the wall.

"I want to know, Carl…If there's something I should know about, then tell me. Because I'm fucking sick of being on the outside of all your inside jokes—and snickers and comments."

Carl grimaced, sighing. "I'll think about it…But in the meantime, stay the hell away from Gabrielle. I'm serious, man. If you have any respect for me as a friend—any trust in me—you'll listen to me and do as I say for once…Wasn't Wiseman enough proof for you? Huh? Look what happened when you didn't listen to me…Well, this…*That* girl gets a hold of you…Sweet Jesus…Alex—she *drove* you to Dennis to get your ass kicked. She handed you over on a platter. What do you *think*? That was innocent? An innocent mistake? And for your information—she knows how you think. She knows you think with your pecker, which is why she's flirting with you in the first place. *Maliciously* flirting with you."

"Fine...Just forget it. Okay?" Alex said finally, unable to hear any more, wishing he could go outside for a smoke to calm his agitation.

After staring into space for a moment, Carl shook his head, throwing his hands up in desperate frustration as if concluding Alex would ignore him anyway. "Yeah...Alright. Catch you later," he mumbled before heading down the hall.

But Alex was too unsettled to concentrate on the rest of his classes, anxious to see Gabrielle and request another library rendezvous or, perhaps, a ride home. He found himself stealing numerous glances and smirks from her throughout his last two periods to ensure nothing had changed between them, to convince himself she was still there for him, as he remembered her.

At the end of the school day, when she turned the corner around the library stacks, he couldn't help but grab her and embrace her, holding her close enough to feel her return the affection. As if sensing his distress, she kissed him and placed his hand on her thigh, under the hem of her dress.

At the soft touch of her skin, he closed his eyes smiling, "That was quite a show you put on today," he whispered.

She smiled. "That was for *you*—"

"Yeah, well—I think the entire table got a hard on..."

She grinned, and they kissed again, when Alex felt a hand roughly grab his shoulder. Completely startled, he stepped back just as Gabrielle was grabbed by the arm and pried away from him.

Carl stood wedged between them, his face flushed with quiet rage.

"What the hell are you doing?" he whispered harshly at Alex.

"What'd you *follow* me here?" Alex asked incredulously.

"Yes—as a matter of fact I did. Somehow, I just knew you were going to ignore me, so I took the liberty of spying on you the remainder of the day. In fact, I'm missing my track practice right now."

"What are you—*my dad*?"

"No—I'm your *best friend*. But I guess you forgot that," Carl said bitterly.

Gabrielle struggled to twist out of Carl's grip to no avail, completely taken aback by the intrusion and struggling to contain an overwhelming surge of nauseous mortification.

Carl turned on her. "Look—I know what you're up to, and I can even understand why you might be—but don't you think he's had enough? Seriously?"

"Leave her out of it," Alex said, his own rage building.

"*Leave her out of it?*" Carl repeated with feigned shock.

Alex stepped up to him. "Let her go. *Now.*"

"What—you're protecting her now?" Carl said caustically. "Well, now that's real ironic coming from the guy who knocked her out and beat her in a fit of rage last summer after a party. Oh, but *you don't remember that,* do you? Well, *I do.* I was there—and I pulled you off and took care of her. Made sure she got home safe. Just like I'm doing again today. Because *I* haven't forgotten—and I'm not living through that again."

There was a brief moment of tense silence, when even the wall clock seemed to stop ticking.

Then, Alex flew at him, knocking Carl against a wall of shelving before hitting him in the stomach and knocking him off balance. He then grabbed Carl by the shirt collar and was moving to punch him when Gabrielle flung herself between them, absorbing Alex's blow with her shoulder.

"Stop it!" she cried.

Not wanting to harm her, Alex drew back.

"For god's sake, Alex—he's your best friend…Just stop it," she pleaded quietly.

The commotion caught the attention of the librarian and a teacher, who came running to the scene, along with a few curious students.

"What is going on here?" the librarian asked, slightly hysterical.

"Carl got dizzy and passed out, but he's okay now…Can somebody get me some water?" Gabrielle said quickly, counting on Carl to play along, which he did.

While Gabrielle tended to Carl, Alex withdrew from the scene, preferring to think she only pretended to care for Carl, only pretended to help him sit up, to give him water, to say something to him, whisper something to him, a hushed conversation Alex could not hear from his vantage. But the ensuing paranoia made him shake.

It took a few minutes for Carl to convince the adults that he was fine, and by then, the students had become disinterested in the drama and wandered off to other points of the library. While Carl collected himself, Gabrielle walked back to Alex.

"Are you okay?" she asked, laying an arm on his shoulder.

"I need a smoke…"

"Okay…Alright…Why don't you go help Carl up first."

"Why should I?"

"Because it's the right thing to do. He's just trying to protect you…I know you can't see that, but I can. And…And I don't want to see your lifelong friendship end over something as stupid and petty as this…" she said quietly.

"What were you saying to him…" he asked, shuffling tensely in place.

She sighed. "I was trying to convince him that I mean you no harm. That I don't wish revenge upon you—that there's no secret evil plan to harm or torture you on prom night."

"Why would you?" he burst, the anger building again.

She smiled to herself, shaking her head. "I don't know…I can't *imagine*… But, come on," she said, taking his hand and leading him to where Carl still sat on the floor, his head buried in his arms.

Carl looked up as they approached, and seeing his pained expression, Alex extended a hand to help him stand, apologizing in the process. But as Carl stood up, Alex's hands and arms had begun to shake uncontrollably.

"Are you okay, bud?" Carl asked, wide-eyed.

"He just needs a cigarette," Gabrielle said, walking over to the back-packs and picking up both hers and Alex's. "Come on—let's take this pleasant exchange outside."

"I think he needs help, not cigarettes," Carl burst, picking up his bag and jogging after them. "He doesn't even smoke—"

"Oh, he smokes…And it may or may not help…Depends on how fast we can get outside and light up," she said, quickening her pace. Alex was happy to keep up, having become increasingly claustrophobic in the school halls and almost wishing they could flee fast enough to leave Carl behind.

After bursting through the metal doors, she walked out near the curb, dropped the bags and fumbled through her purse.

"I don't want your fucking cigarettes, Gabby—I need mine," Alex said.

"I have *yours*—I bought three packs of *Reds* last night, two for the car and one to keep on my person at all times—*okay*?"

"Okay, okay…Thank you…" he mumbled, holding himself to control the trembling, which was only intensifying, but deeply touched and relieved by her gesture. She lit up and handed him the smoke.

"Alex, you need to calm down…Just breathe," she said, rubbing his arms down before walking behind him to massage his shoulders and back.

"Why would he say those things…He's acting like he's some kind of hero— I would have done the fucking same thing had I been there. I would have."

She said nothing, holding him close to herself, hoping the embrace would help, her fear of another attack outweighing the shame over what had just transpired in the library and the insecurity of their relationship being so recklessly displayed. Openly embracing him in spite of the few students still lingering in the parking lot, still coming and going from the building, and in spite of Carl's continued scrutiny from where he stood, twenty or so feet away, arms crossed.

"You wanted his opinion…So what, now?" Alex asked bitterly. "What do we do now?"

She sighed, walking around his person to face him. "What do you want to do?"

"I want to stop this sneaking around shit. I want to stop pretending that we're something we're not. You're my girlfriend, and I don't give a fuck what he thinks about it. I'm taking you to prom, and I will fucking kick anyone's ass who tries to stop me or come between us again—I swear to god. What the fuck…I could understand if the librarian found us and broke us up back there…But *Carl*? Of all people, *Carl*?"

Gabrielle fell quiet, lost in thought and remorse, any pleasure she might feel about being his girlfriend overshadowed by the cost of such a feat and the grief it would bring to his friends, particularly Carl, who had been his friend almost as long as she had.

"I don't want to come between you and Carl," she said sadly, messing with a button on his shirt. "I just don't…I won't be your girlfriend at the expense of your friendship. I'm sorry, Alex. I can't do that. I just can't."

"But I don't understand…Gabby, you can't leave me—you just can't—"

"I'm not leaving you…Jesus, Alex. But can you for once try to see things the way they might—the way Carl or Ron might. Or even Trisha…I know how traumatic it's been for you waking up in this—this strange alternate world, full of people you don't recognize and—and a history you don't remember. But it's just as traumatic for them to see you—someone they loved—who doesn't recognize *them*. Who doesn't even like them. They don't understand how their best friend can just wake up one day hating them—or what they stand for… Their only crime is that they liked Alex Tate. And frankly, I'm just as guilty as they are. He wasn't always an asshole, you know. There was a good fourteen years there where he was the furthest thing from it."

Alex took a deep smoke before hurling the butt to the ground, the glimmer of calm provided by both the nicotine and Gabrielle's soothing rub crushed along with the burning embers, his anxious shaking returning full force. "So—so what are you saying? What do you want me to do?" he asked, barely able to keep his teeth from chattering.

"I want you to talk to him…Just hang out with him and get to know him—*him*. Not Carl Weiss, Carl O'Malley. They're two entirely different people. Just give him a chance…You forget—he was my friend, too. I grew up with him and have known him as long as you have…And it sucks, Alex—it really sucks and hurts to see all this—this bullshit drama between you. It's stupid. I prefer to keep my drama to the stage—the minute that Shakespearean shit starts trickling into my everyday life, I freak. You need to understand that, okay? Because I will not put up with it—I just won't."

"You're not breaking up with me are you?" he asked quietly, feeling ill.

"Have you not heard anything I've said?" she burst. "Oh, *my god*…No—I'm not breaking up with you. No—I will continue to have sex with you. But yes, we will be keeping it under wraps a bit longer, okay? We are going to at least try to show some concern for the other people in our world, okay? Like our *friends*."

He stared at the ground, relieved but disappointed.

Walking to where their bags had been dropped, she picked up hers and started walking away.

"Where are you going?"

"Home."

"I need a ride—"

"Well, get one from Carl," she said, stepping off the curb and into the parking lot, looking forward to a quiet smoke in the privacy of her car to calm her shattered nerves. After hurling her bag into the truck bed of her El Camino, she climbed into the driver's seat and reached for her CD case when a knock sounded on the window. To her surprise, it was Carl.

"*Jesus*…" she breathed, putting the key in the ignition and turning it far enough to roll down the power window.

"What?" she snapped.

"Where are you going?" Carl asked.

"Home…Why?"

"What about him?"

"I thought you could take him home—"

"I'm not taking him home—shaking like that. Did you see him? What the hell, Gabby—he's acting like he's about to have a seizure or something."

"He probably is," she said shrugging. "He has them all the time."

"Are you *kidding me*?" Carl burst. "What do you mean he has seizures all the time—"

"No—I'm not kidding. I've been there when they happen. It's fucking scary…Here," she said, opening the glove compartment and retrieving a pack of *Reds*. "Take this. And you can have my lighter…I have another one around here somewhere."

She held the two items out for Carl to take, but he stood dumbfounded.

"Gabby...I'm seriously freaked out right now. What the hell am I supposed to do if he has a seizure? I mean—do I do CPR—mouth-to-mouth... Jesus," he said, running his hand through his thick, cropped red hair, creating errant, jetting tufts.

"You don't do *anything*. If it looks like he's going to go down, try to get him to sit down first. He'll black out and appear to stop breathing for a minute and then just come to. On his own. My dad says we shouldn't do anything but keep him calm."

"How do you know all this?" he asked suddenly. "I mean—I'm his best friend, and yet I had no idea about all this...What the hell? You're his—his mortal enemy, and yet...yet..."

"*Mortal enemy*? Are you for real? Is that how you see me?"

"Well...Yes—I mean, I would be if I were you. I'd want to kill the son of a bitch."

"Well, you're not me. And he's not who you think he is, and you're not who he thinks you are. Nothing's what it appears to be, Carl. *Nothing*." She extended her hand with the items further out the window.

Sighing in resignation, he took them from her hand. "I'm...I'm sorry about earlier. I'm sorry I brought it up like that."

She rolled her eyes, her face burning in embarrassment at the sudden reminder. "Well, I'm not—okay? I'm relieved, actually. You have no idea."

"No, I actually do...I knew what you thought, and I...I just didn't have the courage to tell you what really happened. I'm sorry."

She shrugged.

"Do you still love him? After all that?" he asked quietly, his one arm on the roof of her car.

She looked down into her lap, wishing he would leave.

"You know, he never loved you, Gabby...He was sexually attracted to you, but that was it. Shit, you scared him. He feared you and eventually loathed you, but he didn't respect you—and he never loved you...Why the hell do you think it's going to be any different this time?"

"Because *he's* different."

"No—*he's* bi-polar, Gabby. He's completely mental—I saw that before the coma. This—this different person you see is one persona in what's clearly some kind of multiple personality disorder. You're just seeing half of a split personality. Where's the other half, Gabby? Where? Have you thought about that? What's going to happen when you're at prom with him—or, or go fuck him in the back seat of a car one night, and he gets his memory back, huh? And then wonders what the hell you're doing there? What's going to happen then? Cause I may not be around next time to stop it."

She shuddered inwardly, looking in her rearview mirror at Alex's lone figure, now seated on the curbside, hearing the logic in Carl's words but opting for instinct.

"I have to go...Call me if you need any help, okay? I'll be at home the rest of the night," she said, starting the engine, quickly moving the gear from park to drive and pulling forward out of the space, across the near empty lot, trying to stem the tide of tears until she reached the privacy of her bedroom.

Alex watched her drive away, his heart heavy, still confused by their conversation and fearful that the main source of happiness in his new existence had just driven off into the proverbial sunset, never to be seen again. Numbness replaced the tension, and he sat slumped on the curb, arms limp at his sides, head hanging, suddenly too tired to even acknowledge Carl, who soon plunked down next to him.

"Do you...need a smoke?" Carl asked, extending a hand that clutched a pack of cigarettes, nearly crushing the container.

Alex shook his head.

Carl sighed, stuffing the items into his jacket pocket. "Look, I'm...I'm sorry if I upset you earlier. I—I meant to, actually. I just didn't know...I didn't know it would, you know...Trigger some sort of attack."

Alex said nothing.

"You know," Carl continued, "I was thinking it was Gabrielle messing with you, but...But now I have to wonder if you're not messing with her—"

"Of course not," Alex interrupted. "I love Gabrielle...But I don't...I'm not sure she feels the same. Not yet..."

"Jesus, Alex—why the hell would she? Shit—she gave her heart to you last year. She gave more than that, actually. You could have just gone out with her then, you know...In fact, if you'd a just gone out with her then—if you'd a done the right thing and broken up with Trisha—all this mess could have been avoided."

"You...You knew about that?"

"Of course I did, you dumb ass."

Alex shrugged defensively. "Sorry—Gabby said nobody knew. It was a big secret."

"You're my fucking best friend—we're like brothers. We've always been like brothers. You wouldn't keep something like that from me…You couldn't. You were too freaked out about it…That—that damn party where you two hooked up the first time and made out…It freaked you out, man…You'd been so insecure with Trisha, you know, because the relationship hadn't changed after three years…You started to think she didn't love you…I had to hear all about that, too…And then you met Gabby…Or, *re-met* Gabby, since you grew up together. But you acted as if you hadn't—as if she was some strange new being plopped into Polson. As if you'd never seen her before—or noticed her before."

Carl sniffed, wiping his face with his sleeve.

"Maybe it's all my fault, you know…" he continued. "You came to me… all freaked out about making out with her…feeling as if you betrayed Trisha, which, honestly, I didn't think you really did—not just with a make-out session…And I told you so…But then you came to me over the next days or weeks, I don't even remember, still obsessed with Gabby, and I…I told you to go talk to her—to Gabby…To just meet her in private and see if the feelings were still there…And maybe that was bad advice…Selfish advice, because on some level…On some level I wanted you to leave Trish…to give me a chance with her."

Alex's hands began to shake again, and he knew it wouldn't be long before the trembling spread through his entire person. He tried to sit on them. "Did… Did he love Trisha?" he asked hoarsely.

"He? You mean *you*. Oh, yeah…She was the center of your world," Carl said, staring out over the blacktop. "I have never seen anyone work as hard as you did to win her over…It was almost embarrassing to watch…Couple months after she moved here, she said you had girly curls, and that's when you chopped all your hair off and never let it grow back…She had some crush on this kid in the next grade, and you did anything and everything that kid did, but better—whether you liked it or not. That's how you got into wrestling, and chess club and student council. Shit—you even went to services at her church just to be seen by her…But you did it, man…You won her over, and she finally went steady with you…"

Carl picked up a loose stone on the ground near him and threw it into an empty expanse of parking lot.

"The problem is she's not a very physical person, you know," he continued. "She just isn't…I mean, she'll kiss and hug, but…She's not going to put out much…It freaks her out…And, I think after a few years of the same routine, you just…you just started to doubt that she loved you. I know you did…

Part of you thought she was repulsed by you, and it freaked you out…So you started pressuring her, you know—almost guilt-tripping her, but…That just freaked her out and pushed her even further away…"

Carl looked at Alex, but Alex could barely meet his stare, his entire focus on trying to calm his severe shaking and avoid another black-out.

"Jesus, Alex—are you okay?" Carl said, jumping up and kneeling in front of him.

"I—I think I could use that cigarette now…It might help…"

"Yeah—sure…I'm sorry…Of course," Carl said, groping into his pocket to retrieve the pack and lighter. He started to hand them to Alex but stopped suddenly, shaking his head. He then took the package and tapped out a cigarette, lighting it and getting it started.

"I thought you didn't smoke," Alex said, trying to smile as he took the smoke from Carl.

"Yeah, well…I don't anymore, but I did after my dad died. A lot, actually…But you helped me kick the habit…"

"I'm sorry…About your dad. When did that happen?"

"A little over two years ago…Cancer…Actually, you helped me cope with the whole thing…Survive…I wouldn't have made it through without you…I didn't have anyone else. Just my mom and my little sister. And my grandparents, but…I was a mess…Not as bad as you right now, but…It was bad."

"So…I was a friend to you, then…I wasn't a complete asshole?" Alex said, taking a deep drag, the nicotine and change of topic having a calming effect.

"Are you kidding me? How can you even ask that? You were the best friend anybody could ever ask for…I told you—you were like a brother to me. I'm serious, man…Everything I am today is because of you…You—you always pushed me to be the best. You always told me I could be the best… You believed in me as much as you believed in yourself…And pretty soon, I believed it…I have straight As because of you. You made it like a competition between us, but it was good, you know—friendly. And wrestling—shit…I know we didn't do that well this season, but I placed higher than anyone. And it was tough, too, because you're like, the team captain, and—and we didn't have you there. So…So I would just remember what you would normally say, you know. What kind of encouragement you would give everyone. And I tried to…You know. Fill in. Substitute…"

Alex took another drag but remained quiet.

"West Point…That was your idea, man," Carl continued. "You said we could get there…You said we could go anywhere we want and be anything we want to be, and I...I believed you. There was nothing you couldn't do if you didn't put your mind to it—no sport or game or puzzle—math problem, ski course—even car repair. Whatever. You just never quit until you conquered it—I think that was it. I think it was because you would never quit until you got what you wanted."

They sat in silence for a minute, Alex trying to sort through his conflicting emotions, both relieved and irked by what he heard, his mind trying to process the other side of the person who was Alex Tate, having only seen him as a self-centered, egotistical and vile human being, refusing to believe he had any redeeming qualities and oblivious to any pain or struggle he may have experienced.

"But he didn't get what he wanted..." Alex said finally.

"What do you mean?"

"He wanted Trisha to love him, and she didn't..."

"No, she *did* love him—just not the way he wanted to be loved."

"So what's the difference? There's no difference to him. He wanted physical affection as an affirmation of love, and he didn't get it. You just told me that Trisha was the center of his world, and yet he couldn't get what he wanted from her."

"You do realize you're talking about yourself don't you? Because you keep speaking as if he's a separate person—and now I'm starting to do it. Christ."

"Because he *is* a separate person...I told you—*I'm not him*. Jesus, I hate the mother-fucker. I'd kill him if I saw him...I tried, actually...."

"Jesus, you're talking crazy, Fahlstrom. Seriously...What is your point?"

"Did he love Gabrielle?" Alex asked, taking another deep drag.

Carl shook his head. "No...*You* never loved Gabrielle."

"Why?"

"Because she wasn't Trisha—she would never be Trisha. And quite frankly, she scared you. I mean—you thought she was hot, and she drove you crazy sexually, but she scared the shit out of you."

"But why?"

"Because you couldn't control her. You had absolutely no control over what she did or thought or—or how she behaved. You used to compare her to a stallion—you would say she was like a wild horse that you couldn't rein in. And since you weren't committed to her, you figured she felt the same about you. That you were just some casual fuck in a long line of fucks...And you were convinced she was shacking up with Wiseman. I told you they were just friends, but you didn't believe it. Shit, we were all friends—we all grew up together, but...You didn't buy it, and it pissed you off."

Alex winced. "So…If Trisha had, you know—put out. What would Alex Tate have thought about that? Huh? Would she have been a slut, too? I mean, maybe anyone who put out for him was a slut."

Carl shook his head vehemently. "No—hell no. Trisha was sacred—and anything you would have done with her would have been treated as such. Shit—you told the girl you'd marry her. You told her you'd go off and become an officer, get a powerful job somewhere and give her everything she ever wanted. But you wanted her to feel the same about you, mentally and physically, to—to put out for you like Gabrielle did, but she wouldn't. She won't. She just won't… And don't think I didn't try to get you to fall in love with Gabrielle instead… Shit. I all but begged you at one point. In fact, I warned you that if you didn't, Gabby would cut it off. And that's exactly what she did…She wasn't going to be your *whore*, even though that's what you tried to turn her into…That's what you saw her as…" Carl said, putting his head in his hands.

"Yeah, well *I don't* see her as that…I told you. I love her. I want to take her to prom."

"Well that's just effing ironic, now, isn't it? And it's effing too late, Alex… *Take her to prom*…You're a dumb ass. You really are."

Alex winced inwardly, crushing the cigarette butt into the ground and lighting another.

"And while we're airing out your dirty laundry—cataloging all the shit that you left behind, it's fucked up enough that you assault your childhood friend and probably the only girl who could ever love you the way you needed to be loved—after calling her a whore— you have to go and make it exponentially more fucked up by hooking up with that effing skank at the convenience store…Unbelievable," Carl said, shaking his head.

Alex choked, physically coughing on his latest drag.

"And if you hadn't hooked up with that slut, none of this would have happened—none of it. But somehow, you couldn't keep your pecker in your pants…It's unbelievable…It truly is, because when I look back at all that you accomplished, it's…it's truly amazing. I mean—you could have gone to the Olympics if you wanted…You could have done anything you wanted, and everything you did was tops. Smartest in the class…Athletic honors all over the place…Headed to West Point or the Naval Academy…And what is your Achilles heel? What brought the entire dream to a crumbling ruin? Your fucking pecker…I mean, look at you…In fact, next time you look in the mirror at your sorry ass self with your hippie hair and homeless attire, you can just thank your Johnson."

"I'll assume you mean Jennifer Hicks…" Alex said wryly, still trying to contain a lingering cough.

"Jennifer Hicks…Fucking Jennifer Hicks…Of all people, Alex, why… Why her? I have yet to figure that one out…I thought it was because she was blond, I really did…But she doesn't look or act a thing like Trisha, so I don't know…Christ—the girl's twenty-one…When you told me you were messing around with her, I wanted to pop you—I almost effing did…I should have…And next time you go screwing around with someone else's girl, you should seriously consider driving a different car. I mean, come on…I know that's why he went after you two on New Year's…I mean, yeah—she's like fucked half the guys in Polson, but none of them drive sapphire blue Camaros. He probably drove by the store to check on his girl, piss drunk, and saw your damn car parked out front—a car he probably remembered seeing one too many times in the recent past… But we'll never know."

"I thought Alex Tate *worked* at the convenience store—"

"Yeah—*you* did for the summer, which is when you first hooked up with the skank. But you continued to mess with her well into the fall…Finally ended it around Thanksgiving, when she started seriously showing."

Alex took another smoke, deliberating over whether to ask the next question but knowing it had to be asked if he were to have any peace of mind.

"You don't think that was his kid, do you?"

Carl grinned, shaking his head. "Shit…Why—you worried about that? Are you seriously worried about that? What'd she do—stop by with the baby?"

Alex remained silent.

"Shit…." Carl repeated, chuckling. "Well, if it's any consolation, you told me all you did was get blow jobs from her…You never admitted to banging her…I've never heard of a girl getting pregnant from a blow…Not to mention, there are at least twenty other candidates for fatherhood besides you… You were just the unlucky bastard parked outside the convenience store that night…But thank god your dad was with you…You'd a both been dead. You and the skank…And your reputation might have been dead with it, shit… This town would have shit."

Alex closed his eyes and breathed a huge sigh of relief.

"She didn't ask for child support, did she?" Carl joked, hitting him in the shoulder.

"That is so not funny right now…"

"She didn't name it after you, did she?"

"Yes, she did fucking name it after me, actually. Why the fuck do you think I'm so freaked out?"

"I don't know, man…" Carl said, whistling. "That is seriously messed up…Then again, she did try to turn you into a hero. Said you saved her life… Whatever. I don't believe any of it. Your sorry ass was just the first to get shot."

"She's moving to Billings," Alex said, wanting to end the subject.

"Yeah, well…I guess you're off the hook then."

They sat in silence for awhile.

"Is there anything else…" Alex said finally.

"Anything else what?"

"Anything else I should know about—about his past. Because I seriously can't take this anymore…I'm not kidding…This has been fucking hell—today has been fucking hell, and if there is any more shit that he left behind, I would seriously appreciate knowing about it before I step into it again. Jesus…"

Carl mused a moment, then shook his head. "No…That's everything… Unless you were hiding something from me, that's everything."

"Good…Alright then…So, once again, I'd like to talk to you about Gabrielle and me. I've already asked her to prom, and she's already said yes. And for your fucking information, no I didn't ask her to prom first, after finding out what an asshole my predecessor was. I fucking asked her to marry me, because she's the love of my life—she was my girlfriend in the life I remember, the life you so willingly trash as being delusional. And while she won't marry me—at least not today—she said she'd go to prom."

Carl eyed him in complete bafflement, unable to retort.

"And I don't know why the fuck you haven't asked Trisha yet. For fuck's sake, I asked her for you—I asked on your behalf. She didn't tell you that?"

Carl continued to stare dumbly at him. "I…I don't think she's over you yet…Or she feels guilty…Shit, I don't understand women…I really effing don't."

"Christ…Look, do you want to know who Trisha is to me? Who I remember her as being? 'Cause I'd love to tell you, man. I really would. In fact, if you would—even for a few minutes—suspend all judgment and just listen to my story, you might…I don't know—actually be relieved. Okay with things. Able to move on."

"What—about your *other life*? What good is that, Alex? It's temporary. I mean—you can tell me and you can even continue to believe it until you wake up one day and it's gone. Replaced by the truth—by reality. And who says that won't happen as violently as this. I mean, it's a nightmare…"

"It's not temporary…I haven't even had a flashback—a dream, a clue about this life. And I should have by now. Surely, something would have triggered by now, but no. Nothing. I've had to start completely over...I feel like an exchange student."

For some reason, this made Carl laugh.

"An exchange son...An exchange friend, even—huh?"

Carl nodded. "Yeah...That's kind of what it feels like."

"Look," Alex said, putting out his cigarette. "I appreciate your saving our lives...Both our lives, but...We need to move on. I need to move on, and so do you. And, I'm moving on with Gabrielle. I just am. And I hope one day you can accept that and—and forgive me for the horrible things he did. I'm sorry...I really am. And if—if that's what you want—Trisha, West Point, to be rich and powerful one day, then go for it. There's no reason you can't have everything you want. And you don't need me anymore to do it...I have my own path...Not sure what that is right now..."

"So...West Point's out, then," Carl said sadly.

"Carl, I didn't even know where West Point was on a map...I didn't know where Annapolis was, either. Never heard of it...I'm flunking a class—barely passing my other courses...I hate school. It's fucking boring...It drives me crazy, sitting there all day when I could be skiing or riding horses or—or playing guitar or even fucking working at a grocery store or something, *anything*."

"Dude, you don't play guitar."

"I do play guitar."

"No, you don't."

"I fucking do—shut the fuck up and come watch me. Jesus...Saturday night."

"What are you talking about?"

"Gabby's having a party Saturday night...We're gonna play music and stuff...I don't know...She called it a *Jam Off*...Whatever the fuck that is..."

"As opposed to a jerk off," Carl joked.

"Shit...Probably."

"Alex, you've never picked up a guitar in your life. I just...I just don't want you embarrassing yourself, you know? I mean—why don't you think about it first?"

"No—why don't you just fucking stop telling me what I can and can't do? Why don't you just accept that maybe I've just changed my mind about what I *want* to do? It's allowed, you know. There's no fucking universal law against changing your mind."

"Alright...Okay...I'll stop by. Ron and I will stop by."

They talked a bit more before Carl suggested they grab a bite to eat at the diner. And somewhere over the course of the next few hours, Alex learned more about Polson and Carl learned more about Kansas. By the end of the evening, Alex had agreed to start working out with Carl in the mornings, attend track practice and baseball practice and learn how to wrestle. While he refused to cut his hair or continue with his application to West Point, he did concede to a group study period a few nights a week to get his grades up. In exchange, Carl gave him permission to take Gabrielle to prom.

∞

Gabrielle woke the next morning to the sound of buzzing, at first thinking it was their alarm but soon dismissing that thought, as they set their radio to wake with music. At times, the buzzing would get very loud, as if just outside her ear before quieting altogether. At other moments, it sounded like a biplane passing over their house, fading into the distance as it headed to Missoula or some other destination.

She opened her eyes and, once adjusted to the light, looked at the alarm clock. There were still ten minutes before they had to get up and get ready for school, a prospect she dreaded, having gone to bed in a foul mood, depressed and annoyed that Alex had not bothered even to call and let her know what transpired with Carl. Part of her fearful that Carl might have already undone the fragile relationship she and Alex had built from scraps over the past week.

Closing her eyes, she tried to let sleep's peace envelop her for a few more minutes.

But the buzzing continued, followed by pings. She thought she heard the blinds lightly banging against the windowpane and tried to cover her ears with her extra pillow.

Just as her thoughts began to drift off into the confusion of a light sleep, a blood curdling scream sounded from the other side of the room.

"*Get it off of me...Get it off...*"

She sat up in bed with a start to see her sister Brooke standing next to the bed, hair flying, arms flailing, still shrieking at the top of her lungs.

The buzzing grew extremely loud again, and she barely had time to duck out of the way of an angry wasp that dove at her head before flying to the ceiling and circling the room.

"*It's in my hair—it's in my hair—Get it off—*"

Her sister continued to shriek, nearly crying.

"Jesus, Brooke—calm down. It's not on you anymore."

Her sister stopped, peering wide-eyed through her thick bangs and massive strands of hair that had flown in front of her face. "Where is it? Where the fuck is it?"

Gabrielle pointed to the wall where the wasp had landed, right next to the window. But Brooke screamed again, antagonizing it and causing it to whizz around the room, dive bombing them, before landing on the window pane, just below the blinds.

"Kill it—" Brooke shrieked.

"Would you shut up? Your screaming's just scaring it…Jesus."

"Kill it," she hissed. "I mean it, Gabby—get rid of it."

"Why do *I* have to get rid of it?"

"Because I'm allergic to them."

"You are *not*," Gabrielle said indignantly.

"Because I hate them…They scare me…Do you think they're in New York?"

"They're everywhere," she burst. "Jesus, Brooke," she breathed, scrambling around for her flip flop before creeping towards the window.

As she got closer to it, she could see it was large and black with a striped abdomen. She wondered if it was male or female and then began musing on whether or not it had a family and what it did with its day. Flip flop poised in the air, she focused her mind on the target, knowing she would only have one shot before it tore off and around the room. But then she thought about it from the wasp's perspective, imagining herself against a glass imprisonment, able to see freedom but unable to reach it—the sun, the wind, the fresh air and pollen. Then, exploding into hundreds of microscopic pieces as a huge, unknown object came bearing down upon her fragile body, every cell screaming in pain as it was destroyed.

"Get me a glass," she breathed.

"*What?*"

"I said get me a glass…I'm gonna capture it, not kill it," she hissed.

"*Why?* What if you miss?"

"I could miss either way—just do it."

Brooke scurried to the bathroom, returning within seconds with an empty glass. She then rummaged around to retrieve a piece of paper, and Gabrielle was able to complete her rescue operation, carrying the entrapped wasp through the house and flinging it out the front door. But instead of giving thanks, Brooke blamed her for the wasp getting inside, accusing her of leaving a door or window open. She then yelled at her for taking a blouse she wanted to wear that day, even though Gabrielle hadn't worn a blouse at all the past two days. By the time Gabrielle had showered, her mood was black, and she chose attire to match, viewing the entire morning as an omen of the remainder of her day.

She walked into home room and, seeing Alex in the second row, took a deep breath and strode over to him, occupying the empty desk next to his, where Ron typically sat.

After raising an eyebrow, he grinned. "Good morning," he said cheerfully.

"What's good about it?" she snapped, studying his attire in dismay. Gone were the jeans and flannel shirt, replaced by sweats. "What'd you just get out of bed?" she asked.

"No, actually, I worked out this morning."

"You *what*?"

"With Carl…It was good."

For some reason, her heart fell, a dark shadow clouding her internal thoughts and even her external environment, the light suddenly blocked by the hulking figure of Ron.

"Um…I think you're in my seat," he said.

She felt her face flush as a surge of rage coursed through her system. Bolting up from the desk, she knocked back the chair in the process, it hit the tile floor with a clamor, and Gabrielle stood in front of Ron, her face mere inches from his. "I didn't think there were assigned seats," she said between her teeth.

Ron stepped back, wide-eyed. "There—there aren't, I just…"

"You just *what*?"

"Always sit here…" he mumbled, backing away. "But I'll find another one."

Alex set the chair upright for her, chuckling. "You're in a mood today."

"Hmmm…Yes, well—and it has nothing to do with the fact that my boyfriend never called me last night to let me know how things went. Never followed up at all."

"Jesus, Gabby…I don't even know your number."

She didn't know whether to laugh or hit him. "Oh, my god…And you wouldn't think to look it up, either. Or maybe you're not even aware that it's taped to the side of your frigerator and has been for the past ten years…Do you know *her* number? Hmm? *Do you?*"

"Whose?" he asked wryly.

"Danielle's—do you still know her number? Still have it memorized—do you?"

He blushed. "Not really…913 something…"

"913—Is that the area code? *Is it?*"

He smirked.

"Do you even know *our* area code? *Do you?*"

He leaned over and whispered in her ear. "Are you having your period?"

Gabrielle saw a flash of light before slapping his arm as hard as she possibly could. But the gesture just made him laugh. Angry, hurt and completely unable to read his intentions, she attempted to give him the silent treatment for the remainder of home room and first period, relieved she would have a break from seeing him for a few hours and wondering if sitting next to him was such a great idea after all, if being clandestine about it wasn't the wiser way to go.

But he kicked her playfully, at times reaching out and grabbing her hair, at other times passing her notes with stupid comments or smiley faces. As she stood up to leave at the sound of the bell, he pulled her back down next to him. "You look nice today," he said, grinning.

"Oh, please…"

"No, you do—you look hot. I just have to be careful, you know…I have sweats on…. Won't be making that mistake again, not if you're gonna keep dressing like this…"

She rolled her eyes.

"Will you have lunch with me?" he asked.

"Maybe."

"What do you mean *maybe?*"

"Maybe I'll have lunch with you and *maybe* we'll get together after school and jam like you promised…but that's only if you haven't scheduled something with Carl."

He crossed his arms, musing a moment. "It's Wednesday, right…Nope, I'm good for tonight. Study group is Tuesday and Thursday."

"*Study group?*"

"Yes, you see, in exchange for his *permission* for us to be together, which was so fucking important for you to receive, I committed to spending the majority of my mornings, evenings and weekends playing every male sport offered in the state of Montana and attempting to keep a B average. Ironic, isn't it, since now I will have less time than ever to spend with you. But, hey…he's okay with us now. *Peace on.*"

She bit her lip, trying to hold back the tears.

He grinned. "*Psyche…*" Then kissed her on the cheek before getting up and heading for his next class.

But by lunch, her nerves were still in tatters and she had no appetite, opting for a plate of fries, a small bowl of grapes and a soda. Alex eyed her plate curiously.

"Are you okay?" he asked.

She shrugged. "Yes...I'm fine...I just don't know where we should sit," she said, scanning the lunch room.

"Well, we can sit at my table—"

"I don't want to sit at your table."

"Well then how 'bout your table?"

"I don't want to sit at my table, either...We'll sit at our own table," she said, making her way towards a half-empty one in-between.

They had just sat down to eat, and Alex was finally getting her to spill the details of her dreadful morning with Brooke, when a tray slammed down next to Gabrielle's with a loud bang. Startled, she turned to see Dennis Wiseman sliding onto the lunch bench next to her.

"Do we have a new friend, Gabby? Please—why don't you introduce me," Dennis said caustically, his black eyes piercing, his shoulder nearly touching hers.

She slid closer to Alex, who placed a hand on her leg, squeezing it reassuringly.

"Um...." She shook her head, speechless.

"He looks like a faggot—is he a faggot?" Dennis asked loudly.

At this, Alex wadded his napkin and threw it on the table. Gabrielle put her head in her hands.

"Wiseman," Alex said between his teeth.

"*Fahlstrom*," Dennis matched.

"Want to fucking take this outside?"

"Well, I'm sure *you do*—wouldn't want to embarrass yourself in front of your girl, here."

Alex spun around on the bench. "I'll be back in five," he whispered to Gabby, before abruptly standing up and heading for the exit.

Gabrielle watched numbly as Dennis strode after Alex, wondering if the drama would ever end, suddenly longing for those endless stretches of days that offered nothing but routine simplicity. She then watched as two of Dennis's friends headed out, trailed by Carl and Ron, finally concluding that she may never see Alex again due to his likely expulsion by the end of the day, followed by his banishment to the mental ranch in Billings. But before she could sink into complete depression, her girlfriends swarmed the now vacant half of the table to get the scoop while offering support, soon having her laughing about the comic absurdity of it all.

After five minutes had passed without incident or update, the discussion turned to prom night planning, the group taking an assessment of who still needed a date. A few minutes later, the lunch door burst open, and Alex strode through, heading for the table, a smirk on his face. Gabrielle's friends grabbed their trays and plates, scattering away as quickly as they had arrived.

He slid onto the bench next to Gabrielle, kissing her cheek. "See—told you I'd be back in five."

"Actually, it's been closer to ten," she said wryly.

He shrugged. "It's the walk—doesn't count. I needed to make sure we were off school property when I did it."

"When you did *what* exactly?"

"Kicked his fucking ass…"

She groaned.

"Don't worry—I didn't hurt him. Well, not too badly…Look—I knocked him on his ass and then invited him to your jerk off party."

"You mean *Jam Off*?"

He shrugged, biting into his burger. "He had it coming to him, Gabs. I want to be friends, but I'm not gonna put up with that shit forever…" he continued in between bites. "I paid my dues with that guy. As far as I'm concerned, I've paid my dues with *everyone*. Jesus H."

Minutes later, Carl and Ron showed up, walking by and slapping Alex on the back as they headed back to their table. Gabrielle did not see Dennis or his friends return for the remainder of lunch, but by last period, her nerves had settled and she was able to focus on her studies, content with Alex sitting next to her, and Alex also seemingly content for once, refraining from the kicks and jabs he inflicted earlier in the day. So calm was she, that when two wasps began circling the ceiling, having wandered in from the classroom window that had been deliberately left wide open to let in the fresh, spring air, she watched bemusedly, relieved that her classmates remained oblivious to the buzzing dance overhead.

And at the end of the school day, after she and Alex had climbed into her car to head to her house for some music practice, any doubt regarding his feelings for her vanished as quickly as his restraint. She had barely gotten the key in the ignition, when he leaned over and began kissing her, soon embracing her, his hands roving up her stockinged leg, looking for skin before venturing on to other territory.

She grabbed his hand, "Why don't we take this to my bedroom," she whispered.

"I don't know if I can wait," he said, grabbing her hand and placing it on his groin, the bulge through his thin cotton sweat pants sending a shudder through her person.

"Jesus, Alex…" she breathed.

It was a good thing the house was empty of family members, Gabrielle thought to herself, her back pushed flat against the wall next to the front door, her jacket and panties already on the floor, she and Alex locked in such a heated embrace, she thought he might try to make love to her standing up. But she was able to maneuver him down the hall to the bedroom and behind a locked door, where she felt more comfortable completely losing herself in the moment. After he had undressed enough of himself, he barely had the patience to undress her, entering her with vehemence once the skirt came off and they had fallen onto the bed. It was rougher than the other day in the stable but not as excruciating, the pleasure outweighing the pain and leading to a faster climax for her, one that lingered, nearly duplicating itself a few minutes later, when he came.

As she lay holding him, her body pressed tight against the mattress under his weight, his head on her chest, she tried to mentally capture every sensation, from his scent, to the feel of the skin on his arms, his neck, his back, to the slightly abrasive touch of his thick curls on her breast. Even his breathing she tried to memorize so she could recreate it later that night, when he would no longer be physically present and she would have to rebuild the moment with mental imprints.

Later, as they began to dress themselves, he gently grabbed her by the shoulders from behind, pushing aside the strap of her camisole. "Is that a tattoo?"

She froze momentarily, shaking off the déjà vu. "Maybe…"

"*Maybe*? It either is or it isn't," he said, laughing. "It looks like a sideways eight."

"Yes…It's the sign for infinity."

"Infinity…" he echoed, lightly tracing it with his finger, tickling her and causing her to twitch slightly. "So, why'd you get it?"

"The tattoo?"

"Well, yeah…The sign, mostly, though. Why'd you get this sign?"

She shrugged, blushing. "I don't know…I was really, really happy at the time. I guess—I guess a part of me was hoping it would last forever. But, nothing does…At least not here."

"Not where?" he asked, kissing the tattoo, his lips slowly moving from there to her neck.

"The world of dreams."

"Am I still dreaming?" he asked playfully, kissing her ear. "This doesn't feel like I'm still dreaming. This feels very real."

"I know," she said sadly.

"So when do we wake up?"

"I don't know...When we want to, I guess."

"But I don't want to," he said, holding her.

"Exactly...None of us do, really...I don't. Not right now...Maybe when I'm old and worn and you've tired of me."

He laughed. "I thought you found the future scary."

"I do...It's horrifying."

"So why are you going there, then? Come back. I'm happy being in the present with you. Where we're young and horny and happy. Where I'll never tire of you or *this*...Come back to the infinite present."

She smiled to herself.

"I might just have to get me a tattoo," he said finally.

"Really?" she said skeptically.

"Yep...I'm going to get the symbol for *pi*."

"Pi? Do you even know what *pi* is? Mr. I'm Flunking Math..."

"Jesus, Gabby—I'm not a complete moron...It's an irrational number... It's an irrational number that spans into *infinity*...And, yeah, I would say it pretty much represents my life right now."

They laughed and made out a bit before heading to the garage to practice a few songs together for Saturday night's party.

CHAPTER EIGHTEEN

Alex woke up on Saturday morning as he did every morning, slightly apprehensive of his surroundings and straining to adjust his eyes until a familiar object came into focus, one that confirmed the world in which he had awaken, be it the dog, the plain gray walls or the photo of the five children taped to his wall.

He then stretched, thinking about the day ahead and the moments he planned to create with his time. Spending another few minutes reliving past moments, especially ones with Gabrielle, which usually provided the impetus to propel him out of bed and into action, as they did today. Being the weekend and therefore a non-workout day with Carl, who had a track meet anyway, he took his dog on a mile-long walk, savoring the surrounding landscape.

The sky was extraordinarily bright that morning, the sun bathing everything in a gentle white glow. In the near distance rose the snow-capped peaks of the Mission Mountains, and as he walked down his street, he enjoyed breathtaking views of Flathead Lake and the surrounding meadows and hillsides. It was during moments like these that he felt a deep sense of gratitude towards whatever force in his mind or his universe had created such beauty and peace, knowing perfectly well its equal power to create the complete opposite.

After showering, he joined his parents for breakfast, his sister nowhere to be found, as usual, and proudly announced that he would be taking Gabrielle to the Junior Prom. After receiving relieved and congratulatory smiles and comments from his parents, he asked to have his car returned, if not that very afternoon, at least in time for the dance, which was three weeks away.

He had seen the vehicle, a gorgeous piece of machinery covered and parked safely in the back of the Trahan's massive garage, a garage built for tractors and other farming equipment and the same garage in which the *Jam Off* party would be held that evening. Though unlocked, Gabrielle did not know where her parents had hidden the spare keys, and all they could do was sit inside the pristine, all black leather interior and imagine themselves on the open highway, listening to music in the high-end Delco-Bose sound system, subwoofers reverberating through the seats. Alex Tate had put extraordinary care and expense into every detail of the car, from its gleaming paint job to the polished engine beneath the hood, and as Alex sat behind the steering wheel, he couldn't help but feel a kinship with the previous owner, a sense of sadness at his passing, making an internal vow to keep the car immaculate as a respectful memorial.

Even without keys, the car was an ideal hideaway for lovemaking, and he and Gabrielle christened it twice, once on Wednesday evening after they had jammed together for a few hours and again just the previous evening, right before Alex had headed off in his parent's station wagon to another night of Rock n' Bowl with his friends, an activity for which Gabrielle had no inclination to participate.

Though he lost the battle for the car in the short-term, his father promised him the keys by prom night as long as he stayed out of trouble. After completing his chores by lunch, he collected his allowance and scraped together all the rest of the money he had leftover from his shopping spree as well as some cash he had found hidden in various books and crannies in his predecessor's room. Money in hand, Alex waited for Gabrielle to pick him up so they could drive to Missoula and pay for the rest of his guitar.

"How 'bout letting me drive today?" he asked, after she had pulled into his driveway.

She smirked. "I guess that means no car today, hmm?"

"You have no idea how emasculating it is having your girlfriend drive you everywhere," he said, opening the driver's side door for her and waiting for her to climb out, curious as to what she was channeling today, a rugged, out-doorsy, olive green jacket covering a tight fitting gray T-shirt paired with dark brown cotton shorts, tall brown boots and blue knit leg warmers which extended beyond the boots to just below the knee. Her thick hair flowed freely in loose waves, and he wondered if she had curled it.

She slid into the passenger seat, and he slid into the driver's seat.

"Do you want to go for a hike or fuck—I really can't tell with that get-up," he asked.

She stared at him wide-eyed.

"Or do you want to go for a hike and then fuck? I'm happy either way," he burst, not expecting a throbbing erection to so quickly disrupt the flow of their day.

"Neither," she said, staring at him incredulously. "I want to go to Missoula to pay for your fucking guitar. And then we need to head back to get ready for our party."

"How the fuck am I supposed to drive for the next hour with you looking like that—"

"Like *what*? Jesus, Alex…It's one o'clock in the afternoon—I just got here. Really…"

He put his head on the steering wheel.

"Do you want a blow job? I'm happy to give you one if that'll calm you down so we can get going with our day…"

"No…Why the fuck would I want a blow job if I can get the real thing? If I can bang *that*—" he said, eyeing her body.

"That?…*That*, as in my body, which has now been objectified into a *that*?" She sighed, shaking her head. "You're a piece of work…If you weren't so fucking hot, I wouldn't put up with your shit."

"Well, if you weren't so hot I wouldn't put up with yours, either…Where are we going?"

"To Missoula, goddamit. Let's go."

"No—where are we going to fuck? I'm not going to Missoula until we've consummated this day. Look at it outside—it's fucking perfect. This is the most perfect day ever, but it's not complete until we've done it. And the last thing I want is to get into some fucking accident on the highway without having made love to you first."

"*Why would we*? What is wrong with you?"

"Nothing's wrong with me—that's how the universe works. You're driving along in life, all happy and thinking things are great, when bam—you get hit with something. A truck. A bullet. A disease. I don't know. And I've decided that I'm not going to let a day go by without getting what I want out of it—fresh air, a view of the mountains, some good food and an incredible fuck with you—and not necessarily in that order...I'm never dying again with any regrets."

She mused a moment. "Wow...That's really profound, actually...Hmmmm...I don't know what I want out of my day...Let's see—"

"Jesus, Gabby—do you have any blankets?"

"Um, no...They haven't been washed yet from the last time we used them... Which was only a week ago, but it could be a year, a decade...an eon, even."

"Fuck..." he said, leaving the car on while running back into the house, emerging a few minutes later with a couple of blankets or towels, she couldn't tell.

Fifteen minutes later they had pulled off the highway near Pablo, parking in a wooded area on the outskirts of the wildlife refuge.

He turned off the car and looked at her. "You're not in the mood, are you?"

She blushed, shaking her head. "I'm just tired today...I don't know why," she said, yawning.

"Well...We have had a lot of sex this week," he offered.

She nodded. "Yeah...more than some people do in a month, a year even.... It's like we were making up for lost time or something ..."

"Well, we were, weren't we," he said quietly.

She smiled. "I wouldn't mind sitting outside with you for a little bit... Maybe we can take a nap."

"A *nap*?"

"Yeah...outside in the sunshine...like cats do. At least my cats do...I get jealous of them sometimes. Especially when I have a lot of homework or just stuff to do and I see them lying there in the sun—always in the sun. Nothing to do and not a care in the world."

Alex chuckled. "Mr. Kitty...Stupidest fucking name for a cat I have ever heard."

"That's not his name, you know," she said laughing. "It's the only thing he answers to, but it's not his name."

"What is his name?"

"Bilbo."

"Bilbo?"

"After the hobbit. Because he's fat like a hobbit...Shit, we tried Bilbo,

Frodo, Sam and Hobbit, but he only comes to Mr. Kitty...And sometimes he'll answer to *Gimli*...He's not even my cat...He's Nate's cat, but he took to me after Nate went to college."

They eventually made their way outside, spreading out the assortment of odd throws and towels Alex had grabbed from his house, some far too decorative and nice to be used outdoors and in the manner Alex wanted to use them, but Gabrielle just smirked to herself, figuring he could take that up with his mother when she came looking for them. For the next hour, they alternated between making out and staring up at the sunlit blue sky through the tree leaves. At some point she fell asleep in his arms, her head resting on his shoulder.

"Hey...Wake up," he said, shaking her gently.

"Do we have to..."

"It's after two."

She sat up stretching and yawning, her dark hair glistening in the sunlight. "But we haven't even had sex yet..."

"I thought you didn't want it," he said wryly, still lying on his back, using one arm as a headrest, the other caressing the skin of her exposed thigh.

"I never said that...I said I was tired...For future reference, that's a code for, *if anything's going to happen, you'll have to take the lead.*"

"Are you kidding me? I thought *tired* was a code word for no sex. I could swear that's what the books say—"

"What books? Not *my* book...the code word—or words—for no sex in my book are *headache, stomach ache, depressed* or *on the rag. Tired* means I'm not really thinking about it, but I could be convinced. *Tired* means you'll have to do all the work—that's all."

"How is that any different than every time we do it? I have to do all the work, anyways. You just lie there," he said, smirking, waiting for the spark in her eye that would be followed by a slap or punch that would trigger an instant erection and intense embrace. But this time, she was the aggressive one, taking off her shorts and unzipping his pants before straddling him.

"How 'bout I do all this work this time and you just lie there," she whispered, kissing his ear, her hair spilling over his exposed chest.

He smiled. "You know I like to be on top," he said, moving to get up.

She resisted. "I know—and it's my turn."

"Gabby you can't," he said quietly, his expression clouding with dark memories, horrific images.

She smiled sadly. "You have a bad memory, don't you?"

He looked away.

"Let me rewrite it for you…"

"You can't…"

"Yes, I can…" She kissed him gently on the lips. "Alex, I love you…There, I said it. I love you, and I want to make love to you…And I want you to be so happy and the memory of this to be so wonderful that you can't possibly think of anything else…"

He closed his eyes, wanting to trust her but scared of his own mind.

"Alex, look at me…You did it for me…Let me return the favor…Please."

After a moment's hesitation, he nodded, smiling, before taking a deep breath and letting himself go, relinquishing all control and following her lead, focusing on the beauty of his surroundings, the light floral scent of her hair, the smooth skin of her thighs pressed tightly against his own, the soft wet touch of her lips as they kissed his stomach, chest and neck. Even the faint sound of her uneven breathing as she poured all of her being into every movement, every lingering pull, each contraction of her muscles a heartfelt embrace. By the time he came, his position, his senses and even time itself dissolved into the explosive bliss as he clutched her waist tightly and thrust upwards and deeply, as far into her as he could go, releasing only when she gasped sharply.

For the next ten minutes, they lay quietly together, letting their labored breathing and the cacophony of birds from the trees and nearby refuge speak for them.

"I don't understand…" he said finally. "This is, like, the best day of my life…Every day is like, the best day…How is it possible to go from such hell to this…"

"Is this what you wanted?"

"Yeah…I guess…I don't know. I hadn't thought about it. I don't remember thinking about it. Maybe…"

She smiled, holding him close. "Well, this is what I wanted…When you know what you want, the universe provides…The universe can't help a conflicted mind…Chaos ensues."

"I love the universe," he said simply. "It's much kinder than god."

She laughed. "How do you know they aren't one and the same?"

He shrugged. "Pictures…History…Creepy old mean guy with a beard or the peace of infinite empty space and possibility…You tell me."

"I think that's unfair to God…I think everyone has him all wrong. And, if you change your definition of God to mean the peace of infinite empty space and possibility, then they *are* one and the same...A rose by any other name smells as sweet."

He exhaled loudly. "Okay...I'm way too spent right now to argue with you," he joked.

On the way to Missoula, they listened to Nirvana, in part to get them inspired for the *Jam Off* and in part to honor the memory of Kurt Cobain, who had died earlier in the month. To change it up, Gabrielle threw in some tracks from the new Beck and Soundgarden. Alex increasingly noticed that she did not carry on lengthy conversations but engaged in spurts—chatting excitedly about a topic for a few minutes before falling into a long stretch of silence. But her silence was calming, and he refrained from asking her where her mind went during those times, as interested as he was in going there with her.

It was during one of these stretches that he threw a thought at her, startling her out of her reverie like a rock knocking a bird off a tree limb.

"Do you have a blue dress by any chance?"

She stared blankly at him.

"Do you?"

"Why?" she asked, her body tensing.

"What's it look like?"

"*Why?*"

"Well, I was thinking maybe you could wear it to prom..."

"No," she said flatly. "I'm not wearing it to prom—"

"Why?"

"Because it's not a prom dress. It's—it's a cocktail dress...or something."

"Is it strapless?"

"No—it's not. It's sleeveless, but it has straps...Oh, my god—why? Why are you asking? Why do you do this?"

"Do what—"

"You know damn well...*Blue dress*...What—did she wear it? Did she?"

"Who?"

"Danielle. Did she get you all hot and horny in it?"

"No, actually—she didn't..." he mumbled. While Danielle had worn the dress, it was not she who had sexually stirred him.

"Well then who did?"

"You did," he said quietly, staring out the windshield, trying to keep part of his mind focused on the road ahead.

"I thought I wasn't in your other life..."

"You weren't…It was a picture…A painting…I saw it in a painting."

"A painting…Like in a museum? A gallery?"

"Something like that."

Gabrielle shook her head and stared out the passenger window.

"Anyway, I'd like to see you in it."

"I bet you would," she snapped.

"I'm serious…I want to take you to prom in that dress, and I want our picture taken—together. As a couple."

"Why?" she burst.

"Because pictures are important to me, okay? They're like frozen moments—shadows of moments. And they tell a story. And I…I want that picture, okay? You do, too…You need that picture as badly as I do."

She sighed, brushing an errant tear from her cheek, unsure from where it stemmed as no others followed. "Fine…I'll wear it…How 'bout the shoes? Do you have an opinion on those? Hmmm? And my hair—do you want it done a certain way, too? Long and flowing, perhaps—curled? Why don't you just come dress me yourself."

"I don't give a shit how you wear your hair or if you wear shoes at all…And frankly, it's the undressing I'm interested in…Which is why I want you to wear a dress like that blue one…Prom dresses are dumb. They're like wedding dresses—which are also dumb. Completely nonconducive to fucking."

She laughed. "Okay—okay. Well, I have a request of my own. No matching cummerbund—I'm serious. I think that's so gay…No cummerbund at all, actually. They're just stupid…And I don't like bow ties, either. In fact, I don't ever want to see you in a bow tie. *Ever*."

"What the fuck's a cummerbund?"

"They're those stupid wide sash looking belts guys wear with tuxes. And they come in different colors…A lot of guys get colors to match their dates' dresses."

"Who said anything about a tux? I'm not getting a tux—I can't afford it, for one."

"Thank god," she breathed.

"And two—since when did prom become about the clothes? And a bunch of clothes that are completely nonconducive to fucking…Prom is about dancing and fucking…Wait, I forgot dinner…It's about eating, dancing and fucking. And the faster we can get out of our clothes, the better… Cummerbunds…Jesus."

She laughed, and they fell quiet for a minute.

"Look...if the blue dress is going to be that traumatic for you, there is another dress I might entertain..."

"I can't imagine," she said wryly.

"That one you wore in a *Westside Story.*"

She burst out laughing. "*What?* Are you serious?"

"I'm dead serious...I want a piece of that chick...*Maria.* We might just have to recreate Tony and Maria's wedding night..."

"Yeah—right...You forget, I'm no longer a virgin."

"You played one quite well...Anyway, we can just pretend that you are... Jesus, I'm getting a hard on just thinking about it...Goddamn it."

"You're insane."

"And you're a good actress...In fact, I can get into this acting career you have...As long as I can fuck all your characters, I am a happy man... And frankly, you're a different person every day, anyway. I don't know who I'm fucking half the time...Like today...You look like *Playboy*'s version of a park ranger."

She stared out the window, utterly speechless but on the verge of hysterics.

"So what's next year's play going to be?"

"Uh...*Sound of Music,* I think..."

"What's it about?"

"Well...There's another Maria—"

"Is she hot?"

"Um...I don't...No, I wouldn't consider her character hot. She's a nanny."

"So...Nanny's can be hot...Who's the guy?"

"Captain von Trapp."

"Sounds like a stud...So what's the plot?"

Gabrielle turned red. "Um...Well, Maria gets kicked out of a convent and goes to work as a nanny for Captain von Trapp, who has seven children. The mother had died."

"Seven children...So he's a horny mother fucker...That guy'll fuck anything that moves. So he bangs the nanny, and then what?"

"He doesn't bang the nanny," Gabrielle burst. "He marries her...In fact he chooses her over some rich, countess who he was previously engaged to."

"Was the countess hot?"

"Well...in the movie she kind of was supposed to be, I think...I guess."

"And who played the nanny?"

"Julie Andrews."

"Jesus Christ...Are you fucking kidding me? If the rich countess was hotter than the nanny, then he wouldn't have married the nanny. And no offense, but Mary Poppins is not hot...at least not as Mary Poppins...Jesus, I'm going to have nightmares now...You'll be rewriting a lot of memories for me after this conversation...And for the record—I don't want to see you in a Mary Poppins outfit ever. *Ever*...You can just walk away from that play... Anyway, they got the story all wrong. You're going to have to fix that."

"How?" she burst, laughing. "Please enlighten me..."

"Well for one—make sure they give you a hot nanny outfit...If the skirt is supposed to be long, modernize it...Cut it above the knee...And unbutton the blouse...And wear your hair down—or part of it down...Or up with lots of strands falling down...And heels...Heels are important..."

"Jesus, Alex—she's supposed to be babysitting seven kids—seven very naughty kids, by the way. They're like, awful. Chased all their other nannies away."

"Well by the end of a day, her blouse would be undone and her hair a mess now, wouldn't it? Skirt might be ripped, too..."

Gabrielle buried her head in her hands, laughing so hard her eyes began tearing.

"I'm trying out for this play..." Alex continued. "I'm gonna be Captain von Trapp—you watch me...Fuck—is this a musical? It's a musical, isn't it... Does he have to sing and dance and shit? You know I have a very limited singing voice..."

"Actually and, interestingly enough...He just plays acoustic guitar and sings one song..."

"Like Nick Drake?"

"Something like that..." she said, giggling.

"Yeah, well—you and I are going to rewrite that play...Everyone's going to know exactly why he chose the nanny over the countess...We'll add our own little subliminal moves and gestures...And by the end of the night, every male in that audience is gonna have a hard on...They won't know why, either...But the birth rate in Polson is going to jump twenty percent nine months from then...You watch."

She wiped the tears from her eyes.

"He wears a uniform, too, doesn't he? *Captain* von Trapp..."

Gabrielle nodded, unable to speak.

"Yeah...Fuck West Point...I'll show Carl...I don't need to go to some fucking military academy to get into a uniform. And then you can fulfill any bizarre fantasy you and half the other women in the universe have about fucking a guy in a uniform...In fact, I'll just keep my costume...Take it out and wear it whenever you want."

It was late in the afternoon by the time they reached Missoula, so they quickly made their exchange, both extremely pleased with the outcome, the pristine condition of Nate's saxophone not only paying for the guitar but netting them an extra seventy-five dollars. Alex felt she should give the money to her brother, but Gabrielle felt otherwise, using five of it to buy sodas and snacks for the long drive home. But the caffeine could not keep Gabrielle awake, and fifteen minutes into the car ride home, she fell asleep, leaving Alex in control of the music and alone with this thoughts.

The truck was running low on gas, and Alex decided to stop in St. Ignatius to refuel, pulling into a convenience store on the side of the highway. As irrationally panicked as he felt, he did not want to disturb her, she looked so peaceful and happy slumped against the passenger door, so he got out of the car to pump gas and face his overwhelming sense of foreboding, a foreboding that he found irritating, invasive, like a toxin. After putting ten dollars worth into the tank, he took a deep breath and strolled up to the building to pay.

The door opened with a chime, not unlike a doorbell. Like most gas stations, the store was tiny and cramped, the floor tiles a bit grimy and the shelves unevenly stocked. A small TV played on the counter, and the attendant, an elderly man in a plaid hunting jacket, was watching a hockey game and chatting with another patron, who leaned over the counter.

They greeted Alex warmly and updated him on the score, as if he had known them all along and cared about the game. After taking his money, the attendant commented on the beautiful day and wished Alex a pleasant afternoon before returning his attention to the game.

Alex walked back out into the still brightly lit day with an enormous sense of gratitude.

It was just after five-thirty when they arrived at the Trahans, and the family was sitting down for a spaghetti and meatball dinner to the background noise of CNN, Dr. Trahan's favorite channel. Alex was seated across from Brooke and Gabrielle, in Nate's spot, he guessed, and the family brought him into their lively discussions on world events, President Clinton and local politics as if he had always sat there and cared about what they were discussing.

In the middle of dinner, there was a quick knock on the front door, but before anyone could answer, it burst open and in strolled Dennis Wiseman.

"Am I late Mrs. T.?" he asked, stopping short upon seeing Alex seated at the table.

"No, honey…Not at all…" Mrs. Trahan said, getting up from the table to grab another chair.

"What's he doing here?" Dennis burst. "And what's he doing in my spot?"

"Now, Dennis—there's room for both of you…Alex, can you scoot over a bit?" she asked, placing the empty chair next to him.

"How is that your spot, Dennis? That's my brother's spot…You're just squatting for a free meal," Brooke said irritably.

"No, I'm not…I'm like family. I'm part of the *tribe*, remember? This is an Indian reservation last time I checked. Even though we're increasingly becoming the minority," he said caustically, throwing Alex a look.

"Dennis, on a molecular level we are all exactly the same…Cut us open, and we all bleed red," Dr. Trahan said dryly.

Dennis sat stiffly, mere inches from Alex, arms crossed, seemingly unable to eat. To break the tension, Alex grabbed the salad bowl and extended it to him.

"Dennis," Alex said, nudging him with the bowl

"Alex," Dennis said, arms still crossed.

"*Dennis…*"

"*Alex…*"

"*Dennis*," Alex said, jamming the bowl into his arm, causing a piece of lettuce to fly out.

"What is this—*Beavis and Butthead* come to dinner?" Brooke snapped.

Gabrielle bit her lip, staring down at her plate and trying not to laugh.

"Seriously…" Brooke continued. "And I don't understand why you're letting her have a party at all," she said, addressing her parents. "Especially if these two ass clowns are going to be there…I mean—they can't stop knocking each other out. All we need is Carl to join the fray. Is he coming? Is he? Throw Carl into the mix, and we have the three stooges. And then we just might have some entertainment tonight if you don't kill each other or trash the place first."

"Now, Brooke—Gabby knows the rules…No alcohol, no drugs—and *no fights*…They're just going to drink sodas and play music…Right, Gabby? Right boys?" her mother asked sweetly, but there was a smirk in her tone, a hint of knowing in her look.

Gabrielle shifted uncomfortably in her chair before smiling and nodding, as that was her intention. But she also knew she had absolutely no control over the thirty or so odd friends who would show up armed with both.

Brooke threw her hands in the air. "That's it…I'm leaving…I can't take this anymore…I'm going to the Fahlstroms," she said dramatically.

"But I thought you were going to jam with us later—you and Danielle," Gabrielle protested, sounding genuinely unhappy about her sister's abandonment.

"With you amateurs? Please…We'll *consider* gracing you with our presence later in the evening…And, by the way," she said, glaring at Alex. "If there is even one broken guitar string on my guitar—just *one*—you're mine. And you better leave it tuned as you found it." Brooke then swept out of the room, her hair blowing behind her.

Alex had remained frozen through the entire exchange, salad bowl still poised mid air between he and Dennis's arm. He turned to Dennis. "Is she always like that?"

"Yep."

"Salad?"

"Why thank you," Dennis said, taking the bowl from him.

Gabrielle's friends started showing up after dinner, many with instruments and some with serious sound equipment—speakers, mixers, amplifiers and even dance lights. The garage had been completely cleared of vehicles and equipment with the exception of the Camaro, which sat covered in the back corner, away from most of the activity. Alex sat on the hood of his car, tuning his acoustic guitar, not even wanting to touch Brooke's until he, Gabrielle and whomever they could recruit to play bass jammed to Nirvana's "Breed" later that evening.

"Protecting your car?" Dennis asked wryly, joining him.

He smiled. "Sort of…It's a damn fine piece of equipment…I got to hand it to the guy—he had taste."

"What are you—complimenting yourself now?" Dennis said.

"Not me…It's not my car…I just inherited it from the asshole."

Dennis scrutinized him, his black eyes getting beady momentarily. "What's your name again?"

"Alex Michael Fahlstrom," Alex said simply, strumming the beginnings of "Road."

"And what's my name?"

"Dennis Wiseass…" Alex said, grinning, starting to play the song in earnest.

Dennis shook his head, trying to contain the beginnings of a smile. "You really know how to play that thing?" he asked, leaning against the door.

"I'm playing it right now…"

"Well I can't tell…I don't know that song…For all I know you're bullshitting…"

Alex rolled his eyes before launching into "Dust in the Wind," one of the few well-known tunes that seemed to impress people who knew little about acoustic and rhythm guitar. It worked on Dennis, who launched into a conversation about music he liked, most of it rock and metal, and begged Alex to grab Brooke's electric guitar so he could listen to some *real* music. He then offered Alex a hand rolled cigarette, which Alex gladly accepted, having left his smokes in Gabrielle's car.

But upon his first inhale, he could tell they were not the average cigarette.

"Shit…" he burst, eyes widening at the intensity of the first puff. "What do you grow this stuff yourself?"

"Why yes I do, actually…That's the real deal there."

"Jesus, Wiseman…" Alex said, taking another drag. "Fuck…"

"And since when have you become a connoisseur of marijuana?" Dennis asked dryly.

Alex looked at him incredulously. "Are you kidding me? I've been smoking this shit since I was fifteen…Fourteen…I don't even remember, that's how much I've smoked."

Dennis shook his head, a bemused look on his face.

But Alex heard his name called and looked up to see Gabrielle heading their direction along with a handful of people, girls and guys, all dressed in artsy attire, including a guy with a purple Mohawk and a girl with pink hair that Alex recognized as being one of Gabrielle's close friends. He shoved the joint into Dennis's hands. "*Get rid of it…Now,*" he whispered hoarsely.

"I'm not getting rid of it."

"Then go smoke it—just *get it out of here*. Jesus."

Alex was then introduced to the group and eventually encouraged to bring his guitar over to where the other musicians were setting up. By the time things got going, there were a handful of guitarists, two bass players, three keyboardists, two drummers, a violinist and a saxophone player. Everyone else insisted they could sing, depending on the song, including Dennis Wiseman. There was also a DJ who brought mixing equipment and had begun to churn electronic dance tunes and other alternative sound to get the mood going and keep it going in-between riffs.

It was kind of like musical improv, Alex thought to himself, with individual musicians or groups of musicians playing a dedicated piece, inviting other musicians to join in if they wished or had something to offer, the goal being to create something new or different at the end from what existed at the beginning. And the music ranged from alternative to hard core punk, from bluegrass to classical, from folk to jazz. There were even a few pop songs. The only rules were to try to keep it under five minutes so everyone would get decent playing time and to refrain from criticizing whatever was played.

As Alex would later realize, while the improv was happening in the back part of the garage with people who actually wanted jam together, a much different scene was going on in the front part of the garage and out into the lawn, where anyone and everyone who had heard about the party had just shown up looking for a place to hang out and get wasted. During the course of the next few hours, he would travel between both worlds, enjoying both the free flow of beer, hard liquor and pot that the masses had to offer and the company of fellow musicians as he riffed along on either his acoustic guitar or Brooke's electric, whichever fit the song.

At some point Carl and Ron showed up, and it was after they did that Alex asked Gabrielle if they could play their Nirvana tune, Nirvana being the subject of a number of performances that evening and, when played, receiving party-wide attention, as everyone was still a bit broken up about Cobain's suicide. The guy with the purple Mohawk volunteered to play bass and some other guy volunteered to sing.

Alex stepped up to the microphone. "This is for my friend, Carl…Carl—if you're out there, please pay attention. And also in honor of the late, great Kurt Cobain—may he find some peace next time round."

He played the teaser chord of "Breed" before launching headlong into the song. Gabrielle stayed with him, playing her opening drum riff flawlessly. The song offered plenty of opportunity for Alex to show off his electric guitar skills, for Gabrielle to flaunt her drumming and for the other two stage volunteers to just look and sound cool, Alex thought to himself, enjoying every minute and smiling inwardly as shouts of *Fahlstrom, you crazy mother fucker* rose from somewhere in the audience.

And when the song was finished and they received cheers and clapping instead of the hoots and beer bottles from New Year's Eve, Alex again thanked the universe before venturing into the drunk, spirited but friendly crowd to find Carl and give him hell. Instead, he ended up giving him a drink, and then another, as Carl's tidy world, constructed of perfectly uniform black and white squares had shattered into uneven fragments of silver-gray with each stroke of his guitar string.

By eleven-thirty, things had wound down, and many of the musicians began packing up their instruments and gear. A few crowds lingered in and out of the garage, and Gabrielle ended up on one side with her friends while Alex ended up on the other side, his friends gathered around his car, the cover having been lifted and the driver's side door opened.

Carl had been drinking heavily since ten and showed no signs of wanting to stop, raising a beer to toast *Alex Michael* and pay homage to *Alex Tate, may he rest in peace with Kurt Cobain*. Alex was on his third joint, preferring marijuana to liquor at that point, though he had his fair share of beers and shots throughout the night, having drunk anything handed to him. Dennis had been wasted since Carl arrived and was in the process of taking Ron down with him, Ron having never smoked pot in his life. Somebody had found the cooler containing what was left of the alcohol and beer and placed it in the center of the group, and when this ran dry well after midnight, Dennis broke out the rest of his marijuana.

Alex remembered climbing into the driver's seat of his car at some point and reclining it as far as it would go. Groping around, he found a cool pair of shades behind the visor and put them on, closed his eyes and lay back, letting his mind drift in and out of the conversation.

"All I'm saying, Carl, is that you should live a little before going and getting your ass shot off in the Middle East somewhere…Ron knows what I'm talking about—don't you, Ronny, boy."

"I have no intention of getting my ass shot off Wiseman…I'm gonna be an officer."

"What the fuck does that matter? Officers get shot all the time…"

"Goddammit—I just want another beer."

"We don't have any beer, you fuck…We have this—which is much better than beer, trust me."

"I ain't smoking that shit, Wiseman…I'm going to West Point…And then I'm going to the Middle East to protect your pansy asses…Goddammit…But I don't want to go alone, man…Jesus Christ…He was supposed to go with me…We were supposed to go together…I can't do it without him…Fucking Jennifer Hicks…I can't do this anymore…I can't…Stupid skank."

"Oh, for fuck's sake..."

"And do you know why we were going to West Point instead of the Naval Academy? The uniforms...Fahlstrom thinks the navy guys look like faggots in their white pants and shit... But I know...I know it's really because he's got a perpetual hard on and those white cotton pants just weren't going to work."

"What the fuck are you talking about, Carl? If he gets a hard on in the navy, *he's* a faggot. What the fuck—"

"There are *women* in the navy, you effing moron. Fahlstrom gets a hard on at anything with tits and an ass...Fucking Jennifer Hicks...She ruined our lives...I can't do this...Where the eff is Alex Tate? Where?"

"He's right there," Ron said numbly.

"That's not Alex Tate, you dumb ass—that's Alex Michael," Carl burst.

"Who the fuck is Alex Michael?" Ron asked.

"*Him*—the dumb ass hippie guitarist laying there in the effing shades."

"O'Malley, you need to calm down...For the love of Jesus, just smoke this."

"What—so you can turn me in? Get revenge on all of us? Ruin my senior year? I need a goddamn beer..."

"You need a goddamn fuck, that's what you need...Jesus, Carl...For your information, I'm not an asshole, and I have no intention of turning anyone in...You just better be sure you get a fuck and get high before you head on out to the Middle East and get your ass blown off. And right now, I can help you with one of your two last requests."

"You're a good man, Wiseman..."

"Damn straight."

"We need you back, Wiseman...The team needs you...Goldilocks there says he's never wrestled in his life...Can you believe that shit?"

"I woulda believed it if he didn't kick my ass this week...Fucker let me beat the shit out of him the first time. Not that he didn't deserve it, 'cause he fucking did...I would have done some serious damage, too, if Gabby hadn't jumped in and saved his ass...Saved by a girl...It was awful...And what the fuck was up with that circle of protection shit? I was disturbed, man—that disturbed me for days...I thought he went faggot on all of us...You have no idea how relieved I was when my ass hit the ground this week..."

"Yeah, well I need you on the team, Wiseman...Ron and I need all the effing help we can get. We got nothing coming up from the middle school... Fucking Jennifer Hicks...She's gonna ruin our senior year."

"How the hell am I supposed to get back on the team?"

"Stop smoking that shit for a few weeks and pass a drug test."

"Fuck...Fucking asshole."

"Who?"

"Alex Tate...He's a fucking asshole...Drug test my ass..."

There was a minute or so of silence.

"You going to prom, Dennis?" Ron asked.

"Yep."

"Who you going with?"

"Cherise."

"Is she the one with the pink hair?"

"No, that's Kelly...Cherise has blond and black striped hair."

"Oh, her...Yeah, she's hot. But those chicks scare me, man...Is she scary?"

"What the fuck are you talking about?"

"I don't know, man...I want to ask Jamie, but she wants to go with Alex."

"Yeah, what the eff is up with that? Word hits the street that he and Trisha have split, and half the girls in school suddenly want to go out with him...Jesus, even Trisha still wants to go with him...Goddammit...Where's a fucking beer when you need one?"

"I thought you were going with Trisha."

"So did I...Fucking Jennifer Hicks...It's all her fault...But seriously, since when did Fahlstrom get game? Jesus..."

"It's the hair, O'Malley...Chicks dig the hair...He's got the Kurt Cobain thing going, too, may he rest in fucking peace."

"I thought he was going to prom with Gabrielle...He said he was."

"Gabby's a wench..."

"No shit...I don't get what's up with those two. I effing caught them getting it on in the library...I mean, Jesus Christ..."

"It's that fucking birthday thing."

"What birthday thing?"

"They share the same birthday and time."

"So? Lots of people do."

"No...You don't understand...They were born at the exact same time—like next to each other. It's fucking weird if you ask me."

Carl burst out laughing. "Are you serious? At the same time?"

"Fucking serious...Ask his mother. Shit, ask her mother...They're like best friends and love talking about how they had their fucking babies at the same time..."

"Shit...I knew they had the same birthday, but...Shit...I forgot about the time thing. I wish I would have remembered that tidbit. It'd a saved me a lot of grief and introspection."

"What the fuck are you talking about Carl?"

"Hell...They were probably fucking each other when they died last lifetime...*Born at the same time*. That explains everything."

"What do you mean last lifetime? Aren't you fucking Catholic, O'Malley?"

"I was...I'm not anything anymore...Not after tonight...Not after all this shit I've seen the past year...My effing best friend goes into a coma and wakes up a guitar-playing hippie...What the *fuck*. He's never touched a guitar in his life..."

"Yeah...And then there's all that shit about Kansas."

"Don't even go there Wiseman."

"He has pictures, Carl—pictures of places in Kansas that match up to his memory. Like addresses and shit."

"How do you know?"

"Gabby told me, the wench...He has an album in his room...She said I lived in a mansion. Can you believe that shit?"

"What the fuck are you talking about Wiseman?"

"What was she doing in his room?" Ron asked.

"What the fuck do you think she was doing in his room, you dumb ass... Jesus, Ron—you seriously need to get laid. Both of you. You're both gonna go faggot if you don't get your asses laid."

"Getting laid is highly overrated, Dennis...Look at Fahlstrom...Look at him. Couldn't keep his effing pecker in his pants, and look where it got him."

"What the fuck are you talking about Carl? There is nothing overrated about getting laid...Your problem is your choice in women. Trisha Kurtz—for fuck's sake...Your balls will fall off waiting for that girl to put out...You need to go get yourself a wench. We all need a good wench."

"I'll smoke to that..." Ron said. "I want a wench, Wiseman...Can you find me one? I want Jamie..."

"Jamie's not a wench, Ron...She's too much like Trisha. You need someone like Kelly."

"But Kelly has pink hair."

"What the fuck does that matter? You think your dick cares?"

"I need a goddamn beer...What the eff happened to all the goddamn beer?"

"You drank it, you dumb ass...Here, smoke this, you dumb shit...And you can thank me for saving your life later."

"What the eff are you talking about?"

"Carl—you don't smoke this joint right now and go find yourself some ass, you're gonna end up just like him. Alex Michael Tate whoever the fuck he is…You hear me? Fucking mental…Trisha Kurtz…Jesus Christ…The two of you lost your minds and your balls the day you fell in love with that piece of work. He was fucking whipped man—and I don't mean pussy whipped, because that would imply there was pussy, which there wasn't…And there won't be any for you, either, O'Malley."

But Alex drifted off to sleep before finding out whether or not Dennis had convinced Carl to get high with him.

∞

"What are you doing here?" Brooke snapped as Gabrielle entered their bedroom around midnight.

Gabrielle blinked, her eyes adjusting to the light in the room and her mind trying to process why Danielle Fahlstrom was sitting on her bed reading a magazine. "Well…This is my bedroom, and I'm going to bed."

"Not in here, you're not—you can sleep in Nate's room."

"Did Alex get home okay?" Danielle asked.

"No—he's still there…Hanging out with his friends."

"Well take him home," Danielle ordered.

"Why? You're his sister—you take him home…I'm not his keeper."

"If you're fucking him, you are."

Gabrielle saw white and nearly flew at her sister in a fit of rage, feeling she had utterly betrayed her confidence.

But Brooke thwarted her with a pillow. "Calm down, Gabs…Danielle's fucking our brother…We're all family around here…In a few generations, we'll be marrying our cousins, for Christ's sake."

Gabrielle plopped herself on the floor, comforted by her sister's attitude. "What's wrong Gabs?"

"There's some seriously weird male bonding going on out there…"

"Is alcohol involved?" Danielle asked.

Gabrielle nodded.

"Pot?" Brooke added.

She nodded.

"Yeah, well—you might as well just turn in for the night…" Brooke said, sighing.

"But make sure Alex gets home by nine tomorrow morning for church," Danielle said, her tone parental.

"Why do I have to make sure he gets home for church?"

"I'm sorry—do you have short-term memory loss? What the hell…"

"But aren't you going to church tomorrow? Why can't you just bring him home with you?"

"Because I'm eighteen, and I don't have to go to church anymore unless I feel like it…And tomorrow, I just don't."

"Fine…" Gabrielle said, her face flushing with anger. But fighting them was useless. She never won and only left the room feeling even more humiliated than when she entered.

The next morning, Gabrielle got up early to take care of her horses and get a start on her chores. Before walking to the barn, she stopped by the garage, relieved to see the four of them were alive and sleeping, sprawled in and around the Camaro. But by eight-thirty, they had not woken up and at eight forty-five, she was desperately trying to revive them.

Dennis was the first to respond, finally sitting up, groggy but semi-coherent.

"You need to help me…We need to get Alex home by nine."

"What time is it?"

"It's almost nine."

"Shit…That ain't gonna happen…Look at him."

"But he has to go to church…Seriously, Dennis—help me get him up."

"I hate to tell you this, Gabby, but he ain't going to church. Not today."

But after more pleading, Dennis conceded to help her rouse Alex, in the process also waking up Carl and Ron, who stumbled around for a few minutes before falling into small panic attacks about not getting home, and then falling to their knees feeling ill.

"Jesus Christ…" Dennis breathed.

"Look—I can get everyone home…Just help me get them into the back of my car."

"What the hell are you talking about Gabby?"

"They can fit in my truck bed, and I'll drive them all home."

"That's a terrible idea…One of them will fall out…Jesus…Carl's car is here—"

"So? He can get it later. Or you can drive it for him. Yeah—let's do that instead."

After another five minutes of stumbling confusion, Alex was propped into the front seat of Gabrielle's car, Ron was lying in the back of her truck bed, and Carl was lying in the back seat of his Buick, Dennis still groggy but conscious enough to drive Carl's car. The caravan headed to the Fahlstroms' house, arriving there by quarter after nine.

Alex, shades still covering his eyes, could barely walk. Gabrielle supporting one arm and Dennis supporting his other, the two guided him up the driveway and up the front steps. Before Gabrielle could reach the handle, the front door flew open.

Mrs. Fahlstrom stood, coat on and purse in hand, a surprised look on her face.

"Well...I see you've brought my son home. And just in time for church."

At that moment, Ron flung himself over the side of Gabby's truck bed and vomited onto the driveway.

Gabrielle looked at Mrs. Fahlstrom in mortified horror, but Mrs. Fahlstrom simply raised an eyebrow and invited them inside.

It was a struggle getting Alex over the threshold, and they had barely taken two steps when Gabrielle could no longer support him, Alex collapsing on the floor on his back, face up, shades still intact. His mother delicately stepped over his person and kneeling down next to him, took off his shades.

"Alex Michael," she said sternly.

He grinned. "Hi mom...You look so pretty."

Mrs. Fahlstrom closed her eyes, pursing her lips, and Gabrielle wanted to crawl into her skin.

"Would somebody like to explain to me why my son has come home piss drunk and smelling of illegal substances?" she asked sweetly. "Dennis? Gabrielle? Perhaps that gentleman out in the driveway?"

Gabrielle and Dennis stood in frozen silence, the subsequent presence of Mr. Fahlstrom's looming figure in the hallway making her nauseous with fear and shame.

Mr. Fahlstrom stood over his son, his gaze slowly moving from Alex's person to that of Dennis and Gabrielle.

"Bill, honey, there's a young man out in the driveway who needs some assistance. Can you go collect him, please?"

"There's another in the car," Dennis said hoarsely.

"Well, thank you, Dennis. And now if you would help to get Alex Michael to the living room, we can all have a nice little chat."

Five minutes later, the five of them were lined up on the living room sofa, which was only large enough to hold three comfortably. Gabrielle was practically hanging off the end, Alex having flung himself on top of her, half asleep, his head on her shoulder. Dennis was in the middle supporting Ron, and Carl was hanging off the other end, holding his stomach.

Mr. Fahlstrom stood, arms crossed, while Mrs. Fahlstrom paced thoughtfully in front of the group, coat still on and purse still in hand. "Hmmm... Who do we have here...Gabrielle Trahan, Alex Michael, Dennis Wiseman, Ron Smith and Carl O'Malley. What an interesting group. And there's five of them, too, Bill—don't you think that's curious."

"Oh, it's curious all right," he said gruffly.

"Is there anyone who's not hung over?" she asked. "Please raise your hand."

Gabrielle looked down the length of the sofa, hoping at least Dennis would raise his hand, but he did not. Swallowing hard, she timidly raised the one that wasn't covered by Alex's person.

"Gabrielle...Would you care to tell us what happened last night?"

"I don't know," she burst. "I had a party. We played some music, and everyone went home. I was in bed by midnight."

"Well not everyone went home, honey. You mean you didn't check on them? You just left your own party?"

"Why would I check on them? They can take care of themselves—"

"Well obviously not," Mrs. Fahlstrom said with mock indignation. "And you're the hostess. Don't you think you share some responsibility for this?"

"No—I don't."

Alex stirred, mumbling her name and how good her hair smelled. Gabrielle tried to hush him, her face reddening.

"Well...I know where the pot came from," she said, eyeing Dennis. "But what about the alcohol. Hmmm? Carl, Ron—any ideas?"

"I'm gonna be sick," Carl groaned. "May I be excused, Miss J?"

"Yes, Carl—you know where the bathroom is. Please return when you're finished. I'm not done with you yet."

Carl stumbled off the sofa, before flying down the hallway.

"I'm really sorry, Miss J..." Ron cried. "Please don't tell my parents... Please," he said before bursting into tears.

Dennis swore under his breath.

Mrs. Fahlstrom turned to her husband. "I don't know, honey, what do you think we should do with them?"

"Honestly, Jayne, it's your call. I'm off duty, or I'd haul the entire sorry lot of them down to the station and have their parents pick them up there. And Alex I would just leave overnight."

Gabrielle watched with dread as Mrs. Fahlstrom resumed her pacing for another minute. Alex's mom then excused herself, promising to return with a solution or a punishment, Gabrielle could not tell which, her nerves in tatters and her shoulder aching under the weight of Alex, who continued to mumble inappropriate comments.

Carl slumped back to the sofa moments before Mrs. Fahlstrom entered the room, having exchanged the purse for a small Kodak camera.

"Alright, everyone, I want you to all squeeze together and give me a big smile," she said sweetly.

They all stared at her in dumb shock.

"Come on…This is for your memory books."

"Are you serious, Miss J?" Dennis asked.

"You're not going to give them to our parents, are you?" Ron asked before bursting into another round of sobs.

"Well, I hadn't thought of that Ron, but thank you for the suggestion."

"*Dumb shit,*" Dennis said under his breath, slapping Ron upside the head.

A flash went off. And then another. Gabrielle wincing, as if each one were a blow to her sense of pride and self, still struggling to keep Alex propped up, still hushing him as he made lewd, suggestive comments to her in front of his parents, mumbling but loud and coherent enough for them to hear. After a minute, it felt like torture, and Gabrielle fought hard not to burst into tears herself.

But the camera stopped finally, and Mrs. Fahlstrom cleared her throat.

"Okay…I've made my decision. You're all grounded until four o'clock today, at which time you will be free to leave or join us for dinner—your choice. Until that time, I have a list of chores I want completed by those of you well enough to do so. Those of you who are unwell are to retire to bed. If you make a mess, you're to clean it up. I want no trace of it in my house, understood?"

"Why am I being grounded?' Gabrielle burst. "I didn't even drink—I didn't do anything. I just played music all night."

"Gabrielle, honey, it was *your party*. Now buck up and take care of your friends. Had you done so last night, you wouldn't be here today, now, would you?"

"*Yeah, take care of me, Gabby,*" Alex murmured, trying to kiss her.

"So you're not going to tell our parents?" Ron asked.

"No, Ron…I'll leave that up to you."

He collapsed on Dennis's lap in relief. Dennis roughly pushed him away, calling him a faggot, then helped Mr. Fahlstrom walk Alex upstairs to his bedroom. Gabrielle watched as the two of them next helped Carl to Danielle's bedroom, leaving Ron to fall asleep on the sofa. Mrs. Fahlstrom then entered the living room with a slip of paper, handing it to Gabrielle.

"Here you go, dear. We'll be home around two," she said, smiling sweetly.

But Gabrielle felt too ashamed to smile back, staring at the floor in utter despair, viewing the next few hours of her life as a prisoner waiting for judgment, imagining Mrs. Fahlstrom calling her mother, imagining her mother's mortification, imagining the two of them grounding her and Alex for the summer. No car. No prom. No phone calls. No chance to be together. By the time Dennis joined her in the living room, she had burst into tears.

"What the hell is wrong with you?" he asked.

"I've ruined everything…Everything…"

"Oh, for fuck's sake…Jesus, Gabby—collect yourself. You haven't ruined shit. Nothing's ruined at all."

"Yes it is…They'll ground us for life…I'll never see him again."

"What are you talking about? Shit—you need a joint. Seriously. But I don't have a goddamn one on me right now…"

But Gabrielle curled herself up into a fetal position, continuing to sob.

"Goddammit, Gabrielle—I am not going to be locked up here for the next six hours with these ass clowns and a hysterical female. Now get your shit together…Where's that fucking list?"

She extended her arm, the list wadded up in her hand. Dennis pried it out, smoothing the paper so he could read it.

"Shit…" he said, laughing. "You can stop your crying now…She ain't mad at you."

Gabrielle looked up at him, wiping away an errant strand of hair that had gotten plastered to her eyes.

"*How To be a Good Hangover Hostess…*" he began reading aloud, making faces as he went through the list of tips, having Gabrielle laughing by the end of it. They spent the next hour attempting to comply with the list before finding it an act of futility, their three friends too far gone, and settling down in front of the television with the Fahlstrom's dog to eat chips, drink sodas and watch cable movies, their only disruption enraged shrieks from Danielle who had come home to find Carl passed out in her bed.

Alex woke up Sunday afternoon as he did every day, slightly apprehensive of his surroundings and straining to adjust his eyes until a familiar object came into focus, one that confirmed the world in which he had awaken, be it the dog, the plain gray walls or the photo of the five children taped to his wall. Today, there was no dog in sight, and his room was too bright to be able to see the walls clearly, the sun bathing everything in a radiant white glow.

He turned to his side, relieved to see the familiar photo. Only next to it was taped a new photo. Frowning, he reached out to pull it off the wall and study it. Musing at the familiar faces and ridiculous poses, he turned it over. On the back side in neat handwriting was written today's date and the following words, all underscored.

STILL NAUGHTY!!!

Blushing and smiling to himself, he climbed out of bed and hesitantly made his way down the steps, the house eerily quiet. As he approached the living room, he could hear voices coming from the dining room, a conversation, laughing.

Walking into the room, he stopped suddenly, surprised to see the group gathered around his kitchen table, a group that consisted of his parents, his sister, Gabrielle, Carl, Dennis and Ron, along with an empty chair that had been waiting for his arrival.

"Well good evening, Alex…So glad you could make it for dinner," his dad said wryly. "We've been waiting for you."

∞

June 4, 1995

On the morning of his eighteenth birthday, Alex opened his eyes and stared at his surroundings in happy contentment, the previously bare walls now covered with posters and photos, the shelves displaying more framed photos or memorabilia. Each photo holding a memory from the past year. There was the one of him and Gabrielle at Junior Prom and the latest one of them at Senior Prom. There were group photos of the football and wrestling teams, along with two championship trophies. Next to this was a framed playbill from the school musical, *Sound of Music*, where he and Gabrielle had the leading roles. And since his parents had bought him a professional camera for his seventeenth birthday, there was a slew of random, spontaneous photos of Gabrielle, his friends, his dog and the horses, his family, his car and the breathtaking, mountainous countryside.

Today would call for more picture-taking, the Fahlstroms and the Trahans having planned a massive combined birthday-graduation party for him and Gabrielle on the Trahan property, inviting all of their friends, including the entire senior class.

And while he and Gabrielle had mapped out their college and career plans, he didn't think of those that morning, instead focusing his mind on every nuance of the present moment, from the play of dust particles in the streaming sunlight to the soft touch of hair on his dog's ear, to the infinite universe of possibility that awaited his direction.